Danielle Steel

GOLDEN MOMENTS

LOVING

and

SEASON OF PASSION

LONDON   NEW YORK   SYDNEY   TORONTO

This edition published 1993
by BCA by arrangement with
Judy Piatkus (Publishers) Ltd

CN 3447

Printed and bound in Great Britain by
Mackays of Chatham PLC, Chatham, Kent

GOLDEN MOMENTS

To Dan
With endless love
For making me so
happy – and so lukey!
Love,
D.

Acknowledgement
Lines from 'Getting There' by Sylvia Plath are
reprinted from *Ariel* (1965) by Sylvia Plath.
Copyright © 1963 by Ted Hughes. Reprinted by
permission of Harper & Row, Publishers, Inc.,
Faber & Faber, London and Olwyn Hughes.

'I shall bury the wounded like pupas,
I shall count and bury the dead.
Let their souls writhe in a dew,
Incense in my track.
The carriages rock, they are cradles.
And I, stepping from this skin
Of old bandages, boredoms, old faces

Step to you from the black car of Lethe,
Pure as a baby.'

From 'Getting There'
by Sylvia Plath, *Ariel*.

CHAPTER I

Edward Hascomb Rawlings sat in his office and smiled at the morning paper on his desk. Page five showed a large photograph of a smiling young woman coming down the ramp of a plane. The Honourable Kezia Saint Martin. Another smaller photograph showed her on the arm of a tall, attractive man, leaving the terminal for the seclusion of a waiting limousine. The man, as Edward knew, was Whitney Hayworth III, the youngest partner of the legal firm of Benton, Thatcher, Powers, and Frye. Edward had known Whit since the boy got out of law school. And that had been ten years ago. But he wasn't interested in Whit. He was interested in the diminutive woman on his arm. Edward knew her almost jet black hair, deep blue eyes, and creamy English complexion so well.

And she looked well now, even in newsprint. She was smiling. She seemed tanned. And she was finally back. Her absences always seemed interminable to Edward. The paper said that she had just come from Marbella, where she had been seen over the weekend, staying at the Spanish summer home of her aunt, the Contessa di San Ricamini, née Hilary Saint Martin. Before that Kezia had summered in the South of France, in 'almost total seclusion'. Edward laughed at the thought. He had seen her column regularly all summer, with reports from London, Paris, Barcelona, Nice, and Rome. She had had a busy summer, in 'seclusion'.

A paragraph further down the same page mentioned three others who had arrived on the same flight as Kezia. The so suddenly powerful daughter of the Greek shipping magnate, who had left her, his only heir, the bulk of his fortune. And there was mention as well of the Belgian princess, fresh from the Paris collections for a little junket

7

to New York. Kezia had been in good company on the flight, and Edward wondered how much money she had taken from them at backgammon. Kezia was a most effective player. It struck him too that it was once again Kezia who got most of the press coverage. It was that way for her. Always the centre of attention, the sparkle, the thunder, the flash of cameras as she walked into restaurants and out of theatres. It had been at its cruellest peak when she was in her teens; the photographers and reporters were always hungry, curious, prying, then. For years it had seemed that she was followed everywhere by a fleet of piranhas, but that was when she had first inherited her father's fortune. Now they were used to her, and their attention seemed kinder.

At first Edward had tried hard to shield her from the press. That first year. That first, godawful, intolerable, excruciating year, when she was nine. But the scavengers had only been waiting. And they hadn't waited long. It came as a shock to Kezia when she was thirteen, to be followed by a red-hot young woman reporter into Elizabeth Arden's. Kezia hadn't understood. But the reporter had. She had understood plenty. Edward's face grew hard at the memory. Bitch. How could she do that to a child? She had asked her about Liane, right there in front of everyone. 'How did you feel when your mother . . .' The reporter was four years late with her story. And out of a job by noon the next day. Edward was disappointed: he had hoped to have her job by the same night. And that was Kezia's first taste of it. Notoriety. Power. A fortune. A name. Parents with histories. And grandparents with histories and power and money. Nine generations of it on her mother's side. Only three worth mentioning on her father's. History. Power. Money. Things you can't conjure up, or lie about, or steal. You have to be born with them running thick in your veins. All three. And beauty. And style. And then some other magical ingredient dancing in you at lightning speed, then . . . and only then, are you Kezia Saint Martin. And there was only one.

Edward stirred the coffee in the white-and-gold Limoges cup on his desk, and settled back to look at the view. The East River, dotted with small boats and barges, was a narrow grey ribbon far below on his right. He faced north from where he sat, and gazed peacefully over the congestion of midtown Manhattan, past its skyscrapers, to look down on the sturdy residential fortresses of Park Avenue and Fifth, huddled near the clump of browning green that was Central Park, and in the distance, a blur that was Harlem. It was merely a part of his view, and not a part that interested him a great deal. Edward was a busy man.

He sipped the coffee, and turned to 'Martin Hallam's' column to see who among his acquaintances was allegedly in love with whom, who was giving a dinner party where, who would attend, and who would presumably not show up because of the latest social feud. He knew only too well that there would be an item or two from Marbella. He knew Kezia's style well enough to know that she would mention herself. She was thorough and prudent. And he was right. 'On the list of returning refugees after a summer abroad: Scooter Hollingsworth, Bibi Adams-Jones, Melissa Sentry, Jean-Claude Reims, Kezia Saint Martin, and Julian Bodley. Hail, hail, the gang's all here! Everyone is coming home!'

It was September, and he could still hear Kezia's voice of a September seven years before . . .

'. . . All right, Edward, I've done it. I did Vassar, and the Sorbonne, and I just did another summer at Aunt Hil's. I'm twenty-one years old and now I'm going to do what I want for a change. No more guilt trips about what my father would have wanted, or my mother would have preferred and what you feel is "sensible". I've done it all, for them and for you. And now I'm going to do it for me . . .'

She had marched up and down his office with a stormy look on her face, while he worried about the 'it' she was referring to.

'And what exactly are you planning to do?' He was dying inside. But she was awfully young and very beautiful.

'I don't know exactly. But I have some ideas.'

'Share them with me.'

'I plan to, but don't be disagreeable, Edward.' She had turned towards him with fiery amethyst lights in her rich blue eyes. She was a striking girl, even more so when she was angry. Then the eyes would become almost purple, the cameo skin would blush faintly under the cheekbones, and the contrast made her dark hair shine like onyx. It almost made you forget how tiny she was. She was barely more than five feet tall, but well proportioned, with a face that in anger drew one like a magnet, riveting her victim's eyes to her own. And the entire package was Edward's responsibility, had been since her parents' deaths. Ever since then, the burden of those fierce blue eyes had belonged to him, and her governess, Mrs. Townsend, and her Aunt Hilary, the Contessa di San Ricamini.

Hilary, of course, didn't want to be bothered. She was perfectly willing, in fact nowadays frankly delighted, to have the girl stay with her in London at Christmas, or come to the house in Marbella for the summer. But she did not want to be bothered with what she referred to as 'trivia'. Kezia's fascination with the Peace Corps had been 'trivia', as had her much-publicized romance with the Argentinian ambassador's son three years before. Her depression when the boy had married his cousin had also been 'trivia', as had Kezia's other passing fascinations with people, places, and causes. Maybe Hilary had a point; it all fell by the wayside eventually anyway. But until it did, it was inevitably Edward's problem. At twenty-one, she had already been a burden on his shoulders for twelve long years. But it was a burden he had cherished.

'Well, Kezia, you've been wearing out the rug in my office, but you still haven't told me what these mysterious plans of yours are. What about that course in journalism at Columbia? Have you lost interest in trying that?'

10

'As a matter of fact, I have. Edward, I want to go to work.'

'Oh?' He had shuddered almost visibly. God, let it be for some charity organization. Please. 'For whom?'

'I want to work for a newspaper, and study journalism at night.' There was a look of fierce defiance in her eyes. She knew what he would say. And why.

'I think you'd be a good deal wiser to take the course at Columbia, get your master's, and then think about working. Do it sensibly.'

'And after I get my master's, what sort of newspaper would you suggest, Edward? *Women's Wear Daily* maybe?' He thought he saw tears of anger and frustration in her eyes. Lord, she was going to be difficult again. She grew more stubborn each year. She was just like her father.

'What sort of paper were you considering, Kezia? *The Village Voice* or the *Berkeley Barb*?'

'No. *The New York Times*.' At least the girl had style. She had never lacked that.

'I heartily agree, my dear. I think it's a marvellous idea. But if that's what you have in mind, I think you'd be far wiser to attend Columbia, get your master's, and . . .' She cut him off, rising from the arm of the chair where she'd been perched, and glared at him angrily across his desk.

'And marry some terribly "nice" boy in the business school. Right?'

'Not unless that's what you want to do.' Tedious, tedious, tedious. And dangerous. She was that too. Like her mother.

'Well, that's not what I want to do.' She had stalked out of his office then, and he found out later that she already had the job at the *Times*. She kept it for exactly three and a half weeks.

It all happened precisely as he had feared it would. As one of the fifty wealthiest women in the world, she became the puppy of the paparazzi again. Every day in some newspaper, there was a mention or a photograph or a blurb or a quote or a joke. Other papers sent their society reporters over to catch glimpses of her. *Women's Wear* had a field day. It was a continuation of the nightmare that had shadowed her: the fourteenth-birthday party broken into by photographers. The evening at the opera with Edward, over the Christmas holidays when she was only fifteen, which they had turned into such a horror. A pigsty of suggestion about Edward and Kezia. After that he had not taken her out publicly for years ... and for years after that, there were the photographs of her that were repressed, and those that were not. The dates she was afraid to have, and then had and regretted, until at seventeen she had feared notoriety more than anything. At eighteen she had hated it. Hated the seclusion it forced on her, the caution she had to exercise, the constant secretiveness and discretion. It was absurd and unhealthy for a girl her age, but there was nothing Edward could do to lighten the burden for her. She had a tradition to live up to, and a difficult one. It was impossible for the daughter of Lady Liane Holmes-Aubrey Saint Martin and Keenan Saint Martin to go ignored. Kezia was 'worth a tidy sum', in common parlance, and she was beautiful. She was young, she was interesting. And she made news. There was no way to avoid that, however much Kezia wanted to pretend she could change that. She couldn't. She never would. At least that was what Edward had thought. But he was surprised at her skill at avoiding photographers when she wanted to (now he even took her to the opera again) and the marvellous way she had of putting down reporters, with a wide dazzling smile and a word or two that made them wonder if she was laughing at them or with them, or about to call the police. She had that about her. Something threatening, the raw edge of power. But she had something gentle too. It was that that baffled everyone. She was a peculiar combination of her parents.

Kezia had the satiny delicacy of her mother and the sheer strength of her father. The two had always been an unusual couple. A surprising couple. And Kezia was like both of them, although more like her father. Edward saw it constantly. But what frightened him was the resemblance to Liane. Hundreds of years of British tradition, a maternal great-grandfather who was a duke – although her paternal grandfather had only been an earl – but Liane had such breeding, such style, such elegance of spirit. Such stature. Edward had fallen head over heels in love with her right from the first. And she had never known. Never. Edward knew that he couldn't . . . couldn't . . . but she had done something so much worse. Madness . . . blackmail . . . nightmare. At least they had averted a public scandal. No one had known. Except her husband, and Edward . . . and . . . him. Edward had never understood it. What had she seen in the boy? He was so much less a man than Keenan. And so . . . so coarse. Crude almost. She had made a poor choice. A very poor choice. Liane had taken Kezia's French tutor as her lover. It was almost grotesque, except that it was so costly. In the end, it had cost Liane her life. And it had cost Keenan thousands to keep it quiet.

Keenan had had the young man 'removed' from the household, and deported to France. After that it took Liane less than a year to drown herself in cognac and champagne, and, secretly, pills. She had paid a high price for her betrayal. Keenan died ten months later in an accident. There had been no doubt it was an accident, but such a waste. More waste. Keenan hadn't given a damn about anything after Liane died, and Edward had always suspected that he had just let it happen, just let the Mercedes slide along the barrier, let it career into the oncoming highway traffic. He had probably been drunk, or maybe only very tired. Not really a suicide, just the end.

No, Keenan hadn't cared about anything in those last months, not even, really, about his daughter. He had said as much to Edward, but only to Edward. Everyone's confidant, Edward. Liane had even told him her ugly stories, over tea one day, and he had nodded sagely and prayed not to get sick in her drawing room. She had looked at him so mournfully, it had made him want to cry.

13

Edward always cared. He cared too much – for Liane, who had been too perfect to be touched (or so he had thought) and for her child. Edward had always wondered if it excited her to have someone so far from her own class, or maybe it was just that the man was young, or maybe because he was French.

At least he could protect Kezia from that kind of madness, and he had long ago promised himself that he would. She was his duty now, his responsibility, and he was going to see to it that she lived up to every ounce of her breeding. He had sworn to himself that there would be no disasters in Kezia's life, no blackmailing, boy-faced French tutors. With Kezia it would be different. She would live up to her noble ancestry on her mother's side and to the powerful people on her father's side. Edward felt he owed that much to Keenan and Liane. And to Kezia, as well. And he knew what it would take. How he would have to inculcate her with a sense of duty, a sense of the mantle of tradition she wore. As she grew up, Kezia had jokingly referred to it as her hair shirt. but she understood. Edward always saw to it that she did. That was the one thing he could give her objectively, he thought: a sense of who and what she was. She was Kezia Saint Martin. The Honourable Kezia Holmes-Aubrey Saint Martin, offspring of British nobility and American aristocracy, with a father who had used millions to make millions, in steel, copper, rubber, petroleum, and oil. When there was big money to be made on unthinkable scales, Keenan Saint Martin was there. It had made him an international legend, and a kind of American prince. His was the legend Kezia had inherited with the fortune. Of course, by some standards Keenan had had to get his hands a little bit dirty, but not very. He was always so spectacular, and such a gentleman, the kind of man whom people forgave anything, even the fact that he made much of his own money.

Liane, on the other hand, was Kezia's threat, her terror ... her reminder that if she crossed the invisible boundaries into forbidden lands, she, like her mother, would die.

14

Edward wanted her to be more like her father. It was so much less painful for him that way. But so often ... too often ... she was the image of Liane, only stronger, and better, smarter, and so much more beautiful even than Liane.

Kezia was born of extraordinary people. She was the last surviving link in a long chain of almost mythical beauty and grace. And it was up to Edward now to see that the chain was not broken. Liane had threatened it. But the chain was still safe, and Edward, like all lonely people who never quite dare, who are never quite beautiful, who are never quite strong – was impressed by it. His own modestly elegant family in Philadelphia was so much less impressive than these magical people to whom he had given his soul. He was their guardian now. The keeper of the Holy Grail: Kezia. The treasure. His treasure. Which was why he had been so glad when her plan to work at the *Times* had failed so dismally. Everything would be peaceful again. For a while. She was his to protect, and he was hers to command. She did not yet command him, but he feared that one day she would. Just as her parents had. He had been trusted and commanded, never loved.

In the case of the *Times*, he had not had to command. She had quit. She had gone back to school for a while, fled to Europe for the summer, but in the fall, everything had changed again. Mostly Kezia. For Edward it had been almost terrifying.

She had returned to New York with something crisper about her manner, something more womanly. This time she didn't consult Edward, even after the fact, and she didn't make claims to being grown-up. At twenty-two she had sold the co-op on Park Avenue where she had lived with Mrs. Townsend – Totie – for thirteen very comfortable years, and rented two smaller apartments, one for herself, and the other for Totie, who was gently but firmly put out to pasture, despite Edward's protests and Totie's tears. Then she had gone about solving the problem of a job as resolutely as she had the matter of the

15

apartment. The solution she chose was astonishingly ingenious.

She had announced the news to Edward over dinner in her new apartment, while serving him a very pleasant Pouilly Fumé '54 to soften the blow.

Kezia had acquired a literary agent, and stunned Edward by announcing that she had already published three articles that summer, which she had sent in from Europe. And the amazing thing was that he had read them all, and rather liked them. He remembered them – a political piece she had written in Italy, a haunting article about a nomadic tribe she had come across in the Middle East, and a very funny spoof on the Polo Club in Paris. All three had appeared in national publications under the name of K. S. Miller. It was the last article that had set off the next chain of events.

They had opened another bottle of wine, and Kezia had suddenly begun to look mischievous, as she tried to extort a promise from him. Suddenly, he had that sinking sensation in his stomach again. There was more, he could tell. He got that feeling every time she got *that* look in her eyes. The look that reminded him so acutely of her father. The look that said the plans had been made, the decisions taken, and there wasn't a hell of a lot you could do about it. Now what?

She had pulled out a copy of the morning's paper, and folded it to a page in the second section. He couldn't imagine what he might have missed. He read the paper thoroughly every morning. But she was pointing to the society column by Martin Hallam, and that morning he hadn't bothered to read it.

It was a strange column, actually, and had begun appearing only a month before. It was a well-informed, slightly cynical, and highly astute account of Jet Set doings in their private haunts. No one had any idea who Martin Hallam was, and everyone was still trying to guess who the traitor might be. Whoever he was, he wrote without malice – but certainly with a great deal of inside

16

information. And now Kezia was pointing to something at the top of the column.

He read it through, but found no mention of Kezia.

'So?'

'So, I'd like you to meet a friend of mine. Martin Hallam.' She was laughing openly, and Edward felt faintly foolish. And then she stuck out a hand to shake his, with a gurgle of laughter and those familiar amethyst lights in her eyes. 'Hello, Edward. I'm Martin. How do you do?'

'What? Kezia, you're joking!'

'I'm not. And no one will ever know. Even the editor doesn't know who writes it. Everything goes through my literary agent, and he's extremely discreet. I had to give them a month of sample columns to show that I knew what I was talking about, but word came back to us today. The column will now run as a regular feature three times a week. Isn't it divine?'

'Divine? It's ungodly. Kezia, how could you?'

'Why not? I don't say anything I could get sued for, and I don't let out any secrets that will destroy anyone's life. I just keep everyone ... well, "informed", shall we say ... and amused.'

And that was Kezia. The Honourable Kezia Saint Martin, K. S. Miller, and Martin Hallam. And now she was home after another summer away. Seven summers had passed since her career began. She was successful now, and it only added to her charm. To Edward, it gave her a mysterious sparkle, an almost unbearable allure. Who but Kezia could pull it off? And for such a long time. Edward and her agent were the only two people she had entrusted with the secret that the Honourable Kezia Saint Martin had another life, other than the one so lavishly depicted in *WWD, Town and Country,* and occasionally in the 'People' column of *Time.*

Edward looked at his watch again. He could call her now. It was just past ten o'clock. He reached for the phone. This was one number he always dialled himself. It rang

17

twice, and she answered. The voice was husky, the way she always sounded in the morning. The way he liked best. There was something very private about that voice. He often wondered what she wore to bed, and then reprimanded himself for the thought.

'Welcome home, Kezia.' He smiled at the newspaper photograph still lying on his desk.

'Edward!' He felt warm at the delight in her voice. 'How I've missed you!'

'But not enough to send me so much as a postcard, you little minx! I had lunch with Totie last Saturday, and she at least gets an occasional letter from you.'

'That's different. She'd go into a decline if I didn't let her know I'm alive.' She laughed, and he heard the clink of a cup against the phone. Tea. No sugar. A dash of cream.

'And you don't think I'd go into a decline?'

'Of course not. You're far too stoic. It would be bad form. *Noblesse oblige,* et cetera, et cetera.'

'All right, all right.' Her directness often embarrassed him. She was right, too. He had a distinct sense of 'form'. It was why he had never told her that he loved her. Why he had never told her mother that he had loved her.

'And how was Marbella?'

'Dreadful. I must be getting old. Aunt Hil's house was absolutely crawling with all sorts of eighteen-year-old children. Good God, Edward, they were born eleven years after I was! Why aren't they at home with their nannies?' He laughed at the sound of her voice. She still looked twenty. But a very sophisticated twenty. 'Thank God I was only there for the weekend.'

'And before that?'

'Didn't you read the column this morning? It said I was in seclusion in the South of France for most of the summer.' She laughed again, and he smiled. It was so good to hear her voice.

'Actually, I was there for a while. On a boat I rented, and it was very pleasant. And peaceful. I got a lot of writing done.'

18

'I saw the article you did on the three Americans imprisoned in Turkey. Depressing, but excellent. Were you there?'

'Of course I was. And yes, it was depressing as hell.'

'Where else did you go?' He wanted to get her off the subject. Disagreeable issues were unnecessary.

'Oh, I went to a party in Rome, to the collections in Paris, to London to see the Queen . . . Pussycat, pussycat, where have you been? I've been to London to see the . . .'

'Kezia, you're impossible.' But delightfully so.

'Yeah.' She took a long swallow of tea and hiccuped in his ear. 'But I missed you. It's a pain in the ass not being able to tell anyone what I'm really doing.'

'Well, come and tell me what you really did. Lunch at La Grenouille today?'

'Perfect. I have to see Simpson, but I can meet you after that. Is one all right with you?'

'Fine. And Kezia . . .'

'Yes?' Her voice was low and gentle, suddenly not quite so brisk. In her own way, she loved him too. For almost twenty years now, he had softened the blow of the absence of her father.

'It really is good to know you're back.'

'And it really is good to know that someone gives a damn.'

'Silly child, you make it sound as though no one else cares.'

'It's called the Poor Little Rich Girl Syndrome, Edward. Occupational hazard for an heiress.' She laughed, but there was an edge to her voice that troubled him. 'See you at one.'

She hung up, and Edward stared out at the view.

Twenty-two blocks from where he sat, Kezia was lying in bed, finishing her tea. There was a stack of newspapers on her bed, a pile of mail on the table next to her. The curtains were drawn back, and she had a peaceful view of the garden behind the townhouse next door. A bird was

19

cooing on the air conditioner. And the doorbell was ringing.

'Damn.' She pulled a white satin robe off the foot of the bed, wondering who it might be, then suspecting quickly. She was right. When she opened the door, a slim, nervous Puerto Rican boy held out a long white box.

She knew what was in the box even before she traded the boy a dollar for his burden. She knew who the box was from. She even knew the florist. And knew also that she would recognize his secretary's writing on the card. After four years, you let your secretary write the cards: 'Oh, you know, Effy, something like "You can't imagine how I've missed you", et cetera.' Effy did a fine job of it. She said just what any romantic fifty-four-year-old virgin would say on a card to accompany a dozen red roses. And Kezia didn't really care if the card was from Effy or Whit. It didn't make much difference anymore. None at all, in fact.

This time Effy had added 'Dinner tonight?' to the usual flowery message, and Kezia paused with the card in her hand. She sat down in a prim blue velvet chair that had been her mother's, and played with the card. She hadn't seen Whit in a month. Not since he had flown to London on business, and they had partied at Annabel's before he left again the next day. Of course he had met her at the airport the night before, but they hadn't really talked. They never really did.

She leaned pensively towards the phone on the small fruitwood desk, the card still in her hand. She glanced across the neat stacks of invitations her twice-weekly secretary had arranged for her – those she had missed, and those that were for the near and reasonably near future. Dinners, cocktails, gallery openings, fashion shows, benefits. Two wedding announcements, and a birth announcement.

She dialled Whit's office and waited.

'Up already, Kezia darling? You must be exhausted.'

'A bit, but I'll live. And the roses are splendid.' She

allowed a small smile to escape her and hoped that it wouldn't show in her voice.

'Are they nice? I'm glad. Kezia, you looked marvellous last night.' She laughed at him and looked at the tree growing in the neighbouring garden. The tree had grown more in four years than Whit had.

'You were sweet to pick me up at the airport. And the roses started my day off just right. I was beginning to gloom over unpacking my bags.'

She had had the bad judgment to arrive on one of the cleaning woman's days off. But the bags could wait.

'And what about my dinner invitation? The Orniers are having a dinner, and if you're not too tired, Xavier suggested we all go to Raffles afterwards.' The Orniers had an endless suite in the tower at the Hotel Pierre, which they kept for their annual trips to New York. Even for a few weeks it was 'worth it': 'Yo7 know how ghastly it is to be in a different room each time, a strange place.' They paid a high price for familiarity, but that was not new to Kezia. And their dinner party was just the sort of thing she ought to cover for the column. She had to get back into the swing of things, and lunch at La Grenouille with Edward would be a good start, but ... damn. She wanted to go downtown instead. There were delights downtown that Whit would never dream she knew. She smiled to herself and suddenly remembered Whit in the silence.

'Sorry, darling. I'd love to, but I'm so awfully tired. Jet lag, and probably all that wild life at Hilary's this weekend. Can you possibly tell the Orniers I died, and I'll try to catch a glimpse of them before they leave. For you, I will resurrect tomorrow. But today, I'm simply gone.' She yawned slightly, and then giggled. 'Good Lord, I didn't mean to yawn in your ear. Sorry.'

'Quite all right. And I think you're right about tonight. They probably won't serve dinner till nine. You know how they are, and it'll be two before you get home after Raffles ...' Dancing in that over-decorated basement, Kezia thought, just what I don't need ...

21

'I'm glad you understand, love. Actually, I think I'll put my phone on the service, and just trot off to bed at seven or eight. And tomorrow I'll be blazing.'

'Good. Dinner tomorrow then?' Obviously, darling. Obviously.

'Yes. I have a thing on my desk for some sort of gala at the St. Regis. Want to try that? I think the Marshes are taking over the Maisonette for their ninety-eighth wedding anniversary or something.'

'Nasty sarcastic girl. It's only their twenty-fifth. I'll take a table at La Côte Basque, and we can go next door late.'

'Perfect, darling. Till tomorrow, then.'

'Pick you up at seven?'

'Make it eight.' Make it never.

'Fine, darling. See you then.'

She sat swinging one leg over the other after she hung up. She really was going to have to be nicer to Whit. What was the point of being disagreeable to him? Everyone thought of them as a couple, and he was nice to her, and useful in a way. Her constant escort. Darling Whitney . . . poor Whit. So predictable and so perfect, so beautiful and so impeccably tailored. It was unbearable really. Precisely six feet and one inch, ice-blue eyes, short thick blond hair, thirty-five years old, Gucci shoes, Dior ties, Givenchy cologne, Piaget watch, apartment on Park and Sixty-third, fine reputation as a lawyer, and loved by all his friends. The obvious mate for Kezia, and that in itself was enough to make her hate him, not that she really hated him. She only resented him, and her need of him. Despite the lover on Sutton Place that he didn't know she knew about.

The Whit and Kezia game was a farce, but a discreet one. And a useful one. He was the ideal and eternal escort, and so totally safe. It was appalling to remember that a year or two before she had even considered marrying him. There didn't seem any reason not to. They would go on doing the same things they were doing, and Kezia would tell him about the column. They would go to the same parties, see the same people, and lead their own lives. He'd

22

bring her roses instead of send them. They would have separate bedrooms, and when Kezia gave someone a tour of the house Whit's would be shown as 'the guest room'. And she would go downtown, and he to Sutton Place, and no one would have to be the wiser. They would never mention it to each other, of course; she would 'play bridge' and he would 'see a client' and they would meet at breakfast the next day, pacified, mollified, appeased, and loved, each by their respective lovers. What an insane fantasy. She laughed thinking back on it now. She still had more hope than that. She regarded Whit now as an old friend. She was fond of him in an odd way. And she was used to him, which in some ways was worse.

Kezia wandered slowly back to her bedroom and smiled to herself. It was good to be home. Nice to be back in the comfort of her own apartment, in the huge white bed with the silver fox bedspread that had been such an appalling extravagance, but still pleased her so much. The small, delicate furniture had been her mother's. The painting she had bought in Lisbon the year before hung over the bed, a watermelon sun over a rich countryside and a man working the fields. There was something warm and friendly about her bedroom that she found nowhere else in the world. Not in Hilary's palazzo in Marbella, or in the lovely home in Kensington where she had her own room – Hilary had so many rooms in the London house that she could afford to give them away to absent friends and family like so many lace handkerchiefs. But nowhere did Kezia feel like this, except at home. There was a fireplace in the bedroom too, and she had found the brass bed in London years before; there was one soft brown velvet chair near the fireplace, and a white fur rug that made you want to dance barefoot across the floor. Plants stood in corners and hung near the windows, and candles on the mantel gave the room a soft glow late at night. It was very good to be home.

She laughed softly to herself, a sound of pure pleasure as she put Mahler on the stereo and started her bath. And tonight ... downtown. To Mark. First, her agent, then

23

lunch with Edward. And finally, Mark. Saving the best till last . . . as long as nothing had changed.

'Kezia,' she spoke aloud to herself, looking in the bathroom mirror as she stood naked before it, humming to the music that echoed through the house, 'You are a very naughty girl!' She wagged a finger at her reflection, and tossed back her head and laughed, her long black hair sweeping back to her waist. She stood very still then and looked deep into her own eyes. 'Yeah, I know. I'm a rat. But what else can I do? A girl's got to live, and there are a lot of different ways to do it.' She sank into the bathtub, wondering about it all. The dichotomies, the contrasts, the secrets . . . but at least no lies. She said nothing to anyone. But she did not lie. Almost never anyway. Lies were too hard to live with. Secrets were better.

As she sank into the warmth of the water, she thought about Mark. Delicious Marcus. The wild crazy hair, the incredible smile, the smell of his loft, the chess games, the laughter, the music, his body, his fire. Mark Wooly. She closed her eyes and drew an imaginary line down his back with the tip of one finger and then traced it gently across his lips. Something small squirmed low in the pit of her stomach, and she turned slowly in the tub, sending ripples gently away from her.

Twenty minutes later she stepped out of the bath, brushed her hair into a sleek knot, and slipped a plain white wool Dior dress over the new champagne lace underwear she had bought in Florence.

'Do you suppose I'm a schizophrenic?' she asked the mirror as she carefully fitted a hat into place and tilted it slowly over one eye. But she didn't look like a schizophrenic. She looked like 'the' Kezia Saint Martin, on her way to lunch at La Grenouille in New York, or Fouquet's in Paris.

'Taxi!' Kezia held up an arm and dashed past the doorman as a cab stopped a few feet away at the kerb. She smiled at the doorman and slid into the cab. Her New York season had just begun. And what did this one have in store?

24

A book? A man? Mark Wooly? A dozen juicy articles for major magazines? A host of tiny cherished moments? Solitude and secrecy and splendour. She had it all. And another 'season' in the palm of her hand.

In his office, Edward was strutting in front of the view. He looked at his watch for the eleventh time in an hour. In just a few minutes he would watch her walk in, she would see him and laugh, and then reach up and touch his face with her hand . . . 'Oh Edward, it's so good to see you!' She would hug him and giggle, and settle in at his side – while 'Martin Hallam' took mental notes about who was at what table with whom, and K. S. Miller mulled over the possibility of a book.

CHAPTER II

Kezia fought her way past the tight knot of men hovering between the cloak room and the bar of La Grenouille. The luncheon crowd was thick, the bar was jammed, the tables were full, the waiters were bustling, and the decor was unchanged. Red leather seats, pink tablecloths, bright oil paintings on the walls, and flowers on every table. The room was full of red anemones and smiling faces, with silver buckets of white wine chilling at almost every table while champagne corks popped demurely here and there.

The women were beautiful, or had worked hard at appearing so. Cartier's wares were displayed in wild profusion. And the murmur of conversation throughout the room was distinctly French. The men wore dark suits and white shirts, and had grey at their temples, and shared their wealth of Romanoff cigars from Cuba via Switzerland in unmarked brown packages.

La Grenouille was the watering hole of the very rich and the very chic. Merely having an ample expense account to pay the tab was not adequate entree. You had to belong. It had to be part of you, a style you exuded from the pores of your Pucci.

'Kezia?' A hand touched her elbow, and she looked into the tanned face of Amory Strongwell.

'No darling. It's my ghost.' He won a teasing smile.

'You look marvellous.'

'And you look so pale. Poor Amory.' She gazed in mock sympathy at the deep bronze he had acquired in Greece, as he squeezed her shoulder carefully and kissed her cheek.

'Where's Whit?'

Probably at Sutton Place, darling. 'Working like mad, presumably. Will we see you at the Marsh party tomorrow night?' The question was rhetorical, and he nodded absently in answer. 'I'm meeting Edward just now.'

'Lucky bastard.' She gave him a last smile and edged through the crowd to the front, where the head waiter would be waiting to shepherd her to Edward. As it happened, she found Edward without assistance; he was at his favourite table, a bottle of champagne chilling nearby. Louis Roederer 1959, as always.

He saw her too and stood up to meet her as she walked easily past the other tables and across the room. She felt eyes on her, acknowledged discreet greetings as she passed tables of people she knew, and the waiters smiled. She had grown into it all years ago. Recognition. At sixteen it had agonized her, at eighteen it was a custom, at twenty-two she had fought against it, and now at twenty-nine she enjoyed it. It amused her. It was her private joke. The women would say 'marvellous dress', the men would muse about Whit; the women would decide that with the same fortune they could get away with the same sort of hat, and the waiters would nudge each other and murmur in French, 'Saint Martin'. By the time she left, there might, or there might not, be a photographer from *Women's Wear* waiting to snap her photograph paparazzi-style as she came through the door. It amused her. She played the game well.

'Edward, you look wonderful!' She gave him a searching look, an enormous squeeze, and sank onto the banquette at his side.

'Lord, child, you look well.' She kissed his cheek gently, and then smoothed her hand over it tenderly with a smile.

'So do you.'

'And how was this morning with Simpson?'

'Pleasant and productive. We've been discussing some ideas I have for a book. He gives me good advice, but let's not . . . here . . .' They both knew that there was too much noise to allow anyone to piece much together. But they rarely spoke of her career in public. 'Discretion is the better part of valour,' as Edward often said.

'Right. Champagne?'

'Have I ever said no?' He signalled the waiter, and the ritual of the Louis Roederer was begun. 'God, I love that stuff.' She smiled at him again and gazed slowly around the room as he began to laugh.

'I know what you're doing, Kezia, and you're impossible.' She was checking out the scene for her column. He raised his glass to her, and smiled. 'To you, mademoiselle, welcome home.' They clinked glasses and sipped slowly at the champagne. It was precisely the way they liked it, a good year and icy cold.

'How's Whit, by the way? Seeing him for dinner tonight?'

'Fine. And no, I'm going to bed to recover from the trip.'

'I don't think I believe that, but I'll accept it if you say so.'

'What a wise man you are, Edward. That's probably why I love you.'

He looked at her for a moment then, and took her hand. 'Kezia, be careful. Please.'

'Yes, Edward. I know. I am.'

The lunch was pleasant, as all their lunches were. She inquired about all his most important clients, remembered all their names, and wanted to know what he had done about the couch in his apartment that so desperately

27

needed re-upholstering. They said hello to everyone they knew, and were joined for brief moments by two of his partners in the firm. She told him a little about her trip, and she kept an eye on the comings and goings and pairings of the natives.

She left him outside at three. The 'surprise' photographer from *Women's Wear* dutifully took their photograph, and Edward hailed her a cab before he walked back to his office. He always felt better when he knew she was back in town. He could be there if she needed him, and he felt closer to her life. He never really knew, but he had an idea that there was more to her life than Raffles and parties given by the Marshes. And much more to her life than Whit. But she didn't tell Edward, and he didn't ask. He didn't really want to know as long as she was all right – 'careful', as he put it. But there was too much of her father in her to be satisfied with a man like Whit. Edward knew that only too well. It had taken more than two years to settle her father's will discreetly, and execute the arrangements for the two women no one had known about.

The cab took Kezia home and deposited her at her door with a flourish of brakes and scattered kerbside litter, and Kezia went upstairs and hung the white Dior dress neatly in the closet. Half an hour later she was in jeans, her hair hanging free, the answering service instructed to pick up her calls. She was 'resting' and didn't want to be disturbed until the following noon. A few moments later, she was gone.

She walked away from her house and slipped quietly into the subway at Seventy-seventh Street and Lexington Avenue. No make-up, no handbag, just a coin purse in her pocket and a smile in her eyes.

The subway was like a concentrated potion of New York, each sound and smell magnified, each character more extreme. Funny old ladies with faces made up like masks, gay boys in pants so tight one could almost see the hair on their legs, magnificent girls carrying portfolios on their way to modelling engagements, and men who smelled of sweat

28

and cigars, whom one wanted not to be near, and the occasional passenger for Wall Street in striped suit, short hair, and hornrims. It was a symphony of sights and odours and sounds conducted to the shrieking background beat of the trains, brakes screaming, wheels rattling. Kezia stood holding her breath and closing her eyes against the hot breeze and flying litter swept up by the oncoming train, then moved inside quickly, sidestepping the doors as they closed.

She found a seat next to an old woman carrying a shopping bag. A young couple sat down next to her at the next stop, and furtively shared a joint, unobserved by the transit patrolman who moved through the car, eyes fixed ahead of him. Kezia found herself smiling, wondering if the old woman on her other side would get high from the smell. Then the train screeched to a halt at Canal Street and it was time to get off. Kezia danced quickly up the steps and looked around.

She was home again. Another home. Warehouses and tired tenements, fire escapes and delicatessens, and a few blocks away the art galleries and coffee houses and lofts crowded with artists and writers, sculptors and poets, beards and bandannas. A place where Camus and Sartre were still revered, and de Kooming and Pollock were gods. She walked along with a quick step and a little throb in her heart. It shouldn't matter so much ... not at her age ... not the way things were between them ... it shouldn't feel so good to be back ... it might all be different now. ... But it did feel good to be back, and she wanted everything to be the same.

'Hey girl. Where've you been?' A tall, lithe black man wallpapered into white jeans greeted her with surprise delight.

'George!' He swept her off her feet in a vast embrace and whirled her around. He was in the ballet corps of the Metropolitan Opera. 'Oh, it's good to see you!' He deposited her, breathless and smiling, on the pavement beside him, and put an arm around her shoulders.

'You've been gone for a mighty long time, lady.' His eyes

29

danced and his grin was a long row of ivory in the bearded midnight face.

'It feels like it. I almost wondered if the neighbourhood would be gone.'

'Never! SoHo is sacred.' They laughed and he fell into step beside her. 'Where're you going?'

'How about The Partridge for coffee?' She was suddenly afraid to see Mark. Afraid that everything was different. George would know, but she didn't want to ask him.

'Make it wine, and I'm yours for an hour. We have rehearsal at six.'

They shared a carafe of wine at The Partridge. George drank most of it while Kezia played with her glass.

'Know something, baby?'

'What, George?'

'You make me laugh.'

'Terrific. How come?'

'Because I know what you're so nervous about, and you're so damn scared you won't even ask me. You gonna ask or do I have to volunteer the answer?' He was laughing at her.

'Is there something that maybe I don't want to know?'

'Shit, Kezia. Why don't you just go on up to his studio and find out? It's better that way.' He stood up, put a hand in his pocket, and pulled out three dollars. 'My treat. You just go on home.' Home? To Mark? Yes, in a way . . . even she knew it.

He shooed her out the door with another ripple of laughter, and she found herself in the familiar doorway across the street. She hadn't even looked up at the window, but instead nervously searched strangers' faces.

Her heart hammered as she ran up the five flights. She reached the landing, breathless and dizzy, and raised a hand to knock at the door. It flew open almost before she touched it, and she was suddenly wrapped in the arms of an endlessly tall, hopelessly thin, fuzzy-haired man. He kissed her and lifted her into his arms, pulling her inside with a shout and a grin.

30

'Hey, you guys! It's Kezia! How the hell are you, baby?'

'Happy.' He set her down and she looked around. The same faces, the same loft, the same Mark. Nothing had changed. It was a victorious return. 'Christ, it feels like I've been gone for a year!' She laughed again, and someone handed her a glass of red wine.

'You're telling me. And now, ladies and gentlemen ...' The endlessly tall young man bowed low, and swept an arm from his friends to the door. 'My lady has returned. In other words, you guys, beat it!' They laughed good-naturedly and murmured hellos and goodbyes as they left. The door had barely closed when Mark pulled her into his arms again.

'Oh baby, I'm glad you're home.'

'Me too.' She slid a hand under his ragged, paint-splattered shirt and smiled into his eyes.

'Let me look at you.' He slowly pulled her shirt over her head, and she stood straight and still, her hair falling across one shoulder, a warm light in her rich blue eyes, a living reflection of the sketch of a nude that hung on the wall behind her. He had done it the previous winter, soon after they had met. She reached out to him slowly then, and he came into her arms smiling at the same moment that there was a knock at the door.

'Go away!'

'No, I won't.' It was George.

'Shit, motherfucker, what do you want?' He pulled open the door as Kezia darted bare-chested into the bedroom. George loomed large and smiling in the doorway with a small split of champagne in one hand.

'For your wedding night, Marcus.'

'George, you're beautiful.' George danced down the stairs with a wave, and Mark closed the door with a burst of laughter. 'Hey, Kezia! Could you dig a glass of champagne?' She returned to the room smiling and naked, her hair swinging loose down her back, the vision of champagne at La Grenouille in the Dior dress bringing laughter to her eyes now. The comparison was absurd.

31

She lounged in the doorway, her head to one side, watching him open the champagne. And suddenly she felt as though she loved him, and that was absurd too. They both knew she didn't. It wasn't that kind of thing. They both understood ... but it would have been nice not to understand, just for a moment. Not to be rational, or make sense. It would have been lovely to love him, to love someone – anyone – and why not Mark?

'I missed you, Kezia.'

'So did I, darling. So did I. And I also wondered if you had another lady by now.' She smiled and took a sip of the too-sweet, bubbly wine. 'I was queasy as hell about coming up. I even stopped and had some wine at The Partridge with George.'

'Asshole. You could have come here first.'

'I was afraid to.' She walked towards him and traced a finger across his chest as he looked down at her.

'You know something weird, Kezia?'

'What?' Her eyes filled with dreams.

'I've got syphilis.'

'WHAT!' She stared at him, horrified, and he chuckled.

'I just wondered what you'd say. I don't really have it.' But he looked amused at his joke.

'Jesus.' She settled back into his arms with a shake of the head and a grin. 'I'm not so sure about your sense of humour, kiddo.' But it was the same Mark.

He followed her into the bedroom and his voice sounded husky as he spoke from behind her. 'I saw a picture of some girl in the paper the other day. She looked sort of like you, only older, and very uptight.' There was a question in his voice. One she was not planning to answer.

'So?'

'Her last name was French. Not "Miller", but her first name was blurred. I couldn't read it. You related to anyone like that? She looked pretty fancy.'

'No, I'm not related to anyone like that. Why?' And now the lies had even begun with Mark. Not just sins of omission; now they were sins of commission too. Damn.

32

'I don't know. I was just curious. She was interesting looking, in a fierce, unhappy sort of way.'

'And you fell in love with her, and decided that you had to find her and rescue her, so you could both live happily ever after. Right?' Her voice was light, but not as light as she wanted it to be. His answer was lost as he kissed her and eased her gently onto the bed. There was at least an hour of truth amid the lifetime of lies. Bodies are generally honest.

CHAPTER III

'Ready?'

'Ready.' Whit smiled at her across the last of their coffee and mousse au chocolat. They were two hours late for the Marshes' party at the St. Regis, but no one would notice. The Marshes had invited more than five hundred guests.

Kezia was resplendent in a blue-grey satin dress that circled her neck in a halter and left her back bare to show her deep summer tan. Small diamond earrings glistened at her ears, and her hair was swept into a neat knot high on her head. Whit's impeccable evening clothes set off his classic good looks. They made a very spectacular couple. By now, they took it for granted.

The crowd at the entrance to the Maisonette at the St. Regis was enormous. Elegantly dinner-jacketed men whose names appeared regularly in *Fortune*; women in diamonds and Balenciagas and Givenchys and Diors whose faces and living rooms appeared constantly in *Vogue*. European titles, American scions of society, friends from Palm Beach and Grosse Pointe and Scottsdale and Beverly Hills. The Marshes had outdone themselves. Waiters circulated through the ever-thickening crowd, offering Moët et Chandon champagne and little platters boasting caviar and pâté.

There was cold lobster on a buffet at the back of the room, and later on there would appear the pièce de résistance, an enormous wedding cake, a replica of the original served a quarter of a century before. Each guest would be given a tiny box of dream cake, the wrapping carefully inscribed with the couple's name and the date. 'More than a little tacky,' as Martin Hallam would note in his column the next day. Whit handed Kezia a glass of champagne from a passing tray and gently took her arm.

'Do you want to dance, or circulate for a while?'

'Circulate, I think, if it's humanly possible.' She smiled quietly at him, and he squeezed her arm.

A photographer hired by their hosts snapped a picture of them looking lovingly at each other, and Whit slipped an arm about her waist. She was comfortable with him. After her night with Mark, she felt benign and benevolent, even with Whit. It was odd to think that at dawn that morning she had wandered the streets of SoHo with Mark, then left him reluctantly at three that afternoon to phone in her column to her agent, clear her desk, and rest before the onslaught of the evening. Edward had called to see how she was, and they had chuckled for a few moments about her mention of their lunch in the morning's column.

'How in God's name can you call me "dashing," Kezia? I'm over sixty years old.'

'You're a mere sixty-one. And you *are* dashing, Edward. Look at you.'

'I try very hard not to.'

'Silly man.' They had moved on to other topics, both of them careful not to mention what she had done the night before. . . .

'More champagne, Kezia?'

'Mm?' She had drifted through the first glass without even noticing it. She had been thinking of other things: Edward; the new article she'd just been commissioned to write, a piece on the outstanding women candidates in the upcoming national elections. She had forgotten all about Whit, and the Marshes' party. 'Good Heavens, did I finish

34

that already?' She smiled at Whit again, and he looked at her quizzically.

'Still tired from the trip?'

'No, just a little dreamy. Drifting, I suppose.'

'That's quite a knack in a furore like this.' She exchanged her empty glass for a full one, and they found a secluded corner where they could watch the dance floor. Her eyes took in all the couples and she made rapid mental notes as to who was with whom, and who was wearing what. Opera divas, bankers, famous beauties, celebrated playboys, and an extravagance of rubies and sapphires and diamonds and emeralds.

'You look more beautiful than ever, Kezia.'

'You flatter me, Whit.'

'No. I love you.'

It was foolish of him to say it. They both knew otherwise. But she inclined her head demurely with a slender smile. Perhaps he did love her, after a fashion. Perhaps she even loved him, like a favourite brother or a childhood friend. He was a sweet man; it wasn't really difficult to like him. But love him? That was different.

'It looks as though the summer did you good.'

'Europe always does. Oh, no!'

'What?' He turned in the direction that had brought a look of dismay to her face, but it was too late. The Baron von Schnellingen was bearing down on them, with perspiration pouring from his temples, and a look of ecstasy at having spotted the pair.

'Oh Christ, tell him you've got the curse, and you can't dance,' Whit whispered.

Kezia burst into laughter, which the chubby little German Baron misinterpreted as delight.

'I am zo happy to zee you too, my dear. Good evening, Vitney. Kee-zee-ah, you are exquisite tonight.'

'Thank you, Manfred. You're looking well.' And hot and sweaty. And obese, and disgusting. And lecherous, as usual.

'It is a valtz. Chust for us. *Ja*?' *Nein*, but why the hell not? She couldn't say no. He was always sure to remind her

35

of how much he had loved her dear departed father. It was simpler to concede one waltz with him, for her 'father's sake.' At least he was a proficient dancer. At the waltz in any case. She bowed her head gently and extended a hand to be led to the floor. The Baron patted her hand ecstatically and led her away, just as Whit whispered in her ear, 'I'll rescue you right after the waltz.'

'You'd better, darling.' She said it through clenched teeth and a well-practised smile.

How could she ever explain something like this to Mark? She began to laugh to herself at the thought of explaining Mark and her anonymous forays into SoHo to anyone at the Maisonette that night. Surely the Baron would understand. He probably crept off to far more unusual places than SoHo, but he didn't expect Kezia to. No one did. Not Kezia, a woman, *the* Kezia Saint Martin . . . and that was different anyway. Like the other men she knew, the Baron conducted his adventures differently, and for different reasons . . . or was it different? Was she simply being a poor little rich girl running away to get laid and play with her Bohemian friends? Were any of them real to her? Sometimes she wondered. The Maisonette was real. Whit was real. The Baron was real. So real it made her feel hopeless at times. A gilded cage from which one never escapes. One never escapes one's name and one's face and one's ancestors and one's father or one's mother, no matter how many years they've been dead. One never escapes all the bullshit about *Noblesse oblige*. Or does one? Does one simply get on the subway with a token and a smile, never to return? The mysterious disappearance of the Honourable Kezia Saint Martin. No, if one leaves, one leaves elegantly and openly. With style. Not fleeing on a subway in total silence. If she really wanted SoHo, she had to say so, if only for her own sake. She knew that much. But was that what she wanted? How much better was SoHo than this? It was zabaglione instead of soufflé Grand Marnier. But neither was very nourishing. What she needed was good, wholesome steak. Counting on Mark's world for sustenance was

36

like hiding with a six-month supply of Oreo cookies and nothing else. She simply had one world to offset the other, one man to complement another, and the worst of it was that she knew it. Nothing was whole. . . . 'Am I?' She didn't realize that she had said it aloud.

'Are you vat?' the Baron cooed in her ear.

'Oh. Sorry. Am I stepping on your foot?'

'No, my beauty. Only my heart. And you dance like an angel.'

Nauseating. She smiled pleasantly and swirled in his arms. 'Thank you, Manfred.'

They swept gracefully about once more, and at last her eye met Whit's, as the waltz drew to a merciful close. She stood slightly apart from the Baron and thanked him again.

'But perhaps they play another?' His disappointment was almost childlike.

'You dance a very handsome waltz, sir.' Whitney was at their side, bowing slightly to the perspiring German.

'And you are a very lucky man, Vitney.' Kezia and Whit exchanged a beatific glance and Kezia bestowed a last smile on the Baron as they glided away.

'Still alive?'

'Very much so. And I've really been hopelessly lazy. I haven't talked to a soul tonight.' She had work to do and the evening was young.

'Want to stop and talk to some of your cronies now?'

'Why not? I haven't seen any of them since I got back.'

'Then onwards, milady. Let us throw ourselves to the lions, and see who's here.'

Everyone was, as Kezia had observed upon entering. And after a round of a dozen tables, and six or seven small groups standing near the dance floor, she was grateful to spot two of her friends. Whitney left her to them, and went to share a cigar with his senior partner. A little congenial talk over a good Monte Cristo never hurt. He waved her on her way, and vanished in a cluster of black and white emitting the pungent fumes of Havana's finest.

37

'Hi, you two.' Kezia joined two tall thin young women who seemed surprised to see her arrive.

'I didn't know you were back!' Cheeks almost met as kisses flew into midair, and the three looked at each other with pleasure. Tiffany Benjamin was more than a little drunk, but Marina Walters looked bright and alive. Tiffany was married to William Patterson Benjamin IV, the number two man in the biggest brokerage house on Wall Street. And Marina was divorced. And loved it that way, or so she said. Kezia knew otherwise.

'When did you get back from Europe?' Marina smiled at her, and appraised the dress. 'Hell of a neat dress, by the way. Saint Laurent?'

Kezia nodded.

'I thought so.'

'And so's yours, Madame Hawkeye.' Marina nodded pleased assent, but Kezia knew it for a copy. 'Christ, I got back two days ago, and I'm beginning to wonder if I was ever away.' Kezia spoke while keeping a casual eye on the room.

'I know the feeling. I got back last week, in time to get the kids back to school. By the time we'd done orthodontists, shoes, school uniforms, and three birthday parties, I forgot I'd ever been away. I'm ready for another summer. Where'd you go this year, Kezia?'

'The South of France, and I spent the last few days at Hilary's in Marbella. You, Marina?'

'The Hamptons all summer. Boring as hell. This was not my most glowing summer.'

Kezia raised an eyebrow. 'How come?'

'No men, or something like that.' She was creeping towards thirty-six and was thinking about having something done about the bags under her eyes. The summer before, she had had her breasts firmed up by 'the most marvellous doctor' in Zurich. Kezia had hinted at it in the column, and Marina had been livid.

Tiffany had been to Greece for the summer, and she had also spent a few days with distant cousins in Rome. Bill

38

had had to come home early. Bullock and Benjamin seemed to require the presence of its director almost constantly. But he thrived on it. He ate it and slept it and loved it. The Dow Jones ticked somewhere in his heart, and his pulse rate went up and down with the market. That was what Martin Hallam said in his column. But Tiffany understood; her father had been the same way. He had been the president of the Stock Exchange when he finally retired to a month of golf before the fatal heart attack. What a way to go, one foot on the Exchange, and the other on the golf course. Tiffany's mother's life was less dramatic. Like Tiffany, she drank. But less.

Tiffany was proud of Bill. He was an important man. Even more important than her father. Or her brother. And hell, her brother worked just as hard as Bill did. Gloria said so. Her brother was a corporate lawyer with Wheeler, Spaulding, and Forbes, one of the oldest firms on Wall Street. But the brokerage house of Bullock and Benjamin was the most important on the Street. It made Tiffany someone. Mrs. William Patterson Benjamin IV. And she didn't mind vacationing alone. She took the children to Gstaad at Christmas, Palm Beach in February, and Acapulco for spring vacation. In summer, they spent a month at the Vineyard with Bill's mother, and then off they went to Europe; Monte Carlo, Paris, Cannes, St. Tropez, Cap d'Antibes, Marbella, Skorpios, Athens, Rome. It was divine. Everything was divine, according to Tiffany. So divine that she was drinking herself to death.

'Isn't this the most divine party you've ever seen?' Tiffany was weaving slightly and watching her friends. Marina and Kezia exchanged a rapid glance, and Kezia nodded. She and Tiffany had gone to school together. She was a nice girl too, when she wasn't drunk. It was something Kezia would not put in the column. Everyone knew she drank, and it hurt to see her like that. It wasn't something amusing to read at breakfast, like Marina's boob lift. This was different, painful. Suicide by champagne.

39

'What's next on your agenda, Kezia?' Marina lit a cigarette, and Tiffany faded back into her glass.

'I don't know. Maybe I'll give a party.' After I write that article I landed today. . . .

'Christ, you've got courage. I look at something like this and I cringe. Meg spent eight months planning it. Are you on the Arthritis Committee again this year?'

Kezia nodded. 'They asked me about doing the Crippled Children's Ball too.' Tiffany awoke at the mention of that.

'Crippled children? How dreadful!' At least she hadn't said it was divine.

'What's dreadful about it? It's as good a ball as any of the others.' Marina was quick to the fiesta's defence.

'But crippled children? I mean really, who could stand to look at them?' Marina looked at her, annoyed.

'Tiffany darling, have you ever seen an arthritic at the Arthritis Ball?'

'No . . . I don't think so. . . .'

'Then you won't see any children at the Crippled Children's Ball either.' Marina was matter-of-fact, and Tiffany seemed appeased, while something slimy turned over in Kezia's stomach.

'I suppose you're right, Marina. Are you going to do the ball, Kezia?'

'I don't know yet. I haven't decided. I'm a little tired of the benefit circuit, frankly. I've been doing that stuff for a hell of a long time.'

'Haven't we all,' Marina echoed ruefully and flicked ashes into the waiter's silent butler.

'You should get married, Kezia. It's divine.' Tiffany smiled delightedly and lifted another glass of champagne from a passing tray. It was her third since Kezia had joined them. A waltz was beginning again at the far end of the room.

'And that, my friends, is my bad luck dance.' Kezia glanced around and inwardly groaned. Where in hell was Whit?

'Bad luck? How come?'

40

'That's how come.' Kezia nodded quickly in the direction of the approaching Baron. He had requested the dance, and had looked high and low for her for half an hour.

'Lucky you.' Marina grinned evilly, and Tiffany did her best to focus.

'And that, Tiffany my love, is why I don't get married.'

'Kezia! Our valtz!' It was useless to protest. She nodded gracefully at her friends and departed on the arm of the Baron.

'You mean she likes him?' Tiffany looked stunned. He was really very ugly. Even drunk she knew that much.

'No, you idiot. She means that with creeps like that hounding her, who has time to find a decent guy?' Marina knew the problem only too well. She had been scouting a second husband for almost two years, and if someone halfway decent didn't hurry along pretty damn soon, her settlement would fizzle out and her tits would fall again, and she'd get waffles on her ass. She figured she had about a year to hit it lucky before the roof fell in.

'I don't know, Marina. Maybe she does like him. Kezia's a little strange, you know. Sometimes I wonder if all that money coming to her so young affected her. I mean, after all, it would affect almost anyone. It's not like you can lead a normal life when you're one of the wealthiest . . .'

'Oh for chrissake, Tiffany, shut up. And why don't you go home and sober up for a change?'

'What a rotten thing to say!' There were tears in Tiffany's eyes.

'No, Tiffany. What a rotten thing to watch.' And with that, Marina turned on her heel and vanished in the direction of Halpern Medley. She had heard that he and Lucille had just broken up. That was the best time to get them. Frightened and bruised, scared to death to manage life on their own, missing the children, lonely at night. She had three children and would be more than happy to keep Halpern busy. He was an excellent catch.

On the dance floor, Kezia was whirling slowly in the

41

arms of the Baron. Whitney was engaged in earnest conversation with a young broker with long, elegant hands. The clock on the wall struck three.

Tiffany went to sit dizzily on a red velvet banquette at the back of the room. Where was Bill? He had said something about calling Frankfurt. Frankfurt? Why Frankfurt? She couldn't remember. But he had gone out to the lobby ... hours ago? ... and things were beginning to whirl. Bill? She couldn't remember if he had brought her tonight, or was he out of town and had she come with Mark and Gloria? Had she ... damn, why couldn't she remember? Let's see, she had had dinner at home with Bill and the children ... alone with the children? ... were the children still at the Vineyard with Mother Benjamin? ... was. . . . Her stomach began to spin slowly with the room and she knew she was going to be sick.

'Tiffany?' It was her brother, Mark, with that look on his face, and Gloria just behind him. A wall of reproach between her and the bathroom, wherever the hell it was at whatever goddamn hotel they were in, or was this somebody's house? She couldn't remember a fucking thing, dammit.

'Mark ... I ...'

'Gloria, take Tiffany to the ladies' room.' He didn't waste time speaking to his sister. He simply addressed his wife. He knew the signs too well. All over the seat of the new Lincoln last time they'd driven her home. And deep within Tiffany something withered further. She knew. That was the trouble. No matter how much she drank, she always knew. She could hear the tone in their voices so clearly. That never faded.

'I ... I'm sorry ... Mark, Bill is out of town and if you could just drive me ...' She belched loudly and Gloria rushed forward nervously while Mark shrank backwards with a look of disgust.

'Tiffany?' It was Bill, with his usual vague smile.

'I thought ... you were ...' Mark and Gloria faded into the background and Tiffany's husband took her arm and

42

escorted her as swiftly as possible from the halls where the last of the party was fading. She was too noticeable in the thinning crowd. 'I thought. . . .' They were moving through the lobby now, and she had left her bag on the banquette. Someone would take it. 'My bag. Bill, my . . .'

'That's right, dear. We'll take care of it.'

'I . . . oh God, I feel awful. I have to sit down.' Her voice was barely a whisper, and her bag was forgotten. He was walking too fast, it made her feel worse.

'You just need some air.' He kept a firm grip on her arm and smiled at passersby, the director on the way to his office . . . good morning . . . morning . . . hello . . . nice to see you. . . . The smile never faded, and the eyes never warmed.

'I just . . . I . . . oh.' The cool night breeze slapped her face and she felt clearer, but her stomach rose menacingly towards her throat. 'Bill. . . .' She turned and looked at him then, but only for a moment. She wanted to ask him a terrible question. Something was forcing her to say it. To ask. How awful. Oh God, she prayed that she wouldn't. Sometimes when she was very drunk she wanted to ask her brother the same thing. Once she had even asked her mother, and her mother had slapped her. Hard. The question always burned in her when she was this drunk. Champagne always did it to her, and sometimes gin.

'We'll just get you into a nice cosy cab, and you'll be all set, won't you dear.' He gently squeezed her arm again, like an overly solicitous headwaiter, and signalled the doorman. A cab stood with open door before them a moment later.

'A cab? Aren't you . . . Bill?' Oh God, and there was the question again, trying to fight its way out of her mouth, out of her stomach, out of her soul.

'That's right, dear.' Bill had leaned over to speak to the driver. He wasn't listening. Everyone spoke over her, around her, past her, never to her. She heard him give the driver their address and she grew more confused by the moment. But Bill looked so sure. 'See you in the morning, darling.' He pecked her cheek and the door slammed shut, and all she could see was the doorman's face smiling at her as the cab pulled away. She reached for the knob to open the window and frantically rolled it down ... and the question ... the question was fighting its way out. She couldn't hold it back any longer. She had to ask Bill ... William ... Billy ... they had to go back so she could ask, but the cab was lunging away from the kerb and the question sailed from her mouth with a long stream of vomit as she leaned out the window. 'Do you love me? ...'

The driver had been paid twenty dollars to get her home, and he did, without a word. He never answered the question. Nor did Bill. Bill had gone upstairs to the room he'd reserved at the St. Regis. Both girls were still waiting. A tiny Peruvian, and a large blonde from Frankfurt. And in the morning, Tiffany wouldn't even remember that she'd gone home alone. Bill was certain of that.

'Ready to go?'

'Yes, sir.' Kezia stifled a yawn and nodded sleepily at Whit.

'It was quite a party. Do you realize what time it is?'

She nodded and looked at the clock. 'Almost four. You're going to be dead at the office tomorrow.' But he was used to it. He was out almost every night in the week. Out, or at Sutton Place.

'And I can't lie in bed till noon like all of you indolent ladies.'

All of them? 'Poor, poor Whit. What a sad story.' She patted his cheek as they swept out the door and onto the deserted street. She couldn't lie in bed in the morning either. She had to start researching that new article, and wanted to be up by nine.

'Do we have anything like this on the agenda tomorrow, Kezia?' He hailed a passing cab and held the door open for her as she gathered up her blue satin skirt and settled onto the seat.

'God, I hope not. I'm out of training after the summer.'

Actually, her summer hadn't been so very different. But at least it had been blissfully devoid of the Baron.

'Come to think of it, I have a partners' dinner tomorrow night. But I think Friday there's something at the El Morocco. Are you going to be in town?' They were speeding up Park Avenue.

'As a matter of fact, I doubt it. Edward is trying to talk me into some deadly dull weekend thing with some old friends of his. They knew my father.' That was always a safe thing to say.

'Monday then. We'll have dinner at Raffles.' She smiled easily and leaned back onto his shoulder. She had lied to Whit after all. She had no plans with Edward, who knew better than to try to rope her into a weekend like the one she had described to Whit. She was going to SoHo. After tonight, she had earned it . . . and what did a little lie to Whitney matter? It was all for a good cause. Her sanity.

'Raffles on Monday sounds fine.' She'd need new material for the column by then anyway. And in the meantime, she could manage to get enough information by calling a few friends for a 'chat.' Marina was always an excellent source. And now she was going to be an excellent item as well. Her interest in Halpern Medley at the Maisonette had not gone unnoticed by Kezia. Nor had Halpern seemed indifferent to Marina. Kezia knew why Halpern was so interesting to her friend, and it was hard to blame her. Going broke was no fun, and Halpern was a most attractive remedy for what ailed her.

'I'll give you a call tomorrow or the day after, Kezia. Maybe we can sneak in a quick lunch. Lutèce, "21," we'll think of some place amusing.'

'I'm sure we will. Want to come up for a quick brandy, or coffee, or eggs or something?' It was the last thing she wanted, but she felt that she owed him something. Eggs if not sex.

'I really can't, darling. I'll be half blind at the office tomorrow as it is. I'd better get some sleep. And you too!' He wagged a finger at her as the cab drew to a halt at her door, and then kissed her ever so gently on the rim of her mouth, barely touching her lips.

'Good night, Whit. It was a lovely evening.' The preceding message was taped in Television City, Hollywood. . . .

'It's always a lovely evening with you, Kezia.' He walked her slowly to the door, and waited for the doorman to unlock it. 'Keep an eye on the papers tomorrow. I'm sure it'll be full of us. Even Martin Hallam will undoubtedly have something to say about that dress.' His eyes smiled at her appreciatively again, and he pecked her on the forehead while the doorman waited patiently. It was fascinating the way they had stopped pretending years before. A peck here and there, a grope, a feel, but she had claimed virginity long since, and he had greedily bought the story.

She waved as he walked away, and rode sleepily up to her floor. It felt good to be home. She unzipped the blue satin dress as she walked through the living room and deposited it on the couch where it could lie until Monday. Until doomsday for all she cared. What an insane way to make a living. It was like a lifetime of Halloween, trick or treat . . . getting all dressed up for a daily masquerade party to spy on your friends. This was the first 'season' when it had rankled right at the beginning. It usually took a few months to get to her. This year, the restlessness had come early.

She smoked a last cigarette, turned off the light, and it seemed as though only a few moments later the alarm was ringing. It was eight o'clock in the morning.

46

CHAPTER IV

Kezia did three hours of work on the new article, outlining, sketching what she thought she knew about the women she wanted to write about, and drafting letters to key people who could tell her something more about them. It was going to be a nice solid K. S. Miller piece, and she was pleased. After that she opened her mail and sifted through it. The usual spate of invitations, a couple of 'fan' letters forwarded to her by a magazine via her agent, and a memo from Edward about some tax shelters he wanted to look into with her. None of it was interesting and she was restless. She had another article in mind; maybe that would help. A piece on child abuse in middle-class homes. It would be a hot and heavy piece if Simpson could find a market for it. She wondered if the Marshes, with their parties for a cast of thousands, ever thought of that. Child abuse. Or the slums. Or the death penalty in California. None of them were 'in' causes. If they had been, surely there would have been a benefit for them, a 'fabulous' ball, or a 'marvellous little vernissage,' something 'absolutely super' staged by a committee of beauties . . . while Marina waited for a sale at Bendel's or hunted a good knock-off at Ohrbach's, and Tiffany announced the cause as 'divine'. . . . What was happening to her, dammit? Why did it matter if Marina tried to palm off her copies as originals? So what if Tiffany was drunk every day long before noon? So fucking what? But it bothered her. Oh God, how it bothered her. Maybe a good piece of ass would calm her nerves. She was in Mark's studio by twelve-thirty.

'Wow, lady, what's with you?'

'Nothing. Why?' She stood watching him work on a gouache. She liked it. She would have liked to buy it from him, but she couldn't do that, and she wouldn't let him give it to her. She knew he needed the money, and that was one commodity she was wise enough not to exchange with him.

'Well, you slammed the door, so I figured something must be bugging you.' He had given her back her keys.

'No, I'm just grumpy, I guess. Jet lag or something.' A smile broke through the anger in her eyes, and she dumped herself into a chair. 'I missed you last night. Sometimes I wish you wouldn't let me go anywhere.'

'Do I have that opinion?' He looked surprised and she laughed and kicked her shoes off.

'No.'

'That's what I thought.' It didn't seem to bother him, and Kezia was beginning to feel better.

'I like the gouache.' She looked over his shoulder as he stepped back to observe the morning's work.

'Yeah. Maybe it'll be okay.' He was demolishing a box of chocolate cookies and looking secretly pleased. Suddenly he turned to face her and slipped his arms around her. 'And what have you been up to since yesterday?'

'Oh, let's see. I read eight books, ran a mile, went to a ball, ran for president. The usual stuff.'

'And somewhere in all that bullshit lies the truth, doesn't it?' She shrugged and they exchanged a smile interspersed with kisses. He didn't really care what she did when she wasn't with him. He had his own life, his work, his loft, his friends. Her life was her own. 'Personally, I suspect that the truth is that you ran for president.'

'I just can't keep any secrets from you, Marcus.'

'No.' He said it while carefully unbuttoning her shirt. 'No secrets at all. . . . Now there's the secret I was looking for.' He tenderly uncovered one breast and leaned down to kiss it, as she slid her hands under his shirt and onto his back. 'I missed you, Kezia.'

'Not half as much as I mi   sed you.' A brief flash of the evening before raced through her mind. Visions of the dancing Baron. She pulled away from Mark then and

48

smiled at him for a long moment. 'You're the most beautiful man in the world, Mark Wooly.'

'And your slave.' She laughed at him, because Mark was no one's slave and they both knew it, and then, barefoot, she darted away from him and ran behind the easel, grabbing his box of chocolate cookies as she went.

'Hey!'

'Okay, Mark, now the truth will out. What do you love more? Me or your chocolate cookies?'

'What are you, crazy or something?' He chased her behind the easel but she fled to the bedroom doorway. 'I love my chocolate cookies! What do you think?'

'Ha ha! Well, I've got them!' She ran into the bedroom and leapt onto the bed, dancing from one foot to the other, laughing, her eyes sparkling, her hair flying around her head like a flock of silky ravens.

'Give me my chocolate cookies, woman! I'm addicted!'

'Fiend!'

'Yeah!' He joined her on the bed with a gleam in his eye, took the cookies from her and flung them to the sheepskin chair, then pulled her into a tight embrace.

'Not only are you a hopeless chocoholic, Mark Wooly, but you're a sex fiend too!' She laughed the laugh of her childhood as she settled into his arms.

'You know, maybe I'm addicted to you too.'

'I doubt it.' But he pulled her down beside him, and wrapped in laughter and her long black hair, they made love.

'What do you want for dinner?' She yawned and cuddled closer to him in the comfortable bed.

'You.'

'That was lunch.'

'So? There's a law that says I can't have for dinner what I had for lunch?' He rumpled her hair, and his mouth sought her lips.

'Come on, Mark, be serious. What else do you want? Besides chocolate cookies?'

49

'Oh ... steak ... lobster ... caviar ... the usual.' He didn't know just how usual it was. 'Oh shit, I don't know. Pasta, I guess. Fettuccine maybe. Al pesto? Can you get some basil? The fresh kind?'

'You're four months late. It's out of season. How about clam sauce?'

'You're on.'

'Then I'll see you in a bit.' She ran her tongue across the small of his back, stretched once more and then hopped out of bed, just out of reach of the hand he held out for her. 'None of that, Marcus. Later. Or we'll never get dinner.'

'Screw dinner.' The light in his eyes was reviving.

'Screw you.'

'That's just what I had in mind. Now you've got the picture.' He grinned broadly as he lay on his back and watched her dress. 'You're really no fun, Kezia, but you're pretty to watch.'

'So are you.' His long frame was stretched out lazily atop the sheets. It occurred to her as she looked at him that there was nothing quite so beautiful as the bold good looks of a very young man, a very handsome young man. . . .

She left the bedroom and returned with her string bag in hand, one of his shirts knotted just under her breasts above well-tailored jeans, her hair tied in a wisp of red ribbon.

'I ought to paint you like that'

'You ought to stop being so silly. I'll get a fat head. Any special requests?' He smiled, shook his head, and she was gone, off to the market.

There were Italian markets nearby, and she always liked to shop for him. Here, the food was real. Home-made pasta, fresh vegetables, oversized fruit, tomatoes to squeeze, a whole array of sausages and cheeses waiting to be felt and sniffed and taken home for a princely repast. Long loaves of Italian bread to carry home under your arm the way they did in Europe. Bottles of Chianti dancing from hooks near the ceiling.

It was a short walk, and it was the time of day when young artists began to come out of their lairs. The end of the day, when those who worked at night began to come alive, and those who worked by day needed to stretch and walk. Later there would be more people in the streets, wandering, talking, smoking grass, drifting, stopping in at the cafés, en route to the studios of friends or someone's latest sculpture show. It was friendly in SoHo; everyone was hard at work. Companions on a shared journey of the soul. Pioneers in the world of art. Dancers, writers, poets, painters, they congregated here at the southern tip of New York, locked between the dying filth and litter of Greenwich Village and the concrete and glass of Wall Street. This was a softer place. A world of friends.

The woman in the grocery store knew her well.

'Ah signorina, comè sta?'

'Bene grazie, e lei?'

'Così così. Un po' stanca. Che cosa vorebbe oggi?'

And Kezia wandered amidst the delicious smells and chose salami, cheese, bread, onions, tomatoes. Fiorella approved of her selections. Here was a girl who knew how to buy. She knew the right salami, what to put in a sauce, how a good Bel Paese should feel. She was a nice girl. Her husband was probably Italian. But Fiorella never asked.

Kezia paid and left with the string bag full. She stopped next door to buy eggs, and down the street she went into the delicatessen for three boxes of chocolate cookies, the kind he liked best. On her way back, she strolled slowly through the ever-thickening groups on the street. The aroma of fresh bread and salami wafted around her head, the smell of marijuana hung close by, the heavy scent of espresso drifted out of the cafés, while a rich twilight sky stretched overhead. It was a beautiful September, still warm, but the air felt cleaner than it usually did, and there were pink lights in the sky, like one of Mark's early water-colours, rich in pastels. Pigeons cooed and waddled down the street, and bicycles leaned against buildings; here and there a child skipped rope.

'What'd you get?' Mark was lying on the floor, smoking a joint.

51

'What you ordered. Steak, lobster, caviar. The usual.' She blew him a kiss and dropped the packages on the narrow kitchen table.

'Yeah? You bought steak?' He looked more disappointed than hopeful.

'No. But Fiorella says we don't eat enough salami. So I bought a ton of that.'

'Good. She must be a trip.' Before Kezia had come into his life, he had existed on navy beans and chocolate cookies. Fiorella was just another part of Kezia's mystery, one of her many gifts to him.

'She is a trip. A good trip.'

'So are you. So are you.' She stood in the kitchen doorway, her eyes alight, a twilight glow filling the room, and she looked back at Mark, sprawled on the floor.

'You know, once in a while I think I really love you, Marcus.'

'Once in a while I think I love you too.'

The look they shared said a multitude of things. There was no unpleasantness there, no pressure, no strain. No depth, but no hassles. There was merit in that, for both of them.

'Want to go for a walk, Kezia?'

'La passeggiata.'

He laughed softly at the word. She always called it that. 'I haven't heard that since you went away.'

'That's what it always is to me, down here. Uptown, people walk. They run. They go crazy. Here, they still know how to live. Like in Europe. *Le passeggiate*, the walks Italians take every evening at dusk, and at noon on Sundays, in funny little old towns where most of the women wear black and the men wear hats and white shirts, baggy suits and no ties. Proud farmers, good people. They check out their scene, greet their friends. They do it right, it's an institution to them. A ritual, a tradition, and I love it.' She looked content as she said it.

'So let's go do it.' He rose slowly to his feet, stretched and put an arm around her shoulders. 'We can eat when we get back.'

52

Kezia knew what that meant. Eleven, maybe twelve o'clock. First they would walk, and then they would run into friends and stop to chat on the street for a while. It would get dark and they would take refuge in someone's studio, so Mark could see the progress of a friend's latest work, and eventually the studio would grow crowded so they would all go to The Partridge for wine. And suddenly, hours later, they would be starving, and Kezia would be serving fettuccine for nine. There would be candles and music, and laughter and guitars, and joints passed around until they were tiny wisps of paper in somebody's roach clip. And Klee and Rousseau and Cassatt and Pollock would come alive in the room as their names flew among them. Paris in the days of the Impressionists must have been like that. Unloved outlaws of the art establishment banding together and forming a world of their own, to give each other laughter and courage and hope ... until one day, somebody found them, made them famous, and offered them caviar to replace the chocolate cookies. It was a shame really. For their sakes, Kezia almost hoped they would never leave the fettuccine and the dusty floors of their studios and their magic nights far behind them, because then they would wear dinner jackets and brittle smiles and sad eyes. They would dine at '21' and dance at El Morocco and go to parties at the Maisonette.

But Park Avenue was far from SoHo. A universe away. And the air was still rich with the last of summer, and the night was filled with smiles.

'Where are you off to, my love?'

'I have to go uptown to do some errands.'

'See ya later.' He wasn't paying attention to her; he was intent on a gouache.

She kissed the nape of his neck on her way past him and looked around the room with a brief, swift glance. She hated to go 'uptown.' It was as though she was always afraid she wouldn't find her way back. As though someone in her world would suspect what she'd been up to, where she had been, and might try to keep her from ever coming back here. The idea terrified her. She needed to come back, needed SoHo, and Mark, and all that they stood for. Silly really. Who could stop her from returning? Edward? Her father's ghost? How absurd. She was twenty-nine years old. Still, leaving SoHo felt like crossing the frontier into enemy territory, behind the Iron Curtain, on a scouting mission for the underground. It amused her to fantasize about it. And Mark's casual way of treating her comings and goings made it easier to float back and forth between both worlds. She laughed to herself as she ran lightly down the stairs.

It was a bright sunny morning and the subway let her out three blocks from her apartment, and the walk down Lexington Avenue and across Seventy-fourth Street was crisp. Nurses from Lenox Hill were dashing out to lunch, afternoon shoppers looked harassed, and traffic bleated angrily. Everything was so much faster here. Louder, darker, dirtier, more.

The doorman swept open the door and touched his cap. There were flowers waiting for her in the refrigerator kept by the building management for instances such as this. God forbid the roses should wilt while Madame was at the coiffeur - or in SoHo. It was the usual white box from Whit.

Kezia looked at her watch and made a rapid calculation. She had the day's calls to make on behalf of 'Martin Hallam,' snooping secretly for tidbits. And she also had the column she'd already finished which she still had to phone in to her agent. A quick bath, and then the meeting for the Arthritis Ball. First meeting of the year, and good meat for Martin Hallam. She could be back in SoHo by five, stop briefly at Fiorella's for provisions, and still be out for the nightly stroll with Mark. Perfect.

She called her service and collected her messages. A call from Edward. Two from Marina, and one from Whit, who wanted to confirm their lunch at '21' the following day. She returned the call, promised him her full attention at lunch.

thanked him for the roses, and listened patiently while he told her how much he missed her. Five minutes later she was in the bathtub, her mind far from Whit, and shortly thereafter she was drying herself in the big white Porthault towels discreetly monogrammed in pink. KHStM.

The meeting was at Elizabeth Morgan's house. Mrs. Angier Whimple Morgan. The third. She was Kezia's age, but looked ten years older, and her husband was trice her age. She was his third wife, the first two having conveniently died, augmenting his fortune handsomely. Elizabeth was still redoing the house. It just took 'forever to find the right pieces.'

Kezia was ten minutes late, and when she arrived, throngs of women were crowded into the hall. Two maids in crisp black uniforms offered tea sandwiches, and there was lemonade on a long silver tray. The butler was discreetly taking orders for drinks. And he was getting a lot more business than the long silver tray.

The couch and Louis XV *fauteuils* ('Imagine, eight of them, darling, from Christie's! And all in one day! You know, the Richley estate, and signed too!') were cluttered with the older women on the committee, enthroned like heads of state, clanking gold bracelets and covered with pearls, wearing 'good' suits and 'marvellous' hats, a host of Balenciaga and Chanel. They eyed the younger women carefully, criticism rich on their minds.

The room had a ceiling the height of two floors; the mantel was French, a 'marvellous' marble, Louis XVI, and the ghastly chandelier had been a wedding present from Elizabeth's mother. Fruitwood tables, an inlaid desk, an ormolu chest, Chippendale, Sheraton, Hepplewhite – it all looked to Kezia like Sotheby's the day before auction.

The 'girls' were given half an hour of grace before coming to order, and then their attention was demanded at the front of the room. Courtnay St. James was in charge.

'Well, ladies, welcome home from the summer. And doesn't everyone look just marvellous!' She was heftily

55

poured into a navy silk suit that crushed her ample bosom and struggled over her hips. A sapphire brooch of considerable size adorned her lapel, her pearls were in place, her hat matched her dress, and three or four rings that had been born with her hands waved her demi-glasses at the 'girls' as she spoke. 'And now, let's get organized for our marvellous, marvellous fete! It's going to be at the Plaza this year.' Surprise! Surprise! The Plaza and not the Pierre. How terribly, terribly exciting!

There was a murmur among the women, and the butler silently circulated his tray at the edge of the crowd. Tiffany was first on line, and seemed to weave as she stood, smiling amiably at her friends. Kezia looked away and let her eyes comb the crowd. They were all here, all the same faces, and one or two new ones, but even the newcomers were not strangers. They had just added this committee to their myriad others. There were no outsiders, no one who didn't belong. One couldn't let just anyone work on the Arthritis Ball, could one? 'But my dear, you must understand, you do remember who her mother was, don't you?' Last year, Tippy Walgreen had tried to introduce one of her strange little friends to the group. 'I mean, after all, everyone knew her mother was half-Jewish! I mean, really, Tippy, you'll *embarrass* the girl!'

The meeting droned on. Assignments were given. Meeting schedules decided. Twice a week for seven long months. It would give the women a reason for living and a motive for drinking – at least four martinis per meeting if they caught the butler's eye often enough. He would continue his rounds, ever discreet, while the pitcher of lemonade remained almost full.

As usual, Kezia accepted her role as head of the Junior Committee. As long as she was in town, it was useful for the column to do it. And it meant nothing more than being sure that all the right debutantes came to the Ball, and that a chosen few of them were allowed to lick stamps. An honour which would enchant their mothers. 'The Arthritis Ball, Peggy? How nifty!' Nifty ... nifty ... nifty....

56

The meeting broke up at five, with at least half of the women comfortably tight, but not so much so that they couldn't go home and face their husbands with the usual 'You know how Elizabeth is, she just forces it on you.' And Tiffany would tell Bill it had all been divine. If he came home. The gossip that Kezia was hearing about Tiffany these days was growing unpleasant.

The echoes she heard brought back other memories, memories that were long gone but would never quite be forgotten. Memories of reproaches she had heard from behind closed doors, warnings, and the sounds of someone violently sick to her stomach. Her mother. Like Tiffany. She hated watching Tiffany now. There was too much pain in her eyes, shoddily wrapped in 'divine' and bad jokes and that vague glazed look that said she didn't know exactly where she was or why.

Kezia looked at her watch in annoyance. It was almost five-thirty, and she didn't want to bother stopping at home to get out of the little Chanel number she'd worn. Mark would survive it. And with luck, he'd be too wrapped up in his easel to notice. If he ever got a chance to notice; at that hour it was almost impossible to catch a cab. She looked at the street in dismay. Not a vacant cab in sight.

'Want a ride?' The voice was only a few feet away, and she turned in surprise. It was Tiffany, standing beside a sleek navy blue Bentley with liveried chauffeur. The car was her mother-in-law's, as Kezia knew.

'Mother Benjamin lent me the car.' Tiffany looked apologetic. In the late afternoon sunlight, away from the world of parties and façades, Kezia saw a so much older version of her school friend, with wrinkles of sadness and betrayal around her eyes, and a sallow look to her skin. She had been so pretty in school, and still was, but she was losing it now. It reminded Kezia again of her mother. She could hardly bear to look into Tiffany's eyes.

'Thanks, love, but I don't want to take you out of your way.'

'Hell, you don't live very far . . . do you?' She smiled a

57

tired smile which made her look almost young again. As though being out with the grown-ups was just too much for her, and now it was time to go home. She had had just enough to drink to make her begin to forget things again. Kezia had lived in the same place for years.

'No, I don't live very far, Tiffie, but I'm not going home.'

'That's okay.' She looked so lonely, so in need of a friend. Kezia couldn't say no. Tears were welling up in her throat.

'Okay, thanks.' Kezia smiled and approached the car, forcing herself to think of other things. She couldn't cry in front of the girl, for God's sake. Cry about what? Her mother's death, twenty years later . . . or for this girl who was already halfway dead? Kezia wouldn't let herself think about it, as she sank into the gentle upholstery in the back seat. The bar was already open. 'Mother Benjamin' kept quite a stock.

'Harley, we're out of bourbon again.'

'Yes, madam.' Harley remained expressionless and Tiffany turned to Kezia with a smile.

'Want a drink?'

Kezia shook her head. 'Why don't you wait 'til you get home?' Tiffany nodded, holding the glass in her hand and gazing out the window. She was trying to remember if Bill was coming home for dinner. She thought he was in London for three days, but she wasn't sure if that was next week . . . or last week.

'Kezia?'

'Yes?' Kezia sat very still as Tiffany tried to make her mind stick to one thought.

'Do you love me?' Kezia was stunned, and Tiffany looked horrified. She had been absent-minded and it had slipped out. The question again. The demon that haunted her. 'I . . . I'm sorry . . . I . . . I was thinking of someone else. . . .' There were tears flooding Kezia's eyes now as Tiffany brought her gaze from the window to rest on Kezia's face.

58

'It's all right, Tiffie. It's okay.' She put her arms around her friend and there was a long moment of silence. The chauffeur glanced into the rearview mirror, then hastily averted his eyes and sat rigid, behind the wheel, patient, imperturbable and profoundly and eternally discreet. Neither of the young women noted his presence. They had been brought up to think that way. He waited a full five minutes while the women in the back seat sat hugged wordlessly and there was the sound of gentle weeping. He wasn't sure which woman was crying.

'Madam?'

'Yes, Harley?' Tiffany sounded very young and very hoarse.

'Where are we taking Miss Saint Martin?'

'Oh . . . I don't know.' She dried her eyes with one gloved hand, and looked at Kezia with a half smile. 'Where are you going?'

'I . . . the Sherry-Netherland. Can you drop me off there?'

'Sure.' The car had already started, and the two settled back in their seat, holding hands between fine beige kid and black suede and saying nothing. There was nothing either could say: too much would have to be said if either of them ever began to try. The silence was easier. Tiffany wanted to invite Kezia home to dinner, but she couldn't remember if Bill was in town, and he didn't like her friends. He wanted to be able to read the work he brought home after dinner, or go out to his meetings, without feeling he had to stick around and make chitchat. Tiffany knew the rules. No one to dinner, except when Bill brought them home. It had been years since she'd tried . . . that was why . . . that was how . . . in the beginning, she had been so lonely. With Daddy gone, and Mother . . . well, Mother . . . and she had thought babies of their own . . . but Bill didn't want them around either. Now the children ate at five-thirty with Nanny Singleton in the kitchen, and Nanny thought it 'unwise' for Tiffany to eat with them. It made the children 'uncomfortable.' So she ate alone in the dining room at seven-thirty. She wondered if Bill would be home for dinner tonight, or just how angry he would be if. . . .

'Kezia?'

'Hm?' Kezia had been lost in her own painful thoughts, and she had had a dull pain in her stomach for the last twenty minutes. 'Yes?'

'Why don't you come to dinner tonight?' She looked like a little girl with a brilliant idea.

'Tiffie . . . it . . . I . . . I'm sorry, love, but I just can't.' She couldn't do that to herself. And she had to see Mark. Had to. Needed to. Her survival came first, and the day had already been trying enough. 'I'm sorry.'

'That's okay. Not to worry.' She kissed Kezia gently on the cheek as Harley drew up to the Sherry-Netherland, and the hug they exchanged was ferocious, born of the longing of one and the other's remorse.

'Take good care, will you?'

'Sure.'

'Call me sometime soon?'

Tiffany nodded.

'Promise?'

'Promise.'

Tiffany looked old again as they exchanged a last smile, and Kezia waved once as she disappeared into the lobby. She waited five minutes and then came out and hailed a cab, and sped south to SoHo, trying to forget the anguish in Tiffany's eyes. Driving north, Tiffany poured herself one more quick Scotch.

'My God, it's Cinderella! What happened to my shirt?'

'I didn't think you'd notice. Sorry, love, I left it at my place.'

'I can spare it. It is Cinderella, isn't it? Or are you running for president again?' He was leaning against the wall, observing the day's work, but his smile told her he was glad she was back home with him.

'State senator, actually. Running for president is so

obvious.' She grinned at him and shrugged. 'I'll get out of this stuff and go get some food.'

'Before you do, Madam Senator . . .' He walked purposefully towards her with a mischievous grin.

'Oh?' The suit jacket was already off, her hair down, her blouse half-unbuttoned.

'Yes, "oh." I missed you today.'

'I didn't even think you'd notice I was gone. You looked busy when I left.'

'Well, I'm not busy now.' He swept her into his arms, her stockinged feet dangling over his arms, her black hair sweeping his face. 'You look pretty all dressed up. Sort of like that girl I saw in the paper while you were gone, but nicer. Much, much nicer. She looked like a bitch.' Kezia let her head fall back gently against his chest as she began to laugh.

'And I'm not a bitch?'

'Never, Cinderella, never.'

'What illusions you have.'

'Only about you.'

'Fool. Sweet, sweet fool. . . .' She kissed him gently on the mouth, and in a moment the rest of her clothes marked a path to his bed. It was dark by the time they got up.

'What time is it?'

'Must be about ten.' She stretched and yawned. It was dark in the apartment. Mark leaned out of bed to light a candle and then snuggled back into her arms. 'Want to go out for dinner?'

'No.'

'Me neither, but I'm hungry, and you didn't buy any food, did you?' She shook her head. 'I was in too much of a hurry to get home. Somehow I was more anxious to see you than to see Fiorella.'

'No big deal. We can sup on peanut butter and Oreos.'

She answered with a choking sound and a hand clasped to her throat. Then she laughed and they kissed and they made their way to the bathtub where they splashed each other generously before sharing his one purple towel. With no monogram. From Korvette's.

61

She was thinking, as she dried herself, that SoHo had come too late for her. Maybe at twenty it would have seemed real, perhaps then she might have believed it. Now it was fun ... special ... lovely ... Mark's, but not hers. Other places belonged to her, all those places she didn't even want, but inadvertently owned.

'Do you dig what you do, Kezia?' She paused for a long moment before answering, and then shrugged.

'Maybe yes, maybe no, maybe I don't even know.'

'Maybe you ought to figure it out.'

'Yeah. Maybe I should figure it out before noon tomorrow.' She had remembered the luncheon engagement with Whit.

'Is there some big deal tomorrow?' He looked puzzled, and she shook her head as they shared a handful of cookies and the last of the wine.

'Nope. No big deal tomorrow.'

'You made it sound like there was.'

'Nope. As a matter of fact, my love, I've just decided that when you reach my age very little is a "big deal." ' Not even you, or your lovemaking, or your sweet delicious young body, or my own bloody life. . . .

'May I quote you, Methuselah?'

'Absolutely. They've been quoting me for years.' And then in the clear autumn night, she laughed.

'What's so funny?'

'Everything. Absolutely everything.'

'I think you're drunk.' The idea amused him, and for a moment she wished that she were.

'Only a little drunk on life maybe ... your kind of life.'

'Why my kind of life? Can't this be your kind of life too? What's so different about your life and my life for christsake?'

Oh Jesus. This wasn't the time.

'The fact that I'm running for state senator, of course!'

He pulled her around to face him as she tried to laugh him off.

'Kezia, why can't you be straight with me? Sometimes

62

you give me the feeling that I don't even know who you are.' His grip on her arm troubled her, almost as much as the question in his eyes. But she only shrugged with an evasive smile. 'Well, I'll tell you, Cinderella, whoever you are, I think you're gassed.' They both laughed as she followed him into the bedroom, and she wiped two silent, unseen tears from her cheeks. He was a nice boy, but he didn't know her. How could he? She wouldn't let him know her. He was only a boy.

CHAPTER V

'Miss Saint Martin, how nice to see you!'

'Thank you, Bill. Is Mr. Hayworth here yet?'

'No, but we have the table waiting. May I show you in?'

'No, thank you. I'll wait at the fireplace.'

The '21' Club was crammed with lunch-hungry bodies. Business executives, high-fashion models, well-known actors, producers, the gods of the publishing world, and a handful of dowagers. The Scions of Meccas. The restaurant was alive with success. The fireplace was a peaceful corner where Kezia could wait before entering the whirling currents with Whit. '21' was fun but she wasn't quite in the mood.

She hadn't wanted to come to lunch. It was strange the way it was all getting a little bit harder. Maybe she was getting too old for a double life. Her thoughts turned to Edward. Maybe she'd see him at '21' for lunch, but he was more likely to be found at Lutèce or the Mistral. His luncheon leanings were usually French.

'How do you suppose the children would feel about it if we took them to Palm Beach? I don't want them to feel I'm pushing out their father.' The wisp of conversation made Kezia turn her head. Well, well, Marina Walters and

Halpern Medley. Things were certainly progressing. Item One for tomorrow's news. They hadn't seen her discreetly folded in one of the large red leather chairs. The advantage of being small. And quiet.

And then she saw Whit, elegant and youthful and tanned, in a dark grey suit and Wedgewood blue shirt. She waved at him and he walked over to her chair.

'You're looking awfully well today, Mr. Hayworth.' She held out a hand to him from her comfortable seat, and he kissed her wrist lightly, then clasped her fingers loosely in his.

'I feel a lot better than I did with a jeroboam of champagne under my belt the other night. How did you weather that?'

'Very nicely, thank you. I slept all day,' she lied. 'And you?' She smiled at him and they began to thread their way towards the dining room.

'Don't make me jealous. Your sleep-ins are an outrage!'

'Ah, Mr. Hayworth! Miss Saint Martin . . .' the head-waiter led them to Whitney's customary table, and Kezia settled in and looked around. Same old faces, same old crowd. Even the models looked familiar. Warren Beatty sat at a corner table, and Babe Paley had just walked in.

'What did you do last night, Kezia?' Her smile was one he could not read.

'I played bridge.'

'You look like you must have won.'

'As a matter of fact, I did. I've been on a winning streak since I got home.'

'I'm glad for you. Me, I've been losing at backgammon consistently for the past four weeks. Bitching rotten luck.' But he didn't look overly worried, as he patted her hand gently and signalled to the waiter. Two Bloody Marys and a double steak tartare. The usual. 'Darling, do you want wine?' She shook her head. The Bloody Marys would be fine.

It was a quick lunch; he had to be back in the office at two. Now that the summer was over, it was business as usual: new wills, new trusts, new babies, new divorces, new season. It was almost like a whole new year. Like children returning to school, socialites marked the years by 'the season', and the season had just begun.

'Will you be in town this weekend, Kezia?' He seemed distracted as he hailed her a cab.

'No. Remember? I have that weekend thing with Edward.'

'Oh, that's right. Good. Then I won't feel like such a meanie. I'm going to Quogue with some business associates. But I'll call you on Monday. Will you be all right?' The question amused her.

'I'll be fine.' She slid gracefully into the cab, and smiled up into his eyes. Business associates, darling? 'Thanks for the lunch.'

'See you Monday.' He waved again as the cab pulled away, and she sighed comfortably from the back seat. Finito. She was off the hook till Monday. But suddenly, there was nothing but lies.

The weekend was perfect. Bright sunny skies, a light breeze, little pollution and a low pollen count, and she and Mark had painted the bedroom a bright cornflower blue. 'In honour of your eyes,' he told her as she worked diligently around the window. It was a bitch of a job, but when they had finished, they were both immensely pleased.

'How about a picnic to celebrate?' He was in high spirits and so was she.

She ran down to Fiorella's for provisions, while he called around to borrow a car. A friend of George's offered his van.

'Where are we going, sire?'

'Treasure Island. My own treasure island.' And he began to sing snatches of absurd songs about islands, interspersed with a great many cackles and guffaws.

'Mark Wooly, you're a madman.'

'That's cool, Cinderella. As long as you dig it.' There was no malice in the 'Cinderella'. They were too happy and it was too fine a day. And Mark had never been malicious.

He took her to a little island in the East River, a nameless gem near Randall's Island. They looped off the highway, and through litter and a bumpy little road that seemed to go nowhere, crossed a small bridge, and suddenly ... magic! A lighthouse and a crumbling castle all their own.

'It looks like the fall of the House of Usher.'

'Yes, and it's all mine. And now it's yours, too. Nobody ever comes here.' New York gazed sombrely at them from across the river, the United Nations, the Chrysler Building and the Empire State looking sleek and polite, as the happy pair lay on the grass and opened a bottle of Fiorella's best Chianti. Tugboats and ferries floated past, and they waved to captains and crewmen and laughed at the sky.

'What a beautiful day!'

'Yeah, it really is.' He put his head in her lap and she leaned down and kissed him.

'Want some more wine, Mr. Wooly?'

'No, just a slice of the sky.'

'At your service, sir.'

Clouds were gathering, and it was four in the afternoon when the first lightning flashed past the clouds.

'I think you're going to get that slice of sky you ordered. In about five minutes. See how good I am to you? Your wish is my command.'

'Baby, you're terrific.' He sprang to his feet and flung out his arms, and in five minutes it was pouring rain and lightning flashed and thunder roared, and they ran around the island together hand in hand, laughing and soaked to the skin.

When they got home, they showered together, and the hot water felt prickly on their chilled bodies. They walked naked into the new blue bedroom, and lay peacefully in each other's arms.

She left him at six the next morning. He slept like a child, his head on his arms, his hair hiding his eyes, his lips soft to her touch.

'Goodbye, my beloved, sleep tight.' She kissed him gently on one temple, and whispered into his hair. It would be noon before he awoke, and she would be far from him by then. In a different world, chasing dragons, making choices.

CHAPTER VI

'Good morning, Miss Saint Martin. I'll tell Mr. Simpson you're here.'

'Thanks, Pat. How've you been?'

'Busy, crazy. Seems like everyone has a new idea for a book after the summer. Or a new manuscript, or a royalty cheque that got lost.'

'Yeah, I know what you mean.' Kezia smiled ruefully, thinking of her own plans for a book.

The secretary took a quick look at her desk, gathered up some papers, and disappeared behind a heavy oak door. The literary agency of Simpson, Wells, and Jones did not look very different from Edward's law firm, or Whit's office, or the brokerage house that had the bulk of her account. This was serious business. Long shelves of books, wood panelling, bronze door handles, and a thick carpet the colour of Burgundy wine. Sober. Impressive. Prestigious. She was represented by a highly reputable firm. It was why she had felt comfortable sharing her secret with Jack Simpson. He knew who she was, and only he and Edward knew of her numerous aliases. And Simpson's staff, of course, but they were unfailingly discreet. The secret had remained well guarded.

'Mr. Simpson will see you now, Miss Saint Martin.'

'Thank you, Pat.'

He was waiting for her on his feet behind the desk, a kindly man close to Edward's age, balding and grey at the temples, with a broad fatherly smile, and comforting hands. They shook hands as they always did. And she settled into the chair across from him, stirring the tea Pat had provided. It was peppermint tea today. Sometimes it was English Breakfast, and in the afternoon it was always Earl Grey. Jack Simpson's office was a haven for her, a place to relax and unwind. A place for excitement about the work she had done. She was always happy there.

'I have another commission for you, my dear.'

'Lovely. What?' She looked up expectantly over the gold-rimmed cup.

'Well, let's talk for a moment first.' There was something different in his eyes today. Kezia wondered what it was. 'This is a little different from what you usually do.'

'Pornography?' She sipped the tea and half suppressed a smile. Simpson chuckled.

'So that's what you want to do, is it?' She laughed back at him and he lit a cigar. These were from Dunhill, not Cuba. She sent him a box every month. 'Well, I'm sorry to disappoint you then. It's definitely not pornography. It's an interview.' He watched her eyes carefully. She so easily got the look of a hunted doe. There were some zones of her life where even he would not dare to tread.

'An interview?' Something closed in her face. 'Well, then I guess that's that. Anything else on the agenda?'

'No, but I think we ought to talk about this a little further. Have you ever heard of Lucas Johns?'

'I'm not sure. The name says something to me, but I can't place it.'

'He's a very interesting man. Mid-thirties, spent six years in prison in California for armed robbery, and served his sentence in Folsom, San Quentin – all the legendary horror spots one hears about. Well, he lived through them, and survived. He was among the first to organize labour unions inside the prisons, and make a lot of noise about prisoners' rights. And he still keeps a hand in it now that he's out. I gather that's his whole life; he lives for the cause of abolishing prisons, and bettering the prisoners' lot in the meantime. Even refused his first parole because he hadn't finished what he'd started. The second time they offered him parole, they didn't give him a choice. They wanted him out of their hair, so he got out and got organized on the outside. He's had a tremendous impact on the public awareness in terms of what really happens in our prisons. Matter of fact, he wrote a very powerful book on the subject when he first got out a year or two ago, can't quite remember when. It got him a lot of speaking engagements, television appearances, that sort of thing. And it's all the more amazing that he'd do that, since he's still on parole. I imagine it must be risky for him to remain controversial.'

'I would think so.'

'He served six years of his sentence, but he's not a free man. As I understand it, they have some sort of system in California called the indeterminate sentence, which means you get sentenced rather vaguely. I think in his case the sentence was five years to life. He served six. I suppose he could have served ten or twenty, at the discretion of the prison authorities, but I imagine they got tired of having him around. To say the least.'

Kezia nodded, intrigued. Simpson had counted on that.

'Did he kill anyone in the robbery?'

'No, I'm fairly certain he didn't. Just hell-raising, I think. He had a rather wild youth, from what I gathered in his book. Got most of his education in prison, finished high school, got a college degree, and a master's in psychology.'

'Industrious in any case. Has he been in trouble since he got out?'

'Not that kind of trouble. He seems to be past that now. The only trouble I'm aware of is that he is dancing a tightrope with the publicity he gets for his agitation on behalf of prisoners. And the reason for this interview now is that he has another book coming out, a very uncompromising exposé of existing conditions, and his views on the subject are sort of a follow-up to the first book, but a good deal more brutal. It's going to create quite a furore, from what I hear. This is a good time for a piece about

69

him, Kezia. And you'd be a good one to write it. You did those two articles on the prison riots in Mississippi last year. This isn't unfamiliar territory to you, not entirely.'

'This isn't a documented piece on a news event either. It's an interview, Jack.' Her eyes sought his and held them. 'And you know I don't do interviews. Besides, he's not talking about Mississippi. He's talking about California prisons. And I don't know anything more about them than what I read in the paper, just like everyone else.' It was a weak excuse, and they both knew it.

'The principles are the same, Kezia. You know that. And the piece we've been offered is about Lucas Johns, not the California prison system. He can tell you plenty about that. You can read his first book for that matter. That'll tell you all you need to know, if you can stomach it.'

'What's he like?'

Simpson restrained a smile at the question. Maybe . . . maybe . . . He frowned and replaced his cigar in the ashtray. 'Strange, interesting, powerful, very closed and very open. I've seen him speak, but I've never met him. One gets the impression that he'll tell anyone anything about prisons, but nothing about himself. He'd be a challenge to interview. I'd say he's very guarded, but appealing in an odd way. He looks like a man who fears nothing because he has nothing to lose.'

'Everyone has something to lose, Jack.'

'You're thinking of yourself, my dear, but some don't. Some have already lost all they care about. He had a wife and child before he went to prison. The child died in a hit-and-run accident, and the wife committed suicide two years before his release. Maybe he's one of those who has already lost. . . . Something like that can break you. Or give you an odd kind of freedom. I think he has that. He's something of a god to those who know him well. You'll hear a lot of conflicting reports about him – warm, loving, kind, or ruthless, brutal, cold. It depends on whom you speak to. In his own way, he's something of a legend, and a mystery. No one seems to know the man underneath.'

'You seem to know a lot about him.'

'He interests me. I've read his book, seen him speak, and I did a little research before I asked you to come in and discuss this with me, Kezia. It's just the kind of piece I think you might be brilliant with. In his own way, he's as hidden as you are. Maybe it'll teach you something. And it's going to be a piece that will be noticed.'

'Which is precisely why I can't do it.' She was suddenly firm again, but for a little while she had wavered. Simpson still had hope.

'Oh? Obscurity is now something you desire?'

'Not obscurity, discretion. Anonymity. Peace of mind. None of this is new to you. We've gone over it before.'

'In theory. Not in practice. And right now you have a chance to do an article that would not only interest you, but would be an extremely good opportunity for you professionally, Kezia. I can't let you pass that up. Not without telling you why I think you ought to do it, in any case. I think you'd be a fool not to.'

'And a bigger fool yet if I did it. I can't. I have too much at stake. How could I even interview him without causing a certain "furore" myself, as you call it. From what you're telling me, he's not a man who passes unnoticed. And just how long do you think it would take for someone else to notice me? Or Johns himself, for that matter. He'd probably know who I am.' She shook her head with certainty now.

'He's not that sort of man, Kezia. He doesn't give a damn about the social register, the debutante cotillions or anything else that happens in your world. He's too busy in his own. I'd be willing to bet he's never even heard your name. He's from California, he bases himself in the Midwest now, he's probably never been to Europe, and you can be damn sure that he doesn't read the social pages.'

'You can't be sure of that.'

'I'd almost swear to it. I can sense what he is, and I already know what he cares about. Exclusively. He's a rebel, Kezia. A self-educated, intelligent, totally devoted

71

rebel. Not a playboy. For God's sake, girl, be sensible. This is your career you're playing with. He's giving a speech in Chicago next week, and you could cover that easily, and quietly. An interview with him in his offices the next day, and that's it. No one at the speech will know you, and I'm certain that he won't. There's no reason at all why K. S. Miller won't cover you adequately. And that's all he'll know or care about. He'll be much more interested in the kind of coverage you're giving him than in what you do with your private life. That's just not the sort of thing he thinks about.'

'Is he a homosexual?'

'Possibly, I don't know. I don't know what a man does during six years in prison. Nor does it matter. The point is what he stands for, and how he stands for it. That's the crux here. And if I thought, even for a moment, that writing this piece would cause you embarrassment, I wouldn't suggest it. You should know that by now. All I can tell you is that I am emphatically sure that he won't have the faintest idea about, or interest in, your private life.'

'But there's no way you can be sure of that. What if he's an adventurer, a sharp con man, who picks up on who I am, and figures out some angle where that could be useful to him? He could turn right around and have me all over the papers just for interviewing him.'

Simpson began to look impatient. He stubbed out the cigar.

'Look, you've written about events, places, political happenings, psychological profiles. You've done some excellent work, but you've never done a piece like this. I think you could do it. And do it well. And I think you should. It's a major opportunity for you, Kezia. And the point is: are you a writer or not?'

'Obviously. But it just seems terribly unwise to me. Like a breach of my personal rules. I've had peace for seven years because I've been totally, utterly, and thoroughly careful. If I start doing interviews now, and if I do this one . . . there will be others, and . . . no. I just can't.'

'Why not at least give it some thought? I have his last book, if you want to read it. I really think you should at least do that much before you make up your mind.'

She hesitated for a long moment and then nodded carefully. It was the only concession she would make; she was still sure she wouldn't do the piece. She couldn't afford to. Maybe Lucas Johns had nothing left to lose, but she did; she had everything to lose. Her peace of mind, and the carefully guarded secret life she had taken so long to build. That life was what kept her going. She wouldn't do anything to jeopardize it, not for anyone. Not for Mark Wooly, not for Jack Simpson, and not for some unknown ex-con with a hot 'cause'. To hell with him. No one was worth it.

'All right, I'll read the book.' She smiled for the first time in half an hour, then shook her head ruefully. 'You certainly know how to sell your arguments. Wretch!'

But Simpson knew he had not yet convinced her. All he could hope was that her own curiosity and Lucas Johns' written words would do the job. He felt in his bones that she had to do this one, and he was seldom wrong.

'Simpson, you really are a first-water wretch! You make it sound like my whole career depends on this . . . or my life even.'

'Perhaps it does. And you, my dear, are a first-water writer. But I think you're getting to a point when you have to make some choices. And the fact is that they're not going to be easy whether you make them now, over this particular article, or later, over something else. My main concern is that you make those choices, and don't just let life, and your career, pass you by.'

'I didn't think that "life" or my career was passing me by." She raised an eyebrow cynically, amused. It was unlike him to be so concerned, or so outspoken.

'No, you've done well until now. There has been a healthy progression, a good evolution, but only to a point. The crunch is bound to come sometime though. That moment when you can't "get by" anymore, when you can't

73

just "organize" everything to suit all your needs. You'll have to decide what you really want, and act on it.'

'And you don't think I've been doing that?' She was surprised when he shook his head.

'You haven't had to. But I think it's time you did.'

'Such as?'

'Such as who do you want to be? K. S. Miller, writing serious pieces that could really further your career, or Martin Hallam tattling on your friends under a pseudonym, or the Honourable Kezia Saint Martin sweeping in and out of debutante balls and the Tour d'Argent in Paris? You can't have it all, Kezia. Not even you.'

'Don't be absurd, Simpson.' He was making her distinctly uncomfortable, and all over this article about an ex-convict labour agitator. Nonsense. 'You know perfectly well that the Hallam column is a joke to me,' she said, annoyed. 'I never really took it seriously, and certainly not in the last five years. And you also know that my career as K. S. Miller is what really matters to me. The deb parties and dinners at the Tour d'Argent, as you put it,' she glowered at him pointedly, 'are something I do to pass time, out of habit, and to keep the Hallam column lively. I don't sell my soul for that way of life.' But she knew too well that that was a lie.

'I'm not sure that's true, and if it is you might well find that sooner or later the price you will have to pay is your soul, or your career.'

'Don't be so dramatic.'

'Not dramatic. Honest. And concerned.'

'Well, don't be "concerned", not in that area. You know what I have to do, what's expected of me. You don't change hundreds of years of tradition in a few short years at a typewriter. Besides, lots of writers work under pseudonyms.'

'Yes, but they don't live under pseudonyms. And I disagree with you about changing traditions. You're right on one score, you don't change traditions in a few years. You change them suddenly, brutally, with a bloody revolution.'

'I don't think that's necessary.'

'Or "civilized", is that it? No, you're right, it's not civilized. Revolution never is, and change is never comfortable. I'm beginning to think you ought to read Johns' book for your own sake. In your own way, you've been in prison for almost thirty years.' His voice softened as he looked into her eyes. 'Kezia, is that how you want to live? At the expense of your happiness?'

'It isn't a question of that. And sometimes there's no choice.' She looked away from him, partly annoyed, partly hurt.

'But that's precisely what we're discussing. And there is always a choice.' Or didn't she see that? 'Are you going to live your life for an absurd "duty", to please your trustee ten years after you come of age? Are you going to cater to parents who have been dead for twenty years? How can you possibly expect that of yourself? Why? Because they died? That's not your fault for God's sake, and times have changed; you've changed. Or is this what that young man you're engaged to expects of you? If that's the case, perhaps the time will come when you'll have to choose between him and your work, and maybe you'd best face that now.'

What man? Whit? How ridiculous. And why was Simpson bringing all of this up now? He had never mentioned any of this before. Why now? 'If you mean Whitney Hayworth, I'm not engaged to him, and never will be. He could never cost me anything except a very dull evening. So you're worrying for naught on that score.'

'I'm glad to hear it. But then what is it, Kezia? Why the double life?' She sighed deeply and looked down at her hands folded in her lap.

'Because somewhere along the way they convince you that if you drop the Holy Grail for even one instant, or put it aside for a day, the entire world will collapse, and it will all be your fault.'

'Well, I'll tell you a well-hidden secret, it won't. The world will not end. Your parents will not haunt you; your

75

trustee won't even commit suicide. Live for yourself, Kezia. You really have to. How long can you live a lie?'

'Is a pseudonym a lie?' It was a weak defence, and she knew it.

'No, but the way you handle it is. You use your pseudonyms to keep two lives totally estranged from each other. Two sides of you. One is duty and the other is love. You're like a married woman with a lover, prepared to give up neither. I think that's an awesome burden to carry. And an unnecessary one.' He looked at his watch and shook his head with a small smile. 'And now, I apologize. I've railed at you for almost an hour. But these are things I've wanted to discuss with you for a very long time. Do what you want on the Johns article, but give a little thought to what we've said. I think it's important.'

'I suspect you're right.' She was suddenly exhausted. The morning had drained her. It was like watching her whole life pass before her eyes. And how insignificant it looked in review. Simpson was right. She didn't know what she'd do about the Johns piece, and that wasn't the point. The point went a great deal deeper than that. 'I'll read the Johns book tonight.'

'Do that, and call me tomorrow. I can hold the magazine off till then. And will you forgive me for preaching?'

She smiled at him, a warmer smile. 'Only if you'll let me thank you. You didn't say anything I wanted to hear, but I think I needed to hear it. I've been thinking along those lines myself lately, and this morning arguing with you was like arguing with myself. Sweet schizophrenia.'

'Nothing as exotic as that. And you're not unique; others have fought the same battle before you. One of them should have written a book on how to survive it.'

'You mean others have survived it?' She laughed over a last sip of her tea.

'Very nicely in fact.'

'And then what did they do? Run off with the elevator man to prove their point?'

'Some. The stupid ones. The others find better solutions.'

76

She tried not to think of her mother.

'Like Lucas Johns?' She didn't know why, but it had just slipped out. The idea was absurd. Almost funny.

'Hardly. I wasn't suggesting that you marry him, my dear. Only interview him. No wonder you made such a fuss.' Jack Simpson knew the real reasons for the fuss. She was afraid. And in his own way, he had tried to calm her fears. Only one interview ... once. It could change so much for her – broaden her horizons, bring her out in the open, make her a writer. If only all went well. It was only because he knew the chances of her being 'found out' were so unlikely that he'd even encouraged it. She would hide forever if she got burned on this one, and he knew it. Neither of them could afford that. He had thought it all over with great care, before suggesting the article to her.

'You know, you made a great deal of sense today, Jack. I must admit, lately the "mystery" has been wearing thin. It loses its charm after a while.' And what he had said had been true. She was like a married woman with a lover. She had just never thought of it that way ... Edward, Whit, the parties, the committees; and then Mark and SoHo and picnics on magical islands; and separate from all that, her work. Nothing fit. It was all separate and hidden, and had long since begun to tear her apart. To what and to whom did she owe her first allegiance? To herself, of course, but it was so easy to forget that. Until someone reminded her, as Jack Simpson had just done. 'Will you tolerate a hug, kind sir?'

'Not tolerate – appreciate, my dear. I would thoroughly enjoy it.' She gave him a brief squeeze and a smile as she prepared to leave.

'It's a damn shame you didn't make that speech ten years ago. It's almost a little late now.'

'At twenty-nine? Don't be foolish. Now go away, and read that book, and call me tomorrow morning.' She left him with a last wave of a brown-kid-gloved hand, and a flurry of long suede coat.

The book jacket in her hand looked unimpressive as

77

she perused it in the elevator. There was no photograph of Lucas Johns on the back, only a brief biography which told her less about him than Simpson had. It was odd, though; from what she had heard that morning, she already had a clear picture of the man. She anticipated something mean in his face, was sure he was short, stocky, hard, and perhaps overweight – and pushy as hell. Six years in prison had to do strange things to a man, and it surely couldn't add to his beauty. Armed robbery too ... a little fat man in a liquor store with a gun. And now he was respected, and she was being offered a chance to interview him. Still, despite all the talk with Simpson, she knew she couldn't do that. He had made some good points about her life ... but an interview with Lucas Johns, or anyone, was still out of the realm of the possible, or the wise.

She did something foolish then. She went to lunch with Edward.

'I don't think you should do it.' He was emphatic.

'Why not?' It was almost like setting a trap for him; she knew what he'd say. But she couldn't resist the urge to bait him.

'You know why not. If you start doing interviews, it's only one step away from someone catching on to what you're up to. You might get away with this one, Kezia. But sooner or later . . .'

'So you think I should hide forever?'

'You call this hiding?' He waved a hand demonstratively around the hallowed halls of La Caravelle.

'In a sense, yes.'

'In the sense you mean, I think that's wise.'

'And what about my life, Edward? What about that?'

'What about it? You have everything you want. Your friends, your comfort, and your writing. Could you possibly ask for more, except a husband?'

'That isn't on my list to Santa Claus anymore, darling. And yes, I could ask for more. Honesty.'

'You're splitting hairs. And what you'd be risking for

78

that kind of honesty would be your privacy. Remember the job you wanted so badly at the *Times* years ago?'

'That was different.'

'How?'

'I was younger. And that wasn't a career, it was a job, and something I wanted to prove.'

'Isn't this the same thing?'

'Maybe not. Maybe it's a question of my sanity.'

'Good heavens, Kezia, don't be ridiculous. You're all wound up with whatever nonsense Simpson levelled at you this morning. Be reasonable, the man has a vested interest in you. He's looking at it from his point of view, not yours. For his benefit, not yours.'

But she knew that wasn't true. And what she also knew now was that Edward was afraid. Even more afraid than she was. But of what? And why? 'Edward, no matter how you slice it, one of these days I'm going to have to make a choice.'

'Over an interview for a magazine? An interview with some jailbird?' He wasn't afraid, he was terrified. Kezia almost felt sorry for him as she realized what it was he so feared. She was slipping away from the last of his grasp.

'This interview really isn't the issue, Edward. We both know that. Even Simpson knows that.'

'Then what in God's name is the issue? And why are you making all these strange noises about sanity and freedom and honesty? None of it makes any sense. Is someone in your life putting pressure on you?'

'No. Only myself.'

'But there is someone in your life I don't know about, isn't there?'

'Yes.' The honesty felt good. 'I didn't know you expected to be kept informed of *all* my doings.'

Edward looked away, embarrassed. 'I just like to know that you're all right. That's all. I assumed that there was someone other than Whit.'

Yes, darling, but did you assume why? Surely not. 'You're right, there is.'

'He's married?' He seemed matter-of-fact about it.

'No.'

'He isn't? I was rather sure he was.'

'Why?'

'Because you're so ... well, discreet, I suppose. I just assumed he was married, or something of the sort.'

'Nothing of the sort. He's free, twenty-three years old, and an artist in SoHo.' That ought to take Edward a while to digest. 'And just for the record, I don't support him. He's on welfare and he loves it.' She was almost enjoying herself now and Edward looked as though he might have a fit of the vapours.

'Kezia!'

'Yes, Edward?' Her voice was pure sugar.

'And he knows who you are?'

'No, and he couldn't care less.' She knew that wasn't entirely true, but she also knew he would never go to any trouble to snoop into the other side of her life. He was just curious in a boyish sort of way.

'Does Whit know about all this?'

'No. Why should he? I don't tell him about my lovers and he doesn't tell me about his. It's an even exchange. Besides, darling, Whitney prefers boys.' She had not anticipated the look on Edward's face; it was not one of total astonishment.

'Yes ... I ... I've heard. I wondered if you knew.'

'I do.' Their voices were quiet now.

'He told you?'

'No, someone else did.'

'I'm sorry.' He looked away and patted her hand.

'Don't be, Edward. It didn't matter to me. That sounds like a harsh thing to say, but I've never been in love with Whit. We're merely a convenience to each other. That's not very pretty to admit, but it's a fact.'

'And this other man – the artist – is it serious?'

'No, it's pleasant, and easy, and fun, and a relief from some of the pressures in my life. That's all it is, Edward. Don't worry, no one's going to run off with the piggy bank.'

80

'That isn't my only concern.'

'I'm glad to hear it.' Why did she suddenly want to hurt him? What was the point of that? But he was appealing to her, tempting her, like an overzealous agent for a resort she had hated, who insisted on luring her back. And there was no way she would go.

He didn't mention the article again until they were waiting for a cab outside the restaurant. This had been one of the rare times they had discussed her business matters in public.

'You're going to do it?'

'What?'

'The interview Simpson discussed with you?'

'I don't know. I want to give it some thought.'

'Give it a lot of thought. Weigh in your mind how much it means to you, and how high a price you're willing to pay for doing it. You might not have to pay that price, or you might well have to. But at least be prepared, know the chances you're taking.'

'Is it such a terrible chance, Edward?' Her eyes were gentle again as she looked up at him.

'I don't know, Kezia. I really don't know. But somehow, I suspect that no matter what I say, you'll do it anyway. Or maybe I can only make matters worse.'

'No. But I may have to do it.' Not for Simpson. For herself.

'That's what I thought.'

CHAPTER VII

The plane landed in Chicago at five in the afternoon, with less than an hour to spare before Lucas Johns' speech. Simpson had arranged the loan of a friend's apartment on Lake Shore Drive. The friend, an elderly widow whose husband had been a classmate of Simpson's, was wintering in Portugal.

Now, as the cab circled the rim of the lake, Kezia began to feel a mounting excitement. She had finally chosen. Taken a first step. But what if it turned out to be more than she could handle? It was one thing to work over her typewriter and call herself K. S. Miller, and quite another to pull it off eye to eye. Of course, Mark didn't know who she was either. But that was different. His farthest horizon was his easel, and even if he knew, he wouldn't really care. It would make him laugh, but it wouldn't matter. Lucas Johns might be different. He might try to use her notoriety to his advantage.

She tried to shrug off her fears as the cab pulled up in front of the address Simpson had given her. The borrowed apartment was on the nineteenth floor of a substantial-looking building across from the lake. The parquet floors in the foyer echoed beneath her feet. Above her head was an elaborate crystal chandelier. And the ghostly form of a grand piano stood silent beneath a dust sheet at the foot of the stairs. There was a long mirrored hall which led to the living room beyond. More dust sheets, two more chandeliers, the pink marble of a Louis XV mantel on the fireplace glowing softly from the light in the hall. The furniture beneath the sheets looked massive, and she wandered curiously from room to room. A spiral staircase led to another floor, and upstairs in the master bedroom she drew back the curtains and pulled up the creamy silk shades. The lake stretched before her, bathed in the glow of sunset, sailboats veering lazily towards home. It would have been fun to go for a walk and watch the lake for a while, but she had other things on her mind. Lucas Johns, and what sort of man he might prove to be.

She had read his book, and was surprised that she liked the sound of him. She had been prepared to dislike him, if only because the interview had become such a major issue between her and Simpson, and Edward. But the issue was herself, and she forgot the rest as she read the book. He

82

had a pleasant way with words, a powerful way of expressing himself, and there were hints of humour throughout the book, and a refusal to take himself seriously, despite his passion for his subject. The style was oddly inconsistent with his history, though, and it was difficult to believe that a man who had spent most of his youth in juvenile halls and jails could be so literate now. Yet here and there he slipped consciously into prison jargon and California slang. He was an unusual combination of dogmas and beliefs and hopes and cynicism, with his own flavour of fun – and more than a faint hint of arrogance. He seemed to be many different things – no longer what he once was, firmly what he had become, a successful blending that he above all respected. Kezia had envied him as she read his book. Simpson had been right. In an indirect way, the book related to her. A prison can be any kind of bondage – even lunch at La Grenouille.

Her mental image of Johns was clearer now. Beady eyes, nervous hands, hunched shoulders, protruding paunch, and thin strands of hair covering a shiny balding forehead. She didn't know why, but she knew that she knew him. She could almost see him speaking as she read the book.

A man of massive proportions was making an introduction to Lucas Johns' speech, sketching in bold strokes the labour-union problems in prisons, the rough scale of wages (from five cents an hour, to a quarter in better institutions), the useless trades that were taught, the indecent conditions. He covered the subject easily, without fire.

Kezia watched the man's face. He was setting the stage and the pace. Low-key, low-voiced, yet with a powerful impact. It was the matter-of-fact way that he discussed the horrors of the prisons that affected her most. It was almost odd that they would put this man on before Johns; it would be a tough act to follow. Or maybe not. Maybe Johns' nervous dynamism would contrast well with the first speaker's easier manner – easy, yet with an intense control. The fibre of this man intrigued her, so much so that she forgot to scan the room to assure herself that there was no one there to recognize her. She forgot herself entirely and was swept into the mood of the speech.

She took out her notebook and jotted quick notes about the speaker, and then began to observe the audience in general. She noticed three well-known black radicals, and two solid labour-union leaders who had shared their knowledge with Johns in the past, when he was getting started. There were a few women, and in the front row a well-known criminal attorney who was often in the press. It was a group that already knew the business at hand for the most part, and one that was already active in prison reform. She was surprised at the large turnout as she watched their faces and listened to the last of the introduction. The room was surprisingly still. There were no rustlings, no little movements in seats, no noisy gropings for cigarettes and lighters. Nothing seemed to move. All eyes stayed fixed on the man at the front of the room. She had been right the first time; this would be tough for Lucas Johns to follow.

She looked at the speaker again. He had the colouring of her father. Almost jet black hair, and fiery green eyes that seemed to fix people in their places. He sought eyes he knew, and held them, speaking only to them, and then moving on, covering the room, the voice low, the hands immobile, the face taut. Yet something about the mouth suggested laughter. Something about the hands suggested brutality. He had interesting hands, and an incredible smile. In a powerful, almost frightening way, he was handsome, and she liked him. She found herself watching him, probing, observing, hungry for details – the shoulders impacted into the old tweed jacket, the long legs stretched lazily out before him, the thickness of his hair, the eyes that roved and stopped, and then moved on again, until they finally sought her out.

She saw him watching her as she watched him. He held her long and hard in the grasp of his eyes, and then dropped her and let his glance move away. It had been a strange sensation, like being backed against the wall with a hand at your throat, and another stroking your hair; you wanted to cringe in fear, and melt with pleasure. She felt warm suddenly, in the room full of people, and quietly looked around, wondering why this man was taking so long. It was hardly an introduction. He had been speaking for almost half an hour. Almost as though he intended to upstage Lucas Johns. And then it dawned on her, and she had to fight not to laugh in the quiet room: this had never been an introduction. The man whose eyes had so briefly stroked hers was Johns.

CHAPTER VIII

'Coffee?'

'Tea, if possible.' Kezia smiled up at Lucas Johns as he poured a cup of hot water, and then handed her a tea bag.

The suite showed signs of frequent guests – half-filled paper cups of coffee and tea, remains of crackers, ashtrays overflowing with peanut shells and stale cigarette butts, and a well-used bar in the corner. It was an unassuming hotel, and the suite was not large, but it was easy and comfortable. She wondered how long he had been there. It was impossible to tell if he'd made his home there for a year, of if he'd moved in that day. There was plenty to eat and drink, but nothing was personal, nothing seemed his, as though he owned the clothes on his back, the light in his eyes, the tea bag he had handed her, and nothing more.

'We'll order breakfast from downstairs.'

She smiled again over her tea, and watched him quietly. 'To tell you the truth, I'm not really very hungry. No rush. And by the way, I was very impressed by your speech last night. You seem so at ease on the stage. You have a nice knack for bringing a difficult subject down to human proportions without sounding self-righteous about what you know first-hand and your listeners haven't experienced. That's quite an art.'

'Thank you. That's a nice thing to say. I guess it's just a question of practice. I've been doing a lot of speaking to groups. Is the subject of prison reform new to you?'

'Not entirely. I did a couple of articles last year on riots in two Mississippi prisons. It was an ugly mess.'

'Yeah, I remember. The real point about the whole subject of "reform" is not to reform. I think that abolition of prisons as we know them now is the only sensible solution. They don't work like this anyway. I'm working on the moratorium on the construction of prisons right now, along with a lot of good people who organized it. I'll be heading down to Washington next.'

'Have you lived in Chicago long?'

'Seven months, as a sort of central office. I work out of the hotel when I'm here, lining up speaking engagements, and some of the other stuff I do. I wrote my new book here, just holed up for a month and got down to work. After that, I lugged the manuscript around with me and wrote the rest on planes.'

'Do you travel a lot?'

'Most of the time. But I come back here when I can. I can dig my heels in and relax here.'

Nothing about him suggested that he did that very often. He didn't seem the sort of man who would know how to stop, or when. For all the stillness, one sensed a driving force inside him. He had a very quiet way of just sitting, barely moving, his eyes watching the person he spoke to. But it was more like the cautious stance of an animal sniffing the air for signs of attack or approach, ready to spring in a moment. Kezia could sense too that he was wary of her, and not totally at ease. The humour she had seen in his eyes the night before was carefully screened now.

86

'You know, I'm surprised they sent a woman out to do the piece.'

'Chauvinism, Mr. Johns?' The idea amused her.

'No, just curiosity. You must be good or they wouldn't have sent you.' There was the hint of arrogance she had sensed in his book.

'I think it's mostly that they liked those two pieces I did for them last year. I suppose you could say I've skirted the subject of prisons before . . . if you'll pardon the pun.'

He grinned and shook his head. 'That's a hell of a way to put it.'

'Then call it "a view from the sidelines".'

'I'm not sure that's an improvement. You can never see from the sidelines . . . or is it that you see more clearly? But with less life. To me, it always feels better to be right in the gut of things. You either get into it, or you don't. The sidelines . . . that's so safe, such a dead way to do anything.' His eyes sparkled and his mouth smiled, but it had been a heavy message. 'Come to think of it, I've read some of your articles, I think . . . could it have been in *Playboy*?' He was momentarily bewildered; she didn't look the type for *Playboy*, not even in print, but he was sure he remembered an article not very long ago.

She nodded assent with a grin. 'It was a piece on rape. In sympathy with the man's side, for a change. Or rather on false accusations of rape, made by neurotic women who have nothing better to do except take a guy home and then chicken out, and later yell rape.'

'That's right. That's the piece I remember. I liked it.'

'Naturally.' She tried not to laugh.

"Now, now. It's funny though, I thought a man had written it. Sounded like a man's point of view. I guess that's why I expected a man to do this interview. I'm not really the kind of guy they usually send women out to talk to.'

'Why not?'

'Because sometimes, dear lady, I behave like a shit.' He laughed a deep, mellow laugh, and she joined him.

'So that's what you do, is it? Is it fun?'

He looked boyishly embarrassed suddenly and took a swallow of coffee. 'Yeah, maybe. Sometimes anyway. Is writing fun?'

'Yes. I love it. But "fun" makes it sound rather flimsy. Like something you do as a hobby. That's not the way I see it. Writing is important to me. Very. It's for real, more so than a lot of other things I know.' She felt strangely defensive before his silent gaze. It was as though he had quietly turned the tables on her, and was now interviewing her.

'What I do is important to me too. And real.'

'I could see that in your book.'

'You read it?' He seemed surprised, and she nodded.

'I liked it.'

'The new one is better.

And so modest, Mr. Johns, so modest. He was a funny sort of man.

'This one is less emotional, and more professional. I dig that.'

'First books are always emotional.'

'You've written one?' The tables turned again.

'Not yet. Soon, I hope.' It irked her suddenly. She was the writer, had worked hard at her craft over the past seven years, and yet he had written not one but two books. She envied him. For that, and a lot of things. His style, his courage, his willingness to follow his guts and jump into what he believed in . . . but then again, he had nothing to lose. She remembered the dead wife and child then, and felt a tremor for something tender in him which must have been hidden somewhere, down deep.

'I have one more question, and then you can get into the piece. What's the "K" for? Somehow "K. S. Miller" doesn't sound like a name.'

She laughed at him, and for the briefest of moments was about to tell him the truth: *Kezia. The 'K' is for Kezia, and the Miller is a fake.* He was the sort of man to whom you gave only the truth. You couldn't get away with less, and you wouldn't have wanted to. But she had to be sensible. It would be foolish to throw it all away for a moment of honesty. Kezia was an unusual name after all, and he might see a picture of her, somewhere, someday, and the next thing you'd know. . . .

'The "K" is for Kate.' Her favourite aunt's name.

'Kate. Sensible name. Kate Miller. Kate Sensible Miller.' He grinned at her, lit another cigarette, and she felt as though he were laughing at her, but not unkindly. The look in his eyes reminded her again of her father. In odd ways they were similar . . . something about the way he laughed . . . about the uncompromising way he looked at her, as though he knew all her secrets, and was only waiting for her to give them up, to see if she would, as though she were a child playing a game and he knew it. But what could this man possibly know? Nothing. Except that she was there to interview him, and her first name was Kate.

'Okay, lady, let's order breakfast and get to work.' The fun and games were over.

'Fine, Mr. Johns, I'm ready if you are.' She pulled out the pad with the scribbled notes from the evening before, drew a pen from her bag, and sat back in her chair.

He rambled on for two hours, talking at length, and with surprising openness, about his six years in prison. About what it was like to live under the indeterminate sentence, which he explained to her: a California phenomenon which condemned men to sentences of 'five years to life' or 'three to life', leaving the term served to be determined by the parole board or the prison authorities. Even the sentencing judge had no control over the length of time a man spent in prison. Once committed to the claws of the indeterminate sentence, a man could languish in prison literally for life, and a lot of men did, forgotten, lost, long past rehabilitation or the hope of freedom until they no longer cared when they might be set free. There came a time when it didn't matter anymore.

'But me,' he said with a lopsided grin, 'they couldn't

wait to get rid of me. I was the ultimate pain in the ass. Nobody loves an organizer.' He had organized other prisoners into committees for better working conditions, fairer hearings, decent visiting conditions with their wives, broader opportunities for study. He had, at one time, been spokesman for them all.

He told her too of what had gotten him sent to prison, and spoke of it with surprisingly little emotion. 'Twenty-eight years old, and still stupid. Looking for trouble, I guess, and bored with the life I had. I was piss-eyed drunk and it was New Year's Eve, and well . . . you know the rest. Armed robbery, not too cool to say the least. I held up a liquor store with a gun that didn't even shoot, and got away with two cases of bourbon, a case of champagne, and a hundred bucks. I didn't really want the hundred but they handed it to me, so I took it. I just wanted the hooch to have a good time with my buddies. I went home and partied my ass off. Till I got hauled off to jail, a little after midnight. . . . Happy New Year!' He grinned sheepishly and then his face grew serious. 'It sounds funny now, but it wasn't. You break a lot of hearts when you do something like that.'

It seemed all wrong to Kezia. Admittedly it was an outrageous thing to do. But six years and his wife's life for three cases of liquor? Her stomach turned over slowly as her mind flashed back to scenes of La Grenouille and Lutèce and Maxim's and Annabel's. Hundred-dollar lunches and fortunes spent on rivers of wine and champagne. But then, at those exalted watering holes, no one ordered his champagne with a shotgun.

Luke passed gracefully over his youth in Kansas. An uneventful period, when his worst problems were his size and his curiosity about life, both of which were out of proportion with his age and his 'station in life'. Despite Simpson's warning that Luke might be closed to personal probing, Kezia found him open and easy to talk to. By the end of the morning, she felt as though she knew all about him, and she had long since stopped taking notes. It was easier to hear the soul of the man just by listening – the political views, the interests, the causes, the experiences, the men he respected and those he abhorred. She would recapture it all later from memory with more depth.

What surprised her most was his lack of bitterness. He was determined, angry, pushy, arrogant, and tough. But he was also passionate in his beliefs, and compassionate about the people he cared about. And he liked to laugh. The baritone laughter rang out often in the small living room in his suite, as she questioned him and he regaled her with stories of years long since past. It was well after eleven before he stretched and rose from his chair.

'I hate to say this, Kate, but we're going to have to stop. I'm addressing another group at noon, and I have a few things to take care of first. Can I interest you in another speech? You're a good audience. Or do you have to get back to New York?' He circled the room, putting papers and pens in his pockets, and looked over his shoulder at her with the look one reserves for a friend.

'Both really. I should get back. But I'd like to hear you talk. What's the group?'

'Psychiatrists. The subject is a firsthand report on the psychological effects of being in prison. And they'll probably want to hear how real the threat of psychosurgery in prison is. They always ask about that.'

'You mean like frontal lobotomies?'

He nodded.

'Is there a lot of that?' She was momentarily stunned.

'Even a little "of that" is too much. But I don't think it happens often. Maybe occasionally. Lobotomies, shock treatment, a lot of ugly shit.'

She nodded sombrely and looked at her watch.

'I'll go pick up my things and meet you there.'

'Are you staying at a hotel around here?'

'No, my agent got me someone's apartment.'

'That's convenient.'

'Very.'

'Want a ride?' He said it easily as they walked towards the door.

'I . . . no . . . thanks, Luke. I've got a few other stops to make on the way. I'll meet you at your speech.'

He didn't press the point, but nodded absently as they waited for the elevator. 'I'll be interested to see this piece when it comes out.'

'I'll have my agent send you tear sheets as soon as we get them.'

He left her in front of the hotel and she walked to the corner and hailed a cab. It was a nice day to walk, and if she had had more time, she would have walked all the way back to the apartment on Lake Shore Drive. It was a warm autumn day with a bright sky overhead, and when she reached the apartment building, she could see sailboats skimming over the lake.

The ghostly apartment echoed her footsteps as she ran up the stairs for her suitcase, pulled the dust sheet over the tidily made bed, and pulled down the shade. She laughed, wondering what Luke would have said if he'd seen it. It didn't fit the image of Kate. Something told her he would not have approved. Or maybe he would have been amused, and together they might have pulled the sheets from all the furniture, lit the fire, and she could have played honkytonk on the grand piano downstairs – put a little life in the place. Funny to think of doing something like that with Luke. But he looked like a good man to have fun with, to giggle at and tease and chortle with and chase. She liked him, and he had no idea who she was. It was a safe, happy feeling, and the makings of the article already felt good in her head.

Luke's speech was interesting, and the group was receptive. She made a few notes, and nibbled absently at the steak on her plate. Luke was sitting at a long, flowerstrewn table at the front of the room, and she had been seated nearby. He looked over at her now and then, with mischievous laughter in the emerald green eyes. Once, silently raising his glass towards her, he winked. It made her want to laugh in the midst of the psychiatrists' general sobriety. She felt as though she knew Luke better than anyone there, maybe even better than anyone else. He had shared so much of his story with her all morning; he had given her the peek into the inner sanctum that Simpson had prophesied she'd never get. It was a shame she could not reciprocate.

Her flight was at three, and she had to leave the luncheon at two. He had just finished speaking when she rose. He had taken his seat at the dais, the usual crowd of admirers around him. She thought about just leaving quietly, without troubling him with thanks and goodbyes, but it didn't feel right. She wanted to say at least something to him before leaving. It seemed so unkind to pry into a man's head for four hours, and then simply vanish. But it was nearly impossible to get through the crowd near his table, and when she finally did, she found herself standing directly behind him, as he spoke animatedly to someone from his seat. She put a light hand on his shoulder and was surprised when he jumped. He didn't seem the kind of man to be frightened.

'That's a heavy thing to do to someone who spent six years in the joint.' His mouth smiled, but his eyes looked serious, almost afraid. 'I get nervous about who stands behind me. By now it's a reflex.'

'I'm sorry, Luke. I just wanted to say goodbye. I have to catch my plane.'

'Okay, just a sec.' He rose to walk her out to the lobby, and she went back to her table to pick up her coat. But Luke was waylaid on the way, and he was locked into another cluster of men as she fidgeted near the door, until she couldn't wait any longer. Unkind or not, she had to go. She didn't want to miss her plane. With a last look in his direction, she slipped quietly out of the room, crossed the lobby, and retrieved her valise from the doorman as he opened the door to a cab.

She settled back against the seat, and smiled to herself.

It had been a good trip, and it was going to be a beautiful piece.

She never saw Lucas standing beneath the awning behind her, a look of storm clouds and disappointment on his face.

'Damn!' All right, Ms. Kate Miller. We'll see about that. he smiled to himself as he strode back inside. He had liked her. She was so vulnerable, so funny . . . the kind of tiny little woman you wanted to toss up in the air and catch in your arms.

'Did you catch the young lady, sir?' The doorman had seen him run.

'No.' He broke into a broad grin which bordered on laughter. 'But I will.'

CHAPTER IX

'Called me? What do you mean he called me? I just walked in the door. And how did he know how to get hold of you?' Kezia was almost livid with rage at Simpson.

'Calm down, Kezia. He called over an hour ago, and I assume that the magazine referred him to me. There's no harm in that. And he was perfectly civil.'

'Well, what did he want?' She was stepping out of her clothes as she spoke, and the bath was already running. It was five minutes to seven, and Whit had said he'd pick her up at eight. They were due at a party at nine.

'He said he didn't feel the article would be complete unless you covered the meeting for that moratorium against prisons tomorrow in Washington. And he'd appreciate it if you'd hold off turning the piece in until you've added that to the rest. It sounds reasonable, Kezia. If you went to Chicago, you can certainly go to Washington for an afternoon.'

94

'When is this thing he wants me to go to?' Goddamn Lucas Johns. He was being a pest, or at least egocentric. She had written the outline for the piece on the plane, and enough was enough. Her sense of triumph was evaporating rapidly now. A man who called scarcely before she'd stepped off the plane could hardly be trusted not to pry.

'The moratorium meeting is tomorrow afternoon.'

'Hell. And if I go by plane, I'm liable to get spotted by some asshole society reporter who'll think I'm going down there for a party, and he'll try to catch a quick bit of news. And then I'm liable to end up with the paparazzi down my back.'

'That didn't happen on the way to Chicago, did it?'

'No, but Washington is a lot closer to home, and you know it. I never go to Chicago. Maybe I should drive down tomorrow, and . . . oh God, the tub! Hang on!'

Simpson waited while she went to turn off the water. She sounded nervous, and he assumed that the trip had been hectic. But it had been good for her. There was no doubt about that. She had braved it out, done the interview, and no one had recognized her, thank God. If they had, he'd never have heard the end of it. Now there were any number of interviews she could do. And Johns had certainly sounded pleased with her work. He had mentioned spending almost four hours with her. She must have handled it well, and Johns' casual references to 'Miss Miller' showed that he hadn't the faintest idea who she was. So what was her problem? Why so jumpy? She came back on the line with a sigh. 'Are you drowning over there?'

'No.' She laughed tiredly then. 'I don't know, Jack, I'm sorry I jumped on you, but it really makes me nervous to do this kind of thing so close to New York.'

'But the interview today went well, didn't it?'

'Yes. Very. But do you think the moratorium is really important to the piece, or is it that Luke Johns is on a star trip now and wants more attention?'

'I think he made a valid point when he called. It's

95

another sphere of his action, and could add a lot of strength to the piece. Atmosphere, if nothing else. It's up to you, but I don't see any harm in your going. And I know what you're worried about, but you saw for yourself in Chicago that there was no problem with that. No paparazzi, and he hasn't the faintest idea that you're anyone but K. S. Miller.'

'Kate.' She smiled to herself.

'What?'

'Nothing. Oh, I don't know. Maybe you're right. What time does the meeting start? Did he say?'

'Noon. He'll be flying in from Chicago in the morning.' She thought about it for a minute, and then nodded at the phone.

'All right, I'll do it. I suppose I could fly down on the shuttle. That's innocuous enough. And I could be back easily by tomorrow night.'

'Fine. Do you want to call Johns yourself to confirm it, or shall I? He wanted confirmation.'

'Why? So he could line up another biographer if I didn't go?'

'Now, now, let's not be nasty.' Simpson chuckled in spite of himself. There were times when she needed a good boot in the ass. 'No, he said something about picking you up at the plane.'

'Shit.'

'What?' Simpson sounded faintly shocked. He was much less used to that from her than Edward, who was of a comparable vintage but a little less proper.

'Sorry. No, I'll call him myself. And I don't want to be met at the plane. Just in case.'

'I think that's wise. And do you want me to arrange someplace for you to stay? If you want to stay at a hotel we could bill it to the magazine, along with your plane fare.'

'No, I'd rather come home. And that place you got me in Chicago was fabulous. Must be quite a home when it's in full swing.'

'Used to be . . . used to be. I'm glad you liked it. I had

96

some good times there, many years ago.' He drifted for a moment and then reverted to his business voice. 'So you'll come home tomorrow night then?'

'Damn right!' She wanted to get down to SoHo, and Mark. It had been days! And tonight she had that damn party at the El Morocco to go to with Whit. Hunter Forbishe and Juliana Watson-Smythe were announcing their engagement, as though everyone didn't already know. Two of the dullest, richest people in town, and worse luck yet, Hunter was her second cousin. The party was sure to be shitful, but at least the El Morocco was fun. She hadn't been since before the summer.

And not only were the dumb bastards getting engaged, but they had decided to have a theme for their party. Black and White. What fun it would have been to appear with George, her dancer friend from SoHo. Black and White . . . or Lucas for that matter, with his black hair to match Kezia's, and their equally white skin. How absurd – and worth a mountain of news for a year. No, she'd have to settle for Whitney, but it was a shame. Luke might have been fun at a party like that. Fun and outrageous. She laughed aloud as she sank into her bath. She would call him after she dressed, to tell him that she'd meet him in Washington tomorrow. But first she had to dress, and she needed time for a party like the one they were going to. She had long since decided what to wear for their charming soiree in black and white. The creamy lace dress was already laid out on her bed, fiercely décolleté and gently empire, with a black moire cape, and the new David Webb choker and earrings she'd bought herself last Christmas: an onyx set with a generous supply of handsome stones, diamonds of course. At twenty-nine she had stopped waiting for someone else to buy that sort of thing for her. She bought them herself.

'Lucas Johns, please.' She waited while they rang his room. He sounded sleepy when he answered. 'Luke? Kee . . . Kate.' She had almost said it was Kezia.

97

'I didn't know you stuttered.'

She laughed and his own laughter answered.

'I don't. I'm just in a hurry. Jack Simpson called me. I'll come down to cover that moratorium thing tomorrow. Why didn't you mention this morning that you thought I should be there?'

'I didn't think of it till after you left.' He smiled to himself as he spoke. 'I think you'll need it, though, to round out the rest. Want me to pick you up at the plane?'

'No, thanks. I'll be fine. Just tell me where to meet you.' He did and she wrote down the address, standing at her desk in the white lace dress and the black moire cape, delicate black silk sandals on her feet and one of her mother's diamond bracelets on each arm. And then she started to laugh.

'What's funny?'

'Oh, nothing really. It's just what I'm wearing.'

'And just what are you wearing, Ms. Miller?' He sounded vastly amused.

'Something terribly silly.'

'Sounds very mysterious to me. I'm not sure if you mean leather hip boots and a whip, or a rhinestone-studded peignoir.'

'A little of both. See you tomorrow, Luke.' She hung up on a last gurgle of laughter as the doorbell rang, and Whitney appeared, as crisp and elegant as ever. For him, of course, the black and white had been easy. He was wearing a dinner jacket and one of the shirts he had made four times a year in Paris.

'Where were you all day? And my ... don't you look splendid!' They exchanged their standard dry little kiss, and he held out her hands. 'Is that something new? I don't remember seeing that dress before.'

'Sort of. I don't wear it often. And I spent the whole day with Edward. We did up my new will.' They smiled at each other and she picked up her bag. Lies, lies, lies. It had never been like this before. But she knew as she swirled out to the hall that it was going to get worse. Lying to Whit, lying to Mark, lying to Luke. 'Is that why you write, Kate? For fun?' She remembered Luke's question as the elevator swept them down to the lobby, and her brows knit as she thought of the look in his eyes. It had not been accusing, only curious. But no, dammit! She didn't just write for fun. It was real. But how real could anything be, when whatever you did, you draped in lies?

'Ready, darling?' Whit was waiting for her outside the elevator, and she had stood there for a moment, not moving, just looking at him, but seeing Luke's eyes, hearing his voice.

'Sorry, Whit. I must be tired.' She squeezed his arm as they walked out to the waiting limousine..

By ten she was drunk.

'Christ, Kezia, are you sure you can walk?' Marina was watching her pull her stockings up and her dress down as they stood in the ladies' room at the El Morocco.

'Of course I can walk!' But she was weaving badly and couldn't stop laughing.

'What happened to you?'

'Nothing since Luke. I mean, Duke . . . I mean breakfast dammit.' She had hardly had time to touch her lunch before catching the plane at O'Hare, and she hadn't bothered with dinner.

'Kezia, you're a nut. Want some coffee?'

'No, tea. No . . . coffee. No! Chaaaaamppagggne.' She dragged the word out and Marina laughed.

'At least you're a friendly drunk. Vanessa Billingsley is crocked out of her mind and just called Mia Hargreaves a raving bitch.' Kezia giggled and Marina lit a cigarette and sat down, while Kezia tried desperately to remember what Marina had just said. Mia called Vanessa a . . . no, Vanessa called Mia . . . if she could just hang on to it, it would be good for the column. And what had she heard earlier about Patricia Morbang being pregnant? Or was that right? Was it someone else who was pregnant? It was all so hard to remember.

'Oh Marina, it's so hard to remember it all.'

Marina looked at her with a half smile and shook her head.

'Kezia, my love, you are smashed. Well, hell, who isn't? It must be after three.'

'Christ, is it really? And I have to get up so early tomorrow. Crap.'

Marina laughed again at the sight of Kezia sprawled on the white wall-to-wall in the ladies' boudoir, looking like a child just home from school, the white lace dress frothed around her like a nightgown. the diamonds glittering on her wrists, like something borrowed from her mother to dispel the boredom of a rainy day.

'And Whit's going to be very cross if I'm drunk.'

'Tell him it's the flu. I don't think the poor bastard would know the difference.' They both laughed at that, and Marina helped her to her feet. 'You really ought to go home.'

'I think I'd much rather dance. Whit dances very nicely, you know.'

'He ought to.' Marina looked at her hard and long, but the implication of the message was lost on Kezia. She was too drunk to hear, or to care.

'Marina?' Kezia looked still more childlike as she stood watching her friend.

'What, love?'

'Do you really love Halpern?'

'No, baby, I don't. But I love the peace of mind he could give me. I've about had it with trying to make it on my own with the kids. And in another six months I'd have had to sell the co-op.'

'But don't you love him a little?'

'No. But I like him a lot.' Marina looked cynical and amused.

'But don't you love anyone? A secret lover maybe? You have to love someone.' *Don't you?*

'Do you? Well, fancy that. Do you love Whit?'

'Of course not.' Some small alarm went off in her head then. She was talking too much.

'Then who do you love, Kezia?'

'You, Marina. I love you lots and lots and lots and lots!' She threw her arms around her friend's neck and started to giggle. And Marina laughed back and gently untwined her from her neck.

'Kezia sweet, you may not love Whitney, but if I were you, I'd get him to take me home. I think you've about had it.' They walked out of the ladies' room arm in arm. Whitney was waiting just outside. He had noticed the ominous sway in Kezia's walk as she left the room half an hour before.

'Are you all right?'

'I'm wonderful!' Whit and Marina exchanged glances, and Whitney winked.

'You certainly are wonderful. And I don't know about you, darling, but I'm also wonderfully tired. I think we'll call it a night.'

'No, no, no! I'm not tired at all. Let's call it a morning!' Kezia found everything suddenly terribly funny.

'Let's call it a get-your-ass-out-of-here, Kezia, before you wind up in Martin Hallam's column tomorrow: "Kezia Saint Martin, drunk as a skunk as she left El Morocco last night with . . ." Wouldn't that be lovely?' Kezia roared with glee at Marina's warning.

'That couldn't happen to me!' Whitney and Marina laughed again and tears began to slide down Kezia's face as she giggled.

'Oh, couldn't it? It could happen to any of us.'

'But not to me. I'm . . . I'm a friend of his.'

'And so is Jesus Christ, I'll bet.' Marina patted her on the shoulder and went back to the party, while Whitney put an arm around Kezia and piloted her slowly towards the door. He had draped her black cape over his arm, and was carrying her small black beaded bag.

'It's really my fault, darling. I should have taken you to dinner before we came here.'

'You couldn't.'

'Of course I could. I left the office early today to play squash at the Racquet Club.'

101

'No you couldn't. I was in Chicago.' He rolled his eyes and placed the cape over her shoulders.

'That's right, darling. That's right. Of course you were.' She went into another fit of giggles as he gently led her outside. She patted his cheek sweetly then and looked at him strangely.

'Poor Whitney.' He was not paying attention. He was far more concerned with getting her into a cab.

He deposited her in her living room and gave her a gentle slap on the bottom, hoping to propel her into the bedroom. Alone.

'Get some sleep, mademoiselle. I'll call you tomorrow.'

'Late! Very late.' She had just remembered that she would be in Washington all day. With a terrible hangover.

'You bet "late"! I wouldn't dare call you before three.'

'Make it six!'

She giggled at him as he closed the door behind him, and she sank into one of the blue velvet living room chairs. She was drunk. Hopelessly, totally, wonderfully drunk. And all because of a stranger named Luke. And she was going to see him tomorrow.

CHAPTER X

The print was blurred and the features were indistinct but it was definitely Kate. The way she carried herself was unmistakable, the tilt of her head, her size. The Honourable Kezia Saint Martin in what looked like some sort of black-and-white outfit. By Givenchy, the paper said, and wearing her late mother's famed diamond bracelets. Heiress to several fortunes; in steel, oil, etc. No wonder she had laughed when she called him and said she was wearing 'something funny.' It looked pretty funny to Luke too. But

102

she looked beautiful. Even in the papers. He had seen her in the papers before, but now he paid close attention to what he saw. Now that he knew her, it mattered to him. And what an odd life she must lead.

He had sensed the turmoil beneath the poise and perfection. The bird in the gilded cage was dying inside, and he knew it. He wondered if she knew it too. And what he knew most acutely was that he wanted to touch her, before it was too late.

Instead they had that damn meeting to go to, and he would have to go on playing her game. He knew that she would have to be the one to end the game of 'K. S. Miller' between them. Only she could do that. All he could do was give her the chance. But how many more chances? How many more excuses could he dream up? How many more towns? How many more meetings? All he knew was that he had to have her, however long it took. The problem was that he didn't have much time. Which made it all the more crazy.

When Kezia arrived, she found Luke in an office, surrounded by unfamiliar faces. Phones were ringing, people were shouting, messages were flying, the smoke was thick, and he hardly seemed to know she was there. He waved once and didn't look at her again all afternoon. The press conference had been rescheduled for two o'clock, and the rooms were chaotic all day long. It was six before she found a place to sit down, shoved her notebook into her bag, and gladly accepted the other half of a stranger's ham sandwich. What a day to survive with a hangover. Her head had gotten worse by the hour. Phones, people, speeches, statistics, photographs. It was all too much. Action, emotion, and pressure. She wondered how he stood it as a regular diet, with or without a hangover.

'Want to get out of here?'

'That's the best offer I've had all day.' She smiled up at him and his face softened for the first time in hours.

'Come on, I'll get you something decent to eat.'

'I really ought to get out to the airport.'

103

'Later. You need a break first. You look like you were hit by a truck.' And she felt it. Rumpled, tired, dishevelled. Lucas did not look much better. He looked tired and he had worn a scowl for most of the afternoon. He had a cigar in one hand, and his hair looked as though he had been running his hands through it for hours.

But he had been right. The day had been a total contrast to the two meetings she had seen in Chicago. This was the meat of it, the gut, as he called it. Impassioned, frenzied, fervent. This was more intense, less polite, and far more real. Luke seemed totally in charge here. He was almost a kind of god. There was a fierceness about him she'd only glimpsed in Chicago. The air was electric with his special kind of energy, and the toughness in him was no longer muted. But his face gentled a little as he looked at her on their way out.

'You look tired, Kate. Too much for you?' It wasn't a put-down; he looked concerned.

'No, I'm fine. And you were right. It was an interesting day. I'm glad I came down to see it.'

'So am I.' They were walking down a long busy corridor, among streams of homebound people. 'I know a quiet place where we can have an early dinner. Can you spare the time?' But his tone told her he expected her to.

'Sure. I'd like that.' Why rush back? For what? For Whitney? . . . or for Mark? But suddenly even that didn't seem so important. They walked out onto the street, and he took her arm.

'What did you do last night, by the way?' He wondered if she'd tell him.

'As a matter of fact, I got drunk. And I haven't done that in years.' It was crazy, this urge to tell him everything, without really doing so. She could have told him the whole of it, but she knew she wasn't going to.

'You got drunk?' He looked down at her with amusement all over his face. So she had gotten drunk in that black-and-white number with her mother's diamond bracelets . . . and with that faggoty-looking dude she was

104

with no doubt scowling his disapproval. He could just see
her. Drunk on champagne. Was there any other way to go?

They were walking briskly, side by side now, and she
looked up at him pensively after a brief silence.

'You really care about the prison thing, don't you? I
mean, in your gut.'

He nodded carefully. 'Can't you tell?'

'Yes. I can. It just amazes me a little, how much of
yourself you pour into it. Seems like a lot of energy
expended in one place.'

'It's worth it to me.'

'It must be. But aren't you taking a hell of a chance just
being involved in these issues, and being so outspoken
about them? Seems to me I've heard they can revoke a
parole for less.'

'And if they do, what have I lost?'

'Your freedom. Or doesn't that matter to you?' Maybe
after six years in prison it no longer mattered to him,
although it seemed to her that that would only make
freedom more dear.

'You miss the point. I never lost my freedom, even when
I was in the joint. Oh sure, for a while, but once I found it
again I kept it. It sounds corny, but no man can take your
freedom from you. They can limit your mobility, but that's
about all they can do.'

'All right, then let's say they try and limit your mobility
again. Aren't you taking a heavy chance with the kind of
agitating you do on the outside – speeches, conferences,
your books, the prison labour-union issues? Seems to me
like you're walking a tightrope.' Unconsciously, she was
echoing Simpson's speech to her.

'Seems to me that a lot of people are. In prison and out.
Maybe you're even walking a tightrope, Miss Miller. So
what? It's cool as long as you don't fall off.'

'And no one pushes you off.'

'Lady, all I know is how fucked up that whole system is.
I can't keep my mouth shut about it. If I did, my life
wouldn't mean a damn thing to me. It's as simple as that.

105

And if I pay a price in the end, it was my own choice. I'm willing to take that chance. Besides, I'd say the California Department of Corrections is not exactly dying to invite me back for a return engagement. I gave them one giant, jumbo, A-Number-One pain in the ass.'

'You're really not afraid of getting revoked?'

'Nah. Never happen.' But he didn't look at her as he said it, and something about him seemed to stiffen. 'You like Italian food, Kate?'

'Sounds lovely. I'm not sure, but I think I'm starving.'

'Then pasta it is. Come on, let's catch that cab.' He raced across the street holding her hand, and dutifully held open the door for her, before following her inside and cramping his legs into the narrow back seat. 'Man, they must build these for midgets. And Jesus, you look so comfortable. You should thank God you're a pygmy.' He gave the driver the address of the restaurant over her outraged protests.

'Just because you're a freak of nature, Lucas Johns, does not mean you vent your problems on . . .'

'Aww, now now. Nothing wrong with being a pygmy.'

She looked at him awesomely and sniffed. 'I ought to punch you in the eye, Mr. Johns, but I'm afraid I might hurt you.'

That set the tone for the evening. Light, playful, companionable. He was easy to be with. And it wasn't until the espresso was served that they both grew more pensive.

'I like this town. Do you come down here often, Kate? I would if I lived in New York.'

'I come down once in a while.'

'What for?' He wanted her to tell him the truth. They couldn't even begin till she did.

And she wanted to tell him that she came down for parties, for balls, for dinners at the White House. For inaugurations. For weddings. But she couldn't say any of it. No matter what.

'I come down on stories occasionally, like this. Or just to see friends.' She caught a glimpse of something dis-

106

appointed in his eyes, but it was fleeting. 'Don't you get tired of travelling so much, Luke?' She was once again the poised Miss Saint Martin. He was beginning to think it was hopeless.

'No, travelling is a way of life for me by now, and it's for a good cause. How about some brandy?'

'Oh God, not tonight!' She cringed at the memory of the headache that had finally left her at dinner.

'Tied one on that bad last night, huh?'

'Worse!' She smiled and took another sip of coffee.

'How come? Having a good time?'

'No. Trying to numb myself through a lousy one, and I guess I had a lot on my mind. Everything kind of got away from me.'

'Like what did you have on your mind?'

You, Mr. Johns. . . . She smiled at her own thought. 'Can I blame it on you and say it was the interview?' A look of sheer female teasing danced in her eyes.

'Sure, you can blame it on me if you want, I've been accused of a lot worse.' So she had to 'numb' herself to get through the party. Interesting. Very interesting. At least she wasn't in love with that asshole. 'You know something, Katie? I like you. You're a very nice woman.' He sat back and smiled, looking deep into her eyes.

'Thank you. I've thoroughly enjoyed the last couple of days. And should I make a terrible confession?'

'What? You flushed your notebook down the toilet back at the office? I wouldn't blame you a bit, and we could start all over. I'd like that.'

'God forbid. No, my "terrible confession" is that this was my first interview. I've always done more general pieces. But this was a new experience for me.' She wondered if all writers fell a little bit in love with the first person they interviewed. Inconvenient if the first person happened to be the tattooed lady at Ringling's.

'How come you've never done an interview before?' He was intrigued.

'Scared to.'

'Why would you be scared? You're a good writer, so that doesn't make any sense. And you're not shy.'

'Yes, I am. Sometimes. But you're difficult to be shy with.'

'Is that something I should correct?'

She laughed and shook her head. 'No, you're just fine the way you are.'

'So what's so scary about interviews?'

'It's a long story. Nothing you'd want to hear. What about you? What frightens you, Luke?'

Damn. She just wouldn't give. He wanted to stand up and shake her. But he had to look cool. 'Is this part of the interview? What frightens me?'

She shook her head, and wondered what he was thinking.

'A lot of things frighten me. Fears can create a lot of confusion. Cowardice frightens me, it can cost someone a life . . . usually someone else's. Waste frightens me, because time is so short. Otherwise, nothing much. Except women. Oh yeah, women scare me to death.'

After a moment of tension, there was laughter in his eyes again, and Kezia was relieved. For a minute she had felt him coming at her with both barrels, but she decided that was only her own paranoia. He didn't know she was lying. He couldn't possibly know, or he would have let on by now if he did. He wasn't a man to play games. She was sure of it.

'Women frighten you?' She was smiling at him again.

'They terrify me.' He tried to cower in his seat.

'Like hell they do.' She started to laugh.

'Yeah, okay. You're right.' They laughed and talked easily for another hour, as the brief tension between them eased again. She succumbed to a glass of brandy at last, and then followed it with another espresso. She wanted to sit there with him forever.

'There's a place I go to in SoHo in New York. The atmosphere reminds me of this. It's called The Partridge, and it's a funny little hangout for poets and artists and just

108

nice people.' Her face lit up as she told him about it, and he watched her talk.

'Is it an "in" place?'

She laughed out loud at the thought. 'Oh no, it's an "out" place. Very "out." That's why I love it.'

So, the lady had her haunts, did she? The places where she went to get away, where no one knew who she was, where. . . . 'Then I'd probably like it, Kate. You'll have to take me there sometime.' He slipped the suggestion in casually as he lit another cigar. 'What do you do with yourself in New York?'

'Write. See friends. Go to parties sometimes, or the theatre. I travel a bit too. But mostly, I write. I know a lot of artists in SoHo, and sometimes I hang out with them.'

'And the rest of the time?'

'I see other people . . . depends on my mood.'

'You're not married, are you?'

'No.' She shook her head decisively, as though to confirm it.

'I didn't think so.'

'How come?'

'Because you're careful, the way women are who're used to taking care of themselves. You think about what you do and say. Most married women are used to having someone else do that kind of thinking, and it shows. How's that for a classic male chauvinist remark?'

'Not bad. But it's also a very perceptive thing to say. I'd never thought of it that way, but I think you might be right.'

'Okay. Back to you now. My turn to interview.' He seemed to be enjoying it. 'Engaged?'

'Nope. Not even in love. I have a virgin soul.'

'I'm overwhelmed. If I had a hat, I'd take it off.' They both laughed again. 'But I'm not sure I believe you,' Luke went on. 'Are you trying to tell me that you don't even have an old man?' What about the faggot in the newspaper picture, baby? But he could hardly ask her about that.

'Nope. No old man.'

'Is that true?'

Her eyes rose to his then, and she looked almost hurt. 'Yes, it's true. There's someone I enjoy a lot, but I . . . I just kind of visit him . . . when I can.'

'Is he married?'

'No . . . just sort of in another world.'

'In SoHo?'

Lucas was quick to pick up on things left unsaid. She nodded again. 'Yes. In SoHo.'

'He's a lucky guy.' Luke's voice was oddly quiet.

'No, he's a funny guy actually. A nice guy. I like him. Sometimes I even like to imagine that I love him, but I don't. It's not very serious between us, and never will be. For a lot of reasons.'

'Like what?'

'We're just very different, that's all. Different goals, different views. He's quite a bit younger than I am, and headed in another direction. It really doesn't matter. Mostly, it's just that we're different.'

'Is that so bad? Being different?'

'No, but there are different kinds of "different." ' She smiled at her own words. 'In this case, different backgrounds, different interests . . . just different enough to make it *too* different, but I still like him. And what about you? An "old lady"?' The term always seemed funny to her, as though it should refer to someone's grandmother, and not his inamorata.

'Nope. No old lady. I move around too much. A few good women here and there. But I put my energy into the cause, not into my relationships. I haven't put out that kind of effort in a long time. I think the time for that is past for me. And you pay a price for the kind of work that goes into shit-kicking like this. You can't have it all ways. You have to make choices.' He said a lot of things like that. In his own way, he was a purist. And his cause came first. 'I meet a lot of good people to talk to, travelling around. That means a lot to me.'

'It means a lot to me too. People you can talk to, in

110

depth, are a rarity.' And he was one of those rare people.

'You're right. Which brings up a question. I'd like to look you up when I come to New York sometime, Kate. Would that be okay? We could go to The Partridge.' She smiled at him; it would be nice to see him. She felt as though she had made a new friend, and it was incredible how much of her soul she had shown him at dinner. She hadn't planned to; in fact she had planned to be rather guarded. But one forgot to be guarded with Luke. That was a very dangerous thing, and she reminded herself of it now.

'It would be fun to see you again sometime.' She was purposely vague.

'Will you give me your number?' He held out a pen and the back of an envelope. He didn't want to give her time to back off. But she made no move to retreat. In a sense, he had her cornered, and she knew it. She took the pen and wrote down her number, but not her address. There was no harm in his having the phone number.

He pocketed the envelope, paid the check, and helped her on with her jacket.

'Can I take you to the airport, Kate?' She seemed to take a long time buttoning her jacket, without looking up, and then at last she met his gaze, looking almost shy.

'That wouldn't be too much trouble?'

He pulled gently at a loose wisp of her hair, and shook his head at her. 'I'd like to.'

'That's really very nice.'

'Don't be a jerk, you're good company.'

He watched her leave, and she turned to give him a last wave at the gate. Her hand rose high above her head and impulsively she blew him a kiss as she walked away down the ramp. It had been a beautiful evening, a great interview, a marvellous day. She was feeling sentimental about the success of it, and strange about Luke.

She boarded the plane and took a seat at the front, accepting the New York and Washington papers from a passing tray. Then she settled back in her seat and switched on the light. There was no one next to her whom she might disturb as she read. It was the last flight to New York, and it would be past one when she got in. She had nothing to do the following day. Work on the Lucás Johns article maybe, but that was all. She had wanted to go to SoHo to see Mark tonight, but now she wasn't in the mood. It wasn't too late. Mark would still be up. But she didn't want to see him. She wanted to be alone.

She felt a gentle sadness wash slowly over her. An unfamiliar, bittersweet feeling of having touched someone who had moved on. She knew she wouldn't see Lucas Johns again. He had the number, but he probably wouldn't have the time, and if he ever did come through town, she would probably be in Zermatt or Milan or Marbella. He would be busy for the next hundred years with his unions and his cause and inmates and moratoriums . . . and those eyes . . . he was such a good man, such a likable man . . . so gentle . . . it was hard to imagine him in prison. Hard to imagine that he'd been tough or mean, had perhaps stabbed a man in a fight in the yard. She had met a different man. A different Luke. A Luke who haunted her all the way home. He was gone for good, from her now, so she could allow herself the luxury of turning him over in her mind . . . just for tonight.

The flight was too short and she almost hated to get off the plane and fight her way through the terminal to a cab. Even at that hour La Guardia was busy. So busy that she never saw the tall, dark-haired man follow her to within yards of the cab. He watched her slide into the taxi from only a few feet away. And then, turning away to conceal his face, he looked at his watch. He had time. It would take her half an hour to get home.

And then he would call her.

112

CHAPTER XI

'Hello?'

'Hi, Kate.' She felt a warm rush come over her at the sound of his voice.

'Hello, Lucas.' Her voice was tired and smoky. 'I'm glad you called.'

'Did you get home all right?'

'I did. It was a quiet flight. I was going to read the paper, but I didn't even bother.' He wanted to say 'I know,' but he didn't, and stifled the urge to laugh.

'What are you up to now, Ms. Miller?' There was mischief in his voice.

'Not much. I was just going to take a hot bath and go to bed.'

'Can I talk you into a drink at The Partridge? Or P.J. Clarke's?'

'Bit of a ride from your hotel in Washington, wouldn't you say? Or did you plan to walk?' She was amused at the thought.

'Yeah, I could. But it's not a bad ride from La Guardia.'

'Don't be silly. I took the last flight in.' What a madman he was to consider flying all the way up to New York for a drink.

'I know you took the last flight. But as it happens, so did I.'

'What?' And then she understood. 'You wretch! And I didn't even see you!'

'I should hope not. I almost broke my shoulder once, ducking down in my seat.'

'Lucas, you're crazy.' She laughed into his ear and lay her head on the back of the chair. 'What a perfectly nutty thing to do.'

'Why not? I have a free day tomorrow, and I was going

113

to take it easy anyway. Besides, I felt lousy watching you leave.'

'I felt pretty lousy leaving. I don't know why, but I did.'

'And now we're both here, and there's no reason to feel lousy. Right? So what'll we do? P. J.'s or The Partridge, or somewhere else? I'm not all that familiar with New York.'

She was still laughing and shaking her head. 'Luke, it's one-thirty in the morning. There isn't all that much we can do!'

'In New York?' He was not going to be put off that easily.

'Even in New York. You are too much. Tell you what, I'll meet you at P. J.'s in half an hour. It'll take you that long to get into the city, and I want to take a quick shower and change clothes at least. You know something?'

'What?'

'You're a nut.'

'Is that a compliment?'

'Possibly.' She smiled gently at the phone.

'Good. I'll meet you at P. J.'s in half an hour.' He was pleased with himself for what he had done. It was going to be a beautiful night. He didn't care if all she did was shake his hand. It was going to be the best night of his life. Kezia Saint Martin. It was impossible not to be impressed. But in spite of the fancy label, he liked her. She intrigued him. She was nothing like what he had imagined those women to be. She wasn't aloof and secretly ugly. She was warm and gentle and lonely as hell. He could read it all over her.

And half an hour later, there she was, in the doorway at P. J.'s, and in jeans. Not even tailor-made ones, just good old regular Levi's, with her silky black hair in two long little-girl braids. More than ever, she looked like a very young girl to him.

The bar was jammed, the lights were bright, the sawdust was thick on the floor, and the jukebox was blaring. It was his kind of place. He was having a beer, and she came over with a gleam in her eye.

'My God, you're sneaky! No one's ever followed me onto

114

a plane in my life. But what a neat thing to do!' That wasn't entirely true but she was laughing again.

She ordered a Pimm's Cup, and they stood at the bar for half an hour while Kezia glanced over his shoulder at the door. There was always the chance that someone she knew would wander in, or a group of late-night partygoers would arrive after a stop at Le Club or El Morocco, and blow the 'Kate Miller' story to pieces.

'Expecting someone, or just nervous?'

She shook her head. 'Neither. Just stunned, I guess. A few hours ago we had dinner in Washington, said goodbye at the airport, and now here you are. It's a bit of a shock.' But a pleasant one.

'Too much of a shock, Kate?' Maybe he had gone too far, but at least she didn't look angry.

'No.' She was careful with the word. 'What do you want to do now?'

'How about taking a walk?'

'That's funny, I thought of that on the plane. I wanted to go for a walk along the East River. I do that once in a while, late at night. It's a nice way to think.'

'And get killed. Is that what you're trying to do?' The idea of her walking along the river unprotected unnerved him.

'Don't be so silly, Lucas. You shouldn't believe all the myths you hear about this town. It's as safe as any other.' He glowered and finished his beer.

They began to walk slowly up Third Avenue, past restaurants and bars, and the clatter of occasional late-night traffic on Fifty-seventh Street. New York was not in any way like any other town. Not like any American city. Like a giant Rome maybe, with its thirst for life after dark. But this was bigger, more, wilder, crueller, and far less romantic. New York had its own romance, its own fire. Like a bridled volcano, waiting for its chance to erupt. They both felt the vibes of the town as they wandered its streets, out of step with its mood, refusing to feel pushed or shoved; they felt oddly at peace. They passed little groups

115

of people, and male streetwalkers carrying pug dogs and French poodles, and wearing tight sweaters and crotch-clutching jeans. Women walked lap dogs, and men lurched drunkenly towards cabs. It was a city that stayed alive round-the-clock.

They cut east on Fifty-eighth Street, and walked through the slumbering elegance of Sutton Place, sitting like a dowager next to the river. Kezia wondered for a moment if they would meet Whit, leaving his lover's apartment – if he still left it.

'What are you thinking about, Kate? You look all dreamy.'

She looked up at him and smiled. 'I guess I am. I was just letting my mind wander ... thinking about some people I know ... you ... nothing much really.' He took her hand and they walked quietly next to the river, making their way slowly north, until a question interrupted her thoughts. 'I just thought of something. Where are you going to sleep tonight?'

'I'll work it out. Don't worry about it. I'm used to arriving in cities in the middle of the night.' He looked unconcerned.

'You could sleep on my couch. You're a bit tall for it, but it's comfortable. I've slept there myself.'

'That sounds fine to me.' Better than fine, but he couldn't let her see how happy he was, or how surprised. It was all so much easier than even his wildest dreams.

They exchanged another smile and kept walking. She felt comfortable with him, and hadn't felt this peaceful in years. It didn't matter if she let him sleep on her couch. So what if he knew where she lived? In the end, what did it really matter? How long could she hide – from him, from herself, from strangers and friends? The precautions were becoming an unbearable burden. At least for one night, she wanted to see the burden aside. Luke was her friend; he wouldn't harm her, even if he knew her address.

'Do you want to go home now?' They were at Seventy-second and York.

116

'Do you live near here?' The neighbourhood surprised him. It was middle-class ugly.

'Not too far from here. A few blocks over and a couple more blocks up.' They headed west on Seventy-second Street, and the neighbourhood began to improve.

'Tired, Kate?'

'I must be, but I don't feel it.'

'You're probably still numb from the drunk you tied on last night.' He grinned.

'What a rotten thing to bring up! Just because I get drunk once a year . . .'

'Is that all?'

'It certainly is!'

He pulled one of the pigtails and they crossed the deserted street. Downtown, traffic would still be blaring, but here there was no one in sight. They had reached Park Avenue now, divided by neat flower beds and hedges.

'I wouldn't say you live in the slums, Katie Miller.' For a while, as they had strolled along York, he wondered if she'd take him to a different apartment to keep secret the place where she lived. Thank God, she wasn't as frightened as that. 'You must do well with your articles.' A look of open teasing passed between them, and they both started to laugh.

'I can't really complain.'

She was playing it right till the end. She wasn't going to cop to a thing. It amazed him. So secretive, and what in hell for? He pitied her for the agonies of her double life. Or maybe she didn't spend enough time on his side of the tracks to make it a strain. But there was SoHo, the place she went to 'get away.' From what? Herself? Her friends? He knew her parents were dead. What could she have to get away from? Surely not the guy he'd seen with her in the paper.

They turned a corner onto a tree-lined street, and she paused with a smile at the first door. An awning, a doorman, an impressive address.

'This is it.' She pressed the bell, and the doorman fought with the lock. He looked sleepy and his hat was tilted back

117

on his head. It was a relief man, she observed, and all he ventured was a vague, 'Good evening.' Providentially, he couldn't remember her name.

Luke smiled to himself in the elevator. She turned the key to her apartment and pushed open the door. There was mail neatly stacked on the hall table, the cleaning woman had been there, and the place looked impeccably neat and smelled of fresh wax.

'Can I offer you some wine?'

'Champagne, I presume.'

She turned to look at him, and he was smiling gently at her, mischief in his eyes. 'It's quite a pad, baby. Class, by the barrel.' But he didn't say it cruelly; it was more like a question.

'I could tell you it's the home of my parents . . . but I wouldn't want to do that.'

'Is it . . . or was it?'

She raised an eyebrow. 'Nope, it's mine. I'm old enough to put together something like this for myself now.'

'As I said, you must do well with your work.'

She shrugged and smiled. She wanted to make no excuse. 'What about that wine? It's pretty lousy actually. Would you rather have a beer?'

'Yes. Or a cup of coffee. I think I'd rather have that.' She left him to put on the kettle, and he ambled after her, his voice reaching her from the doorway as she clattered cups in the kitchen. 'Hey, do you have a roomie?'

'A what?' She wasn't paying attention; she would have grown pale if she had.

'A roommate. Do you have one?'

'No. Why? Do you take cream and sugar?'

'No, thanks. Black. No roommate?'

'Nope. What makes you ask?'

'Your mail.' She paused with the kettle in her hand, and looked around at him.

'What about my mail?' She hadn't thought of that.

'It's addressed to a Miss Kezia Saint Martin.' Time seemed to stand still between them. Neither moved.

'Yes. I know.'

'Anyone you know?'

'Yeah.' The weight of the world seemed to fall from her shoulders with one word. 'Me.'

'Huh?'

'I'm Kezia Saint Martin.' She attempted a smile but looked almost stricken, and he tried to feign shock. Had she known him a little bit better she'd have laughed at the look in his eyes.

'You mean you're not Kate S. Miller?'

'Yeah, I'm K. S. Miller too. When I write.'

'Your pen name. I see.'

'One of many. Martin Hallam is another.'

'You collect aliases, my love?' He walked slowly towards her.

She put the kettle down on the stove, and turned deliberately away. All he could see was the dark hair and her narrow shoulders bent over.

'Yes, aliases. And lives. There are three of me, Luke. Four actually. No, five now, counting "Kate." K. S. Miller never needed a first name before. It's all more than a little schizophrenic.'

'Is it?' He was right behind her now, but he did not reach out to touch her. 'Why don't we go sit down and talk for a while?'

His voice was low and she turned to face him with a barely perceptible nod. She needed to talk, and he'd be a good man to talk to. She had to talk to someone before she went mad. But now he knew she was a liar ... or maybe that didn't matter with Luke. Maybe he'd understand.

'Okay.' She followed him into the living room, sat primly on one of her mother's blue velvet chairs, and watched him lean back on the couch.

'Cigarette?'

'Thanks.' He lit it for her and she took a long, deep pull at the unfiltered cigarette, collecting her thoughts.

'It sounds sort of crazy when you tell someone about it. And I've never tried to tell anyone before.'

119

'Then how do you know it sounds crazy?' His eyes were unwavering.

'Because it is crazy. It's an impossible way to live. I know, I've tried. "My Secret Life," by Kezia Saint Martin.' She tried to laugh, but it was a hollow sound in the silence.

'Sounds like it's time you got it off your chest, and I'm handy. I'm sitting here and I've got nowhere to go and no time to be there. And all I know is that it's an insane life you seem to lead, Kezia. You deserve better than that.' Her name sounded unfamiliar on his lips, and she looked at him through the smoke. 'Worse than crazy, this must be a mighty lonely way to live.'

'It is.' She felt tears well up at the back of her throat. She wanted to tell Luke all of it now. K. S. Miller, Martin Hallam, Kezia Saint Martin. About the loneliness and the hurt and the ugliness of her world draped in gold brocade, as though they could hide it by making it pretty outside, or make their souls smell better by drenching them in perfume . . . and the intolerable obligations and responsibilities, and the stupid parties, and the boring men. And the victory of her own byline on her first serious article, and no one to share it with except a middle-aged lawyer and a still older agent. She had a lifetime to show him, a lifetime she had hidden deep in her heart, until now.

'I don't even know where to begin.'

'You said there are five of you. Pick one, and take it from there.'

Two lone tears slid down her face and he stretched out a hand to her. She took it, and they sat that way, their hands reaching across the table, the tears running slowly down her face.

'Well, the first me is Kezia Saint Martin. The name you saw on the letters. Heiress, orphan . . . isn't that a romantic vision?' She smiled lopsidedly through her tears. 'Anyway, my parents both died when I was a child, and left me a great deal of money and an enormous house, which my trustee sold and turned into a large co-op on Eighty-first

Street and Park, which I eventually sold to buy this. I have an aunt who's married to an Italian count, and I was brought up by my trustee and my governess, Totie. And of course, the other thing my parents left me was a name. Not just a name. But a *Name*. And it was carefully impressed on me before they died, and after they died, that I wasn't just "anybody." I was Kezia Saint Martin. . . . Hell, Luke, don't you read the papers?' She brushed the tears away and pulled back her hand to blow her nose on a mauve linen handkerchief, edged in grey lace.

'What in God's name is that?'

'What?'

'That thing you're blowing your nose in?' She looked at the bit of pale purple in her hand and laughed.

'A handkerchief. What do you think it is?'

'Looks like a vestment for a pint-sized priest for chrissake. Talk about fancy. Now I know you're an heiress!'

She laughed and felt a little bit better.

'And yes, I do read the papers, by the way. But I'd rather hear this story from you. I don't like to just read about people I care about.'

Kezia was momentarily confused. People he cared about? But he didn't even know her . . . but he had flown up from Washington to see her. He was there. And he looked as though what she had to say mattered to him.

'Well, every time I set foot anywhere, I get my photograph taken.'

'It didn't happen tonight.' He was trying to show her something, that she was freer than she knew.

'No, but it could have. That was just luck. That's why I was watching the doors - that, and the fact that I was afraid I'd see someone I knew, and they'd call me Kezia instead of Kate.'

'Would that have mattered so much, Kezia? If someone had blown your cover? So what?'

'So . . . I would have felt like a fool. I would have felt

121

'Frightened?' He finished for her, and she looked away.

'Maybe.' Hers was a small voice now.

'Why, love? Why would it frighten you if I knew who you really were?' He wanted to hear it from her. 'Were you afraid that I'd hurt you then? Pursue you for your money? Your name? What?'

'No ... it's ... well, possibly. Other people might want me for those things, Lucas, but I'm not worried about that with you.' Her eyes sought his squarely and she made sure he understood her. She trusted him, and she wanted him to know that. 'But the worst of it is something else. Kezia Saint Martin isn't just me. She's "someone." She has something to live up to. When I was twenty, I was considered the most eligible girl on the market. You know, sort of like Xerox stock. If you bought me, your investment was bound to go up.' He watched her eyes as she spoke and there were years of hurt embedded in them. Lucas was silent, his hand gently holding hers. 'And there was more to it than just being noticed. There was history ... good history, bad history, grandparents, my mother....' She paused and seemed to forget to go on. Lucas' voice finally stirred her.

'Your mother? What about your mother?'

'Oh ... just ... things....' Her voice was trembling and her eyes avoided his. She seemed to be having trouble continuing.

'What kind of things, Kezia? How old were you when she died?'

'I was eight. And she ... she drank herself to death.'

'I take it "things" got to her too?' He sat back for a moment and watched Kezia, whose eyes now rose slowly to his with a look of unfathomable sorrow and fear.

'Yeah. Things got to her too. She was The Lady Liane Holmes-Aubrey before she married my father. And then she was Mrs. Keenan Saint Martin. I'm not sure which must have been worse for her. Probably being Daddy's wife. At least in England she knew how it all worked. Here, things were different for her. Quicker, sharper, brasher.

122

She talked about it sometimes. She felt more "public" here than she had at home as a girl. They didn't jump all over her the way they do me. But then, she didn't have Daddy's fortune either.'

'Was she rich too?'

'Very. Not as rich as my father, but directly related to the Queen. Fun, isn't it?' Kezia looked away bitterly for a moment.

'I don't know, is it fun? It doesn't sound like it yet.'

'Oh, it gets better. My father was very rich and very powerful and very envied and very hated, and occasionally very loved. He did crazy things, he travelled a lot, he . . . he did whatever he did. And Mummy was lonely, I think. She was constantly spied on, written about, talked about, followed around. When she went to parties, they reported what she wore. When Daddy was away, and she danced with an old friend at a charity ball, they made a thing of it in the papers. She got to feeling hunted. Americans can be brutal that way.' Her voice trailed off for a moment.

'Only Americans, Kezia?'

She shook her head. 'No. They're all as bad. But they can be more direct about it here. They're gutsier, or less embarrassed. They show less "deference," I don't know . . . maybe she was just too frail. And too lonely. She always looked as though she didn't quite understand "why." '

'She left your father?' He was interested now. Very. He was beginning to feel something for the woman who had been Kezia's mother. The frail British noblewoman.

'No. She fell in love with my French tutor.'

'Are you kidding?' He looked almost amused.

'Nope.'

'And it made a big stink?'

'I guess so. It must have. It killed her.'

'That, directly?'

'No . . . who knows? That and a lot of other things. My father found out, and the young man was dismissed. And I guess it got to her after that. She was a traitor, and she sentenced herself to death. She drank more and more, and

123

ate less and less, and finally she got what she wanted out of it. Out.'

'You knew? About the tutor, I mean.'

'No, not then. Edward, my trustee, told me later. To be sure that the "sins of the mother would never be visited on the daughter." '

'Why do you call it a "betrayal"? Because she cheated on your father?'

'No, that would have been forgivable. The unforgivable was that she betrayed her ancestry, her heritage, her class and her breeding by falling in love – and having an affair – with a "peasant." ' She tried to laugh, but the sound was too brittle.

'And that's a sin?' Lucas looked confused.

'That, my dear, is the cardinal sin of all! Thou shalt not screw the lower classes. That applies to the women of my set anyway. For the men it's different.'

'For them it's okay to screw the "lower classes"?'

'Of course. Gentlemen have been balling the maid for hundreds of years. It's just that the lady of the house is not supposed to get laid by the chauffeur.'

'I see.' He tried to look amused but he wasn't.

'That's nice. My mother didn't see. And she committed an even worse crime. She fell in love with him. She even talked about running away with him.'

'How in hell did your father find out? Did he have her followed?'

'Of course not. He never suspected. No, Jean-Louis simply told him. He wanted fifty thousand dollars from my father not to make a scandal, not very much, all things considered. My father paid him twenty-five and had him deported.'

'Your trustee told you all this?' Lucas looked stormy now.

'Of course. Insurance. It's meant to keep me in line.'

'Does it?'

'In a way.'

'Why?'

124

'Because in a perverted way I'm afraid of my destiny. It's sort of "damned if you do, and damned if you don't." I think that if I lived my life the way I'm supposed to, I'd hate it enough to drink myself to death like my mother. But if I betray my "heritage," then maybe I'll end up like her anyway. A betrayer betrayed, in love with a two-bit low-class jerk who blackmailed her husband. Pretty, isn't it?'

'No. It's pathetic. And you really believe that crap about betrayal?'

She nodded. 'I have to. I've seen too many stories like that. I've ... in small ways it has happened to me. When people know who you are they ... they treat you differently, Lucas. You're no longer a person to them. You're a legend, a challenge, an object they must have. The only ones who understand you are your own kind.'

'Are you telling me they understand you?' He looked stunned.

'No. That's the whole trouble. For me, none of it works. I'm a misfit. I can't bear what I'm supposed to be. And I can't have what I want ... I fear it anyway. I ... oh hell, Lucas, I don't know.' She looked distraught as she folded a matchbook between her fingers.

'What happened to your father?'

'He had an accident, and not because he was heartsick over my mother. He had a healthy number of women after she died. Even though I'm sure he missed Mummy. But he was very bitter then. It seemed as though he didn't believe in anything anymore. He drank. He drove too fast. He died. Very simple really.'

'No, very complicated. What you're telling me is that a "betrayal," as you call it, of your "heritage," your world, leads to suicide, death, accidents, blackmail and heartbreak. But what does following the rules lead to? What happens if you play it straight, Kezia, and never "betray your class," as you'd put it? What happens if you just go along with their rules ... I mean you, Kezia. What would it do to you?'

125

'Kill me slowly.' Her voice was very soft but she sounded very certain.

'Is that what's been happening to you?'

'Yes. I think so, in a small way. I still have my escapes, my freedoms. They help. My writing is my salvation.'

'Stolen moments. Do you ever take those freedoms openly?'

'Don't be ridiculous, Lucas. How?'

'Any way you have to. Just do what you want to, openly for a change?'

'I couldn't.'

'Why not?'

'Edward. The press. Whatever I did that was even the least out of line, would be all over the papers. And I mean something as simple as going out with someone "different," ' she looked at him pointedly, 'going somewhere "inappropriate," saying something unguarded, wearing something indiscreet.'

'All right, so you get bad press. And then what? Chicken Little, the sky would not fall in.'

'You don't understand, Lucas. It would.'

'Because Edward would raise hell? So what?'

'But what if he's right . . . and . . . what . . . what if I end up . . .' She couldn't say it but he could.

'Like your mother?'

She looked up, her eyes swimming in tears, and nodded.

'You wouldn't, babe. You couldn't. You're different. You're freer, I'm sure. You're probably more worldly, and maybe even more intelligent than she was. And hell, Kezia, what if you did fall in love with the tutor, or the butler, or the chauffeur, or me for that matter? So fucking what?'

She didn't answer the question. She didn't know how. 'It's a special world, Lucas,' she said finally, 'with its own special rules.'

'Yeah. Like the joint.' He looked suddenly bitter.

'You mean prison?'

He nodded quietly in answer. 'I think you may be right. A silent, invisible prison, with walls built of codes and

126

hypocrisies and lies and restrictions, and cells padded with prejudice and fear, and all of it studded with diamonds.'

He looked up at her suddenly and laughed.

'What's funny?'

'Nothing, except that nine-tenths of the world are out there beating each other over the head to get into that elite little world of yours, and from the sound of it, they won't dig it when they get there. Not much.'

'Maybe they will. Some do.'

'But what happens to the ones who don't, Kezia? What happens to the ones who can't live with that bullshit?' He held tightly to her hand as he spoke, and her eyes rose slowly to his.

'Some of them die, Lucas.'

'And the others? The ones who don't die?'

'They live with it. They make peace with it. Edward is like that. He accepts the rules because he has to. It's the only way he knows, but it's ruined his life too.'

'He could have changed all that.' Luke sounded gruff and Kezia shook her head.

'No, Lucas, he couldn't have. Some people can't.'

'Why not? No balls?'

'If you want to call it that. Some people just can't stomach the unknown. They'd rather go down with a familiar ship than drown in unfamiliar seas.'

'Or get saved. There's always the chance that they'd find a lifeboat, or wash up on an island paradise. How about that for a surprise?'

But Kezia was thinking of something else. It was minutes before she spoke again, her eyes closed, her head resting on the back of the chair. She sounded very tired, and almost old. She wasn't entirely sure Luke understood. Maybe he couldn't. Maybe no outsider could. 'When I was twenty-one, I wanted to have a life of my own. So I tried to get a job at the *Times*. I swore to Edward that I could pull it off, that no one would bother me, that I wouldn't disgrace my name, all that bullshit. I lasted for seventeen workdays, and I almost had a nervous breakdown. I heard every joke, was the butt of every kind of hostility, curiosity, envy and obscenity. They even had paparazzi in the ladies' room when I had to pee. It amused them to hire me and watch the fun. And I tried, Luke, I really tried, but there was no way I could stick with it. They didn't want me. They wanted my fancy name and then to try and bring me down, just for kicks, to see if I was human too. I never came out in the open again. That was the last job anyone knew about, the last glimpse of the real me that the world out there had. From then on it was all underground, with pseudonyms, hiding behind agents, and ... well, it's all been just the way it was when I met you. And this is the first time I've taken a chance on being found out.'

'Why did you?'

'Maybe I had to. But as far as anyone knows, I go to all the right parties, am on all the right committees, vacation in all the right places, know all the right people, and everyone thinks I'm lazy as hell. I have a reputation for partying all night and sleeping till three in the afternoon.'

'And don't you?' He couldn't suppress a grin.

'No, I do not!' She wasn't amused, she was angry. 'I work my bloody ass off, as a matter of fact. I take every decent article I can get, and I have a good name in my field. You don't get that by sleeping till three.'

'And that doesn't fit with all the "right" people? Writing isn't "right" either?'

'Of course not. It's not respectable. Not for me. I'm supposed to be looking for a husband and having my hair done, not snooping around prisons in Mississippi.'

'Or ex-cons in Chicago.' There was a hint of sadness in his eyes. She had made it all so clear now.

'Their objection would not be to whom I write about, it would be the fact that I'm betraying my heritage.'

'That again. Jesus, Kezia, isn't that notion a little out-of-date? A lot of your kind of people work.'

'Yes, but not like this. Not for real. And ... there's more.'

128

'I figured that much.' He lit another cigarette and waited, and was surprised when she smiled.

'Aside from everything else, I'm a traitor. Have you ever read the Martin Hallam column? It's syndicated so you might have seen it.'

He nodded.

'Well, I write that. I started it as a kind of a fun thing, but it worked, and . . .' She shrugged and threw up her hands as he started to laugh.

'You mean you write that crazy goddamn column?'

She nodded, grinning sheepishly.

'And you rat on all your fancy friends like that?'

She nodded again. 'They lap it up. They just don't know that I'm the one who writes it. And to tell you the truth, in the last couple of years it's gotten to be a drag.'

'Talk about being a traitor! And no one suspects it's you?'

'Nope. No one ever has. They don't even know it's written by a woman. They just accept it. Even my editor doesn't know who writes it. Everything goes through my agent, and of course I'm listed as K. S. Miller on the agency roster.'

'Lady, you amaze me.' Now he looked stunned.

'Sometimes I even amaze myself.' It was a moment of light-hearted laughter after the painful start of the conversation.

'I'll say one thing, you certainly keep yourself busy. The K. S. Miller articles, the Hallam column, and your "fancy life." And no one even suspects?' He seemed dubious.

'No. And that part hasn't been easy. That's why I panicked at the idea of interviewing you. I thought you might have seen my photograph somewhere, and would recognize me, as me, not as "Kate Miller" obviously. All it would take to blow my whole trip would be one person seeing me at the wrong place at the wrong time, and zap, the whole house of cards would go down. And the truth of it is that the writing part of my life, the serious work, is the only part I respect. I won't jeopardize that for anyone, or anything.'

129

'But you did. You interviewed me. Why?'

'I told you. I had to. And I was curious, too. I liked your book. And my agent pressured me. He was right, of course. I can't go on hiding forever if I want a serious literary career. There are times when I'll have to take chances.'

'You took a big one.'

'Yes, I did.'

'Are you sorry?' He wanted an honest answer.

'No. I'm glad.' They smiled at each other again, and she sighed.

'Kezia. what if you told the world, *that* world, to go screw, and just openly did what you want for a change? Couldn't you at least be K. S. Miller out front?'

'How? Look at the stink it would make, what they'd say in the papers. Besides, it would muddy the waters. People would be requesting articles not because of K. S. Miller, but because of Kezia Saint Martin. I'd be back where I was eight years ago, as a gofer on the *Times*. And my aunt would have fits, and my trustee would be heartbroken, and I'd feel as though I had betrayed everyone who came before me.'

'For chrissake, Kezia. All those people are dead, or as good as.'

'The traditions aren't. They live on.'

'And all on your shoulders, is that it? You have the sole responsibility of holding up the world? Don't you realize how insane that is? This isn't Victorian England, and Jesus, that's your life you're hiding in the closet. Yours, one shot at it and it's gone. If you respect what you're doing, why not take your chances, drag it out of the closet and live it with pride? Or is it that you're too fucking scared?' His eyes burned holes in hers.

'Maybe. I don't know. I've never felt I had the choice.'

'That's where you're wrong. You always have a choice. About anything you do. Maybe you don't want a choice. Maybe you'd rather hide like a neurotic and live ten different screwed-up lives. It doesn't look worth a damn to me though, lady, I'll tell you that much.'

130

'Maybe it isn't. It doesn't look like much to me either right now. But what you don't understand is the matter of duty, obligation, tradition.'

'Duty to whom? What about yourself, dammit? Didn't you ever think of that? Do you want to sit around alone here for the rest of your life, writing in secret, and then going out to those asinine parties with that faggoty asshole?' He stopped suddenly and she frowned.

'What faggoty asshole?'

'The one I saw you with in the paper.'

'You mean you knew?'

He eyed her squarely and nodded. 'I knew.'

'Why didn't you tell me?' Her eyes blazed for a moment. She had let him so far into the inner sanctum of her life, a traitor already

'How could I tell you? "Hey, lady, before you do the next interview I'd like to tell you that I know your real name because I read about you in the paper"? So what? And I figured that you'd tell me when you were ready to, or maybe never. But if I slapped you in the face with it, you'd have run like the devil and I didn't want that.'

'Why? Afraid I might not write the article? Don't worry, they'd have sent someone else out to do it. You wouldn't have lost your story.' She almost sneered at him, and he grabbed her arm so suddenly it stunned her.

'No, but I might have lost you.'

She waited a long moment before speaking, and he still held her arm. 'Would it have mattered?'

'Very much. And what you have to decide now is whether or not you want to live lies for the rest of your days. Seems like a bummer to me . . . terrified about who's going to see you when and where and with whom and doing what. Who gives a shit? Let them see you! Show them who you really are, or don't you even know, Kezia? I think that's the crux of it. Maybe K. S. Miller is as big a phony as Martin Hallam or Kezia Saint Martin.'

'Oh to hell with you, dammit!' she shouted, wresting her arm free. 'It's so goddamn easy for you to sit there

131

and make speeches. You have absolutely nothing to lose. No one expects a damn thing of you, so how can you know what it's like? You can do anything you bloody well please.'

'Really?' His voice was quiet again and the texture of satin. 'Well, let me tell you something, Miss Saint Martin. I know about duty one hell of a lot more than you do. Only mine isn't to a bunch of upper-class mummies. My duty is to real people, guys I served my time with who have no one to speak out for them, no families to hire lawyers or remember them or give a damn. I know who they are, I remember them, sitting on their ass waiting for freedom, locked up in the hole, forgotten after years in the joint, some of them for as long as you've been alive, Kezia. And if I don't have the fucking balls to go out and do something for them, then maybe no one else will. They're my "duty." But at least they're real, and I guess I'm lucky, because I care about them. I don't just do it because I have to, or becau se I'm scared not to. I do it because I want to. I gamble my own ass for theirs, because every time I shoot my mouth off, I run the risk of winding up right back in there with them. So tell me about duty, and having something to lose. But I'll tell you one more thing before you do. And that's that if I didn't give a shit about them, if I didn't like them, or even love them, I'd say "Goodbye, Charlie" and tell them all to go fuck themselves. I'd get married again, have a bunch of kids, and go live in the country.

'Kezia, if you don't believe in the life you're leading, don't live it. It's as simple as that. Because the price you're trying to avoid paying, you're going to wind up paying anyway. You're going to wind up fucking hating yourself for wasting the years and playing games you should have outgrown years ago. If you dug that life, that would be fine. But you don't, so what are you still doing there?'

'I don't really know. Except I don't think I'm as ballsy as you are.'

'You're as ballsy as you want to be. That's bullshit.

132

You're just waiting for an easy way out. A petition that gives you your freedom, a man to come and take you by the hand and lead you away. Well, maybe it'll happen like that, but it probably won't. You'll probably have to do it all yourself, just like everyone else.'

She was silent in answer, and he found himself wanting to hold her. He had given her a lot to swallow in one dose, but he couldn't help himself. Now that she had opened the doors, he had to tell her what he saw. For both their sakes. But mainly for hers.

'I didn't mean to trample all over you, babe.'

'It needed to be said.'

'You could probably level some things at me that need to be said too. I see what you're going through, and you're right in a sense, it is a lot easier for me. I have an army of people waiting in the wings all the time to tell me how terrific I am. Not the parole board, mind you, but people, friends. That makes a big difference, it makes it kind of an ego trip. What you're trying to do is a lot harder. Causes carry a lot of glory, breaking away from home never does . . . until later. Much later. But you'll get there. You're already more than halfway there, you just don't know it yet.'

'You think so?'

'I know so. You'll make it. But we all know it's a rough road.' As he watched her, he was once again stunned by all that he'd heard. The secrets from the depths of her soul, the confessions about her family and the insane theories about tradition and treason. It was all more than a little new to him, but intriguing nonetheless. She was the product of a strange and different world, yet a hybrid in her own way. 'Where do you think that road to freedom is going to take you, by the way – to SoHo?' He wanted to know, but she laughed at him.

'Don't be ridiculous. I have a pleasant time down there, but that's not the real thing. Even I know that. It just helps get me through the rest of the bullshit. You know, the only thing that isn't bullshit is K. S. Miller.'

133

'That's a byline, not a human being. You're the human being, Kezia. I think that's what you forget. Maybe on purpose.'

'Maybe I've had to. Just look at my life, Luke. It's nowhere, and the games are getting harder and harder to play. It's all one big long game. The game of the parties, the committees, the balls and the bullshit, the game of "artist's old lady in SoHo," the game of the gossip column. It's all a game. And I'm tired of living in a world that's so limited it can only bring itself to include about eight hundred people. And I don't fit in a scene like SoHo.'

'Why? Not your class?'

'No. Just not my world.'

'Then stop poaching on other people's worlds. Make your own. A crazy one, a good one, a bad one, whatever you want, just make it one that suits you, for a change. You make the rules. Be quiet about it if you think you have to, but at least try to respect your own trip. Don't sell out, Kezia. You're too smart for that. I think you realize yourself that you've gotten to a point where you're going to have to make some choices.'

'I know that. I think that's why I had the courage to invite you here. I had to. You're a good man, I respect you. I couldn't insult you with more lies and evasions. I couldn't insult myself like that. Not again. It's a question of trust.'

'I'm honoured.' She looked up to see if he was making fun of her, and was touched when she saw that he wasn't. 'And that makes four,' he announced.

'Four what?'

'You said there were five of you. You've just covered four. The heiress, the writer, the gossip columnist, and the tourist in SoHo. Who's number five? I'm beginning to like this.' He smiled easily again, and stretched out his legs.

'So am I. And I am not a gossip columnist, by the way. It's a "Society Editorial." ' She grinned primly.

'Forgive me, Mr. Hallam.'

134

'Indeed. The fifth me is your doing. "Kate." I've never told all this to anyone before. I think this marks the beginning of a new me.'

'Or the end of all the old ones. Don't just tack another role onto the list, another game. Do it straight.'

'I am.' There was tenderness in her eyes as she watched him.

'I know you are, Kezia. And I'm glad. For both of us. No . . . for you.'

'You've given me a kind of freedom tonight, Luke. That's a very special thing.'

'It is, but you're wrong about my giving it to you. I told you before that no one can take your freedom from you . . . and no one can give it back either. You manage that one all by yourself. Keep it safe.' He leaned over and kissed her on the top of her head and then moved to whisper in her ear. 'Which way's your john?'

She laughed as she looked up into his face. He was such a beautiful man.

'The john's down the hall to your left. You can't miss it, it's pink.'

'I'd be disappointed if it weren't.' His laugh was a slow rumble as he disappeared down the hall, and she went back to the kitchen to see about their coffee. Three hours had passed.

'Still want that coffee, Luke?' He was back and stretching lazily in the kitchen doorway.

'Could I trade it in for a beer?'

'Sure could.'

'Terrific, and you can keep the glass clean, thanks. No class. No class at all. You know how it is with the peasants.' He pulled the tab off the can and took a long swallow. 'Man, that tastes good.'

'It's been a long night. I'm sorry to have chewed your ear off like that, Luke.'

'No, you're not, and neither am I.' They smiled at each other again, and she sipped at a glass of white wine.

'I'll get you set up on the couch.' He nodded and took a

135

long swig of beer, as she stepped easily under the arm he had propped in the doorway.

She had the couch made up as a bed in a matter of moments.

'That ought to keep you till morning. Do you need anything else before I trot off to bed?'

What he needed would have shocked her. She was crisp and matter-of-fact again now. The lady of the house. The Honourable Kezia Saint Martin.

'Yes, as a matter of fact, I do need something before you "trot off to bed." I need a glimpse of the woman I sat here and talked to all night. You've got a poker up your ass again, my love. It's a lousy habit. I'm not going to hurt you, or rape you, or plunder your mind. I won't even blackmail you.'

She looked surprised and a little hurt as she stood across the room. 'I didn't feel you had plundered my mind. I wanted to talk to you, Lucas.'

'So what's different now?'

'I just wasn't thinking.'

'So you closed up.'

'Habit, I guess.'

'And I told you, a lousy one. Aren't we friends?'

She nodded at him, tears bright in her eyes again. It had been an emotional evening. 'Of course we're friends.'

'Good, because I think you're very special.' He crossed the room in three long strides, and gave her a hug and a kiss on the cheek. 'Good night, babe. Have a good sleep.' She stood on tiptoe and returned the kiss to his cheek.

'Thanks, and you too, Lucas. Sleep tight.'

He could hear a clock ticking somewhere in the darkened house, and there was no sound from her room. He had only been lying there for about ten minutes, and he was too keyed up to sleep. It felt as though they had talked for days, and he had been so afraid of frightening her away, of doing something to make her close the door again. That was why he was lying on the couch, and had settled

136

for a kiss on the cheek. She was not a woman you could rush at – not unless you wanted to lose her before you began. But they had come a long way in one night. He was content merely with that. He ran over the hours of talking in his mind . . . the expressions on her face . . . the words . . . the tears . . . the way she reached out for his hand. . . .

'Luke? Are you sleeping?' He had been so intent on his thoughts that he hadn't heard her bare feet pad across the carpeted floor.

'No. I'm awake.' He propped himself up on one elbow and looked at her. She was wearing a soft pink nightgown and her hair fell loose past her shoulders. 'Is anything wrong?'

'No, I can't sleep.'

'Neither can I.'

She smiled and sat down on the floor near the couch. He didn't know what to make of her reappearance. She was not always easy to read. Luke lit a cigarette and handed it to her. She took it, inhaled, and returned it.

'You did a nice thing for me tonight, Lucas.'

'What's that?' He was lying down again, gazing up at the ceiling.

'You let me talk out a lot of things that have been bothering me for years. I needed that so badly.'

And that wasn't all she needed, but the idea of dealing with that almost frightened him. He didn't want to screw up her life; she had enough on her hands.

'Luke?'

'Yeah?'

'What was your wife like?' There was a long silence and she began to regret having asked him.

'Pretty, young, crazy, like me in those days . . . and afraid. She was afraid to go it alone. I don't know, Kezia . . . she was a nice girl, I loved her . . . but it seems like a long time ago. I was different then. We did things, we never said things. It got all fucked up when I went to the joint. You have to be able to talk when something like that happens, and she couldn't. She couldn't even talk when our little girl was killed. I think that's what killed her. It all knotted up inside her till she strangled on it and died. In a way she was dead before she committed suicide. Maybe like your mother.'

Kezia nodded, watching his face. He wore a faraway look, but his voice showed no emotion other than respect for the passing of time.

'What made you ask?'

'Curious, I guess. We talked a lot about me tonight.'

'We talked a lot about me yesterday in the interview. I'd say we're even. Why don't you try and get some sleep?'

She nodded and he stubbed out the cigarette they had shared, as she stood up.

'Good night, Luke.'

' 'Night, babe. See you tomorrow.'

'Today.'

He grinned at her correction, and then swatted one long paw lazily in the direction of her bottom. 'Back-talker. Get your ass to bed now, or you'll be too tired to show me the town tomorrow.'

'Can you spend the day?'

'I plan to, unless you have something better to do.' He had never thought to ask her.

'Nope. I'm free as a bird. G'night, Lucas.' She turned quickly in a flurry of pink silk then, and he watched her go, wanting to reach out and stop her. And then it was out, before he could swallow the words.

'Kezia!' His voice was soft but urgent.

'Yes?' She turned with a look of surprise on her face.

'I love you.'

She stood very still, and neither of them moved. He lay twisted on the couch, watching her face. And she looked awed by his words.

'I . . . you're very special to me, Luke. I . . .'

'Are you afraid?'

She nodded, lowering her eyes. 'A little.'

'You don't have to be, Kezia. I love you. I won't hurt you. I've never known a woman like you.'

138

She wanted to tell him that she had never known a man like him, but somehow she couldn't. She couldn't say anything. She could only stand there, wishing for his arms, and not knowing how to find them.

It was Lucas who went to her, quietly, wrapping himself in the sheet she'd used for his bed. He walked slowly towards her and put his arms around her, holding her close.

'Everything's okay, babe. Everything's just fine.'

'It is, isn't it?' She gazed up at him with a sunny look on her face. This was different from anything she had known. It mattered, it was serious, and to the core of her soul he knew who she was.

'Lucas . . .'

'Yeah, Mama?'

'I love you. I . . . love . . . you. . . .' He swept her up in his arms then, gently, easily, and carried her back to her room in the dark. And as he set her down, she looked up at him and smiled. It was the smile of a woman, mischievous, mysterious, and tender. 'You know something funny, Luke? I've never made love in my own bedroom before.'

'I'm glad.'

'So am I.' Their voices had sunk to whispers.

Her shyness fell away from her as she held out her arms to him, and he carefully pulled the pink silk nightgown down past her shoulders. She unravelled the sheet from his waist. His hands spent the dawn learning her body, and at last she fell asleep in his arms, as the sky was turning pale grey.

CHAPTER XII

'Good morning, my love. What do you want to do today?' She grinned at him with her chin on his chest.

'Oh, you know, the usual ... tennis, bridge, whatever we're supposed to do on Park Avenue.'

'Up your nose.'

'My nose? Why my nose?'

'I love your nose. It's gorgeous.'

'You're crazy. Stark staring cuckoo, Miss Saint Martin. Maybe that's why I love you.'

'Are you sure you love me?' She was playing a game that women only play when they're sure.

'Absolutely certain.'

'How do you know?' She ran a finger along his neck pensively and then let it float down his chest.

'Because my left heel itches. My mother told me I'd know it was true love when my left heel itched. It itches. So you must be the one.'

'Crazy nut.' He silenced her with a kiss, and she tucked herself into his arms, and they lay side by side, enjoying the morning.

'You're beautiful, Kezia.'

'So are you.' He had a lean, powerful body that rippled with healthy muscles, covered by the smoothest of skin. She bit gently at his nipple, and he swatted her small white behind.

'Where'd you get the expensive-looking tan?'

'Marbella, of course. And in the South of France. "In seclusion".'

'You're shitting me.' He looked vastly amused.

'I shit you not. The papers said I was "in seclusion". Actually I went off on my own on a boat I hired in the

Adriatic, and just before Marbella I did some research for a story in North Africa. That was terrific!' Her eyes shone with the memory.

'You sure do get around.'

'Yup. I did a lot of work this summer too. Gee, Luke wouldn't it be neat if we could go to Europe together sometime? I mean the good places like Dakar and Marrakech, Camargue in France, and Brittany, and Yugoslavia. Maybe Scotland too.' She looked up at him dreamily and nibbled his ear.

'Sounds delightful, but unfortunately it'll never happen. Not for a while anyway.'

'Why not?'

'Can't. My parole.'

'What a bore.'

He threw back his head and laughed, pulling her away from his ear carefully, and looking for her lips with his mouth. They kissed hungrily and long, and when it was over he chuckled again.

'You're right, my parole is a bore. I wonder what they'd say if I told them that.'

'Let's tell them and find out.'

'I have a sneaking suspicion you would.'

She grinned wickedly at him and he pulled the sheet from her body to look at her aagain.

'You know what I love?'

'My bellybutton?'

'Better than your big mouth anyway. At least it's quiet. No, be serious for a minute . . .'

'I'll try.'

'Shut up.'

'I love you.'

'Oooh, woman, don't you ever stop talking?' He kissed her fiercely and tugged at a lock of her hair.

'I haven't had anyone to talk to in so long, never like this . . . it just feels so good I can't stop.'

'I know what you mean.' He ran a hand gently up the inside of her thigh with a passionate look in his eyes.

141

'What were you going to tell me?' She lay watching him matter-of-factly.

'Sweetheart, your timing is lousy. I was about to ravish your body again.'

'No, you weren't. You were going to tell me something.' She looked almost angelic.

'Don't be a tease. And I was going to tell you something before you interrupted me. What I was going to say is that it's incredible how last week I didn't even know you, and three days ago you appeared at one of my speeches, and two days ago I told you the story of my life. By yesterday, I had fallen in love with you. And now here we are. I didn't think things like this happened.'

'They don't. But I know what you mean. I feel like I've known you forever.'

'That's what I mean. Feels like we've been hanging out together for years. And I love it.'

'Have you ever felt like this before?'

'Women! What an impertinent question. But for your information, no, I have not. One thing's for damn sure, I've never fallen head over heels in love in three days before . . . and never with an heiress.'

He grinned at her and lit a cigar. Kezia reflected gleefully that her mother would have died. A cigar in the bedroom? Before breakfast? Good lord.

'Lucas, you know what you've got?'

'Bad breath?'

'Aside from that. You've got style.'

'What kind of style?'

'Gorgeous style, sexy style, courageous style, ballsy style . . . I think I'm crazy about you.'

'Crazy, for sure. About me, in that case I'm damn lucky.'

'So am I. Oh, Lucas, I'm so glad you're here. Imagine if I hadn't given you my phone number!' The thought appalled her.

'I'd have found you anyway.' He sounded totally confident.

142

'How?'

'I'd have found a way. Bloodhounds, if I'd had to. I wasn't about to let you slip out of my life in one breath. I couldn't keep my eyes off you all night at that first speech. I couldn't figure out if you were the writer who was coming to interview me.' It was delicious sharing the secrets of their first feelings, and Kezia was smiling as she hadn't in years.

'You scared me that first morning.'

'Did I? Jesus, and I tried so hard not to. I was probably ten times as scared as you were.'

'But you didn't look it. And you looked at me so pointedly, I kept thinking that you could see whatever I thought.'

'I wish to hell I could have. It was all I could do not to jump up and grab you.'

'Masher.' She rolled closer to him, and they kissed again. 'You taste of cigar.'

'Want me to go brush my teeth?'

'Later.' He smiled and rolled onto his stomach, the pink nightgown still tangled near his feet. He kissed her again and held her close in his arms, his body slowly taking hold of hers, his feet pressing her legs wide apart.

'Okay, lady, you said you'd show me the town.' He sat naked in one of the blue velvet chairs, smoking his second cigar of the day, and drinking his first beer. They had just finished breakfast. And she looked at him and started to laugh.

'Lucas, you look impossible.'

'I do not. I look extremely possible. And I feel better than hell. I told you, babe, no class.'

'You're wrong.'

'About what?'

'Having no class. Class is a question of dignity, and pride, and caring, and you happen to have lots of all three. I'm related to an absolute horde of people who have no class at all. And I met some people in SoHo who had tons of it. It's a very strange thing.'

'It must be.' He didn't seem to care one way or the other. 'So what are we doing today? Besides making love.'

'Hmm . . . all right, I'll show you the town.'

And she did. She arranged for a limousine, and they toured Wall Street and the Village, drove up the East River Drive and crossed Forty-second Street to Broadway, pausing at the Stage Delicatessen for cream cheese and bagels. Then they followed their route north to Central Park and swooped past the Plaza, where they stopped for a drink at the Oak Room. Back down Fifth, and up Madison past all the boutiques, and all the way uptown again, where they halted the chauffeur at the Metropolitan Museum and got out and walked in the park. It was six o'clock when they wound up at the Stanhope for drinks, fighting the pigeons for peanuts at the sidewalk cafe.

'You give a good tour, Kezia. Hey, I just thought of something. Want to meet one of my friends?'

'Here?' She looked surprised.

'No, not here, silly girl. Uptown. In Harlem.'

'Sounds interesting.' She looked at him with a long, slow smile. The idea intrigued her.

'He's a beautiful guy. Nicest dude I know. I think you'd like him.'

'I probably would.' They exchanged a sweet sunny look which reflected the warmth of the day.

'It wouldn't be too cool to go up in the limo though, would it?'

He shook his head in answer, and picked up the check. 'We can send Jeeves home, and catch a cab up.'

'Bullshit to that.'

'You want to go in the limo?' He hadn't counted on that. Certainly not for a trip up to Harlem, but maybe she didn't know how to travel any other way.

'Of course not, you dummy. We can go up on the subway. It's faster, and smarter. A lot more discreet.'

'Well, listen to her. "Discreet". You mean you take the subway?' He stood up and looked down at her face as they laughed. She was full of surprises.

144

'How do you think I used to go down to SoHo? By jet?'

'Your own private Lear, I would think.'

'But of course. Come on, Romeo, let's get rid of Jeeves, and go for a walk.' The chauffeur tipped his hat and was instantly gone, and they strolled leisurely towards the subway, where they descended into the bowels of the world, bought tokens, and shared pretzels and a Coke.

They reached the 125th Street station, and Luke held her hand as they climbed the stairs to the street.

'It's just a few blocks.'

'Come to think of it, Luke, are you sure he'll be home?'

'Nope. We're going to the place where he works and I'm sure that he'll be there. You can hardly drag him out of the damn place to feed him.'

Luke seemed broader suddenly as they walked along, and more sure of himself than he had appeared all day. His shoulders seemed to spread, his walk almost rolled, while his eyes kept careful watch on passersby. He was wearing his familiar tweed jacket, and she was in jeans. But this was still Harlem. A long way from home. For her. To him, it appeared to be something he knew. He was wary, but only he knew of what.

'You know something, Lucas? You walk differently here.'

'You'd better believe it. Brings back memories of Q.'

'San Quentin?' He nodded and they turned a corner, as Lucas looked up at a building and stopped.

'Well, baby, this is it.' They were standing in front of a decaying brownstone with a half-burnt-away sign: *Armistice House*. But it didn't look to Kezia as though it had been much of a truce.

He let go her hand and put an arm around her shoulders as they walked up the stairs. Two raucous teen-age black boys and a Puerto Rican girl came roaring out of the door, laughing and shrieking, the girl running away from the boys, but not very hard. Kezia smiled and looked up at Luke.

'So what's so different up here?'

Luke didn't smile back. 'Junkies, pushers, hookers,

145

pimps, street fights, shankings. Same stuff that goes on anywhere in town, in any town in the world these days . . . except the neighbourhood you live in. And don't get any fancy ideas. If you decide that you like Alejandro, don't come up here to visit after I'm gone. Give him a call, and he can come to see you. This isn't your world.'

'But it's yours?' She was almost annoyed at the speech. She was a big girl. She had survived before Luke. Though admittedly not in the middle of Harlem. 'And this is your world, I suppose?' she repeated. He didn't look like he fit any better than she did. Well, not much better.

'Used to be. But not anymore. I can deal with it though. You can't. It's as simple as that.' He held the door open for her and his tone of voice told her he meant business.

The corridor, lined with faded posters, smelled of stale urine and fresh grass. Graffiti doubled as artwork between the posters, and glass shades around light bulbs had been broken, and paper flowers hung limply from fire extinguishers. A tired sign said 'Welcome to Armistice House! We love you!' And someone had crossed out the 'love' and written 'fuck'.

Luke wove his way up a narrow staircase, keeping one hand in Kezia's, but the tenseness was leaving him now. The once-upon-a-time street fighter had come for a visit. A social call. She laughed, suddenly reminded of the legends of the Old West.

'What's so funny, Mama?' He looked at her from his great height as she came up the stairs behind him, light on her feet, smiling and happy.

'You are, Marshal Dillon. Sometimes you're an absolute riot.'

'Oh, is that so?'

'Yes, that's so.' She leaned her face towards him and he bent down to kiss her.

'I like that. I like it a lot.' He ran his hand across her behind as she joined him on the landing, and he gave her a gentle push towards a badly scarred door.

'Are you sure he's here?' Kezia felt suddenly shy.

146

'I'm sure, babe. He's always here, the dumb asshole. He spills his guts in this shithouse. His guts and his heart and his soul. You'll see.' The name on the door said 'Alejandro Vidal.' No promises, no slogans, and this time no graffiti. Only a name.

Kezia waited for Luke to knock, but he didn't. He kicked brutally at the door, and then opened it at lightning speed as he entered.

'*Qué* . . .' A slight Latino man behind a desk rose to his feet with a look of astonishment, and then began laughing.

'Luke, you bastard, how are you? I should have known it was you. For a second, I thought they were finally coming to get me.'

The small, blue-eyed, bearded Mexican looked ecstatic to see him, as Luke strode across the room and threw his arms around his friend.

It was several minutes before Luke remembered Kezia, or Alejandro even took notice, and it was just as long again before Kezia got more than a glimpse of the man, lost in Luke's bear hugs. There had been a wealth of ¿*Qué pasa, hombre?*s and a fast flurry of Mexican curses. Alejandro's pure Spanish, and the pidgin Luke had picked up in the joint. Jokes about 'twice pipes' and someone's 'short', and a variety of unintelligible dialects that were part Mexican, part prison, and pure Californian. The patois was a mystery to Kezia. And then suddenly it all stopped, and the kindest smile and softest eyes imaginable settled on Kezia's face. The smile was a slow spread from the eyes to the mouth, and the eyes were the softest blue velvet. Alejandro Vidal had the kind of face you brought your troubles to, and your heart. Almost like a Christ, or a priest. He looked shyly at Kezia and smiled..

'Hello. This rude sonofabitch will probably never remember to introduce us. I'm Alejandro.' He held out a hand and she met it with hers.

'I'm Kezia.' They shook hands with ceremony and then laughter, and Alejandro offered the room's only two chairs as he perched on his desk.

147

He was a man of average height, but of slight build, and next to Luke he was instantly dwarfed. But it wasn't his frame that caught one's attention. It was his eyes. They were tender and knowing. They didn't reach out and grab you; you went to them gladly. Everything about him was warm. His laughter, his smile, his eyes, the way he looked at them both. He was a man who had seen a great deal, but there was not a trace of the cynic about him. Only the understanding of the sorely tried, and the compassion of a gentle man. His sense of humour allowed his soul to survive what he saw. And while Luke and he made jokes for an hour, Kezia watched him. He was an odd contrast to Luke, but she liked him instantly, and knew why he was Luke's closest friend. They had met long ago in L.A.

'How long have you been in New York?' It was the first time she'd addressed him since they'd met. He had given her tea, and then succumbed to gossip and nonsense with Luke. It had been a year since they'd seen each other and there was much to catch up on.

'I've been here about three years, Kezia.'

'Seems like long enough to me,' Luke broke into the exchange. 'How much shit you gonna take around this dump, Al, before you get smart and go home? Why don't you go back to L.A.?'

'Because I'm working on something here. The only problem is that the kids we treat are outpatient instead of live-in. Man, if we had a resident facility, I could take this shabby operation a long, long way.' His eyes lit up as he spoke.

'You're treating kids with drug problems?' Kezia was interested in what he had to say. If nothing else, it might make a good story. But more than the story, she was intrigued by the man. She liked him. He was the sort of person you wanted to hug, and she had only just met him.

'Yes, drug and minor criminal histories. The two are almost always related.' He came alive as he explained the services the facility offered, showed her charts, graphs, histories, and outlines of future plans. But the real problem

148

remained: lack of control. As long as the kids went back on the streets at night, back to broken homes where a mother was turning tricks on the room's only bed, or a father was zeating his wife, where brothers shot dope in the john, and sisters took reds or sold yellows, there wasn't a lot they could do. 'The whole point is to get them out of their environment. To change the whole life pattern. We know that now, but here it's not easy.' He waved dimly at the peeling walls and amply made his point. The place was in very bad shape.

'I still think you're nuts.' But Luke was, as always, impressed with his friend's determination, his drive. He had seen him beaten, mugged, rolled, kicked, laughed at, spat on, and ignored. But no one could ever keep Alejandro down. He believed in his dreams. As Luke did in his.

'And you think you're any saner, Luke? You're going to stop the world from building prisons? Hombre, you die before you see that one happen.' He rolled his eyes and shrugged, but the respect was entirely mutual. It amused Kezia to listen to them talk. To Kezia, Alejandro spoke perfect English, but with Luke he fell into the language of the streets. A put-on, a remnant, a joke, or a bond, she wasn't quite sure. Maybe a combination of them all.

'Okay, smartass, you'll see. Thirty years from now there won't be a prison functioning in this state, or in any other state for that matter.' She caught 'loco' and 'cabeza' in answer and then Luke flipped up one finger on his right hand.

'Please, Luke, there's a lady present.' But it was all in good fun, and Alejandro seemed to have accepted her. There was the faintest hint of shyness about him. Still, he joked with her, almost as he did with Luke. 'And you, Kezia? What do you do?' He looked at her with wide-open eyes.

'I write.'

'And she's good.'

Kezia laughed and gave Luke a shove. 'Wait until you see the interview before you decide. Anyway, you're pre-

judiced.' They shared a smile three ways and Alejandro
looked pleased for his friend. He had known immediately
that this was no light-hearted fling, no one-night stand or
casual friend. It was the first time he had seen Luke with a
woman. Luke kept his women in bed, and went home when
he wanted some more. This one had to be special. She
seemed different from the others too. Worlds different. She
was intelligent, and she had a certain style. Class. He
wondered where Luke had met her.

'Want to come downtown for dinner?' Luke lit a cigar
and offered one to his friend. Alejandro took it eagerly and
then looked surprised when he lit it.

'Cubano?'

Luke nodded. Kezia laughed.

'The lady's well-supplied.'

Alejandro whistled and Luke looked momentarily proud.
He had a woman who had something no one else on their
block had: Cuban cigars. 'How about dinner, big Al?'

'Lucas, I can't. I'd like to, but . . .' He waved at the
mountain of work on his desk. 'And at seven tonight we're
having a group for the parents of some of our patients.'

'Group therapy?'

Alejandro nodded. 'Getting to the parents helps. Sometimes.'

Kezia suddenly had the feeling that Alejandro was
emptying a tidal wave with a thimble, but you had to give
him credit for trying.

'Dinner another time maybe. How long will you be in
town?'

'Tonight. Tomorrow. But I'll be back.' Alejandro smiled
again and patted his friend on the back.

'I know you will. And I'm happy for you, man.' He
gazed warmly at Kezia and then smiled at them both. It
felt like a blessing.

It was obvious that Alejandro hated to see them leave as
much as Lucas hated to go. And Kezia felt it too.

'You were right.'

'About what?'

150

'Alejandro.'

'Yeah. I know.' Lucas had been lost in his own thoughts all the way to the subway. 'That sonofabitch is going to get himself killed up here one of these days with his goddamn groups and his fucking ideals. I wish he'd get the hell out.'

'Maybe he can't.'

'Oh yeah?' Lucas was pissed. He was worried about his friend.

'It's kind of like a war, Luke. You fight yours, he fights his. Neither of you really cares if you get sacrificed in the process. It's the end result that matters. To both of you. He's not so different from you. Not in the way he thinks. He's doing what he has to do.'

Lucas nodded, still looking disgruntled. but he knew she was right. She was very perceptive. It surprised him sometimes. For someone as dumb as she was about her own life, she had a way of putting her finger right on the spot for others.

'You're wrong about one thing, though.'

'What?'

'He isn't like me at all.'

'What makes you say that?'

'There isn't a mean bone in his body.'

'But there is in yours?' A smile started to light in her eyes. Mr. Macho was talking.

'You'd better believe it, Mama. Lots of them. You don't live through what I did, six years in the California prison system, if you're made like him. Someone turns you into a punk, and if you don't dig it, you die the next day.' Kezia was silent as they started their journey back into the subway.

'He was never in prison then?' She had assumed that he had been, because Luke was.

'Alejandro?' Luke let out a hearty bass laugh. 'Nope. All his brothers were, though. He was visiting one of his brothers at Folsom. And I dug him. When I switched to another joint, he got special permission to come and see me. We've been brothers since then. But Alejandro's not on

151

the same trip, never was. He went the other way from the rest of his family. Magna cum laude at Stanford.'

'Christ, he's so unassuming.'

'That's why he's beautiful, babe. And the dude has a heart of pure gold.'

The arriving train swallowed their words, and they rode home in silence. She tugged at his sleeve at the Seventy-seventh Street stop.

'This is us.' He nodded, smiled, and stood up. He was back to himself again, she could see it. The worry for Alejandro had faded from his face. He had other things on his mind now.

'Baby, I love you.' He held her in his arms as the train pulled away, and their lips met and held. And then suddenly he looked at her, worried again. 'Is this uncool?'

'Huh?' She didn't know what he meant, as he pulled away from her looking embarrassed.

'Well, I can dig your not wanting to wind up in the papers. I made you a lot of speeches last night, but I do understand how you feel. Being yourself is one thing, making page one is another.'

'Thank God I never do that. Page five maybe, page four even, but never page one. That's reserved for homicides, rapes, and stock market disasters.' She laughed up at him again. 'It's okay, Luke. It was "cool". Besides . . .' there was mischief in her eyes . . . 'remarkably, very few of my friends ride the subway. It's silly of them, actually. This is such a marvellous way to travel!' There was pure debutante in her voice as she fluttered her eyelashes at him, and he gave her a severe look from the top of his height.

'I'll be sure to keep that in mind.' He took her hand and swung it as they walked along with matched smiles.

'Want to pick up something to eat?' They were passing a store that sold barbecued chickens.

'No.'

'Aren't you hungry?' She was suddenly famished. It had been a long day.

'Yes. I'm hungry.'

'Well?' He was hurrying her along the street and she didn't understand, and then with a look at his face she understood. Perfectly. 'Lucas, you're awful!'

'Tell me that later.' He took her by the hand, and laughing, they ran over the subway grate, and then turned the corner towards home.

'Lucas! The doorman!' They looked like dishevelled children, running helter-skelter down the street hand in hand. They came to a screeching halt outside the door to her building. He followed her decorously inside, as they both fought to stifle giggles. They stood in the elevator like altar boys, and then collapsed in laughter in the hallway as Kezia dug for her key.

'Come on, come on!' He ran a hand smoothly under her jacket, and slid it inside her shirt.

'Stop it, Luke!' She laughed and searched harder for the elusive key.

'If you don't find the damn thing at the count of ten, I'm going to . . .'

'No, you're not!'

'Yes, I am. Right here in the hall.' He smiled and ran his mouth over the top of her head.

'Stop that! Wait . . . got it!' She pulled the key triumphantly from her bag.

'Nuts. I was beginning to hope you wouldn't find it.'

'You're a disgrace.' The door swung open and he lunged for her as they stepped inside, and swept her into his arms to carry her to their bed. 'No, Lucas, stop!'

'Are you kidding?'

She arched her neck regally, perched in his arms, looked him in the eye and bristled, but there was mirth in her eyes. 'I am not kidding. Put me down. I have to go wee-wee.'

'Wee-wee?' Luke's face broke into broad lines of laughter. *Wee-wee?*

'Yes, wee-wee.' He put her down and she crossed her legs and giggled again.

153

'Why didn't you say so. I mean if I'd known that . . .' His laughter filled the hall as she disappeared towards the pink bathroom.

She was back in a minute, and tenderness had replaced the spirit of teasing. She had kicked off her shoes on the way, and stood barefoot before him, her long hair framing her face, her eyes large and bright, and something happy in her face that had never been there before.

'You know something? I love you.' He pulled her into his arms and gave her a gentle hug.

'I love you too. You're something I've imagined, but never thought I'd find.'

'Neither did I. I think I'd resigned myself to not finding it, and just going on as I was.'

'And how was that?'

'Lonely.'

'I know that trip too.'

They walked silently into the bedroom and he turned down the bed as she stepped out of her jeans. Even the Porthault sheets no longer embarrassed her, they were lovely for Luke.

CHAPTER XIII

'Lucas?'

'Yeah?'

'Are you all right?' It was dark in the bedroom and she was sitting up, looking down at him, with a hand on his shoulder. The bed was damp around them.

'I'm fine. What time is it?'

'Quarter to five.'

'Christ.' He rolled over on his back, and looked up at her, groggy. 'What are you doing up, babe?'

'I wasn't. But you had a bad dream.' A very bad dream.

154

'Don't worry about it. I'm sorry I woke you.'

He stroked one breast tenderly with his eyes half-closed, and she smiled. 'My snoring's worse, though. You got off lucky.'

But she was worried. The bed was drenched from his thrashings.

'I think I'd rather you snored. You sounded so upset. Frightened, I think.' At the last, he'd been trembling.

'Don't worry about it, Mama. You'll get used to it.'

'Do you have dreams like that often?' He shrugged in answer, and reached for his cigarettes.

'Smoke?' She shook her head.

'Do you want a glass of water?'

He laughed as he flicked out the match. 'No, Miss Nightingale, I don't. Cut it out, Kezia. What do you expect? I've been a lot of funny places in my life. They leave their mark.'

But like that? She had watched him for almost twenty minutes before waking him. He acted as though he were being tortured.

'Is that ... is that from when you were in prison?' She hated to ask, but he only shrugged again.

'One thing's for sure. It isn't from making love to you. I told you, don't worry about it.' He propped himself up on one elbow and kissed her. But she could still see terror in his eyes.

'Luke?' Something had just occurred to her.

'What?'

'How long are you staying here?'

'Till tomorrow.'

'That's all?'

'That's all.' And then, as he saw the look on her face, he stubbed out his cigarette and drew her into his arms. 'There'll be more. This is just the beginning. You don't think I want to lose you, after it took me all these years to find you, do you?' She smiled in answer, and they lay side by side, in the dark, silent, until at last they fell asleep. Even Luke slept peacefully this time, which was rarer than

155

Kezia knew. Lately, since they had started following him again, he had nightmares every night.

'Breakfast?' She was pulling on the white satin robe and smiled at him crookedly as she stretched.

'Just coffee, thanks. Black. I hate to rush through breakfast and I don't have much time.' He had leaped from the bed and was already pulling on his clothes.

'You don't?' She remembered again. He was leaving.

'Don't look like that, Kezia. I told you, there'll be more. Lots more.' He patted her bottom and she slipped easily into his arms.

'I'll miss you so much when you go.'

'And I'll miss you too. Mr. Hallam, you're a very beautiful woman.'

'Oh, shut up.' She laughed, but it embarrassed her when he reminded her of the column. 'What time's your plane?'

'Eleven.'

'Shit.' He laughed at her, and ambled slowly down the hall, his large frame rolling easily in his own special gait. She watched him silently, leaning in the bedroom doorway, reflecting that it seemed as if they had been together forever - teasing, laughing, riding subways, talking late into the night, watching each other sleep and wake, and sharing a cigarette and early morning thoughts before coffee.

'Lucas! Coffee!' She set a steaming cup down on the sink for him, and tapped his shoulder through the shower curtain. It all felt so natural, so familiar, so good.

He reached around the curtain for the cup, leaned his head out and took a sip. 'Good coffee. Are you coming in?'

She shook her head. 'No, thanks. I'm a bath person myself.' Given her choice, she always preferred bathing. It was less of a shock first thing in the morning. It was all part of a ritual. Dior Bath Oil, the perfumed water just warm enough and just high enough to cover her chest in the deep pink marble tub, then emerging into warm towels

156

and her cosy white satin dressing gown, and favourite satin slippers with the ostrich plumes and the pink velvet heels. Luke grinned at her as she stood watching him, and extended an arm to invite her to join him.

'Come on in.'

'No, Luke. Really. I'll wait.' She was still in a slow, sleepy mood.

'Nope. You won't wait.' And then with an unexpected, swift, one-handed motion he slipped the robe from her shoulders, and before she could protest, he had lifted her from her feet in the crook of his arm, and deposited her in the cascade of water beside him.

'I was missing you, babe.' He grinned broadly as she spluttered and pulled the strands of wet hair from her eyes. She was naked, save for the ostrich-plumed slippers.

'Oh! You ... you ... bastard!' She pulled the slippers from her feet, tossed them out of the tub, and hit him in the shoulder with the flat of her hand. But she was fighting laughter too, and he knew it. He silenced her with a kiss and her arms went around him as he leaned down to kiss her. He shielded her from the sheets of steaming water, and she found her hands travelling down from his waist to his thighs.

'I knew you'd like it once you got in.' His eyes were bright and teasing.

'You're a miserable, rotten, oversized bully, Lucas Johns, that's what you are.' But the tone did not match the words.

'But I love you.' He oozed male arrogance and a sort of animal sensuality, mixed with a tenderness all his own.

'I love you too,' and as he closed his eyes to kiss her, she ducked him and directed the shower head high full in his face, ducking down to nip playfully at one thigh.

'Hey, Mama, watch that! Next time you might miss!' But where he feared she would bite him, she kissed him, as the shower rippled through her hair and down her back, warming them both. He pulled her up slowly, his hands travelling over her body, and their lips met as he pulled her

157

high into his arms and settled her with legs wrapped around his waist.

'Kezia, you're crazy.'

'Why?' They were comfortably ensconced in a rented limousine, and she looked totally at ease.

'This isn't the way most people travel, you know.'

'Yeah, I know.' She smiled sheepishly at him, and nibbled his ear. 'But admit it, it's fun.'

'It certainly is. But it gives me one hell of a guilt complex.'

'Why?'

'Because this isn't my style. I don't know, it's hard to explain.'

'Then just shut up and enjoy it.' She giggled, but she knew what he meant. She had seen other worlds too. 'You know, Luke, I've spent half of my life trying to deny this way of life, and the other half giving in to it and hating it, or hating myself for being self-indulgent. But all of a sudden, it doesn't bother me, I don't hate it, it doesn't even own me anymore. It just seems like a hell of a funny thing to do, and why not?'

'In that light, it isn't so bad. You surprise me, Kezia. You're spoiled and you're not. You take this stuff for granted, and then again you laught at it like a little kid. I dig it like this. You make it fun.' He looked pleased as he lit a cigar. She had armed him with a box of Romanoff Cubans.

'I dig it like this, too. Like this, my love, it's a whole other trip.'

They held hands in the back of the limousine and JFK Airport appeared much too soon. The glass window had been up between them and the chauffeur, and Kezia pressed the button to lower the window, to remind him which terminal they wanted. Then she buzzed the window back into place.

'Sweetheart, you're a bitch.'

'That's a nice contradiction.'

'You know what I mean.' He looked briefly at the window.

'Yeah. I do.'

They exchanged the supercilious smile of people born to command, one by her heritage, the other by his soul. They rode the rest of the way in silence, holding hands. But something inside Kezia quivered at the thought of his leaving. What if she never saw him again? What if it had all been a fling? She had bared her soul to this stranger, and left her heart unguarded, and now he was going.

But in his own silence, Luke had the same fears. And those weren't his only fears. He had felt it in his gut. Cop cars were all the same, pale blue, drab green, dark tan, with a tall shuddering antenna on the back. He could always feel them, and he had felt this one. And now it was tailing them at a discreet distance. He wondered if they had followed him that night from Washington, if even on the late-night walk to her apartment, he had been tailed. They were doing that more and more lately. It wasn't just near the prisons. It was getting to be everywhere now. The bastards.

The chauffeur checked Luke's bags in for him, while Kezia waited in the car. It was only a few moments before Luke stuck his head back in the car.

'You coming to the gate with me, babe?'

'Is this like the shower or do I have a choice?' They grinned at each other with the memory of the morning.

'I'll let you use your judgment on this one. I trust mine in the shower.'

'So do I.'

He looked at his watch and her smile disappeared.

'Maybe you'd better stay here, and just go back in to the city. It would be stupid for you to get into a lot of hassles.' He shared her concern. He knew what it would do to her to have a fuss made in the papers, in case someone saw them. And he was no Whitney Hayworth III. He was Lucas Johns, and newsworthy in his own right, but not in a way

159

that would have been easy for Kezia. And what if the cops in the blue car approached him? It could ruin everything with her, might scare her off.

She held her arms out to kiss him, and he leaned towards her.

'I'm going to miss you, Lucas.'

'I'll miss you too.' He pressed his mouth down hard on hers, and she stroked the hair on the back of his head. His mouth tasted of toothpaste and Cuban cigars; it was a combination that pleased her. Clean and powerful, like Luke. Straightforward, and alive.

'God, I hate to see you go.' Tears crept close to her eyes, and suddenly he withdrew.

'None of that. I'll call you tonight.' And in a flash, he was gone. The door thumped discreetly shut, and she watched his back as he strode away. He never turned back to look, as silent tears slid down her cheeks.

She left the window to the chauffeur as it had been. Closed. She had nothing to say to him. The drive back to the city was bleak. She wanted to be alone with the cigar smoke, and her thoughts of the day and two nights before. Her thoughts rambled back to the present. Why hadn't she gone to the gate with him? What was she afraid of? Was she ashamed of him? Why hadn't she had the balls to . . .

The window sped down abruptly and the driver looked in the rearview mirror in surprise.

'I want to go back.'

'Excuse me, miss?'

'I want to go back to the airport. The gentleman forgot something in the car.' She pulled an envelope from her handbag and clutched it importantly in her lap. A flimsy excuse, the guy had to think she was nuts, but she didn't give a damn. She just wanted to get back there in time. A time for courage had come. There was no turning back now, and Luke had to know that. Right at the start.

'I'll take the next exit, miss, and double back as soon as I can.'

She sat tensely in the back seat, wondering if they would

160

get there too late. But it was hard to argue with the chauffeur's driving, as he weaved in and out of lanes, passing trucks at terrifying speeds, all but flying. They pulled up outside the terminal twenty minutes after they had left it, and she was out the door almost before the driver had brought the car to a full stop at the kerb. She darted through travelling executives, old women with poodles, young women with wigs, and tearful farewells, and breathlessly she looked up to check the gate number for the flight to Chicago.

Gate 14 E. Damn ... at the far end of the terminal, almost the last gate. She was racing, and her hair pulled free of its tight, elegant knot. Talk about a story! She laughed at herself as she pushed through people and came close to knocking down children. The paparazzi would have a field day with this - heiress Kezia Saint Martin dashing through airport, knocking people down, for a kiss from ex-con agitator Lucas Johns. She choked on a bubble of laughter as she covered the last yards of the race and saw that she had made it in time. The vast expanse of his shoulders and back was filling the open doorway at the gate. She had just made it.

'Luke!'

He turned slowly, his ticket in his hand, wondering who was in New York that he knew. And then he saw her, her hair falling free of its pins, hanging loosely over the bright red coat, her face glowing from the dash from the car. A broad grin swept over his face, and he carefully removed himself from the line of impatient travellers, and made his way to her side.

'Lady, you're crazy. I thought you'd be back in the city by now. I was just standing here thinking about you as we got ready to board.'

'I was ... halfway ... back ... to the ... city ...' She was happy and breathless as they stood looking into each other's eyes. 'But ... I ... had to ... Come back.'

'For chrissake, don't have a heart attack on me now. You okay, babe?'

She nodded vigorously and folded into his arms. 'Fine.'

He took the last of her breath away with a kiss that brought her to her toes, and a hug that threatened her shoulders and neck.

'Thank you for coming back, crazy lady.' He knew what it meant. And she glowed as she looked up at him. He knew what she was, and what the papers could do with a kiss like the one they'd just indulged in, in broad daylight, with a sea of people around them. She had come back. Out in the open. And at that moment, he knew what he had hoped, but not quite believed. She was for real. And now she was his. The Honourable Kezia Saint Martin.

'You took a hell of a chance.'

'I had to. For me. Besides, I happen to love you.'

'I knew that, even if you hadn't come back ... But I'm glad you did.' His voice was gruff as he held her again. 'And now I have to catch that plane. I have to be in a meeting in Chicago at.three.' He pulled gently away.

'Luke ...'

He stopped and looked at her for a long moment. She had almost asked him not to go back. But she couldn't do it. She couldn't ask for something like that. And he would never have stayed ...

'Take good care!'

'You too. We'll get together next week.' She nodded and he walked through the door at the gate. All she could see was one long-armed wave before he disappeared down the ramp.

For the first time in her life, she stayed at the airport, and watched the flight take off. It was a good feeling, watching the thin silver plane rise into the sky. It looked beautiful and she felt brand new. For the first time she could remember, she had taken her fate in her hands and publicly taken her chances. No more hiding in SoHo or vanishing somewhere near Antibes. No clandestine nothing. She was a woman. In love with a man. She had finally decided to gamble. The only hitch was that she was a novice, and she was playing with her life, without

162

knowing how high the stakes had been set. She didn't see the plain-clothesman stubbing out his cigarette near the gate. She looked straight at him, and then walked away, unaware of the threat he was to them both. Kezia was a child walking blindly into a jungle.

CHAPTER XIV

'Where in God's name have you been?' Whit sounded annoyed, a luxury he rarely allowed himself with Kezia.

'I've been here, and for Heaven's sake, Whit, you sound like someone ripped ten inches out of your knitting.'

'I don't think that's amusing, Kezia. I've been calling you for days.'

'I had a migraine, and I put the phone on the service.'

'Oh darling, I am sorry! Why didn't you tell me?'

'Because I couldn't speak to anyone.' Except Lucas. She had spent two days entirely alone since he'd left. Two glorious days. She had needed the time alone to absorb what had happened. He had called her twice a day, his voice gruff and full of laughter and loving and mischief. She could almost feel his hands on her as they spoke.

'And how are you feeling now, darling?'

'Wonderful.' Ecstatic. That new sound crept into her voice. Even with Whit.

'You certainly sound it. And I assume you remember tonight?' He sounded prissy and irritated again.

'Tonight? What's tonight?'

'Oh for God's sake, Kezia!'

Oh shit. Duty was calling. 'Well, I can't remember. Migraines do that to me. Remind me. What's tonight?'

'The dinners for the Sergeant wedding start tonight.'

'Jesus. And which one is this?' Had she already missed some of the frivolous fetes? She hoped so.

'Tonight is the first one. Cassie's aunt is giving a dinner in their honour. Black tie. Now do you recall, my love?'

Yes, but she wished to hell she didn't. And he spoke to her as though she were retarded. 'Yes, Whit. Now I remember. But I don't know if I'm up to it.'

'You said you felt marvellous.'

'Of course, darling. But I haven't been out of bed for three days. The dinner might be quite a strain.' And it was also a must, and she knew it. She had to go, for the column if nothing else. She had had plenty of time off. She had even run roughshod over the column for the past few days. Now back to work, and reality. But how? How, after Luke? The idea was absurd. What reality? Whose? Whit's? What utter bullshit. Luke was reality now.

'Well, if you're not up to it, I suggest you explain it to Mrs. FitzMatthew,' Whit was saying petulantly. 'It's a sit-down dinner for fifty, and she'll want to know if you're planning to disrupt her seating arrangement.'

'I suppose I should go.'

'I think so.'

Asshole. 'All right, darling, I will.' There was a hint of the martyr in her voice, as she stifled a giggle.

'You're a good girl, Kezia. I was really awfully worried about where you were.'

'I was here.' And so was Luke, for a while.

'And with a migraine, poor thing. If I'd known, I'd have sent you flowers.'

'Jesus, I'm glad you didn't.' It had slipped out.

'What?'

'The smell of roses makes the headache worse.' Reprieve.

'Oh. Then it's just as well I didn't know you were ill. Well, rest up for tonight. I'll come and get you around eight.'

'Black tie or white tie?'

'I told you, black. Friday night is white tie.'

'What's Friday?' Her whole social calendar had slipped her mind.

'Those headaches do make you forgetful, don't they? Friday is the rehearsal dinner. You *are* going to the wedding, aren't you?'

The question was purely rhetorical. But he was in for a shock. 'Actually, I don't know. I'm supposed to go to a wedding in Chicago this weekend. I don't know which I should do.'

'Who's getting married in Chicago?'

'An old friend from school.'

'Anyone I know?'

'No one you know, but she's a very nice girl.'

'That's nice. Well, do what you feel best.' But the annoyance was back in his voice again. She was so tiresome at times. 'Just let me know what you decide. I had rather counted on your being at the Sergeants'.'

'We'll work something out. See you later, love.' She blew him a glib kiss and hung up the phone, pirouetting on one bare foot, the satin robe hanging open to reveal still-suntanned flesh. 'A wedding in Chicago.' She laughed over her shoulder as she walked down the hall to run her bath. Hell, it was better than a wedding. She was flying out to meet Luke.

'Good Lord, you look spectacular, Kezia!' This time even Whit looked impressed. She was wearing a filmy silk dress that draped over one shoulder *à la grecque*. It was a pale coral shade and the fabric seemed to float as she walked. Her hair was done in two long looped braids threaded with gold, and her sandals were a dull gold that barely seemed to hang on her feet. She moved freely like a vision, with coral and diamonds brilliantly at her ears and throat. But there was something about the way she moved that troubled Whit as he watched her. She was so striking tonight that it was almost unsettling. 'I've never seen you look so well, or so beautiful.'

'Thank you, darling.'

She smiled at him mysteriously as she whisked past him out the door. The scent of lily of the valley hung close to

165

her. Dior. She looked simply exquisite. And it was more than just looks. Tonight she seemed more a woman than ever before. The change would have frightened him, had they not been such old friends.

There was a butler waiting for guests in the entrance to the house of Cassie's aunt. Two parking attendants had been on hand to relieve them of Whit's car, had he not brought the limousine. Beyond the indomitable butler, Georges, who had once worked for Pétain in Paris in the 'good old days', were two maids in starched black uniforms, waiting expressionlessly to collect wraps and direct ladies to the appropriate bedroom to tend to their faces and hair before making an 'appearance'. A second butler intercepted them on their way, to begin the evening with a round of champagne.

Kezia had a white mink jacket to offer the black uniform that approached her, but no need or desire to 'fix her face'.

'Darling?' Whit held a glass of champagne out to her, and that was the last time he saw her at close range. For the rest of the evening, he caught glimpses of her, laughing at the centre of a circle of friends, dancing with men he hadn't seen on the circuit in years, whispering into someone's ear, and once or twice he thought he saw her alone on the terrace, looking out over the autumn night on the East River. But she was elusive tonight. Each time he approached, she floated away. It was damn annoying in fact, that feeling of watching a vision, or simply a dream. And people were talking about her. The men were, at least, and in an odd way that troubled him. It was what he wanted, though, or thought he did - 'Consort to The Kezia Saint Martin'. He had planned it all carefully years ago but he didn't like the taste of it lately, or the sound of her voice, or the remark she had made to him that morning. He thought they had an understanding, unspoken but mutually understood. Or was it that you had to put it to them after all? At least everyone thought he did. Kezia was good about that. She didn't care about that sort

of thing anyway. Whit knew that. He was certain ... or
was it ... Edward? Suddenly the idea shot into his mind
and wouldn't be banished. Kezia, sleeping with Edward?
And the two of them making a fool of him?

'Good evening, Whit.'

The object of his newly formed suspicions had appeared
at his side. 'Evening,' he muttered.

'Beautiful party, isn't it?'

'Yes, Edward, it is. Dear Cassie Sergeant is going out in
style.'

'You make her sound like a ship. Though I must say the
allusion is not entirely inept.' Edward looked virtuously as
their gazes fell on the more than slightly rotund form of
the soon-to-be bride, poured like cement into pink satin.

'Mrs. FitzMatthew is certainly doing her best.' Edward
smiled vaguely at the crowd around them. The dinner had
been superb. Bongo Bongo Soup, Nova Scotia salmon,
crayfish flown in from the Rockies, Beluga caviar smuggled
in from France in appalling quantities ('You know,
darling, France doesn't have those absurd regulations
about putting all that nasty salty stuff in it. Such a
frightful thing to do to good caviar!'). The fish course had
been followed by rack of lamb and an almost depressing
number of vegetables, salade d'endives, and soufflé Grand
Marnier – after the Brie, an enormous wheel of it from
Fraser Morris on Madison, the only place in town to buy it.
'And only Carla FitzMatthew could possibly have a staff
equal to organizing the task of soufflé for fifty.'

'Hell of a dinner, wasn't it, Whit?'

Whit nodded grimly. He'd had more than a bit too much
to drink, and he didn't like the new thoughts his mind had
turned up.

'Where's Kezia, by the way?'

'You ought to know.'

'I'm flattered that you think so, Whit. Matter of fact, I
haven't talked to her all evening.'

'Then save it for bed tonight.' Whitney spoke into his
drink, but the words were not lost upon Edward.

'I beg your pardon?'

'Sorry ... I suppose she's here somewhere. Flitting about. Looks rather handsome tonight.'

'I'd say you could do better than "handsome", Whitney.' Edward smiled into the last of his wine, musing about Whit's comment. He didn't like the tone of Whit's voice, and he couldn't have meant what it sounded like. Besides, he was obviously plastered. 'The child looks quite extraordinary. I saw you two come in together.'

'And you won't see us going out together. How's that for a surprise?' Whitney was suddenly ugly as he leered a smile at Edward, turned on his heel and then stopped. 'Or does that please rather than surprise you?'

'If you're planning to leave without Kezia, I think you might tell her. Is anything wrong?'

'Is anything right? Good night, sir. I leave her to you. You can bid her good evening for me.'

He was instantly gone in the crowd, depositing his empty glass in Tiffany Benjamin's hand as he left. She was conveniently standing in his path to the door, and gazed rapturously into the empty glass, waving it instantly for a refill, never noticing that she now had two in her hands.

Edward watched him go, and wondered what Kezia was up to. Whatever it was, it was clear that Whit didn't like it, though why, he couldn't imagine. Polite inquiries had confirmed years of suspicion. Whitney Hayworth III was determinedly gay, though not publicly. Bit of a shabby setup for Kezia, even if she did have that boy in the Village, not that that was a comforting thought. But Whitney ... why did he have to ... you just couldn't tell with people anymore. Of course those things had gone on in his youth too, especially among the prep school boys. But it was never taken as seriously then. It was a stopgap measure, so to speak; no one thought of it as a way of life. Just a passing stage before everyone settled down, found a wife, and got married. But not anymore ... not anymore
. . .

168

'Hello, love. Why so gloomy?'

'Gloomy? Not gloomy, just thinking.' Edward roused a smile for Kezia's benefit, and she was easy to smile for. 'And by the way, your escort just left. In his cups.'

'He's been in a bad mood all day. Practically lost his temper with me on the phone this morning. He'll get over it. Probably very quickly.' They both knew that Mrs. FitzMatthew's home was within a few short blocks of Whit's lover's. Edward chose to ignore the suggestion.

'And what have you been up to?'

'Nothing much. Catching up with a few people here. Cassie's wedding certainly dragged us all out of hiding. There are people here I haven't seen in ten years. It's really a beautiful night, and a very nice party.' She swirled around him, patted his arm, and planted a kiss on his cheek.

'I thought you didn't like these gala events.'

'Once in a great while I do.' He looked at her sternly, and then felt irresistibly pulled into laughter. She was impossible, and so incredibly pretty. No, more than pretty. She was extravagantly beautiful tonight. Whitney's feeble 'handsome' had been hopelessly inadequate as praise.

'Kezia . . .'

'Yes, Edward?' She looked angelic, artlessly keeping her eyes on his, and he tried to resist the urge to smile back.

'Where have you been lately? Whitney's not the only one who hasn't been able to reach you. I was a little worried.'

'I've been busy.'

'The artist? The young man in the Village?'

Poor thing, he actually looked worried. Visions of money fleeing from her frail little hands. . . . 'Not the Village. SoHo. And no, it wasn't that.'

'Something else? Or someone else, should I say?'

Kezia could almost feel her back begin to bristle. 'Darling, you worry too much.'

'Perhaps I have reason to.'

'Not at my age, you don't.' She tucked his hand into her arm, and walked him into a circle of his friends, curtailing the conversation, but not allaying his fears. He knew her too well. Something had happened. Something that had never happened before, and she was already subtly altered. He felt it. Knew it. She looked much too happy and much too calm, and as though she had finally flown free from his reach. She was gone now. She wasn't even at Carla FitzMatthews' elaborate party. And only Edward knew that. The only thing he didn't know was where she really was. Or with whom.

It was half an hour later before Edward noticed that Kezia had left the party. An inquiry here and there told him that she had left alone. It disturbed him. She was not dressed to go gallivanting around the city alone, and he wasn't sure that Whit had left her the car. Rotten little faggot, he could at least have done that much for her.

He said his goodnights and hailed a cab to take him to his own apartment on East Eighty-third but somehow he found himself giving the driver Kezia's address. He was horrified. He had never done that before. Such foolishness ... at his age ... she was a grown woman ... and perhaps she wasn't alone ... but ... he simply had to.

'Kezia?' She answered on the first ring of the house-phone, as Edward stood in embarrassment next to the doorman.

'Edward? Is something wrong?'

'No. And I'm sorry to do this, but may I come up?'

'Of course.' She hung up and he was upstairs a moment later.

She was waiting for him in the open doorway, as he emerged from the elevator. She looked suddenly worried as she stood barefoot in her evening gown, her hair loose, and her jewellery put away. And Edward found himself feeling like a fool.

'Edward, are you all right?' He nodded and she let him into the apartment.

'Kezia ... I ... I'm so sorry. I shouldn't have come, but I had to make sure you'd gotten home all right. I don't like to think of you dripping in diamonds and going home unescorted.'

'Darling, darling worrywart, is that all?' She laughed softly and her face broke into a smile. 'Good God, Edward, I thought something dreadful had happened.'

'Maybe it did.'

'Oh?' Her face grew serious again for a moment.

'I think I finally became senile tonight. I suppose I should have called instead of dropping by.'

'Well, now that you're here, how about a drink?' She didn't deny that he should have called, but she was always gracious. 'Some poire, or framboise?' She waved him into a chair and went to the Chinese inlaid chest where she kept the liquor. Edward remembered it well; he had been with her mother when she had bought it at Sotheby's.

'Poire, thank you, dear.' He sank tiredly into one of the familiar blue velvet chairs, and watched her pour the potent transparent liqueur into a tiny glass. 'You really are a good sport about your old Uncle Edward.'

'Don't be silly.' She handed him the drink with a smile and sank to the floor near his feet.

'Do you have any idea how beautiful you are?' She waved the compliment away and lit a cigarette, as he sipped at his poire. She was beginning to wonder if he'd already had too much to drink. He seemed a bit doleful as the moments ticked on. And she was waiting for a phone call from Luke.

'I'm glad you're all right,' he began. And then he couldn't stop himself anymore. 'Kezia, what are you up to?' He simply had to know.

'Absolutely nothing. I'm sitting here next to you and I had been about to get undressed and do some work on the column. I want to phone it in in the morning. . . . I don't think Carla's going to like me when I do. She's too easy to poke fun at. I couldn't resist.'

Kezia was trying to keep things light but Edward looked older and more tired than she had ever seen him.

'Can't you be serious for a moment? I didn't mean what

you were doing right now. I meant ... well, you look different lately.'

'How lately?'

'Tonight.'

'Do I look worried, sick, unhappy, undernourished? What kind of different?' She didn't like his questioning and now she was going to turn it around on him quickly. It was high time to stop this kind of nonsense. And she didn't want any more unannounced late night visits.

'No, no, nothing like that. You look extremely well.'

'And you're worried?'

'Yes, but ... all right, all right, dammit. You know what I mean, Kezia. And you're just like your bloody father. You don't tell anyone anything until after the fact. And then everyone else has to pick up the pieces.'

'Darling, I assure you, you will never have to pick up any pieces, not for me. And since we both agree that I look rested, healthy, and well-fed, my account is not overdrawn, and I have not appeared naked at the Oak Room ... what is there to worry about?' Her voice was only a trifle sharp.

'You're being evasive.' He sighed. He didn't have a chance and he knew it.

'No, darling. I'm enjoying the right to a little privacy, no matter how much I love you, or how good a father you've been to me. I'm all grown up now, love. I don't ask if you sleep with your maid or your secretary, or what sort of things you do alone in the bathroom at night.' Something about Edward told her he'd perform rituals like that in the bathroom, where they 'belonged'.

'Kezia! That's shocking!' He looked angry and pained. Nothing went his way anymore. Not with her.

'It's no more shocking than what you're basically asking me. You just say it more gently than I do.'

'All right. I understand.'

'I'm glad.' It was high time. 'But just to put your fidgety old soul to rest, I can honestly tell you that there's nothing for you to worry about right now. Nothing.'

'Will you tell me when there is?'

172

'Would I cheat you of an opportunity to worry?'

He laughed and sat back in his chair. 'All right. I'm impossible. I know it, and I'm sorry. No . . . I'm not sorry. I like knowing that all's right with your life. And now I'll let you finish your work. You must have gotten some good items for the column tonight.' The room had been ripe with gossip. And he was embarrassed at having probed, at being in her apartment at all, at this unsuitable hour. It wasn't easy being a surrogate father. And even less so being in love with your surrogate child.

'I got some very good items, as a matter of fact, along with tales of Carla's orgy of opulence. It really is a disgrace to spend thousands on a party.'

She sounded like the old Kezia again, the one who didn't frighten him, the one he knew so well and who would always be his.

'And of course I'll include me in the gossip,' she announced with a bright smile.

'Little wretch. What are you going to say about your-self? That you looked stunningly beautiful, I hope.'

'No, well, maybe a mention of the dress. But actually I've written up Whit's charming exit.'

Was she angry? Could she possibly care? 'But why?'

'Because, to put it bluntly, the time for fun and games is over. I think it's time Whit went his way and I went mine. And Whit hasn't got the balls to do it, and maybe neither have I, so if I run something embarrassing, his friend on Sutton Place will do it for us. If he's anyone at all, he won't tolerate Whit being publicly ridiculed.'

'My God, Kezia. What did you write?'

'Nothing indecent. I'm certainly not going to make scandalous accusations in the press. I wouldn't do that to Whit. Or myself. The point is really that I haven't time to play these games after all. And it isn't good for Whit either. All I said in the column was that . . . here, I'll read it to you.' She put on a businesslike voice and went to her desk. He watched her, feeling hunger in his heart.

' "The usual lovebirds were thick in the flock; Francesco

173

Cellini and Miranda Pavano-Casteja; Jane Roberts and Bentley Forbes; Maxwell Dart and Courtney Williamson, and of course Kezia Saint Martin and her standby consort Whitney Hayworth III, although this couple was seldom seen together last night as they each appeared to take flight on their own. It was also noticed that in what appeared to be a fit of pique, Whitney made an early solo exit, leaving Kezia 'midst the rest of the doves, hawks, and parrots. Perhaps the elegant Whitney grows tired of following in her wake? Heiresses can be such demanding people. Also of interest in Carla FitzMatthew's baronial halls. . . .'' Well, how does it sound?' She sounded suddenly chirpy and unaffected by what she had written; the business voice was put away with the column. And news was news and gossip was gossip, and Edward knew it all bored her anyway.

He looked over at her with a dubious smile. 'It sounds rather uncomfortable. Frankly, I don't think he'll like it.'

'He's not meant to. It's supposed to be somewhat demeaning. And if he doesn't have the balls to tell me to go to hell after what I'm doing to his public image, then his boyfriend will tell him he has no guts. I think this will get to him.'

'Why don't you just tell him it's over?'

'Because the only good reason I have is the one I'm not supposed to know. That, and the fact that he bores me. And hell, Edward, I don't know . . . maybe I'm cowardly. I'd rather leave it to him. With a good prod in the right direction from me. It seems as though anything I could say to him directly would be too insulting.'

'And what you said in the column is better?'

'Of course not. But he doesn't know I said it.'

Edward laughed ruefully as he finished his drink and stood up. 'Well, let me know if your plot has any effect.'

'It will. I'd bet on it.'

'And then what? You announce that in the column too?'

'No. I thank God.'

'Kezia, you confuse me. But on that note, my dear, I bid you good night. Sorry to have called on you so late.'

'I'll forgive you this time.'

The phone rang as she walked him to the door and she looked suddenly excited.

'I'll let myself out.'

'Thanks,' she smiled, pecked his cheek and ran back to her desk in the living room with a broad smile, leaving Edward to shut the door softly and wait for the elevator alone.

'Hi, Mama. Too late to call?' It was Luke.

'Of course not and I was just thinking about you.' She smiled, holding the phone.

'So was I. I miss the hell out of you, babe.'

She unzipped her dress and walked the phone into the bedroom. It was so good to hear his voice in the room again. It was almost as though he were there. She could still feel his touch . . . still . . . 'I love you and miss you. A whole bunch.'

'Good. Want to come to Chicago this weekend?'

'I was praying you'd ask.'

He laughed gruffly into her ear and took a puff on one of the Cuban cigars. He gave her the number of the flight he wanted her on, blew her a kiss and hung up.

She slipped happily out of the dress, and stood smiling for a moment before getting ready for bed. What a marvellous man Lucas was. Edward had fled entirely from her mind. As had Whit, whose call was the first she got the next morning.

CHAPTER XV

'Kezia? Whitney.'

'Yes, darling. I know.' She knew a lot more than he did.

'What do you know?'

175

'I know that it's you, silly. What time is it?'

'Past noon. Did I wake you?'

'Hardly. I just wondered.' So, it had run in the morning's second edition. She had gotten up at the crack of dawn to phone it in.

'I think we ought to have lunch.' He sounded very crisp and very businesslike, and very nervous.

'Right this minute? I'm not dressed.' It was rotten but she was amused. He was so easy to play with.

'No, no, when you're ready, of course. La Grenouille at one?'

'How delightful. I wanted to call you anyway. I've decided to go to that wedding in Chicago this weekend. I really think I should go.'

'I think you probably should. And Kezia . . .'

'Yes, darling, what?'

'Have you seen the papers today?'

Obviously, darling. I wrote them. At least the part you mean. . . . 'No. Why? Is the nation at war? Actually, you sound quite upset.'

'Read the Hallam column. You'll understand.'

'Oh dear. Something nasty?'

'We'll discuss it at lunch.'

'All right, darling, see you then.'

As he hung up, he chewed on a pencil. Christ, he hoped she'd be reasonable. It was really getting to be a bit too much. Armand wasn't going to put up with much more of this nonsense. He had thrown the front section at Whitney at breakfast, along with a terrifying ultimatum. Above all Whit couldn't lose him. He couldn't. He loved him.

Once settled at their table at La Grenouille, their conversation was staccato but direct. Or rather, Whit's was direct, and Kezia kept quiet. It was simply that he had gotten far too attached to her, felt far too possessive about her, and knew he had no right to. She had made that much clear. And how did that make him look? And what's more, he had so little to offer her at this point in his life; he

176

wasn't even a partner in the firm, and in light of who she was . . . and it was all getting so painful for him . . . and did she understand his position at all? It was just that he knew she would never marry him, and while she would always be the love of his life, he simply had to get married and have children, and she wasn't ready and . . . oh God, wasn't it awful?

Kezia nodded mutely and gulped her Quenelles Nantua. What was a girl to do? And yes, she understood perfectly, and he was quite right of course, she was light-years away from marriage, and possibly because of the death of her parents and being an only child, she'd probably never marry, to preserve her name. And children were not something she could even faintly imagine anyway, and she felt just awful if she'd hurt him, but this was probably all for the best. For both of them. She granted him the kindness of being right. And they would always remain the 'dearest friends alive'. Forever.

Whitney made a mental note to have Effie send her flowers once a week until she was ninety-seven. Thank God, she had taken it well. And hell, maybe he had had the right idea when he suspected she had something going with Edward. You never knew with Kezia, you only sensed that there was a lot more to her than she let on to, underneath all the poise and perfection. But who gave a damn? He was free! Free of all those intolerable evenings being the man on her arm. And naturally, to recover from the 'terrible pain of it all', he wouldn't be seen socially for months . . . and he could finally live a life on Sutton Place with Armand. It was about time too. Armand had made that much clear over breakfast. After three years of waiting, he had had it. And now with Whitney humiliated in the newspapers . . . Hallam had made him sound like a puppy nipping at Kezia's skirts, and maybe it was a good thing after all. He had finally done it. No more pretence, no more Kezia. Not for him.

Kezia walked away from La Grenouille with a spring

in her step and wandered down Fifth Avenue to peek in the windows at Saks. She was going to Chicago ... Chicago ... Chicago! And she was finally free of Whit, and she had done it in the best possible way. Poor bastard, he had been ready to cry with relief. She almost hated to look so sombre about it. She wanted to congratulate him and herself. What they should have been doing was clinking champagne glasses and shouting with glee, after all the years they'd wasted putting on a show for their friends, and hell, they weren't even married. But they had been a good front for each other. A front. Thank God, she had never married him. Jesus. The very thought made her tremble.

And then another tremor went through her. It had been days, a week ... a long time ... she didn't even know how long. She hadn't even thought of him. Mark. But all in one day? In one fell swoop like that? Clean slate? Both of them? Wasn't that too much to handle? She cared a hell of a lot more about Mark than she did about Whit. Whit was in love. He had a man of his own. But Mark? God, it was like having two wisdom teeth pulled in one day.

But her feet carried her irreversibly towards the subway at Fifty-first Street and Lexington. She had to. She really had to. And she knew it.

The train bumped along on its route pointing south, and she wondered why. For Luke? But that was crazy. She hardly knew him. And what if he cancelled the weekend and never saw her again? Or what if she went to Chicago for the weekend, but he never saw her again after that? What if ... but she knew it wasn't for Luke. It was for Kezia. She had to. She couldn't play games anymore. Not with Whit, or Mark, or Edward, or anyone ... or herself. The many skins of the snake that was Kezia Saint Martin were peeling away. Now *there* would be a piece for the column.

It was a lot harder with Mark. Because she cared.
'You're going away?'

178

'Yes.' She held his eyes and wanted to stroke his hair, but she couldn't do that to him. Not to Mark.

'But that didn't make any difference this summer.' He looked hurt and confused and even younger than he was.

'It makes a difference now, though. Maybe I'll stay away for a very long time. A year, two years, I don't really know.'

'Kezia, are you getting married?' The question was suddenly blunt and she wanted to say yes, just to make it easier, but she didn't want to tell him that either. It was enough to say that she was going away. That was simpler.

'No, baby. I'm not getting married. I'm just going. And in my own way, I love you. Too much to screw you up. I'm older than you are, we both have things to do with our lives. Different things, separate things. It's time now, Marcus. I think you know that too.' He had finished the bottle of Chianti before she had finished her second glass. They ordered another.

'Can I ask you something crazy?'

'What?'

He smiled at her, hesitating; the boyish half smile she loved so much was all over his face. But that was the trouble. She loved the smile, the hair, The Partridge, and the studio. She didn't really love Mark. Not way down deep. Not the way she loved Luke. Not enough.

'Are you the chick I saw in the paper that time?'

She waited a long moment before answering. Something pounded in her ears, and then she looked at him. Straight in the eye. 'Yes. Probably. So?'

'So, I was curious. What's it feel like to be like that?'

'Lonely. Scary. Dull a lot of the time. It's not so hot.'

'Is that why you kept coming down here? Because it was dull and you were bored?'

'No. Maybe originally, just to get away. But you've been someone very special to me, Mark.'

'Was I an escape?'

Yes. But how could she tell him that? And why tell him

179

now? *Oh, please, don't let me hurt him . . . Not more than I have to.*

'No. You're a person. A beautiful person. A person I loved.'

'Loved? Not "love"?' He looked at her, tears swimming bleakly in the childlike eyes.

'Times change, Marcus. And we have to let them change, for both our sakes. It only gets ugly when people try to hang on. It's too late then. For both our sakes, I have to go.'

He nodded sadly into his wine, and she touched his face for one last time before she stood up and walked away. She half ran once she got out of the door. Mercifully, a cab was cruising down the street. She hailed it and slipped inside, so he couldn't see the tears running down her face. Nor could she see the tears on his. He never saw her again. Only in the papers, now and then.

The phone was ringing as she came through the door. She felt wrung out. It had been like two wisdom teeth after all. Four wisdom teeth. Nine. A hundred. And now what? It couldn't be Whit. Edward? Her agent?

'Hi, Mama.' It was Luke.

'Hi, love. Oh God, it's good to hear your voice. I'm beat.' She had needed the sound of him so badly . . . his touch . . . his arms . . .

'What'd you do today?'

'Everything. Nothing. It was a horrible day.'

'Christ, you make it sound like it.'

'I just "took care of business", as you'd say. I planted a nasty little piece in the column last night, designed to make Whit's lover jealous.' She had no secrets from Luke. He knew her whole life now. 'Which it did, so we had lunch and got that squared away. No more Whitney to squire me to parties.'

'You sound upset. Is that the way you wanted it?'

'Yes, that's why I did it. I just wanted to do it in some way that wouldn't ruin his ego. I felt I owed him that after

180

all these years. We played a game till the end. And then I went down to SoHo, and got that all cleared up. I feel like the bitch of the year.'

'Yeah. Those things never feel good. I'm sorry you had to deal with all that in one day.' But he didn't sound sorry, and she knew that he was relieved. It made her glad she had done it.

'It had to be done. and it's a relief. I'm just tired. And what about you, love? Busy day?'

'Not as busy as yours. What else you been up to, babe? No fancy benefit meetings?' He chuckled in the phone and she groaned. 'Now what did I say?'

'The magic word . . . oh shit. You just reminded me. I'm due at a goddamn Arthritis meeting at five, and it's already that now. Oh Fuck And Shit!' He laughed at her and she giggled.

'Martin Hallam should only hear that!'

'Oh shut up.'

'Well, I've got more good news for you. I hate to hit you with it on a day like today. You can't come to Chicago this weekend, babe. Something came up and I have to go the coast.'

'What coast?' What in hell did he mean?

'The West Coast, my love. Christ, Kezia, I hate to do this to you. Are you okay?'

'Yeah, I'm terrific.'

'Now come on, be a big girl.'

'Does that mean I can't see you?'

'Yes. It does.'

'Couldn't I fly out to meet you there?'

'No, babe, you can't. It wouldn't be cool.'

'Why not, for chrissake? Oh Luke, I had a perfectly horrible day, and now this . . . please let me come out.'

'Baby, I can't. I'm going to be organizing a heavy little business deal, you might say. It's touchy for me, and it's not a scene I want you involved in. It's going to be a rough couple of weeks.'

'That long?' She wanted to cry.

'Maybe. I'll see.'

She took a deep breath, and swallowed, and tried to untangle her mind. What a bitch of a day.

'Luke, will you be all right?'

He hesitated for just a moment before he said, 'I'll be fine. Now you just go to your colitis meeting, or whatever the fuck it is, and don't worry your pretty little head about me. This is one dude who can take care of himself. That much you should know.'

'Famous last words.'

'I'll let you know as soon as I'm back. Just remember one thing.'

'What?'

'That I love you.' At least there was that.

They hung up and Luke paced the length of his suite in Chicago. Shit, he was crazy to get involved with her. And now of all times, when things were starting to get hot. She was starting to depend on him, and she wanted more than he could give. He had other things to think about, the commitments he had made, the men he wanted to help, and he had his own ass to think of now, and the fucking pigs who'd been following him for weeks. Days, years, it felt as though he had always had them on his tail, like vultures swooping down on him, coming just close enough to let him know they were there, and then disappearing again behind a cloud. But he always knew they were there. He could always feel it.

He walked to the bar and poured himself a long tall bourbon in a water glass. No water, no soda, no ice, and swallowed it without putting the glass down. And then, as though he had to know, he took three long strides to the door of his suite and yanked it open with a jerk that should have pulled it off its hinges, but didn't. It shuddered briefly in his hand, and he stood there, and so did the man in the corner. He looked shocked to see Luke, and had jumped when the door opened. He was wearing a hat, and walked down the corridor trying to look like a man going somewhere, but he wasn't. He looked every

182

inch what he was, a cop on an assignment. The tail on Luke Johns.

Kezia's feet felt like lead as she stepped into the cab. The meeting was being held on upper Fifth Avenue. With a view of the park. At Tiffany's apartment. Three floors on Ninety-second and Fifth. And bourbon or scotch. No mickey-mousing around with lemonade or sherry at her place. There would also be gin and vodka for those who preferred that. At home, Tiffany stuck to Black Label.

She was standing near the door when Kezia arrived, with a double scotch on the rocks in one hand.

'Kezia! How divine! You look fabulous, and we were just getting started. You haven't missed anything!' That was for sure.

'Goodie.' Tiffany was too far gone to notice the tone of Kezia's voice or the blurry look around her eyes where her mascara had run when she'd cried. The day had taken its toll.

'Bourbon or scotch?'

'Both.'

Tiffany looked momentarily baffled. She was already drunk, and had been since noon.

'I'm sorry, love. I didn't mean to confuse you. Make it scotch and soda, but don't bother. I'll make it myself.' Kezia strode to the bar, and for this rare occasion she matched Tiffany drink for drink. It was the second time she had gotten drunk because of Luke, but at least the last time she'd been happy.

CHAPTER XVI

'Kezia?' It was Edward.

'Hi, love. What's new?'

'That's what I wanted to ask you. Do you realize that I haven't seen or heard from you in almost three weeks?'

'Don't feel alone. No one has. I've been hibernating.' She was munching on an apple as she talked to him, with her feet on the desk.

'Are you ill?'

'No. Just busy.'

'Writing?'

'Yup.'

'I haven't seen you anywhere. I was beginning to worry.'

'Well, don't. I've been fine. I've been out a couple of times, just to keep my hand in the game for the column. But my "appearances" have been brief and sporadic, I'm sticking pretty close to home.'

'Any particular reason?' He was probing again, and she continued to munch on her apple noncommittally.

'No particular reason. Just work. And I wasn't in the mood to go out more than I absolutely had to.'

'Afraid to run into Whit?'

'No . . . well . . . maybe a little. I was more afraid to run into all the local big mouths. But actually, I've just been snowed under with work. I'm doing three articles, all with deadlines next week.'

'I'm glad you're all right then. Actually, my dear, I was wondering if you wanted to have lunch.'

She made a face and put down the apple core. Shit. 'Well, love, I'll tell you . . .' Then she started to laugh. 'Okay. I'll have lunch with you. But not at any of the usual spots.'

'My God, I do believe the girl's becoming a recluse.' He

laughed back but there was still a hint of worry in his voice. 'Kezia, are you sure you're all right?'

'Wonderful. Honest.' But she'd have been a lot happier if she could have seen Luke. They were still burning the long distance wires twice a day, but he couldn't have her around. There was still too much happening. So she had been burying herself in her work.

'All right. Then where do you want to have lunch?'

'I know a nice natural foods bar on East Sixty-third. How does that sound to you?'

'You want the truth?'

'Sure, why not?'

'Repulsive.'

She laughed at the sound of his voice. 'Be a sport, darling. You'll love it.'

'For you, Kezia . . . even a natural foods bar. But tell me the truth, is it dreadful?'

'What if it is! You order a baggie from Lutèce and bring it along.'

'Don't be absurd.'

'Then give this a try. It's really not bad.'

'Ahhh . . . youth.'

They agreed to meet at twelve-thirty, and she was already there when he arrived. He looked around, and it wasn't as bad as he'd thought. The people at the small wooden tables were a healthy mix of midtown Eastsiders. Secretaries, art directors, hippies, pretty girls in blue jeans with portfolios at their sides, boys in flannel shirts and shoulder-length hair, and here and there a man in a suit. Neither he nor Kezia stood out in their midst, and he was relieved. It was certainly not La Grenouille, but thank God it wasn't Horn & Hardart's either . . . not that there was anything wrong with their food . . . but the people. The people! They just weren't Edward's style. And one never knew what Kezia had up her sleeve. The girl had a fiendish sense of humour.

She was sitting at a corner table when he approached, and he could see that she was wearing jeans. He smiled a

185

long smile into her eyes and he leaned down to kiss her when he got to the table.

'I have missed you so, child.' He never realized quite how much until he saw her again. It was the same feeling he got every year at their first lunch after the summer. It had been almost a month this time too.

'I've missed you too, love. Hell, I haven't seen you in ages. And it's almost Halloween.' She giggled mischievously and he searched her face as he settled into a chair. There was something different about her eyes ... that same something different he had noticed the last time he'd seen her. And she was suddenly thinner.

'You've lost weight.' It was a fatherly accusation.

'Yes, but not very much. I eat funny when I write.'

'You ought to make it a point to eat well.'

'At Le Mistral perhaps? Or is it healthier to feed one's face at La Côte Basque?' She was teasing him again, not unkindly, but nevertheless with a new vehemence.

'Kezia, child, you're really too old to consider becoming a hippie.' He was teasing her back. But not entirely.

'You're absolutely right, darling. I wouldn't even consider it. Just a hard-working slave to my typewriter. I suddenly feel as though I've come into my own with my work. It's a beautiful feeling.'

He nodded silently and lit a cigar. He wondered if that's what it was. Maybe she would eventually simply retire into her work. At least it was respectable. But it didn't seem likely. And he was still troubled by the subtle alterations he sensed, but couldn't quite see. He could see that she was thinner, more angular, more intense. And she spoke differently now, as though she had finally taken her place in her beliefs, in her work. But the change went deeper than that. Much deeper. He knew it.

'Do they serve anything to drink in this place?' He looked mournfully at the menu chalked up on a board on the wall. There was no mention of cocktails, only carrot or clam juice. His stomach rebelled at the thought.

'Oh, Edward, I didn't even think of a drink for you. I

186

am sorry!' Her eyes were laughing again and she patted his hand. 'You know, I've really missed you too. But I've needed to be left alone.'

'I'd say it had done you good, but I'm not entirely sure of that either. You look as though you've been working too hard.' She nodded slowly.

'Yes, I have. I want to get into it now. And you know, it's becoming a strain to get out that damn column. Maybe I ought to retire.' Here, she felt no qualms about discussing the doings of Martin Hallam. No one would have cared.

'Are you serious about giving it up?. The prospect troubled him. If she gave up the column, how often would he see her among the familiar faces at all the city's gala events?

'I'll see. I won't do anything rash. But I'm giving it some thought. Seven years is a very long time. Maybe it's time for Martin Halam to quit.'

'And Kezia Saint Martin?'

She didn't answer, but quietly met his eyes.

'Kezia, you're not doing anything foolish, are you, dear? I was relieved to hear of your decision about Whitney. But I rather wondered if it meant . . .'

'No. I ended it with my young friend in SoHo too. On the same day in fact. It was sort of a purge. A pogrom. And a relief, in the end.'

'And you're all alone now?'

She nodded, but what a pest he could be. 'Yes. Me and my work. I love it.' She gave him a radiant smile.

'Perhaps that's what you need for a while. But don't get all severe and intense. It wouldn't become you.'

'And why not?'

'Because you're far too pretty and far too young to waste yourself on a typewriter. For a while, yes. But don't lose yourself for too long.'

'Not "lose" myself, Edward? I feel like I've finally "found" myself.'

Oh lord, this was going to be one of those days when her face looked just like her father's. Something told him the

187

girl had made up her mind. About something, whatever it was. 'Just be cautious, Kezia.' He relit his cigar, keeping his eyes deep in hers. 'And don't forget who you are.'

'Do you have any idea how often I've heard that?' And how sick it makes me by now. 'And don't worry, darling, I couldn't possibly forget. You wouldn't let me.'

There was something hard in her eyes now, which made him uncomfortable.

'Well, shall we order?' She smiled flippantly and waved at the board. 'I suggest the avocado and shrimp omelette. It's superb.'

'Shall I catch you a cab?'

'No. I'll walk. I'm in love with this town in October.'

It was a crisp autumn day, windswept and clear. In another month it would be cold, but not yet. It was that exquisite time of year in New York when everything feels clean and bright and alive, and you want to walk from one end of the world to the other. Kezia always did, at least.

'Call me in a bit, will you, Kezia? I worry when I don't hear anything from you for weeks on end. And I don't want to intrude.'

Since when, darling? Since when? 'You never do. And thanks for the lunch. And you see . . . it wasn't so bad!' She hugged him briefly, kissed his cheek, and walked away, turning to wave as she stopped for the light at the corner.

She walked down Third Avenue to Sixtieth Street and then cut west to the park. It took her out of her way, but she was in no rush to go home. She was well ahead in her work, and it was too nice a day to hurry indoors. She took deep breaths and smiled at the pink-cheeked children on the street. It was rare to see children look healthy in New York. Either they had the greyish-green tinge of deep winter, or the hot pale sweaty look of the blistering summers. Spring came so fleetingly to Manhattan. But fall . . . fall, with its crisp crunchy apples, and pumpkins on fruit stands waiting to have faces carved on them for Halloween. Brisk winds that swept the sky clean of grey.

And people walking along with a quickened pace. New Yorkers didn't suffer in October, they enjoyed. They weren't too hot or too cold or too tired or too cross. They were happy and gay and alive. And Kezia walked in their midst, feeling good.

Leaves brushed the walks in the park, swirling about her feet. Children bounced in the carriage at the pony stand, squealing for another ride. The animals at the zoo bobbed their heads as she walked past, and the carillon began its tune as she approached. She stopped and watched it with all the mothers and children. It was funny. That was something she had never thought of before. Not for herself. Children. How strange it would be to have a little person beside you. Someone to laugh at and giggle with and wipe chocolate ice cream from his chin, and tuck into bed after reading a story, or snuggle close to as he climbed into your bed in the morning. But then, you'd have to tell him who he was, and what was expected of him, and what he'd have to do when he grew up 'if he loved you'. That was the reason she had never even remotely wanted children. Why do that to someone else? It was enough that she had to live with it for all these years. No, no children. Never.

The carillon stopped its tune, and the dancing gold animals stopped their mechanical waltz. The children began to drift away or rush towards hovering vendors. She watched them, and suddenly wanted a red balloon for herself. She bought one for a quarter and tied it to the button on her sleeve. It danced in the wind, high above her head, just below the branches of towering trees, and she laughed; she wanted to skip all the way home.

Her walk took her past the model boat pond, and at Seventy-second Street she reluctantly left the park. She ambled out slowly, the balloon bobbing as she walked behind nannies who prowled the park sedately, pushing oversized English prams covered with lace. A clique of French nurses moved like a battalion down the walk, towards an oncoming gaggle of British nannies. It amused her to watch the obvious though sugar-coated hostility

189

between the two national tribes. And she knew too that the American nurses were left to their own devices, shunned by both the British and French. The Swiss and Germans willingly kept to themselves. And the black women who cared for equally sumptuously outfitted babies did not exist. They were the untouchable caste.

Kezia waited for the traffic to ebb, and eventually wandered over to Madison to stroll past the boutiques on her way home. She was glad she had walked. Her mind wandered slowly back to Luke. It seemed forever since she had seen him. And she was trying so hard to be good about it. Working hard, being a good sport, laughing with him when he called, but something was curling up tighly inside her. It was like a small, dark kernel of sad, and no matter what she did she couldn't get rid of it. It was heavy and tight. Like a fist. How could she miss him so much?

The doorman swept open the door for her, and she pulled her balloon down low beside her, feeling suddenly silly, as the elevator man attempted not to notice.

'Afternoon, miss.'

'Afternoon, Sam.' He wore his dark winter uniform and the eternal white cotton gloves, and he looked at a spot on the wall. She wondered if he didn't ever want to turn and face the people he carted up and down all day long. But that would have been rude. And Sam wasn't rude. God forbid. For twenty-four years, Sam had never been rude, he simply took people up and down ... up ... and ... down ... without ever searching their eyes ... 'Morning, madam' ... 'Morning, Sam' ... 'Evening, sir' ... 'Good evening, Sam'. ... For twenty-four years, with his eyes rooted to a spot on the wall. And next year they'd retire him with a gold-plated watch and a bottle of gin. If he didn't die first, his eyes politely glued to the wall.

'Thank you, Sam.'

'Yes, miss.' The elevator door slipped shut behind her, and she turned her key in the lock.

She picked up the afternoon paper on the hall table, on her way in. It was her habit to keep abreast of the news,

190

and on some days it amused her. But this was not one of those days. The papers had been full of ugly stories for weeks. Uglier than usual, it seemed. Children dying. An earthquake in Chile, killing thousands. Arabs and Jews on the warpath. Problems in the Far East. Murders in the Bronx. Muggings in Manhattan. Riots in the prisons. And that worried Kezia most of all.

But now she glanced lazily past the front page, and then stopped with one hand still on the door. Everything grew very still, she suddenly understood. Her heart stopped. Now she knew. The headline on the paper read: *Work Strike at San Quentin. Seven Dead.* Oh God . . . let him be all right.

As though in answer to the prayer she had spoken aloud, the phone came to life, and dragged her attention away from the riveting headline. Not now . . . not the phone . . . what if . . . Mechanically, she moved towards it, the paper still in one hand, as she distractedly tried to read on.

' 'Lo . . .' She couldn't take her eyes away from the paper.

'Kezia?' It didn't sound like her.

'What?'

'Miss Saint Martin?'

'No, I'm sorry, she's . . . Lucas?'

'Yes, dammit. What the hell's going on?' They were both getting thoroughly confused.

'I . . . I'm sorry, I . . . oh God, are you all right?' The sudden terror still caught in her throat, but she was afraid to say anything too precise on the phone. Maybe he was in a bad place to talk. That article suddenly had told her a great deal. Before she had suspected, but now she knew. No matter what he told her, she knew.

'Of course, I'm all right. You sound like you've seen a ghost. Anything wrong?'

'That's a fairly apt description, Mr. Johns. And I don't know if anything's wrong. Suppose you tell me.'

'Suppose you wait a few hours, and I'll tell you anything you want to know, and a lot more besides. Within reason,

191

of course.' His voice sounded deep and husky, and there was laughter peppered in with the unmistakable fatigue.

'What exactly do you mean?' She held her breath, waiting, hoping. She had just had the fright of her life, and now it sounded like ... she didn't dare hope. But she wanted it to be that.

'I mean get your ass out here, lady. I'm going crazy without you! That's what I mean! How about catching the next plane out here?'

'To San Francisco? Do you mean it?'

'Damn right, I do. I miss you so much I can hardly think straight anymore, and I'm all through out here. And it's been too fucking long since I've had my hands on your ass. Mama, this has seemed like five hundred years!'

'Oh darling, I love you. If you only knew how much I've missed you, and just now I thought ... I picked up the paper and ...' He cut her off quickly with something brittle in his voice.

'Never mind, baby. Everything's okay.' That was what she had wanted to hear.

'What are you going to do now?' She sighed as she spoke.

'Love the shit out of you and take a few days off to see some friends. But you are the first friend I want to see. How soon can you be here?'

She looked at her watch. 'I don't know. I ... what time's the next plane?' It was just after three in New York.

'There's a flight that leaves New York at five-thirty. Can you make it?'

'Jesus. I'd have to be at the airport no later than five, which means leaving here at four, which means ... I have an hour to pack, and ... screw it, I'll make it.' She jumped to her feet and looked towards the bedroom. 'What should I bring?'

'Your delicious little body.'

'Aside from that, silly.' But she hadn't smiled like this in weeks. Three weeks, to be exact. It had been that long since she'd seen him.

192

'How the hell do I know what you should bring?'

'Is it hot or cold, darling?'

'Foggy. And cold at night, and warm in the daytime. I think ... oh shit, Kezia. Look it up in the *Times*. And don't bring your mink coat.'

'How do you know I have one? You've never seen it.' She was grinning again. To hell with the headlines. He was all right and he loved her.

'I just figured you had a mink. Don't bring it.'

'I wasn't planning to. Any other instructions?'

'Only that I love you too goddamn much, woman, and this is the last time I let you out of my sight.'

'Promises, promises! I wish. Hey ... will you meet me?'

'At the airport?' He sounded surprised.

'Uh huh.'

'Should I? Or would it be cooler if I didn't?' It was back to that again. Being cautious, being wise.

'Screw being cool. I haven't seen you in almost three weeks and I love you.'

'I'll meet you.' He sounded ecstatic.

'You'd damn well better.'

'Yes, ma'am.' The baritone laugh tickled her ear, and they hung up. He had fought his own battles with his conscience during the last three godawful weeks, and he had lost ... or won ... he wasn't yet sure. But he knew he had to have Kezia. Had to. No matter what.

CHAPTER XVII

The plane landed at 7.14 p.m., San Francisco time. She was on her feet before the plane had come to a full stop at the gate. And despite earnest pleadings from the stewardesses, she was one of a throng in the aisles.

She had travelled coach to attract less attention, and

she was wearing black wool slacks and a black sweater; a trench coat was slung over her arm, dark glasses pushed up on her head. She looked discreet, almost too discreet, and very well-dressed. Men checked her out with their eyes, but decided she looked rich and uptight. Women eyed her with envy. The slim hips, the trim shoulders, the thick hair, the big eyes. She was not a woman who would ever go unnoticed, whatever her name, and in spite of her height.

It was taking forever to open the doors. The cabin was hot and stuffy. Other people's bags bumped her legs. Children started to cry. Finally, they swung open the doors. The crowd began to move, only imperceptibly at first, and then in a sudden rush, the plane blurted its contents like toothpaste onto the ramp. Kezia pressed through the other travellers, and as she turned a corner, she saw him.

His head was well above all the others. His dark hair shone, and she could see his eyes from where she stood. He had a cigar in his hand. His whole being wore an air of expectation. She waved and he saw her, joy sweeping his face, and carefully he eased through the crowd. He was at her side in a moment, and swept her high off the ground in his arms.

'Mama, is it good to see you!'

'Oh Lucas!' She grinned in his arms, and their lips met in a long, hungry kiss. Paparazzi be damned. Whatever they saw, they could have. She was finally back in his arms. The other travellers moved round them like water around rocks in a stream, and there was no one left by the time they moved on.

'Let's get your bags and go home.'

They gave each other the smile usually exchanged by people long used to sharing one bed and took the escalator down to the baggage claim, her small hand clasped firmly in his large one. People caught sight of them and watched them go hand in hand. Together, they were the sort of people you notice. With envy.

'How many bags did you bring?'

'Two.'

'Two? We're only staying three days.' He laughed and gave her another hug. And she tried not to show the flash of pain in her eyes. Three days? That was all? She hadn't asked him before. But at least it was that much. At least they were together again.

He plucked her bags from the turntable like a child snatching furniture out of a dollhouse, propped one suitcase under his arm, grasped the other by the handle in the same hand, and kept his other arm around Kezia, squeezing her tight.

'You haven't said much, Mama. Tired?'

'No. Happy.' She looked up at him again, and nestled in close. 'Christ, it's been such a long time.'

'Yeah, and it won't ever be that long again. It's bad for my nerves.' But she knew it might be that long again. Or longer. It might have to be. That was the way his life was. But it was over now. Their three-day honeymoon had just begun.

'Where are we staying?' They were waiting outside for a cab. And so far, so good. No cameras, no reporters; no one even knew she had left New York. She had made one brief call saying that was taking two days off from the column before she'd call in to report. They could run some of the extra tidbits she hadn't had room for in the column that week. That would tide them over until she got her mind back on Martin Hallam again.

'We are staying at the Ritz.' He said it with grandeur as he tossed her bags into the front seat of a cab.

'Is that for real?' She laughed as she settled back in his arm.

'Wait till you see it.' And then he looked worried. 'Baby, would you rather stay at the Fairmont or the Huntington? They're a lot nicer, but I thought you'd worry about . . .'

'Is the Ritz more discreet?' He laughed at the look on her face.

195

'Oh yeah, Mama. It sure is discreet. That's one thing I like about the Ritz. It is *discreet!*'

The Ritz was a large fading grey house in the heart of the mansions of Pacific Heights. It had once been an elegant home, and now housed castoffs; little old ladies and fading old men, and circulating in their midst the occasional 'overflow' of houseguests from the sumptuous homes nearby. It was an odd mixture, and the decor was the same: crooked chandeliers with dusty prisms, fading red velvet chairs, flowered chintz curtains, and here and there an ornate brass spitoon.

Luke's eyes danced as he led her inside towards a twittering old woman who hovered nervously at the desk. She wore a cup of braided hair over each ear, and her false teeth looked as though they would glow in the dark.

'Good evening, Ernestine.' And the beauty of it was that she looked like an Ernestine.

'Evening, Mr. Johns.' Her eyes took in Kezia with approval. She was the sort of guest they liked. Well-dressed, well-heeled, and well-polished. After all, this was the Ritz!

He led her into a decaying elevator run by a tiny old man who hummed 'Dixie' to himself as they rose, swaying, to the second floor.

'Usually, I walk. But I thought I'd give you the full show.'

A sign in the elevator announced breakfast at seven, lunch at eleven, and dinner at five. Kezia giggled, holding tight to his hand.

'Thank you, Joe.' Luke gently patted his back and picked up the bags.

'Carry the bags for you, sir?'

'No, thanks.' But he quietly slipped a bill into the man's hand, and led Kezia down the hall. It was carpeted in dark red, and the walls were lined with elaborate sconces. 'To your left, babe.' She followed his nod to the end of the hall. 'Wait till you see the view.' He fitted his key in the lock, turned it twice, set down the bags, and then pulled her close. 'I'm so glad you came out. I was afraid you'd be busy or something.'

'Not for you, Luke. After all this time, you must be joking! Well, are we going to stand here all night?'

'Nope. We sure as hell aren't.' He picked her up easily, and carried her over the threshold into a room that made her gasp and then laugh. She had never seen so much blue velvet and satin all in one place.

'Luke, it's a riot. And I love it.' He set her down with a smile, and she looked at the bed with wide eyes. It was a huge four-poster with blue velvet hangings and a blue satin spread. There were blue velvet chairs and a blue satin chaise longue, an old-fashioned dressing table, a fireplace, and a flowered blue rug that had seen better days. And then she noticed the view.

It was a dark expanse of bay, lit on the other side by the hills of Sausalito, the lights on the Golden Gate twinkling as traffic sped by.

'Luke, what a fabulous place!' Her face glowed.

'The Ritz. At your feet.'

'Darling, I love you.' She walked into his arms and kicked off her shoes.

'Lady, you couldn't love me half as much as I love you. Not even a quarter.'

'Oh shut up.'

His mouth came down gently on hers and he lifted her onto the blue satin bed.

'Hungry?'

'I don't know. I'm so happy I can't think.' She rolled sleepily onto her side, and kissed him on the side of his neck.

'How about some pasta?'

'Mmmm . . . sure . . .' But she made no move to get up. It was one in the morning, her time, and she was content where she lay.

'Come on, Mama, get up.'

'Oh God, not a shower!' He laughed and slapped her on the behind as he pulled back the sheets.

'If you don't get up in two minutes, I'll bring the shower to you.'

'You wouldn't dare.' She lay with her eyes stubbornly closed and a sleepy smile on her face.

'Oh wouldn't I?' He was looking down at her, love and tenderness rich in his eyes.

'Christ, you would. You're such a meanie. Can't I take a bath instead of a shower?'

'Take whatever you want, but get up off your ass.' She opened her eyes and looked up at him, without moving an inch.

'In that case, I'll take you.'

'After we eat. I didn't have time for lunch today and I'm starving. I wanted to wrap everything up before you got out.'

'And did you?' She sat up on one elbow and reached for a cigarette. This was the opening she had been waiting for, and suddenly there was tension in her voice, mirrored in his eyes.

'Yeah. We wrapped everything up.' The faces of the dead men flashed through his head.

'Lucas ...' She had never directly asked him, and he had not yet volunteered.

'Yeah?' Everything about him seemed suddenly guarded. But they both knew.

'Should I mind my own business?' He shrugged and then slowly shook his head. 'No. I know where you're going, Mama. And I guess it's your business to ask. You want to know what I've been up to out here?' She nodded. 'But you already know, don't you?' He looked almost old and very tired as he spoke. The holiday atmosphere had suddenly faded.

'I think so. I think I knew without knowing, but then this afternoon ...' Her voice trailed off. This afternoon? Only then? It seemed years ago. 'This afternoon I saw the paper, and the headline ... the San Quentin work strike, that was your doing, wasn't it, Luke?' He nodded very slowly. 'What will they do to you for that, Lucas?'

'Who? The pigs?'

'Among others.'

'Nothing. Yet. They can't pin anything on me, Mama. I'm a pro. But that's part of the problem, too. I'm too much of a pro. They can never pin anything on me, and one day they're going to screw me royally. Out of vengeance.' It was a first warning.

'Can they do that?' She looked shocked, but not really as though she understood.

'They can if they want to. Depends how badly they want to. Right now, I figure they're pretty pissed.'

'And you're not scared, Lucas?'

'What would that change?' He smiled a cynical little smile, and shook his head. 'No, pretty lady, I'm not scared.'

'Are you in danger, Lucas? I mean real danger?'

'You mean my parole, or other kinds of danger?'

'Either.'

He knew that she had to know, so he answered her. More or less. 'I'm not in real danger, babe. There are some very angry people involved, but the ones who're the most pissed are the least sure I had anything to do with it. That's the way I run things. The parole pricks won't even try to do anything to me for a while, and by then they'll have cooled off. And any of the hotheads involved in the strike who don't dig my views are too pissy-eye scared of me to even flip me the bird. So, no, I'm not really in danger.'

'But you could be, couldn't you?' It hurt her to think of it, to realize it . . . to admit it. She had known that about him from the first. But now she was in love with him. It was different. She didn't want him to be some hotshot troublemaker. She wanted him to lead a peaceful life.

'What are you thinking of? You looked a thousand miles away for a minute there. You didn't even hear me answer your question.'

'What was your answer?'

'That I could be in danger crossing the street, so why

199

get paranoid now? You could be in danger. You could get kidnapped for a fat ransom. So? So why go crazy about could I be in danger, or could I not be in danger. I'm sitting here, I'm fine, I love you. That's all you need to know. Now what were you thinking?'

'That I wish you were a stockbroker or an insurance agent.' She grinned and he let out a burst of laughter.

'Oh Mama, have you got the wrong number!'

'All right, so I'm crazy.' She shrugged in momentary embarrassment and then looked at him seriously again. 'Luke, why do you still get involved in the strikes? Why can't you let it go? You're not in prison anymore. And it could cost you so much.'

'Okay. I'll tell you why. Because some of those guys make three cents an hour for the work they do in there. Backbreaking work, in conditions you wouldn't let your dog live in. And they have families, wives and children just like the rest of the world. Those families are on welfare, but they wouldn't have to be if the poor bastards inside could earn a decent wage. Not even a high wage, just a decent one. There's no reason why they shouldn't be able to put some money aside. They need it as much as everyone else. And they work for their bread. They work damn hard. So, we set up work strikes. We design them so that the system we use can be implemented by inmates at any prison. Like this one. Folsom is going to be pulling almost the same thing, with some minor alterations in style. Probably next week.' He saw the look on her face and then shook his head. 'No. They don't need me for that one, Kezia. I did my bit here.'

'But why in hell do you have to be the one to do it?' She sounded almost angry and it surprised him.

'Why not?'

'Your parole for one thing. If you're on parole, then you still "belong" to the State. Your sentence was five to life, wasn't it?'

'Yeah. So?'

'So they own you for life, officially. Right?'

200

'Wrong. Only for another two and a half years, when my parole runs out, smartass. Sounds like you've been doing some reading on the subject.' He lit another cigarette and avoided her eyes.

'I have, and you're full of shit with your two and a half years. They could revoke your parole any time they want to, and then they've got you for life again, or another five years.'

'But Kezia ... why would they want to do that?' He was trying to pretend he didn't know.

'Oh for chrissake, Luke. Don't be naive, or is that just for my benefit? For agitation in the prisons. That's got to be in violation of your parole agreement. You don't need me to tell you that. And I'm not as dumb as you think.' She had been doing more reading than he'd anticipated. And this was a tough one to argue. She was right on the money.

'I never thought you were dumb, Kezia.' His voice was subdued. 'But neither am I. I told you, they could never pin this work-strike thing on me.'

'Who says so? What if one of the people you do this stuff with says something? Then what? What if some asshole just gets fed up and kills you? Some "radical", as you put it.'

'Then we worry. Then. Not now.' She was silent for a moment, her eyes bright with tears.

'I'm sorry, Lucas. I can't help it, though. I do worry.' And she knew she had good reason to. Lucas was not about to give up his work in the prisons, and he was in danger. They both knew it.

'Come on, Mama, let's forget this and go eat.' He kissed her on the eyes and the mouth, and pulled her firmly by both arms. He had had enough heavy talk for a while. The tension between them eased away slowly, but Kezia's fears were not over. She only knew that she was fighting a losing battle if she hoped to make him give up what he was doing. He was a born gambler. She just hoped he'd never lose.

They were downstairs in the lobby again half an hour later.

'Where are we going?'

'Vanessi's. Best pasta in town. Don't you know San Francisco?'

'Not very well. I was here as a child, and once about ten years ago for a party. But I didn't see very much. We had dinner someplace Polynesian, and stayed at a hotel on Nob Hill. I remember the cable car, and that's about it. I was out here with Edward and Totie.'

'That doesn't sound like much fun. Jesus, you don't know this town at all.'

'Nope. But now I've seen the Ritz, and you can show me the rest.' She hugged his arm and they exchanged a peaceful smile.

Vanessi's was crowded, even at ten. Artists, writers, newspaper people, an after-theatre crowd, politicians, and debutantes. It was jammed with a fair sampling of everything there was in town. And Luke had been right. The pasta was great. She had gnocchi, and he had fettuccine, and for dessert they shared an unforgettable zabaglione.

She sat back with her espresso and took a lazy look around.

'You know, it kind of reminds me of Gino's, in New York, only better.'

'Everything in San Francisco is better. I'm in love with this town.'

She smiled at him and took a sip of the hot coffee.

'The only trouble is that the whole city goes dead at midnight.'

'Tonight I think I might too. Christ, it's already two-thirty in the morning, my time.'

'Are you beat, babe?' He looked almost worried. She was so small and looked so fragile. But he knew she was a lot tougher than she looked. He had already glimpsed that.

'No. I'm just relaxed. And happy. And content. And that bed at the Ritz is like falling asleep on a cloud.'

'Yeah. Isn't it though?' He reached across the table and took her hand, and then she saw him glance at something over her shoulder with knit brows. She turned around to see what it was. It was only a table of men.

'People you know?'

'In a way.' His whole face had hardened, and his hand had seemed to lose interest in hers. It was a group of five men, with short, well-trimmed hair, double-knit suits, and light ties. They looked faintly like gangsters.

'Who are they?' She turned to face him again.

'Pigs.' He said it matter of factly.

'Police?'

He nodded. 'Yeah, special detail investigators, assigned to digging up trouble for people like me.'

'Don't be so paranoid. They're just having dinner here, Luke. Like we are.'

'Yeah. I guess so.' But they had dampened his mood, and shortly after, they left.

'Luke ... you have nothing to hide. Do you?' They were walking down Broadway now, past the barkers at all the topless bars. But the table of cops still weighed on their minds.

'No. But that guy who was sitting at the end of the table has been on my ass since I got into town. I'm getting sick of it.'

'He wasn't following you tonight. He was having dinner with his friends.' The group of policemen had shown no interest in their table. 'Wasn't he?' Now she was worried too. Very.

'I don't know, Mama. I just don't like their trip. A pig is a pig ... is a pig.' He licked one end of a cigar, lit it, and looked down at her face. 'And I'm a sonofabitch to throw my bad vibes on you. I just don't like cops, baby. That's the name of the game. And let's face it, I've been playing heavy games with the strike at San Quentin. Seven guards were killed during the three weeks.' For a moment, he wondered if he had been wrong to stick around.

203

They wandered into porn bookstores, watched tourists on the street, and finally ambled onto Grant Avenue, cluttered with coffeehouses and poets, but the police stayed on their minds, however little they showed it to each other. And Luke was once again aware of being tailed.

Kezia tried to lighten his mood by playing tourist.

'It looks rather like SoHo, only more funky somehow. You can tell it's been around for a while.'

'Yeah, it has. It's the old Italian neighbourhood, and there are a lot of Chinese. And kids, and artists. It's a good scene.' He bought her an ice cream cone, and they took a cab to the Ritz. It was four in the morning for Kezia by then, and in the arms of her lover she slept like a child. Something troubled her only faintly as she drifted off to sleep – something about police . . . and Luke . . . and spaghetti. They were trying to take away his spaghetti . . . or . . . she couldn't figure it out. She was too tired. And much, much too happy.

She had fallen asleep as he watched her, a smile on his face as he stroked the long black hair that rippled past her naked shoulders and down her back. She looked so beautiful to him. And he was already so goddamn in love with her.

How was he ever going to tell her? He slipped quietly out of bed after she fell asleep, and went to look at the view. He had blown it, blown all his own rules. What a fucking stupid thing to do. He had no right to someone like Kezia. He had no right to anyone until he knew. But he had wanted her, had to have her – as an ego trip at first because of who she was. And now? Now it was all different. He needed her. He loved her. He wanted to give her something of himself . . . even if only the last golden hours before sunset. Moments like that don't come every day, at most they come once in a lifetime. But now he knew he would have to tell her. The question was, how?

204

'Lucas, you're a beast!' She groaned as she turned over in bed. 'For God's sake, it's still dark.'

'It's not dark, it's just foggy. And breakfast in this joint is at seven.'

'I'll go without.'

'No, you won't. We have things to do.'

'Lucas ... please ...' He watched her struggle out of sleep. His hair was combed, his teeth were brushed, his eyes were bright. He had been up since five. He had a lot on his mind.

'Kezia, if you don't get off your ass, I'll keep you on it all day. And then you'll be sorry!' He ran his hand smoothly from her breast to her belly.

'Who says I'll be sorry?'

'Don't tempt me. But come on, babe. I want to show you the town.'

'In the middle of the night? Can't it wait a few hours?'

'It's seven-fifteen.'

'Oh God, I'm dying.'

And then, laughing at her, he picked her up out of bed, and deposited her in the bathtub of warm water he had run while she slept.

'I figured you wouldn't be up to a shower this morning.'

'Lucas, I love you.' The hot water lulled her gently, as she lay looking sleepily into his eyes. 'You spoil me. No wonder I love you.'

'I figured there had to be a reason. And don't take too long. They close the kitchen at eight, and I want some food in my stomach before I drag you around town.'

'Drag me, eh?' She closed her eyes and sank deeper into the tub. It was an ancient bathtub that stood high

205

off the floor on gold-leaf claw feet. It would have been large enough for both of them.

They breakfasted on pancakes and fried eggs and bacon. And for the first morning in years, Kezia didn't even bother to read the paper. She was on holiday, and she didn't give a damn what the world had to say. 'The world' would only complain, and she was not in the mood for complaints. She felt too good to be bothered with that.

'So where are you taking me, Lucas?'

'Back to bed.'

'What? You got me up, just to go back to bed?' She looked incensed and he laughed.

'Later. Later. First, we take a look at the town.'

He drove her through Golden Gate Park and they walked around its lakes and kissed in hidden corners under still-flowering trees. Everything was still green and in bloom. The rusty look of the East in November was so different, and so much less romantic. They had tea in the Japanese Garden, and then drove out to the beach before driving back through the Presidio to look out over the bay. She was having a ball: Fisherman's Wharf, Ghiradelli Square, The Cannery. . . .

They ate fresh crab and shrimp at the stands at the wharf, and revelled in the noise of Italian vendors. They watched old men playing boccie in Aquatic Park, and she smiled watching one very old man teach his grandson how to play. Tradition. Luke smiled too, watching her. She had a way of seeing things that he had never thought of before. She always had a sense of history, of what had come before and what would come later. It was something to which he'd never given much thought. He lived with his feet firmly planted in *now*. It was an exchange they gave to each other. She gave him a sense of her past, and he taught her to live where she was.

As the fog lifted, they left their borrowed car down at the wharf, and took the cable car to Union Square. It made her laugh as they rolled down the hills. For the first time in her life she felt like a tourist. Usually she moved

206

across a regulated map between familiar houses in cities she had known all her life, from the homes of old friends to the homes of other old friends, wherever she was, the world over. From one familiar world to another. But with Luke being a tourist was fun. Everything was. And he loved the way she enjoyed what he showed her. It was a fun town to show – pretty, and easy, and not too crowded at that time of year. The rugged natural beauty of the bay and the hills made a pleasing contrast to the architectural treasures of the town: skyscrapers all politely herded downtown, the gingerbread Victorians nestled in Pacific Heights, and the small colourful shops of Union Street.

They drove over the Golden Gate Bridge just because she wanted to see it 'up close', and she was enchanted.

'What a handsome piece of work, isn't it, Luke?' Her eyes scanned far above to its spires piercing the fog.

'So are you.'

They dined that night at one of the Italian restaurants on Grant Avenue. A place with four tables for eight, where you sat next to strangers, and made friends as you shared soup and broke bread. She talked to everyone at their table; this was new to her too. Luke grinned as he watched her. What would they have said if they had known she was Kezia Saint Martin? The idea made him laugh more. Because they wouldn't have known. They were plumbers and students, bus drivers and their wives. Kezia Saint Who? She was safe. With him, and with them. That pleased him; he knew that she needed a place where she could play, without fear of reporters and gossip. She had blossomed in the brief time since she'd flown into town. She needed that kind of peace and release. He was glad it was something he could give her.

They stopped for a drink at a place called Perry's on Union Street, before going home. It reminded her a bit of P. J.'s in New York. And they decided to walk home from there. It was a pleasant walk over the hills, dotted with small parks along the way. The foghorns were bleating at

207

the edge of the bay, and she kept stride beside him, holding his hand.

'God, Luke. I'd love to live here.'

'It's a good place. And you don't even know it yet.'

'Not even after today?'

'That's just the tourist stuff. Tomorrow we see the real thing.'

They spent the next day driving north on the coast. Stinson Beach, Inverness, Point Reyes. It was a rugged coastline that looked much like Big Sur farther south. Waves crashing against the cliffs, gulls and hawks soaring high, long expanses of hills, and sudden sweeps of beaches, unpopulated and seeming almost to be touched by the hand of God. Kezia knew what Luke had meant. This was a far cry from the wharf. This was real, and incredibly beautiful, not merely diverting.

They had an early dinner in a Chinese restaurant on Grand Avenue, and Kezia was in high spirits. They were seated in a little booth with a curtain drawn over the doorway and you could hear giggles and murmurs in other booths, and beyond, the clatter of dishes and the tinkling sound of Chinese spoken by the waiters. Kezia loved it, and it was a restaurant Luke knew well, one of his favourite hangouts in town. He had been there the night before she arrived, to tie up the loose ends about the strike at San Quentin. It was an odd thing, talking about dead men and inmates over fried wonton. It seemed immoral somehow, when he gave it much thought, but mostly he didn't. They had learned to accept what they lived with. The realities of men in prison, and the cost of changing that system. It cost some men their lives. Luke and his friends were the generals, the inmates were the soldiers, the prison administrators the enemy. It was all very simple.

'You're not listening to me, Lucas.'

'Hm?' He looked up to see Kezia watching him with a smile.

'Something wrong, darling?'

208

'Are you kidding? How could there be?' She was watching his eyes, and he pushed thoughts of San Quentin from his mind, but something was bothering him. A sense of foreboding, of . . . something. He didn't know what. 'I love you, Kezia. It was a beautiful day.' He wanted to chase the painful thoughts away, but it was getting harder to do.

'Yes, it was. You must be tired from all that driving though.'

'We'll get a good night's sleep tonight.' He chuckled at the thought and leaned forward for a kiss.

It wasn't until they left that he saw the same face he had seen too often during the weeks he'd spent in San Francisco. As he looked around and saw the man darting back into one of the booths with a newspaper under his arm, it was suddenly too much for him.

'Wait for me up front.'

'What?'

'Go on. I have some business to take care of.'

She looked suddenly surprised, and frightened by the expression on his face. Something had happened to him; it was as if a dam had broken, or like the moment before an explosion . . . like . . . it was frightening to watch.

'Go on, dammit!' He gave her a firm shove towards the front of the restaurant and headed quickly back towards the booth he had seen the man enter. It took him only a moment to reach it, and he pulled back the aged, fading curtain with such force that it tore at the top. 'Okay, sweetheart, you've had it.' The man looked up from his newspaper with an overdone expression of unknowing surprise, but his eyes were wary and quick.

'Yes?' He was greying at the temples but he looked almost as solid as Luke. He sat poised in his seat, like a tiger ready to pounce.

'Get up.'

'What? Look, mister . . .'

'I said get up, motherfucker, or didn't you hear me?' Luke's voice was as sweet and smooth as honey but the

209

look on his face was terrifying, and as he spoke, he lifted the man from his seat with a hand on each lapel of his ugly plaid double-knit sportcoat. 'Now what is it exactly that you want?' Luke's voice was barely more than a whisper.

'I'm here for dinner, Mack, and I suggest you lay off right now. Want me to call the cops?' The man's eyes were menacing and his hands were starting to come up slowly and with well-trained precision.

'Call the cops ... you fucking ... whatcha got, a radio in your pocket, motherfucker? Listen, man, I'm having dinner with a lady and I don't dig being tailed night and day, everywhere I go. It makes me look bad, got that? Nice and clear?' And then he gasped. Luke's victim had removed both of Luke's hands from his lapels and delivered a swift punch to his middle all in one flashing gesture.

'That'll make you look worse, Johns. Now how about going home like a nice boy, or you want me to run you in for attempted assault? That'd look good to your parole board, wouldn't it? You're just fucking lucky they don't get you with a murder beef one of these days.' There was hatred in his voice.

Luke caught his breath and looked up into the man's eyes. 'Murder? They'd have a bitch of a time sticking me with that. A lot of things, but not murder.'

'What about the guards at Q. last week, or don't they count? You might as well have killed them yourself, instead of having your punks do the job.' The conversation was still carried on in an undertone, and Luke lifted one eyebrow in suprise as he stood up slowly and painfully.

'Is that to what I owe the honour of your company everywhere I go? You're trying to stick me with the murder of those Bulls in Quentin?'

'No. That's not my problem. Not my detail. And believe it or not, babyface, I don't like tailing you any more than you like having me on your ass.'

210

'Watch out, you may make me cry.' Luke picked up a glass of water from the table and took a long swallow. 'So what's with the tail?' Luke put down the glass and watched him carefully, wondering why he hadn't punched the man back. Jesus, he was getting soft ... dammit ... she was changing everything, and that could really cost him.

'Johns, you may find it hard to believe, but you're bring tailed for protection.'

Luke answered with a shout of cynical laughter. 'How sweet. Whose protection?'

'Yours.'

'Really? How thoughtful. And just who do you think is going to hurt me? And just exactly why do you care?' He looked doubtful; they could have thought of a better story.

'I don't care, and that's upfront, but the assignment is to follow you until further notice and keep my eyes open for assailants.'

'Bullshit.' Luke was angry now. He didn't like the idea.

'Is it bullshit?'

'Sure it is. Oh, what the fuck do I know?' That was all he needed, with Kezia around. Shit.

'The word is that some of the hothead left-wing reform groups don't like your trip, don't like you floating in and out of their scene like some kind of visiting hero. They want your ass, man.'

'Yeah? Well, let's put it this way: if they ask for it, I'll call you. Till I do, I can do without company.'

'I could do without you too, but we don't have a choice. Nice place for dinner though. Great egg rolls.'

Lucas shook his head with a look of restrained aggravation and shrugged. 'Glad you liked it.' He paused for a long moment in the doorway then and watched the man who had punched him. 'You know something, man? You're a lucky motherfucker. You'd hit me like that some other time and I'd have pulverized you. And enjoyed it.' They eyed each other for a long moment and the other man shrugged and folded his newspaper.

211

'Suit yourself. But that would buy you a one-way ticket back to the joint. Save us all a lot of trouble if you ask me. But anyway, watch your ass, man. Somebody's out to get you. They didn't tell me who, but it must've been a hot tip because they had me out on the street an hour later.'

Luke started to leave the booth then, and suddenly turned with a question in his eyes. 'You guys tailing anyone else?' That might tell him something.

'Maybe.'

'Come on, man, don't tell me half-assed stories without telling me the rest!' There was fire in his eyes again and the other man nodded his head slowly.

'Yeah. Okay. We're tailing some other dudes.'

'Who?'

The cop heaved a slow sigh, looked at his feet and then back at Luke. There was no point playing games and they both knew it. And he felt that he had already pushed Luke as far as he should, farther possibly. Lucas Johns was not a man you played with. He looked up slowly, and reeled off the names expressionlessly.

'Morrissey, Washington, Greenfield, Falkes, and you.'

'Jesus.' The five of them were the all-time heavies in prison agitation. Morrissey lived in San Francisco, Greenfield in Vegas. Falkes had come out from New Hampshire, but Washington was local and the only black in the group. All radicals of a kind, but none of them heavy left-wingers. They just wanted to fight for their ideals, and change a system that should have died years ago. None of them had wild illusions about changing the world. Washington took the most flak from those who opposed them. The black factions thought he should be fighting with them; he wasn't enough of a rebel for them. But Luke thought he was the best of both worlds.

'You're tailing Frank Washington?'

'Yeah.' The plainsclothesman nodded.

'Then you better tail him good.' The other man nodded knowingly, and Luke turned his back and left.

212

Kezia was waiting nervously at the front door.

'Are you all right?'

'Of course I'm all right. Why shouldn't I be?' He wondered if she had heard something, or worse yet seen. Remarkably, no one had walked by during the brief fracas and the waiters had been too busy to notice the intensity of the subsequent exchange.

'You were gone for so long, Lucas. Is something wrong?' She searched his face but found nothing.

'Of course not, I just saw someone I know.'

'Business?' Her face had the intense look of a wife.

'Yes, silly lady, business. I told you. Now mind your own, and let's go back to the hotel.' He gave her a fierce hug and walked her out into the night fog with a smile. She knew something was amiss, but he covered it well. There was never anything she could put her finger on. And Luke was going to see that it stayed that way.

But the next morning over breakfast there was no mistaking that something was very wrong. She had awakened him this time, after ordering a sumptuous breakfast for them to share. She shook him gently with a kiss after the tray had been delivered to the room.

'Good morning, Mr. Johns. It's time to get up, and I love you.' He rolled over with a sleepy smile and half-opened eyes, and pulled her down to kiss him.

'Sure is a nice way to start the day, Mama. What are you doing up so early?'

'I was hungry, and you said you had a lot to do today, so I got up and got organized.' She sat on the edge of the bed with a smile.

'Want to come back to bed and get unorganized again?'

'Not until after breakfast, hot pants. Your eggs'll get cold.'

'Jesus, you're practical. Such a cold-hearted woman.'

'No. Just hungry.' She patted his behind, kissed him again, and got up to take the covers off their breakfast.

'Boy, that smells good. Did they send up the paper too?'

'Yes, sir.' It was neatly folded on the tray, and she

213

picked it up and unfolded it, handing it to him with a small curtsy. 'At your service, monsieur.'

'Lady, how did I live without you before?'

'With difficulty, undoubtedly.' She smiled at him again and turned to pour him a cup of coffee. When she looked up she was shocked by the expression on his face. He was sitting naked on the side of the bed, with the newspaper open on his lap, and tears starting down his face, contorted with anger and grief. His hands were clenched in fists.

'Lucas? Darling, what is it?' She went to him hesitantly and sat down next to him, searching the headlines quickly to see what had happened. It was the main feature in the paper: *Ex-Priest Prison Reformer Shot and Killed*. The killing was thought to have been done by a radical left-wing group, but the police were not yet sure. Joseph Morrissey had been shot eight times in the head while leaving his house with his wife. The photographs on the front page showed a hysterical woman leaning over the shapeless form of the victim. Joe Morrissey. His wife was reported to be seven months pregnant.

'Shit.' It was the only sound she heard from Luke as she ran a hand gently around his shoulders, with tears running from her own eyes. They were tears for the man who had died, and tears of fear for Luke. It could have been Lucas.

'Oh darling. I'm so sorry.' They seemed such empty words, for what she felt. 'Did you know him well?'

He nodded silently and then closed his eyes. 'Too well.'

'What do you mean?' Her voice was a whisper.

'He was my front man. Remember, I told you I never go into the prisons, and no one can pin anything on me?'

She nodded.

'Well, they can't pin anything on me because of guys like Joe Morrissey. He was a chaplain in four of the joints before leaving the priesthood. He stuck around with some of the hard-core reformers after that. And he fronts for the heavies. Mostly me. And now ... we killed him. I

214

killed him. Goddamn fucking . . .' He got up and walked angrily across the room, wiping the tears from his face. 'Kezia?'

'Yes?' Her voice was a frightened little sound from across the room.

'I want you packed and dressed right now. And I mean *right now*. I'm getting the hell out of here.'

'Lucas . . . you're afraid?'

He hesitated for a moment and then nodded. 'I'm afraid.'

'For me? Or yourself?'

He almost smiled then. He was never afraid for himself. But this was no time to get her involved. 'Let's just say I want to be smart. Now come on, baby. Let's get moving.'

'You're leaving too?' She was talking to his back now though.

'Later.'

'What are you going to do before that?' She was suddenly terrified. Oh God, what if they killed him?

'I'm going to take care of business, and then get my ass back to Chicago tonight. And you're going to go to New York, like a nice girl, and wait there. Now shut up and get dressed, dammit!' He turned towards her with an attempted snarl, but then his face softened as he saw the look of terror on her face. 'Now, Mama, come on. . . .' He walked back across the room and took her in his arms as she began to cry again.

'Oh Lucas, what if . . .'

'Shhh . . .' He held her tight and kissed the top of her head gently. 'No "what if", Mama. Everything's going to be cool.'

Going to be cool? Was he out of his mind? Someone had just been killed! His front man, for chrissake. She looked at him with shock in her eyes and he pulled her gently up off the bed.

'Now I want you to get ready.' Too many people could figure out where he was staying. And Kezia was one gold mine he didn't want in his pocket if someone was laying for him. Maybe killing Morrissey was just a warning. Some warning. His stomach turned over again at the thought.

She started to get dressed while throwing things into her suitcase and casting sidelong glances at Luke. He suddenly looked so businesslike, so foreign to her, so angry.

'Where will you be today, Lucas?'

'Out. Busy. I'll call you when I get to Chicago. And you're not going to a birthday party for chrissake. Just put on some clothes. Hurry up.'

'I'm almost ready.' And a moment later she was, looking very sober, with large dark glasses concealing the lack of makeup.

He looked at her for a long moment, tension rippling through his body, and then nodded. 'Okay, lady. I'm not going to ride with you. I'm going to call a cab, and get the hell out of here. You're going to wait in Ernestine's office downstairs and wait for a cab with her. She will take you to the airport.'

'Ernestine?' Kezia looked surprised. The proprietress of the Ritz didn't look the sort to play nursemaid to grown guests. And Luke was wondering about it himself. But he figured that for fifty bucks she'd do almost anything.

'That's right. Ernestine. Go to the airport with her. And get on the first goddamn plane out. I don't give a shit if it stops fifteen times on the way to New York. But I want you out of here. I don't want you hanging around the airport. Is that clear?' She nodded silently. 'It damn well better be, 'cause Kezia, I'm not kidding. I'll tear your hide off if you fool around somewhere. *Get out of this town!* Is that clear? I'm sorry I brought you here in the first place.' And he looked it.

'I'm not sorry. I'm glad. And I love you. I'm just sorry your friend ...' Her voice trailed off and her eyes grew large as she looked at him, and he softened. He took her in his arms again, once more torn between wanting her and knowing he shouldn't take her down with him. But he needed her too much.

216

'You're quite something, lady.' He kissed her quietly and then straightened up. 'Get ready to go, Mama. I'm going to tell Ernestine to get you out of here within five minutes, and I'll be calling to check. I'll call you in New York tonight. But it may be late. I want to get back to Chicago before I start playing around making phone calls.'

'You'll be okay today?' But it was a pointless question and she knew it. Who knew if he'd be okay? What she really wanted to ask him was when she'd see him again, but she didn't dare. She just watched with large damp eyes as he quietly closed the door to the room. A moment later she saw him leave the hotel in a cab. And ten minutes later, she and Ernestine did the same. Kezia got very drunk on the flight back to New York.

CHAPTER XIX

It had been over a week since she'd left him in San Francisco. Now he was back in Chicago and calling her two or three times a day. But there had been a raw fibre of terror in her gut since she'd left him. He said everything was fine, and he'd be in New York any day. But when? And how was he really? She was aware of a guarded quality to his speech when he called. He didn't trust his phone. And this was far worse than the last time they'd been apart. Then she had only been lonely. Now she was afraid.

She was desperately trying to keep her time, and her mind, as filled as she could. She had even suggested to Luke that she do a piece on Alejandro.

'On that fleabag centre he runs?'

'Yes. Simpson says he might have a market for it. I think I'd like to do it. Think Alejandro would agree?'

'He'd love it, and a little publicity might help him get funds.'

'All right. I'll get busy on it.' Either that or go crazy, sweetie pie.

'Okay, now what do I do? I've never been interviewed before.' She laughed at the nervous look on his face. He was such a nice man, with a good sense of humour.

'Well, Alejandro, let's see. Actually, you're only my second personal interview. Usually, I go about it quietly. Kind of sneaky.' She looked like a kid in her pigtails and jeans. But a clean kid. That was rare in those halls.

'Why sneaky? Are you afraid of what you write?' His eyes opened wide. It surprised him. She was so direct; it seemed unlike her to go through any back doors.

'It's mostly because of the crazy life I lead. Luke covered it fairly accurately. I am one way, and live a number of other ways.'

'And what's Luke to you, Kezia? Is he real?'

'Very. It's my old life that isn't real. Never was. And it's even less so now.'

'You don't like it?'

She shook her head in silent answer.

'That's too bad.'

'I'm almost ashamed of it, Alejandro.'

'Kezia, that's crazy. It's part of you. You can't deny it.'

'But it's so ugly.' She toyed with a pencil and looked at her hands.

'It can't all be ugly. And why "ugly"? To most people that life looks pretty good.' His voice was very soft.

'It's an empty life, though. It takes everything out of you, and doesn't put anything back. It's pretence and games, and people cheating on each other, and lying, and thinking how many thousands of dollars to spend on a dress, when they could be putting it into something like this. It just doesn't make a hell of a lot of sense to me. I guess I'm a misfit.'

218

'I'm afraid I don't know much about that world.'

'You're better off.'

'And you're silly.' He reached out and touched her face, pulling her chin up until her eyes met his. 'It's part of you, Kezia. A nice part. A gracious part. You really think you'd be so much better off living up here like this? People lie and cheat and steal here too. They shoot junk. They fuck their children. They beat their mothers and their wives. They get frustrated and angry. They don't have time to learn the things you know. Maybe you should just take that knowledge and use it well. Don't waste your time feeling bitter or sad for the years before this. Just use it well now.'

She smiled at him for a long moment. He made sense. And he was right. Her world had given her something. It was a part of her life. 'I think I hate it so much because I'm afraid I'll get stuck there in the end. It's like an octopus, and it won't let you go.'

'Baby, you're a big girl now. If you don't want it, all you have to do is walk away. Quietly. Not with a bazooka in one hand and a grenade in the other. No one can stop you. Haven't you figured that out yet?' He looked surprised.

'I guess not. I never felt I had a choice.'

'Sure you do. We all have choices. We just don't see them sometimes. Even I have a choice, in this "shithouse" as Luke calls it. Any time it gets me down, I can walk out. But I don't.'

'Why don't you?'

'Because they need me. And I love it. I feel like I *can't* walk out, but the point is, I can. I just don't want to. Maybe you didn't want to walk out of your world either. Maybe you still don't want to. Maybe you're not ready to yet. Could be you feel safe there. And why not? It's familiar. And familiar is easy. Even if it's the shits, it's easy, because you know it. You never know the hell that is going to be out there.' He gestured vaguely with one arm as she nodded. He understood very well.

'You're right. But I think I'm ready to leave the womb

219

now. I also know that until now I haven't been ready. That's embarrassing to admit. Seems like at my age, I should have all that behind me, and be all squared away.'

'Bullshit. That takes a hell of a long time. I was thirty before I had the balls to leave my little Chicano world in L.A. and come here.'

'How old are you now?'

'Thirty-six.'

'You don't look it.' She was surprised.

'Maybe not, *querida*, but I sure as hell feel it.' He laughed his soft velvety laugh, and the warm Mexican eyes danced. 'Some days I feel eighty.'

'I know what you mean. Alejandro . . .' Her face grew serious.

'What, babe?' He thought he knew what was coming.

'You think Luke's okay?'

'In what way?' Oh God, don't let her ask. He couldn't tell her. Luke had to do that himself, if he hadn't already . . . but he should have by now.

'I don't know. He's so . . . well . . . so bold, I guess that's the right word. He just does what he does and that's it. I worry about his parole, about his safety, his life, everything. But he doesn't seem to.' She wasn't looking at him and he watched her hands; they were nervous and taut, playing games with her pen.

'No, he doesn't worry about his parole, or his ass, or much of anything. That's just Luke.'

'Do you think he's going to get his ass in a jam one day? Like maybe killed?' She couldn't help thinking of Morrissey. Her eyes came back to him, full of questions, and fear.

'If he has problems, Kezia, he'll tell us.'

'Yeah. The day before the ceiling comes down.' She had learned that much about him. He never said a word till the last minute, about anything. 'He doesn't give one much warning.'

'No, Kezia. He doesn't. That's just his way.'

'One has to respect it, I suppose.'

220

He nodded very quietly, and wanted to reach out and touch her hand. But he couldn't. All he could do was talk to Luke. He thought it was time.

'And that, my friend, ought to finish the story. Thank you.' With a sigh, she sat back in the chair in Alejandro's office. It had been a long day. They'd been talking for hours.

'You think you've got it all?' He looked pleased. She was fun to work with. Lucas was one hell of a lucky man, *and* he knew it.

'All, and then some. Can I lure you downtown for dinner? You ought to have something to make up for my picking your brain all afternoon.'

He smiled at the thought. 'I don't know about that. Hell, Kezia, if you get us some decent publicity for this place, it might change a lot of things. Community acceptance, if nothing else. That's been one of our biggest problems. They hate us worse up here than they do at City Hall. We get it at both ends.'

'It really seems like that.'

'Maybe your story will change the trend.'

'I hope so, love. I really hope so. So, what about dinner?'

'You're on. I'd take you to dinner up here, but Lucas would kill us both. I don't think he wants you hanging around this part of town.'

'Snob.'

'No, for once in his life he's using his head. Kezia, he's right. Don't just come up here like it's the cool thing to do. It isn't. It's dangerous. Very.'

She was amused at their collective concern. The two rough guys protecting the delicate flower. 'Okay, okay. I get the message. I got a whole speech from Luke on the phone. He wanted me to come up here today in a limo.' She laughed.

'Did you?' Alejandro's eyes grew wide. Talk about heat from the neighbourhood!

'Of course not, you ass. I came up by subway.' He answered her laugh with his own. They had fallen into the easy banter and jovial insults of friends, and she was glad. He was a very appealing man. Deeply sensitive, and at the same time fun. Above all, what struck her again about him was his kindness. And he was right about her too. Her past was a part of her life. The grandeur, the money . . . running away from it wouldn't solve anything. She was tempted to with Luke, and that wouldn't do it. She was Kezia Saint Martin and he was Lucas Johns and they loved each other. He couldn't become another Whit, and she was no street girl. They had come from different places and met when the time was right. But now what? What about the future? She hadn't figured that one out yet. She hadn't figured that out at all. And maybe neither had Luke.

'Hey, Kezia, tell you what . . . how about dinner down in the Village?'

'Italian?' It was all she ever ate with Luke, and pasta was coming out of her ears. She had cooked spaghetti for him the night before.

'No. Fuck Italian. That's Luke's trip. Spanish! I know a great place.' She laughed at him and shook her head.

'Don't you guys ever eat hamburgers or hot dogs or steak?'

'No way. Right about now I'd sell my soul for a burrito. You don't know what it does to a Mexican to live in this town. Everything's kosher or pizza.' He made a face and she laughed again as she followed him out.

'Tell the truth. It's fantastic, isn't it?' She had settled on a tostada while he ate paella.

'I've got to admit, it's not bad. And it's a change from fettuccine.'

'This place is run by a Mexican bandit, and his old lady's from Madrid. Great combination.'

She smiled and sipped at her wine. It had been a nice evening. She enjoyed Alejandro's company and it took the

222

edge off her yearning for Luke. All she wanted to do was go home and wait for his call.

'Kezia . . .' Alejandro seemed to hesitate.

'Yeah?'

'You're good for him. You're the best thing he's ever had. But do me a favour . . .' He paused again.

'What, love?' How she liked this funny Mexican man. He cared so much about everything. The kids at his centre, his friends, and especially Luke. And now her.

'Please don't get hurt. He lives a hard life. It's a long way from home for you. Lucas is a gambler. He plays and he pays. But if he loses . . . you'll pay too. Through the teeth, kid – worse than anything you know.'

'Yeah. I know.' They sat silent for a moment in the light of the candle on their table, and thought their own thoughts.

And when Alejandro took her home, Luke was waiting for her in the living room.

'Lucas!' She ran into his arms and was instantly swept off the ground. 'Oh darling, you're home!'

'You'd better believe it! And what's this lecherous Mexican bandit doing with my woman?' But there was no fear in his eyes, only delight at having Kezia in his arms again.

'We did the interview today.' Her words were muffled as she buried her face in his chest. She held him as tightly as a child would, clutching all her security in those arms, in those shoulders, in that man.

'I wondered where you were. I got home two hours ago.'

'You did?' She looked more childlike than ever, the days of worry slipping away from her like rain. Alejandro stood by and watched the scene with a smile. 'We had dinner at a nice little Spanish place in the Village.'

'Oh God, he took you to that place? How bad is the heartburn?'

She grinned up at him again as she slid out of her shoes and stretched, a look of mischief coming into her eyes. Lucas was home and he was safe!

'Not bad. And it was lovely. Alejandro is very good to me.'

'Best dude I know.' Lucas sprawled on the couch with an appreciative look towards his friend, who was getting ready to leave them.

'Don't you want some coffee, Alejandro?'

'Nope, I'll leave you lovebirds alone.'.

'Smart man, Al. She has some packing to do anyway. We're leaving for Chicago in the morning.'

'We are? Oh Lucas, I love you! How long are we staying?' This time she wanted to know how long they had.

'How about till Thanksgiving?' He looked at her happily through half-closed eyes.

'Together? Three weeks? Lucas, you're crazy! How can I stay away that long? The column . . .' Oh shit.

'You do it in the summer, don't you?' She nodded.

'Yeah, but I cover things over there, and there's no one here in the summer.' He laughed, and she looked a question into his eyes.

'What's so funny?'

'The way you say "no one". Can't you cover a couple of posh parties in Chicago?'

'Yeah. I guess I could.' And she wanted to go. Oh God, how she wanted to go!

'Then why don't you? And maybe I can wind things up there in less than three weeks. There's no reason why I can't work out of New York. What the hell . . . and all I really need is a week there to work out some things. I can commute, if I have to.'

'Could we both commute?' Her eyes were filled with stars.

'Sure we could, Mama. The two of us. I made up my mind on the plane coming back here tonight. I told you it would never be like that last stint again, and it won't be. I can't stand it without you.'

'Lucas, my love, I adore you.' She bent quickly to kiss him.

224

'Then take me to bed. Good night, Alejandro.'

Their friend chuckled to himself as he let himself out. Lucas was asleep before she turned the lights out. She looked at him, sound asleep on his side. Lucas Johns. Her man. The hub of her life. And here she was, following him from town to town like a gypsy. It was fun, she loved it, but she knew that sooner or later she'd have to make some decisions . . . the column . . . she hadn't been to a party in weeks . . . and now she was off to Chicago . . . and what then? But at least Lucas was with her. And safe. Who cared about parties? She had been afraid for his life.

CHAPTER XX

'Kezia, when are you coming back?'

She had been on the phone long-distance to Edward in New York for over half an hour. 'Probably some time next week. I'm still working on that story out here.' And she had appeared at two social galas, but it was harder out here. This wasn't her town. It took a lot more research to come up with the dirt. 'Besides, darling, I'm enjoying Chicago.' That confirmed the worst of his suspicions. She sounded so happy. And she was not the sort to be thrilled by Chicago; it was not her milieu. Too Midwest, too American, too Sears Roebuck, and not enough of the rarefied air of Bergdorf's and Bendel's. There had to be someone in Chicago. Someone new? He only hoped it was someone worthwhile. And respectable.

'I saw your last article in *Harper's*. Nice piece. And I heard from Simpson the other day that you've got something coming out in a few weeks in the Sunday *Times*.'

'I do? Which one?'

'Something about a drug rehabilitation centre in Harlem. I didn't know you'd done that.'

'That was just before I left town. Save it for me when it comes out.' But suddenly there was an unspoken awkwardness between them. They both felt it.

'Kezia, are you all right?'

And now it was back to that again. 'Yes, Edward, I'm fine. Honest. We'll have lunch next week when I get back, and you can see for yourself. I'll even meet you at La Côte Basque.'

'Dear lady, how kind you are.'

She laughed at him and they hung up after a few moments of business: they had some new tax shelters to discuss.

Luke looked up from his reading with a quizzical eye.

'Who was that?' He knew it had to be Edward or Simpson.

'Edward.'

'You can tell him you'll have lunch with him sooner. If you want.'

'Are you sending me back?' They had been gone for ten days.

'No, you jerk.' He grinned at the look on her face. 'I just thought we'd go back tomorrow. You've got your work to consider, and I have to commute to D.C. for the rest of the week. There's a series of closed meetings for the moratorium that I want to attend, and I can catch another speaking engagement or two down there. Washington seems to love me.' The checks had been coming in with pleasing regularity. 'I just thought we'd settle down in New York for a couple of weeks.'

She laughed at him, relieved. 'Are you sure you can stand staying any place for that long?'

'I'll sure try.' He slapped her behind as he walked to the bar and poured himself a bourbon and water.

'Luke?' She was lying on the bed, looking pensive.

'Yeah?'

'What am I going to do about the column?'

'That's up to you, babe. You've got to make up your own mind on that. Do you dig writing it?'

'Once in a while. But not lately. Not for a long time, in fact.'

'Then maybe it's time to quit, for your own sake. But don't give it up for me. Do what you want. And if you've got to stick around New York covering fancy parties, then you do that. You've got to take care of your business too. Don't forget that.'

'I'll see how I feel about it after next week. I'll do my usual thing when we go back to New York. Then I'll see how it feels.' With Luke commuting to Washington, she'd have plenty of time to hit her old circuit.

After four days in New York, she had been to the opening of a play, the closing of a theatre, two lunches for ambassadors' wives, and a charity fashion show. Her feet hurt, her mind ached, and her ears were numbed by the constant flow of idle gossip. Who gave a damn? Kezia didn't. Not any more.

'Lucas, if I ever hear the word "divine" again, I think I'm going to throw up.'

'You look tired.' She looked more than tired. She looked drained, and she felt it.

'I am tired, and I hate all that fucking shit.' She had even made it to a meeting of the Arthritis Ball that day. Tiffany had passed out in the john. And she couldn't even use it for the column. The only good piece of information she'd picked up was that Marina and Halpern were getting married. But so what? Who cared?

'What are we doing this weekend?' If he told her that they were going to Chicago, she would have a fit of hysterics. She didn't want to go anywhere, except bed.

'Nothing. Maybe I'll go up and see Al. Want to have him for dinner?' He was sitting on the edge of the bed and looked as tired as she.

'That, I would love. I'll cook something here.' He smiled at the domestic exchange and she picked up on

227

what he was thinking. 'It's neat, isn't it, Luke? Sometimes I wonder if you love it all as much as I do. I've never lived like this before.'

He grinned at her, knowing how true that was.

'You know what I mean.'

'Yes, I do. And I probably love it even more than you do. I'm beginning to wonder how I survived without you before this.' He slipped into bed beside her, and she turned off the light. He had his own keys to the apartment, and used the answering service as his, she had cleaned out a closet for him, and the maid had finally even smiled at him. Once. She called him 'Mister Luke.'

'You know something, darling? We're lucky. Incredibly lucky.' She was pleased with herself, as though she had caught a falling star in her hands.

'Yes, baby, we are.' Even if only for now. . . .

'Well, gentlemen, I propose a toast to the demise of Martin Hallam.'

'Lucas, what does she mean?' Alejandro looked puzzled and Luke looked at her curiously. This was the first he had heard of it.

'Kezia, does this mean what I think?'

'Yes, sir. It does. After seven years of writing the Martin Hallam column, I quit. I did it today.'

Luke looked at her, shocked. 'What did they say?'

'They don't know yet. I told Simpson today, and he's going to handle the rest. They'll know tomorrow.'

'Are you sure?' It wasn't too late to reverse the decision.

'I have never been so sure in my life. I don't have the time for that garbage any more. Or the inclination to waste my time doing it.' She saw a strange look pass between Luke and Alejandro, and wondered why no one seemed impressed. 'Well, you two are certainly a lousy audience for my big announcement. Phooey on both of you.'

Alejandro smiled and Luke laughed.

'I guess we're just kind of shocked, babe. And I suddenly wondered if you're doing it because of me.'

'Not really, darling. It's my decision. I don't want to have to go to those shitty parties for the rest of my life. You saw how tired I was this week. And for what? It's just not my thing any more.'

'Have you told Edward?' He looked worried, and Alejandro was looking daggers at him.

'No. I'll call him tomorrow. You're the first two to know after Simpson. And you're a couple of creeps.'

'I'm sorry, baby. It's just sort of a shock.' He lifted his glass to her then, a nervous smile on his face. 'To Martin Hallam then.' Alejandro raised his glass in response, but his eyes never left Lucas' face.

'To Martin Hallam. Rest in peace.'

'Amen.' Kezia drained her glass in one gulp.

'No, Edward. I'm sure. And Simpson agrees. It's a diversion I don't really have time for any more. I want to stick with serious writing.'

'But it's such a drastic step, Kezia. You're used to the column. Everyone's used to it. It's become an institution. Have you given this decision adequate thought?'

'Of course I have. For months. And the fact is, darling, that I don't want to be an "institution." Not that kind of institution. I want to be a writer, a good one, not a gossip-monger amongst fools. Really, darling, you'll see. It's the best possible decision.'

'Kezia, you're making me nervous.'

'Don't be ridiculous. Why?' She swung her foot as she sat at her desk. She had called him right after Luke left the house for a morning of meetings. At least Luke had come around, after the first shock. And Simpson had applauded the decision, and said it was high time.

'I wish I knew why you make me nervous. I think it's because I get the feeling I don't know what you're up to, not that it's really any of my business.' But he wanted it to be. That was the rub.

229

'Edward, you're going to make yourself senile worrying about nothing.' He was beginning to annoy her. Constantly.

'What are you doing for Thanksgiving?' It was almost an accusation.

'Going away.' But he didn't dare ask where. And she didn't volunteer the information. They were going back to Chicago.

'All right, all right. Dammit, Kezia, I'm sorry. It's just that, in my mind, you will always be a child.'

'And I will always love you, and you will always worry too much. Over nothing.'

He had made her uncomfortable, though. After they hung up, she sat silently and wondered. Was she crazy to stop writing the column? At one time, it had been so important to her. But not any more. But still . . . was she losing touch with who and what she was? In a way, she had done it for Luke. And for herself. Because she wanted to be free to move around with him, and besides, she had outgrown the column years ago.

But suddenly, she wanted to discuss it with Luke. He was gone for the day. She could call Alejandro, but she hated to bother him. It was a queasy feeling, like leaving the dock in the fog, headed for an unknown destination. But she had made her decision. She would live by it. Martin Hallam was dead. It was a simple decision really. The column was over.

She sat back at her desk and stretched, and decided to go for a walk. It was a grey November day, and there was a nip of winter in the air. It made her want to throw a long wool scarf around her neck and run to the park. She felt suddenly free of an old wearisome burden. The weight of Martin Hallam had finally slipped from her shoulders.

Kezia grabbed an old sheepskin jacket from her closet and slipped tall black custom-made boots under her carefully pressed jeans. She dug a small knitted red cap from the pocket of her jacket, and took a pair of gloves from a shelf. She felt new again now. A writer of

230

anything she wanted, not a scavenger of social crumbs. A small smile hovered on her lips, and there was a mischievous gleam in her eye as she headed for the park, with long strides. What a marvellous day, and it wasn't even lunchtime yet. She thought about buying a picnic to eat in the park, but decided not to bother. Instead, she bought a small bag of hot roasted chestnuts from an old gnarled man pushing a steaming cart along Fifth Avenue. He grinned at her toothlessly and she waved at him over her shoulder as she walked away. He was sweet really. Everyone was. Everyone suddenly looked as new as she felt.

She was well into the park and halfway through the chestnuts when she looked ahead and saw the woman trip and fall on the kerb. She had spun out into the street close to the clomping feet of an ageing horse pulling a shabby hansom carriage through the park. The woman lay very still for a moment, and the driver of the carriage stood and pulled at the horse's reins. The horse seemed not even to have noticed the bundle near his hoofs. She was wearing a dark fur coat and her hair was very blond. It was all Kezia could see. She frowned and quickened her pace, shoving the chestnuts into her pocket, and then breaking into a trot as the driver of the hansom jumped from his platform, still holding the reins. The woman stirred then, knelt and lurched forward, into the horse's legs this time. The horse shied, and his owner pushed the woman away. She sat down heavily on the pavement then, but mercifully free of the horse's legs at last.

'What the hell'sa matta wi'youse? Ya crazy?' His eyes bulged furiously as he continued to back his horse away and stare at the woman. Kezia could only see the back of her head, as she shook her head mutely. He mounted his platform then, and clucked his horse back into motion, with a last flick of his middle finger at the still-seated woman, and a 'Stupid bitch!' His passengers were obscured beyond a scratched and smoky window in the carriage, and the ancient horse continued plodding, so used to his route that bombs could have shattered near his feet and he would have continued in the well-worn groove he had travelled for years.

Kezia saw the woman shake her head fuzzily and kneel slowly on the pavement. She ran the last few steps then, wondering if the woman had been hurt, and what had caused her to fall. The dark fur coat was fanned out behind her now, and it was obvious that it was a long and rather splendid mink. Kezia heard a dry little cough from the woman just as she reached her, and then she saw her turn her head. What she saw made her stop, shocked by who it was and how stricken she looked. It was Tiffany, her face gaunt yet swollen, her eyes puffy, yet her cheeks were pulled inward, with painful lines near her eyes and mouth. It wasn't yet noon, and she was already drunk.

'Tiffany?' Kezia knelt beside her and smoothed a hand over her hair. It was uncombed and dishevelled and there was no makeup on the ravaged face. 'Tiffie ... it's me. Kezia.'

'Hi.' Tiffany seemed to look somewhere past Kezia's left ear, unknowing, unseeing, uncaring. 'Where's Uncle Kee?'

Uncle Kee. Jesus, she meant Kezia's father. Uncle Kee. She hadn't heard that in so long ... Uncle Kee ... Daddy ...

'Tiffie, are you hurt?'

'Hurt?' She looked up vaguely, seeming not to understand.

'The horse, Tiff. Did it hurt you?'

'Horse?' She wore the smile of a child now, and seemed to understand. 'Oh, horse. Oh, no, I ride all the time.' She stood up shakily then, and dusted off her hands and the front of her long black mink coat. Kezia looked down and saw torn grey stockings and one bruised black suede Gucci shoe. The coat gaped a little and Kezia caught a glimpse of a dressy black velvet skirt and a white satin shirt, with several rows of large grey and white pearls. It was no outfit to be roaming the park in, nor was it an

232

outfit for that time of day. Kezia wondered if she'd been home the night before.

'Where are you going?'

'To the Lombards'. For dinner.' So that was where she'd been. Kezia had been invited there too, but had turned down the invitation weeks ago. The Lombards. But that had been last night. What had happened since?

'How about if I take you home?'

'To my house?' Tiffany looked suddenly wary.

'Sure.' Kezia tried to put an easy tone in her voice, while holding Tiffany up firmly by one elbow.

'No! Not my house! No. . . .' She bolted from Kezia's grip then and stumbled, and was instantly sick at Kezia's feet and over her own black suede shoes. She sat down on the pavement again and began to cry, the black mink trailing sadly in her own bile.

Kezia felt hot tears burn her eyes as she reached down to her friend and tried to pull her up again.

'Come on, Tiffie . . . let's go.'

'No . . . I . . . oh God, Kezia . . . please . . .' She clutched at Kezia's denim-clad legs, and looked up at her with eyes torn by a thousand private demons. Kezia reached gently down to her and pulled her up again, as she saw a cab swoop around the bend from which the hansom cab had appeared only moments before. She held up a hand quickly and hailed it, and then pulled Tiffany closer. 'No!' It was the anguished wail of a heartbroken child, and Kezia felt her friend trembling in her arms.

'Come on, we'll go to my place.'

'I'm going to be sick.' She closed her eyes and sank toward Kezia again, as the cabbie darted out and threw open the door.

'No, you're not. Let's get in.' She managed to slide Tiffany onto the seat and gave the driver her own address as she rolled down both windows to give her friend air. It was then that she noticed that Tiffany wasn't carrying a handbag.

'Tiffie? Did you have a bag?' The girl looked around

233

blankly for a moment and then shrugged, letting her head fall back onto the seat as both eyes closed and the air rushed in over her face.

'So what?' The words were so low Kezia had barely heard her.

'Hm?'

'Handbag ... so what?' She shrugged, and seemed almost to fall asleep, but a moment later her hand blindly sought Kezia's and gripped it tightly as two lone tears squeezed down her face. Kezia patted the thin cold hand and looked down with horror at the large pear-shaped emerald flanked by diamond baguettes. If someone had taken Tiffany's handbag, he had missed the best part. The thought made Kezia shudder. Tiffany was ripe prey for anyone. 'Walked ... all ... night....' The voice was almost a painful croak, and Kezia found herself wondering if it wasn't more likely 'drank' all night. It was obvious she hadn't gone home after the Lombards.

'Where did you walk to?' She didn't want to get into a heavy conversation in the cab. First she'd put Tiffany to bed, call her home and tell the housekeeper that Mrs. Benjamin was fine, and then they'd talk later. No drunken hysterics in the cab.... The cabbie might decide he had a hot story and ... Christ, that Kezia did not need.

'Church ... all night ... walking ... slept in church....' She kept her eyes closed and seemed to drift off between words. But the grip on Kezia's hand never slackened. It was only a few minutes before they drew up in front of Kezia's building, and with no explanations required or proffered, the doorman helped Kezia get Tiffany into the elevator, and the elevator man helped get her inside. The apartment was empty; Luke was out, and the cleaning woman wasn't due. Kezia was grateful for the solitude as she led her friend into the bedroom. She didn't want to explain Luke, even in Tiffany's current state. She had taken a hell of a chance bringing her there, but she couldn't think of any place else.

Tiffany sat sleepily on the edge of Kezia's bed and looked around. 'Where's Uncle Kee?'

Her father again ... Christ. 'He's out, Tiff. Why don't you lie down, and I'll call your place and tell them you'll be home later.'

'No! ... Tell them. ... Tell. ... Tell her to go to hell!' She began to sob then and shake violently from head to foot. Kezia felt a cold chill run up her spine. Something about the words, the tone of voice ... something ... it had struck a chord in her memory, and she suddenly felt frightened. Tiffany was looking at her now with wild eyes, shaking her head, tears pouring down her face. Kezia stood near the phone and looked at her friend, wanting to help, but fearing to go near her. Something inside Kezia turned over.

'Shouldn't I tell them something?' The two women stayed that way for a moment, with Tiffany slowly shaking her head.

'No ... divorce. ...'

'Bill?' Kezia looked at her stunned.

Tiffany nodded.

'Bill asked for a divorce?'

She nodded yes and then no. And then she took a deep breath. 'Mother Benjamin. ... She called last night ... after the Lombards' dinner. Called me a ... a ... lush ... an alcoholic ... a ... the children, she is going to take the children, and make Bill ... make Bill ...' She gasped, choking back more sobs, and then retched briefly, but dryly.

'Make Bill divorce you?'

Tiffany gasped again and nodded while Kezia continued to look on, still dreading to go near her.

'But she can't "make" Bill divorce you, for Christ's sake. He's a grown man.'

But Tiffany shook her head and looked up with empty, swollen eyes. 'The trust. The big trust. His whole life ... depends ... on it. And the children ... their trust ... He ... she could ... he would ...'

'No, he wouldn't. He loves you. You're his wife.'

'She's his mother.'

'So what, dammit? Be reasonable, Tiffany. He's not going to divorce you. . . .' But suddenly Kezia wondered. Would he? What if the bulk of his fortune depended on it? How much did he love Tiffany? Enough to sacrifice that? As Kezia watched her, she knew Tiffany was right. Mother Benjamin held all the cards. 'What about the children?' But she saw the answer in Tiffany's eyes.

'She . . . she . . . they . . .' She was racked by fresh sobs, and clutched the bedspread beneath her as she fought to finish. 'She has . . . them. . . . They were gone last night after the . . . Lombards' dinner . . . and . . . Bill . . . Bill . . . in Brussels . . . she said . . . I . . . oh God, Kezia, someone help me please. . . .'

It was a death wail and Kezia found herself trembling as she stood across the room and finally, painfully, slowly began to walk toward her friend. But it was like hearing it again . . . hearing it . . . things began to come back to her. There were tears on her own face now and there was this horrible, terrible urge to slap the girl sitting filthy and broken on her bed . . . an urge to just sweep her away, to shake her, to . . . oh God, no. . . .

She was standing in front of her and the words seemed to rip through her soul, as though they were someone else's, hurled by and at a long vanished ghost. 'Then why are you such a fucking drunk, dammit . . . why . . . why?' She sank down on the bed beside Tiffany then, and the two women held each other tight as they cried. It seemed like years before Kezia could stop, and this time it felt as though Tiffany were comforting her. There was a timelessness about the arms veiled by black mink. They were arms that had held Kezia before. Arms that had heard those words before, twenty years before. Why?

'Jesus. I'm . . . I'm sorry, Tiffie. It . . . you brought back something so painful for me.' She looked up to see her friend nodding tiredly, but looking more sober than she had in an hour. Maybe in days.

'I know. I'm sorry. I'm a bad trip all around.' The tears continued to fan out from her eyes, but her voice sounded almost normal.

'No, you're not. And I'm so sorry about the kids, and about Mrs. Benjamin. What a stinking thing to do. What are you going to do?'

She shrugged in answer, looking down at her hands.

'Can't you fight it?' But they both knew otherwise. Not unless she cleaned up radically overnight. 'What if you go to a clinic?'

'Yeah, and when I come out, she'll have a grip on those kids that will never loosen, no matter how sober I get. She's got me, Kezia. She's got my soul ... my heart ... my ...' She closed her eyes again then, and the look of pain on her face was intolerable. Kezia put her arms around her again. She seemed so thin and frail, even in the thick fur coat. There was so little one could say. It was as though Tiffany had already lost. And she knew it.

'Why don't you lie down and try to get some sleep?'

'And then what?' Her eyes were almost haunting.

'Then you can take a bath, have something to eat, and I'll take you home.'

'And then?' There was nothing Kezia could say. She knew what the other girl meant. Tiffany stood up slowly and walked shakily to the window. 'I think it's time I went home.'

She seemed to be looking far beyond and far away, and Kezia berated herself silently for the wave of relief that she felt. She wanted Tiffany out of her house. Before Luke came home, before she fell apart again, before she said something that brought even one instant of horror back, she wanted her gone. Tiffany made her unbearably nervous. She frightened her. She was like a living ghost. The reincarnation of Liane Holmes-Aubrey Saint Martin. Her mother ... the drunk. ... She did not argue with Tiffany.

'You want me to take you home?' But she found herself hoping not.

Tiffany shook her head and brought her gaze back from the window with a small, gentle smile, and quietly shook her head. 'No. I have to go alone.' She walked out of the bedroom, through the living room, and stopped at the front door, looking back at Kezia hovering uncertainly in the bedroom doorway. Kezia wasn't sure if she should let her leave alone, but she wanted her to. She just wanted her to go home. To go away. Their eyes held for a moment, and Tiffany lifted one hand in a mock military salute, pulled her coat more tightly around her, and said, 'See ya,' just as they had when they were in school. 'See ya,' and then she was gone. The door closed softly behind her, and a moment later Kezia heard the elevator take her away. She knew she had no money to go home with, but she knew that Tiffany's doorman would pay for the cab. The very rich can travel almost anywhere empty-handed. Everyone knows them. Doormen are delighted to pay for their cabs. They double their money in tips. Kezia knew Tiffany was safe. And at least she was out of her house. There was a heavy scent left hanging in the air, a smell of perfume mixed with perspiration and vomit.

Kezia stood at the window for a long time, thinking of her friend, and her mother, loving and hating them both. After a while, the two seemed to blend into one. They were so much alike, so ... so ... It took a long hot bath and a nap to make Kezia feel human again. The excitement and the freedom of the morning, of ditching that damn column, was tarnished by the agony of seeing Tiffany sprawled in the street at the feet of that horse, shouted at by the hansom cab driver, puking and crying and wandering lost and confused ... and screwed over by her mother-in-law ... bereft of her children, with a husband who didn't give a damn. Hell, he probably would let his mother talk him into a divorce. And it probably wouldn't take much talking. It made Kezia's stomach turn over again and again, and when at last she lay down for a nap she slept badly, but at least when she awoke,

238

things looked better again. Much better. She looked up to see Luke standing at the foot of the bed. She glanced at the clock by her bed. It was much later than she'd thought.

'Hi, lazyass. What did you do? Sleep all day?' She smiled at him for a moment and then grew serious as she sat up and held out her arms. He leaned over to kiss her and she nuzzled his neck.

'I had kind of a rough day.'

'An assignment?'

'No. A friend.' She seemed unwilling to say more. 'Want something to drink? I'm going to make some tea. I'm freezing.' She shivered gently and Luke looked at the window and the night sky beyond.

'No wonder, with the windows open like that.' She had opened all of them wide, to banish the smell. 'Make me some coffee, babe?'

'Sure thing.' They exchanged a haphazard kiss and a smile, and she took the newspaper from the foot of the bed where he'd left it when he leaned over to kiss her hello.

'That girl in the paper anyone you know?'

'Who?' She was wandering barefoot through the living room now, yawning as she went.

'The socialite on the front page.'

'I'll look.' She flicked on the kitchen light, and looked down at the paper in her hands. The room spun around as she did. 'It ... it ... I ... oh God, Lucas, help me ...' She slid slowly down the side of the doorway, staring at the photograph of Tiffany Benjamin. She had jumped from the window of her apartment shortly after two. '*See ya ... see ya....*' Suddenly the words rang in her ears. 'See ya.' With that little salute they had done all through school. Kezia scarcely felt Luke's arms around her as he led her to the couch to sit down.

239

CHAPTER XXI

'Do you want me to come with you?' Kezia shook her head as she zipped up the black dress and then slipped on the black alligator shoes she had bought the summer before in Madrid.

'No, love, thanks. I'll be okay.'

'Promise?'

She smiled at him as she put on her mink hat. 'Swear.'

'I'll say one thing, you sure as hell are looking fancy.'

He looked at her appreciatively and she smiled again.

'I'm not sure that I'm supposed to.' But she knew that she looked just right. She was trying to decide if she should wear her mink coat or her black Saint Laurent. She decided on the black.

'You look fine. And listen, lady, if it gets too heavy for you, you split, right?'

'I'll see.'

'That's not what I said.' He walked to the mirror and pulled her around to face him. He still didn't like the look in her eyes. 'If it gets heavy, you come home. Either that, or I come with you.' He knew that was out of the question. Tiffany's funeral was going to be one of the 'events' of the season. But all he wanted to know was that Kezia knew the score. It wasn't her fault Tiffany had committed suicide. She had not killed Tiffany. She had not killed her mother. She had done her best. They had been over it and over it and over it, and he wanted to be sure that she wouldn't backslide now. It was a bitch of a thing to happen but it wasn't her fault. She slid quietly into his arms as they stood in front of the mirror, and she held him tighter than usual.

'I'm glad you're here, Lucas.'

'So am I. Now do I have that promise from you?' She nodded silently and held her face up to him to kiss, which he did with a vengeance.

'Goodness, at that rate, Mr. Johns, I may never leave here in the first place.'

'That would suit me just fine.' He ran a hand inside the V-neck of her dress and she backed off with a giggle.

'Lucas!'

'At your service, madam.'

'You're awful!'

'Awful horny!' He was eyeing her with a smile as she clipped on simple pearl earrings. He knew he was being irreverent, but it lightened the mood. He tried to sound casual as he sat down and watched her put on lipstick and a last dab of perfume. 'Is Edward going with you?' She shook her head and picked up the black alligator bag and short white kid gloves. The thick black and white silk scarf from Dior provided the only brighter spot to her outfit.

'I told Edward I'd met him there. And stop worrying about me. I'm a big girl, and I'm fine, and I love you and you take care of me better than anyone in this world.' She faced him with a smile that looked more like the Kezia who could take care of herself and he began to feel better.

'Jesus, you look good. If you weren't in a hurry . . .'

'Lucas, you're all talk.' She had turned away and was crossing the living room on her way to get her coat, when he came up silently behind her and picked her up off her feet.

'All talk am I? Listen here, wench . . .'

'Lucas! Lucas dammit, put me down! Lucas!' He spun her around back down to the ground and she fell giggling and breathless into his arms as he chuckled. 'You are the worst, most miserable, impossible . . .' He met her lips with his own and after a moment she pushed him gently away with a look both happy and sad on her face. 'Luke . . . I have to go.'

241

'I know.' He was sober now too, and helped her on with her coat. 'Just take it easy.' She nodded, kissed him, and was gone.

The church was already filled when she got there, and Edward was waiting discreetly near a door. He signalled silently to her, and she joined him, slipping a hand inside his arm.

'You look lovely.' His voice was a whisper and she nodded, as he tightened his grip on her arm. They were ushered up the main aisle, and Kezia tried not to see the casket draped in a blanket of white roses. Mother Benjamin sat piously in the front pew with her widower son and his two children. Kezia felt the breath catch in her throat as she saw them, and she wanted to scream 'Killer!' at the bowed head of her friend's mother-in-law. 'Killer! You killed her, with your fucking threats of divorce and taking the children . . . you . . .'

'Thank you.' She heard Edward's subdued voice as the usher showed them to a pew near the middle. Whit was standing three pews ahead.

He looked thinner, and suddenly more openly effeminate in an over-tailored Cardin suit that clutched at his waist, and seemed to hang too closely across his back. She suspected the suit had been a gift from his friend. It was not the sort of thing Whit would have bought for himself.

Marina was there too, with Halpern, looking embarrassingly happy in spite of the setting. They were getting married at New Year's in Palm Beach. Marina looked as if her troubles were over.

Kezia found it hard not to cast the eye of Martin Hallam about, looking for people, tidbits, stories. But she couldn't hide behind him any more. Now he was dead too. And she was simply Kezia Saint Martin, mourning her friend. The tears ran freely down her face as they carried the casket down the aisle, to the maroon limousine that waited outside. Two policemen had been detailed to redirect traffic around the long snaking line of limousines, not a single one of which was rented. It was all the real thing. And as was to be expected, an army of press lay in wait for the mourners as they left.

It was hard to believe that it was all over. They had had so much fun in school, had written to each other from their respective colleges. Kezia had been Tiffany's maid of honour when she married Bill, had laughed at her when she was pregnant. When did the end start? When did the drinking make her a drunk? Was it then, after the first baby? Or after the second? Was it later? Had she been before? The awful part was that now it seemed as though she had always been that way, always lurching, vague, dropping 'Divine's like rabbit pellets everywhere she went. It was this Tiffany that leapt to mind, the drunken, vomiting, confused Tiffany . . . not the funny girl in school . . . that mock salute at the door that last day . . . that . . . see ya . . . see ya . . . see ya. . . .

Kezia found herself staring blankly at the backs of people's heads and felt Edward guiding her slowly out of the pew. It was a long wait at the line where she shook hands with assorted relatives. Bill looked officious and solemn, dispensing small smiles and understanding nods like an undertaker instead of a husband. The children looked confused. Everywhere people were looking around, checking out who was there, what they had worn, and clucking and shaking their heads over Tiffany . . . Tiffany the drunk . . . Tiffany the lush . . . Tiffany the . . . friend. And it was all so much like Kezia's mother's funeral that it was unbearable. Not only to her, but to Edward. He looked grey when they left the church at last. Kezia took a deep breath, patted his hand and looked up at the sky.

'Edward, when I die, I want you to see to it that I'm tossed into the Hudson, or something equally simple and pleasant. If you do one of these numbers for me, I'll haunt you for the rest of your life.' She was not entirely joking. But Edward looked at her with an unhappy expression.

'I hope I won't be around to worry about it. Do you want to go to the cemetery?' She hesitated for a moment, and then shook her head, remembering her promise to Luke. This had been bad enough.

'No, I don't. Are you going?'

He nodded painfully.

'Why?' Because he ought to. She knew the answer too well. That's what killed people like Tiffany. Ought to's.

'Really, Kezia. One ought . . .' She didn't wait to hear the end of it. She merely leaned over, kissed his cheek, and started down the steps.

'I know, Edward. Take care.'

He had wanted to ask her what she was doing later, but he never got the chance, and he didn't want to impose on her. He never did. It didn't seem right to trouble her. She had her own life to live, but it had been such a wretched day. Such a bad day for him. It all reminded him so much of Liane. Of that godawful, unbearable day when. . . . He watched Kezia slip easily into a cab, and wiped a tear quickly from his cheek. He was smiling a small, appropriate smile when she looked back at him from the rear window.

'How was it?' Luke was waiting for her with hot tea.

'Horrible. Thanks, darling.' She took a sip of the tea before she took off the black Saint Laurent coat, and with her free hand pulled the dark mink hat from her head. 'It was ghastly. Her mother-in-law even had the bad taste to bring the kids.' But Kezia had been at her mother's funeral too. Maybe that was just the way things had to be. As painful as possible to make them seem real.

'Do you want to go out to dinner, or have something sent in?'

She shrugged, not really caring. Something was bothering her. Everything was.

'Baby, what's wrong? Did it hit you that hard? I told you. . . .' He looked at her unhappily.

'I know. I know. But it's upsetting . . . and maybe something else is bothering me. I don't know what. Maybe it's seeing all those fossils who still think they own

244

me. Maybe it's growing pains. I'll be okay. I'm probably just depressed about Tiffany.'

'You sure it's not something else?' He was troubled, more than she knew.

'I told you, I don't know. But it's no big deal. There have just been a lot of changes lately ... quitting the column ... you know. It's time to grow up, and that's never easy.' She tried to smile but his eyes didn't answer.

'Kezia, am I making you unhappy?'

'Oh, darling, no!' She was horrified. What a ridiculous thought. And what the hell had he been worrying about all afternoon, she wondered. He looked lousy.

'Are you sure?'

'Of course I'm sure. I'm positive, Lucas. Really.' She leaned over to kiss him and saw sadness in his eyes. Maybe it was compassion for her, but what she saw touched her deeply.

'Are you sorry about having given up the column?'

'No, I'm glad. Honestly glad. It just feels odd when things change. Makes one insecure. It does me, anyway.'

'Yeah.' He nodded and stayed silent for a long time as she finished her tea, her coat now tossed on a chair, the black dress she wore making her look more severe. He watched her and it was a long time before he spoke again. There was an odd note in his voice when he did. The bantering of earlier in the day was gone.

'Kezia ... there's something I have to tell you.'

She looked up, all innocence, trying to smile. 'What is it, love?' And then she joked, 'You're secretly married and have fifteen children?' She spoke with the confidence of a woman who knows that there are no secrets ... only one.

'No, you jerk. I'm not married. But there's something else.'

'Give me a hint.' But for once she didn't look worried. It couldn't be important or he wouldn't be bringing it up now. He knew she was upset about Tiffany.

'Babe, I don't know any way to tell you, except to put it to you straight. But I have to tell you. It just can't wait

245

any more. I'm up for a revocation hearing.' The words fell into the room like a bomb. Everything smashed and then stopped.

'A what?' She couldn't have heard him correctly ... couldn't have. She was dreaming. This was one of his nightmares and she'd overheard by mistake.

'A hearing. I'm up for a hearing. About my parole. They want to revoke me for conspiracy to provoke disturbances in the prisons. In other words, agitation.'

'Oh God, Lucas. . . . Tell me you're joking.' She closed her eyes and sat very still, as though she were waiting, but he could see her clenched hands shake in her lap.

'No, babe, I'm not kidding. I wish I were, but I'm not.' He reached out and took both her small hands in his. Her eyes opened slowly, drowning in tears.

'How long have you known?'

'There's been a threat of it for a while. Since before I met you, in fact. But I never believed it would happen. I got confirmation of the hearing today. What really did it, I think, was the San Quentin work strike. They got pissed enough to grab my ass this time.' That, and kill Morrissey.

'Jesus. What'll we do?' Her face looked limp as the tears flowed in silence. 'Can they prove you were involved in that strike?'

He shook his head in answer, but he didn't look encouraged. 'No. But that's why they're so pissed. Now they'll try to get me on anything they can. But we'll do our damnedest. I have a good lawyer. And I'm lucky. A few years ago, you couldn't have an attorney at hearings to revoke your parole. Just you and the board. So, cheer up, things could have been worse. We have a good lawyer, we have each other. And they can't object to our life-style, it's as clean as they come. We'll just have to do what you do with these things. Wait it out till the hearing, and then put up a good fight.'

But they both knew that the key issue was neither the fight, nor his life-style. He was accused of agitation. And

246

it was all true. 'Come on, Mama, hang tough.' He leaned over to kiss her, taking her into his arms, but her body was stiff and unyielding, her face bent as the tears continued to flow. He saw her knees shake as he looked down at her lap. He felt as though he had killed her. And in a way, he was right.

'When is the hearing?' She expected to hear that it was the next day.

'It's still more than six weeks away. January eighth, in San Francisco.'

'And then what?'

'What do you mean, "and then what?" ' She was sitting so still that she frightened him.

'What if they make you go back?'

'That won't happen.' His voice was deep and subdued.

'But what if it does, dammit, Luke?' Her shriek of pain and fear slashed through the silence.

'Kezia, it won't!' He lowered his voice and tried to calm her, while fighting his own desperation. This was not at all what he'd planned. But what could he expect? He should have known this from the beginning. He had led her gently away from her home, into his, and now he was sitting there telling her that their house might burn down. The look in her eyes made her an orphan again. And her pain was his doing. He felt the weight of it like a cement sack around his heart.

'Darling, it's not going to happen like that. And if it does – and that's only an "if" – then we live with it. We both have the balls to do that. If we have to.' He knew he did. But did she? Not the way she looked then.

'Lucas . . . no!' Her voice was a barely audible whisper.

'Baby, I'm so sorry. . . .' There was nothing more he could say. The thing that he'd feared for so long had finally happened. Only the joke of it was that before Kezia he hadn't feared it in the same way. Hadn't feared it at all. He had regarded it as a potential price to pay, a possible inconvenience. He had had nothing to lose . . . and now he had it all . . . and it was all on the line. And she had to pay the price with him. But she had to be told. Alejandro had told him that for weeks, and he had stalled, and evaded, and lied to himself. There was no lying now. The notice lay crumpled in a ball on the desk. They had taken the matter out of his hands ... and now look at the mess.... He lifted her chin gently with one hand, and sought her lips tenderly with his. It was all he could give her, what he felt, what he was, how he loved her. They still had another six weeks. If no one murdered him first.

CHAPTER XXII

For Thanksgiving, they had hot turkey sandwiches in their room at the hotel in Chicago. The revocation hung over their heads, but they had fought hard to ignore it. They rarely discussed it, except once in a while, late at night. They had six weeks till the hearing, and Kezia was determined not to let the threat of it ruin their life. She fought for gaiety with an almost unbearable determination. Lucas knew what was happening to her, but there was so little he could do. He couldn't wish the hearing away. His own nightmares were back, and he didn't like the way Kezia looked. She was already losing weight. But she was game. She made the same old jokes, they had a good time. They suddenly made love two and three times a day, sometimes four, as though to stock up on what they might lose. Six weeks was so short. When they went back to New York, there were only five left.

'Kezia, you don't look well. You don't look well at all.'
'Edward, my darling, you're driving me mad.'
'I want to know what you're up to.' The waiters

swished past them and poured more Louis Roederer champagne.

'You're prying.'

'YES, I am.' He looked sour, and old. She looked tired, and far older than she had so briefly before.

'All right. I'm in love.'

'I assumed that much. And he's married?'

'Why do you always assume that the men I go out with are married? Because I'm discreet? Hell, I have a right to be that, I've learned that much over the years.'

'Yes, but you don't have a right to indulge in sheer folly.'

No, just a right to misery, darling, and shitty rotten luck. Right, Edward? Of course. Or is it just a right to duty and pain? 'Folly, in this case, dear Edward, is a beautiful man whom I adore. We have more or less lived and travelled together for more than two months now. And just before Thanksgiving, we found out ... that ...' Her voice caught and her heart trembled as she wondered what she was doing ... 'We found out that he's sick. Terribly sick.'

Edward's face suddenly looked pinched. 'What sort of sick?'

'We're not sure.' She was into it now. She almost believed it herself. It was easier than the truth, and it would get him off her back for a while. 'They're attempting treatment, and at this point he has about a fifty-fifty chance of living. Which is why I don't "look well." Satisfied?' Her voice was ripe with bitterness, her eyes dulled with tears.

'Kezia, I'm so sorry. Is he ... is he ... anyone I know?'

Not on your ass, sweetheart. She almost wanted to laugh. 'No, he isn't. We met in Chicago.'

'I wondered about that. Is he young?'

'Young enough, but he's older than I am.' She was quiet now. In a way she had told him the truth. Sending Lucas back to prison would be like condemning him to

249

death. Too many men hated or loved him, he was too well known, had stirred up too much. San Quentin would kill him. Someone would. If not an inmate, a guard.

'I don't know what to say.' But his face said what his words couldn't. There was a ghost in his eyes. The ghost of Liane Saint Martin. 'This man ... is he ... would ... does he come to New York?' He was groping for a criterion that Kezia wouldn't leap at in fury but there were none. Where did he go to school? What does he do? Where does he live? Who is he? Kezia would have exploded at any of those questions. But he wanted to know. Had to. He owed it to her ... to himself.

'Yes, he comes to New York. He's been here with me.'

'He stays in your apartment?' He suddenly remembered her saying that they had lived together. My God, how could she?

'Yes, Edward. In my apartment.'

'Kezia ... is he ... is he ...' He wanted to know if this was someone decent, respectable, not some fortune hunter, or ... or 'tutor,' but he simply couldn't ask, and she wouldn't have let him. Edward felt as though he was on the verge of losing her forever. 'Kezia. ...'

She looked at him then with tears on her cheeks and quietly shook her head. 'Edward ... I ... I can't do this today. I'm sorry.' She kissed him gently on the cheek then, picked up her handbag, and slid to her feet. He didn't stop her. He couldn't. He merely watched her retreat towards the door and clenched his hands very tightly for a moment before signalling for the check.

In the bitter cold of the winter afternoon, she rode the subway to Harlem. Alejandro was the only one who could help. She was beginning to panic. She had to see him.

She walked quickly from the subway to the centre, oblivious of how she looked in the long red Paris coat and the full white mink hat. She didn't give a damn how she looked. On the streets where she slalomed between garbage cans and scampering children, they looked at her as if she were a strange apparition, but the wind was bitingly cold and there was snow in the air. No one had time to be bothered. They left her alone.

There was a girl in Alejandro's office when Kezia arrived, and they were laughing. Kezia paused in the doorway. She had knocked, but their laughter had muffled the sound.

'Al, are you busy?' It was rare that she called him by the nickname Luke used.

'I ... no ... Pilar, will you excuse me?' The girl bounced from the chair and scraped past Kezia with a look of wonderment in her eyes. Kezia looked like a vision fresh out of *Vogue*, or someone in a movie.

'I'm sorry to break in on you like this.' Her eyes looked agonized beneath the white fur.

'It's all right. I was ... Kezia?'

She had crumbled into tears in front of his eyes, and now she stood there, broken, holding out both arms, her handbag askew on the floor, the last of her control dissolved.

'Kezia ... *pobrecita* ... babe ... take it easy ...'

'Oh, Christ, Alejandro.... I can't stand it!' She let herself fall into his arms and buried her face on his shoulder. 'What can we do? They're going to take him back. I know it.' She sniffed and pulled away to see his eyes. 'They will, won't they?'

'They might.'

'You think they will too, don't you?'

'I don't know.'

'Yes, you do, godammit. Tell me! Somebody tell me the truth!'

'I don't know the truth, damn you!'

She was shouting and he was shouting still louder. The walls seemed to echo with what they had both penned up – fear and anger and frustration.

'Yeah, maybe they will take him back. But for chris-sake, lady, don't give up till they say it. What are you going to do? Let yourself die now? Give him up? Destroy

251

yourself? Wait till you hear, for chrissake, then figure it out.' The room had been full of his voice and she could hear tears creeping up on him too, but she was quiet. He had brought her back to her senses, to a point of control.

'Maybe you're right. I'm just so fucking scared, Alejandro. I don't know what to do to hang on anymore. . . . I get this rising panic like bile in my guts.'

'There's nothing you can do, except try to be reasonable and hang in. Try not to panic.'

'What if we run away? Do you think that they'd find him?'

'Yes, eventually, and then they'd kill him on sight. Besides, he'd never do that.'

'I know.' He came close to her again and held her in his arms. She was still wearing the coat and fur hat, and her face was streaked with mascara and tears. 'The worst of it is that I don't know what to do to help him, how to make it easier for him. He's under so damn much strain.'

'You can't change that. All you can do is stand by him. And take care of yourself. It's not going to help anyone if you fall apart. Remember that. You can't give up your whole life for him, or your sanity. And Kezia . . . don't give up yet. Not till they say the word, if they do, and not even then.'

'Yeah.' She nodded tiredly at him and leaned back against the desk. 'Sure.'

'I didn't know you were a quitter.'

'I'm not.'

'Then don't act like one. Get your shit together, woman. You've got a rough road ahead, but nobody said it was the end of the road. It isn't to Luke.'

'Okay, mister big mouth, I get your point.' She tried to muster a smile.

'Then start acting like you ain't going to quit. That big dude loves you one hell of a lot.' And then he walked back to her and hugged her again. 'And I love you too, little one . . . I do too.' Tears started to squeeze from her eyes again and she shook her head at him.

'Don't be nice to me, or I'll cry again.' She laughed through her tears and he rumpled her hair.

'You're looking mighty fancy, lady. Where've you been? Shopping?' He had just noticed.

'No. To lunch with a friend.'

'It couldn't have been heroes and Cokes from the look of it.'

'Alejandro, you're nuts.' But they shared the moment of honest laughter, and he reached for his coat on the back of the door.

'I'll take you home.'

'All the way downtown? Don't be silly!' But she was touched at the thought.

'I've done enough here for one day. Want to play hooky with me?' He looked young as he made the offer, his eyes dancing, his smile that of a playful boy.

'As a matter of fact, that sounds just fine.'

They walked away from the centre arm in arm, her red coat linked with his drab army surplus jacket and hood. He gave her a squeeze and she laughed into the warm eyes. She was glad she had come up to see him. She needed him, differently but almost as much as she needed Luke.

They got off the subway at Eighty-sixth Street and stopped in one of the German coffeehouses for a cup of hot chocolate 'mit schlag': great clouds of whipped cream. An oom-pah-pah band was doing its best, and outside, Christmas lights were already blinking hopefully. They said nothing of the revocation, but talked of other times. Christmas, California, his family, her father. It was funny; she had thought about her father a lot lately, and wanted to share it with someone. It was so hard to talk to Luke now; every conversational path led them back to the tangled emotional maze of the revocation.

'Something tells me you're a lot like your father, Kezia. He doesn't sound all that much of a conformist either, if you scratch the surface a little.'

She smiled at the melting whipped cream on her hot chocolate. 'He wasn't. But he had a nice way of pulling it all off, judging from what I've been told and what I remember. I suspect he wasn't as compelled to make choices.'

'Those were different times. He didn't have the same choices. That might have had something to do with it. What's your trustee like?'

'Edward? He's lovely. And solidly to the bone everything he was brought up to be. And I think he's lonely as hell.'

'And in love with you?'

'I don't know. I never gave it much thought. I don't think he is.'

'I'll bet you're wrong.' He smiled and took a swallow of the warm sweet drink, his lips frothed with the cream. 'I think there's a lot you don't see, Kezia. About yourself and your effect on other people. You're naive in that sense.'

'Is that so?' She smiled at him. He was nice to be with. And she had needed someone to talk to. Years ago, she had talked so well with Edward, but not now. In an odd way, Alejandro was replacing him now. It was Alejandro she had turned to, when she couldn't talk to Edward, or even Luke. Alejandro who gave her solace and fatherly advice. And then she had a funny thought. She looked up, and giggled. 'And I suppose you're in love with me too?'

'Maybe so.'

'You nut.' She knew he didn't mean it, and they sat back and listened to the pounding of the old-fashioned music. The restaurant was crowded but they sat apart from the noise and the movement, as isolated as the old men reading German newspapers alone at their tables.

'What are you guys doing for Christmas?'

'I don't know. You know Luke. I don't think he's made up his mind. Or if he has, he hasn't told me. Are you staying here?'

'Yeah. I wanted to go home to L.A., but I've got too much to do at the centre, and the trip is expensive. There's a facility I want to check out in San Francisco, though. Maybe next spring.'

'What kind of facility?' She lit a cigarette and relaxed in her chair. The afternoon had metamorphosed into something delightful.

'They call them therapeutic communities out there. Same as the centre, except the patients live in, which gives you a much better chance of success.' He looked at his watch and was surprised at the time. It was just after five.

'Want to join us for dinner?'

He shook his head regretfully. 'No. I'll leave you two lovebirds in peace. Besides, there's a "little piece" of my own I want to check into, closer to home.' He cackled evilly, and she chuckled.

'Havoc in Harlem? Who is she?'

'A friend of a friend. She works at a day-care centre and probably has big tits, bad breath and acne.'

'You've got something against big tits?' She grinned again.

'Nope. Just the other two. But it's a type. There are two or three like that who work at the centre. And yeah, I'm a snob. About women.' He signalled for the check.

Kezia laughed at him. 'How come you don't have an old lady?' She had never asked him before.

'Either because I'm too ugly, or too mean. I'm not quite sure which.'

'Bullshit. What's the real story?'

'Who knows, *hija*. Maybe my work. You were right way back when - Luke and I have a lot in common that way. The causes come first. That's hard for a woman to live with, unless she's got a heavy trip of her own. Anyway, I'm picky.'

'I'll bet you are.' And therein most likely lay the truth. Because he was assuredly neither ugly, nor mean. She found him strangely attractive, and cherished the relationship that had blossomed between them. 'So what's with this lady tonight?'

'I'll see.' He was gently evasive, but Kezia was curious.

'How old is she?'

'Twenty-one, twenty-two. Something like that.'

255

'I hate her already.'

'You should worry.' He looked up at the porcelain skin framed by the white fur hat. Her eyes stood out like sapphires.

'Yeah. But I'm staring at thirty. That's a far cry from twenty-two.'

'And you're a lot better off.' She thought about it for a moment and nodded. Twenty-two hadn't been very much fun. It had started to be, though, after she began writing. Before that, it was the shits. Unsure of where she was going, what she was doing, and who she wanted to be, while having to present an outward appearance of unshakable certainty and poise.

'You should have known me ten years ago, Alejandro. You would have laughed.'

'You think I was better off at that age?'

'Probably. You were freer.'

'Maybe, but still not very cool. Hell, ten years ago I wore a crew cut cemented into place with "greasy kid stuff." Talk about funny! And I'll bet you weren't wearing a crew cut.'

'No. A pageboy. And pearls. I was adorable. The hottest thing on the market. Come and get it, ladies and gentlemen, one untouched, unused, near-perfect heiress. She walks, she talks, she sings, she dances. Wind her up and she plays "God Bless America" on the harp.'

'You played the harp?'

'No, dummy. But I did everything else. I was absolutely "mahvelouss," but not very happy.'

'So now you're happy. That's a lot to be grateful for.'

'I am.' Her thoughts flew back to Lucas ... and the hearing. Alejandro watched the transitions in her eyes, and moved quickly to bring her back to the easy chatter of the last hour.

'How come you don't play the harp? Aren't heiresses supposed to?' He was all innocence.

'No, that's angels. They're the ones who play the harp.'

'You mean they're not the same thing?'

256

She threw back her head and laughed at the thought. 'No, darling. They are most emphatically not the same thing. I do play the piano, though. That's a prerequisite for your heiress wings. A few play the violin, but most of us tackle the piano at an early age, and give it up by the time we're twelve. Chopin.'

'I still kind of wish you could play the harp.'

'Up your ass, Mr. Vidal.' She grinned and he feigned shock.

'Kezia! And you're an heiress? How shocking! Up my . . . what?'

'You heard me, mister. Now come on, let's go home. Lucas will worry.' They slipped into their coats, he left the tip on the table, and they walked out into the cold air, arm in arm. The afternoon had been well spent. She felt restored.

When they got home, Luke was waiting in the living room, bourbon in hand and with a smile on his face.

'Well, what have you two been up to?' He liked to see them together, but Kezia noticed something pinched about his eyes. Jealousy?

'We went out for a cup of hot chocolate.'

'A likely story. But I'll forgive you both. This time.'

'That's big of you, darling.' Kezia walked to his side and bent to kiss him.

He pulled a cigar out of his pocket and winked at Alejandro, as he slid his arm around her waist. 'Why don't you get our friend a beer?'

'Probably because he'd throw up after all the hot chocolate he drank . . . mit schlag!' She grinned over at Alejandro.'

'What's that?' Luke's voice sounded unusually loud. As though he was terribly nervous.

'Whipped cream.'

'Puke. Nah, get him a beer.'

'Lucas . . .' She wondered suddenly if he had something to say to Alejandro, he looked so odd – and a little bit crocked.

257

'Go on.'

Kezia looked at him strangely and then turned to Alejandro. 'You want a beer?'

Their friend threw up both hands and shrugged. 'No, but with a dude that size, who argues?' All three of them laughed and Kezia vanished into the kitchen.

She called back over her shoulder as she flicked on the light. 'I'll make you coffee. I can't stand the idea of beer after all that good chocolate.'

'Right on.' Alejandro sounded distracted as he answered and Kezia wondered what was afoot. Lucas had the look of a small boy. Or the look of a man with a secret. She grinned to herself, wondering if it was something to do with her. Maybe a present, something silly, an outing, a dinner. Luke was like that. She wouldn't allow herself to wonder if it was something to do with the hearing. It couldn't be. He looked much too pleased with himself, and a little bit punchy.

She went back to the living room a few moments later with the coffee. Two cups. Luke looked as if he could use one.

'Look at that, man, she wants to sober us up.' Luke's tone was jovial, but Alejandro didn't look as if he needed sobering. He looked tense and unhappy, as though something drastic had happened in the moments she was out of the room. Kezia looked at his face, then at Luke's, and then she put down the two cups and sat down on the couch.

'Okay, sweetheart, game's over. What's up?' Her voice was light and nervous and brittle, and her hands had begun to tremble. It was something to do with the hearing. It wasn't anything fun after all. Now she could tell. 'What's wrong?'

'Why the hell should something be wrong?'

'For one thing,' she cast a glance away from him, and apologetically at their friend, 'if you'll forgive me,' and then she turned back to Luke, 'because you're drunk, Lucas. How come?'

258

'I am not.'

'You are. And you look scared. Or pissed. Or something. And I want to know what the hell's happening. You told Al, now tell me.'

'What makes you think I told Al anything?' Now he looked visibly nervous, and Kezia was beginning to look angry.

'Look, dammit! Don't play games with me. I'm having just as tough a time coping with all this crazy bullshit as you are. Now tell me! What's wrong?'

'Oh, for chrissake. Will you listen to that, Al?' He looked around at them both with a plastic smile on his face, and crossed one leg over the other and then back again, while Alejandro looked very upset.

Kezia looked from Lucas to him. 'Okay, Alejandro, will you tell me what's going on?' Her voice was rising to an uncomfortable level, nearing hysteria. But Lucas broke in with a look of impatience, and pushed himself forcefully out of his chair, growing instantly pale as he stood.

'Just keep it together, Mama. And I'll tell you myself.' But as he turned to face her the room swam, and he sank almost to his knees. Alejandro rushed to his side and took the half-empty glass from his hand. Most of the bourbon had sloshed into the carpet, and Luke's face was now frighteningly pale.

'Take it easy, brother.' He supported him with one arm, as Kezia rushed to his side.

'Lucas!' Her eyes were frantic as Luke sat down heavily on the floor next to her, and rested his head on his knees. He was drunk and in shock. But slowly he turned his face towards her with a gentle expression.

'Mama, it's no big deal. Someone tried to shoot me today. They missed by an inch.' He closed his eyes on the last words, as though afraid of her eyes.

'Someone what?' She held his face with both her hands and slowly he looked up at her again. It had not yet registered in her face.

'Someone tried to kill me, I guess, Kezia. Or scare the

259

piss out of me. Either way, but everything's cool. I'm just a little punchy, that's all.'

She thought instantly of Morrissey now, and knew Lucas had too. 'My God ... Lucas ... who did it?' She was sitting next to him, trembling, and her stomach felt as though it were riding a wave.

'I don't know who. Hard to tell.' He shrugged and suddenly looked very tired.

'Come on, man, let's get you to bed.' Alejandro helped him slowly to his feet, and he wasn't sure if he should be supporting Lucas or Kezia. She looked almost worse. 'Can you make it, Luke?'

'Are you kidding? I'm not hurt, man. I'm gassed.' He chuckled proudly for a moment, as he walked into the bedroom. Alejandro shook his head with a worried frown on his face, as Kezia settled Luke against the pillows. 'For chrissake, Kezia, I'm not dying. Don't overdo it. And get me another drink, will you?'

'Should you?'

He laughed at the question and crossed both eyes with a grin. 'Oh Mama, should I!' The smile she returned to him was her first in ten minutes, but she could feel her knees shaking as she sank onto the edge of the bed.

'My God, Lucas, how did it happen?'

'I don't know. I went up to talk to some guys in Spanish Harlem today, and we were walking down the street after the meeting and whap, someone almost winged me. The motherfucker must have been aiming for my heart, but he took lousy aim.'

Kezia sat staring at him in shocked disbelief. It could have been like Morrissey. He could have been dead. There were chills on her spine as she thought of it.

'Anyone else knew about the meeting?' Alejandro looked frightened as he continued to stand there and look at his friend.

'A few people.'

'How few?'

'Not few enough.'

260

'Oh God, Lucas . . . who did it?' Suddenly Kezia's head was bowed, and she was sobbing as she sat there. Luke leaned forward and circled her with his right arm, pulling her towards him.

'Come on, baby, take it easy. It could have been anyone. Just some crazy kid out for a laugh. Or maybe someone who knew me. Could have been some heavy-weight right-winger up there who doesn't dig prison reform. Could have been some pissed off left-winger who doesn't think I'm enough of a "brother". What the hell difference does it make? They tried. They didn't get me. I'm okay. You're okay. I love you. So . . . no big deal, please. Okay?' He sank back on the pillows then with a dazzling smile. But neither Kezia nor Alejandro was swayed by the bravado.

'I'll get you another drink.' Alejandro left the room, and had a drink of his own in the kitchen. Shit. It was coming to that now. And with Kezia in the picture. Terrific. He heaved a long sigh as he walked back to the bedroom with a tall glass of straight bourbon for Luke. Kezia was crying again when he walked in, but this time softly. The two men exchanged a long look over her head and Luke nodded slowly. It had been quite a day. And they were both wondering if it was going to be like this all the way till the hearing. It could have been a cop for all they knew, and they both realized it, even though they didn't tell that to Kezia. But the reality was that Lucas was popular only with those he worked with on the outside or the men in prison all over the country who benefited directly from all he did. Not many others really understood. And as loved as he was, he was equally hated.

'I'm going to hire you a bodyguard.' She looked up with a sniff, as Luke took a long sip of his bourbon and Alejandro sat down in a chair near the bed. She was still sitting near Luke.

'No, you're not, pretty lady. No bodyguard, no bullshit. This happened once. It won't happen again.'

'How do you know?'

261

'Baby, don't push me. Let me run this show. All I want from you is your beautiful smile and your love.' He patted her hand and took a long sip of bourbon Alejandro had handed him. 'All I want from you is what you already give me.'

'Yeah, and not my advice.' She said it sadly, her shoulders sagging. 'Why don't you let me hire a body-guard?'

'Because I already have one.'

'You hired someone?' Why didn't he tell her anything anymore?

'Not exactly. But I've been followed by the cops for a while now.'

'By the cops? Why by them?'

'Why the hell do you think, Mama? Because they think I'm a threat.' It put an aspect on things that she didn't like. And it suddenly brought home to her that in a sense Luke was considered an outlaw, and that in living with him, she was on that same ill-favoured side of the law. She somehow hadn't totally absorbed her position in all this before. 'And don't kid yourself, sweetheart, it could just as well have been a cop who tried to get a piece of me today.'

'Are you serious?' Her face grew even paler. 'Would they do that to you, Luke?'

'Damn right. If they thought they could get away with it, they'd do it in a hot second. And enjoy it.'

'Oh God.' The police taking potshots at Luke? They were supposed to give decent citizens protection. But that was the whole point. And Kezia finally knew it. To the cops, Lucas wasn't 'decent'. He was only that in her eyes, and Al's, and his friends', not in the eyes of the rednecks, and the Adult Authority, and the law.

Luke exchanged a rapid look with Alejandro, who slowly and unhappily shook his head. Bad things were coming. He could feel it. 'But I'll tell you one thing, Kezia. I don't want any bullshit from you. You do exactly what I tell you from now on. No visits to Al up in Harlem, no traipsing through the park alone, no dis-

262

appearing into the subway. Nothing except what I tell you you can do. Is that clear?' He was wearing the face of a general again as he said it. 'Is it?'

'Yes, but . . .'

'No!' He was roaring now. 'Just listen to me for once in your life, damn you! Because if you don't, you goddamn stupid naive asshole . . . because if you don't,' his voice began to tremble and Kezia was shocked to see tears in his eyes, 'maybe they'll get you instead of me. And if they did . . .' His voice began to crack and grow soft as he lowered his eyes, 'if they did . . . I couldn't . . . take it. . . .' She went to him with tears on her own cheeks as she put her arms around him and let him rest his head on her chest. They stayed like that for what seemed like hours, with Luke crying in her arms, and what she did not know was that he was torturing himself for what he was doing to her. Oh God . . . how could he have done this to a woman he loved . . . Kezia. . . . At last he fell asleep in her arms as they sat there, and when Kezia slid him down onto the pillow and turned off the light, she suddenly remembered Alejandro sitting in the chair. She turned to find him, but he was long since gone, with heartaches of his own, and no Kezia whose arms he could cry in. And like Luke, the tears that he cried were for her.

CHAPTER XXIII

Lucas put down the phone with a look of dismay, and Kezia instantly knew.

'Who was it?' But she didn't need to ask. She knew, whatever the name, whatever the city, it didn't really matter. He always wore that face, and sounded the way he had, for calls about prisons. But now, when Christmas was so close. . . .

263

'It was one of my crazy friends out in Chino.'

'And?' She wasn't létting him off the hook.

'And ...' He ran a hand through his hair and bit the end of a cigar that had been lying on the desk. It was almost midnight and he had been strolling the house in his shorts, barefoot and bare-chested. And ... they want me to come out. Think you can handle that, Mama?'

'You mean come out with you?' It was the first time he had asked her.

'No, I mean stay here. I'll be back by Christmas. But ... it looks like they need me. Or at least they think they do.' There was something gruffer in his voice, pure macho, all man. And a vibrant chord of excitement that ran through his words, no matter how careful he was to conceal it. He loved what he did. The meetings, the men, the riots, the cause. He loved getting back at the 'pigs', and helping his brothers. It was what he lived for. And there was no room for Kezia in that world. It was a world of men who had lived without women for long enough to know that they could do without them, if they had to. They had a hard time learning to include them again. And this was one place where Luke wouldn't budge. He wouldn't have considered taking her with him, not for a moment. Not when there was danger involved. Not after last time in San Francisco. Not after he'd almost been shot. She knew she had been crazy to hope that he was inviting her this time. He wasn't.

'Yes, I can handle it, Luke. But I'll miss you.' She tried to keep the sadness from her voice, and the terror, but he knew. She looked at him and shrugged. 'So it goes. You're sure you'll be home by Christmas?'

'As sure as I can be. They're afraid riots might start. But I think we'll probably get everything straightened out before that happens.' Maybe. If. She wondered if he really wanted to, or if he'd rather play with the fireworks. But she knew that wasn't fair. 'I'm sorry, Mama.'

'Me too, but I'll be okay.' She walked over to him and slid her arms around his neck. She kissed him gently on

264

the back of the head and smelled the fresh richness of the cigar. He was going to 'war'. Again. 'Lucas ...' She hesitated about saying it, but she had to.

'What, babe?'

'You're crazy to do this now. With the hearing pending. And ...' She was afraid to voice all her fears, but he knew them. He had the same ones.

'Oh Christ, Kezia, don't start that.' He pulled away from her and stood up to walk across the room, half naked and puffing on his cigar, with a ferocious look on his face. 'You just be sure you take care of yourself. And what fucking difference does it make what I do now, with the backlog of bullshit they're going to throw at me at the hearing anyway? I've been doing this kind of thing since I got out of the joint. You think one more time will make a difference?'

'Maybe.' She stood very still and kept her eyes on his. 'Maybe this one time could make the difference between revocation and freedom. Or between living and dying.'

'Bullshit. And anyway ... I have to, that's all.' He slammed the door to the bedroom and she wondered how close she was to the truth. He had no right to do this to her, jeopardize his own life and hers with it. If this trip cost him his freedom, or his life, what did he think it would do to her, or didn't he think? The bastard. ...

Kezia followed him into the bedroom and stood looking at him as he pulled a suitcase out of his closet. She watched him with fire in her eyes, and a lead weight on her heart.

'Lucas ...' He didn't answer. He knew. 'Don't go ... please, Luke ... not for me. For you.' He turned to look at her then, and without exchanging another word with him, she knew she had lost.

It was the twenty-third before Kezia got the call she had feared. He would not be home for Christmas. He'd be gone for at least another week. Four men had already died in the Chino strike, and the last thing on his mind was Christmas, or home. For one brief moment Kezia found herself wanting to tell him what a bastard he was, but she couldn't. He wasn't. He was simply Luke.

She didn't want to admit to Edward that she was going to spend Christmas alone. It was such a lonely admission, an admission of defeat. He would have tried to be sweet to her, and insisted she spend it with him in Palm Beach, which she would have hated. She wanted to spend the holiday with Luke, not with Edward or Hilary. She had toyed with the idea of flying out to California to surprise him, but she knew she wouldn't have been welcome. When he was involved in his work, that was it. He wouldn't have been amused or pleased by the gesture, and he probably wouldn't have been able to spend any time with her anyway.

So she was alone. With a stack of engraved invitations, and red and green inked notes suggesting she stop by for a drink, or drop in on the city's 'best' holiday parties, the sort of invitations people would have given right arms and eyeteeth for. Eggnog, punch, champagne, caviar, pâté, amusing little stocking gifts from Bendel's or Cardin. The cotillions were in full swing, if she wanted to check out the season's debs, which she didn't. There was a rash of charity balls, a white tie party at the Opera, and a skating fete at Rockefeller Centre to celebrate the alliance of Halpern Medley and Marina Walters. The El Morocco would be alive with the holiday spirit. Or there was always Gstaad or Chamonix ... Courchevelles or Klosters ... Athens ... Rome ... Palm Beach. But none of it appealed. None of it.

After mulling it all over in cursory fashion, Kezia decided it would be less lonely to be alone, than to be lost in the midst of empty hilarity. She was not feeling very festive. She thought briefly about inviting some friend over to help her spend Christmas day, but she never got up enough steam to ask anyone in particular, and could think of no one she really wanted to ask ... only Lucas. And the others would be busy with whatever they had planned, just as right now they were busy at Bergdorf's and Saks buying shocking pink slippers and parrot green robes, or drinking rum in the Oak Room, or helping their mothers 'get ready' in Philadelphia or Boston or Bronxville or Greenwich. Everyone was bound to be somewhere, and she was actually alone. She and an army of doormen and maintenance men, each of whom had received his Christmas dues. The superintendent discreetly left a mimeographed sheet in the mail around the fifteenth of December. Twenty-two names, all waiting for bribes. Merry Christmas.

It was the afternoon of the twenty-fourth, and Kezia had nothing to do. She walked the length of the apartment in her cream satin robe, and smiled to herself. There was a mist of snow on the ground outside.

'Merry Christmas, my love.' The whispered words were for Lucas. He had kept his word and called every day, and she knew he'd call again later. Christmas by telephone. It was better than nothing. But not much. The silver-wrapped boxes on her desk were for him – a tie, a belt, a bottle of cologne, a briefcase, and two pairs of shoes. A collection of mundane gifts, except that she knew they would all make him laugh. She had explained all the 'in' symbols to him when they first met, like translating the language of the country she lived in. Status-ese. The Dior ties, the Gucci shoes, the Vuitton luggage, and its ugly LV's plastered all over the mustard and mud coloured surface. It had made him laugh when she told him. 'You mean those guys all wear the same shoes?' She had laughed back, nodding, and explained that the women wore them too. One style for the women, and one for the men. Varied styles would have created insecurity, so there was just one. One had a choice of colours, of course. It was all terribly, terribly original, wasn't it? But it had become a standard joke with them, and neither of them could keep a straight face anymore as they passed a pair of Guccis on the street, or a Pucci dress on a woman. The Pucci-Gucci Set. It was something else they shared from their private

267

vantage point. So that's what she had bought him for Christmas. A Pucci tie, a Gucci belt, Monsieur Rochas cologne (which she actually decided she liked quite a lot), a Vuitton briefcase, and the indomitable Gucci shoes in black leather, standard model, and of course, a duplicate pair in brown suede. She smiled to think of him opening them all, and the look on his face.

But her smile deepened as she thought of the real presents she had bought him, the ones hidden in the pocket of the Vuitton case. Those were the ones that mattered to her, and would undoubtedly matter to him. The signet ring with the dark blue stone carved with his initials, and her initials and the date engraved in tiny letters on the inside of the setting. Carefully wrapped in tissue paper was a leather-bound book of poems that had been her father's, and had occupied a place of honour on his desk for as long as Kezia could remember. It made her happy to know that now it would be Luke's. It meant a great deal to her. It was a tradition.

She drank a cup of hot chocolate as she stood looking out at the snow. It was cold out, very cold, the way only New York and a few other cities can be. The kind of chill that makes you feel as though you've been slapped when you walk out the door. The freezing winds swept your legs and brushed your cheeks like steel wool, and the ice on the windowsill was frozen in patterns of lace.

The phone rang as she stood alone in the silent room. It could be Luke. She dared not ignore it.

'Hello?'

'Kezia?' It wasn't Luke's voice, and she wasn't quite sure whose it was. There was the merest hint of an accent. 'What are you doing here?'

'Oh, Alejandro!'

'Who were you expecting? Santa Claus?'

'In a way. I thought it might be Luke.'

He smiled at the comparison. Only she could come up with that. 'I had a suspicion you'd be here. I saw the papers, and have an idea of what it must be like in Chino.

268

I figured he wouldn't want you out there. So what are you up to? Ten thousand parties?'

'No. Nary a one. And you're right. He didn't want me out there. He's too busy.'

'That, and it's not a cool scene.' Alejandro was grave.

'No. But it isn't a cool scene for him either. He's a fool to get sucked into that now. It'll just add more fuel to their fires at the hearing. But Luke never listens.'

'So what else is new? What are you doing for Christmas?'

'Oh, I think I'll hang my stocking up on the fireplace and put out cookies and a glass of milk for Santa, and . . .'

'Milk? *Qué* horror!'

'And what would you suggest?'

'Tequila, of course! Jesus, if that poor sonofabitch has to drink milk all over the world, it's a wonder he bothers with the trip.'

She laughed at him and switched on some lights. She had been standing in the early darkness of the winter dusk.

'Do you suppose it's too late to pick up some tequila?'

'Baby, it's never too late for that!'

She laughed again at the earnest sound of his voice. 'And what are you up to for Christmas? More work at the centre?'

'Yeah, some. It's better than sitting at home. Christmas with my family is always a big deal. It kind of depresses me to be away from all that, unless I keep busy. How come you're not going to all those big fancy parties?'

'Because that would depress me. I'd rather be alone this year.' She was thinking of the hearing on the eighth again. It was strange though, lately things with Luke had seemed nearly normal. The first shock of the hearing was gone. It almost didn't seem real. Just a meeting they would have to go to, nothing more. Nothing could touch the magic circle around Kezia and Luke. Certainly not a hearing.

'So you're sitting around there all by yourself?'

269

'Sort of.'

'What do you mean "sort of"?'

'Well, okay. Yeah. I am all by myself. But it's not like I'm crying my eyes out. I'm just enjoying being peaceful at home.'

'Sure. With presents for Luke all over the house, and a Christmas tree you haven't bothered to decorate, and not answering the phone, or only when you think it might be Luke. Listen, lady, that's one stinking way to spend Christmas. Am I right?' But he knew he was. He knew her by now.

'Only partially, Father Alejandro. Boy, you sure like to lecture!' She laughed at the tone of his voice. 'And the presents for Luke are not "all over the house", they're neatly stacked on my desk.'

'And what about the tree?'

'I didn't buy one.' Her voice was suddenly meek.

'Sacrilege!'

She laughed again and felt silly. 'All right. I'll go buy one. And then what do I do?'

'You don't do anything. Do you have any popcorn?'

'Hmmm . . . yes. As a matter of fact, I do.' There was still some left from the last time she and Luke had made popcorn in the bedroom fireplace at three in the morning.

'Okay. Then cook up some popcorn, make some hot chocolate or something, and I'll be there in an hour. Or do you have other plans?'

'Not a thing. Just waiting for Santa.'

'He'll be on the subway and down in an hour.'

'Even if I don't have tequila in the house?' She was teasing him; she was glad he was coming.

'Don't worry. I'll bring my own. Imagine not having a tree!' Friendly outrage crept into his voice. 'Okay, Kezia. See you later.' He already sounded busy as he hung up the phone.

He arrived an hour later with an enormous Scotch pine dragging behind him.

270

'In Harlem, you get them cheaper, particularly on Christmas Eve. Down here this would cost you twenty bucks. I got it for six.' He looked chilled and ruffled and pleased. It was a beautiful tree; it stood a head taller than he, and its branches reached out furrily when he pulled off the ropes that had bound them. 'Where'll I put it?' She pointed to a corner, and then unexpectedly reached up and kissed his cheek.

'Alejandro, you are the best friend in the world. It's a beautiful tree. Did you bring your tequila?' She hung his coat in the closet and turned back to look at the tree. Now it was beginning to look like Christmas. With Luke not planning to come home, she hadn't done any of the things she usually loved. No tree, no wreath, no decorations and very little Christmas spirit.

'My God, I forgot the tequila!'

'Oh no . . . how about cognac?'

'I'll take it.' He smiled at the offer with obvious pleasure.

She poured him a glass of cognac, and went to ferret out the box of Christmas tree ornaments from the top shelf of a closet. They were old ones, some of which had been her grandfather's. She took them out tenderly, and held them up for Alejandro to see.

'They look pretty fancy to me.'

'No, just old.'

She joined him in a glass of cognac and together they strung lights and hung baubles until there were none left in the box.

'It really looks beautiful, doesn't it?' Her face lit up like a child's, and he reached over and gave her a hug. They sat side by side on the floor, their cognac glasses and a huge crystal bowl full of popcorn beside them.

'I'd say we did a damn good job.' He was a little merry from the drinks, and his eyes looked soft and bright.

'Hey . . . you want to make a wreath?' She had just thought of the ones she had made every year as a child.

Make one? With what?'

'All we need is a branch from the tree . . . and some fruit . . . and . . . let's see, wire. . . .' She was looking around, getting organized. She went to the kitchen and came back with a knife and some scissors. 'You cut off a branch, one of the lower ones in the back so it won't show. I'll get the rest.'

'Yes, ma'am. This is your show.'

'Wait till you see.' The light in his eyes had been contagious and now hers shone too, as she gathered what they would need. They were going to have Christmas! In a few minutes, it was all spread out on the kitchen table. She wiped her hands on her jeans, rolled up the sleeves of her sweater, and set to work, as Alejandro watched, amused. She looked a lot better than she had two hours before. She had looked so lost and sad when he arrived, and he hadn't liked the sound of her voice on the phone. He had cancelled a date, a dinner, and two promises to "drop in," but he owed this one to Luke. And to Kezia. It was crazy; there she was in her fancy apartment, with all her millionaire friends, and she was alone on Christmas. Like an orphaned child. He wasn't about to let it stay that way either. He was glad he had cancelled his plans and come down. For a moment, he hadn't been sure she would let him.

'You going to make a fruit salad?' She had apples, pears, walnuts, and grapes spread out near the branch.

'No, silly. You'll see.'

'Kezia, you're crazy.'

'I am not . . . or maybe I am. But I know how to make a wreath anyway. I used to make ours every year.'

'With fruit?'

'With fruit. I told you, you'll see.' And he did. With deft fingers, she tied the branch together with wire, and then carefully wired each piece of fruit and attached it to the wreath. The finished product looked like something in a Renaissance painting. The thick pine branch was covered with a neat circle of fruit, the nuts scattered here and there, the whole thing held together with an invisible

272

network of fine wire. It was a handsome ornament, and Alejandro loved the look on her face. 'See! Now where'll we put it?'

'On a plate? It still looks like a fruit salad to me.'

'You're a barbarian.'

He laughed and pulled her into his arms. It was warm and comfortable there.

'You'd never get away with a wreath like that in a poor neighbourhood. It'd be picked clean in an hour. But I will admit . . . I like it. It's a beautiful wreath – for a fruit salad.'

'Asshole.'

'Yup. That's me.' But she was still comfortably lodgēd in his arms as they spoke. She felt safe there; she liked it. She pulled reluctantly away after a few moments, and their eyes met with laughter.

'What about some dinner, Kezia? Or are you serving the wreath?'

'You take one bite out of that and I'll brain you! One of my friends' brothers did that one year and I cried for a week.'

'He must have been a sensible kid, but I can't stand women in tears. We'd better go get a pizza.'

'On Christmas?' She was shocked.

'Well, they don't sell tacos in this part of the world, or I would have suggested that. Can you suggest anything better?'

'I certainly can!' She still had the two Rock Cornish game hens she had been saving for Luke's Christmas dinner, just in case he came home. 'How about a real Christmas dinner?'

'How about saving that for tomorrow? Will the invitation still be good?'

'Sure? Why . . . do you have to go now?' Maybe he was in a hurry, and thus the suggestion of pizza. Her face suddenly fell, and she tried to look as though nothing had happened. But she wanted him to stay. It had been such a nice evening.

'No, I don't have to go. But I just had an idea. Want to go skating?'

'I'd love it.'

She put another sweater on over the one she already wore, thick red wool socks, brown suede boots, and buried herself in a lynx jacket and hat.

'Kezia, you look like someone in a movie.' She had the kind of beauty which appealed to him. Luke was a damn lucky man.

She told the answering service when they'd be back, in case Lucas called, and together they braved the biting night air. There was no wind, only a bitter frost which seared the lungs and eyes.

They stopped for hamburgers and hot tea, and she laughed as he told her of the chaos of Christmas in a Mexican home. A thousand children underfoot and all the women cooking, their husbands drunk, and parties in every home. She told him the things she had liked about her Christmases as a child.

'You know, I never got the purple-sequined gold dress.' She still looked almost surprised. She had seen it in a magazine when she was six, and had written all about it to Santa.

'What did you get instead? A mink coat?' He said it teasingly, without malice.

'No, darling, a Rolls.' She looked down her nose at him from beneath the big furry hat.

'And a chauffeur, of course.'

'No, I didn't get him till I was seven. My own, of course, with two liveried footmen.' She giggled at him again from under the hat. 'Shit, Alejandro, they used to drop me three blocks from school when I was a kid, and then follow me. But I had to walk the last bit of the way because they didn't think it was cool for me to arrive at school with a chauffeur.'

'That's funny. My parents felt the same way. I had to walk too. It's really rough what kids have to go through, isn't it?' His eyes laughingly mocked her.

274

'Oh shut up'

He threw back his head and laughed. Plumes of frost flew from his mouth in the cold night air.

'Kezia, I love you. You are really one crazy lady.'

'Maybe I am.' She was thinking of Lucas.

'Man, I wish I had bought some tequila. It's gonna be colder than shit on the ice.' She giggled at him then, looking like a child with a secret. 'I'm glad you think it's so funny. Me, I'm not wearing fur, and if I fall on my ass, which I will, I'll wind up with a good case of frostbite.' She giggled again, and with a white cashmere mittened hand pulled a flat silver flask from her pocket. 'What's that?'

'Instant insulation. Cognac. The flask was my grandfather's.'

'The dude was no dummy. That's a mighty thin flask. Hell, you could wear that in your suit and no one would spot it . . . pretty cool.' Arm in arm, they walked into the park, and began to sing 'Silent Night.' She unscrewed the cap on the flask and they each took a sip before she put it back in her pocket, feeling much better. It was one of those rare nights in New York when the city seemed to shrink. Cars had all but disappeared, buses seemed quieter and fewer, people were no longer rushing and actually took the extra second or two to smile at passersby. Everyone was either at home or away, or hiding from the fierce winter cold, but here and there groups were walking or singing. Kezia and Alejandro smiled at the other couples they passed, and now and then someone joined in their songs. By the time they got on the ice at the skating rink they had all but exhausted their collective knowledge of Christmas carols, and had had several sips from the flask.

'That's what I like, a woman who travels equipped. A flask full of cognac. Yep, you are crazy . . . but good crazy, definitely good crazy.' He sailed past her on the ice with a broad grin, intending to show off, and winding up instead on his ass.

'Mister, I think you're drunk.'

275

'You ought to know, you're my barman.' He grinned at her good-humouredly as he got up.

'Want some more?'

'No. I just joined A.A.'

'Party pooper.'

'Lush.'

They laughed at each other, sang 'Deck the Halls,' and skated a few turns arm in arm. The rink was almost deserted, and the other skaters shared in the Christmas spirit. The piped music was merry and light, carols intermingled with waltzes. It was a beautiful night. And it was past eleven before they decided the 'd had enough. Despite the cognac, their faces were numb from the cold.

'How about midnight mass at Saint Patrick's? Or would that be a bad trip? You're not Catholic, are you?'

'Nope. Episcopal, but I have nothing against Saint Patrick's. Your mass isn't that different from ours. I'd really enjoy it.' There was a moment of worry in her face, as she thought of missing a call from Luke. But the prospect of church appealed to her, and Alejandro swept her along. He suspected what she'd been thinking. And going home to sit by the phone would negate all they'd done. It was turning into a passable Christmas, and he wasn't going to let her spoil it. Even for Luke.

They walked down a deserted Fifth Avenue, past all the ornate window dressings, the lights and the trees. It had a carnival air. Saint Patrick's was jammed, hot, and smelled strongly of incense. They wedged their bodies in way at the back of the church; they could not approach the front pews, short of standing on shoulders and walking on heads. People had come from miles. Midnight mass at Saint Patrick's was a tradition for many.

The organ was somber and majestic, the church dark except for the light shed by thousands of candles. It was a high mass, and one-thirty when they got out.

'Tired?' He held her arm as they made their way down the steps. The cold air was a shock after the scented warmth of the church.

276

'More like sleepy. I think it's the incense.'

'Of course the cognac and the skating have nothing to do with it.' His eyes laughed at her, but kindly.

He hailed a cab, and the doorman at her place lurched his way to the door.

'Looks like he's been having a good time.'

'So would you if you raked in as much money as he and the other guys do. They each get an envelope from everyone in the building.' She thought of what Alejandro must make at the centre and cringed at the comparison. 'Want to come up for a drink?'

'I shouldn't. . . .' He knew she was tired.

'But you will. Come on, Al, don't be a drag.'

'Maybe I'll just stay for a minute, and have a bite of the fruit salad.'

'Touch my wreath and you'll regret it! And don't say I didn't warn you!' She brandished the nearly empty flask at him and he ducked. They giggled sleepily as they walked out of the elevator arm in arm. The apartment was warm and cozy and the tree looked pretty all lit up in the corner. She went out to the kitchen, as he sat down on the couch.

'Hey Kezia!'

'What?'

'Make that another hot chocolate!' He had had more than enough cognac, and so had she.

'I was.'

She came out with two steaming cups covered with rapidly dissolving marshmallows, and they sat side by side on the floor, looking up at the tree.

'Merry Christmas, Mr. Vidal.'

'Merry Christmas, Miss Saint Martin.' It was a solemn moment, and for what felt like a very long time neither spoke. Their thoughts were drifting separately to other people, other years, and in their own ways, they each found their minds wandering back to Luke and the present.

'You know what you ought to do, Alejandro?'

'What?' He had stretched out on the floor, his eyes

277

closed, his heart warm. He was growing very fond of her and he was glad he had made a change of plans. This was turning into a beautiful Christmas. 'What should I do?'

'Sleep on the couch. It seems stupid for you to go all the way uptown at this hour. I'll give you some sheets and a blanket and you can stay here' And then I won't have to wake up in an empty house tomorrow morning, and we can giggle and laugh, and go for a walk in the park. Please, please stay . . . please. . . .

'Wouldn't it be a pain in the ass for you if I stay?'

'No. I'd love it.' The look in her eyes said she needed his presence there, and he didn't know why, but he needed that too.

'Are you sure?'

'Very sure. And I know Lucas won't mind.' She knew she could trust him, and it had been such a nice evening that now she desperately didn't want to be alone. It was Christmas. It had finally dawned on her. Christmas: a time for families and friends and people you love. A time for children and big sloppy dogs to come lumbering into the house and play with the wrappings from the gifts that were being opened. Instead, she had sent Edward a set of colourless books for his library, and French place mats from Porthault to Aunt Hil, to add to the towering stack already in her London linen closets. And in turn, Hilary had sent her perfume, and a scarf from Hardy Amies. Edward had given her a bracelet that was too large and not her style. And Totie had sent her a hat that she'd knitted, that didn't go with anything Kezia owned, and might possibly have fit her when she was ten. Totie had aged. Hadn't they all? And the exchange of gifts had all been so meaningless this year, by mail, via stores, to people she owed by ritual and tradition, not really by heart. She was glad she and Alejandro had not tried to drum up gifts for each other that night. They had given each other something far better. Their friendship. And now she wanted him to stay. Aside from Luke, it suddenly felt as though he were her only friend.

278

'Will you stay?' She looked down at him lying on the floor beside where she sat.

'With pleasure.' He opened an eye, and held out a hand for one of hers. 'You may be crazy, but you're still a beautiful lady.'

'Thank you.'

She kissed him gently on the forehead, and went down the hall to get him some sheets. A few minutes later, she gently closed the door to the room with a last whispered 'Merry Christmas,' which meant 'thanks.'

CHAPTER XXIV

Kezia had been out shopping. She had stopped sitting in her apartment, just waiting for Luke. It had been driving her crazy. So she foraged around Bendel's and wandered through the boutiques on Madison Avenue for an hour that afternoon, and when she opened the door, Luke's suitcase was spilling its contents nervously across the floor, brush, comb, razor, rumpled shirts, sweaters lying about, two broken cigars tangled with a belt, and one shoe, whose mate was missing: Lucas was home.

He waved at her from the desk as she walked in. He was on the phone, but a broad grin spread over his face, and she walked swiftly to his side, matching his smile, and wrapped her arms around his broad shoulders. It felt so good just to hold him again. He felt so big and so beautiful, his hair smelled fresh and felt like silk under her hand. Black silk, and soft on his neck. He hung up the phone and turned around in his chair to hold her face in his hands and look into the eyes that he loved.

'God, you look good to me, Mama.' There was something fervent in his eyes and his hands were almost rough.

'Darling, how I missed you!'

'Baby, me too. And I'm sorry about Christmas.' He buried his face in her chest, and gently kissed her left breast.

'I'm so glad you're home ... and Christmas was lovely. Even without you. Alejandro took care of me like a brother.'

'He's a good man.'

'Yes, he is.' But her thoughts were far from Alejandro Vidal. They were filled with the man she was looking at. Lucas Johns was her man. And she was his woman. It was the best feeling she knew. 'Oh Jesus, but how I missed you, Lucas!' He laughed with pleasure at the catch in her voice, and pulled her off her feet, standing up and sweeping her into his arms like a child. He kissed her firmly on the mouth, said not a word, and walked her straight into the bedroom as she giggled. He marched right over the suitcase, the clothes, the cigars, kicked the bedroom door shut with his foot, and made his presence rapidly and amply known. Lucas was very much home.

He had brought her a turquoise Navajo bracelet of elaborate and intricate beauty, and he laughed at the Christmas presents she gave him ... and then grew silent over the book that had been her father's. He knew what it must have meant for her to give it to him, and he felt something hot at the back of his eyes. He only looked up at her and nodded, his eyes quiet and grave. She kissed him gently, and the way their lips met told them both what they already knew, how much he loved her, and she him.

He was back at the phone in an hour, bourbon in hand. And half an hour later he announced that he had to go out. When he did, he didn't come back to the apartment until nine, and then got back on the phone again. When he finally got to bed at two in the morning, Kezia had long since gone to sleep. He was up and dressed when she awoke the next morning. These were hectic days. And tense ones. And now there were always plainclothesmen wherever Luke was. Even Kezia spotted them now.

'Jesus, darling, I feel like I didn't even get to talk to you yesterday. Are you already going out now?'

'Yeah, but I'll be back early today. I just have so much to do, and we've got to get back out to San Francisco in three days.' Three days. Where had she gotten the idea that they would be spending time alone in New York? Time to walk in the park, and talk, to lie in bed at night and think aloud, time to smile at the fire, and giggle over popcorn. It wasn't going to be like that at all. It already wasn't. The hearing was less than a week away now, and at his insistence, she was sticking close to home. He had been adamant about that. He had enough to think about without worrying about her.

He left ten minutes later, and the promise that he'd be back early went by the wayside. He walked in at ten that night, looking tired and nervous and worn, reeking of bourbon and cigars, with dark rings under his eyes.

'Luke, can't you take one day off? You need it so much.' He shook his head as he threw his coat over the back of a chair. 'Just an afternoon? Or one evening?'

'Goddammit, Kezia! Don't press me! I have too fucking much to do as it is.' Gone the dream of peace before the hearing. There would be no peace, no time alone, no rest, no candlelight dinners. There would be Luke coming and going, looking ravaged, up at dawn, drunk by noon, and sober again and spent by the end of the evening. And nightmares when he finally allowed himself a few hours of sleep.

A canyon had opened between them, a space around him which she couldn't even begin to approach. He wouldn't let her.

On their last night in New York she heard Luke's key in the door and turned in her seat at the desk. He looked pathetically tired, and he was alone.

'Hi, Mama. What's doing?'

'Nothing, love. You look like you had a bitch of a day.'

281

'Yeah, I did.' The smile was old and rueful, the lines around his eyes had deepened noticeably in the last few days. Luke sagged visibly in his chair. He was beat.

'Want a drink?' He shook his head. But tired as he was, there was a familiar light in his eyes. It was as though the old Luke had finally come home ... the one she'd waited weeks, and now days for. He was worn out, exhausted, but sober and alone. She went to him and he put his arms around her.

'I'm sorry I've been such a sonofabitch.'

'You haven't been. And I love you ... a whole bunch.' She looked down into his face, and they smiled.

'You know, Kezia, the funny thing is that no matter how hard you run, you can't run away from it. But I got a lot done. I guess that's something at least.' It was the first hint he'd given her that he was scared too. It was like a train heading straight for their life, and their feet were rooted to the tracks while it just kept coming at them ... and coming and coming and coming ... and ...

'Kezia ...'

'Yes, love?'

'Let's go to bed.' He took her by the hand, and they walked quietly into the bedroom. The Christmas tree still stood tall in a living room corner, shedding needles all over the floor, the branches beginning to droop dryly from the weight of the ornaments. 'I wanted to take that down for you this week.'

'We can do it when we get back.' He nodded and then stopped in the doorway, looking at something over her head, but still holding her hand.

'Kezia, I want you to understand something. They might take me away at the hearing. I want you to know that, and accept it, because if that happens, it happens, and I don't want you falling apart.'

'I won't.' But her voice was shaken and tiny.

'Noblesse oblige?' His accent was funny and she smiled. The words meant 'Nobility obliges'; she'd grown up with it all of her life. The obligation to keep your chin up, no

282

matter who sawed off your legs at the knee; the ability to serve tea with the roof coming down around your ears; the charm of developing an ulcer while wearing a smile. Noblesse oblige.

'Yeah, noblesse oblige, and partly something else maybe.' Her voice was strong again now. 'I think I could keep it together because I love you as much as I do. Don't worry. I won't fall apart.' But she didn't understand it either, nor could she accept it. It couldn't happen to them. And maybe it wouldn't . . . or maybe it would.

'You're a beautiful lady, sweet Kezia.' He put his arms around her again, and they stood in the doorway for a long, long time.

CHAPTER XXV

Their mood on the plane was almost hysterically festive. They had decided to travel first-class.

'First-class all the way. That's my girl.' He was prominently carrying his new Vuitton briefcase, and ostentatiously wearing the brown suede Gucci shoes. They had agreed that the brown suede were the wealthier looking.

'Lucas, pull your feet in.' She giggled at him; he was deliberately dangling one foot in the aisle.

'Then they won't see my shoes.' He lit a cigar from the new shipment from Romanoff, and flapped the Pucci tie in her face.

'You're a nut, Mr. Johns.'

'So are you.' They exchanged a honeymoon smooch and the stewardess looked over and smiled. They were a good-looking couple. And so happy they were almost ridiculous.

'Want some champagne?' He was fumbling around in his briefcase.

'I don't think they'll serve it till we're off the ground.'

'That's their business, Mama. Me, I bring my own.' He grinned broadly at her.

'Lucas, you didn't!'

'I most certainly did.' He pulled out a bottle of vintage Moët et Chandon and two plastic glasses, also a small tin of caviar. In four months he had developed a fondness for much of her way of life, while still keeping his own view and perspective. Together they filtered out the best of both worlds and made it their own. Mostly, the 'posh' things amused him, but there were certain things he truly liked. Caviar was one of them. And so was pâté. The Gucci shoes were a lark, and she knew that's how he'd feel, which was why she had bought them.

'Want some champagne?' She nodded, smiling, and reached out for one of the two plastic glasses.

'What are you looking so funny about?'

'Who, me?' And then she started to laugh, and leaned over and kissed him. 'Because I brought some too.' She opened her tote bag, and pointed at the bottle lying on the top. Louis Roederer, though not quite as vintage a year as his Moët. But still, not a bad one. 'Darling, aren't we chic?'

'It's a wine-tasting party!' Stealthily they guzzled champagne and devoured the caviar; they necked during the movie, and traded old jokes, which got sillier by the hour and the glass. It was like leaving on a vacation. And he had promised her that he would be all hers the next day. No appointments, no meetings, no friends. They would have the day to themselves. She had taken reservations at the Fairmont, just for the hell of it; a suite in the tower, for a hundred and eighty-six dollars a day.

The plane landed smoothly in San Francisco, just before three o'clock. They had the rest of the afternoon and the evening before them. Their rented limousine was waiting, and the chauffeur took their baggage stubs, so they could head for the car. Luke was as anxious as Kezia to avoid any publicity. This was no time for that.

'Do you think they noticed my shoes?'

She looked down at them pensively for a moment. 'You know, maybe I should have bought them in red.'

'Maybe I should have made love to you during the movie. No one would have seen.'

'How about in the car?' She settled back on the seat, and automatically pressed the button to raise the glass between their seat and the chauffeur's. He was still hunting for their bags.

'Baby, that may cut out the sound track, but if we're going to make love he'll still get a wide-angle view.'

She laughed with him at the thought. 'Want some more champagne, Lucas?'

'You mean there's more left?' She nodded, smiling, and produced the remaining half bottle of Roederer. They had polished off the Moët et Chandon. He produced the plastic glasses from his briefcase, and they poured another healthy round.

'You know, Lucas, we really have a great deal of class. Or is it panache? Possibly . . . style.' She was thinking it over, the glass tilted slightly in one hand.

'I think you're drunk.'

'I think you're gorgeous, and what's more, I think I love you.' She made a passionate lunge at him, and he groaned as her champagne flew at the window, and his splashed on the floor.

'Not only are you drunk, but you're a sloppy drunk. Just look at the Honourable Miss Kezia Saint Martin.'.

'Why can't I be Kezia Johns?' She sank back into the corner with her empty champagne glass, and waited for him to refill it, a pout taking over her face. He eyed her curiously for a long moment and cocked his head to one side.

'Are you serious or drunk, Kezia?' This was important to him.

'Both. And I want to get married.' She looked as though she were going to add, 'And so there!' but she didn't.

'When?'

'Now. Let's get married now. Want to fly to Vegas?' She brightened at the thought. 'Or is it Reno? I've never gotten married before. Did you know I'm an old maid?' She smiled primly, as though she had revealed a marvellous secret.

'Jesus, baby, you're shitfaced.'

'I most certainly am not! How dare you say such a thing?'

'Because I've been supplying the champagne. Kezia, be serious for a minute. Do you really want to get married?'

'Yes. Right now.'

'No. Not right now, you nut. But maybe later this week. Depending on ... well, we'll see.' The accidental reference to the impending hearing had gone over her head, and he was grateful for that. She was thoroughly plastered.

'You don't want to marry me.' She was getting close to champagne-induced tears, and he was trying hard not to laugh.

'I don't want to marry you when you're drunk, stupid. That's immoral.' But there was a special smile on his face. My God, she wanted to marry him. Kezia Saint Martin, the girl in the papers. And here he was in a limo wearing Gucci shoes, on his way to a suite at the Fairmont. He felt like a kid with ten electric trains. 'Lady, I love you. Even if you are shitfaced.'

'I want to make love.'

'Oh God.' Luke rolled his eyes, and the chauffeur slid into his seat behind the wheel. A moment later the car pulled away from the kerb. Neither of them had seen the unmarked car drive up behind them. They were being followed again, but by now they were used to it. It was a fixture.

'Where are we going?'

'To the Fairmont, remember?'

'Not to church?'

'Why the fuck would we want to go to church?'

286

'To get married.'

'Oh, that kind of church ... Later. How about getting engaged?' He looked at the signet ring on his hand again. He had been so pleased with the gift. But she saw the look in his eyes, and anticipated what he had in mind.

'You can't give me that. I gave it to you. That would be Indian giving, not a proper engagement ... an Indian engagement? In any case, I don't believe it would be for real.' She looked haughty and was listing badly to one side.

'I don't believe you're for real, Mama. But okay, if this one won't do it, let's stop and get a "proper" engagement ring. What would you consider proper? I hope it's something smaller than a ten-carat diamond.'

'That would be vulgar.'

'That's a relief.' He grinned at her, and she dropped the haughty look for a smile.

'I think I'd like something blue.'

'Oh. Like a turquoise?' He was teasing, but she was too drunk to see it.

'That would be pretty ... or a lapis patchouli. ...'

'I think you mean lapis lazuli.'

'Yes, that's who I mean. Sapphires are nice too, but they're too expensive, and they crack. My grandmother had a sapphire that ...' He shut her up with a kiss, while pressing the button to lower the window separating them from the chauffeur.

'Is there a Tiffany's here?' He knew all the right names now. For a man who hadn't known the difference between a Pucci and a lap dog four months ago, he had learned the private dialect of the upper classes with astonishing speed. Bendel's, Cartier's, Parke Bernet, Gucci, Pucci, Van Cleef, and of course ... Tiffany, everyone's favourite supermarket for diamonds. And comparable stones ... undoubtedly, they would have something blue, other than turquoise.

'Yes, sir. There's a Tiffany's here. On Grant Avenue.'

'Then take us there before the hotel. Thanks.' He

rolled the window back into place. He had learned that one too

'My God, Lucas, we're getting engaged? For real?' Tears sprang to her eyes as she smiled.

'Yes, but you're going to stay in the car. The papers would really love this one. Kezia Saint Martin gets engaged at Tiffany's, and the bride was noticeably inebriated.'

'Noticeably shitfaced,' she corrected.

'Excuse me.' He gently relieved her of the empty glass she'd been holding, and kissed her. They rode into town sitting close together in the back of the car, his arm around her, a beatific smile on her face, and a look of peace on his that hadn't been there for weeks.

'Happy, Mama?'

'Very.'

'Me too.'

The driver stopped in front of the grey marble façade of Tiffany's on Grant Avenue, and Luke gave her a hasty kiss and dashed from the car, with a sobering admonition that she stay there.

'I'll be right back. Don't leave without me. And don't under any circumstances get out of the car. You'd fall flat on your ass.' Then, as an afterthought, he stuck his head in the window and wagged a finger at her slightly hazed eyes. 'And stay out of the champagne!'

'Go to hell!'

'I love you too.' He gave her a quick wave over his shoulder as he dashed into the store. It seemed like only five minutes before he was back.

'Show me what you got!' She was so excited she could hardly sit still. Unlike other women at her age, this was the first time she'd gotten engaged.

'I'm sorry, baby. They didn't have anything I liked, so I didn't get anything.'

'Nothing?' She looked crushed.

'No . . . and to tell you the truth, they didn't have a thing I could afford.'

288

'Oh shit.'

'Darling, I'm sorry.' He looked crestfallen and held her close.

'Poor Lucas, how awful for you. I don't need a ring, though.' She suddenly brightened and tried to keep the disappointment out of her voice, but she was so tipsy that it was hard to keep it all in control.

'Do you suppose we could get engaged without a ring?' He sounded almost humble.

'Sure. I now pronounce thee engaged.' She waved an imaginary wand at him, and smiled happily into his eyes. 'How does it feel?'

'Fantastic! Hey, far out! Look what I found in my pocket!' He pulled out a dark blue velvet cube. 'It's something blue, isn't that what you wanted? A blue velvet box.'

'Oh you . . . you! You did get me a ring!'

'No. Just the box.' He dropped it into her lap and she snapped the lid open and gasped.

'Oh Lucas, it's gorgeous! It's . . . it's incredible! I love it!' It was an emerald-cut aquamarine with a tiny diamond chip set on either side. 'It must have cost you a fortune. And oh darling, I love it!'

'Do you, babe? Does it fit?' He took it from the box for her and carefully slipped it on her finger. Doing that was a heady feeling for both of them, as though when it reached the base of her finger something magic would happen. They were engaged. Christ, what a trip!

'It fits!' Her eyes danced as she held out her hand, looking at the ring from every possible angle. It was a beautiful stone.

'Shit. It looks like it's loose. Is it too big?'

'No, it isn't. No, it isn't! Honest!'

'Liar. But I love you. We'll get it sized tomorrow.'

'I'm engaged!'

'Hey, that's funny, lady. Me too. What's your name?'

'Mildred. Mildred Schwartz.'

'Mildred, I love you. That's funny though, I thought

your name was Kate. Didn't it used to be?' He had a tender light in his eye, remembering the first day he'd met her.

'Isn't that what I told you when we met?' She was a little too drunk to be sure.

'It was. You were already a liar way back then.'

'I already loved you then, too. Right away, just about.' She sank back into his arms again, with her own memories of their first days.

'You loved me then?' He was surprised. He thought it had taken longer. She had been so evasive at first.

'Uh huh. I thought you were super. But I was scared you'd find out who I was.'

'Well, at least now I know. Mildred Schwartz. And this, my love, is the Fairmont.' They had just pulled up in the driveway, and two porters approached to assist the chauffeur with their bags. 'Want me to carry you out?'

'That's only when you get married. We're only engaged.' She flashed the ring at him with a smile which enchanted him.

'Please forgive the impertinence. But I'm not sure you can walk.'

'I beg your pardon, Lucas. I most certainly can.' But she wove badly when her feet touched the pavement.

'Just keep your mouth shut, Mama, and smile.' He picked her up in his arms, nodded to the porters and mentioned something about a weak heart, and a long plane trip, while she quietly nibbled his ear. 'Stop that!'

'I will not.'

'You will, or I'll drop you. Right here. How'd you like a broken ass for an engagement present?'

'Up your ass, Lucas.'

'Shh ... keep your voice down.' But he wasn't much more sober than she; he only held it a mite better.

'Put me down, or I'll sue you.'

'You can't. We're engaged.' He was halfway through the lobby with Kezia in his arms.

'And it's such a pretty ring too. Lucas, if you only knew how much I love you.' She let her head fall onto his shoulder and studied the ring. He carried her easily, like a rag doll, or a very small child.

'Due to Mrs. Johns' weak heart, and her weakened condition from the flight,' would they send the registration forms up to the room? The couple rode quickly up in the elevator, with Kezia carefully propped up in a corner. Luke watched her with a grin.

'I'll walk to the room, thank you.' She looked at him imperiously, and tripped as she got out of the elevator. He caught her before she fell, and he offered her his arm, trying hard to keep a straight face.

'Madam?'

'Thank you, sir.' They walked gingerly down the hall, with Luke supporting most of her weight, and at last arrived at the room.

'You know what's funny, Lucas?' When she was drunk, she had the voice of Palm Beach, London, and Paris.

'What, my dear?' Two could play that game.

'When we came up in the elevator, I felt like we could see the whole world, even the sky, the Golden Gate Bridge . . . everything. Is that what being engaged does to you?'

'No. It's what being in a glass elevator does to you, when it runs along the outside of the building, and you ride in it when you're drunk. You know, sort of like special effects.' He gave her his most charming smile.

'Go to hell.'

The porter was waiting for them in the door of the suite, and Luke tipped him solemnly and closed the door behind him.

'And I suggest that you lie down, or take a shower. Probably both.'

'No, I want to . . .' She walked slowly towards him, an evil gleam in her eye, and he laughed.

'As a matter of fact, Mama, so do I.'

'Hey, lady, it's a beautiful day.'

'Already?'

'It has been for hours.'

'I think I'm going to die.'

'You're hung over. I ordered coffee for you.' He smiled at the look on her face. They had made matters worse with a third bottle of champagne after dinner. It had been a night for lengthy celebration. Their engagement. It was more than a little mad. He knew only too well that by the following day he could be in jail, which was why he hadn't jumped at the thought of Reno or Vegas. But that was one thing he wouldn't do to her. If they revoked him, that was it. He wasn't going to take her down with him, as his wife. He loved her too much to do that to her.

She struggled with the coffee, and felt better after a shower.

'Maybe I'm not going to die after all. I'm not quite sure yet.'

'You never know with a weak heart like yours.'

'What weak heart?' She looked at him as though he were crazy.

'That's what I told them when I carried you into the lobby.'

'You carried me?'

'You don't remember?'

'I don't remember being carried. I do remember feeling like I was flying.'

'That was the elevator,.

'Jesus. I must have really been bombed.'

'Worse than that. Which reminds me ... do you remember getting engaged?'

'Several times.' She grinned wickedly and ran a hand up his leg.

'I mean with a ring, you lewd bitch. Shame on you!'

'Shame on me? If I remember correctly ...'

'Never mind that. Do you remember getting engaged?'

But her face softened as she saw how earnest he was. 'Yes, darling, I remember. And the ring is incredible.' She flickered it at him, and they both smiled as she kissed him. 'It's a magnificent ring.'

292

'For a magnificent woman. I wanted to buy you a sapphire, but they were waaaaaayyyy over my head.'

'I like this better. My grandmother had a sapphire that . . .'

'Oh not that again!' He started to laugh and she looked surprised.

'I already told you?'

'Several times.' She grinned and shrugged her slim shoulders. She was wearing only his ring. 'Now, are we going to sit here all day, making love and being lazy, or are we going to go out?'

'Do you suppose we ought to go out?' But she looked as if she liked the first idea better.

'It might do us good. We can come back for more of this later.'

'Is that a promise?'

'Do you usually have to force me, my love?'

'Not exactly.' She smiled primly and walked to the closet. 'Where are we going?'

'What do you want to do?'

'Can we go for a drive? I'd love that. Up the coast, or something nice and easy like that.'

'With the chauffeur?' The idea didn't have much appeal. Not with the chauffeur.

'No, silly, alone of course. We can rent a car through the hotel.'

'Sure, babe, I'd like that too.'

She was forking out vast sums of money for this trip. The suite at the Fairmont, the first-class seats on the trip out, the limousine, the elaborate room service meals, and now yet another car, for his pleasure. She wanted it all to be special. She wanted to soften the blow of the hearing, or at least provide some diversion from the reason they were there. Underneath the holiday air was the kind of gaiety one produces for a child who is dying of cancer – circus, puppet shows, dolls, colour TV, Disneyland, and ice cream all day long, because soon, very soon . . . Kezia longed for the days of their first trip to San Francisco, for

293

their early days in New York. This time nothing was natural; it was all terribly luxurious, but it wasn't the same. It was forced.

The concierge rented a car for them, a bright red Mustang with a stick shift that pleased Luke. He roared up the hills on his way to the bridge.

It was a pleasant drive for a sunny winter afternoon. It was never very cold in San Francisco. There was a brisk breeze, but the air was warm, and everything around them was green, a far cry from the barren landscape they'd left.

They drove all afternoon, stopped here and there at a beach, walked to the edge of the cliffs, sat on rocks and talked, but neither spoke of what weighed on their hearts. It was too late to talk and there was nothing to say. The hearing was too close. They had both said it all, in all the ways they knew how, with their bodies, with gifts, with kisses, with looks. All they could do now was wait.

A light green Ford trailed them all day long, and it depressed Luke to realize they were being followed that closely. He didn't say anything to Kezia, but something in her manner led him to suspect that she knew too. There was more than a faint air of bravado, of each trying to reassure the other, by pretending not to see all the terrors around them ... or simply the passing of time. The hearing was right in front of their faces, and Lucas noticed that the cops stuck much closer now, as though they thought he'd suddenly bolt and run. But to where? He knew enough not to run. How long could he have gotten away with something like that? Besides, he couldn't have taken Kezia. And he couldn't have left her. They had him; they didn't have to breathe down his neck.

They stopped for dinner at a Chinese restaurant on their way back, and then went to the hotel to relax. They had to meet Alejandro's plane at ten o'clock that night.

The plane was on time and Alejandro was among the first through the doors.

294

'Hey, brother, what's your hurry?' Lucas stood lazily propped against the wall.

'It must be New York. It's getting to me. How's it going, man?' Alejandro looked worried and tired, and felt suddenly out of place when he saw the look on their faces, happy, relaxed, with windburn tans and pink cheeks from the sun. It was almost as though he had come out for no reason. What could be wrong in the lives of two people who looked like that?'

'Hey! Guess what?' Kezia's eyes glowed. 'We're engaged!' She held out the ring for his inspection.

'Beautiful. Congratulations! We're going to have to drink to that!' Luke rolled his eyes and Kezia groaned.

'We did that one last night.'

' "We", my ass. She did. Shitfaced to the gills.'

'Kezia?' Alejandro looked amused.

'Yop, on champagne. I drank about two bottles all by myself.' She said it with pride.

'From your flask?'

She laughed at the memory of Christmas and shook her head, as they went to claim his bags. They had brought the limousine; the Mustang had been returned.

The banter in the car on the way into the city was light and easy, bad jokes, silly memories, Alejandro's account of his trip, complete with a woman in labour and another woman who had smuggled her French poodle aboard under the coat and then threatened hysterics when the stewardess tried to take the dog away.

'Why do I always get on those flights?'

'You should try flying first-class.'

'Sure, brother, you bet. Hey, what's with the fruity brown shoes?' Kezia laughed and Lucas looked pained.

'Man, you ain't got no class at all. They're Guccis.'

'Look like fruit shoes to me.' The three of them laughed and the car pulled up in front of the hotel.

'It's not much, but we call it home.' Luke was in high spirits as he waved grandly to the towering palace that was the Fairmont.

'You guys certainly travel in style.' They had offered him the couch in the living room of their suite. It pulled out to make an extra bed.

'You know, Al, they've got a little old guy who walks around in the lobby just making "F"'s in the sand in the ashtrays.' Alejandro rolled his eyes, and the three of them chuckled again. 'It's the little things that make the difference.'

'Up your ass, man.'

'Please, not in front of my fiancée.' Luke looked mock prim.

'You guys really engaged? For real?'

'For real.' Kezia confirmed it. 'We're going to get married.' There was steel in her voice, and hope, and life, and tears, and fear. They would get married. If they got the chance.

None of them mentioned the hearing and it wasn't until Kezia started to yawn that Luke began to look serious.

'Why don't you go on to bed, babe? I'll be in, in a bit.' He wanted to talk to Alejandro alone, and it was easy to know what about. Why couldn't he share his fears with her? But it wouldn't do to look hurt. It wouldn't have served any purpose.

'Okay, darling. But don't stay up too late.' She kissed him gently on the neck and blew a kiss to Alejandro. 'Don't get too drunk, you guys.'

'Look who's talking.' Luke laughed at the thought.

'That's different. I was celebrating my engagement.' She tried to look haughty, but started to laugh as he swatted her behind and gave her a kiss.

'I love you. Now beat it.'

' 'Night, you guys.'

She lay awake in their bed and watched the line of light under the bedroom door until three. She wanted to go out there, to tell them that she was scared shitless, too, but she couldn't do that. She couldn't do it to Luke. She had to keep a stiff upper lip. Noblesse oblige, and all that shit.

She saw the next morning that Luke hadn't gone to bed all that night. At six in the morning, he had finally fallen asleep where he sat, and Alejandro had quietly laid down on the couch. They all had to be up by eight.

The hearing was at two, and Luke's attorney was due at the Fairmont at nine for a briefing. It would probably be the first time that Alejandro would hear it all straight. Luke had a way of clouding the issues, to spare his friends fear. And he knew that Kezia wouldn't let herself speak what she thought. Alejandro got nothing from Kezia now, and nothing from Luke except bullshit and bravado. The only real thing he had heard was to 'take care of Kezia, in case.' And that was going to be no easy task. That girl was going to take it harder than hell if he fell.

For a brief moment before he went to sleep, Alejandro almost wished that he hadn't come. He didn't want to see it. Didn't want to watch it happen to Luke, or see Kezia's face when it did.

CHAPTER XXVI

The attorney arrived at nine, bringing tension with him. Kezia greeted him with a formal 'good morning', and made the introduction to 'Our friend, Mr. Vidal.' She poured coffee and commented what a beautiful day it was. That's when things started to go sour. The attorney gave a terse little laugh that set Kezia's nerves on edge. She was suspicious of him anyway. He was renowned for his skill at hearings like Luke's, for which he charged five thousand dollars. Lucas had insisted on paying it himself with his savings. He had set aside money for that, 'just in case'. But Kezia didn't like the man's style - over-confident, overpaid, and overbearing. He assumed far too much.

The attorney looked around the room and felt the chill vibes from Kezia, and then made matters worse by putting his foot in his mouth. She was a most unnerving young woman.

'My father used to say on mornings like this, "Could be a beautiful day to die".' Her face grew ashen and taut and Luke gave her a look that said 'Kezia, don't blow it!' She didn't, for Luke's sake, but she smoked twice as much as she ordinarily did. Luke made no pretense: at nine in the morning, he was drinking bourbon straight up. Alejandro chain-drank cold coffee. The party was over.

The meeting lasted two hours, and at the end of it they knew nothing more than they had before. No one did. There was no way to know. It all depended on the Adult Authority and the judge. No one could read their minds. Lucas was in danger of being revoked for instigating 'unrest' in the prisons, agitating, and basically meddling in what the parole board and prison authorities felt was no longer his business. They had the right to revoke him for less, and there was no denying Luke's agitating. Everyone knew of it, even the press. He had been less than discreet in the years he'd been out. His speeches, his book, his meetings, his role in the moratorium against prisons, his hand in prison labour strikes across the country. He had gambled his life on his beliefs, and now they'd have to see what the price was. Worse, under the California indeterminate sentence laws, once he was revoked, the Adult Authority could keep him for as long as they liked. The attorney's 'probably not more than two or three years' only added to their collective gloom. No one held out much hope. For once, not even Luke. And Kezia was silent.

The lawyer left them shortly after eleven, and they agreed to meet at the courthouse at one-thirty. Until then, they were free.

'Want to have lunch?' It was Alejandro's suggestion.

298

'Who can eat?' Kezia was having increasing trouble playing the game. She had never looked as pale, and suddenly she wanted to call Edward or Totie, even Hilary, or Whit. Someone ... anyone ... but someone she knew well. This was like waiting in a hospital corridor to find out if the patient would live ... and what if ... what if he didn't ... what if ... oh God.

'Come on, you guys, let's go out.' Luke had the situation in control, except for the almost imperceptible tremor of his hands.

They had lunch at Trader Vic's. It was nice, it was pretty, it was 'terribly posh' as Luke said, and the food was probably excellent, but none of them noticed. It didn't feel right. It was all so fancy, so overdone, so false, and such a goddamn strain to keep up the pretense of giving a damn where they ate. Why the Fairmont and Trader Vic's? Why couldn't they just eat hot dogs, or have a picnic, or go on living after today? Kezia felt a weight settle over her like a parachute dipped in cement. She wanted to go back to the hotel to lie down, to relax, to cry, to do something, anything but sit in this restaurant eating a dessert she couldn't even taste. The conversation droned on; all three of them talked, saying nothing. By the time the coffee was served, they had sunk into silence. The only sound was of Luke, drumming the fingers of one hand softly on the table. Only Kezia heard; she felt the sound rippling through her like a triphammer pulse. She felt wired to the marrow of his bones, to his brain, to his heart. If they took him, why couldn't they take them together?

Alejandro looked at his watch, and Luke nodded.

'Yeah. It's about that time.' He signalled for the check and Alejandro made a gesture to reach for his wallet. With a sharp look in his eyes, Luke shook his head. And this wasn't a day to argue with him. He left the money on the small wicker platter the waiter had left with the bill, and they pushed the table away. Kezia felt as though she could hear a drum roll as they walked outside to the limousine. She felt like a costar in a B movie. They couldn't be real people, this couldn't be an hour before Luke's hearing, it couldn't be happening to them. None of it seemed real. And then, as the limousine rolled them inexorably away, she started to laugh, almost hysterically.

'What's funny?' Luke was tense, and Alejandro was silent now. Her laughter rang out jarringly. There was something shattering about it, something unbearably painful. It wasn't real laughter.

'Everything's funny, Luke. All of it. It really is, it . . . I . . . it's all so absurd.' She laughed on, until he took her hand and held it too hard. Then she stopped, tears suddenly trying to rush into the space where the laughter had been. It was all so absurd, all those ridiculous people at Trader Vic's - they'd be going to a concert after lunch, or the hairdresser, or to board meetings, or I. Magnin's, or to tea parties and dressmakers . . . leading their perfectly normal lives. But what could be normal, that, or this? None of it made any sense. The laughter tried to bubble back into her mouth, but she wouldn't let it. She knew that if she laughed again she would cry, and maybe even howl. That was what she wanted to do. Howl like a dog.

They drove west into the pale afternoon sun, and then south on Van Ness Avenue, past used cars and new cars and the blue plastic of the Jack Tar Hotel. The ride seemed to go on forever. People were busy, were running, were going, were living, and all too soon the dome of City Hall loomed before them. It stuck out like a proud gilded onion, a dowager's tit, noble and overdressed in patina and gold. Terrifying. City Hall. And within so few feet, other limousines were beginning to arrive for the symphony at the Opera House. Nothing made any sense.

Kezia felt vague and confused, almost drunk, though she'd had only coffee. And only the steadying presence of Luke on one side and Alejandro on the other kept her feet moving. Up the steps, through the doors, into the building, past the people . . . oh God . . . oh God, no!

'I need a pack of smokes.' Luke strode away from them and they followed, through the vast marble halls and under the dome. He walked with the determined rolling gait she knew so well, and silently she reached for Alejandro's hand.

'You okay, Kezia?'

She answered with a question in her eyes: *I don't know. Am I?*

'Yes.' She gave him a small wintry smile and looked up at the dome. How could ugly things happen here? It looked like Vienna or Paris or Rome, the columns and friezes and arches, the lofty swoop of the dome, the echo, the gold leaf. The day was really here. January eighth. The hearing. She was nose to nose with it now. Brutal reality.

She held tight to Luke's hand as they rode up in the elevator, and she stood as close to him as she could . . . closer . . . tighter . . . nearer . . . more. . . . She wanted to slip inside his skin, bury herself in his heart.

The elevator stopped on four, and they followed the corridors to the law library where the attorney had said he would meet them. They passed a courtroom, and suddenly Luke pushed her aside, almost thrusting her at Alejandro.

'What . . .'

'Fucking bastards.' Luke's face was suddenly angry and red, and Alejandro understood before she did. They quickened their pace, and he put an arm around her shoulders.

'Alejandro, what . . .'

'Come on, babe, we'll talk about it later.' The two men exchanged a look over her head, and when she saw the television cameras waiting, she knew. So that was it. Lucas was going to make news. Either way.

They detoured the reporters unnoticed, and slipped into the law library to wait. The attorney joined them after a few minutes, a thick file in his hand, a tense look on his face. But something about his demeanor impressed Kezia more than it had at the hotel.

'Everyone ready?' He tried to look jovial and failed dismally.

'Now? Already?' It wasn't two o'clock yet, and Kezia was beginning to panic, but Alejandro still had a tight grip on her shoulders. Luke was pacing in front of a book-lined wall.

'No. It'll be a few minutes. I'll meet you back here, and let you know when the judge is in court.'

'Is there any other way into the courtroom?' Alejandro was troubled.

'I . . . is . . . why?' The attorney looked puzzled.

'Have you walked past the courtroom yet?'

'No. Not yet.'

'It's crawling with reporters. Television cameras, the works.'

'The judge won't let them inside. Not to worry.'

'Yeah. But we'll still have to walk through them.'

'No, we won't.' Luke was back in their midst. 'Or Kezia won't in any case, if that's what you're worried about, Al.'

'Lucas, I most certainly will!' Small as she was, she looked as though in the heat of the moment she might hit him.

'You will not. And that's that.' This was no time to argue with him. The look on his face made that much clear. 'I want you here. I'll come and get you when it's over.'

'But I want to be in there with you.'

'On TV?' His voice dripped irony, not kindness.

'You heard what he said. They won't be in court.'

'They don't need to be. They'll get you coming and going. And you don't need that. And neither do I. I am not going to argue with you, Kezia. You're staying here in the library, or you can go back to the hotel. Now. Is that clear?'

'All right.'

The attorney left them, and Luke began to pace again, and suddenly he stopped and walked slowly towards her,

302

his eyes fixed on hers, everything about him familiar and dear. It was as though the barbed wire had gone from his spine. Alejandro sensed the mood and moved slowly towards a distant row of maroon and gold books.

'Baby . . .' Luke was only a foot away from her, but he didn't reach out to touch her, he only looked, watching her, as though counting every hair on her head, every thread in her dress. He took in all of her, and his eyes bore through to her soul.

'Lucas, I love you.'

'Mama, I have never ever loved you more. You know that, don't you?'

'Yes. And you know how much I love you?'

He nodded, his eyes still digging deep.

'Why are they doing this to us?'

'Because I decided to take my chances a long time ago, before I knew you. I think I'd have done it differently if I'd known you all along. Maybe not. I'm a shitkicker, Kezia. You know it. I know it. They know it. It's for a good cause, but I'm a thorn in their side. I've always thought it was worth it, if I could change something for the better . . . but I didn't know then that I'd be doing this to you.'

'Is it still worth it, for you, not counting me?' Even without considering her, how could it have been now? But his answer surprised her.

'Yes.' His eyes didn't waver, but there was something sad and old about them that she had never seen before. He was a man paying a heavy price, even if they didn't revoke him. It had already cost him a great deal.

'It's worth it even now, Lucas?'

'Yes. Even now. The only thing I feel like shit about is you. I should never have dragged you through it. I knew better right at the start.'

'Lucas, you're the only man I've ever loved, maybe the only human being I've ever loved. If you hadn't "dragged me through this," my life would never have been worth a good goddamn. And I can live with what's happening.

303

Either way.' For a moment she was as powerful as he; it was as though his strength had filled her to catalyze her own.

'And what if I go?'

'You won't.' I won't let you. . . .

'I might.' He seemed almost detached, as if he was ready to go if he had to.

'Then I'll handle that too.'

'Just handle yourself, little lady. You're the only woman I've ever loved like this. I won't let anything destroy you. Not even me. Remember that. And whatever I do, you've got to know that I know what's best. For both of us.'

'Darling, what do you mean?' Her voice was a whisper. She was afraid.

'Just trust me.' And then, without another word, he bridged the last foot between them, pulled her into his arms and held her breathlessly close. 'Kezia, right now I feel like the luckiest man in the world. Even here.'

'Just the most loved.' There were tears brushing her lashes, as she buried her face in his chest. Alejandro was forgotten, the law library had faded around them. The only thing they had that mattered and was real was each other.

'Ready?' The lawyer's face looked like a vision from a bad dream. Neither of them had heard him coming. Nor had they seen Alejandro watching them with tears streaming down his face. He wiped them away as he walked towards them.

'Yeah. I'm ready.'

'Lucas . . .' She clung to him for a moment, and he pushed her ever so gently away.

'Take it easy, Mama. I'll be back in a minute.' He gave her a lopsided smile and squeezed her hand tight. She wanted so desperately to reach out to him, to keep him from going, to stop it, to hold him close and never let him go. . . .

'We'd best be . . .' The attorney looked pointedly at his watch.

'We're going.' He signalled to Alejandro, gave Kezia a last ferocious squeeze, and strode to the door, his attorney and his friend right behind him. Kezia was standing where he had left her.

'Lucas!' He turned at the door as her voice echoed in the silent rows of books. 'God be with you!'

'I love you.' His three words rang in her ears as the door whooshed slowly closed.

There was no sound, not even that of a clock ticking. Nothing. Silence. Kezia sat in a straight-backed chair and watched a sliver of sunlight asleep on the floor. She didn't smoke. She didn't cry. She only waited. It was the longest half hour of her life. Her mind seemed to doze like the sun on the floor. The chair was uncomfortable but she didn't feel it. She didn't think, didn't feel, didn't see, didn't hear. Not even the footsteps that finally came. She was numb.

She saw his feet pointing at hers before she saw his face. But they were the wrong feet, the wrong shoes, a different colour and too small. Boots . . . Alejandro . . . where was Luke?

Her eyes ran up the legs until they reached his face. His eyes were dark and hard. He said nothing, only stood there.

'Where is Lucas?' The words were small and precise. Her whole body had stopped. And he answered all in one breath.

'Kezia, they revoked him. He's in custody.'

'What?' She flew to her feet. Everything had started again, only now it was all going too fast instead of too slowly. 'My God, Alejandro! Where is he?'

'He's still in the courtroom. Kezia, no . . . don't go . . .' She was on her way to the door, her feet racing over the grey marble floor. 'Kezia!'

'Go to hell!' She flew out the door just as he caught her arm. 'Stop it, damn you! I have to see him!'

'Okay. Then let's go.' He held her hand tightly in his.

305

and hand in hand they ran down the hall. 'He may be gone now.'

She didn't answer, she only ran faster, her shoes beating like her heart, pounding the floor as they ran. The reporters had already thinned out. They had their story. Lucas Johns was on his way back to Quentin. So it goes. Poor sonofabitch.

Kezia shoved her way past two men blocking the door of the courtroom, and Alejandro slipped in beside her. The judge was leaving the bench, and all she could see was one man, sitting quietly, alone, his back to her, facing straight ahead.

'Lucas?' She slowed to a walk and approached him slowly. He turned his head towards her, and there was nothing on his face. It was a mask. A different man than she knew. An iron wall with two eyes. Two eyes that held tears, but said nothing.

'Darling, I love you.' She had her arms around him then, and he leaned slowly against her, letting his head rest on her chest, letting his weight go, his whole body seeming to sag. But his arms never moved to go around her, and then she saw why. He was already in handcuffs. They hadn't wasted much time. His wallet and change lay on the table before him, and among them were the keys to the New York apartment, and his ring, the one she had given him for Christmas. 'Lucas, why did they do it?'

'They had to. Now you go home.'

'No. I'll stay till you go. Don't talk. Oh Christ, Lucas . . . I love you.' She fought back the tears. He would not see her cry. He was strong, so was she. But she was dying inside.

'I love you too, so do me a favour and go. Get the hell out of here, will you?' The tears had gone from his eyes and she covered his mouth with her own as her answer. She was bending towards him, her thin arms and small hands trying to envelop the whole of his body, as though he were a child and had grown too big for her lap. Why had they done it? Why couldn't she take this away from

306

him? Why couldn't she have bought them? Why? All this pain and the ugliness and the handcuffs . . . why was there nothing she could do? Fucking goddamn parole board, and the judge and . . .

'Okay, Mr. Johns.' There was a nasty inflection on the 'Mr.,' and the voice came from right behind her.

'Kezia, go!' It was the command of a general, not a plea from the defeated.

'Where are they taking you?' As her eyes flew open wide with anger and fear, she felt Alejandro's hands on her shoulders, pulling her back.

'To county jail. Alejandro knows. Then to Quentin. Now get the fuck out of here. Now!' He rose to his full height and faced the guard who was about to lead him away.

She stood on tiptoe briefly and kissed him, and then almost blindly she let Alejandro lead her out of the court. She stood for a moment in the hall, and then as though in a distant vision far off down the hall she saw him go, a guard on either side, his hands shackled in front of him. He never looked back and it seemed as though, long after he was gone, she felt her mouth open, and a long piercing sound filled the air. A woman was screaming but she didn't know who. It couldn't be someone she knew. Nice people don't scream. But the sound wouldn't end and someone's arms were holding her tight, as flashbulbs began to explode in her face and strange voices assailed her.

And then suddenly she was flying over the city in a glass cage, and after that she was led into a strange room and someone put her to bed and she felt very cold. Very cold. A man piled blankets on her, and another man with funny glasses and a moustache gave her a shot. She started to laugh at him because he looked so funny, but then that terrifying sound came back again. The woman was screaming. What woman? It was a long, endless howl. It filled the room until all the light was squeezed out of her eyes and everything went black.

CHAPTER XXVII

When Kezia woke up, Alejandro was sitting in the room with her, watching her. It was dark. He looked tired and rumpled and was surrounded by empty cups. He looked as though he had spent the night in the chair, and he had.

She watched him for a long time; her eyes were open and it was hard to blink. Her eyes felt bigger than they ever had before.

'You awake?' His voice was a hoarse whisper. The ashtrays were filled to the brim.

She nodded. 'I can't close my eyes.'

He smiled at her. 'I think you're still stoned. Why don't you go back to sleep?'

She only shook her head, and then tears washed the too-open eyes. Even that didn't help her to close them. 'I want to get up.'

'And do what?' She made him very nervous.

'Go pee pee.' She giggled and choked on fresh tears.

'Oh.' The smile was brotherly and tired.

'You know something?' She looked at him curiously.

'What?'

'You look like hell. You stayed up all night, didn't you?'

'I dozed. Don't worry about me.'

'Why not?' She staggered out of bed and headed for the john, pausing in the doorway. 'Alejandro, when can I see Luke?'

'Not till tomorrow.' So she already remembered. He had been afraid that he would have to start from scratch after the shot they'd given her the night before. It was now six in the morning.

'You mean today or tomorrow?'

'I mean tomorrow.'

'Why can't I see him till then?'

'County only has two visiting days. Wednesday and Sunday. Tomorrow is Wednesday. Them's the rules.'

'Bastards.' She slammed the bathroom door and he lit another cigarette. He was into his fourth pack since the night had begun. It had been one hell of a night. And she still hadn't seen the crap in the papers. Edward had called four times that night. He'd seen the news in New York. He was half out of his mind.

When she came back, she sat on the edge of the bed and lit a cigarette from his pack. She looked tired, haggard, and pale. The tan seemed to have instantly faded, and dark rims framed her eyes all the way around, like purple eye shadow gone wild.

'Lady, you don't look so hot. I think you ought to stay in bed.' She didn't answer, but only sat there, smoking and swinging her foot, her head turned away from him.

'Kezia?'

'Yeah?' She was crying again when she turned to face him, and she felt like a very small child melting into his arms. 'Oh God, Alejandro. Why? How can they do this to us? To him?'

'Because sometimes it happens that way. Call it fate, if you want.'

'I'd call it fucked.' He smiled tiredly and then sighed.

'Babe . . ' She had to know, but he hated to tell her.

'Yeah?'

'I don't know if you remember, but the newspaper boys took a bunch of pictures as they led Luke away.' He held his breath and watched the look on her face. He could see that she didn't remember.

'Those shits, why couldn't they leave him his last shred of dignity? Miserable, rotten . . .'

Alejandro shook his head. 'Kezia . . . they took pictures of you.' The words dropped like a bomb.

'Of me?'

He nodded.

'Jesus.'

'They just thought you were his old lady, and I had Luke's attorney call them and ask them not to run the pictures or your name. But by then, they knew who you were. Somebody spotted the pictures when they were developing them. That's a lot of bad luck.'

'They ran the pictures?' She sat very still.

'Out here, you're page one. Page four in New York. Edward called a few times last night.' Kezia threw back her head and started to laugh. It was a nervous, hysterical laugh, and not the reaction he had expected.

'Man, we really bought it this time, didn't we? Edward must be dying, poor thing.' But she didn't sound very sympathetic. She sounded distracted.

'That's putting it mildly.' Alejandro almost felt sorry for the man. He had sounded so stricken. So betrayed.

'Well, you plays, you pays, as they say. How bad are the pictures?'

About as bad as you could get. She had been hysterical when the photographers had spotted them. Alejandro pulled the evening edition of the *Examiner* from under the bed and held it out to her. On the front page was a photograph of Kezia collapsing in Alejandro's arms. She cringed as she saw it, and glanced at the text. 'Socialite heiress Kezia Saint Martin, secret girlfriend of ex-con Lucas Johns, collapses outside courtroom after . . .' It was worse than they had feared.

'I think Edward is mainly concerned with what kind of shape you are in now.'

'My ass, he is. He's having a heart attack over the story. You don't know Edward.' She sounded almost like a child afraid of her father. It seemed odd to Alejandro.

'Did he know about Luke?'

'Not like this he didn't. Actually, he knew I had interviewed him, and he also knew there's been someone important in my life for the last few months. Well, sooner or later, I guess it had to come out. We were lucky till now. It's a bitch that it had to be like this though. Have the papers called since?'

310

'A few times. I told them there was no story, and you were flying back to New York today. I thought that might get them off your back, and they'd keep busy watching the airport.'

'And the lobby.'

He hadn't thought about that. What an insane way to live.

'We'll have to call the manager and arrange to get out of here. I want to move to the Ritz. They won't find us there.'

'No, but you can count on some coverage tomorrow if you want to see Luke at the jail.'

She stood up and faced him, an icy look in her eyes. 'Not "if", Alejandro, "when". And if they want to be pigs about it, fuck them.'

The day slipped by in a haze of silence and cigarette smoke. Their move to the Ritz passed uneventfully. A fifty dollar 'gift' to the manager encouraged him to show them out through a back door, and keep his mouth shut about it later. Apparently, he had. There were no calls for them at the Ritz.

Kezia sat lost in her own thoughts, rarely speaking. She was thinking of Luke, and how he had looked when they led him away . . . and before that, how he had looked in the law library. He had been a free man then, for those last precious moments.

She called Edward from the Ritz and struggled through a brief, anguished conversation with him. They both cried. Edward kept repeating, 'How could you do this?' He left the words 'to me' unspoken, but they were there, nevertheless. He wanted her to fly home or let him fly out. He exploded when she refused.

'Edward, please, for God's sake, don't do this to me. Don't pressure me now!' She shouted through her tears and wondered briefly why they kept throwing guilt at each other. Who cared 'who was doing what to whom'. It had been done unto Kezia, and Luke, but not by Edward.

311

And Kezia had done nothing to Edward, not intentionally. They were all caught in the teeth of a maniacal machine, and no one could help it, or stop it.

'You have to come home, Kezia! Think of what they'll do to you out there.'

'They've already done it, and if it's in the papers in New York it won't make any difference where I am. I could fly to Tangiers for chrissake, and they'd still want a piece of the action.'

'It's really unbelievable. I still don't understand ... and Kezia ... good God, girl, you must have known this would happen to him. That story you told me about his being sick ... this was what you meant, wasn't it?' She nodded silently at the receiver and his voice came back sharper. 'Wasn't it?'

'Yes.' Her voice sounded so small, so broken and hurt.

'Why didn't you tell me?'

'How could I?' There was a long moment of silence when they both knew the truth.

'I still don't understand how you could involve yourself. You said in your own article about him that there was a possibility of this. How ...'

'Oh shut up, damn you, Edward, I did. That's all, I did. And stop clucking like a bloody mother hen about it. I did, and I got hurt, we both got hurt, and believe me, he's hurting one hell of a lot more sitting in jail right now.' There was deadly silence and Edward's voice came back with a measured venom that was totally foreign to him ... except for once before.

'Mr. Johns is used to jail, Kezia.' She wanted to hang up on Edward then, but she didn't quite dare. Severing the connection would sever something more, something deeper, and she still needed that tie, maybe only a little bit, but she needed it. Edward was all she had in a way, except Luke.

'Do you have anything else to say?' Her voice was almost as vicious as his had been a moment before. She was willing to kick at him, but not dismiss him entirely.

'Yes. Come home. Immediately.'

'I won't. Anything else?'

'I don't know what it will take to bring you to your senses, Kezia, but I suggest you make an effort to become rational as quickly as possible. You may regret this for a lifetime.'

'I will, but not for the reasons you think, Edward.'

'You have no idea how something like this can jeopardize ...' His voice trailed off unhappily. For a moment he hadn't been speaking to Kezia, but to the ghost of her mother, and they both knew it. Now Kezia was certain. Now she knew why he had told her about her mother and the tutor. Now she knew it all.

'Jeopardize what? My "position"? My "consequence", as Aunt Hil would say? Jeopardize my chances of finding a husband? You think I give a damn about all that now? I care about Luke, Edward. I care about Lucas Johns. I love him!' She was shouting again.

Three thousand miles away, silent tears were sliding down Edward's face. 'Let me know if there's anything I can do for you.'

It was the voice of her attorney, her trustee, her guardian. Not her friend. Something had finally snapped. The gap between them was broadening to a frightening degree, for both of them.

'I will.' They exchanged no goodbye and Edward severed the connection. Kezia sat for a long moment holding the dead phone in her hands, while Alejandro watched her.

Tears of farewell slid down her cheeks. That had been two in two days. In one way or another, she had lost the only two men she had ever loved, since her father. Three lost men in a lifetime. She knew that somehow she had just lost Edward. She had betrayed him. What he had sought most to prevent had finally come.

Edward, sitting in his office, knew it too. He walked solemnly to the door, locked it carefully, walked back to his desk, and flicked the switch on his intercom,

313

informing his secretary in the driest of tones that he did not want to be disturbed until further notice. Then, having carefully put aside the mail on his desk, he lay his head down on his arms and broke into heart-rending sobs. He had lost her ... lost them both ... and to such unworthy men. As he lay there he wondered why the only two women he had ever loved had such a brutal flaw in their characters ... the tutor ... and now this ... this ... jailbird ... this nobody! He found himself shouting the word, and then, surprised at himself, he stopped crying, lifted his head, sat back in his chair, and stared at his view. There were times when he simply did not understand. No one played by the rules anymore. Not even Kezia, and he had taught her himself. He shook his head slowly, blew his nose twice, and went back to his desk to look over the mail.

Jack Simpson was sympathetic when he called her. But Kezia's agent didn't help matters by feeling guilty for introducing her to Luke. She assured him that he'd given her the best gift of her life, but the tears in her voice didn't console either of them.

Alejandro tried to coax her into a walk, but she wouldn't move, and sat in the hotel room with the shades drawn, smoking, drinking tea, coffee, water, scotch, scarcely eating, just thinking, her eyes filling with tears, her hands shaking and frail. She was afraid to go out now, afraid of the press and afraid of missing a phone call from Luke.

'Maybe he'll call.'

'Kezia, he can't call from county jail. They won't let him.'

'Maybe they will.'

It was pointless to argue with her; it was almost as though she didn't hear. And whatever she heard, she didn't listen to. The only sounds that penetrated were her own inner voices, and the echoes of Luke.

It was midnight before Alejandro finally got her to bed.

314

'What are you doing?' She could see his outline in the chair in the corner. Her voice sounded strangely odd.

'I thought I'd just sit here for a while. Will it keep you from sleeping?' She wanted to reach out in the darkness and touch his hand. She couldn't find the words again, all she could do was shake her head and cry. It had been an unbearable day, not as tense as the previous day, but more wearing. The endless pressure of pain.

He heard muffled sobs in the pillow and came closer to sit on the edge of the bed. 'Kezia, don't.' He stroked her hair, her arm, her hand, as her body shook with sobs. She was keening for Luke. 'Oh baby ... little girl, why did this happen to you?' She was so unprepared, so unused to anything she could not control, and she had seen nothing like this. There were tears in his own eyes again, but she couldn't see them.

'It didn't happen to me, Alejandro. It happened to him.' The voice was bitter and tired through her tears.

He stroked her hair for what seemed like hours, and at last she fell asleep. He smoothed the covers around her, and touched her cheek ever so gently. She looked young again as she slept; the anger had left her thin face. The bitterness of what can happen to a life out in the big, bad, ugly world had come as a shock to her. She was learning the hard way, with her heart, and her guts.

He heard her knock gently on his door, and raised his head from the pillow. Sleep had taken a long time to come to him the night before, and now it was only five after six.

'Who is it?'

'Me. Kezia.'

'Is anything wrong?'

'I just thought maybe we should get up.' Today was the day she was going to see Lucas. Alejandro smiled tiredly as he got up to open the door, pulling on his pants as he went.

'Kezia, you're crazy. Why don't you go back to sleep

315

for a while?' She was standing there in a blue flannel nightgown and her white satin robe, her feet bare, her hair loose and long and dark. Her eyes looked alive again in the much too pale face.

'I can't sleep and I'm hungry. Did I wake you?'

'No, no, of course not. I always get up at six. In fact, I've been up since four.' He looked at her chidingly and she laughed.

'Okay, okay. I get the message. Is it too early to get you some coffee, and me some tea?'

'Sweetheart, this ain't the Fairmont. Do you really want to get moving that bad?'

She nodded. 'How soon can I see him?'

'I don't think they let you visit till eleven or twelve.' Christ, they could have had another four hours of sleep. Alejandro silently mourned the lost hours. He was half dead.

'Well, we're up now. We might as well stay up.'

'Wonderful. That's just what I wanted to hear. Kezia, if I didn't love you so much, and if your old man weren't such a fucking giant, I think right about now I'd kick your ass.'

She smiled delightedly at him. 'I love you too.'

He grinned at her, sat down, and lit a cigarette. She already had one in her hand, and he saw that the hand was still shaking, but aside from that and the pale, pointed look of her face, she looked better. Some sparkle had come back to her eyes, a hint of life and the old Kezia. The girl was a fighter for sure.

He vanished into the bathroom and came out with combed hair, brushed teeth, and a clean shirt.

'My, don't you look pretty.' She was wide awake and full of teasing this morning. It was a far cry from the condition she'd been in the morning before. At least that was a relief.

'You're just looking for trouble this morning, aren't you? Hasn't anyone ever told you not to bug a man before his first cup of coffee?'

'Pobrecito!'

He flipped her the finger and she laughed at him.

'And now that you've dragged me out of my warm bed, I suppose you're going to take two hours to dress.' He waved at the nighgown and robe.

'Make that five minutes.'

She was as good as her word. She was moving very quickly this morning, like a kid waiting for her first trip to the circus, up at dawn, nervous, jumpy, and already tired by breakfast. And they still had five hours to kill before they could see Luke.

Alejandro's thoughts drifted constantly to Luke now. How was he taking it? Was he all right? What was he thinking? Was he already back to the jailhouse living, the cold indifference of lost hopes, or was he still Luke? And if he had already reverted to what he'd once been, how big a shock would it be for Kezia? And how would she adjust to the visit? Alejandro knew it only too well, but he knew that she didn't. Visiting through a thick glass window, speaking on a static-ridden phone, with Luke wearing a filthy rumpled orange overall that would barely reach to his elbows and knees. He would be living in a cell with half a dozen other men, eating beans and stale bread and an imitation of meat, drinking coffee grinds and shitting with no toilet paper. It was one hell of a place to take Kezia, visiting with pimps and hookers and thieves and distraught mothers and hippie girls who would bring ragged children in their arms or on their backs. There would be noise and stench and agony. How much could she take? How far into this world would Luke lead her? And now it was on *his* back. It was Alejandro's baby. Taking care of Kezia.

There was a knock on his door that broke into his thoughts. Kezia again. Dressed and ready to go.

'Boy, you sure look gloomy as hell.'

His thoughts must have showed. 'Morning is not my best hour. I can't say the same for you, though. You look pretty sharp for tea at a truck stop.' She was, as usual, expensively dressed. And there was a brittle cheeriness about her which was beginning to make him nervous. What if she cracked?

'Shouldn't we call a cab?' They had dispensed with the limousine when they checked into the Ritz, again with an oversized tip to buy the chauffeur's silence.

'We can walk. I know a place a few blocks away.'

They headed south in the damp air, and crept down the steep hills hand in hand.

'It's really such a beautiful city, isn't it, Al? Maybe we can go for a walk later today.'

He hoped not. He hoped Luke would tell her to get her ass on a plane to New York. By the end of the week, Luke would be back in Quentin, and there was no point in her staying for that. She couldn't visit him until she got clearance anyway, and that could take weeks. And sooner or later, she'd have to go home. Better sooner than later.

The truck stop was full but not crowded, the room was warm, and the jukebox was already alive. The aroma of coffee mingled with the odour of tired men, cigarette smoke and cigars. She was the only woman in the place, but invited only a few uninterested glances.

Alejandro made her order breakfast, and she made a face. He was unyielding. Two fried eggs, bacon, hash browns, and toast.

'For chrissake, Alejandro, I don't eat that much for dinner.'

'And you look it. Skinny upper-class broad.'

'Now don't be a snob.' She ate one piece of bacon, and played with the toast. The untouched eggs stared up at her like two jaundiced eyes.

'You're not eating.'

'I'm not hungry.'

'And you're smoking too much.'

'Yes, Daddy. Anything else?'

'Up yours, lady. Listen, you'd better take care of yourself, or I'll squeal to the boss.'

'You'd tell Lucas?'

318

'If I have to.' A flicker of worry flashed through her eyes.

'Listen, Alejandro, seriously. . . .'

'Yes?' He laughed at the way she was beginning to squirm.

'I'm serious. Don't upset Luke about anything. If he saw it, that hideous picture in the paper will be bad enough.'

Alejandro nodded, sobered, no longer teasing. They had both seen the small item on page three of the *Chronicle* that morning: Miss Saint Martin had not yet returned to New York; it was assumed that she was 'hiding' somewhere in the city. There was even some speculation about whether she had been hospitalized for nervous collapse. She had certainly looked well on her way to it in the pictures. But they also suggested that if she were in town, she'd probably show up on a visiting day to see Luke, 'unless Miss Kezia Saint Martin has pulled strings for private visiting privileges with Mr. Johns.'

'Gee, I never thought of that.'

'Want to give it a try? It may spare you some hassles with the press. It seems pretty clear they'll be watching for you on visiting days.'

'So let them. I'll go on the same day as everyone else, and visit just like everyone else does.'

Alejandro nodded. The remaining hours until visiting began to grind by. It seemed like weeks before it was a quarter to twelve.

Chapter XXVIII

'Ready to go?' She nodded and picked up her handbag. 'Kezia, you're amazing.' She looked like an extremely pretty young woman without a care in the world. The makeup helped, but it was the way she carried herself, the mask she had slipped into place.

'Thank you, sir.' She looked tense but beautiful, and totally different from the sobbing woman he'd held in his arms in the City Hall corridor two days before. She was every inch a lady, and every ounce in control.

Only the tremor of her hands gave her away. If it weren't for that, she would have looked completely unruffled. Alejandro mused as he watched her. So that's what it was, the hallmark of class, to never show what you feel, as though you've never known a moment of sorrow. Just comb your hair, put it back in an elegant little knot, powder your nose, smack a smile on your face, and speak in a low subdued voice. Remember to say 'thank you' and 'please' and smile at the doorman. The mark of good breeding. Like a show dog, or a well-trained horse.

'Are you coming, Alejandro?' She was in a hurry to leave the hotel.

'Christ, woman, I can hardly keep my mind straight, and you stand there like you're going to a tea party. How do you do it?'

'Practice. It's a way of life.'

'It can't be healthy.'

'It's not. That's why half the people I grew up with are now alcoholics. The others live on pills, and in a few years a whole bunch of them will drop dead from heart attacks. Some of them have already managed to die.' A vision of Tiffany flashed through her mind. 'You cover up all your life, and one day you explode.'

'What about you?' He was following her down the hotel's ill-lighted stairs.

'I'm okay. I let off steam with my writing. And I can be myself with Luke . . . and now you.'

'No one else?'

'Not till now.'

'That's no way to live.'

'You know, Alejandro,' she said, when she had climbed into the cab, 'the trouble with pretending all the time is that eventually you forget who you are, and what you feel. You become the image.'

'How come you didn't then, babe?' But, as he watched her, he wondered. She was frighteningly cool.

'My writing, I guess. It helps me spill the grief in my guts. Gives me a place where I can be me. The other way, keeping it all in, sooner or later rots your soul.' She thought once more of Tiffany. That's what had happened to her, and others in the course of the years. Two of Kezia's friends had committed suicide since college.

'Luke'll feel better when he sees you, anyway.' And that was worth something. But Alejandro knew why she had worn the well-tailored black coat, the black gabardine slacks, the black suede shoes. Not for Lucas. But to make sure that the next picture in the paper showed her with it all in control. Elegant, uptight, and distinguished. There would be no collapse at the jail.

'You think there'll be press when we get there?'

'I don't think so, I know it.'

There was. Kezia and Alejandro got out of the cab at the front entrance of 850 Bryant Street. The Hall of Justice. It was an unimpressive grey building with none of the majesty of City Hall. Outside, a pair of sentries from the *Examiner* scouted her arrival. Another pair were pacing at the building's rear entrance. Kezia had a nose for them, like Luke did for police. She clung tightly to

Alejandro's arm while looking as though she barely held it, and quietly pulled her dark glasses over her eyes. There was a faint smile on her face.

She brushed quickly past a voice calling her name, while a second reporter spoke into a pocket-sized transmitter. Now they knew what lay ahead. Alejandro studied her face as a guard searched her handbag, but she looked surprisingly calm. A photographer snapped their picture, and with bowed heads they stepped quickly into an elevator in the salmon marble halls. It struck Kezia, as the doors closed, that the walls were the same colour as the gladioli at Italian funerals, and she laughed.

On the sixth floor, Alejandro led her quickly through another door and up a flight of strangely drafty stairs.

'A breeze from the River Styx perhaps?' There was irony and mischief in her voice. He couldn't get over it. Was this the Kezia he knew?'

She kept the glasses in place and he took her hand as they waited in line. The man in front of them smelled and was drunk, the black woman in front of him was obese and crying. Farther up the line, a few children were wailing and a bunch of hippies leaned back against the wall, laughing. They stood in a long thin line on the stairs, one by one reaching a desk at the top. Identification of visitor, name of inmate, and then a little pink ticket with a window number and a Roman numeral indicating a group. They were in Group II. The first group had already been herded inside. The stairs were crowded but there were no reporters in sight.

They moved inside, to a neon-lit room which boasted another desk, two guards, and three rows of benches. Beyond it they could see a long hall lined with windows, along which ran a shelf with a telephone every few feet, and a stool to sit on as you visited. It was awkward and uncomfortable. Group I was in the midst of its visit, destined to last five minutes or twenty, depending on the mood of the guards. Faces were animated, women giggled and then cried, inmates looked urgent and determined

322

and then let their faces relax at the sight of a three-year-old son. It was enough to tear your heart out.

Alejandro glanced at Kezia uncomfortably. She looked undaunted. Nothing showed. She smiled at him and lit another cigarette. And then suddenly the photographers swarmed them. Three cameramen and two reporters, even the local rep from *Women's Wear* was with them.

Alejandro felt a wave of claustrophobia engulf him. How did she stand it? The other visitors looked astonished and some backed away while others pressed forward to see what was happening. Suddenly, there was chaos, with Kezia in the eye of the storm, dark glasses in place, mouth set, looking stern but unshakably calm.

'Are you under sedation? Have you spoken to Luke Johns since the hearing? Are you. . . . Did you. . . . Will you. . . . Why?' She said nothing, only shaking her head.

'I have no comment to make. Nothing to say.' Alejandro felt useless beside her. She remained in her seat, bowed her head, as though by not seeing them, they might disappear. But then unexpectedly, she stood up and spoke to them in a low, subdued voice.

'I think that's enough now. I told you, I have nothing to say.' A burst of flashes went off in her face, and two guards came to the rescue. The press would have to wait outside, they were disrupting the visiting. Even the inmates having visits had stopped talking and were watching the group around Kezia and the flashes of light that went off every few seconds.

A guard called her aside to the desk, as the photographers and reporters reluctantly exited. Alejandro joined her, realizing he hadn't said a word since the onslaught began. He felt lost in the stir. He had never even thought of dealing with something like that, but she handled it well. That surprised him. There had been no trace of panic, but then again it wasn't new to her either.

The head guard leaned close to them and made a suggestion. A guard could accompany them when they left. They could take an elevator straight into the police garage in the basement, where a cab could be waiting. Alejandro leapt at the idea, and Kezia gratefully agreed. She was even paler than she had been, and the tremor in her hands was now a steady fluttering. The paparazzi attack had taken its toll.

'Do you suppose I might see Mr. Johns in a private room somewhere up here?' She was rapidly abandoning her determination to shun special favours. The curious crowd was becoming almost as oppressive as the press. But her request was denied. Nevertheless, a young guard was assigned to hover nearby.

A voice called out the end of the first visit, and guards ushered Group I into a cage where they could wait for the elevator without disturbing the next group. It was strange to watch the difference in faces as they left – pained, shocked, silent. Their moment of laughter had ended. Women clutched little slips of paper with orders, requests: toothpaste, socks, the name of a lawyer a cellmate had suggested.

'Group Two!' The voice boomed into her thoughts, and Alejandro took her elbow. The pink slip of paper in her hand was crumpled and limp, but they checked it for the number of the window where they'd visit Luke.

There would be other visitors at close range on either side, but the promised guard was standing beside them. It seemed like a very long wait. Ten minutes, maybe fifteen. It felt endless. And then they came. From behind a steel door, a line of dirty wrinkled orange suits, unshaven faces, unwashed teeth, and broad smiles. Luke was fifth on the line. Alejandro took one look at his face and knew he was all right, and then he watched Kezia.

Unconsciously, she got to her feet as she saw him, stood very straight, to her full tiny height, a blistering smile on her face. Her eyes came alive. She looked incredibly beautiful. And she must have looked even better to Luke. Their eyes met and held and she almost danced on the spot. Until finally he got to the phone.

'Why's the goon standing behind you?'

'Lucas!'

'All right, the *guard*.' They exchanged a smile.

'To keep away the curious.'

'Trouble?'

'Paparazzi.'

Luke nodded. 'Someone said there was a movie star out here, and a lot of reporters took her picture. I take it that's you?'

She nodded.

'Are you okay?'

'I'm fine.' He didn't question that, and she wouldn't have confessed to being other than "fine," if he had. His eyes momentarily sought Alejandro, who nodded and smiled.

'That picture of you in the paper was the shits, Mama.'

'Yeah, it was.'

'I freaked out when I saw it. Looked like you were having a stroke.'

'Don't be a jerk. And I'm all back together now.'

'Did that scoop hit New York?'

She nodded again.

'Jesus. You must have heard about it from Edward.'

'You might say that. But he'll survive.' She smiled ruefully.

'Will you?'

She nodded as he searched her face.

'What did he say?'

'Nothing unexpected. He was just worried.'

'What a bitch for you to have to go through that on top of everything else.' It was odd the way they were talking, as though they were sitting side by side on the couch.

'Bullshit. Besides, Lucas, we've really been lucky till now. It could have happened long before this.'

'Yeah, but we could have gotten press coverage in a lot better circumstances.'

She nodded and smiled, anxious to turn to other subjects. They had so little time.

325

'Are you all right, darling? Really?'

'Baby, I'm used to this shit. I'm A-l okay.'

'We're still engaged, you know, Mr. Johns.'

'Mama, I love you.'

'I adore you.' Her whole face glowed as she melted into his eyes.

They discussed legal technicalities, and he gave her a list of calls to make, but basically he had taken care of all his own business before they came out for the hearing. He had known what the chances were, better than she had.

The rest of their visit was spent on banalities, jokes, teasing, sarcastic descriptions of the food, but he looked surprisingly well. The grimness was not unfamiliar to him. He spoke to Alejandro for a few minutes, and then pointed back at Kezia. She removed an earring again and picked up the phone as Luke looked over his shoulder towards a voice she couldn't hear.

'I think this is going to be it. Visiting is about over.'

'Oh.' A dim light flickered in her eyes. 'Luke . . .'

'Listen, babe, I want you to do something for me. I want you to go back to New York tonight. I already told Alejandro.'

'Lucas, why?'

'What are you going to do here? Hang out till I get to Q, and then wait three weeks till I get clearance for visits, and see me once a week for an hour? Don't be an ass, babe. I want you at home.' Besides, it was safer. Even though now, she wasn't really in danger. Now that he was on ice, all the factions warring against him would be appeased. Kezia was of no real interest. Still, he didn't want to take chances with her.

'Go to New York, and then what, Luke?'

'Do what you do, Mama. Write, work, live. You're not in here, I am. Don't forget that.'

'Lucas, you . . . darling, I love you. I want to stay here in San Francisco.'

She was fierce, but he was more so. 'You're going. I'm

326

leaving for Quentin on Friday. And I'll put the forms in for you to visit. When they get processed, you can come back. Figure about three weeks. I'll let you know when.'

'Can I write to you?'

'Does a bear shit in the woods?' He grinned at her.

'Lucas!' The tenseness broke into laughter. 'You must be all right.'

'I am. So you be fine too. And tell that idiot friend of mine that he'd better take care of you or he'll be one dead Mexican when I get out.'

'How charming. I'm sure he'll be thrilled.'

And then it was suddenly over. A guard called something on Luke's side of the glass wall, and another guard told them they'd had it on the visitors' side. She felt Alejandro's hand on her arm, and Lucas stood up.

'That's it, Mama. I'll write.'

'I love you.'

'I love you, too.' The entire world seemed to stop with those words. It was as though he placed them one by one in her heart via his eyes. He said them, and held her close with a look, and then gently he put down the phone. Her eyes never left him as he walked back through the door, and this time he looked back, with a jaunty grin and a wave. She answered with a wave and her most valiant smile. And then he was gone.

The guard who had stood behind them now took them aside and showed them the way to the separate elevator. A cab had been called and was already waiting in the garage. There were no reporters in sight. In a moment, they were in the cab and speeding from the building and Luke. They were alone again, Alejandro and Kezia, and now she had nothing to look forward to. The visit was over. And his words rang in her ears, as his image filled her mind's eye. She wanted to be alone just then, with the dreams of the recent and distant past. The still new aquamarine sparkled on her trembling hand as she lit a cigarette and fought for control.

'He wants us to go back to New York.' She spoke to

Alejandro without looking at him and her voice sounded hoarse.

'I know.' He had expected a fight. It surprised him to hear her say it so bluntly. 'Are you up to the trip?' It would be best if she was, to just get the hell out and let her pick up the pieces at home, and not at the Ritz.

'I'm fine. I think there's a plane at four. Let's catch it.'

'We'll have to run like the devil.' He looked at his watch, and she discreetly blew her nose.

'I think we can make it.' Her voice kept him a thousand miles away, and it was the last time they spoke until they boarded the plane.

CHAPTER XXIX

The voice on the phone had grown familiar and dear.

'I'm hungry. Any chance that you'll feed me?' It was Alejandro. They had been back in New York for a week. A week of constant calls from him, unexpected visits, small bunches of flowers, problems he supposedly needed her help to resolve, ruses and excuses and tenderness.

'I suppose I might drum up some tuna surprise.'

'That's what they eat on Park Avenue? Shit, I eat better uptown. But the company's not as good there. Besides, I've got a problem.'

'Another one? Bullshit. Honest, love, I'm okay. You don't have to come down here again.'

'What if I want to?'

'Then I shall rejoice at the pleasure of seeing you.' She smiled into the phone.

'So formal. And serving tuna surprise yet. Any news from Luke?'

'Yep. Two great big fat letters. And a visiting form for me to fill out. Hallelujah! Fifteen more days and then I can visit.'

328

'Keep your shirt on. Did he say anything else? Or just a lot of corny shit I don't want to hear?'

'Lots of that. And he also said he was in a four-by-nine cell with another guy. Sounds cosy, doesn't it?'

'Very. Any other good news?' He didn't like the sound of her voice when she told him. Bitterness had begun to replace grief.

'Nothing much otherwise. He said to send you his love.'

'I owe him a letter. I'll do it this week. And what did you do today? Write anything sexy?'

She laughed at the thought. 'Yeah, I wrote a very sexy book review for the Washington *Post*.'

'Fantastic. You can read it to me when I get there.'

He arrived two hours later, with a small plant and a bag of hot chestnuts.

'How are things at the centre? Mmm ... yummy ... have another one.' She was shelling the hot nuts in her lap in front of the fire.

'The centre's not bad. It's been worse.' But not much. He didn't want to tell her that now. The way things were going, he'd be gone in a month, maybe two. But she'd had enough of her own changes recently, without having to listen to his.

'So what's this alleged problem you want to discuss with me?'

'Problem? Oh! *That* problem!'

'Liar ... but you're a sweet liar. And a good friend.'

'All right. I'll confess. I just wanted an excuse to see you.' He hung his head like a kid.

'Flattery, dear Alejandro ... I adore it.' She grinned up at him and tossed him another chestnut. He watched her as she leaned her back against a chair, warming her feet by the fire. There was a smile on her lips. But the spark had gone dead in her eyes. Daily, she was looking worse. She had lost a lot of weight, she was deathly pale, and her hands still shook almost constantly. Not a lot, but enough. He didn't like it. He didn't like it at all.

'How long has it been since you've been out, Kezia?'

'Out of what?'

'Don't play dumb with me, asshole. You know what I mean. Out of this house. Outdoors. In the fresh air.' He eyed her directly, but she avoided his gaze.

'Oh that. Actually, not for a while.'

'How long is a while? Three days? A week?'

'I don't know, a couple of days, I guess. Mainly, I've been worried about being swarmed by the press.'

'Bullshit. You told me three days ago that they didn't call anymore, and they haven't been hanging around the building. The story is dead, Kezia, and you know it. So what's keeping you home?'

'Lethargy. Fatigue. Fear.'

'Fear of what?'

'I haven't figured that out yet.'

'Look, babe, a lot of things have changed for you, and very brutally and suddenly at that. But you have to get back to doing something with yourself. Go out, see people, get some air. Hell, go shopping if that's what turns you on, but don't lock yourself up in here. You're beginning to turn green.'

'How terribly chic.' But she had gotten the point.

'Want to go for a walk now?'

She didn't, but she knew that she ought to. 'Okay.'

They wandered towards the park in silence, holding hands, and she kept her eyes down. They were almost at the zoo before she spoke.

'Alejandro, what am I going to do?'

'About what?' He knew, but he wanted to hear it from her.

'My life.'

'Give yourself time to adjust. Then figure it out. It's still much too fresh. In a sense, you're in shock.'

'That's what it feels like. Like I'm wandering around in a daze. I forget to eat. I forget if the mail has come, I can't remember what day of the week it is. I start to work, and then my mind wanders and I look up and it's two hours later and I haven't finished the sentence I was typing. It's crazy. I feel like one of those little old ladies who burrow into their houses, and someone has to keep reminding them to put the other stocking on, and to finish their soup.'

'You're not that bad yet. You cleaned up those chestnuts pretty quick.'

'No. But I'm getting there, Alejandro. I just feel so vague . . . and so lost . . .'

'All you can do is be good to yourself, and wait till you feel more yourself.'

'Yeah, and in the meantime I look at his stuff in the closet. I lie in bed, and wait to hear his key in the door, and I kid myself that he's in Chicago and he'll be back in the morning. It's driving me goddamn nuts.'

'No wonder. Look, babe, he's not dead.'

'No. But he's gone. And I've come to rely on him so much. In thirty years, or ten adult ones anyway, I've never relied on a man. But with Luke, I let myself go, I tore down all the walls. I leaned all over him, and now . . . I feel like I'm going to fall over.'

'Now?' He tried to tease her a little.

'Oh shut up.'

'All right, seriously. The fact is that he's gone and you're not. You're going to have to pick up your life. Sooner or later.'

She nodded again, dug her hands deeper into her pockets, and they walked on. They had reached the horse carri-ges at the Plaza before she looked up.

'It must be quite a hotel,' Alejandro said. In a way, it reminded him of the Fairmont.

'Haven't you ever been in it? Just for a look?' She was surprised when he shook his head.

'Nope. No reason to. This isn't exactly my part of town.' She smiled at him and slipped her hand through his arm.

'Come on, let's go in.'

'I'm not wearing a tie.' The idea made him nervous.

'And I look like a slob. But they know me. They'll let us in.'

331

'I bet they will.' He laughed at her, and they marched up the steps to the Plaza, looking as though they had decided to buy the place on a lark.

They walked past the powdered dowagers eating pastry to the strains of violins in the Palm Court, and Kezia guided him expertly down the mysterious halls. They heard Japanese, Spanish, Swedish, a flurry of French, and the music that reminded Alejandro of old Garbo movies. The Plaza was more grandiose than the Fairmont, and much more alive.

They stopped at a door while Kezia peeked inside. The room was large and opulent with the endless oak panelling that had given it its name. There was a long elaborate bar, and a lovely view of the park.

'Louis?' She signalled to the headwaiter as he approached with a smile.

'Mademoiselle Saint Martin, *comment ça va! Quel plaisir!*'

'Hello Louis. Do you suppose you could squeeze us into a quiet table? We're not dressed.'

'*Aucune importance.* That is not a problem!' He assured them so magnanimously that Alejandro was convinced they could have arrived stark naked, and possibly should have.

They settled at a small table in the corner, and Kezia dug into the nuts.

'Well, do you like it?'

'It's quite something.' He looked a bit awed. 'Do you come here a lot?'

'No. I used to. As much as one can. Women are only allowed in at certain times.'

'A stag bar, eh?'

'You're close. Rhymes with ...' She giggled. 'Fags, darling, fags. I suppose you might say this is the most elegant gay bar in New York.' He laughed in answer and took a look around. She was right. There were a number of gay men scattered here and there - a very large number as he took a second look. They were by far the most elegant men in the room. The others all looked like solid businessmen, and dull.

'You know, Kezia, when I look around a place like this, I know why you wound up with Luke. I used to wonder. Not that there's anything wrong with Lucas. But I'd expected you to hang out with some Wall Street lawyer.'

'I tried that for a while. He was gay.'

'Jesus.'

'Yeah. But what did you mean when you said "when you look around a place like this"?'

'Just that the men in your set don't knock me out.'

'Oh. Well, they don't knock me out either. That was always the trouble.'

'And now what? You go back to the old world?'

'I don't know if I can, or why I should bother. I think most likely I'll wait for Luke to get out.' He didn't say anything, and they ordered another round of scotch.

'What about your friend Edward? Have you made peace with him?' Alejandro still shuddered at the memory of the half-crazed voice on the phone at the Fairmont after the hearing.

'After a fashion. I don't think he'll ever really forgive me for the scandal. It makes him feel like a failure, since in a sense he brought me up. But at least the papers have cooled it. And people forget. I'm already old news.' She shrugged and took another swallow of scotch. 'Besides, people let me get away with a lot. If you have enough money they call you eccentric and think you're amusing. If you don't have the bucks they call you a perverted pig and an asshole. It's disgusting, but it's true. You'd be aghast at some of the things my friends get away with. Nothing as mundane as my "outrageous" love affair with Luke.'

'Do you care if people get upset about Lucas?'

'Not really. It's my business, not theirs. A lot has changed in the last few months. Mostly me. It's just as well Edward, for instance, had this illusion of me as a child.'

333

Alejandro wanted to say 'So do I,' but he didn't. She had that quality about her; it had something to do with her size and her seeming fragility.

They left after their third round of scotch, on equally empty stomachs, both high as kites.

'You know what's funny?' She was laughing so hard she could barely stand up, but the cold air had sobered them both a little.

'What's funny?'

'I don't know ... everything is ...' She laughed again, and he wiped tears of cold and mirth from his eyes.

'Hey, you want a buggy ride?'

'Yes!' They piled aboard and Alejandro instructed the driver to take them to Kezia's. It was a cosy carriage with an old raccoon lap robe. They snuggled under it and giggled all the way home, insulated by the raccoon and the scotch.

'Can I tell you a secret, Alejandro?'

'Sure. I love secrets.' He held her close so she wouldn't fall out. That was as good an excuse as any.

'I've been drunk every night since I got back.'

He looked at her through his own haze of scotch and shook his head. 'That's dumb. I won't let you do that to yourself.'

'You're such a nice man. Alejandro, I love you.'

'I love you too.'

They sat side by side and rode the rest of the way to her house in silence. He paid for the hansom cab and they rode up to her apartment, giggling in the elevator.

'You know, I think I'm too drunk to cook.'

'Just as well. I think I'm too drunk to eat.'

'Yeah. Me too.'

'Kezia, you should eat. . . .'

'Later. Want to come to dinner tomorrow?'

'I'll be there. With a lecture.' He tried to look grave but couldn't master the expression and she laughed at him.

'Then I won't let you in.'

'Then I'll huff and I'll puff and I'll blow ...' They both collapsed in the kitchen with mirth, and he tipsily kissed the tip of her nose. 'I've got to go. But I'll see you tomorrow. And make me a promise?'

'What?' All of a sudden he had looked so serious.

'No more drinking tonight, Kezia. Promise?'

'I ... uh ... yeah ... okay.' But it was a promise she was not planning to keep.

She saw him to the elevator, and waved cheerily as the door closed, before coming back to the kitchen and bringing out the rest of last night's fresh bottle of scotch. She was surprised that there was only an inch or so left.

It was odd, but as she poured what was left into a tumbler with one ice cube, the vision of Tiffany's funeral flashed into mind. It was a dumb way to die, but the others all left such a big mess. At least drinking wasn't messy ... not really ... not very ... or was it? She didn't really give a damn, as she smiled to herself and drained the full glass.

The phone was ringing but she didn't bother to answer it. It couldn't have been Luke. Even drunk she knew that much. Luke was away on a trip ... in Tahiti ... on a safari ... and there were no phones there ... but he'd be back at the end of the week. She was sure of it. Friday. And let's see ... what was today? Tuesday? Monday? Thursday! He'd be home tomorrow. She opened a fresh bottle. Bourbon this time. For Lucas. He'd be coming home soon.

CHAPTER XXX

'Child, you look awfully thin.'

'Marina just called it "divinely svelte". She and Halpern just walked by.' The wedding had been held over the New Year's holiday in Palm Beach.

Edward slid onto the banquette beside her. It was their first lunch in almost two months. And now she looked so different it shocked him.

Her eyes were sunken into her head, her skin looked taut on her cheekbones, and there was not even lustre where once there had been fire. What a price she had paid. And for what? It still horrified him, but he had promised her not to discuss it. That was the condition on which she'd accepted his invitation to lunch. And he wanted so much to see her. Maybe there was still a chance to regain what they'd lost.

'Sorry I was late, Kezia.'

'Not to worry, love. I had a drink while I waited.' And that was new too. But at least she was still impeccably groomed. Even more so than usual, in fact. She looked almost formal. The mink coat she so seldom wore was thrown over the back of a chair.

'Why so dressed up today, my dear? Going somewhere after lunch?' Normally, she played it down, but not today, and the rare appearance of the mink coat surprised him.

'I'm turning over a new leaf. Coming home to roost, as they say.' Luke's letter that morning had insisted that she at least try her old stamping grounds again. It was better than sitting home sulking – or drinking, a new habit he didn't know about. But she had decided to try his advice. That was why she had accepted the luncheon with Edward, and dragged out the fur coat. But she felt like an ass. Or like Tiffany, trying to dress up disaster with breath mints and fur.

'What do you mean by "turning over a new leaf"?' He didn't dare mention the Luke Johns affair, she might have walked out on the spot. And he was afraid of that. He signalled the waiter to order their usual Louis Roederer champagne. The waiter looked harassed but showed he understood, with a smile.

'Oh, let's just say that I'm making an effort to be a nice girl, and see some of my old friends.'

'Whitney?' Edward was a little taken aback.

'I said I was being nice, not ridiculous, darling. No, I just thought I'd "come back" and take a look around.' The champagne arrived, the waiter poured, Edward tasted and nodded approval. The waiter poured again for both of them, and Edward lifted his glass in a toast.

'Then allow me to say welcome home.' He wanted to ask if she had learned her lesson, but he didn't dare. Perhaps she had, though ... perhaps she had. And in any case, her little misadventure had certainly aged her. She looked five years more than her age, particularly in a simple lilac wool dress and her grandmother's remarkable pearls. And then he noticed the ring. He glanced at it and nodded approval. 'Very pretty. Something new?'

'Yes. Luke got it for me in San Francisco.' Something pinched in his face again. Bitterness. Anger.

'I see.' There was no further comment, and Kezia finished her drink while Edward sipped his champagne.

'How is the writing these days?'

'It'll do. I haven't written anything I like in a while. And yes, Edward, I know. But looking at me like that won't change a damn thing. I know all about it.' She was suddenly sick of the constant arch in his brows. 'That's right, darling, I'm not writing as well as I should. I've lost twelve pounds since you last saw me, I lock myself up at home because I'm terrified of reporters, and I look ten years older. I know all about it. We both know I've had a rough time. And we both know why, so stop looking so fucking shocked and disapproving. It's really a dead bore.'

'*Kezia!*'

'Yes, Edward?'

He realized then from the look in her eyes that she had had more to drink than he'd thought. He was so stunned that he half turned in his seat and eyed her intensely.

'Okay, darling, what now? Is my mascara on crooked?'

'You're drunk.' His voice was barely a whisper.

'Yes, I am,' she whispered back with a bitter little

337

smile. 'And I'm going to get drunker. How's that for a fun day?' He sat back in his seat with a sigh, searching for the right words to say, and then he saw her. The reporter from *Women's Wear Daily*, eyeing them from across the room.

'Damn.'

'Is that all you can say, love? I'm turning myself into an alcoholic and all you can think of is "damn"?' She was playing with him now, evilly, meanly, but she couldn't help herself. She was shocked when she felt his grip on her arm.

'Kezia, that woman from *Women's Wear* is over there and if you do anything, anything to catch her attention or antagonize her, I'll ... you'll regret it.' Kezia laughed a deep-throated laugh and kissed his cheek. She thought it was funny, and Edward felt the sinking feeling of events slipping away from him, out of control. She wanted to bait everyone; she didn't want to 'come home'. She didn't even know where home was. And she was worse than Liane had ever been. So much more brazen, so much stronger, tougher, more wilful ... and so much more beautiful. He had never loved her more than now, at this instant, and all he wanted to do was shake her, or slap her. And then make love to her. Right in the middle of La Grenouille if he had to. The ideas suddenly running through his mind shocked him, and he shook his head as though to clear it. As he did, he felt Kezia patting his hand.

'Don't be afraid of silly old Sally, Edward, she won't bite you. She just wants a story.' He found himself wondering if they should leave now, before they had lunch. But that might make a scene too. He felt trapped.

'Kezia. ...' He was almost trembling with fear, and all he could do was take her hand in his, look into her eyes and pray that she'd behave herself and not create a scene. 'Please.' Kezia saw the pain in his eyes, and it was like scalding oil on her soul. She didn't want to see his feelings, not now. She couldn't handle her own, let alone his.

'All right, Edward. All right.' She looked away, her voice subdued again, and noticed the WWD reporter making little notes on a pad. But there would be no further story. Only that they had been seen. She was not going to make trouble. They'd all had enough. 'I'm sorry.' She said it with the sigh of a child, leaning back against the banquette, as relief swept over Edward. It made him feel tender again.

'Kezia, why can't I help you?'

'Because nobody can.' There were tears trembling on her lashes. 'Just try to accept that there isn't a hell of a lot you can do for me right now. The present is what it is, and the past happened, and the future ... well, I don't see it too clearly right now. Maybe that's the trouble.' She often found herself wondering now if this was what Tiffany had felt. As though someone had stolen the future. They had left her the large emerald ring and the pearls, but no future. It was hard to explain it to Edward. He was always so certain of everything. It made him seem far away too.

'Do you regret the past, Kezia?' But he looked up with horror at the reaction in her eyes. He had said the wrong thing again. Lord, it was hard to talk to the girl. Crucifixion over lunch.

'If you are referring to Lucas, Edward, of course I don't regret it. He's the only decent thing that's happened to me in the last ten or twenty, or maybe even thirty years. What I regret is the revocation. There's nothing I can do about it now. There's nothing anyone can do. You can't appeal a revocation of parole. It's totally pointless.'

'I see. I didn't realize you were still that involved in this ... this problem. I thought that after ...'

She cut him off, with a look of extreme aggravation.

'You thought wrong. And just so you don't die of the shock if you see it in the papers, I'm going back out there shortly.'

'What in God's name for?' He was speaking to her

339

sotto voce so no one would hear, but Kezia was speaking in her normal voice.

'To visit him, obviously. And I told you, I don't want to discuss it. And do you know something, Edward? I'm finding this entire subject inappropriate with you, and this lunch unbearably boring. As a matter of fact, darling, I think I've about had it.' Her voice was rising to an unpleasant timbre, and Edward could feel himself squirm inside the starch in his collar. He was hating every minute of it. She drained her glass, looked around the room for a minute, and then looked back at him strangely.

'Kezia, are you all right? You looked rather pale for a moment.' He looked terribly worried.

'No, really, I'm fine.'

'Shall I have them get you a cab?'

'Yes, maybe I ought to go. To tell you the truth, it's a hell of a strain. That bitch from *Women's Wear* has been watching us since we sat down, and all of a sudden I feel like the whole goddamn place is watching me to see what kind of shape I'm in. It's all I can do not to stand up and tell them all to go fuck themselves.'

Edward blanched. 'No, Kezia. I don't think you ought to do that.'

'Oh hell, darling, why not? For a laugh?'

She was playing with him again, and so cruelly. Why? Why did she have to do that to him? Didn't she know that he cared? That it tore him apart to see her this way . . . that he was not made merely of white shirts and dark suits . . . that someone lived inside the elegant tailoring, a heart . . . a body . . . a man. Tears burned his eyes and there was a gruffness in his voice as he quietly stood and took Kezia's arm. He looked different now, and she sensed it too. The games were over.

'Kezia, you're leaving now.' She could hardly hear his words, but she could have read his tone from across the room. She was being dismissed like a naughty child.

'Are you very angry?' She whispered it to him as he helped her into her mink. She was frightened now. She

340

had only wanted to play ... wanted to ... hurt. They both knew it.

'No. Only very sorry. For you.' He guided her towards the door, keeping a firm grip on her elbow. She was going to have no chance to misbehave between the table and the door. The fun was over. And she felt oddly submissive at his side. He cast a few frosty smiles left and right as they made their way out. He didn't want anyone to think there was trouble, and Kezia looked dreadful.

They stood for a moment at the cloakroom while he waited for the girl to retrieve his coat and homburg.

'Edward, I ...' She had started to cry now and held tightly to his arm.

'Kezia, not here.' Enough was enough. He couldn't bear it anymore.

She swept the tears away with one hand gloved in black suede, and tried out a wintry smile.

'Where are you going from here? Home to lie down, I hope.' And get hold of yourself. He didn't say it, but it was in his eyes, as he settled the homburg into place.

'Actually, I was going to show up at the Arthritis Ball meeting today. But I don't know if I'm up to it.'

'I don't think you are.'

'Yes. But I haven't been there in so long.' And now there's Tiffany's place to fill as the local socialite lush. ... Motherfucking old bags. Oh God, what if she said ... what if ... what if. ... She felt a rush of heat follow the wave of pale green and wondered if she was going to faint or throw up. That would make a story for *WWD*.

Edward took charge of her elbow again and led her out to the street. The cold air seemed to restore her. She took a deep breath and felt better.

'Do you have any idea what it's like to watch you do this to yourself? And for ... for ...' Her eyes sought his but he couldn't stop himself anymore. 'For nothing. For that ... that no one. Kezia, for God's sake, stop now. Write to him, tell him you don't want to see him again. Tell him. ...'

341

Her words stopped him cold. 'Are you telling me this is a choice?' She stood still, watching him.

'What do you mean?' He felt ice trickle slowly down his back.

'You know exactly what I mean. Is this a choice, Edward? Your friendship or his love?'

No, little girl, my love or his. But he couldn't say that to her.

'Because if that's what you're saying ... then I'm saying goodbye.' She held out her arm before he could answer and stopped a cab that was passing. It came to a screeching halt just beyond the canopy.

'No, Kezia, I . . .'

'See you soon, darling.' She pecked at his cheek before he could regain his composure and slipped quickly into the cab. Before he knew it she was gone. Gone. '. . . then I'm saying goodbye.' How could she? And so heartlessly, without any emotion in her eyes.

But what he didn't know was that she couldn't give up Luke. Not for anyone. Not even for him. Luke was her route to escape from the world that had haunted her. Luke had shown her the way out; now she had to stick with him. She couldn't turn back. Not even for Edward. And alone in the cab, she wanted to die. She had done it. She had killed him. Killed Edward. It was like killing her father ... like killing Tiffany again. Why did someone always have to get mutilated, Kezia wondered as she drove uptown, fighting back sobs. And why Edward? Why him? He only had her, and she knew it. But maybe it had to be. She couldn't leave Luke, and if it was a question of loyalty ... Edward could take it. He was so sturdy. He would always weather what had to be borne. He was good about those things. He understood.

Kezia did not know that he would spend the rest of the day walking, looking into faces, looking at women, and thinking of her.

The cab drew up outside the Fifth Avenue address

342

Kezia had given. She was right on time for the meeting. The committee would be beginning to gather. She thought of their faces as she paid the driver the fare. . . . All those faces . . . and mink coats . . . and sapphires . . . and emeralds . . . and . . . she felt a wave of panic sweep over her. The lunch with Edward had left her drained, and she didn't feel able to cope. She paused for a moment before going inside the building. And then she knew. She couldn't go in. The prying eyes at La Grenouille had been bad enough. But at least they had to keep their distance. The women on the committee didn't, and they'd be all over her in an instant, with snide questions and sneering asides. And of course they had all seen the newspaper photographs of her collapsing in court, and read every word of the story. It was simply too much to handle.

The snow crunched beneath her feet as she walked to the corner to hail another cab and go home. She wanted to flee. She had unthinkingly walked back into the insanity of her life before Luke. And even for a day it unnerved her. From cab to cab, from luncheon to meeting to nowhere to nothing to drink to drank to drunk. She wondered what in God's name she was doing.

It was snowing and she was hatless and without boots, but she pulled the mink coat tightly around her and sank her gloved hands into her pockets. It was only a twelve-block walk to her house, and she needed the air.

She trudged all the way home, her suede shoes soaking wet on her feet, her hair damp, and when she got home her cheeks were aflame and her legs felt icy and numb, but she felt alive and sober again. She had pulled her hair from its knot and let it fall around her shoulders, gathering a mantilla of snow.

The doorman rushed to her side with his half-broken umbrella as he saw her loom from the snow and darkness, and she laughed as he approached.

'No, no, Thomas. I'm fine!' She felt like a child again, and the sodden shoes didn't matter at all. It was the sort

343

of performance that would have won her days of scolding as a child. Totie might even have reported her to Edward for something like that. But Totie was a thing of the past now, as was Edward. She had seen that today. She could walk in the snow all night now if she wanted. It didn't really matter. Nothing did. Except Luke.

But at least the buzzing sound had left her head, her shoulders didn't feel quite so heavy, her spirit felt clean. Even the drinks had been washed away by the cold and the snow.

The doorbell rang just as she peeled off her stockings and struck her cold feet under the hot water tap in the tub. They tingled and hurt and turned red. She debated answering the door, and decided rapidly not to. It was obviously just the elevator man with a package; had it been a visitor they would have called from downstairs for permission to send someone up. But the bell was persistent, and finally she dried her feet in one of the big monogrammed towels, and ran to the door.

'Yes? Who is it?'

'Cesar Chavez.'

'Who?'

'It's Alejandro, you dummy.'

She pulled open the door. 'Good lord, you look like Frosty the Snowman. Did you walk?'

'All the way.' He looked terribly pleased with himself. 'I think I love New York after all. When it snows anyway. Isn't it great?'

She nodded with a broad smile of agreement. 'Come on in.'

'I was hoping you'd say that. They rang from downstairs for ages, but you didn't answer. The guy said you were home, and I must have looked honest or cold, because he let me come up.'

'I had the water running in the tub.' She looked down at her bare feet which were now almost purple from the return of circulation after the shock of the tub. 'I walked home too. It felt great.'

344

'What happened? Couldn't find a cab?'

'Nope. I just felt like walking. It was sort of a crazy day, and I needed to unwind.'

'What happened?' He looked faintly worried.

'Nothing much. I had one of those unbearably fancy lunches with Edward, and it was a hell of a strain. Between his dismal failure at not looking disapproving, and the stares of the rest of the people there, not to mention a *Women's Wear* reporter creeping up on us . . . I got a bad case of the freaks. And then to make matters worse, I took myself off to a benefit meeting, and flaked out before I walked in the door. That's when I decided to walk home.'

'Sounds like you needed it.'

'Yeah. I just can't play the old games anymore. I can't even begin to tackle the double life nonsense again, and I won't do it. That life just doesn't suit me. I'd rather be here by myself.'

'Are you telling me to leave?'

'Don't be a jerk.'

He chuckled, and she took his sopping wet coat, and hung it on the kitchen door.

'I must admit, that whole trip sounds pretty bad.'

'Worse . . . but dahling, how divine you look, isn't that the wet look by Cardin . . . oh, and your ring!' She picked up the hand where he had a large rough Indian turquoise. 'But the ring is David Webb of course . . . his nnneeewwww collection, daaahhhling? Ah, and of course sneakers by Macy's. What an exquisite idea!' She made a face and rolled her eyes. 'I mean, Jesus, Alejandro, how can anyone breathe under all that shit?'

'Wear a snorkel?'

'You're impossible. I'm being serious.'

'Forgive me.' He settled down on the couch after having dumped his sneakers with his coat in the kitchen. 'Hell, you used to live that life fairly successfully, didn't you?'

'Sure. As long as I was sneaking around on subways to

345

meet my lover in SoHo, or flying off to meet Luke in Chicago. Besides, I had to do all that dumb shit for the column.'

'Bullshit. You didn't just "have to," you wanted to, or you wouldn't have done it.'

'That's not necessarily true. But in any case, I don't want to do it anymore, and I won't. Besides, everyone knows I won't play the game now, so why try to pretend? But the point is what do I do now? I don't fit there, and Luke's not here, which leaves me feeling . . . aimless, I guess is the best way to put it. Any suggestions?'

'Yeah. Make me a cup of hot chocolate. Then I'll solve all your problems.'

'That's a deal. Want some brandy in it?'

'Nope. I'll take it straight, thanks.' He didn't want to give her an excuse to start drinking. She didn't need much of an excuse, but he thought she might balk at drinking alone. He was right.

'You're not much fun, but in that case I'll have mine straight too. I think I've been drinking too much lately.'

'No kidding. When did you figure that out? After A.A. called you with a free subscription, or before?'

'Don't be nasty.'

'What do you want me to do? Keep my mouth shut till you wind up with cirrhosis?'

'That sounds fine.'

'Jesus, Kezia, that's not even funny. You really piss me off!' And he looked it as she vanished into the kitchen.

She appeared a few minutes later with two steaming mugs of hot chocolate. 'And how was your day?'

'Stinking, thanks. I had a minor altercation with my board of directors. At least they thought it was minor. I almost quit.'

'You did? How come?'

'The usual garbage. Allotment of funds. I got so annoyed I told them I was taking two days off.'

'That must have pleased them. What are you going to do with the two days?'

346

'Fly out to San Francisco with you to see Luke. When are you going?'

'Good lord, Alejandro! Can you do that?' She was delighted, but he had just spent so much money coming out with them to the hearing.

'Sure I can do it. But not in first-class. Are you willing to sit with the peasants at the back of the bus?'

'I think I can stand it. Do you play backgammon? I can bring my small set.'

'How about poker?'

'You're on. To tell you the truth, I'm glad you're coming. . . . I was thinking about it this morning, and I think I'm scared to death of this trip.'

'Why?' That surprised him.

'San Quentin. It sounds so awful. And I've never been any place like it.'

'It's not exactly a joy ride, but it's not a dungeon either. You'll be okay.' But just to be sure, he was going. Luke had urgently requested that he come out with her. And Alejandro knew he wouldn't ask unless there was a damn good reason. Something was happening.

'Listen, are you coming out just because you figured I was afraid to do it alone?' The idea amazed her.

'Don't be so egocentric. He happens to be my friend too.' She blushed faintly and he tugged at a lock of the rumpled black hair. 'Besides, after what I've seen you come through, I have the feeling that if they were firing M-16's over your head, you'd just tighten your earrings, put on your gloves, and march right on in.'

'Am I as bad as all that?'

'Not bad, baby - impressive. Goddamn impressive. And by the way, while we're out there I want to interview for a job at a therapeutic community I mentioned to you once.'

'You're serious about looking for a new job?' So much was changing.

'I don't know yet. But it's worth looking into.'

'Well, whatever your reasons, I'm glad we're going out

there together. And Luke will be so pleased to see you. What a super surprise for him!'

'When are we going?'

'When can you get away from the centre?'

'Pretty much any time I want.'

'How about tomorrow night? I got a letter from Luke this morning that said I'll be cleared in two days. So tomorrow night would be just right, for me anyway. How about you?'

'Sounds perfect.'

They settled back with their hot chocolate, and snuggled into the couch, telling old stories and talking about Luke. She laughed again as she hadn't in weeks, and at midnight she lured him into almost an hour of dice.

'You know what I can't handle anymore?'

'Yeah, dice. Lady, you play lousy.' But she loved it, and he was having a good time too.

'No, shut up. I'm being serious.'

'Excuse me.'

'Really, I am. The thing that I can't handle is the pressure of pretence, and that whole way of life I grew up with is pretence to me now. I can't talk openly about Luke without creating a scandal. I can't show anyone that I hurt. I can't even be me. I have to be The Honourable Kezia Saint Martin.'

'Maybe that's because you happen to be the Honourable Kezia Saint Martin. Ever think of that?' He rolled the dice in his hands.

'Yes, but I'm not "that" Kezia Saint Martin. Not anymore. I'm me. And I keep worrying, thinking I'm going to blurt it all out or call someone an asshole, or throw a quiche Lorraine in somebody's face.'

'Sounds like fun. Why not try it?' She roared with laughter as they sat in front of the fire, her legs tucked under her.

'Someday I might just try it. But that, my friend, would be the ultimate grand finale. Can't you see it in

Time magazine? "Kezia Saint Martin flipped out at a party on Friday and threw a lemon meringue pie that sprayed five guests. The victims of Miss Saint Martin's temporary insanity were the Countess von . . ." et cetera, et cetera, et cetera.'

'Do they serve lemon meringue pies at those parties?' He looked faintly curious.

'No. I guess I'd have to settle for baked Alaska.'

He chuckled at the thought, and reached out and stroked her now dry hair. It was warm from the fire.

'Kezia, love, you've got to gain back some weight.'

'Yeah. I know.' They shared a small tender smile, and then with a gleam in his eyes, he rolled the dice in his hands, blew on them and threw, closing both eyes.

'Snake eyes, or bust!'

Kezia chuckled at the results, pinched his nose, and whispered in his ear, 'In that case, Mr. Vidal, it's bust. Hey, you asshole, open your eyes.' But instead he reached out unexpectedly and swept an arm around her waist. 'What are you doing, you nut?' His face was barely a breath away from hers, and she thought it was funny. It wasn't funny to him.

'What am I doing? Making an ass of myself of course.' He opened both eyes and made a clown's face, checked out the dice and shrugged, but there was a hint of pain in his eyes. How dense could she be? But it was, perhaps, for the best.

He got to his feet and stretched slowly in front of the fire, watching the flames lick at the logs. He had his back to the still chuckling Kezia. 'You know what, little one? You're right. I can't stand the pressure of pretence anymore either.'

'It's a bitch, isn't it?' She was sympathetic as she munched on a cookie. It was the first time in weeks that she hadn't had a drink all evening.

'Yeah . . . it's a bitch. "The pressure of pretence," how well you put it.' She thought he was referring to his job.

'I'm an expert on the subject.' But she wasn't in the

mood to be serious. Not with him; they had had too happy an evening. 'What brought that into your mind?' The words were garbled in cookie crumbs. She looked up but his back was still turned to her.

'Nothing. Just a thought.'

CHAPTER XXXI

They travelled in coach and the flight was dull. The movie was one Kezia had already seen with Luke, and Alejandro had brought some professional journals to read. They spoke during the meal, but the rest of the time he left her alone. He knew how tense she was, and this time he was not amused when she brought out the flask.

'Kezia, I don't think you should.'

'Why not?' She looked almost hurt.

'Drink what they serve you, that ought to be enough.' He wasn't preaching, but he sounded very firm. The tone of his voice embarrassed her more than his words, and she put it away. When the drinks came around, she ordered one scotch, and turned down the second.

'Satisfied?'

'It's not my life, sister. It's yours.' He went back to his reading, and she to her own thoughts. He was an odd man at times. Independent, lost in his own doings, and then at other times he took such pains with her. She more than suspected that he was making the trip mostly for her, to be sure she would be all right, and he could have lost his job for that.

They had made reservations at the Ritz, and she felt a thrill of excitement ripple through her as they drove towards the city. The skyline began to show as they cleared the last bend, and then suddenly there it was. The new modern cathedral on Gough, the brown licorice

350

silhouette of the Bank of America building, and the lick of fog rolling in from the bay. She realized now how she had longed to see it again. The bay, and the Golden Gate Bridge, with Sausalito and Belvedere and Tiburon twinkling like a forest of Christmas trees at night, if there wasn't too much fog. And if there was, she would close her eyes, breathe deeply of the fresh sea air, and listen to the lonely bleating of the fog horns. She knew that when she heard them again, Lucas would be listening to them too.

Alejandro watched her as they drove, and it touched him to see her like that. Excited, tense, combing the city with her eyes as though looking for something precious she had left there.

'You love this town too, don't you, Kezia?'

'Yes, I do.' She sat back and looked at it with pleasure, as though she had built it herself.

'Because Luke brought you here?'

'Partly. But it's something else too. Just the town, I guess. It's so damnably pretty.' He smiled and looked over at her.

'Damnably, huh?'

'Okay, okay, so make fun of me. All I know is that I'm happy here.' Despite the brutal things that had happened there, she loved it. It had something no other city she knew had. Her thoughts drifted back to Luke again, and she couldn't suppress a smile. 'You know, it's incredible, I've come three thousand miles to see him for an hour.'

'And something tells me you'd have come six thousand miles if you'd had to.'

'Maybe even twelve.'

'Even twelve? Are you sure?' He was teasing again, and she liked it. He was an easy companion.

'Alejandro, you're a pest. But a nice pest.'

'I love you too.'

It was one in the morning in San Francisco, and four in the morning for them, but neither of them was sleepy.

'Want to go out for a drink, Alejandro?'

'No, I'd rather go for a ride.'

'The temperance society at my beck and call. How delightful.' She set her mouth primly and he laughed. 'Mind your own business. After we drop off the stuff at the hotel, let's go down to the bay.' They had rented a car at the airport and Alejandro was driving.

'At your service, madam. Isn't that what you're used to?'

'Yes and no. But one thing's for sure. I'm not used to remarkable friends like you. You really are amazing.' Her voice had grown very soft. 'I don't think anyone's ever done as much for me as you have. Not even Edward. He used to watch over me, but we were never this at ease with each other. I love him, but very differently. He always expected so much of me.'

'Like what?'

'Oh ... to be everything I was born to, and more, I suppose.'

'And you are.'

'No, not really. The computer must have blended it all differently in me. Some of the pieces don't fit, by his standards.'

'You miss the point. It's your head that matters, your soul, your heart.'

'No, love. You miss the point. It's the parties you go to, the clothes you wear, which committees you belong to.'

'You're crazy.'

'Not anymore. But I used to be.' She was suddenly serious, but the moment fled as they arrived at the Ritz. Ernestine, wearing a green plaid flannel bathrobe, checked them in, looking faintly disapproving to see Kezia with Alejandro, and not Luke. But their separate rooms at opposite ends of the hall seemed to appease her. She padded back to bed, and they went back outside to the car.

'To the bay!' He was as excited as she.

'Thank you, Jeeves.'

'Certainly, madam.' They giggled together, and let the

352

car bump over the hills on Divisadero Street. It felt like a roller coaster as the sharp swoops and drops lifted them off the seat.

'Want to stop for a taco?'

She smiled in answer and nodded her head. 'Me, I get turned on by the bay. You, it's the tacos. Welcome home.'

'And not a pizza in sight.'

'Don't they have pizza out here?'

He made a face in response. 'Yes, but we keep them under control. Not like New York. One of these days, a mad onslaught of crazed pizzas will take over the town.' He made fierce monster faces and she laughed.

'You're a nut. Good heavens, look at that car!' They rolled into a drive-in food place on Lombard, and waiting at the window was a hot rod with the back all jacked up. 'You'd think they'd fall on their faces.'

'Of course not. What a beauty ... vrooommm ... rooom!' He made the appropriate sounds and grinned broadly. 'Haven't you ever seen one like that?'

'Not that I can remember – and I daresay I'd remember – except maybe in a movie. What a horror!'

'Horror? It's a beauty! Wash your mouth out with soap!'

She was laughing and shaking her head. 'Don't tell me you had one like that! I'd be shocked!'

'Well, I did. A lowrider special. My first car. After that I screwed up my image and got a secondhand VW. Life was never the same.'

'It sounds tragic.'

'It was. Did you have a car as a kid?' She shook her head, and his eyes opened wide in disbelief. 'You didn't? Christ, all kids in California have cars by the time they're sixteen. I bet you're lying. I'll bet you had a Rolls. Come on, tell the truth!' She giggled, furiously shaking her head, as they drove up to the window to order their tacos.

'I'll have you know, Mr. Vidal, that I did not have a Rolls! I borrowed a crumbling old Fiat when I stayed in Paris, and that was it. I've never owned a car in my life.'

353

'What a disgrace. But your family had one, right?' She nodded. 'Aha! And it was . . .' He waited.

'Oh, just a car. You know, four wheels, four doors, steering column, the usual stuff.'

'You're telling me it was a Rolls?'

'It was not.' She grinned at him broadly and handed him the tacos that had just appeared at the window. 'It was a Bentley. But my aunt has a Rolls, if that makes you feel any better.'

'Much. Now hand over those tacos. You may have come three thousand miles to see your old man. I came for the tacos. A Bentley . . . Jesus.' He took a bite of his taco and sighed rapturously. Kezia leaned back in her seat and began to unwind. It was comfortable being with him; she didn't have to pretend. She could just be herself.

'You know something funny, Alejandro?'

'Yeah. You.' He was into his third taco.

'No, I'm being serious.'

'Yeah? How come?'

'Oh, for chrissakes, put a taco in you and you get all full of yourself.'

'No, I get gas.'

'Alejandro!'

'Well, I do. Don't you ever get gas? Or is that bred out of you?'

She blushed as she laughed. 'I refuse to answer that question on the grounds that . . .'

'I'll bet you fart in bed.'

'Alejandro, you're awful. That's a highly unsuitable remark.'

Pobrecita.' He was a ceaseless tease when he was in a good mood, but she liked it. He had been so quiet on the plane, but now the atmosphere was festive again.

'What I was trying to tell you, Mr. Vidal, before you got outrageous . . .'

'Outrageous? Fancy that!' He had switched from tacos to root beer and took a long swallow.

'What I'm trying to tell you . . .' she lowered her voice,

354

'is that the weird thing is, I have really come to need you. Isn't that strange? I mean, I'd be totally lost without you. It's so nice knowing you're around.'

He was silent, with a distant look in his eyes. 'Yeah. I feel that way too,' he said, finally. 'It feels funny when I don't see you for a couple of days. I like knowing you're okay.'

'It's nice to know that you care. I guess that's what I feel, and it feels good. And I worry that maybe someone's killed you on the subway when you don't call.'

'You know, that's one of the things I like best about you.'

'What?'

'Your unfailing optimism. Your faith in the human race ... killed on the subway. ... Asshole. Why would I get killed on the subway?'

'Everyone else does. Why shouldn't you?'

'Gee. Terrific. You know what I think, Kezia?'

'What?'

'That you fart in bed.'

'Oh, so we're back on that again, are we? Alejandro, you're a shit. And a rude, outrageous shit at that! Now drive me to the bay. And what's more I do *not* fart in bed!'

'You do!'

'I don't!'

'You do!'

'Ask Luke!'

'I will!'

'You dare!'

'Aha! Then he'd tell me the truth, wouldn't he! You do!'

'I do not! Damn you!'

The debate continued as he backed out of the drive-in, and finally dissolved in gales of their laughter. They chuckled and giggled and teased the remaining few blocks to the bay, and then they fell silent. It lay stretched before them like a bolt of darkest blue velvet, and there was a veil of fog high overhead, not low enough to obstruct the view from across the bay, but just enough so that it sat suspended on the spires of the bridge. A foghorn hooted sadly far off in the distance, and the lights around the rims of the shore sparkled.

'Lady, one of these days I'm going to move back here.'

'No, you won't. You're in love with your work at the centre in Harlem.'

'That's what you think. That bullshit is getting to be more than I want to have to deal with every day. People just don't get as crazy out here. You never know, maybe that interview I have lined up out here will pan out.'

'And then what?'

'We'll see.'

She nodded pensively, unnerved by the idea that he might leave New York. But it was probably just talk, to let off some steam. She decided to ignore what he had said. It was safer that way.

'When I see it like this, I want to stop time and stay in this moment forever.'

'Crazy girl. Don't we all wish we could do that. Did you ever come down here at dawn?' She shook her head. 'It's much better then. This city is like a beautiful woman. It changes, it has moods, it gets all grey and baggy-eyed, and then turns beautiful and you fall in love with her all over again.'

'Alejandro, who do you love?' She hadn't thought of that since the day they'd shared hot chocolate in Yorkville. He was almost always alone, or with her.

'That's a strange question.'

'No, it's not. Isn't there someone? Even an old flame from the past?'

'No, none of those. Oh, I don't know, Kezia. I love a lot of people. Some of the kids I work with, you, Luke, other friends, my family. A whole bunch of people.'

'And too many. It's so safe to love lots of people. It's a lot harder to love just one. I never did . . . until Luke. He taught me so much about that. He isn't afraid of that the

356

way I was ... and maybe you are. Isn't there even one woman you love, as a woman? Or maybe a few?' She had no right to ask, and she knew it, but she wanted to know.

'No. Not lately. Maybe one of these days.'

'You ought to give it some thought. Maybe you'll meet someone out here sometime.' But deep in her heart, she hoped he wouldn't. He deserved the best sort of woman there was, one who could give him back all that he gave. He deserved that, because he gave so much. But secretly, she knew that she hoped he wouldn't find her just yet. She wasn't ready to lose him. Things were so lovely just as they were. And if he had someone, she would lose him; it would be inevitable.

'What are you thinking about, little one? You look so sad.' He thought he knew why, but he didn't.

'Just silly stuff drifting through my head. Nothing much.'

'Don't worry so much. You'll see him tomorrow.'

She only smiled in response.

CHAPTER XXXII

They saw it as they rounded a bend on the freeway. San Quentin. Across a body of water, a finger of the bay that had poked its way inland, it stood at the water's edge, looking ugly and raw. Kezia kept it in view the rest of the way, until finally it vanished again as they left the freeway and followed an old country road around a series of bends.

The mammoth fortress that was San Quentin took her breath away when they saw it again. It seemed to stand with its body jutting into her face, like a giant bully or an evil creature in a hideous dream. One felt instantly dwarfed beneath the turrets and towers, the endless walls that soared upwards, dotted only here and there by tiny windows. It was buillt like a dungeon, and was the colour of rancid mustard. It was not only fearsome, but it reeked of anger and terror, loneliness, sorrow, loss. Tall metal fences topped with barbed wire surrounded the encampment, and in all possible directions stood gun towers manned by machine-gun-toting guards. Guards patrolled the entrance, and people emerged wearing sad faces, some drying their eyes with bits of handkerchief or tissue. It was a place one could never forget. It even boasted a long dry moat, with still active drawbridges to the gun towers that kept the guards safe from potential 'attack.'

As she looked at the place, Kezia wondered how they could be so fearful. Who could possibly get free of that place? Yet now and then people did. And seeing the place made her suddenly know why they'd try anything, even death, to escape. It made her understand why Luke had done what he had to help the men he called his brothers. Prisoners of places like that had to be remembered by someone. She was only sorry it had been Luke.

She also saw a row of tidy houses with flowers beds out front. The houses stood inside the barbed wire fences, in the shadow of the gun towers, at the feet of the prison. And she guessed, accurately, that they were the houses of guards, living there with their wives and their children. The thought made her shudder. It would be like living in a graveyard.

The parking lot was rutted with potholes and strewn with litter. There were only two parking spaces left when they got there, and a long line of people snaked past the guardhouse at the main gate. It took them two and a half hours to reach the head of the line, where they were superficially searched and then herded on to the next gate, to have their pockets ransacked again.

The gun tower stood watchfully over them as they walked into the main building to sit with the rest of the visitors in a smoke-filled, overheated waiting room that looked like a train station. There were no sounds of

358

laughter in that room, no whispered snatches of conversation, only the occasional clinking of coins in the coffee
machine, the whoosh of the water fountain or the brief
spurt of a match. Each visitor hugged to himself his own
fears and lonely thoughts.

Kezia's mind was filled with Luke. She and Alejandro
hadn't spoken since they entered the building. There was
nothing to say. Like the others, they were preoccupied
with the business of waiting. Another two hours on those
benches . . . and it had been so long since she'd seen him,
touched his hand, his face, kissed him, held him, or been
held the way only Luke knew how to hold her. Kisses are
different when they come from such a great height, or
that's how it had seemed. Everything was different. He
was a man she could look up to, in myriad ways. The first
man she had looked up to.

In all, she and Alejandro waited almost five hours, and
it felt like a dream when a voice on the intercom
squawked out his name.

'Visit for Johns . . . Lucas Johns. . . .' She sprang to
her feet and ran to the door of the room where they
would visit. Luke was already there, filling the doorway, a
quiet smile on his face. He stood in a long, barren grey
room, whose only decor was a clock. There were long
refectory tables with inmates on one side and visitors on
the other, while guards wandered and patrolled, their
guns displayed prominently. One could kiss hello and
goodbye, and hold hands during the visit. That was all.
The whole scene had an eerie unreality to it, as if this
couldn't exist, not for them. Luke lived on Park Avenue
with her, he ate with a fork and a knife, he told jokes, he
kissed her on the back of the neck. He didn't belong here.
It didn't make sense. The other faces around them looked
ragged and fierce, angry and tired and worn. But now so
did Luke. Something had changed. As she walked into his
arms, she felt a wave of claustrophobic terror seize her
throat . . . they were lost in the bowels of that tomb . . .
but once in Luke's arms, she was safe. And the rest

359

seemed to fade. She was oblivious of all but his eyes. She completely forgot Alejandro beside her.

Luke swept her up in his arms and the force of his embrace flushed the air from her chest in one breath. He held her aloft for a moment, not releasing his grip, and then gently set her down, hungrily seeking her lips once again. There was a quiet desperation about him, and his arms felt thinner. She had felt bones in his shoulders where weeks before there had been so much flesh. He was wearing blue jeans and a workshirt, and coarse shoes that looked too small for his feet. They had shipped the Guccis and everything else back to New York. Kezia had been there when the package arrived, everything crumpled, and his shirt badly torn. It gave you an idea of how it had come off his back. Not with a valet, but at the point of a gun. At the time she had cried, but now there were no tears. She was too glad to see him. Only Alejandro had tears in his eyes as he watched them, a radiant smile sweeping over her face, hiding the panic, and a look of intense need in the eyes of his friend. After a moment, Luke's gaze swept over her head, and acknowledged Alejandro. It was a look of gratitude Alejandro didn't remember seeing before. Like Kezia, he saw that something was different, and he remembered the urgent plea in Luke's letters to come out with Kezia. Alejandro knew something was coming, but he didn't know what.

Luke led Kezia by the hand to one of the long refectory tables, and went around to his side to sit down, while Alejandro took another chair next to her. She smiled even more as she watched Luke take his seat.

'Jesus, it's so good to just watch you walk. Oh, darling, how I've missed you.' Luke smiled quietly at her and gently touched her face with his work-roughened hand. The callouses had come back quickly.

'I love you, Lucas.' She said the words carefully, like three separate gifts she had wrapped for him, and his eyes shone strangely.

'I love you too, babe. Do me a favour?'

360

'What?'

'Take your hair down for me.' She smiled and quickly pulled out the pins. There was so little pleasure she could give him, each minute gesture suddenly meant so much more. 'There, that's better.' He stroked the silky softness of her hair, and looked like a man running his hands through diamonds or gold. 'Oh Mama, how I love you.'

'Are you all right?'

'Can't you tell?'

'I'm not sure.' But Alejandro could. He could tell a lot more than either of them, each was so blinded by what he wanted to see. 'I guess you look okay, but you've gotten thin.'

'Look who's talking. You look like shit.' But his eyes said she looked better than that. 'I thought you told me you were going to take care of her, Al.' He looked from one to the other, and at last there was a hint of long-forgotten laughter back in his eyes. He looked almost like Lucas again.

'Listen, man, do you know how hard this woman is to push around?'

'You're telling me!' The two men laughed and exchanged an old familiar smile. And Luke's eyes lit up as he looked at Kezia again. She held so tightly to his hands that her fingers ached until they were numb.

It was an odd visit, full of conflicting vibrations. Luke seemed to have a passionate and hungry need for Kezia, which was amply mutual. Yet, there was a rein on him somewhere. She sensed it, and didn't know what it was. A hesitation, a withdrawal, and then he would say something and she would feel the floodgates open again.

Suddenly the hour was over. The guard signalled, and Luke stood up quickly and led her back to the front of the room for their one regulation farewell kiss.

'Darling, I'll be back as soon as they'll let me.' She was thinking of staying out for the week, and coming back to see him again. But right now she was nervous at the sight of the guard, and Alejandro seemed to edge closer. It was

361

all happening too fast. She wanted more time with Lucas
. . . the moments had flown by.

'Mama . . .' Luke's eyes seemed to devour every inch of
her face. 'You won't be coming back here.'

'Are they transferring you?'

He shook his head. 'No. But you can't come back
anymore.'

'That's ridiculous. I . . . aren't the papers in order?'
She was suddenly terrified. She had to come back again.
She needed to see him. They had no right to do this.

'The papers are in order. For today. But I'm taking
you off my visiting list tonight.' His voice was so low she
could barely hear it. But Alejandro could, and he knew
what Lucas was doing. Now he understood why Luke had
wanted him to come out.

'Are you mad? Why are you taking me off your list?'
Hot tears burned her eyes and she clung to his hands. She
didn't understand. She hadn't done anything wrong. And
she loved him.

'Because you don't belong here. And this is no life for
you. Baby, you've learned a lot in the last few months,
and done a lot of things you'd never have done if you
hadn't met me. Some of it was good for you, but this
isn't. I know what this does, what it'll do to you. By the
time I get out, you'd be burnt out. Look at you now, thin,
nervous . . . you're a wreck. Go back to what you have to
do. And do it right.'

'Lucas, how can you do this?' The tears began to roll
down her face.

'Because I have to . . . because I love you . . . now be a
good girl, and go.'

'No, I won't. And I'll come back. . . . oh Lucas! Please!'
Luke's eyes sought Alejandro's over her head and there
was a barely perceptible nod. Luke bent quickly to kiss
her, squeezed her shoulders, and then quickly turned and
took a step towards the guard.

'Lucas! No!' She reached out her arms, ready to cling to
him, and he turned back to her with a face carved in stone.

362

'Stop it, Kezia. Don't forget who you are.'

'I'm nothing without you.' She stepped towards him and looked into his eyes.

'That's where you're wrong. You're Kezia Saint Martin, and you know who she is now. Treat her well.' And then with a nod at the guard, he was gone. An iron door swallowed the man she had loved. He never turned back for a last look or another goodbye. He had said nothing to Alejandro as he left. He hadn't had to. The short nod at the end said it all. He was committing her into his care. He would know that she was safe and that was all he could do. It was all he had left to give.

Kezia stood in the visiting area, numb, unaware of the eyes that turned towards her. It had been an agonizing scene for the few who had overheard it. It made the men squirm, and their visitors blanch. It could have happened to them, but it didn't. It happened to her.

'I . . . Alej . . . I . . . could . . .' She was disoriented, stunned, lost.

'Come on, love, let's go home.'

'Yes, please.' She seemed to have shrunk in those last shattering minutes. Her face looked frighteningly pale. This time he knew there was no point in asking how she was. It was easily seen.

He walked her out of the building and to the main gate as rapidly as he could. He wanted to get her the hell out of there before she fell apart. He guided her quickly around the potholes in the parking lot and eased her into the car. He was feeling almost as shocked as she. He had known something was wrong, but he had had no idea what Luke had in mind. And he knew what a bitching tough thing it had been to do. Lucas needed her there, her visits, her love, her support. But he knew what it would do to her too. She would have hung on for years, destroying herself, maybe even drinking herself to death while she waited. It couldn't have gone on, and Luke knew it. Kezia had been right way at the beginning. Lucas Johns was a man with incredible guts. Alejandro knew he wouldn't have had the courage to do it. Damn few men would, but damn few men faced what Luke was now facing – survival in a place where his life had been marked. And with who Kezia was, they could have gotten to her first. That had been the worst of Luke's fears, but now that was over. Everything was, for Luke.

'I . . . where are we going?' Kezia looked frighteningly vague as Alejandro started the car.

'Home. We're going home. And everything's going to be fine.' He spoke to her as one would to a very small child, or a very sick one. Right then, she was both.

'I'm going to come back here, you know . . . I'll come back. You know that, don't you? He doesn't really mean it . . . I . . . Alejandro?' There was no fire in her voice, only confusion. Alejandro knew she wouldn't be back. Luke was a man of his word. By that afternoon, her name would be inexorably cancelled from his list. It would leave him no choice. He couldn't have had her reinstated for six months, and by then much would have changed. Six months could change a lot in a life. Six months before, Kezia had met Luke.

She was no longer crying as they drove away. She merely sat very still in the car, and then in the hotel room, where he left her under the careful guard of a maid, while he attended to the interview he could no longer keep his mind on. It was a hell of a day to have to worry about that. He rushed through it, and got back to the Ritz. The maid said she hadn't moved, or even spoken. She had merely sat there, in the same chair she'd been in when he left her, staring at nothing.

With misgivings, he made plane reservations for six o'clock that night and prayed she wouldn't come out of shock until he got her home to her own bed. She was like a child in a trance, and one thing was for sure, he didn't want to be in San Francisco with her when she came out of it. He had to get her back to New York.

She ate nothing on the tray the stewardess put before her, and nodded uncomprehendingly when Alejandro

364

offered her the earphones for music. He settled them on her head, and then watched her remove them dreamily five minutes later. She sang to herself for a little while, and then lapsed back into silence. The stewardesses eyed her strangely, and Alejandro would nod with a smile, hoping no one would make any comments, and praying that no one would recognize her. She looked sufficiently vague and dishevelled by then to be less easily recognized. He could barely handle her as it was, without worrying about the press. They might set her off, and unleash the flood of reality she was holding in abeyance by staying in shock. She looked drugged or drunk, or more than a little crazy. The flight was a nightmare he longed to see end.

Today had been the last straw, and he ached thinking of Lucas. He ached for them both.

'You're home, Kezia. Everything is all right.'

'I'm dirty. I need a bath.' She sat on a chair in her living room, seeming not to understand where she was.

'I'll run a bath for you.'

'Totie will do it.' She smiled at him vaguely.

He bathed her gently, as he had his nieces long ago. She sat staring at the ornate gold dolphin faucets on the white marble wall. It didn't even strike him that it was she he was bathing. He wanted to reach out to her, hold her, but she wasn't even there. She was gone, somewhere, in some distant world hidden from the broken one she had left.

He wrapped her in a towel, she dutifully put on her nightgown, and he led her to bed.

'Now you'll sleep, won't you?'

'Yes. Where's Luke?' The vacant eyes sought his, something in them threatening to break and pour all over the floor.

'He's out.' She wasn't ready to deal with the truth, and neither was he.

'Oh. That's nice.' She smiled vapidly at him, and climbed into bed, clumsily as children do, her feet struggling to find their way into the sheets. He helped her in, and turned off the lights.

'Kezia, do you want Totie?' He knew he'd find her number in Kezia's address book, if he had to. He had been wondering if he should hunt through it for the name of her doctor, but everything seemed under control, for the moment.

'No, thank you. I'll wait for Luke.'

'Okay. Call if you need me. I'll be right here.'

'Thank you, Edward.' It was a shock to realize that she didn't know who he was.

He settled down for a long night's vigil on the couch, waiting for the scream he was sure would come. But it never did. Instead she was up at six, and in the living room in her nightgown and bare feet. She didn't seem to question how she'd gotten home, or who had put her to bed. And he was stunned when he realized how lucid she was. Totally.

'Alejandro, I love you. But I want you to go home.'

'Why?' He didn't trust her alone.

'Because I'm all right now. I woke up at four this morning, and I've been thinking everything over for the last two hours. I understand what happened, and now I have to learn to live with it. And the time to do that is right now. You can't sit here and treat me like an invalid, love; that's not right. You have better things to do with your life.' Her look told him she meant it.

'Not if you need me.'

'I don't . . . not like that . . . look, please. Go away. I need to be by myself.'

'Are you telling me you're throwing me out?' He tried to make it sound light, but it didn't. They were both much too tired for games. She looked worse than he did, and he hadn't slept.

'No. I'm not throwing you out, and you know it. I'm just telling you to go back to what you have to do. And let me do this.'

366

'What are you going to do?' He was frightened.

'Nothing drastic. Don't worry about that.' She sank into one of the velvet chairs and took one of his cigarettes. 'I guess I'm not ballsy enough to commit suicide. I just want to be alone for a while.'

He got up tiredly from the couch, every bone and muscle and fibre and nerve ending aching.

'All right. But I'll call you.'

'No, Alejandro, don't.'

'I've got to. I'll be goddamned if I'm going to sit uptown and wonder if you're dead or alive. If you don't want to talk to me, then tell your answering service how you are and I'll call them.' He turned to face her, with his coat in his hand.

'Why does it matter so much? Because Luke told you to do that?' Her eyes poured into his.

'No. Because I want to. You may not have noticed it yet, but I happen to care what happens to you. You might even say that I love you.'

'I love you too . . . but I want you to leave me alone.'

'If I do, will you call me?'

'Yes, in a while. When I get it together a little. I guess in my heart I knew it was over the day he walked out of the law library at the hearing. That's when it should have been over. But neither of us had the guts to let go. I didn't anyway. And the bitch of it is that I still love him.'

'He loves you too or he wouldn't have done what he did yesterday. I think he did it because he loves you.'

She stood in silence and turned away from him then, so he couldn't see her face. 'Yeah, and all I have to do now is learn to live with it.'

'Well, if you need someone to talk to . . . yell. I'll come running.'

'You always do.' She turned, and a small smile appeared on her lips and then vanished.

He walked to the door with bent shoulders, carrying his valise from their trip, his jacket and coat slung over

367

his back. He turned at the door and knew for only the briefest of seconds how Luke must have felt the day before when he sent her away.

'Take it easy.'

'Yeah. You too.'

He nodded and the door shut gently behind him.

She was drunk day and night for five weeks. Even the cleaning woman stopped coming, and she had sent her secretary away the first week. She was alone with her empty bottles, and plates caked with half-eaten food, wearing the same filthy robe. Only the delivery boy from the liquor store was a regular 'visitor' anymore. He would ring twice and deposit the bag outside her door.

Alejandro didn't call her till the news hit the papers. He had to call then. He had to know how she was. She was drunk when he called, and he told her he'd be right down. He took a cab, terrified she would see the papers before his arrival. But when he got to her door, he saw five weeks of newspapers unread and stacked in the foyer. He was stunned by the condition of what had once been her home. Now it looked like a barnyard . . . bottles . . . filth . . . plates . . . overflowing ashtrays . . . chaos and disorder. And Kezia. She didn't even look like the same girl. She was tear-stained, reeling, and drunk. But she still didn't know.

He sobered her up long enough to tell her. As best he could. But after her fourth cup of coffee, and opening the windows for air, the headlines did it for him, as her eyes scanned the type. She looked up into his face, and he knew that she understood. It couldn't get much worse for her now. It already had.

Luke was dead. Stabbed on the yard, so they said. 'A racial disturbance . . . well-known prison agitator, Lucas Johns. . . .' His sister had claimed the body, and the funeral was being held in Bakersfield the day Kezia was reading the news. It didn't matter. It didn't change anything. Funerals weren't Luke's style. Neither were sisters. He had never even mentioned her to Kezia. The only thing that mattered was that he was gone.

'Do you know when he died, Alejandro?' She still sounded drunk, but he knew she was coherent.

'Does it matter?'

'Yes.'

'No, I don't know exactly. I guess I could find out.'

'I already know. He died in court at the hearing. They killed him. But that day, the day he really died, he died beautiful and proud and strong. He walked into that hearing like a man. What they did to him after that is on their hands.'

'I suppose you're right.' Tears had begun to stream down his face. For what had happened to Luke. For what had happened to her. She was already as dead as Lucas, in her own way. Drunk, dirty, sick, tired, ravaged by memories, and now his death. He remembered that day in the law library, before Lucas walked into the hearing. She was right, he had walked tall and proud, and she had been so sure, so powerful beside him. They had had something he'd never seen before. And now, one was dead, and the other was dying. It made him feel sick. It was all like living a nightmare; his best friend was dead and he was in love with Luke's woman. And there was no way he could tell her now. Not now that Lucas was dead.

'Don't cry, Alejandro.' She smoothed a hand across his cheeks to wipe off the tears, and then ran a hand over his hair. 'Please don't cry.' But he was crying for himself as much as for them, and she couldn't know that. She tilted his face up to hers then, and held him so gently he hardly felt her hands on his shoulders. She looked into his eyes, and then slowly, quietly, she bent over and kissed him, carefully, on the mouth. 'The funny thing is that I love you too. It's really very confusing. In fact, I've loved you for a very long time. Isn't that strange?'

She was still more than a little bit drunk and he didn't know what to say. Maybe she had finally gone crazy from the constant shocks and the grief. Maybe she was mad now. Or perhaps he was. Maybe she hadn't even kissed him . . . maybe he was only dreaming.

'Alejandro, I love you.'

'Kezia?' Her name felt strange on his lips. She was Luke's. And Luke was dead now. But how could Luke be dead? And how could she love them both? It was all so totally crazy. 'Kezia?'

'You heard me. I love you. As in, I'm in love with you.'

He looked at her for what seemed like a very long time, the tears still wet on his cheeks.

'I love you too. I loved you the first day he brought you up to meet me. But I never thought . . . I just . . .'

'I never thought either. It's like all the stuff you read in bad novels. And it's very, very confusing.' She led him to the couch and sat down beside him, leaned her head back and closed her eyes.

'It's just as confusing for me.' He watched her as she sat there.

'Then why don't we leave each other alone for a while?'

'So you can drink yourself to death a little faster?'

His voice was suddenly loud and bitter in the quiet room. She had shown him everything he wanted, but she wanted to destroy it before she would give it to him. What a horrible joke.

'No. So I can think.'

'No drinking?'

'Mind your own business.'

'Then get fucked, lady. Just get fucked!' He was on his feet and shouting. 'I don't need to fall in love with you to watch you fucking die! To watch you commit suicide like some pathetic skid-row alcoholic. If that's what you plan to do with your life, then leave me alone! Oh God, Kezia . . . God damn you!' He pulled her to her feet and shook her until she felt the world shake under her, and she had to protest.

'Stop it! Leave me alone!'

'I love you! Don't you understand that?'

370

'No. I don't understand that. I don't understand anything anymore. I love you too. So fucking what? We get attached to each other and love each other and need each other and then the sky falls in all over again? Who needs it, goddamn you . . . who fucking needs it?'

'I do. I need you.'

'Okay, Alejandro, okay . . . and now will you do me a favour and just leave me alone? Please?' Her voice was trembling and there were tears in her eyes again.

'Okay, baby. It's up to you now.'

The door closed quietly behind him, and five minutes later there was the sound of shattering glass. She had taken the newspaper with the ugly article on the front page and thrown it at the window with such force that it had gone through the glass.

'Fuck you, world! Go to hell!'

CHAPTER XXXIII

At the end of that week, Alejandro saw the same picture as Edward. Edward saw it with pain, Alejandro with shock. Edward had known. *Women's Wear* carried it too. Kezia Saint Martin boarding a plane for Geneva. 'For a rest from the rigours of the social season.' The papers already seemed to have forgotten her association with Lucas. How quickly people forget.

The papers said she was planning to go skiing, but it didn't say where, and her hat was pulled so low over her face that Alejandro would never have known her if he hadn't seen the name. As he looked at the picture, he marvelled again at the absence of reporters on their last trip to San Francisco and back. In the state she'd been in, that would really have made news.

He sat for a long time in the small office with the paint

371

peeling off the walls, looking at the picture, at the hat pulled low over the face. At the word, Geneva. And what now? When would he hear from her again? He still remembered the kiss of the last morning he'd seen her, only a few days ago. And now she was gone. He felt heavy, as though he were nailed to the chair, glued to the floor, part of the building and crumbling like the rest of it. Everything was going to pot in his life. His job stank, he hated the city, his best friend was dead, and he was in love with a girl he knew he could never have. Even if Luke had wanted it that way, as Alejandro suspected he might have. ... There was something about Luke's insistent summons to come out with Kezia that last time. Luke knew she'd need help. But it was never meant to be. He knew that, and Kezia must know it too. It was all very crazy, and he had to work out his own life. But he kept staring at the word, hating it. Geneva.

'Someone here to see you, Alejandro.' He looked up to see one of the kids poke his head in the door.

'Yeah? Who?'

'Perini's probation officer, I think.'

'Tell him to get fucked.'

'For real?' The boy looked thrilled.

'No, not for real, asshole. Give me five minutes, and send him in.'

'What'll I do with him for five minutes?'

'I don't know, dammit. Do whatever you want to do. Beat him up, roll him, kick him down the stairs. Give him coffee ... I don't give a shit what you do.' Alejandro threw the newspaper off his desk and into the garbage.

'Okay, man. Okay. Don't get all pissed off.' He had never seen Alejandro like that before. It was scary.

The hotel in Villars-sur-Ollon suited her purposes perfectly, high up in the mountains and in a town that was crawling with schools. There were virtually no tourists there, except a few visiting parents. She stayed in a huge hotel that was mostly uninhabited, and took tea with seven old ladies to the sound of violins and a cello. She went for long walks, drank a lot of hot chocolate, went to bed early, and read. Only Simpson and Edward knew where she was, and she had told them both to leave her alone. She didn't plan to write until further notice, and even Edward had respected her wishes. He sent her weekly papers to keep her abreast of her financial news, and expected no response, which was just as well, because he got none. It was the middle of April before she was ready to leave.

She took the train to Milan, spent a night, and then went on to Florence. She mingled with the early spring tourists, toured the museums, wandered in and out of shops, walked along the Arno, and tried not to think. She did the same in Rome, and by then it was easier. It was May. The sun was warm, the people were lively, the street musicians were funny, and she ran into a few friends. She had dinner with them, and found that the urge to jump up and scream had finally left her. Little by little, she was healing.

In the early weeks of June, she rented a Fiat and drove north to Umbria, and to Spoleto where later in the summer the music festival would be held. And then she drove through the Alps, and eventually into France.

She danced in St. Tropez in July, and gambled in Monte Carlo, boarded the yacht of friends in St. Jean-Cap Ferrat for a weekend, and bought new Gucci luggage in Cannes. She began to write again when she drove up through Provence, and spent three weeks lost in a tiny hotel, where the terrine was superb, better than any pâté she had eaten.

Luke's book reached her there, hesitantly sent to her by Simpson, with the reviews. She opened the package unsuspectingly one morning, bathed in sunshine as she stood barefoot in her nightgown on the little balcony outside her room. She could see hills and fields beyond, and for almost an hour she simply sat cross-legged on the balcony floor with the book in her lap, holding it, running

373

her fingers over the cover, but unable to open it. The jacket design was good, and there was a marvellous photograph of him on the back. It had been taken before she had met him, but she had a copy of the same photo on her desk in New York. He was walking down a street in Chicago, wearing a white turtleneck sweater, his dark hair blown by the wind, his raincoat slung over his shoulder. One eyebrow raised, he was looking sarcastically into the camera with the beginnings of a smile. She had squeezed the photograph out of him the first time she had seen it.

'What the hell do you want that for?'

'You look so sexy in it, Luke.'

'Jesus. You nut. I hope my readers don't think so.'

'Why not?' She looked up, a little surprised, and he had kissed her.

'Because I'm supposed to look brilliant, not sexy, silly lady.'

'Well, you happen to look both. Can I have it?' He had waved an embarrassed hand at her, and gone off to answer the phone. But she had taken the photograph, and framed it in silver. It was a glimpse of the real Luke, and she was glad it was on the book jacket. People should see him as he was . . . people should . . .

She had looked up after what seemed like hours, the book still cradled in her lap, unfelt tears rolling steadily down her face, misting the view. But she had been looking into the past, not at the fields in the distance.

'Well, babe, here we are.' She spoke aloud and smiled through her tears, using the hem of her nightgown to wipe her face. She could almost see Lucas smiling at her. It didn't matter where she went anymore, she carried him with her in a warm, tender way. Not in the agonizing way that she had; now she could smile at him. Now he was with her, forever. In New York, in Switzerland, in France. He was a part of her now. A comfortable part.

She looked far into the fields with a soft shrug and leaned back against the legs of a chair, still holding the book in her hands. A voice seemed to tell her to open it, but she couldn't, and then as she watched the face in the photograph yet again, almost expecting him to move along that long-forgotten street in Chicago, it was as though she could see his face growing stern, his head shaking in teasing annoyance.

'Come on, Mama, open it, dammit!'

She did, gingerly, carefully, not wanting to breathe or to look or to see. She had known, known it when she touched the book, but seeing it would be different. She wondered if she could bear it, but she had to. Now she wanted to see, and she knew he had wanted her to. He had never told her, but now it was as though she had always known. The book was dedicated to her.

Fresh tears ran down her face as she read it, but they were not tears of grief. Tears of tenderness, of gratitude, of laughter, of loving. Those were the treasures he had given her, not sorrow. Luke had never been a man to tolerate sorrow. He had been too alive to taste even a whisper of death. And sorrow is death.

To Kezia, who stands by my side wherever I go. My equal, my solace, my friend. Brave lady, you are the bright light in a place I have long sought to find, and now at last we're both home. May you be proud of this book, for now it is the best I can give you, with thanks and my love.

L.J.

'. . . and now at last we're both home.' It was true, and it was late August by then, and she had one final test. Marbella. And Hilary.

'My God, darling, you look divine! So brown and healthy! Where on earth have you been?'

'Here and there.' She laughed and brushed her hair from her eyes. It was longer now, and the harsh angularity of her face had melted again. There were small

375

lines on either side of her eyes, from the sun, or whatever, but she looked well. Very well.

'How long can you stay? Your cable didn't even give me a hint, naughty child!'

Yes, she was back in that old familiar world. Dear, darling Hilary. But it amused her to be called a naughty child. Hell, why not? Her birthday had come and gone in late June. She was thirty now.

'I'll be here for a few days, Aunt Hil, if you have room.'

'That's all? But darling, how awful, and of course I have room, how absurd.' She was currently having room for at least fourteen others, not to mention the staff. 'Why don't you think about staying longer?'

'I've got to get back.' She accepted an iced tea from the butler. They stood near the tennis courts where the other guests played.

'Get back to where? My, Jonathan has improved his serve, hasn't he?'

'Undoubtedly.'

'Of course, how silly of me. You don't know him. Perfectly beautiful man.'

He looked like a carbon copy of Whitney. It made Kezia smile.

'So where is it you're going back to?' Hilary returned her attention to Kezia, over a well-chilled martini.

'New York.'

'At this time of year? Darling, you're mad!'

'Maybe so, but I've been away for almost five months.'

'Then another month can't possibly hurt.'

'I'm going back to do some work.'

'Work? What sort of work? Charity? But no one's in town in the summer for heaven's sake. Besides, you don't work, do you?' For a moment Hilary looked slightly confused. Kezia nodded.

'Yes, I do. Writing.'

'Writing? What on earth for?' She was quite bemused, and Kezia was trying hard not to laugh. Poor Aunt Hil.

'I guess I write because I enjoy it. Very much, as a matter of fact.'

'Is this something new?'

'No, not really.'

'Can you write? Decently, I mean.' But this time Kezia couldn't help it; she laughed.

'I don't know. I certainly try to. I used to write the Martin Hallam column. But that wasn't my best work.' Kezia wore a mischievous grin. Hilary gaped.

'You what? Don't be insane! You ... Good God, Kezia, how could you!'

'It amused me. And when I had enough of it, I retired. And don't look so upset, I never said anything mean about you.'

'No, but you ... I ... Kezia, you really amaze me.' She relieved the butler of another martini and stared at her niece. The girl was really quite strange. Always had been, and now this. 'In any case, I think you're a fool to go back in August.' Hilary had not yet recovered. 'And that column doesn't run anymore.' Kezia giggled; it was as though Hilary were trying to trap her into admitting that she hadn't actually written it. But that was wishful thinking.

'I know, but I'm going back to discuss the terms on a book.'

'A book based on gossip?' Hilary blanched.

'Of course not. It's sort of a political theme. It's really too long to go into.'

'I see. Well, I'd be thrilled if you wanted to stay ... as long as you promise not to write naughty things about all my guests.' She tittered sweetly, as it occurred to her that this might make for some very amusing gossip of her own. 'Did you know my niece used to be Martin Hallam, dear?'

'Don't worry, Aunt Hil, I don't write that kind of thing anymore.'

'What a pity.' Her third martini had softened the blow. Kezia watched her as she accepted her second iced tea. 'Have you seen Edward yet?'

'No. Is he here?'

'You didn't know?'

'No, I didn't.'

'You have been off the beaten track, haven't you?
Where did you say you'd been all this time?' Hilary was
watching Jonathan's serve again.

'Ethiopia, Tanzania. The jungle. Heaven. Hell. The
usual spots.'

'How nice, darling ... how really very nice. See
anyone we know?' But she was too engrossed in Jonathan's game to listen or care. 'Come darling, I'll introduce you to Jonathan.' But Edward appeared on the
scene before Hilary could sweep her away. He greeted
Kezia with warmth, but also with caution.

'I never thought I'd see you here!' It was an odd
greeting after so much and so long.

'I never thought you would either.' She laughed and
gave him a hug that reminded him of old times.

'How are you, really?'

'How do I look?'

'Just the way I'd want to see you. Tanned, healthy,
and relaxed.' And also sober. That was a relief.

'And that's how I am. It's been a long bunch of
months.'

'Yes, I know.' He knew that he would never know the
full story, but he was certain it had come close to
destroying her. Much too close. 'You're staying for a
while?'

'Just a few days. Then I have to go back. Simpson is in
the midst of making a deal for me, for a book.'

'How perfectly marvellous!'

'That's how I feel.' She smiled happily, and hooked her
arm in his, as he prepared to lead her away for a walk.

'Come. Tell me about it. Let's go sit down under the
trees over there.' He removed two more iced teas from a
silver tray and headed for a gazebo far from the courts.
They had a lot to catch up on, and for the first time in
years she seemed willing to talk. He had missed her very

378

badly, but the time had done him good as well. He had realized at last what she represented in his life, and what she could never be. He too had made peace with himself and the people he dreamed of, as much as he ever would. Most of all he had accepted what seemed to be his role. Acceptance. Understanding. As life's trains passed him by. The last lonely gentleman standing on the platform.

Kezia was almost sorry to leave Marbella, for the first time in her life. She had come to terms with a thousand ghosts in the months she'd spent alone, not only Luke's ghost, but others. She was even free of the ghost of her mother. At last. And now she had to go home.

It was funny, on the plane home from Spain she remembered something Alejandro had said a long time ago. 'That whole life is a part of you, Kezia. You can't deny it.' Though she didn't want to live it anymore, she no longer needed to exorcise it either. She was free.

It was a pleasant flight, and New York was hot and muggy and beautiful and throbbing when she arrived. Hilary was wrong. It was exciting even in August. Maybe no one who mattered was there, but everyone else was. The city was alive.

There were no photographers to greet her, nothing, no one, only New York. And that was enough. She had so much to do. It was late Friday night. She had to go home and unpack, wash her hair, and first thing the next morning, she would take the subway to Harlem. First thing. She had flown home from Spain for her book, but to see Alejandro too. It was time now. For her anyway. She had planned it for a long time. And she was ready. For him. For herself. He was part of her past, but not the part she had put away. He was the part she had saved for the present.

And the present looked and felt splendid. She was unfettered now, unbound and happy and free. She tingled with the excitement of all that lay ahead ... people, places, things to do, books to write, her old conquered

379

world at her feet, and now new worlds to conquer. Above all, she had conquered herself. She had it all now. What was there to fear? Nothing, and that was the beauty of what she had found. No one owned her anymore, not a life-style, not a man, no one. Kezia owned Kezia, for good.

The days with Luke had been treasured and rare, but a new dawn had come . . . a silver and blue morning filled with light. And there was room for Alejandro in her new day, if he was around, and if not, she would ride laughing and proud into noon.

LOVING

TO BEATRIX

May you always be
Proud to be
yourself,
because you
happen to be
the loveliest lady
I know.
   With all my love,
     Mommy

Ever hopeful,
  filled with dreams,
    bright new,
      brand-new
    hopeful schemes,
pastel shades
    and Wedgwood skies,
first light
    of loving
      in your eyes,
soon to dim
      and then you flee,
        leaving me
          alone
            with me,
the things I fear,
    the things you said
      burning rivers
        in my head,
    bereft of all
        we shared,
my soul
    so old,
      so young,
        so bare,
afraid of you,
    of me,
      of life,
        of men . . .

until
    the bright new
        dreams
            begin again.
the landscape never
        quite the same,
    eventually
        a different game,
    aware at last
        of what I know,
            and think,
                and am,
                    and feel,
    the gift of love
        at
            long
                last
                    real.

DANIELLE STEEL

'Real isn't how you are made,' said the Skin Horse. 'It's a thing the happens to you. When a child loves you for a long, long time, not just to play with, but REALLY loves you, then you become Real.'

'Does it hurt?' asked the Rabbit.

'Sometimes,' said the Skin Horse, for he was always truthful 'When you are Real you don't mind being hurt.'

'Does it happen all at once, like being wound up,' he asked, 'or bi by bit?'

'It doesn't happen all at once,' said the Skin Horse. 'You become It takes a long time. That's why it doesn't often happen to peopl who break easily, or have sharp edges, or who have to be carefully kept. Generally, by the time you are Real, most of your hair has beer loved off, and your eyes drop out and you get loose in the joints and very shabby. But these things don't matter at all, because once you are Real you can't be ugly, except to people who don't understand . . . but once you are Real you can't become unreal again. It lasts for always.'

from 'The Velveteen Rabbit'
by Margery Williams

Chapter 1

Bettina Daniels looked around the pink marble bathroom with a sigh and a smile. She had exactly half an hour. She was making remarkable time. Usually she had much less time in which to make the transition from girl, student, and ordinary mortal to bird of paradise and hostess extraordinaire. But it was a metamorphosis she was thoroughly used to making. For fifteen years she had been her father's aide-de-camp, going everywhere with him, fielding off reporters, taking telephone messages from his girl friends, even sitting backstage to lend him support as he did late-night talk shows to promote his latest book. He scarcely needed to make the effort to do the promotions. His last seven books had automatically spiralled up *The New York Times* Bestseller List, but still, promotion was something one did. Besides which, he loved it. He loved the preening and parading, the food for his ego, and the women who found him irresistible, confusing him with the heroes in his books.

It was easy to confuse Justin Daniels with the hero in a novel. In some ways Bettina herself had done it for years. He was so blatantly beautiful, so unfailingly charming, so witty, so funny, so delightful to be with. Sometimes it was difficult to remember how selfish, how egotistical, how ruthless he could also be. But Bettina knew both sides of the man, and she loved him anyway.

He had been her hero, her companion, and her best friend for years. And she knew him well. She knew all the flaws and the foibles, all the sins and fears, but she knew too the beauty of the man, the brilliance, the gentleness of his soul, and she loved him with every ounce of her being, and knew that she always would. He had failed her and hurt her, he had forgotten to be at school for almost every important moment,

I

had never shown up for a race or a play. He had assured her that young people were boring, and dragged her along with his friends instead. He had hurt her over the years, mainly in the pursuit of his own shimmering dreams. It never occurred to him that she had a right to a childhood, and picnics and beaches, birthday parties, and afternoons in the park. Her picnics were at the Ritz or the Plaza-Athénée in Paris, her beaches were South Hampton and Deauville, her birthday parties were with his friends at 21 in New York or the Bistro in Beverly Hills; and rather than afternoons in the park he would insist she accompany him on the yacht cruises he was constantly being invited to share. Hers was hardly a life to be pitied, and yet Justin's trusted friends often reproached him for how he brought up his child, what he had deprived her of, and how lonely it was to tag along constantly with a bachelor father eternally on the prowl. It was remarkable that in some ways even at nineteen she was still so youthful, still so innocent, with those enormous emerald eyes; yet there was the wisdom of the ages lurking there too. Not because of what she had done, but rather because of what she had seen. At nineteen she was still in some ways a baby, and in other ways she had seen an opulence, a decadence, an existence that few men or women twice her age had ever seen.

Her mother had died of leukemia shortly after Bettina's fourth birthday and was nothing more than a face in a portrait on the dining-room wall, a laughing smile with huge blue eyes and blonde hair. There was something of Tatianna Daniels in her daughter, but not much. Bettina looked like neither Tatianna nor Justin. She looked mainly like herself. Her father's striking black hair and green eyes were partly passed down to his daughter, whose green eyes were not wholly unlike his. However, her hair was rich auburn, the colour of very old, very fine cognac. His tall angular frame was in sharp contrast to Bettina's, which was narrow, minute, almost elfin in its delicate proportions. It served to give her an aura of fragility as she brushed the auburn hair into a halo of soft curls, as she did now, looking at her watch once again.

Bettina made a rapid calculation. Twenty minutes. She would be on time. She sank rapidly into the steaming water in the tub and sat there for a moment, trying to unwind as she watched the snow falling outside. It was November, and this was the first snow.

It was also their first party of the 'season', and for that reason it had to be a success. And it would be. She would see to that too. She mentally checked over the guest list again, wondering if there were some who would fail to arrive because of the snow. But she thought it unlikely. Her father's parties were too celebrated, the invitations awaited too breathlessly for anyone to want to miss the occasion or risk not being invited again. Parties were an essential part of the life of Justin Daniels. When he was between books, he gave them at least once a week. And they were noteworthy for the people who came and the costumes they wore, the incidents that happened, the deals that were made. But above all they were special, and an evening at the Danielses' was like a visit to a faraway, once-dreamed-of land.

The parties were all spectacular. The luxurious surroundings sparkled in seventeenth-century splendour, as butlers hovered and musicians played. Bettina, as hostess, floating magically between groups, always seemed to be everywhere that she was wanted or needed. She was a truly haunting creature; elusive, beautiful, and very, very rare. The only one who did not fully realise how remarkable she was, was her father, who thought every young woman was naturally as gracious as Bettina. His casual acceptance of her was something that had long since irritated his closest friend. Ivo Stewart adored Justin Daniels, but it had irked him for years that Justin never saw what was happening to Bettina, never understood how she worshipped him, and how much his attention and praise meant to her. Justin would only laugh when Ivo made comments, which he did frequently, shaking his head and waving a well-manicured hand at his friend.

3

'Don't be ridiculous. She loves what she does for me. She enjoys it. Running the parties, going to shows with me, seeing interesting people. She'd be embarrassed if I made a point of telling her how I appreciate what she does. She knows I do. Who wouldn't? She does a marvellous job.'

'Then you should tell her that. Good God, man, she's your secretary, your housekeeper, your publicity girl – she does everything a wife would do and more.'

'And better!' Justin pointed out as he laughed.

'I'm serious.' Ivo looked stern.

'I know you are. Too much so. You worry too much about the girl.' Ivo hadn't dared to tell Justin that if he didn't worry about her, he wasn't sure if Justin would himself.

Justin had an easy, cavalier way about him, in sharp contrast to Ivo's more serious view of the world. But that was also the nature of Ivo's business, as publisher of one of the world's largest newspapers, the *New York Mail*. He was also older than Justin, and not a young man. He had lost one wife, divorced another, and purposely never had children. He felt it was unfair to bring children into such a difficult world. And at sixty-two he did not regret the decision . . . except when he saw Bettina. Then something seemed always to melt in his heart. Sometimes seeing Bettina, he wondered if remaining childless had been a mistake. But it didn't matter now. It was too late to think about children, and he was happy. In his own way he was as free as Justin Daniels.

Together, the two men went to concerts, operas, parties. They went to London for an occasional weekend, met in the South of France for a few weeks in July, and shared a remarkable number of illustrious friends. It was one of those solid friendships that forgives almost all sins and allows the free expression of disapproval, as well as delight, which was why Ivo was so open in voicing his opinions of Justin's behaviour with his child. Recently the subject had come up at lunch at La Côte Basque.

4

Ivo had chided Justin, 'If I were in her shoes, old boy, I'd walk out on you. What's she getting from you?'

'Servants, comfort, trips, fascinating people, a twenty-thousand-dollar wardrobe.' He prepared to go on, but Ivo cut him off.

'So what? Do you think she really gives a damn? For chrissake, Justin, look at the girl – she's lovely, but half the time she's in another world, dreaming, thinking, writing. Do you really think she gives a damn about all the showy bullshit that means so much to you?'

'Of course she does. She's had it all her life.' Her childhood was completely different from Justin's, who had grown up poor and made millions on his books and movies. There had been good times and bad times, and some very hard times, but Justin's spending had only gone in one direction over the years: up. The opulence he surrounded himself with was vital to him. It reassured him of who he was. He was looking at Ivo now over a demitasse of strong coffee at the end of lunch. 'Without all that I give her, she wouldn't be able to make it for a week, Ivo.'

'I'm not so sure.' Ivo had more faith in her than her father. One day she would be a truly remarkable woman, and whenever he thought of it, Ivo Stewart smiled.

Drying herself off quickly with a large pink monogrammed towel, Bettina knew she would have to hurry. She had already laid out her dress. It was a beautiful watered-silk sheath of the palest mauve, which fell from her shoulders to her ankles like a soft slinky tube. She slipped rapidly into the appropriate laces and silks, climbed into the dress, and stepped carefully into the matching mauve sandals with tiny gold heels. On its own the dress would have been splendid. She admired it again as she fluffed her burnt-caramel hair for the last time, making sure that the mauve on her eyelids was exactly the same as the dress. She clasped a rope of amethysts around her neck and another to her left wrist as tiny diamonds sparkled in her ears. And then, carefully, she

5

lifted the heavy green velvet tunic from its hanger and slipped it over the mauve silk of the dress. The tunic was lined in the same shimmering mauve, and she looked like a symphony in lilac and deep Renaissance green. It was a breathtakingly beautiful outfit, which her father had brought her from Paris the winter before. But she wore it with the same ease and unaffected simplicity that she would have worn a pair of old faded jeans. Having paid the outfit due homage in the mirror, she could forget that she had it on. And that was precisely what she was planning to do. She had a thousand other things on her mind. She cast a glance around the cosy French provincial bedroom, made sure that she had left the screen in front of the still roaring fire, and glanced out the window for the last time. It was still snowing. The first snow was always so pretty. She smiled to herself as she made her way quickly downstairs.

She had to check the kitchen and make sure everything looked right for the buffet. The dining-room was a masterpiece, and she smiled at the perfection of the canapés that marched along countless silver platters like overgrown confetti scattered everywhere for a holiday feast. In the living-room everything was in order, and in the den the furniture had been removed as she'd ordered and the musicians were tuning up. The servants looked impeccable, the apartment looked divine, with room after room of museum-quality Louis XV furniture, marble mantels, overwhelming bronzes, and inlaid wonders at which one could only stare in awe. The damasks were in soft creamy colours, the velvets leaned to café au lait or apricot and peach. The whole apartment was a splendour of warmth and loving, and it was Bettina's taste that was exhibited everywhere, Bettina's caring that so lavishly showed.

'My God, you look pretty, darling.' She wheeled at the sound of his voice and stood for a moment, her eyes warm and smiling. 'Isn't that the thing I got you in Paris last year?' Justin Daniels smiled at his daughter and she smiled back.

6

Only her father would call the exquisite Balenciaga he had bought her for a king's ransom 'a thing'.

'It is. I'm glad you like it.' And then, hesitantly, almost shyly, 'I like it too.'

'Good. Are the musicians here?' He was already looking past her, into the wood-panelled sanctum of the large den.

'They're tuning up. I think they'll be starting any minute. Would you like a drink?' He never thought of her needs. It was always she who thought of his.

'I think I'll wait for a minute. Christ, I'm tired today.' He sprawled for a moment in a comfortable bergère as Bettina watched him. She could have told him that she was tired too. She had got up at six that morning to work out the details of the party, gone to school at eight thirty, and then rushed home to bathe, dress, and see that everything was just right. But she didn't say anything to him about it. She never did.

'Are you working on the new book?' She looked at him with devotion and interest as he nodded and then looked over at her with a smile.

'You always care about the books, don't you?'

'Of course I do.' She smiled gently.

'Why?'

'Because I care about you.'

'Is that the only reason?'

'Of course not. They're wonderful books, and I love them.' And then she stood up and laughed softly as she bent down to kiss him on the forehead. 'I also happen to love you.' He smiled in answer and patted her arm gently as she swept away at the sound of the door. 'Sounds like someone's arriving.' But she was worried suddenly. He did look unusually tired.

Within half an hour the house was jammed with people laughing, talking, drinking, being witty or amusing or unkind, and sometimes all three. There were miles of evening dresses, in rainbow hues, and rivers of jewels, and a veritable army of men in black tie, their white shirts studded

7

with mother of pearl and onyx and tiny sapphires and diamonds. And there were almost a hundred well-known faces in the crowd. Aside from the hundred of relative celebrities were another two hundred unknowns, drinking champagne, eating caviar, dancing to the music, looking for Justin Daniels or others they had hoped to glimpse or even meet.

Through it all Bettina passed unnoticed, darting, moving, watching that everything went smoothly, that people were introduced, had champagne, had been fed. She was careful to see that her father had his Scotch, and then later his brandy, that his cigars were always near at hand. She was careful to keep her distance when he seemed to be flirting with a woman and quick to bring him an important guest who had just arrived. She was a genius at what she was doing. And Ivo thought she was more beautiful than any woman in the room. It wasn't the first time that he had wished she was his child and not Justin's.

'Doing you usual number, I see, Bettina? Exhausted? Or only ready to drop?'

'Don't be silly, I love it.' But he could see that beneath her eyes there was the faintest hint of fatigue. 'Would you like another drink?'

'Stop treating me like a guest, Bettina. Can I interest you in sitting down somewhere?'

'Maybe later.'

'No, now.'

'All right, Ivo. All right.' She looked up into the deep blue eyes in the kind face that she had come to love over the years and let him lead her to a seat near a window, where for a moment they silently watched the snow, and then she turned her eyes back to him. His full white mane looked more perfectly groomed than ever. Ivo Stewart always looked perfect. He was just that kind of man. Tall, lean, handsome, youthful, with blue eyes that always seemed about to laugh and the longest legs she'd ever seen. She had called him Ivo Tall when she was a child. Slowly she gave way to a small worried frown. 'Have you noticed that Daddy looks very tired tonight?'

Ivo shook his head. 'No, but I notice that you look tired. Anything wrong?'

She smiled. 'Just exams. Why is it that you notice everything?'

'Because I love you both, and sometimes your father is a complete moron and doesn't notice a damn thing. Writers! You could drop dead at their feet and they'd march over you, muttering something about the second part of chapter fifteen. Your father's no different.'

'No, he just writes better.'

'I suppose that's an excuse.'

'He doesn't need an excuse.' Bettina said it very gently, and Ivo's eyes met hers. 'He's marvellous at what he does.' *Even if he isn't the most wonderful father,* she thought, *he's a brilliant writer!* But they were words she would never have said out loud.

'You're marvellous at what you do too.'

'Thank you, Ivo. You always say the nicest things. And now' – she stood up reluctantly and smoothed her dress – 'I have to get back to playing hostess.'

It had gone on until four in the morning, and her whole body ached as she walked slowly upstairs. Her father was still in the den with two or three of his cronies, but she had done her job. The servants had already whisked away most of the mess, the musicians had been paid and sent home, the last guests had been kissed and thanked before they departed, the women bundled in their minks as their husbands led them to limousines waiting outside in the snow. And as she walked slowly to her room Bettina stopped for a moment and looked outside. It was beautiful; the city looked peaceful and silent and white. And then she went to her room and closed the door.

She carefully hung the Balenciaga back on its hanger and slipped into a a pink silk nightgown before sliding between the flowered sheets that one of the maids had turned down

9

earlier that night. And as she lay in bed a moment later she ran over the evening again in her head. It had gone smoothly. It always did. She sighed sleepily to herself, wondering about the next party. Had he said next week, or the week after that? And had he liked the musicians tonight? She had forgotten to ask. And the caviar . . . what about the caviar . . . was it as good as . . . ? Looking very small and fragile, she sighed once more and fell asleep.

Chapter 2

'Care to join us for lunch today? Twenty-one, at noon.' She read the note as she finished her coffee and picked up the heavy red coat she wore to school. She was wearing navy gabardine slacks and a navy-blue cashmere sweater and boots that she hoped would resist the snow. Quickly she picked up a pen and jotted a note to him on the other side of his.

'Wish I could, but I'm sorry . . . exams! Have a good time. See you tonight. Love, B.'

She had been telling him about her exams all week. But he couldn't be expected to remember the details of her life. He was already thinking of his next book, and that was enough. And nothing in her college life had thus far been worthy of his attention. This was easy to understand. It didn't fascinate her either. In contrast to the life she led with him, everything else was so flat. She did feel secretly that the normalcy of her college life was refreshing, but it seemed somewhat remote to her. She always felt like an observer. She never joined in. Too many people had already figured out who she was. It made her a curiosity, and an object of stares and fascination. But she didn't feel worthy of their interest. She wasn't the writer. She was only his child.

The door closed softly behind her as she went off to school, mentally running over the notes she had made for herself to prepare for the exam. It was difficult to feel lively about it on two-and-a-half hours' sleep. But she'd come out all right, she always did. Her grades were quite high, which was another thing that frequently set her apart from the others. She wasn't even sure now why she had let her father talk her into going on with school. All she wanted to do was find a corner somewhere to write her play. That was all. Just that . . . And then she grinned to herself as the elevator reached the ground floor. There was more to the fantasy after all. She wanted to write a *hit* play. That would take more time . . . like twenty or thirty years.

'Morning, miss.' She smiled at the doorman as he tipped his hat, and for a moment she almost ran back into the building. It was one of those stunningly cold days when the first breath of air feels like nails being inhaled. She hailed a cab and climbed in. Today was not a day to prove anything by taking the bus. To hell with it. She would rather stay warm. She settled back against the seat and looked long and hard at her notes.

'Bettina couldn't come?' Ivo looked up in surprise as Justin joined him at the huge bar that was always their meeting spot at 21.

'Apparently not. I forgot to ask her last night, so she left me a note this morning. Something about exams. I hope that's all it is.'

'What's that supposed to mean?'

'It means I hope she's not involved with some little fool at college.' Both of them knew that up until now there had been no man in her life. Justin didn't give her time.

'You expect her to stay unattached for the rest of her life?' Ivo looked at him dubiously over his martini.

'Hardly. But I expect her to make an intelligent choice.'

'What makes you think she won't?' Ivo watched his friend with interest and he could see the tired look about his eyes that Bettina had mentioned the night before.

'Women don't always make wise choices, Ivo.'

'And we do?' He said it with amusement. 'Do you have any reason to suspect she's met someone?'

Justin Daniels shook his head. 'No, but you never know. I abhor those little bastards who go to college just to screw girls.'

'Like you, you mean.' Ivo was now grinning broadly as Justin shot him an evil look and ordered a Scotch.

'Never mind that. I feel like hell today.'

'Hung over?' Ivo didn't look impressed.

'I don't know. Maybe. I've had indigestion since last night.'

'It's obviously old age.'

'Aren't you the smart one today?' Justin gave him a look that Ivo knew meant he'd had enough and then they both laughed. Despite their diverging views about Bettina, the two men never failed to get along. She was the only subject on which they almost never agreed and the only bone of contention between them. 'By the way, can I interest you in a brief trip to London next weekend?'

'For what?'

'What do I know? Chasing girls, spending money, going to the theatre. The usual.'

'I thought you were already working on the new book.'

'I am, but I'm stuck and I want to play.'

'I'll have to see. You may not have noticed, but there are several minor wars, not to mention political coups, breaking out all over the world. The paper may want me here.'

'It won't change a damn thing if you're gone for the weekend. Besides, you *are* the paper, you can call your own shots.'

'Thank you, sir. I'll keep that in mind. Who's joining us for lunch by the way?'

'Judith Abbott, the playwright. Bettina's going to have a fit that she missed her.' He looked sombrely at Ivo then and ordered another Scotch. But Ivo had not missed the frightened look in his eyes.

For a moment Ivo wondered, and then he gently touched his friend's arm and spoke barely above a whisper. 'Justin . . . is something really wrong?'

There was a pause for a moment. 'I don't know. I feel strange all of a sudden . . .'

'Do you want to sit down?' But it was already too late; a moment later he slumped to the floor and two women looked down and screamed. His face was hideously contorted, as he seemed to wrestle with intolerable pain.

Frantically Ivo issued orders, and it was only moments before the paramedics arrived, moments when Ivo held his friend in his arms and prayed that it wasn't too late. But it was. Justin Daniels's hand fell limply to the floor the moment Ivo let it go, as police on the scene pushed the curious away and the paramedics fought on for almost half an hour. But it was useless. Justin Daniels was dead.

Ivo watched helplessly as they pounded his heart, gave him artificial respiration, oxygen, everything, while Ivo gave him prayers. But it made no difference. At last they covered his face as tears rolled down Ivo's cheeks. They asked him if he wanted to come with the body to the hospital morgue. The morgue? Justin? It was unthinkable. But it wasn't. And they went.

Ivo felt grey and trembling as he walked out of the hospital an hour later. There was nothing more to be done except tell Bettina. He felt sick when he thought of it. Jesus . . . how was he going to tell her? What could he say? What did this leave her? And who? She had no one in the world except Justin. No one. She had the best guest list in New York and knew more celebrities than the society writer at the *Times*, but that was all she had. Other than that she had nothing. Except Justin. And now he was gone.

Chapter 3

The clock on the mantelpiece ticked interminably as Ivo sat in the den, staring bleakly out over the park. It was already late in the afternoon and the light was slowly failing. In the street below, the usual angry snarl of traffic crawled south along Fifth Avenue. It was rush hour and there was snow on the ground, to add an extra impediment to Bettina's getting home at the end of the day. The cars barely moved as drivers honked angrily. In the Danielses' apartment the distant honking was a muted sound. Ivo didn't even hear it as he sat there, waiting to hear Bettina's footstep in the hall, her voice calling out, her laughter as she came home from school. He found himself looking around the room, at the trophies, the artifacts handsomely displayed on shelves in the bookcase along with the leather-bound volumes Justin had treasured. Many of them had been bought at auction in London when Ivo had been with him on occasional trips over the years. Just like their trips to Munich and Paris and Vienna. There had been so many years, so many moments, so many good times they had shared. It was Justin who had celebrated and cried and cavorted with him for the thirty-two years of their friendship, over love affairs and divorces and victories of all kinds . . . Justin who had asked Ivo to sit with him at Doctor's Hospital the night Bettina was born, as they both got blind drunk on champagne, and then went on to celebrate afterwards on the town . . . Justin . . . who was suddenly no more. So swiftly gone. Ivo's thoughts wandered soberly back to the moments in the hospital that afternoon. It all seemed so unreal. And then Ivo realised that it was Justin he was waiting for, not Bettina . . . Justin's voice in the long empty hall . . . his elegant frame in the doorway with a smile in his eyes and laughter on his lips. It was Justin, not Bettina, whom Ivo expected to see as he sat in the quiet, wood-panelled room staring at the cold cup of coffee the butler had brought him an hour before. They knew. They all knew. Ivo had told the servants shortly after he arrived at the house. He had also called Justin's lawyer and his agent. But no one else. He didn't want anything in the press or on the radio before Bettina knew. The servants knew also that they were to say nothing to her when she arrived. They were only to direct her to Ivo in the den . . . where he waited . . . in the stillness . . . for one of them to come home . . . If only Justin would come home, then it would all be a lie after all and he wouldn't have to tell her . . . he wouldn't have to . . . it wouldn't be . . . He felt tears sting his eyes again as he fingered the delicate blue and gold Limoges cup set before him.

Absently Ivo touched the lace on the edge of his napkin as he suddenly heard the front door open. There was a hushed voice, the butler's, and then her brighter one. Ivo could almost see her, smiling, open, shrugging out of the heavy red coat, saying something to the butler, who smiled for no one else except 'Miss'. For 'Miss', everyone smiled. Except Ivo; this afternoon he couldn't smile. He stood and walked slowly to the door, feeling his heart pound as he waited for her. Oh God, what would he say?

'Ivo?' She looked surprised as she came towards him across the hall. They had just told her that he was waiting for her in the den. 'Is something wrong?' She looked instantly sympathetic and reached out both hands. It was too early for him to leave the office and she knew it. He rarely left his desk before seven or eight. It made him difficult to have as a dinner guest sometimes, but it was a foible everyone easily forgave. The publisher of the *New York Mail* had a right to keep long hours, and he was still sought out by every hostess in town. 'You look tired.' She looked at him reproachfully and held his hand as they sat down. 'Isn't Daddy home?'

He shook his head dumbly, and his eyes filled with tears as she kissed his cheek. 'No. Bettina . . .' And then, hating himself, he heard himself add, 'Not yet.'

16

'Would you like a drink, instead of that miserable-looking cup of coffee?' Her smile was so warm and gentle that it tore at his heart, as her eyes took in every detail. She was worried about him and that made him smile. She looked so incredibly young and lovely and innocent that he wanted to tell her anything but the truth. Her auburn hair looked like a halo of curls as it floated around her head. Her eyes were bright and her cheeks pink from the cold, and she looked tinier than ever. But her smile faded as she watched him. Suddenly she knew that something was terribly wrong. 'Ivo, what is it? You've hardly said a word since I came in.' Her eyes never left his, and then slowly he reached for her hand. 'Ivo?' She grew pale as she watched him, and in spite of himself tears filled his eyes as he pulled her gently into his arms. She didn't resist him. It was as though she knew that she would need him, and he her. She found herself holding tightly to Ivo as she waited for the news.

'Bettina . . . it's Justin . . .' He felt a sob rise in his throat, and he fought it. He had to be strong. For Justin. For her. But she had gone tense in his arms now, and suddenly she pulled away.

'What do you mean? . . . Ivo . . .' Her eyes were frantic, her hands like frightened little birds. 'An accident?' But Ivo only shook his head. And then slowly he looked at her, and in his eyes she saw the full force of her fear.

'No, darling. He's gone.' For an instant nothing moved in the room as the shock washed over her like a wave, and her eyes stared into his, not fully understanding, and not wanting to know.

'I – I don't understand . . .' Her hands fluttered nervously, and her eyes seemed to dart from his face to her hands. 'What do you mean, Ivo? . . . I – ' And then, in anguish and horror, she jumped to her feet and crossed the room, as though to get away from him, as though by fleeing him, she could flee the truth. 'What the hell do you mean?' She was shouting at him now, her voice tremulous and angry, her eyes filled with tears. But she looked so fragile, so frail, that he wanted to take her in his arms again.

'Bettina . . . darling . . .' He went to her, but she fought him off, unthinking, unknowing, and then suddenly she reached out to him and clung to him as her whole body was wracked by sobs.

'Oh, God . . . oh, no . . . Daddy . . .' It was a long, slow, childlike wail. Ivo held her tightly in his arms. He was all she had.

'What happened? Oh, Ivo . . . what happened?' But she didn't really want to know. All she wanted to know was that it wasn't true. But it was. Ivo's face told her again and again that it was.

'It was a heart attack. At lunch. They sent an ambulance immediately, but it was too late.' He sounded anguished as he said it.

'Didn't they do anything? For God's sake . . .' She was sobbing now, her narrow frame shaking, as he kept an arm around her shoulders. It was impossible to believe. Only the night before they had danced in this room.

'Bettina, they did everything. Absolutely everything. It was just – ' God, what an agony it was to tell her all of it. It was almost unbearable for him. 'It happened very quickly. It was all over in a matter of moments. And I promise you, they did everything they could. But there wasn't much they could do.' She closed her eyes and nodded, and then slowly she left the comfort of his arms and crossed the room. She stood with her back to him, looking down at the snow and the gnarled, naked trees across the street in Central Park. How ugly it looked to her now, how lonely, how bare, when only the night before it had looked beautiful and fairylike as she stood at her bedroom window, dressing for the party and waiting for the first guests to arrive. She hated them now, all of them, for having robbed her of her last night alone with him . . . her last night . . . he was gone now. She closed her eyes again tightly and braced herself for the question she had to ask.

'Did he – did he say anything, Ivo . . . I mean . . . for me?' Her voice was a tiny mouse sound from her vigil at the window, and she didn't see Ivo shake his head.

'There wasn't time.'

She nodded silently, and a moment later took a deep breath. Ivo didn't know whether to go to her, or let her stand there alone. He felt he might break her in half with the merest touch of his hand, so taut and brittle and fragile she seemed as she stood there, aching and alone. She was alone now, and she knew it. For the first time in her life. 'Where is he now?'

'At the hospital.' Ivo hated to say it. 'I wanted to speak to you before making any arrangements. Do you have any idea what you'd like to do?' He approached her slowly and turned her around to face him. He looked down at her. Her eyes seemed suddenly a thousand years old, and it was the face of a woman she turned up to him, not the face of a child. 'Bettina, I – I'm sorry to press you about this, but . . . do you have any idea what your father would have wanted?'

She sat down again, softly shaking the halo of auburn curls. 'We never talked about – about things like that. And he wasn't religious.' She closed her eyes and two huge tears rolled sombrely down her face. 'I suppose we ought to do something private. I don't want' – she could barely go on speaking – 'a lot of strangers there to stare at him and –'. But then all she could do was bow her head as her shoulders shook pathetically, and Ivo took her once again in his arms. It took her fully five minutes to compose herself, and then she looked up at Ivo with a bleak look in her eyes. 'I want to see him now, Ivo.' He nodded, and she stood up and walked silently to the door.

She was terrifyingly quiet on the way to the hospital and she was dry-eyed and poised as she sat in the back seat of Ivo's limousine. She seemed to shrink as she sat there, huddled into a silver fox coat, her eyes huge and childlike beneath a matching fur hat.

She stepped out of the car ahead of him at the hospital,

and she was instantly through the door, waiting impatiently for Ivo, wanting to be taken to her father's side. In her heart she had not yet understood the reality, and somehow she expected to find him anxious to see her and very much alive. It was only when they came to the final doorway that she seemed to slow down, the staccato of the heels of her black kid boots silenced on the hospital floor, the light beyond the doorway dim, and her eyes suddenly huge as she stepped slowly inside the morgue. He was there, covered with a sheet, and on tiptoe she went to him, and stood there, trying to get up the courage to pull the sheet down so she could see his face. Ivo watched her for a moment, and then walked softly to her side.

He whispered to her and gently took her arm. 'Do you want to go now?' But she only shook her head. She had to see him. Had to. She had to say goodbye. She wanted to tell Ivo that she wanted to be alone with her father, but she didn't know how, and in the end she was just as glad.

With a trembling hand she reached out and touched the corner of the sheet, and slowly, slowly, pulled it back until she could see the top of his head. For an instant it seemed as though he was playing with her, as though she were a child again and they were playing peekaboo. More quickly now she pulled the sheet down until she dropped it on his chest. The eyes were closed, the face peaceful and eerily pale as she looked down at him, her eyes wide and filled with pain, but she understood now. It was as Ivo had said – her father was gone. The tears poured steadily down her face as she bent to kiss him and then took a step back, as firmly Ivo put an arm around her again and led her out of the room.

Chapter 4

But the truth of it didn't hit Bettina until after the funeral. Between her father's death and his final ritual were two days of frantic surrealism, picking out something for him to wear, checking constantly with the secretary she had hired to help with the arrangements, talking to Ivo about who had been called and who must be, organising servants, and reassuring friends. There was something wonderfully comforting about 'arrangements'. They were a place to flee from her emotions, from the truth. She hurried between the apartment and the funeral home, and finally stood in the cemetery, a fragile figure in black, carrying one long, white rose, which she laid silently on her father's coffin as the rest of the group stood apart from her. Only Ivo hovered somewhere near her. She could see his shadow falling across the snow near her own. Only Ivo had bridged the gap again and again in the painful days after her father's death. Only Ivo had been able to reach out and touch her. Only Ivo was there to let her know that someone still cared, that she was not totally un-protected in the world now, frightened and alone.

He took her hand silently and led her back to his car. Half an hour later she was secure in her apartment again, locked in the safe little world she had always known. She and Ivo were drinking coffee, and outside a bright November sun shone on the fresh snow. The winter snow had come early, and the only place it looked lovely was in the park. The rest of the city had lain beneath a blanket of slush for three days. Bettina sighed to herself, sipped her coffee, and looked absently at the brightly burning fire. It was an odd comparison, but she felt the way her father used to when he finished a book. Suddenly she had lost her 'people' and she was out of a job. There was no one to care for and fuss over,

21

to order cracked crab for, to make sure his cigars were at hand, the guest list was to his liking, and the plane reservations to Madrid were exactly as he wanted. There was no one to take care of now except herself. And she wasn't quite sure how to do that. She had always been so busy taking care of him.

'Bettina.' There was a long pause as Ivo set down his cup and slowly ran a hand through his white hair. He only did that when he felt very awkward, and she wondered why he should feel that way now. 'It's a bit early to bring it up to you, darling, but we ought to meet with the lawyers this week.' He felt his heart sink as she turned her wide green eyes to his.

'Why?'

'To discuss the will, and . . . there are several other points of business that we ought to talk to them about.' Justin had left him as executor, and the lawyers had already been clawing at him for two days.

'Why now? Isn't it too soon?' She looked puzzled as she stood and walked to the fire. She was feeling tired and restless all at the same time. She wasn't sure whether to run around the block a hundred and fifty times or just go to bed and cry. But Ivo was looking distressingly businesslike as his eyes followed her to the fire.

'No, it's not too soon. There are some things you'll have to know, some decisions to be made. Some of it should get rolling now.'

She sighed in answer and nodded as she went back to the couch. 'All right. We'll see them, but I don't understand the rush.' She looked at Ivo with a quiet smile and he nodded and reached out a hand. Even Ivo didn't know the full extent of what the lawyers had on their minds. But twelve hours later they did.

Ivo and Bettina looked at each other in shock. The lawyers looked at her gravely. No stock. No investments. No capital. In brief, there was no money. According to his attorneys,

Justin hadn't been upset about it because he always expected things to 'come around', but the turnaround had not yet come. In fact it hadn't come in several years, and he had been living on credit for too long. Everything he owned was heavily mortgaged or had been put up as collateral and it turned out that he had fabulous loans to repay. His last advances had all been spent, on cars – like the new Bentley, and then shortly afterwards the 1934 Rolls – antiques, racehorses, women, trips, houses, furs, Bettina, himself. The winter before he had bought the country's most extravagant thoroughbred from a friend. Two point seven million he had paid for it, the papers had said. In fact it had been slightly more, and the friend had allowed him to defer payment for a year. The year wasn't yet over, and the debt was still unpaid. He knew he would cover it, there would be more advances, and he had his royalties, which never failed to come in, in six-figure cheques. What Ivo and Bettina then learned as they sat there was that even his future royalties had been borrowed against, from some of his wealthier friends. He had borrowed to the hilt from everyone, bankers, as well as friends, against real property, future income, and dreams. What had happened to his investments, to the snatches of conversations she had heard about 'sure things'? As the hours with the attorneys wore on, it became clear that there were no sure things, except his astronomical debts, they were sure. He had kept much of his borrowing private. He had dispensed with his investment advisers years ago, calling them fools. It became increasingly confusing and Bettina sat baffled and stunned. It was impossible to make heads or tails out of what they were saying except that it would take months to sort it all out and that the vast estate of the illustrious, charming, celebrated, much adored Justin Daniels amounted not to a king's ransom, but to a mountain of debt.

Bettina looked at Ivo in confusion, and he looked at her in despair. He felt as though he had just aged another ten years.

'And the houses?' Ivo looked at the senior attorney with fear.

'We'll have to look into that, but I assume that they'll all have to be sold. We've been recommending that course of action to Mister Daniels for almost two years now. As a matter of fact it's quite possible that once we sell the houses, and ... er' – there was an embarrassed cough – 'several of the antiques and artifacts in Mister Daniels's New York apartment, it's possible that we will have brought matters back into the black.'

'Will there be anything left?'

'That's difficult to say at the moment.' But the look on his face told its own tale.

'What you're saying then' – Ivo's voice was tense and angry, and he wasn't sure if he was angrier at Justin or his lawyers – 'is that after all is said and done, there won't be anything left except the apartment here in New York. No stocks, no bonds, no investments, nothing?'

'I believe that will prove to be correct.' The elderly man fingered his glasses uncomfortably, while his junior partner cleared his throat and tried not to look at the slender young girl.

'Was there no provision made for Miss Daniels?' Ivo couldn't believe it.

But the lawyer spoke one word. 'None.'

'I see.'

'Of course there was' – the senior partner checked some papers on his desk – 'a sum of eighteen thousand dollars in Mister Daniels's chequing account on the day he died. We have to clear probate of course, but we would be happy to advance a small sum of money to Miss Daniels in the interim, to enable her to pay whatever living expenses –' But Ivo was steaming by now.

'That won't be necessary.' Ivo snapped closed his briefcase and picked up his coat. 'Just how long do you think it will take to let us know where things stand?'

The two lawyers exchanged a glance. 'About three months?'

'How about one?' Ivo's look was not one to quibble with, and unhappily the elder attorney nodded.

'We'll try. We do understand that the circumstances are somewhat trying for Miss Daniels. We'll do our very best.'

'Thank you.' Bettina shook hands with them and quickly left the office. Ivo said almost nothing on the way to the car, he only glanced anxiously again and again at her face. She was ivory-pale, but she seemed quiet and very much in control. Once they were in his car again, he raised the window between them and his driver and turned to her with a look of sorrow in his eyes. 'Bettina, do you understand what just happened?'

'I think so.' As he watched her he saw that even her lips were frighteningly pale. 'It looks like I'm about to learn a few things about life.'

As they drove up in front of her elaborate building he asked.

'Will you let me help you?'

She shook her head, kissed his cheek, and got out of the car.

He sat watching her until she had disappeared into the building, wondering what would happen to her now.

Chapter 5

The doorbell rang just as Bettina looked at her watch. His timing was perfect and she smiled as she ran to the door. She greeted him with a kiss and Ivo entered and bowed, looking very debonair in a black coat and a homburg. Bettina, on the other hand, was wearing a red flannel shirt and jeans.

'You're looking very lively this evening, Miss Daniels. How was your day?'

'Interesting. I spent the day with the man from Parke-Bernet.' She smiled tiredly, and he thought for a moment how he missed seeing her in her usual elegant clothes. She seemed to have abandoned her other wardrobe in the month since Justin had died. But she also hadn't gone anywhere, except to the lawyers, to hear more bad news. Now all she wanted was to get the hell out of the mess. She was about to start meeting with art dealers, real estate agents, antiquaries, jewellers, anyone and everyone who could take the goods off her hands and leave her with something with which to whittle away the debts.

'They're taking all of this stuff off my hands' – she waved vaguely at the antiques – 'as well as everything out of the house in South Hampton and the one in Palm Beach. They've already had someone to look it all over. The furniture in the South of France I'm getting rid of over there, and' – she sighed absent-mindedly as she hung up his coat – 'I think the house in Beverly Hills will sell with everything in it. Some Arab is buying the place, and he left everything he had in the Middle East. So it should work out well for both of us.'

'Aren't you keeping anything?' Ivo looked appalled, but he was getting used to the feeling and she was getting used to the look on his face.

She shook her head with a small smile. 'I can't afford to. I'm dealing with the national debt, Ivo. Four and a half million dollars is not exactly easy to wipe out. But I will.' She smiled again, and something turned over near his heart. How could Justin do this to her? How could he not have known that something like this might happen, that she would be left to clean up his mess? The unfairness of it tore at Ivo's soul. 'Don't look so worried, love.' She was smiling at him now. 'It'll all be sorted out one of these days.'

'Yes, and in the meantime I sit here helplessly and watch you tear your life apart.' It was hard to remember now that she was only nineteen. She looked and sounded so much older. But there was still an occasional look of mischief in her eyes.

'And what would you like to do, Ivo? Help me pack?'

'No, I wouldn't.' He snapped at her, and then apologised with his eyes. But it was she who spoke first.

'I'm sorry. I know you want to help. I don't know. I guess I'm just tired. I feel like this is never going to end.'

'And when it does end, what then? I don't like your having given up school.'

'Why? I'm getting an education right here. Besides, tuition is expensive.'

'Bettina, stop that!' She sounded so bitter and there was suddenly something so jaded in her eyes. 'I want you to promise me something.'

'What's that?'

'I want you to promise me that when the worst of this is over, when you've taken care of the apartment, the furniture, whatever you have to do, you'll go away for a while, just to restore yourself and get some rest.'

'You make it sound like I'm a hundred years old.' And she didn't ask him how he thought she was going to pay for the trip. There was almost nothing any more. She was cooking for herself in the vast kitchen, and she was not doing much else. She wasn't buying anything, going anywhere. In fact, just that morning, she had been thinking of selling her

27

clothes. The evening clothes at least. She had two closets of them. But she knew that if she told Ivo, he'd have a fit.

'I mean it, I want you to go away somewhere. You need it. This has been an enormous strain. We both know that. If I could, I'd send you away right now, but I know that you have to be here. Will you promise me to think about it?'

'I'll see.' She had survived Christmas by forgetting it entirely, and spent the holidays packing up her father's books. Somehow now she couldn't think of much else. The rare books were going to London, to auction, back whence they had come, and hopefully they would bring a good price. The appraiser said they were worth several hundred thousand dollars. She hoped he was right.

'What did Parke-Bernet tell you?' Now Ivo looked tired too. He came by to see her almost every day, but he hated her news. Selling, packing, getting rid of, it was like watching her unravel her whole life.

'The sale will be in two months. They'll make space for it in the schedule. And they are very pleased with our things.' She handed Ivo his usual Scotch and soda and sat down. 'Can I interest you in some dinner?'

'You know, I'm very impressed with your cooking. I never knew you could cook.'

'Neither did I. I'm discovering that there are a lot of things I can do. Speaking of which' – she smiled at him as he took a long swallow of his Scotch – 'I've been wanting to ask you about something.'

He smiled as he sat back against the couch. 'What's that?'

'I need a job.' The matter-of-fact way she said it almost made him wince.

'Now?'

'No, not this minute, but when I finish all this. What do you think?'

'At the *Mail*? Bettina, you don't want that.' And then, after a moment, he nodded. At least he could do that much for her. 'As my assistant?'

She laughed and shook her head, 'No nepotism, Ivo. I mean a real job that I'm qualified for. Maybe a copy girl.'

'Don't be ridiculous. I won't let you do that.'

'Then I won't ask you for a job.' She looked determined. And the agony of it struck him again and again. But the truth of it was that she would need a job. She had faced it, and he was going to have to face it too. 'We'll see. Let me give it some thought. Maybe I can come up with a better idea than something at the *Mail*.'

'What? Marry a rich old man?' She said it in jest and they both laughed.

'Not unless you audition me first.'

'You're not old enough. Now, how about dinner?'

'You're on.'

They exchanged another smile, and she disappeared into the kitchen to put on some steaks. She quickly set the long refectory table that her father had brought back from Spain, and she set a vase of yellow flowers down on the deep-blue cloth. When Ivo wandered into the kitchen a few minutes later, everything was underway.

'You know, Bettina, you're going to spoil me. I'm getting used to stopping here every night on my way home. It beats the hell out of frozen dinners or sandwiches on stale bread.'

She turned to laugh at him as he said it, pushing back her rich coppery locks with the back of one hand. 'Ha! When did you ever eat a frozen dinner, Ivo Stewart? I'll bet you haven't eaten dinner at home once in ten years! Speaking of which, what's happened to your social life since you started to baby-sit for me? You never go out any more, do you?'

He looked vague as he touched the bright flowers on the table. 'I haven't had time. Things have been awfully busy at the office.' And then, after a moment, he looked at her again. 'And what about you? You haven't been out in a long time either.' His voice was very gentle, and she turned away with a soft shake of her head.

'That's different. I couldn't . . . I can't . . .' The only

invitations were from her father's friends and she couldn't face them now. 'I just can't.'

'Why? Justin wasn't the kind of man to expect you to go into mourning, Bettina.' Or was it something else? Was she embarrassed to face people now that the truth had come out in the papers? Was it that? They had been unable to hide the truth of Justin's finances from the press.

'I just don't want to, Ivo. I'd feel strange.'

'Why?'

'I don't belong in that world any more.' She said it so forlornly that he walked to her side.

'What in hell do you mean?'

Her eyes filled with tears as she looked at him, and suddenly she looked young again.

'I'd feel like a fraud, Ivo. I . . . oh, Christ, Daddy's life was such a lie. And now everyone knows it. I know it. I don't have anything. I have no right to flounce around at fancy parties any more or hang out with the illustrious and the elite. I just want to sell all this stuff, get out of here, and go to work.'

'That's ridiculous, Bettina. Why? Because Justin ran into debt you're going to deprive yourself of the world you've lived in all your life? That's crazy, don't you know that?'

But she shook her head as she wiped her eyes with the tail of her shirt. 'No, it's not crazy. Daddy didn't belong in that world either if he had to run into debt for four million dollars to stay there. He should have led a very different life.' All the pain and disillusionment of the past weeks suddenly came out in her voice, but Ivo pulled her gently towards him and held her in the crook of one arm. It was like being a little girl again. For a moment, she almost wanted to crawl on to his lap.

'Now wait a minute, Justin Daniels was a brilliant author, Bettina. No one can ever take that away from him. He was one of the greatest minds of his time. And he had a right to be in all the places he was, with all the people he was. What he shouldn't have done was let his judgement get so insanely

30

out of hand, but that is entirely another matter. He was a star, Bettina. A rare and special star, just as you are. Nothing will ever change that. No debt, no sin, no failure, no mistake. Nothing will change what he was, or what you are. Nothing. Do you understand?' She wasn't sure that she did, but she looked at him now with a look that blended confusion and pain.

'Why do you say I'm special too? Because I'm his daughter? Is that why? Because that's another thing that makes me feel I don't belong in that world any more, Ivo. My father is gone. What right have I to go back to those people? Especially now, with absolutely nothing. I can't give them fabulous parties any more, or wonderful introductions over lunch to the people they want to meet. I can't do anything, or give them anything . . . I have nothing . . .' And then her voice caught on a sob. 'I *am* nothing now.'

Ivo's voice was sharp in her ears, and his arm tight around her. 'No, Bettina! You're wrong. You *are* something. You always will be, absolutely nothing will change that. And not because you're Justin's daughter, because you're *you*. Don't you realise how many people came here for you? To meet *you*? Not just him? You're something of a legend; you have been since you were a little girl, and you've never even realised it, which was part of your charm. But it's important that now you understand that *you* are Someone. *You*. Bettina Daniels. As a matter of fact I'm not going to accept this recluse act of yours any more.' He looked purposeful as he suddenly strode across the room and picked up a bottle of wine. He helped himself to two glasses, opened the bottle, poured the deep garnet-coloured Bordeaux wine, and handed her a full glass. 'I have just made a decision, Miss Daniels, and that's that. You are coming with me to dinner and the opera tomorrow night.'

'I am? Oh, Ivo, no . . .' She looked horrified. 'I can't. Maybe later . . . some other time . . .'

'No. Tomorrow.' And then he smiled gently at her. 'Child of mine, don't you realise what day tomorrow is?' She shook her head blankly as she took their steaks off the grill. 'It's New Year's Eve. And no matter what else is happening, we are going to celebrate, you and I.'

He held up his glass of wine. 'The year of Bettina Daniels. It's time we realised that your life isn't over. Darling, it has just begun.' She smiled slowly at him as she took the first sip of her wine.

Chapter 6

Bettina stood in the darkened living-room, watching the traffic honk its way impatiently down Fifth Avenue. Cars were crammed side by side and bumper to bumper as the festivities began. Horns blared, sirens whirred, people shouted, and somewhere in the night there was laughing too. But Bettina stood immeasurably still as she waited. It was a strange electrifying feeling, as though her whole life were about to begin again. Ivo was right. She shouldn't have stayed in by herself so much.

Perhaps her strange feelings were due to all the changes going on in her life. She was no longer a child. She was on her own. And she felt oddly grown-up in a way she never had before. Her adulthood was no longer borrowed; it was real.

The bell rang a few moments later, and suddenly all her grown-up feelings seemed silly. It was only Ivo after all, and what was so different about going to the opera with him? She ran to the door and let him in. He stood smiling on the doorstep, tall and handsome, and long and lean, the white mane dusted with snowflakes, and around his neck a rich, creamy silk scarf, which was in sharp contrast to the black cashmere coat he wore over tails. She stood back for a moment, smiling at him, and then clapped her hands together like a child as he stepped inside.

'Ivo, you look lovely!'

'Thank you, my dear, so do you.' He smiled gently down at her as she bent her head gracefully in the monklike velvet hood of her midnight-blue coat.

'Are you ready?' She nodded in answer, and he crooked his arm. With a tiny smile she slipped her white-gloved hand into it and followed him back to the door. The house was

33

eerily quiet. Gone the servants who would have held the door or taken Ivo's coat. Gone the polite bows, the instant service, the protection . . . from reality . . . from the world. For an instant Bettina stood very quietly as she hunted in her small navy silk evening bag for the key. And then she smiled up at Ivo as she found it and locked the door.

'Things have changed, haven't they?' She looked wistful despite the bright smile. He only nodded, feeling her pain.

But she seemed more herself as they chatted, going down in the elevator, and then in his car. The driver urged the car patiently through the endless holiday traffic, and in the back seat Bettina made Ivo laugh with tales of the people she had met a few months before in school.

'And you mean you don't miss it?' He looked at her searchingly, his eyes growing sober. 'How could you not?'

'Very easily.' This time her eyes were serious too. 'In fact not going there any more is a relief.' The look on his face said that he didn't understand her as she looked at him and then turned away. 'The truth of it is, Ivo, that my father saw to it that I never saw people my own age. They're strangers to me now. I don't know what they talk about, what to say. They talk of things I don't even understand. I'm an outsider.'

Listening to her, Ivo realised once again the high price she had paid for being Justin Daniels's daughter.

'But what does that leave you?' He looked troubled, but she laughed a silvery laugh in the darkened limousine. 'I'm serious, Bettina, if you don't belong with people your own age, then whom do you belong with?'

She smiled gently up at him and whispered softly. 'You.' And then she looked away again and patted his hand. And for a moment an odd sensation ran through his entire body. He wasn't sure if it was excitement or fear. But it wasn't pity or regret. Certainly neither of those, and it should have been, he reproached himself. It should have been either, or both. He should have felt sorry for her, worried, concerned, not excited by her, as suddenly he undeniably was. But that

34

was insanity. And worse than that, it was terribly wrong. He fought back what he was feeling and smiled at her while gently patting the gloved hand. There was a twinkle of mischief in his eyes when he spoke.

'You should be out playing with children your own age.'

'I'll keep it in mind.' And then after another pause, which brought them almost to the door of the Metropolitan Opera, she turned to him with a small smile. 'Do you know, Ivo, this will be the first uninterrupted opera I'll have seen in years?'

'Are you serious?' He seemed surprised.

She nodded as she smoothed her gloves over her hands. 'I used to dash out to the Belmont Room to make sure they had everything ready for Daddy and his party. Then, invariably, there were messages. I had to check the supper reservations and make sure everything was right there. That usually wiped out the second half of the first act. During the second act he'd think of thirty-seven things he'd forgotten to tell me during the first act, which meant more calls, more messages. And then I never got to see the end of the third act because he wanted to leave early to avoid the crowd.'

For a moment Ivo looked at her strangely. 'Why did you do it?' Had she loved him that much?

'I did it because it was my life. Because it wasn't all organising and arranging and servitude, as you seem to think now. It was special and exciting and glamorous, and – ' Then she looked embarrassed. 'It made me feel important, as though I mattered, as though without me he couldn't go on – ' And then she faltered and looked away as Ivo's voice grew soft.

'That's probably true, you know, without you he couldn't have gone on. Certainly not as happily and comfortably and smoothly. But no human being deserves to be spoiled like that, Bettina. Certainly not at the expense of someone else.'

The deep green eyes flashed emerald fire now. 'It wasn't at my expense.' And then in irritation as she reached for the

35

door, she snapped at him. 'You don't understand.' But he did. He understood much more than he told her. Much more than she wanted him to know. He understood the loneliness and the pain of the life with her father. It hadn't been all glamour and Arabian nights. For her it had been sorrow and solitude as well.

'May I help you?' He reached out to assist her with the door handle and she turned to him with smouldering eyes, ready to say no, to push his hand away, to insist on doing it herself. It was a symbolic gesture, and he had to fight to keep the smile from his eyes. And then he couldn't resist laughing and reaching out a hand to rumple the soft caramel curls peeking out from her hood. 'It might help if you unlock it, Miss Independence. Or would you rather just break out the window with your shoe and crawl through?'

And then suddenly she was laughing too as she pulled up the door lock and tried to glare at him, but the moment of anger was already gone. The chauffeur was waiting outside to assist them, and she sprang from the car to the street, smoothing her coat and pulling her hood up against the sharp wind.

Ivo held open the door of his box as they reached it and Bettina slipped inside. For a moment she was reminded of the evenings she had spent there with her father, but she forcefully swept aside the memories and looked into Ivo's blue eyes. He looked wonderful and alive and electric, and it felt good just to be looking into those blue eyes. She looked up at him candidly and patted his cheek gently, while he felt something tender inside him stir.

'I'm glad I came with you tonight, Ivo.'

Everything stopped for a moment as he looked at her, and slowly he smiled. 'So am I, little one. So am I.' And then with chivalry and decorum he assisted her with her coat, and this time it was Bettina who smiled. She could still remember the first time he had done that for her, when she had come to the opera with him and her father more than ten years before. She had been wearing a burgundy-coloured coat with a little velvet collar, and a hat to match, white gloves, and Mary Jane shoes. The opera had been *Der Rosenkavalier*, and she had been horrified to see a woman dressed as a man. Ivo had explained it all to her, but she had still been greatly chagrined. Suddenly, as she thought of it, she found herself laughing, while she slipped out of her dark-blue velvet evening coat and turned once again to face Ivo's eyes. 'And may I ask what's so funny?' He looked warm and already amused.

'I was thinking of that first time I came here with you. Remember the woman "trying to fake that she was a man"?' And suddenly at the memory Ivo was laughing with her, and then as the memory faded she saw something very different in his eyes. He was looking at the dress she was wearing, and as he did so the night of *Der Rosenkavalier* seemed to die in his mind. The dress that she had worn beneath the midnight-blue evening coat was of the same deep, deep blue, but it seemed to float about her in a cloud of chiffon; the long full sleeves cast a kind of dreamlike spell about her arms, and the tiny waist exploded into billows of soft flowing fabric that fell to her feet. She looked infinitely delicate and startlingly beautiful as she stood before him, her eyes as bright as the sapphires and diamonds in her ears. 'Don't you like the dress?' She looked up at him innocently in barely concealed disappointment, and suddenly the laughter came back to his eyes as he reached out both arms. How young she still was in some ways. It always surprised him. It was difficult to understand how she had maintained a core of innocence beneath such a knowing veneer, and in spite of her constant exposure to men who couldn't possibly have escaped the kind of thoughts he was having now.

'I love the dress, darling. It's beautiful. I was just . . . a little taken aback.'

'Were you?' She twinkled at him. 'And think, you haven't even seen the half.' And with that she pivoted neatly on one heel to turn her back to him, and in sharp contrast to the

37

long sleeves, high neck, and full skirt, the back of the dress was cut away, and all that Ivo seemed to see dancing before him was the most devastatingly perfect expanse of creamy flesh.

'Good God, Bettina, that's not decent.'

'Of course it is, don't be stupid. Let's go sit down. The music is starting.'

Ivo sighed to himself as he sat there. He wasn't sure which image of her he should be addressing, which he should be holding to in his mind. The child he remembered or the woman sitting there. There were several things he could offer the child. He could make room for her in his home. But as a woman, the problem was a good deal more complicated . . . What then? A job at the paper? An evening at the opera, as her friend? He could help her find an apartment . . . but then what? How would she pay? The problem was truly intolerable. When the first act came to an end, he realised how little of it he had heard.

'Ivo, isn't it marvellous?' Her eyes were still dreamy as the curtain fell.

'Yes, it's lovely.' But he wasn't thinking of the opera, only of her. 'Would you like something from the bar?' The others were already standing and forming a line at the exits. A trip to the bar was a must for all serious operagoers, not so much for what they drank, but whom they saw. But Ivo saw that she seemed to hesitate. 'Would you rather stay here?' Gratefully she nodded, and they both sat back down.

'Do you mind terribly?' She was instantly apologetic, but Ivo waved a nonchalant hand.

'Of course not. Don't be silly. Would you like me to bring you something here?' But she only shook her head again and laughed.

'You're going to have me as spoiled as I had my father, Ivo. Watch out! It becomes damn hard to live with.' They spoke of Justin briefly and then Ivo remembered the stories Justin had shown him. The stories Bettina had written.

38

'One day, if you want to, you can be an even greater writer than Justin.'

'Do you mean that?' She stared at him, as though too terrified to breathe, waiting, wanting to hear his answer, and yet much too afraid. But he was nodding, and she let out a very small sigh.

'I do. Your last four or five stories. You know, the ones you wrote last summer in Greece . . . they're extraordinary, Bettina. You could publish them if you wanted to, in fact I was going to ask you sometime if that was what you had in mind.' He looked at her seriously, and she gazed at him, stunned.

'Of course not. I just wrote them to – to write them. For no reason. Did Daddy show them to you?'

'Yes.'

'Did he think they were good?' Her voice was dreamy and wistful now, and she seemed to have almost forgotten that Ivo was there. But he stared at her in astonishment.

'Didn't he tell you?' Gently she shook her head. 'That's criminal, Bettina. He loved them. Didn't he ever say?'

'No.' And then she looked at Ivo squarely. 'But he wouldn't have actually. That kind of praise wasn't really his style.' No, but hearing it was. Oh, yes, how he loved that, Ivo thought.

Ivo was annoyed again as he thought of it. 'Suffice it to say that he truly loved them.'

She smiled carefully at Ivo again. 'I'm glad.'

Perhaps here was a way he could help her. 'Are you going to try to publish them?'

'I don't know.' She shrugged, suddenly childlike again. 'I told you, I dream about writing a play. But that doesn't mean I will.'

'It could if you wanted it to. One good strong dream is enough. If you hold it, and cherish it, and build on it. If you never give up that dream. No matter what.' For a long time Bettina said nothing, and she averted her eyes. He moved a little closer, and she could feel him next to her, his hand just

39

near hers where they sat. 'Don't give up your dreams, Bettina . . . don't ever, ever do that.'

When she looked up at him at last, it was with wise, tired eyes. 'My dreams are already over, Ivo.'

But he shook his head firmly, with the smallest of smiles. 'No, little one, they've only just begun.' And with that, he leaned forward and kissed her softly on the mouth.

Chapter 7

It had been a strange and wonderful evening with Ivo. After the opera they had gone to dinner at La Côte Basque, and they they had gone dancing at Le Club. Ivo and her father had been members there since it had opened, but years later it was still a nice club and it was the perfect place to spend New Year's Eve. They had reverted to their old easy ways of friendship, only his kiss had confused her for a moment, but she pushed it from her mind. He was a very dear friend. For the most part it had been like old times. They talked and laughed and danced. They drank champagne and stayed on until three, when at last Ivo professed exhaustion and announced that he was taking her home. They were both oddly quiet in the limousine driving back to her apartment, Bettina thinking of her father and how odd it was not to have been with him, or at least called him to wish him a happy new year. They rode slowly up the East Side, until at last they reached her door.

'Do you want to come up for a cognac?' She said it almost by rote, between yawns, but it was very close to four in the morning, and Ivo laughed.

'You make it sound very tempting. Do you suppose you can stay awake long enough to get upstairs?' He helped her from the car and followed her inside.

'I'm not sure . . . mmm . . . all of a sudden I'm so sleepy . . .' But she was smiling as they rode up in the elevator. 'Sure you don't want another drink?'

'Positive.'

And then she grinned at him. 'Good. I want to go to bed.' And as she said it she looked twelve years old again, and they both laughed.

The house was eerily empty as she turned her key and flicked on the light as she opened the door.

'Aren't you afraid to be alone here, Bettina?'

She looked at him honestly and nodded. 'Sometimes.'

His heart ached again as he looked at her. 'Will you make me a promise? If you ever, ever have a problem, you'll call. And I mean immediately. I'd come right over.'

'I know you would. It's a nice feeling.' She yawned again, sat down on a Louis XV chair in the hall, and kicked off her elegant navy-blue satin shoes. He sat down on a chair facing her, and they both smiled.

'You look beautiful tonight, Bettina. And terribly, terribly grown up.'

She shrugged, looking much like the young girl she was. 'I suppose I am grown-up now.' And then with a chortle she tossed one of the navy satin shoes in the air. She caught it again, barely missing a priceless vase that sat on a little marble ledge. 'You know the weirdest thing of all, Ivo?'

'What?'

'I mean aside from the loneliness, it's being responsible for me. There is no one, absolutely no one, to tell me what to do, to give me hell, to give me praise, to figure things out for me . . . none of it . . . If I had just broken that vase, it would have been my problem, no one else's. That's a lonely feeling sometimes too. Like no one gives a damn.' She looked pensively at her shoe, and then dropped it to the floor again, but Ivo was watching her intently.

'I give a damn.'

'I know you do. And I care about you too.'

He said nothing in answer for a moment. He just watched her. 'I'm glad.' Then he stood up and wandered slowly over to where she sat. 'And now, contrary to your theory, I'm going to tell you to go to bed, like a good girl. Shall I walk you upstairs to your room?' She hesitated for a long moment, and then she smiled.

'You wouldn't mind?'

He looked oddly serious when he shook his head. She walked towards the stairs in bare feet, her shoes lying forgotten on the foyer floor, and threw her blue velvet coat over her arm, as Ivo followed the naked oval of her back up to her bedroom. But he was in control now. In the course of the evening he had decided what he was going to do. She turned to look over her shoulder at him when they reached the top of the stairs.

'Are you going to tuck me into bed?' She was half teasing and half serious, and he wasn't quite sure what else he saw in her big green eyes. But he wasn't going to ask questions.

She ran a hand tiredly over her eyes, and she suddenly seemed very old. 'There's so much I have to do, Ivo. Sometimes I'm not sure how I'm going to do it all.' But as she said it he patted her shoulder, and she looked up at him, smiling.

'You will, darling. You will. But what you need first, mademoiselle, is a good night's sleep. So good night, little one. I'll let myself out.' She heard him walk softly down the carpeted hall, and then there was silence as she knew he had reached the stairs, and at last she heard his heels click on the marble floor below, and he called out 'Good night' for the last time before he closed the front door.

Chapter 8

Bettina followed the woman upstairs and down, smiling pleasantly, opening closet doors, and standing by as the real estate agent extolled the apartment's virtues and then unabashedly indicated its flaws. Bettina didn't have to be there for the performance, but she wanted to be. She wanted to know what they were saying about her home.

At last it was over, after almost an hour, and Naomi Liebson, who had been there three times that month, prepared to leave. There had been other visitors as well, with other realtors, but so far this was the most definite bite.

'Aahh just don't know, honey. Aahhm not really, really sure.' Bettina tried to smile again as she watched her, but the charm of showing the apartment was beginning to wear thin. It was exhausting escorting this army of would-be buyers through the place every day. And there was no one to relieve the tension for her. Ivo had been in Europe on business for three weeks. There had been an international conference in China, and as it had been the first of its kind, he had to go. After which he had business appointments in Europe: Brussels, Amsterdam, Rome, Milan, London, Glasgow, Berlin, and Paris. It was going to be a long trip. And it already felt as though he had been gone for years.

'Miss Daniels?' The real estate agent dragged her back from her reverie with a touch on the arm.

'I'm sorry . . . I was dreaming . . . Was there something else?' Naomi Liebson had apparently disappeared into the kitchen again. She wanted to look again, to try to envision how it would look if they broke through two walls. From the sound of what she'd been saying, she was going to gut the place anyway, upstairs and down. It made Bettina wonder why she didn't buy something more to her liking, but apparently this was what she did for fun. She had performed similar mutilation on five co-ops in as many years. But then she sold them again at enormous profits, so maybe she wasn't so crazy after all. Bettina looked curiously at the realtor, and then smiled. 'Think she'll buy it?'

The realtor shrugged. 'I don't know. I'm bringing two more people by later today. I don't think they're right for it though. It's too big for them, and one couple is elderly, and you've got too many stairs.'

'Then why bring them?' Bettina looked at her with fatigue beginning to pull down the corners of her delicate mouth. But she hadn't been able to resist asking. Why did they all come? There were people who wanted more bedrooms, older people who didn't want stairs, large families who needed more servants' rooms than even she had; there had been people for whom the apartment could never have been right, yet the realtors continued to come in droves, showing the place off to only a handful for whom the place made some sense. It seemed like a monstrous waste of time, but it was all part of the game.

And then of course it was Justin Daniels's apartment, and that was always worth a thrill . . . 'Why are they selling? . . .' Again and again Bettina had heard the whispers. And then the answer, 'He died and left the daughter flat broke . . .' The first time she had cringed when she heard it, and angry tears of indignation had stung her eyes . . . *How dare they! How could they?* But they dared and they could. And it didn't matter any more. She just wanted to sell the place and get out. Ivo was right, it was too big and too lonely, and now and then she had been scared. But the worst of it was that she couldn't afford it, and each month when the gargantuan maintenance was due, she trembled as she depleted her dwindling funds still more. It was high time that someone bought it. Naomi Liebson or whoever else.

45

The other houses had all sold after the first of the year. The one in Beverly Hills brought a windfall a few weeks before. The young man from the Middle East had bought it, lock, stock, and barrel, with carpets, dressers, eighteenth-century mirrors, modern paintings, and all. The place had always been an odd mélange of the extremely showy and the very refined and Bettina had never liked it as much as the apartment in New York. It barely hurt at all to sign the papers. Now all that remained abroad was the flat in London, but according to Ivo that was almost empty now. He had called from over there. Her father's London solicitor had also assured her that he had someone to buy the place. He would let her know at the end of the week. Which left only the co-operative apartment on Fifth Avenue in New York. Even that wasn't going to look the same in another two weeks. She sighed to herself again as she thought of the auction. They had moved the date up, as a favour. And in ten days Parke-Bernet was arriving to take it all. Literally everything. She had spent the three weeks of Ivo's absence going over each table, each bookcase, each chair. In the end she knew she could hang on to nothing, only a few mementos, some small objects that had no value, but meant something to her.

But other than that there would be nothing left that was hers after the auction, and she hoped to have sold the apartment by then. Camping out in the empty apartment would be more than she could bear.

The agent looked at her curiously as they both stood patiently, waiting for Mrs Liebson to return. It was unusual for a seller to help show the apartment, but then again Bettina was an unusual girl.

'Have you found anything else yet?' She eyed Bettina with interest. Hell, Naomi thought, even if Bettina were broke, after they sold this palazzo, she could buy herself something small and pretty, maybe a studio, or a little one-bedroom penthouse overlooking the park. That wouldn't cost her more than 100 thou. The woman didn't realise that it was

46

going to take every dime from the sale of the large apartment, as well as all the profits from the auction, to put her father's estate in the black.

Bettina only shook her head. 'I'm not looking yet. I don't want to start until I sell this.'

'That's all wrong. You know how it is when you sell. The buyer drags his feet for three weeks, and then suddenly bango, they buy it, and they want you out overnight.'

Bettina attempted a smile, but it was bleak. She was planning on moving to the Barbizon Hotel for Women at Lexington Avenue and Sixty-third, read *The New York Times* every day and of course the *Mail*, and hoped to find herself an apartment to rent in a matter of days, or maybe even weeks. She was even willing to share, if she had to. And then after that she would look for a job. She had decided not to discuss it with Ivo again. He would just set her up in a fancy office for a salary she didn't deserve and she didn't want that. She wanted to earn her living. She had to find a real job. The prospect of it almost crushed her with exhaustion as Mrs Liebson returned.

'Aahh just don't know what I'm goin' to do with that kitchen. Honey, it's a mess.' She looked reproachfully at Bettina, while still managing a broad smile. She looked at the realtor then and nodded, and with barely a goodbye they left. Bettina stood there for a moment, hating them both, as she softly closed the door. She didn't give a damn if the woman bought the apartment. She didn't want her to have it anyway. She didn't want her touching the kitchen, or anything else. It was *her* home, and her father's, theirs; it didn't belong to anyone else.

She sat down slowly in the winter twilight and stared around her and then down at the richly inlaid floor. How could he do this to her? How could he have left her in this god-awful mess? Didn't he understand what he was doing? Couldn't he have known? The resentment for her father rose up slowly in her throat like bile, and she let the tears start to flow. They were tears of anger and exhaustion, and her

47

shoulders began to shake as she dropped her face in her hands and started to sob. It seemed hours later when she finally heard the phone. She let it ring for a while, but it was persistent, so at last she stood up and crossed the hall to the discreet closet in the entry where it was concealed. She was just getting used to having to answer the phone herself no matter how rotten she felt. Gone were the days of glory, she thought as she wiped her eyes with a handkerchief and sniffed.

'Hello?'

'Bettina?'

'Yes?' She could barely hear the muffled male voice.

'Are you all right, darling? It's Ivo. Is this a good time to call?' Her face lit up as she heard him and she suddenly had to brush away fresh tears.

'Oh, is it!'

'What? I can't hear you, darling, speak up! Are you all right?'

'I'm fine.' And then suddenly she wanted to tell him the truth, all of it . . . . *No, I'm lonely, I'm miserable . . . In a few weeks I won't have a home.*

'What's happening with the apartment? Have you sold it?'

'Not yet.'

'All right. Well, we've sold London. The deal closed tonight.' He quoted a figure. It was enough to make a healthy inroad in her debts.

'That ought to help. How's your trip going?'

'It seems endless.' She smiled into the phone.

'It certainly does. When are you coming home?' She hadn't realised how anxious she was to see him.

'I don't know. I should really have come back days ago, but I got involved in some special meetings over here. I may have to delay it a bit.' She felt herself pouting and didn't give a damn if she sounded like a little girl. She could do that with him. He understood.

'How long?'

48

'Well' – he seemed to hesitate – 'I've just arranged to stay for another two weeks.'

'Oh, Ivo!' He had been gone since two days after their New Year's Eve date. 'That's awful!'

'I know, I know. I'm sorry. I'll make it up to you when I get back, I promise.'

'Will you be back in time for the sale?'

'What sale?'

'The auction.'

'When is it? I thought it wasn't for a while.'

'They moved it up for me. It's two weeks from tomorrow. Friday and Saturday. And it's only Daddy's stuff. It's all of it.'

'And what about you, for God's sake? You go off into the world with one suitcase and your name?'

'Hardly. You haven't seen my closets. It'll take more than one suitcase.' At last she smiled.

'You can't give everything up. What the hell are you going to do? Sleep on the floor?'

'I checked into it and I can rent a bed. It's either that or wait another year for Parke-Bernet to have another date to schedule the sale. And then what? What if this place sells? I'd have to pay storage for the furniture . . . Never mind, Ivo, it's too complicated. It has to be like this.'

'For God's sake, Bettina, I wish you'd waited for me to come back before you got into all this.' He sounded distraught and he was looking around his hotel room with dismay. There wasn't a great deal he could do to stop her from three thousand miles away, and the fact was that she was right to do what she was doing. He just hated to have her face it all alone. But she was good at it. All her life, in a way, Bettina had faced the difficult moments alone.

'Anyway, don't worry about it, Ivo, it's all under control. I just miss you like crazy.'

'I'll be back soon.' He checked his calendar and gave her the exact date of his return.

'What time are you coming in?'

49

'I'm taking a seven a.m. flight out of Paris, which should get me into New York at nine in the morning, New York time. I'll be in the city by about ten.' She had wanted to surprise him by being at the airport, but she suddenly realised that there was no way she could. 'Why?'

'Never mind. That's the day of the Parke-Bernet sale.'

'What time does it start?'

'Ten o'clock in the morning.'

He made a note on his calendar. 'I'll meet you there.'

Suddenly Bettina was smiling. Unlike her father, Ivo never let her down. 'Are you sure you can do that? Don't you have to go to work?'

This time he smiled at her as he held the phone. 'After five weeks, one day can hardly make that much difference. I'll be there as early as I can. And I'll call you long before that, little one. Now you're sure you're all right?' But how all right could she be with realtors crawling all over her apartment and all her belongings about to be sold at auction by Parke-Bernet?

'I'm fine. Honest.'

'I don't like your being there all alone.'

'I told you. I'm all right.'

They spoke a few minutes more. Then it was time for him to go.

'I'll call you. Bettina – ' There was a strange, empty pause as he hesitated, and she held her breath.

'Yes?'

'Never mind, little one. Take care.'

Chapter 9

The phone rang the next morning before Bettina had got out of bed. It was the real estate agent. Five minutes later Bettina sat up in her bed with a look of dismay.

'For God's sake, this is very good news!' The real estate woman spoke to her in obvious irritation, and Bettina nodded. It was good news. But it still came as a shock. She had just lost her home. For a handsome price. But still, it was gone. The moment had come.

'I suppose it is. I just . . . I hadn't . . . I didn't expect it to happen so quickly. When will she . . . how soon – ' She couldn't find her words and suddenly she hated the woman from Texas. She was buying the co-op. And for a sum that should have made Bettina squeal with delight. But she didn't feel like squealing. The agent talked on while Bettina's eyes filled with tears.

'Shall we say we'll close two weeks from tomorrow? That will give you both two full weeks to get organised.'

The arrangements made, Bettina hung up, sitting in silence in her bedroom, looking around her as though for the last time.

She spent the next week alternately packing and stopping to dry her tears. And at last on Wednesday they arrived to remove the countless priceless pieces to the hallowed halls of Parke-Bernet. It was the same day she went to her attorney to finalise the sale of the apartment. She didn't even bother calling to rent a bed. She uncovered an old sleeping-bag she had bought years before and slept on the floor of her room. It was only for three nights; she could have moved to the hotel early, but she didn't want to. She wanted to stay there until the end.

The day of the sale at Parke-Bernet she woke up early. She began to stir as the first light of dawn crept across the floor.

She didn't even bother to close the curtains any more. She liked waking up early and sitting cross-legged with her coffee on the thick carpeting in her room.

But this morning she was even too nervous for coffee, and she paced catlike about the house in her nightgown and bare feet. If she closed her eyes, she could see the apartment as it had been only last week. With her eyes open, it was strangely barren, and the parquet floors cold beneath her feet. She went hastily back to her room shortly after seven and tore through her closet for almost an hour. This wasn't a day for blue jeans. She wasn't going to wear work clothes or hide in a back row. She was going to walk in proudly and hold her head high. For this one last time she was going on view as Justin Daniels's daughter, and she was going to look fabulous. As though nothing had changed.

She emerged at last with a striking black wool Dior suit with padded shoulders, a cinched waist, and a long narrow skirt. Her hair would look like flame atop a black candle. And the jacket buttoned high in a mandarin collar. She didn't need a blouse. She would wear her mink over it, and on her feet, high-heeled black kid Dior shoes.

She bathed in the pink marble bathroom for the last time and emerged smelling faintly of gardenias and roses. She brushed her hair until it shone like dark honey, put on her make-up, and slowly got dressed. When she stood in front of the mirror, she was proud of what she saw. No one would have guessed that she was only a nineteen-year-old girl who had just lost everything she owned.

The auction room was already crowded with row after row of dealers, collectors, gawkers, buyers, and old friends. All conversation stopped as she entered the room. Two men jumped forward and snapped her picture, but Bettina didn't even flinch. She walked regally to one of the first rows, almost in front of a spotter, and threw her mink coat easily over the back of her chair. Her eyes weren't smiling, and she acknowledged none of those who tried to get her attention. She was a startling vision in black, with her copper hair, and her only jewellery was a long strand of her mother's large, perfect pearls. In her ears she wore matching ear-rings, and on her hands, a single onyx and pearl ring. The only thing she hadn't sold in the three months since her father had died were her jewels. Ivo had assured her that she would be able to hang on to them and still clean up the debts, and he was right.

The stage was directly in front of her where she knew she would be able to see the old familiar items appear as they were auctioned. Paintings, couches, end tables, lamps. And in the corners and along the sides of the room she could already see a few pieces, the pieces that would have been too large to carry on and off the stage, highboys, enormous sideboards, his bookcase, and two very large standing clocks. Most of it Louis XV, some Louis XVI, some English, all rare, many signed, it was going to be what the catalogue called an 'important' sale, but that was only fitting, Bettina thought to herself, Justin Daniels had been an important man. And she felt important again now, as she sat there, because this one last time she was there as his daughter, not simply herself.

The bidding began at exactly seven minutes past ten, and Ivo had not yet arrived. Bettina looked at the plain Cartier watch on her left wrist, and then let her eyes wander back to the man at the podium, the spotters, and the huge inlaid Louis XV chest with the marble slab on top of it, which they had just auctioned off for twenty-two thousand five. The circular platform on the stage slowly turned lazy-Susan style and another familiar item was revealed. It was the large ornate seventeenth-century mirror from their front hall.

'The bidding is open at two thousand five . . . two thousand five . . . three, I have three . . . four . . . five . . . six . . . seven . . . seven five on the left . . . eight! . . . Nine at the front of the room . . . nine five . . . ten in the rear! . . . Ten . . . ten . . . do I have . . . eleven! . . . Eleven five . . . and twelve . . . twelve at the front of the room.' And with that he clicked the hammer down. It was all over in less than a minute. It went with lightning speed, and the action was all but invisible. Fingers barely moved, hands were barely raised, there were nods, signals of the eye, the slightest gesture of a pen, a hand, and the spotters were trained to see it all and report it rapidly to the auctioneer, but it was rare that the spectators could see who was doing the bidding. Bettina had no idea at all who had just bought the large antique mirror. She made a notation in her catalogue and settled back in her chair to watch the next item.

There were two beautiful French bergère chairs, upholstered in delicate café-au-lait silks, that had been in her father's bedroom. There was also a matching chaise longue similarly upholstered, which was the next item in the catalogue. Bettina, with pen poised and waiting for the bidding to begin, felt someone slide into the empty seat beside her. Then she heard a familiar voice in her ear.

'Do you want those?' His eyes looked tired and his voice sounded grim. As she turned to see Ivo the funereal air of intensity of the hour before momentarily fled.

She put her arms around his neck for a moment and held him close. Slowly his face broke into a smile. She pulled away from him briefly and whispered in his ear. 'Welcome home, stranger. I'm so glad you could come.'

He nodded and then, sobering, repeated his first question. The bidding was already at nine thousand five. 'Do you want them?' But she only shook her head. And then, leaning closer to her again, he gently took her hand. 'I want you to tell me what you want from all this. Anything that means something to you, tell me. I'll buy it and keep it for you at my place. You can pay me later if you want to and I don't give a damn if that means in twenty years . . .' And then he smiled and leaned towards her again. 'If I'm still around to collect it, which I doubt.' He knew how proud she was and that he had to make the offer as he did.

She whispered again as they closed the bidding at thirteen and a half for the two chairs. 'You damn well better be around, Ivo.'

'At eighty-two? For God's sake, Bettina, give me a break.'
They looked at each other as though they had seen each
other every day for the past month. It was difficult to believe,
suddenly, that he'd been gone for five weeks. 'Are you all
right?'

She nodded slowly. 'I'm fine. Are you exhausted from the
flight?' A couple in front of them shushed them, and Ivo
glared malevolently at the pair. And then he turned to
Bettina with a tired smile.

'It was a long flight. But I didn't want you to be here
alone. How long will this go on today? All day?' He prayed
that it wouldn't, he needed a few hours' sleep.

'Just till lunch. And tomorrow morning and afternoon.'
He nodded and turned his attention to what was being
shown on the stage. Bettina had grown strangely quiet, and
Ivo squeezed her hand. It was Justin's desk.

Ivo leaned quietly towards her and spoke once again in
her ear. 'Bettina?' But she shook her head and looked away.

'Seven thousand . . . seven . . . eight? Seven five! . . . Eight!
. . . Eight . . . Nine! . . .' It went for nine thousand dollars, and
Bettina supposed that to an antique dealer it was worth the
price. It was worth more than that to her though. It had
been the desk where her father worked, where he had
written his last two books, where she had seen him again and
again, poring over manuscripts . . . Her mind drifted
painfully into the past, but Ivo was watching her and still
holding tightly to her hand.

'Relax, little one . . . It's still yours.' He spoke infinitely
gently, and she looked up at him in confusion.

'I don't understand.'

'You don't have to. We can discuss it later.'

'Did you buy it?' She looked at him, stunned, and
wanting to laugh for a moment, he nodded.

'Don't look so surprised.'

'For nine thousand dollars?' She looked horrified, and
someone behind them told her to lower her voice.
Thousands of dollars were being bandied about between

55

bidders, this was no time for distractions from the audience. This was a serious crowd. Like gamblers, they paid attention to what they were doing and little else. But Bettina was still staring at Ivo in astonishment. 'Ivo, you didn't!' This time she whispered more softly, and he smiled.

'I did.' And then he cast an eye towards the stage again and raised an eyebrow questioningly. It was another desk. He leaned towards her again. 'Where was that?'

'In the guest room, but it's not a good one. Don't buy it.' She looked at him seriously, wondering just how many pieces he was planning to buy, and he watched her, amused.

'Thanks for the advice.' Apparently the dealers and collectors shared her sentiments about the piece. It went for only eighteen hundred dollars. By that day's standards it was cheap.

The proceedings seemed to go on for hours, but Bettina didn't let him buy anything more. At last it was over. At least for the day. It was five minutes to twelve. They stood up as the rest of the crowd got up to leave, clutching their catalogues and discussing the bidding with friends. She realised Ivo was staring at her. It made her feel warm inside, though slightly uncomfortable.

'What are you looking at?'

'I'm looking at you, little one. Because it's so good to see you.' His voice was like velvet on the words. And she wanted to tell him that she missed him, but instead, with a faint blush on her cheeks, she bowed her head.

As he watched, a shadow darted into her eyes. Now what was wrong? There was something different about her already. Once again something had changed since he had been gone. But he wasn't sure what this time and he wasn't sure he liked what it was.

He looked at her very seriously. 'Will you come home with me, Bettina, for lunch?' She hesitated for a long moment, and then she nodded.

'That would be nice.'

He beckoned to his driver, who was waiting, and a

moment later they sped away towards his apartment, twelve blocks south of hers, on Park Avenue. It was comfortable there. It was far less grandiose, but filled with lovely things that looked inviting and warm. There were big leather chairs and soft couches, paintings of hunting scenes, and bookcases filled with rare books; there was lots of brass around the fireplace, and the windows were large and inundated with sun. It was clearly a man's apartment, yet it was friendly and cosy and would have been large enough for more than just him. Downstairs he had a living-room, dining-room, and library. Upstairs he had two bedrooms and his private den. There was also a spacious wood-panelled country kitchen. Behind it there would have been room for two maids, but he only kept one. His driver lived elsewhere and was actually employed by the *Mail*. Bettina had always liked coming to his apartment. It was like going to someone's house in the country, or like visiting a favourite uncle in his lair. Everything smelled of tobacco and cologne and fine leather. She liked the feel of his things, their texture, and their smell.

Bettina looked around her with a feeling of homecoming as they walked into the sunny living-room and he checked back over his shoulder. She looked better again, and for a moment the look of terror seemed to have fled. 'It's nice to be back here, Ivo. I always forget how pretty it is.'

'That's because you don't come here often enough.'

'That's only because you don't ask me.' She was teasing now, and happy, as she plunked herself down on the couch.

'If that's all that keeps you away from here, I will ask! And often!' He smiled and tried not to glance at the mountain of mail. 'Oh, God, will you look at that, Bettina . . .'

'I was trying not to. It reminds me of my father's after he'd been away for a few days.'

'And this is nothing. I'm sure it's worse at the office.' He ran a hand across his eyes and then walked into the kitchen. Mathilde seemed to have mysteriously disappeared. He had expected her to be waiting.

'Where's Mattie?' Bettina reflected his thought. She had called her that since she was a very small child.

'I don't know. Can I offer you a sandwich? I'm starved.'

She looked at him sheepishly. 'So am I. I was so nervous during the bidding, and now suddenly I'm ravenous.' And then she remembered. 'Speaking of which, Ivo . . . what about that desk?' She looked at him pointedly, but there was something far softer in her eyes.

'What desk?' He looked nonchalant as he headed for the kitchen. 'I hope there's at least something to eat.'

'Knowing Mattie, enough for an army. But you didn't answer my question, Ivo. What about the desk?'

'What about it? It's yours.'

'No, it was Daddy's. Now it's yours. Why don't you keep it? He'd like you to have it, you know.' She looked at him gently once they arrived in the kitchen, and he reached into the fridge and turned his back.

'Never mind that, you can write your play on that desk. Let's not discuss it.' It was still too soon to talk to her about what he had in mind.

She sighed. They would have to discuss it another time. 'Why don't you let me make the lunch?'

He couldn't resist stretching out a hand to rumple her hair. His voice was hoarse but gentle when he spoke again. 'You look very pretty today, little one . . . in your black suit.'

She said nothing for a long moment, and then she walked past him, preparing to make lunch. His eyes never left her, and when her back was turned, he finally asked. 'What is it that you're not telling me, Bettina? I get the feeling there's something you have on your mind.' He felt stupid once he had said it. Every stick of furniture her father had owned was being sold at auction, it was natural that she should be disturbed. Yet he had the feeling that there was more than that. He had seen something even more painful in her eyes. 'Is there something you're not telling me?'

'I've sold the apartment.'

'What? Already?' Bettina nodded mutely. 'And when does the new owner take possession?'

Bettina looked away and tried to catch her breath. 'Tomorrow. I said I'd be out by tomorrow afternoon. As a matter of fact it's in the contract.'

'And who was the fool who let you do that?' Ivo looked at her ominously and then held out his arms. 'Never mind who, I can guess. It was your father's idiot lawyer. Oh, Christ.' And then all she knew was that he was holding her and it didn't quite feel as though the world had come to an end. 'Oh, baby . . . poor baby . . . all the furniture and now the whole place. Oh, God, it must feel awful.' He held her and swayed softly, and in his arms she felt suddenly safe.

'It does, Ivo . . . it does . . . I feel . . .' And then the tears suddenly crowded into her eyes. 'I feel as though . . . they're taking away . . . everything . . . as though there's . . . nothing left. Just me, alone in the apartment . . . it's already over . . . there is no more past . . . and I have nothing, Ivo . . . nothing at all . . .' She was sobbing in his arms as she said it, and he only held her tight.

'It'll be different one day, Bettina. One day, you'll look back at all this and it will seem like a dream. A dream that happened to somebody else. It will fade, darling . . . it will fade.' But how he wished he could make it fade quickly and make her pain disappear. He had already made a decision before he left for London, but he wondered if this was the right time. He waited until she was quieter before he asked her any questions, but then he brought her into the living-room and sat her down next to him on the couch. 'What are you going to do tomorrow, Bettina, when you move out?'

She took a deep breath and looked at him. 'Go to a hotel.'

'What about tonight?'

'I want to sleep there.'

'Why?'

She started to say Because it's my home, but it sounded ridiculous, it was only an empty apartment. It wasn't

59

anyone's home any more. 'I don't know. Maybe because it's my last chance.'

He looked at her kindly. 'But that doesn't make much sense, does it? You've lived there, you've collected all the good memories it had to give. And now it's all gone, it's empty, like an empty tube of toothpaste, all squeezed out. There's not point keeping it a moment longer, is there?' And then, after only an instant, he looked at her more deeply. 'I think it would make a lot of sense if you moved out today.'

'Now?' She looked startled, and once again like a frightened child. 'Tonight?' She stared at him blankly and he nodded.

'Yes. Tonight.'

'Why?'

'Trust me.'

'But I don't have a reservation . . .' She was clutching at straws.

'Bettina, I've been waiting to ask you this, but I'd like you to stay here.'

'With you?' She looked startled, and he laughed.

'Not exactly. I'm not a masher after all, darling. In the guest room. How does that sound?' But nothing had really registered. Suddenly she felt very confused.

'I don't know . . . . I suppose I could . . . just for tonight.'

'No, that wasn't what I had in mind. I'd like you to stay until you get settled, till you find a nice place of your own. Something decent,' he admonished gently, 'and the right job. Mattie could take care of you. And I'd feel a lot better if I knew you were safe here. I don't think your father would have objected. In fact I'd say it was what he'd have liked best. Now' – he watched her eyes carefully – 'what about you?'

But her eyes were filling slowly with tears. 'I can't, Ivo.' She shook her head and looked away. 'You've been too good to me already, and I could never pay you back. Just today . . . the desk . . . I can't ever – '

'Shh . . . never mind . . .' He took her in his arms again and gently stroked her hair. 'It's all right.' And then he pulled away to look at her and tried to coax her to smile. 'Besides, if you're going to cry all the time, you can't stay at a hotel. They'd throw you out for making too much noise.'

'I don't cry all the time!' She sniffed and accepted his handkerchief to blow her nose.

'I know that. In fact you've been unbelievably brave. But what I don't want you to be is foolish. Going to a hotel would be foolish.' And then more firmly he added, 'Bettina, I want you to stay here. Is that so awful? Would you really hate it, being here with me?' But all she could do was shake her head. She wouldn't hate it. In fact that was one of the things that frightened her most. She wanted to be there with him. Maybe even a little too much.

For a moment she wavered, and then sighed again as she blew her nose. And then at last she let her eyes find his. He was right. It did make more sense than going to a hotel. If she just didn't feel like that . . . if he weren't so damn good-looking in spite of his age. She had to keep reminding herself that he wasn't forty-seven or even fifty-two . . . he was sixty-two . . . sixty-two . . . and her father's very dearest friend . . . it was almost like incest . . . she couldn't let herself feel that way.

'Well?' He turned to look at her from where he stood at the bar while he was reproaching himself for thoughts similar to hers.

She sounded almost breathless as she answered. 'I'll do it. I'll stay.'

Their eyes met and they smiled. It was an end and a beginning, and a promise, and the birth of hope. For them both.

By Saturday it was over. They had to go back to the apartment, to pick up the last of her stuff. She had spent the night before in Ivo's guest room, catered to and pampered by the jovial and warm-hearted Mathilde, who had prepared their dinner and in the morning brought Bettina a tray. Ivo was glad to be able to restore her to comfort again. It had to be a relief from the emptiness of the apartment she had hung on to almost till the end.

'I told Mrs Liebson I'd be out by six.' Bettina looked at her watch nervously, and Ivo took her arm.

'Don't worry, we have time.' He knew how little she had left there. He had gone over with her the night before to pick up one of her bags. And his heart had ached for her when he saw the sleeping-bag stretched out on the floor. Now it was a question of a dozen suitcases, two or three boxes, and that was all. He had assured her that there was room in his storeroom and Mathilde had already cleared two closets for her. It would be more than enough.

As usual Ivo's driver was waiting, and he sped them quickly over to Fifth and was rapidly at Bettina's door. She clambered out quickly, and Ivo was hard on her heels. She looked up at him questioningly. 'Do you really want to come up?'

He realised with a flash of understanding what was on her mind. 'Do you want to be alone?'

Her eyes wavered as she answered. 'I'm not sure.'

He nodded softly. 'Then I'll come.' And she looked somehow relieved.

Two porters were summoned, and a few moments later they all stood in the empty front hall. There were no lights lit and it was dark outside. Ivo watched her as she stared bleakly past the front hall.

She glanced hurriedly over her shoulder at Ivo, and then at the two men. 'Everything is upstairs in the front bedroom. I'll be right back, I want to check around.' But this time Ivo didn't follow her. He knew she wanted to be alone. The two men scurried off to get her things, and he lingered in the hallway, listening to her footsteps as she wandered from room to room, pretending that she was checking to see if anything had been forgotten or mislaid. But it was memories she was collecting, moments with her father that she wanted to touch for one last time.

'Bettina?' Ivo called out softly. He hadn't heard her heels in a long time. But at last he found her, standing tiny and forgotten in her father's bedroom, with tears streaming from her eyes.

He went to her, and she held him, whispering softly into his arms. 'I will never be back here again.' It seemed hard to believe. It was over. But it had been for a while.

Ivo held her gently. 'No, little one, you won't. But there will be other places, other people, who may one day mean almost as much to you as this.'

She shook her head slowly. 'Nothing ever will.'

'I hope you're wrong. I hope that – that there are other men you love at least as much as him.' And then he smiled down at her very gently. 'At least one.' Bettina didn't respond.

'He didn't leave you, little one. I hope you know that. He simply moved on.'

That seemed to reach her, and suddenly she turned around and walked solemnly from the room. She paused in the doorway and held out her hand. He put an arm around her shoulders and walked her to the front door, which she locked for the last time, and slipped her key under the door.

Chapter 10

The sun was streaming in the dining-room windows as Mathilde poured Bettina a second cup of coffee. She had been intently studying the newspaper, and suddenly she looked up with a smile.

'Thank you, Mattie.' The month of living at Ivo's had been restful for her. It had helped heal the wounds. Ivo had made everything easy. She had a beautiful little room, three meals a day of Mathilde's excellent cooking. She had all the books she wanted to read. She joined him in the evening to go to operas, or concerts, or plays. It was not unlike living with her father, yet in many ways it was a far more peaceful way of life. Ivo was a good deal less erratic, and his every thought seemed to centre around her. He had spent the last month with her, almost every evening, going out to interesting places or sitting home by the fire and talking for hours. On Sundays they did the *Times* crossword puzzle together and went for walks in the park. It was March and the city was still cold and grey, but now and then the air smelled of spring.

He looked over his paper at her now with a smile. 'You look embarrassingly cheerful this morning, Bettina. Any reason for it, or were you still thinking about last night?' They had gone to the opening of a new play and they had both loved it. Bettina had talked passionately of it all the way home. Ivo assured her that one day she would write something even better than that. And now she was smiling at him, with her head tilted to one side. She had been reading *Backstage*, the little weekly theatrical paper she had to travel halfway across town to buy.

'There's an ad in here, Ivo.' Her eyes were full of meaning and he gave her his full attention.

'Is there? What kind of ad?'

'There's a new repertory group forming, off Broadway.'

'How far off Broadway?' He was instantly suspicious. And when she gave him the address, he was more so. 'Isn't that a little remote?' It was a grim neighbourhood near the Bowery. One which Bettina had never even seen.

'What difference does that make? They're looking for people, actors, actresses, and technical people, all non-equity. Maybe they'd give me a chance.'

'At doing what?' He felt dread crawl up his spine. He had been afraid of something like this. Twice he had reiterated his offer of a job at the paper, something nice, decent, and slightly overpaid. And both times she had refused. The last time with such vehemence that he no longer dared to mention the offer.

'Maybe I could get some kind of technical job, helping set up the scenery, working the curtain. Anything. I don't know. It would be a terrific opportunity to see how the inside of a theatre works . . . you know, for when I write my play.'

For an instant he almost smiled. She was so incredibly childish at times. 'Don't you think you'd learn more just going to see the successful shows on Broadway, like last night?'

'That's different. It doesn't show me how everything gets put together behind the scenes.'

'And you feel you have to know that?' He was stalling and she knew it. She laughed gently.

'Yes, Ivo, I do.' And then, without saying more, she went to the phone in his study across the hall, the paper still clutched in her hand. She was back five minutes later, beaming at him. 'They said to come down today, around three.'

Ivo sat back in his chair with a discouraged sigh. 'I'll be back from lunch then. You can take the car.'

'To this theatre? Are you crazy? They'll never hire me if I show up in a limousine.'

'That wouldn't be the worst news I'd heard all day, Bettina.'

'Don't be silly.' She leaned down to kiss his forehead and lightly touched his hair. 'You worry too much. It'll be fine. And think, maybe I'll get a job out of it.'

'Then what? You work in that horrendous neighbourhood? How do you propose to get there every day?'

'On the subway, like the rest of the people who work in this town.'

'Bettina – ' He looked almost menacing, except that behind the menace was fear. Fear of what she was doing, where she was going, and of what it might mean for him.

'Now, Ivo . . .' She waggled a finger at him, blew a kiss, and disappeared into the kitchen to say something to Mathilde. Feeling very elderly, Ivo folded his newspaper, called out his goodbyes, and left for work.

At two thirty that afternoon Bettina made her way to the subway, disappeared into its bowels, and stood waiting in the dank chill for a train to arrive. When it did, it was smelly, graffiti-covered, and half empty; the only other passengers seemed to be old women with curling hairs on their chins, thick elastic stockings, and shopping bags, filled with mysterious items, that seemed to pull at their frail shoulders like rocks. There were a few teenaged boys wandering by, and here and there a man nodding off to sleep with his face buried in the collar of his coat. Bettina smiled to herself, thinking of what Ivo would say to all this. But he would have said a great deal more had he seen the theatre at the address given in the ad. It was an old ramshackle building that had been a movie theatre some twenty years before. In the interim it had often stood empty, housed some unsuccessful porno ventures, and at one time been turned into a church. Now it was being reinstated as a theatre, but not in any grand style. The repertory group would do nothing to revive the exterior of the building, they needed the few pennies they had to put on their plays.

As Bettina entered the building with mixed emotions of awe, excitement, and fear, she looked around her. There seemed to be no one around but she heard her footsteps echoing on the bare wooden floors. Everything seemed to be intensely dusty and there was an odd smell that reminded her of an attic.

'Yeah?' A man in blue jeans and a T-shirt was looking her over, with cynical blue eyes and a full, sensual mouth. His hair sprang from his head in a profusion of tight blonde curls and gave his face a softness belied by the toughness of his eyes. 'What is it?'

'I – I came . . . actually I called this morning . . . I . . . there was an ad in the paper . . .' She was so nervous, she could hardly speak, but she took a deep breath and went on. 'My name is Bettina Daniels. I'm looking for a job.' She held out a hand, almost as an offering, but he didn't shake it, he just kept his hands shoved into his jeans.

'I don't know who you talked to. It wasn't me, or I'd have told you not to bother coming down. We're full up. We cast the last female role this morning.'

'I'm not an actress.' She said it with radiant cheer, and for a minute the man with the blonde curls almost laughed.

'At least you're the first one who's honest. Maybe we should have cast you. Anyway, kiddo, sorry.' He shrugged and started to move away.

'No, wait . . . really . . . . I wanted a job doing something else.'

'Like what?' He looked her over unabashedly, and had Bettina been less anxious, she would have wanted to slap his face.

'Anything . . . lights . . . the curtain . . . whatever you've got.'

'You got any experience?'

Her chin went up just a fraction. 'No. I don't. But I'm willing. I'd like to learn.'

'Why?'

'I need the job.'

67

'So how come you don't go to work as a secretary somewhere?'

'I don't want to do that. I want to work in the theatre.'

'Because it's glamorous?' The cynical eyes were laughing at her now and she was slowly getting angry.

'No, because I want to write a play.'

'Oh, Jesus. So you're one of those. I suppose you went to Radcliffe, and now you think you're going to win a Tony in one year.'

'No, I'm a drop-out, and I just want a chance to work in a real theatre. That's all.' But she felt beaten. She knew that she had already lost. The guy hated her. She could tell.

He stood there watching her for a long time, then slowly he took a step closer to where she stood. 'You know anything about lights?'

'A little.' It was a lie but she was desperate now. She felt like it was her last chance.

'How little?' The eyes were boring into her own.

'Very little.'

'In other words you don't know shit.' He sighed and slumped hopelessly. 'All right, so we'll train you. If you don't make a pain in the ass of yourself, I'll train you myself.' And then in a sudden, unexpected motion he stuck out his hand. 'I'm the stage manager. My name's Steve.' She nodded her head, not sure of what he was saying to her. 'Jesus, relax for chrissake, will you? You got the job.'

'I did? Doing lights?'

'Working the dimmer board. You'll love it.' She was to learn later that it was hot, boring, claustrophobic work, but at that moment in time it was the best news she had ever had.

She smiled at him radiantly. 'Thank you so much.'

'Don't worry about it. You just happen to be the first one who came for the job. If you're lousy, I'll fire you. No big deal.'

'I won't be.'

'Good. Then that's one headache I don't have. Be here

68

tomorrow. I'll show you around. I don't have time today.'
As he said it he glanced at his watch. 'Yeah, tomorrow. And
once we go into rehearsals at the end of this week, that's it,
kiddo, seven days a week.'

'Seven?' She tried not to look shocked.

'You got kids?' She quickly shook her head. 'Good. Then
you don't have to worry. Your old man can come to see the
plays at half price. And if we don't make it, you won't have
to worry about working seven days a week. Right? Right.'
Nothing seemed to bother him. 'Oh, by the way you know
we don't pay you. You're lucky to have the job. We split the
box-office take.'

Bettina was shocked again. She was going to have to be
careful with the six thousand dollars she had left.

'So you'll be here tomorrow. Right, kid?' She nodded
obediently. 'Good. If you're not, I'll give someone else the
job.'

'Thank you.'

'You're welcome.' He was making fun of her, but now
there was something softer in his eyes. 'I shouldn't tell you
this, but I got started just like you. It's a bitch. Only at first I
wanted to be an actor, and that's worse.'

'And now?'

'I want to be a director.' The camaraderie of the theatre
had already taken hold; they were making friends.

Bettina smiled at him with a burst of her old spirit. 'If
you're very nice to me, maybe I'll let you direct my play.'

'Never mind the bullshit, kiddo. Get lost, I'll see you
tomorrow.' And then, as the heels of her boots clattered
across the barren floor towards the door, he called out to her,
'Hey, what did you say your name was?'

'Bettina.'

'Right.' He waved, turned away distractedly, and walked
quickly through the theatre towards the stage. For only an
instant Bettina watched him, and then rushing back into the
sunshine, she let out a whoop of delight. She had a job!

Chapter 11

'I keep forgetting that I don't have to look at the want ads any more.' Bettina looked at Ivo over the Sunday paper with a smile. It was the first time she had been able to sit down and relax in three weeks. It was Sunday morning and they had just taken their favourite seats, near a roaring fire. The play was 'up', and Bettina had until the evening before she had to go downtown.

'Do you really like it?' He was still troubled. He hated the neighbourhood, the idea, and the hours. And he didn't like the circles under her eyes. But that was mainly from the excitement. She had come home every night and been too wound up to go to bed much before three.

But she looked at him earnestly now, and he could see that she meant what she said. 'Ivo, I love it. Last night I almost felt' – she seemed to hesitate – 'like Daddy with his books. If I'm going to write for the theatre and put together a decent play, I have to know everything about the theatre. This is the only way that makes sense.'

'I suppose so. But couldn't you just write novels like your father?' He sighed with a small wintry smile. 'I worry about you coming home from the theatre at night, in that stinking neighbourhood, at that appalling hour.'

'It's busy, and I'm safe. It never takes me more than a minute to find a cab.' She didn't dare take the subway at those hours.

'I know, but – ' He shook his head dubiously, and then threw up both hands. 'What can I say?'

'Nothing. Just let me enjoy it. Because I am.'

'How can I argue with anything that makes you that happy?' It was written all over her face. Even he had to admit it. And it had been that way for weeks.

'You can't, Ivo.' And then she looked back at the paper

70

again, but this time more pensively. 'Now all I have to do is to find my own place.'

'Already?' Ivo sounded shocked. 'What's your rush?'

She looked up at him slowly. There was something very quiet in her eyes. She didn't want to leave either, but she knew it was time. 'Aren't you getting a little tired of having me hang around?'

But Ivo shook his head sadly as she asked. 'Never, Bettina. You know better than that.' The very thought of her leaving weighed down his soul. But he had no right to hold on to her.

She didn't dare tell him that there were two apartments she thought she should see. She'd have to take a chance and let them wait until Monday. She at least owed him that. And it was obvious that her going out on her own upset him. Maybe he still felt he owed something more to her father. But he couldn't play nursemaid to her forever. She had got too comfortable living here. It was definitely time she moved on. It would be better that way really. It was too easy like this. She had even learned to control what she had at first felt for him. They were friends now, companions, but nothing more. She had understood that those odd stirrings of hers had had to be squelched.

They went for their usual Sunday walk, putting the conversation about her leaving behind them.

They stopped for a time, watching New Yorkers whirl around them, skating, bicycling, jogging in Central Park. She sat down on the grass and patted a spot next to her. 'Sit down, Ivo.' And then, after a time, 'Something's bothering you. Can I ask what?'

But it was nothing he could tell her. That was the bitch of it. He avoided her eyes. 'Business.'

'You're lying. Now tell me the truth.'

'Oh, Bettina . . .' He closed his eyes and sighed. 'I'm just tired. And once in a while' – he opened his eyes and smiled at her – 'I feel very, very old.' And then, not sure why he let himself tell her, he went on. 'Some things are reserved to special ages. Having babies, getting married, getting grey

71

hair, falling in love. And no matter how smoothly our lives run, now and then we find ourselves in the wrong time slot, the wrong age . . .'

She looked puzzled as she watched him. And then the light of teasing came gently to her eyes. 'All right, Ivo. You're pregnant? Now tell me the truth.' He had to laugh at her as she tenderly patted his hand.

And then, throwing caution to the wind, he told her as he watched her eyes. 'All right. It's your moving out. Suddenly I can't imagine a life without you.' And then he smiled at her. 'Doesn't that sound strange? But you've spoiled me. I can't even remember how it was before.'

'Neither can I.' She played with the grass and spoke barely above a whisper before at last she looked back into his eyes. 'I hate to leave you, but I have to.'

And then he asked the question they both wondered about. 'Why?'

'Because I should be independent, because now I have to grow up. Because I have to support myself. I can't just live in your house forever. That wouldn't be right. And it isn't very proper either, I suppose.'

'What would make it right?' He was pushing. He wanted her to say it – but for the first time in years he was afraid.

'You could adopt me.' They both smiled at that. And then he looked at her seriously again.

'You're going to think I'm crazy, and I probably shouldn't tell you, but when I was in Europe, I came up with what I thought was a splendid plan. In the meantime, of course, I've come to realise that I was out of my mind.' He smiled down at her tensely, and then looked away. 'Do you know what I was going to do, Bettina?' He said it almost to himself as he lay full length on the grass, leaning on his elbows and squinting at the sky. 'I was going to ask you to marry me. In fact I was going to insist. But you were living in Justin's apartment then, and things were different. Suddenly you moved into my place, and I felt as though you were at my mercy. I didn't want to take advantage of you. I didn't – ' He stopped as he heard her sniff and he turned to see her looking at him in stupefaction, with tears running down her face. He smiled gently as he saw her and with one hand touched her wet cheek. 'Don't be so horrified, Bettina. I didn't do it, did I, you big silly? Now stop crying.'

'Why not?'

'Why not what?' He handed her his handkerchief and she dabbed at her eyes.

'Why didn't you ask me?'

'Are you serious? Because you're not quite twenty and I'm sixty-two. Isn't that enough reason? I shouldn't even be telling you this, but it's strange now, with you planning to leave suddenly. I suppose I want to hang on to you. I want to be able to tell you everything I think and feel, as I have in these last weeks, and I want you to be able to do the same.'

'Why the hell didn't you ask me?' She jumped up then and stared down at him as he lay there, somewhat stunned.

'To marry me?' He was astonished. 'Are you crazy? I told you. I'm too goddamn old.' Ivo looked suddenly angry as he pulled his legs towards him and sat up straight.

She sank back down on to the grass next to him, staring at him with flashing eyes. 'Couldn't you at least have given me a chance? Couldn't you have asked me how *I* felt? No, you're so busy treating me like a baby that you have to make all the decisions yourself. Well, I'm not a baby, you moron, I'm a woman and I have feelings too. And I've been in love with you since – since – goddamn it, forever. And do you ask me? No. Do you say anything? No! Ivo – ' But he was grinning at her as they sat there, and he silenced her quickly with a long, powerful kiss.

'Are you crazy, Bettina?'

But now she was smiling too. 'Yes, I am. I'm crazy about you. Jesus, didn't you know it? Didn't you guess? New Year's Eve when you kissed me, everything fell into place. But then, well, you seemed to withdraw – that way.'

'Do you mean to tell me, Bettina, that you love me? I mean really love me, not just as your father's old friend?'

'That is exactly what I mean. I love you. I love you . . .'
And then she leaped to her feet and shouted it to the trees. 'I
LOVE YOU!'

'You're crazy!' He said it laughingly and tackled her to
the ground. But she was lying next to him now and his eyes
found her, and slowly his hands. 'I love you . . . oh, darling, I
love you . . .' And then, gently, his mouth came down slowly
on hers.

Chapter 12

They tiptoed back into the apartment like two thieves, but
Bettina was giggling hopelessly as Ivo tried to help her off
with her coat. And then he whispered at her hoarsely as they
tiptoed up the stairs, 'Mattie said she was going to visit her
sister in Connecticut. I know she won't be back until
tonight.'

'What difference does it make?' She looked up at him
teasingly with those green eyes, and he suddenly didn't give
a damn who knew what he was feeling for her. He didn't
even feel guilty. All he knew was that he wanted her,
desperately, with every part of his body and soul. It was only
when they stood in his bedroom that he came to his senses,
and there was suddenly a gentler light in his eyes. She stood
near the door, watching him, childlike, barefoot, in her blue
jeans and red sweater. Carefully he walked towards her
and took her by the hand. He led her back to a big deep red
easy chair, where he sat down, and pulled her down slowly
on to one of his knees. Fleetingly he thought it was not
unlike the many times she had sat on his lap when she was a
child.

'Bettina . . . darling . . .' His voice was a caress as his hand
touched her neck and his lips rapidly followed suit. But he
pulled away from her quickly and looked into her eyes. 'I
want you to tell me something – and you have to be honest.
Has there ever been a man?' She shook her head slowly,
wearing a small smile.

'No. But that's all right, Ivo.' She wanted to tell him that
she wasn't afraid. That she had wanted him for so long, that
every moment of pain would be worth it, and after the first
time she would give him pleasure for the rest of his life. That
was all she could think of. What she would do for him.

'Are you afraid?' His arms were gentle around her, and

75

she slowly shook her head. And then he laughed softly. 'I am, silly girl.'

She looked at him with those big lovely green eyes and smiled. 'Why?'

'I don't want to hurt you.'

'You won't. You never have.' And then he nodded and took her gently by the hand, and after a moment she looked at him again with a thought. 'Will I get pregnant?' She wasn't afraid of it, she just wondered. She had heard of girls who had got pregnant the very first time. But he was shaking his head and smiling and she was surprised.

'No, darling. Never. I can't have children. Or at least not any more. I had that taken care of a long time ago.' She nodded, accepting, not wanting to know why. He stood up next to her then and scooped her up, doll-like in his arms, and she let him carry her carefully to his bed, where he laid her down and began to undress her slowly. The room darkened and night fell. His eyes and his lips and his fingers caressed her as slowly he bared each inch of her flesh, and at last she lay naked, tiny, perfect. He longed to press against her and feel the satin of her flesh. But instead he covered her gently with the covers and turned to undress himself in the room that was finally dark.

'Ivo?' Her voice was very young and small.

'Yes?' Even in the dark she could hear him smile.

'I love you.' It thrilled him just to hear it, and he slipped into the sheets just behind her back.

'I love you too.' Gently he touched her, his hands covering her body, slowly, achingly, softly, as he could feel his whole body throb. Then gently he turned her to face him, and he kissed her long and hard on the mouth. He wanted her to want him as much, if not more, as he needed her. And at last she was pressed against him, moving, grinding, touching, almost begging, as firmly he held her and then pressed within her, quickly, jabbing, feeling her wrench upward and tense, clutching at his back, as he pressed into her more. He knew it would be painful but he wanted her to know how much he loved her, and as he held her he told her again and again until at last they both lay still. He could feel her warm blood on the sheets, but he didn't care. He only held her very tightly, feeling her tremble and holding her close to him in his arms. 'I love you, darling . . . oh, Bettina, how I love you . . . with all of my heart.' Even in the darkness she turned her eyes up to his in answer, and slowly he kissed her, sharing the moment and wanting to end her pain. 'Are you all right?' She nodded slowly, and then at last she seemed to catch her breath.

'Oh, Ivo . . .' And then, as she smiled at him, tears spilled down her face to her chin.

'Why are you crying, little one?' It had been so many years since he had done something like that, he was suddenly afraid he had hurt her. He looked into her eyes almost with grief. But she was smiling and laughing through her tears.

'Just think what we've been missing all month!' And then suddenly he laughed too.

'You're silly and I love you.' But there was something he wanted to ask her and it was too soon. Yet he wanted to talk to her, to tell her, to ask her What now? And then he smiled down at her again as he turned on to his side and propped himself up on one elbow. As he did Bettina thought to herself that he looked incredibly young. 'Does this mean you won't be moving out, mademoiselle?'

She looked at him impishly, shrugged her shoulders, and smiled at him. 'Is that what you want, Ivo? For me to stay here?'

He nodded, feeling young again. 'What about you? Do you want to stay?'

She lay back among his pillows feeling happier than she ever had before. 'Yes, I want to stay.'

'But have you really thought about it? Bettina, I'm a very old man!'

But at that she laughed at him and stretched out comfortably on the bed. It was extraordinary. She wasn't

77

even embarrassed with him. Exposing her body to him was like opening up to the other half of her soul. 'You know something, Ivo, I think you lie about your age. I think you're really all of about thirty-five and you dye your hair white . . . because no one can tell me after today, least of all you, that you are a very old man.'

He looked at her seriously. 'But I am. Do you care?'

'I don't give a damn.'

But he knew better. 'Now you don't. But one day you will. And when that day comes, when I seem too old to you, when you want a young man, I'll step aside. I want you to remember that, darling. Because I mean it, with all my heart. When your time with me is over, when it is no longer right for you, when you want a younger man, and a different life, and babies, I'll go. And I'll understand, and I'll love you, but I will go.'

Her eyes were filled with tears as she listened. 'No, you won't.' But he only nodded and took her gently back into his arms again.

He whispered softly in her ear. 'Are you terribly sore, my darling?' She shook her head. Gently he took her, and this time she moaned softly and there was pleasure in her eyes. And at last as they lay together, happy and spent, he remembered something and looked at her with a soft smile. 'I assume that you understand, Bettina, that I want to marry you.' She looked up at him this time in surprise. She had hoped, but she hadn't been sure.

Her copper hair was tousled and she looked wonderfully sleepy but there was something very soft and lovely in her eyes. She hugged him. 'I'm glad. Because I want to marry you too.'

'Mrs Stewart.'

And then, laughing softly, she kissed him and muttered, 'The Third.' He looked at her in surprise then and pulled her to him.

'Are you ready?' He knocked softly on the door and waited

on the other side, but Bettina was flying about in a panic, still in her slip, her eyes frantic, her arms flapping wide.

'No, no, wait!' Mathilde went hurriedly to the closet to get the dress and slipped it carefully over Bettina's hair, and then she smoothed it over the narrow shoulders, closing hooks, buttons, snaps, and a zipper that ran imperceptibly up one side. It was a dress Bettina had bought in Paris with her father, but she had never worn it and it was perfect now.

She stood back to look at herself in the mirror, and over her left shoulder the reflection of the elderly Mathilde smiled benevolently too. Bettina looked beautiful in the simple cream satin dress. It was a mid-calf length, high-necked and short-sleeved with perfectly belled cap sleeves, and a jacket with much the same lines. She pulled on little white kid gloves and felt for the pearls in her ears, and then she stared down at her ivory-coloured stockings and the virginal satin shoes. Everything was perfect, and she looked up at Mathilde now with a soft smile.

'You look beautiful, mademoiselle.'

'Thank you, Mattie.' She reached out to kiss the old woman then and after that walked slowly to the door. She hesitated for a long moment, wondering if he was still waiting on the other side. 'Ivo?' She almost whispered it, but he heard her from behind the still closed door.

'Yes. Are you ready?'

She nodded, and then giggled. 'I am. But aren't you supposed to wait to see me until we get there?'

'How do you propose to do that? Blindfold me in the car?' He was amused by her insistence on tradition, considering the circumstances. He was amused by everything she did these days. She was suddenly once again like a very enchanting child. She was free of worry, and the disastrous winter of tragedy had finally come to an end. She was his now, and she had a new life ahead of her, as his much pampered wife. 'Come on, darling. We don't want to be late for Judge Isaacs. How about if I just close my eyes?'

'Okay. Are they closed?'

79

'Yes.' He smiled, and feeling slightly foolish, he closed his eyes. He heard the door open, and a moment later he was aware of her perfume nearby. 'Can I open them yet?'

She looked at him for a long moment, and then nodded slowly. 'Yes.' And he did, sighing softly as he saw her, wondering why the winter of his life should be so blessed, by what right?

'My God, you look lovely.'

'Do you like it?'

'Are you serious? You look exquisite.'

'Do I look like a bride?' He nodded gently, and then took her once more in his arms.

'Do you realise that an hour from now you'll be Mrs Ivo Stewart?' And then he smiled down at her, dwarfed beside him. 'How does that sound?'

'Lovely.' She kissed him again, and then left his arms.

'Oh, that reminds me . . .' He reached suddenly behind him to something enveloped in pale-green tissue on the hall chair. He held it out to her with a look of tenderness. 'For you.'

She took it from him carefully, tearing the paper, and the smell of lilies of the valley suddenly filled the hall. 'Oh, Ivo, where did you get them?' It was a beautiful little bouquet made of white roses and the tiny delicate white flowers from France.

'I had them sent over from Paris. Do you like the bouquet?'

She nodded happily and reached up to kiss him once more. But he stopped her and presented with a flourish a smaller package. She opened it up. There weren't words big enough to describe the nine-carat diamond ring gleaming brilliantly on a bed of midnight-blue velvet.

'Oh, Ivo, I don't know what to say.'

'Say nothing, my love, just wear this ring and be happy and safe and secure forever.'

The ceremony was over in minutes. The words had been

said, the rings exchanged. Bettina was now Ivo's wife. She hadn't even wanted a party. She was still, after all, grieving for her father. They had dinner at Lutèce, at a quiet table in the rear, and afterwards they went dancing, and Bettina stood on tiptoe to whisper in his ear.

'I love you, Ivo.' She looked so tiny, so fragile, and so much like a little girl. But she wasn't, she was his woman. Now. Entirely his. Forever.

Chapter 13

Nervously Bettina fastened diamond clips to her ears and ran a brush through her hair. She swirled it around her hand deftly and wound it into a smooth, ladylike knot. The deep auburn lights shone as she smoothed it, and when she had put the last of the pins in her hair, she stood up. Her body seemed tighter and thinner, and as she stood in a black lace dress, which reached to her ankles and black satin shoes, she could see her reflection across her dressing-room in the long mirrored wall. Ivo had had the room put in especially for her, in the new apartment they'd bought on their first anniversary five months before. It was perfect for their life-style, a duplex with a beautiful view of Central Park. Their bedroom had a large handsome terrace, they each had a dressing-room, and there was a small den for Ivo upstairs. Downstairs there was a living-room, a wood-panelled dining-room, and a kitchen, and behind it a nice-sized room for Mathilde. It was perfect. Not too grandiose, and yet it was far from small. Bettina had done it precisely as she wanted, except for the few touches Ivo had added for her, the little room of closets, the funny little gazebo on the large terrace, and a wonderful old-fashioned swing that he had hooked to the thin lip of overhanging roof. He had teased her that they would sit out there on summer evenings, dreaming and 'necking on their back porch'.

But it was rare for them to spend a night in the city during the summer. The repertory group for which she was now assistant manager and which had become more legitimate and moved up-town, had no performances in July and August and she and Ivo summered in South Hampton now. They had bought their own house. Her life was once more as it had been with her father, with the exception that she was happier than she had ever been before. She only worked five nights a week now, and on Sundays and Mondays, they gave elegant dinners for twelve or fourteen or showed films at home. Ivo had access to all the new movies, and once in a while she was able to sneak away for a ballet, a gala, an opening, or just an evening at Lutèce or Côte Basque. And in spite of it all they managed to spend quite a bit of time alone, after the theatre or in the daytime if Ivo could get away. He never had enough of her, and there were times when he wanted to share her with no one at all. He was lavish with his time, his attention, his affection, and his praise. Bettina was secure in his love. It was like the culmination of a long, happy dream.

She smiled at herself in the delicate black lace dress. It seemed to drift around her like a soft cloud, and she arranged the folds of her skirt before she zipped what little fabric there was in the back. It left her shoulders and arms and back bare, dwindled her waist to almost nothing, and floated up towards her throat, where it clasped with one hook around her neck. It looked like the sort of dress for which only one or two severed threads could have been disastrous, but there was no danger of that, the dress was exquisitely made. Checking the diamond earrings again and glancing at the smooth knot of hair, she squinted at her reflection with a small smile of excitement. 'Not bad for an old broad,' she whispered softly and grinned.

'Hardly that, my love.' She turned in surprise. She hadn't seen her husband smiling at her from the doorway.

'Sneaky. I didn't hear you come in.'

'I didn't intend you to. I just wanted to see how you look. And you look' – he smiled appreciatively and bent to kiss her softly on the mouth – 'ravishing.' He stepped back again and looked at her. She was even more beautiful than she had been a year and a half before. And then his smile deepened. 'Excited, Bettina?' She was about to say no, but then, laughing, she nodded her head.

'Maybe a little.'

'You should be, my darling.' And then he himself had to

laugh. Was it possible that was all she was? Twenty-one? Tonight was her twenty-first birthday. And then, as he watched her, he slipped a hand into his pocket and came out with a dark-blue velvet box. There had been so much of that since they had married. He had showered her with presents and spoiled her since the day they'd got home from their precious honeymoon in East Hampton.

'Oh, Ivo . . .' She looked at him as he handed her the dark blue box. 'What more can you give me? You've already given me so much.'

'Go ahead, open it.' And when at last she did, he smiled at her small gasp.

'Oh, Ivo! No!'

'Oh, yes.' It was a magnificent pearl and diamond choker she had seen and admired at Van Cleef's. She had told him about it after they first married, in a funny, half-joking confidence, when she told him that one knew one had really grown up when one had a choker of pearls. He had been amused by her theory, and she had gone on to describe the elegant women who had worn chokers at her father's parties, sapphires, diamonds, rubies . . . but only the truly 'grown-up' women had had the good taste to wear chokers made of pearls. He had enjoyed the story and, like everything else she told him, he never forgot. He had been waiting impatiently for her twenty-first birthday to give her the choker of pearls. The one he had chosen was also enhanced by diamonds that hung together in a handsome oval clasp, which could be worn in the back or front. As she fumbled to put it on and he watched her, he could see bright tears standing out in her eyes, and then suddenly she was crushed against him, holding tightly to him, as she bowed her head against his chest. 'It's all right, darling . . . Happy birthday, my beloved . . .' He tilted her face towards him then and kissed her ever so softly on the lips.

But there was something more than just gratitude in her face when she kissed him. 'Don't ever leave me, Ivo . . . never . . . I couldn't bear it . . .' It wasn't the diamonds and the pearls that he gave her, it was that he always understood, he always knew, he was always there. She knew that she could always count on him. But the terrifying thing was – what if one day he wasn't there? She couldn't bear to think of it. What if he stopped loving her one day? Or what if he left her helpless and gasping as her father had . . . But as he looked at her Ivo understood the horror he could see hiding in her eyes.

'As long as I can help it, darling, I'll never leave you. Never.'

And then they wandered downstairs, his arm firmly around her shoulders. It was only a few moments later when the doorbell rang with the first guests. Mathilde was being assisted by a bartender and two rented butlers, and a caterer had been arranged for the food. For once Bettina had to do absolutely nothing. Everything had been organised by Ivo. All she had to do was relax, have a good time, and be one of the guests.

'But shouldn't I just take a look in the kitchen?' She whispered it to him softly as they wandered away from a group of guests, but he held on to her firmly with a long, tender smile.

'No, you should not. Tonight I want you out here, with me.'

'As you wish, sire.' She swept a low curtsey and he patted her gently on the fanny as she rose. 'Fresh!'

'Absolutely!' Their love life hadn't dwindled either in the past year. She still found him exciting and appealing, and they spent a remarkable amount of their time in bed.

She stood in tiny, regal splendour, Ivo at her side, a champagne glass in one hand, the other on her choker, surveying her domain. She felt like she had turned a corner. She was a woman, a lover, a wife.

Chapter 14

'Ready to call it a night, little one?' Ivo looked down at her with a gentle smile as they circled the dance floor for a last time. She nodded as she looked up at him. For once the emeralds in her ears shone more than her eyes. She looked tired and troubled, despite the brilliantly beautiful green and gold sari dress she was wearing, and the new emerald earrings, which were an almost perfect match for her mother's ring. Ivo had just bought her the earrings the previous Christmas and she loved them.

As they turned to go back to their table, all of the guests stood and applauded. She was so used to the sound of applause, that she was comforted by it. But tonight the applause wasn't for the repertory group but for Ivo, who was retiring, finally, after thirty-six years at the paper, twenty-one years as its chief. He had decided, after much agony, to end his career at sixty-eight rather than push it all the way to mandatory retirement in two years. Bettina had not yet quite adjusted to what was happening, and he knew that it troubled her more than she would admit. Together they had shared six untroubled, endlessly happy years of winters in the city, summers in the country, trips to Europe, and moments that they shared. And at twenty-five she enjoyed it, and he indulged her, although now when she worked, he had his chauffeur pick her up around the corner from work. He no longer bowed to all of her ideas about her independence, and having proven herself with the rep group, she was less fierce about the little things. Yet it was comfortable to depend on Ivo. He made life so easy and so happy.

'Come on, my darling.' He took her gently by the hand and led her through the crowd of well-wishing friends in evening dresses and tuxedos. In fact as he looked at them he was grateful for the touch of her hand. There was so much that he was leaving, and suddenly he wondered if he had been wrong. But it was too late to reverse his decision. The announcement of the new publisher had already been made. And Ivo was becoming the chief adviser to the chairman of the board. It was an illustrious title, which in fact held very little power. He would simply become now a respected elder, and as he rode home in the limousine with Bettina, he found himself close to tears.

But they had already done some careful planning. She had taken three months off from the rep group and they were leaving the next day for the South of France. He had arranged their passage by ship, since suddenly they had so much spare time.

They drove down in leisurely fashion from Paris to St-Jean-Cap-Ferrat, after a two-week stay at the Ritz, where Bettina teasingly said they did nothing but eat. Cap-Ferrat was heavenly in September, and in October they went on to Rome. And at last, in November, they regretfully returned to the States. Ivo called a vast number of his cronies and arranged to have lunch with everyone at their assorted favourite hang-outs and clubs. And Bettina went back to The Players. Things were on the upswing for them, the previews good, the audiences plentiful, and Bettina was happy with her job. Steve was finally directing, and she had his old job as theatre manager, for which she had got her equity card at last. The play they were doing was an original work, by an unknown playwright, but it had seemed different to her right from the beginning. There was a tension, an excitement, a kind of tangible magic one could feel in the air.

'All right, I believe you.' Ivo had said it teasingly as she told him about it with excited, emphatic eyes.

'Will you come and see it?'

'Sure.' He went back to his paper and his breakfast with a smile. It was rare, but the night before, he hadn't waited up for her. He had had a long day himself. Now and then his age peeked at him around corners, but most of the time nothing much had changed.

'When will you come and see it?'

He looked up at her again with a rueful smile. 'Will you please stop pushing, Mrs Stewart?'

But she grinned at him and firmly shook her head. 'No. I won't. This is the best play I've ever worked on. It's brilliant, Ivo, and it's exactly the kind of play I want to write.'

'All right, all right, I'll see it.'

'You promise?'

'I promise. Now can I read my paper?'

She looked at him sheepishly. 'Yes.'

But by noon she was already anxious to get back to the theatre. She watched Ivo dress for a luncheon at the Press Club, and then she showered and climbed into jeans. She left him a note that she had left early, and she'd see him late that night. She suspected he wouldn't mind it. Since they'd got back from Europe, he'd been very tired, and it would probably do him good to take it easy for the rest of the day. Besides, he was used to her crazy theatre schedule.

She jumped out of the cab hastily and walked the rest of the way, humming to herself and feeling the bitter winter wind in her hair. She still wore it long to please Ivo, and today it flew out past her shoulders, like fine copper thread.

'What's your hurry, lover? You can't be late for work.' As she crossed the street near the theatre she looked over her shoulder in surprise. The voice was British and familiar, and when she saw him, he was wearing a warm tweed coat and a red cap. He was the star of their new play.

'Hi, Anthony. I just thought I'd tie up some loose ends.'

'Me too. And we have a quick rehearsal at four thirty. They're going to change the opening of the second act.'

'Why?' She looked at him with interest, and as they reached the theatre he held open the door.

'Don't ask me.' He shrugged boyishly. 'I just work here. I never understand why playwrights do all that scribbling and switching. Paranoia, if you ask me. But that's the theatre, love.' He stood for a moment in front of his dressing-room and eyed her with a long, friendly smile. He was more than a head taller than she and he had enormous blue eyes and soft brown hair. There was something enchanting and innocent about him, probably due to his very British intonations and the light in his eyes. 'Are you doing anything for dinner tonight?'

She looked pensive, and then shook her head. 'Probably not. I'll just eat a sandwich here.'

'Me too.' He made a face and they both grinned. 'Care to join me?' He waved behind him into the dressing-room, and she hesitated for a moment, and then slowly nodded.

'Sure.'

'And then what?' He was looking at her with fascination over the pastrami. They had been chatting, sitting on two canvas chairs in his dressing-room for half an hour.

'Then I worked on *Fox in the Hen House, Little City*, let's see . . .' She hesitated pensively, and then grinned. 'Oh, and *Clavello*.'

'You worked on that?' He looked impressed. 'Christ, Bett, you've had more work than I've had, and I've been at it for ten years.'

She looked surprised as she surveyed him, nibbling at the remains of her pickle. 'You don't look old enough to have been at it for that long. How old are you?' She wasn't embarrassed to ask him questions. In the past half hour they had somehow become friends. He was easy to be with and fun to talk to, unlike the others she had met in the theatrical world. Despite the camaraderie, jealousy was always thick in the air. But it rarely touched her. She was only the stage manager, after all. Yet she never tired of what she saw in the theatre, and the magic was there for her, every night.

'I'm twenty-six.' He looked at her enchantingly. A small boy in a man's clothes, pretending to be in a play.

'How long have you been in the States?'

'Just since rehearsals. Four months.'

'You like it?' She finished the last of the pastrami and the pickle and cast a jeans-clad leg over the arm of her chair.

'I love it. I'd give my ears to stay.'

'Can't you?'

'Sure, on temporary visas. But, Christ, that's all such a mess. I take it you don't know about the never-ending search for the almighty green card.'

She shook her head. 'What's that?'

'Permanent resident's card, working permit, et cetera. They'd be worth a fortune if you could buy them on the black market. But you can't.'

'What do you have to do to get one?'

'Work a minor miracle, I think. I don't know, it's too bloody complicated. Don't ask. And what about you?' He stirred his coffee and looked at her seriously for a moment. She was startled, she felt almost caressed by the blue eyes.

'What do you mean?'

'Oh, you know,' he shrugged, smiling. 'Vital statistics, age, rank, shoe size, do you wear a bra?'

She grinned back at him, startled, and then shrugged. 'All right, let's see. I'm twenty-five, I wear a size five-and-a-half shoe, and the rest of it is none of your business.'

'Married?' He looked casually intrigued.

'Yes.'

'Damn.' He snapped his fingers regretfully and they both laughed. 'Been married long?'

'Six and a half years.'

'Kids?' But this time she shook her head. 'That's smart.'

'Don't you like children?' She looked surprised, but he was non-committal.

'They're not the greatest thing ever to happen to a career. Distracting little bastards at best.' It reminded her of the egocentricity of most actors and made her think of her father too. And then he smiled at her again. 'Well, Bettina, I'm damn sorry to hear you're married. But' – he looked up at her cheerfully – 'don't forget to give me a call when you get divorced.' But as he said it she stood up with a broad grin.

'Anthony Pearce, my friend, don't hold your breath while you're waiting.' And then with a wave and a smile she walked to the door and saluted. 'See you later, kid.'

She saw Anthony again that night as she left the theatre, and they both pulled their collars up against the cold.

'Jesus, it's freezing. God knows why you want to stay in the States.'

'Sometimes I ask myself that too.'

And then she smiled at him again as they walked towards the corner, trying to avoid the patches of ice. 'Nice performance tonight.'

'Thank you.' He turned to her questioningly. 'Want a lift?' He was about to hail a cab.

But she shook her head at him. 'No, thanks.'

He shrugged and walked on as she turned left at the corner. And she saw Ivo's car waiting for her, with the driver, the motor running, and inside she knew it would be warm. She looked over her shoulder quickly to see if anyone was watching, and then she pulled open the door and slipped inside. But as he crossed the street, seemingly oblivious, Anthony had turned one last time to wave goodnight. All he saw was Bettina, disappearing into a long black limousine. He dug his hands deeper into his pockets, raised an eyebrow, and walked on with a smile.

Chapter 15

'Hi, darling.' It was bright and sunny the next morning at breakfast. Again Ivo had been asleep the night before when she came in. It was unlike him. And they hadn't made love in a week. She felt guilty keeping track of it, but he had spoiled her so much for so long that now she was suddenly aware of any change.

'Missed you last night.'

'Think I'm over the hill, little one?' He said it softly with a kindly light in his eyes. It was clear that he didn't think so, and Bettina rapidly shook her head.

'Not a chance, so don't start counting on using that as an excuse.'

He went back to his paper, and Bettina went upstairs to get dressed. She had wanted to tell him about her dinner with Anthony, but suddenly it didn't seem quite right. She was always careful not to make him feel jealous, even though they both knew he had no reason to be.

Three quarters of an hour later Bettina was wearing grey slacks and a beige cashmere sweater, brown suede boots, and a silk scarf the same colour as her hair. Ivo had just come upstairs in his robe.

'What are you doing today, darling?' She had the urge to slip her hands under his robe. But he was looking at his watch and hadn't noticed the look in her eye.

'Oh, God, I have a board meeting at the paper in half an hour. And I'm going to be late.' That took care of the morning.

'And after that?' She looked hopeful.

'Lunch with my fellow board members. Another meeting. And then home.'

'Damn. By then I'll have left for the theatre.'

His eyes were both wistful and tender. 'Want to quit the play?' But she shook her head emphatically.

'No!' And then in a childlike voice she explained, 'It's just that I miss you so much now that we're back in the States and I'm working. In Europe we were together all the time, and now suddenly it feels like we never see each other any more.' He was touched by the remorseful tone in her voice and he reached out to hold her.

'I know.' And then after stroking her hair for a few minutes, he lifted her face up towards his and kissed her lips. 'I'll see what I can do about not scheduling so many lunches. Want to take another trip?'

'I can't, Ivo . . . the play.'

'Oh, for – ' There was fire for a moment, and then it subsided with the wave of a hand. 'All right, all right.' But then he turned to her more seriously. 'Don't you think after all these years you've absorbed enough to write something of your own? Really, darling, I have visions of you turning eighty-seven and still hobbling down to work the curtain for some off-off-Broadway play.'

'I don't work off-off-Broadway.' She looked insulted, and he laughed.

'No, you don't. But don't you think you've done it for long enough? Think of it, we could go away now for six months and you could write your play.'

'I'm not ready.' She seemed terrified at the thought, and he wondered why.

'Yes, you are. You're just afraid, darling. But there's no reason to be. You're going to write something marvellous when you finally do it.'

'Yes, but I'm just not ready, Ivo.'

'All right. Then don't complain that you never see me. You're down at that damn theatre all the time.' It was the first time that he had complained of it, and Bettina was surprised by the quick anger in his tone.

'Darling, don't say that.' She kissed him, and his voice was gentler when he spoke again.

'Silly girl. I love you, you know.'

'I love you too.' They held each other for a moment, but then he had to leave.

At the theatre everything was already bustling, people were hurrying everywhere, and the stars of the show had begun to arrive. Bettina saw Anthony walking around backstage in jeans, a black turtleneck sweater, and his red cap.

'Hi, Bett.' He was the only member of cast or crew who insisted on shortening her name.

'Hello, Anthony. How's everything?'

'Insane. They want to make more changes.' It was a new play and last-minute rewrites were to be expected. He didn't look especially perturbed. 'I wanted to ask you to dinner again, but I couldn't find you.'

She smiled easily. 'I brought a sandwich from home.'

'Made by your mother?' Bettina laughed but she couldn't very well tell him No, made by our maid. Instead she only shook her head. 'Any chance I can induce you to join me for coffee a little later?'

'Sorry, not tonight.' She had to get home to Ivo. She didn't want to stay out too late. Only once or twice in years of working in the theatre had she gone out after hours with the crew. Last night was enough.

He shot her a disappointed look and disappeared.

She didn't see him again until after the show. He found her setting lights and overseeing the routine house clean-up before she went home.

'What did you think of the changes, Bettina?' He looked at her with interest and sat down on a stool, and she paused for a moment before answering, her eyes narrowed, reliving the scenes in her head.

'I'm not sure I like them. I don't think they were necessary.'

'That's what I thought. Weak. I told you, writers are fucking paranoids.'

She smiled at him again. 'Yeah. Maybe so.'

'Can I lure you out now for that cup of coffee?' But she shook her head.

'Maybe another time, Anthony. I'm sorry. I can't.'

'Hubby waiting?' He sounded flip as he said it, and she squarely met his eyes.

'I hope so.' He looked irritated, and as Bettina put her coat on she was irritated too. He had no right to be annoyed that she wouldn't go out with him. No right at all. It bothered her that he had looked aggravated, but she was strangely afraid that he wouldn't ask again. She picked up her handbag, jammed on her hat, and walked out the door. Screw Anthony Pearce. He didn't mean anything to her.

She walked briskly down the street towards the corner, feeling the wind whistle past her ears. She hastened towards the waiting limousine, grabbed the door handle, and put one foot inside, only to hear a voice behind her. She turned in astonishment. It was Anthony standing behind her, his collar turned up, the red cap on his head.

'Can you give me a lift?'

Despite the cold, she felt herself flush with embarrassment. He was the first person in six years who had discovered her getting into the car. And all she could think of to say was 'Oh.'

'Come on, love, I'm freezing me arse off. And there aren't any cabs.' There was a fine mist of snow starting to filter into the air. And he had seen her now, so what did it matter? She looked at him for a moment, and then answered tersely.

'All right.' She climbed in and he got in beside her, and she turned to him, annoyed at his pushiness. 'Where do you want me to drop you off?' He seemed unperturbed by the embarrassment he had caused her. The address he gave her was in SoHo.

'I have a loft. Want to come up and see it?' She grew angry again at how persistent he was.

'No, thank you, I don't.'

'Why so angry?' And then with a smile he looked at her admiringly. 'But I must say, love, it becomes you.'

In rapid irritation she raised the window between the driver and them. And then she looked at him hotly. 'May I remind you that I'm a married woman?'

'What difference does that make? I didn't say anything out of line. I didn't tear off your clothes. I didn't kiss you in front of the chauffeur. All I did was ask for a ride. Why so touchy? Your old man must be jealous as hell.'

'No, he's not, and that's none of your damn business either. I just . . . it's just that . . . oh, never mind.' She sat in steaming silence as they drove south towards his loft. When at last they reached it, he held out a friendly hand.

'I'm sorry to have upset you, Bettina.' His voice was gentle and boyish as he spoke. 'I really didn't mean to.' And then hanging his head, 'I'd like to be your friend.'

As she looked at him something about him cut straight to her soul. 'I'm sorry, Anthony . . . I didn't mean to be rude. It's just that no one has ever . . . I felt so awkward about the car . . . I'm really so sorry. It isn't your fault.'

He kissed her cheek gently – a friendly kiss. 'Thanks for that.' And then hesitantly, 'Will you slap me if I offer you a cup of coffee just one more time?' He looked so earnest, so anxious, that she didn't dare refuse. But she wanted so much to get home to Ivo. Still . . . she had been very sharp with the young English actor.

She sighed and nodded. 'Okay. But I can't stay long.' She followed him up an endless narrow staircase as her car waited downstairs, and at last when she thought they must have walked to heaven, he unlocked a heavy steel door, and on the other side was revealed to her an apartment filled with charm. He had painted clouds on the ceiling, filled corners with wonderful tall, leafy trees; there were campaign chests and Oriental objects, straw mats and small rugs, and huge comfortable chairs upholstered in a soft blue. It was more than an apartment, it was a haven, a piece of country, a garden in an apartment, a cloud riding in a pale-blue summer sky. 'Oh, Anthony, it's wonderful.' Her eyes widened with pleasure as she looked around.

'Do you like it?' He looked at her innocently again, and they both smiled.

'I adore it. How did you put all this together? Did you bring it from London?'

'Some of it, and some of it I just threw together here.' But nothing about it looked thrown together. It was a beautiful place. 'Now, cream or sugar?'

'Neither, thank you. Black.'

'That must be how you stay so thin.' He glanced appreciatively at her narrow and dancer-graceful body as she let herself down in one of the blue chairs.

He was back in a few minutes with two steaming cups and a plate of cheese and fruit.

It was one thirty when she finally ran panic-stricken down the stairs to her car. What would Ivo say? And suddenly, this time, she was praying that he was asleep. As it turned out, her prayers were answered. He had waited till midnight, and then fallen asleep in their bed. Bettina felt a wild pang of guilt as she watched him, and then wondered why. All she had done was have coffee with a member of the cast. What harm could there be in that?

Chapter 16

'Did he beat you?' Anthony teased.

'Of course not. He's wonderful and understanding. He doesn't do things like that.'

'Good. Then let's have coffee again sometime. As a matter of fact how about dinner tonight before the show?'

'We'll see.' She was purposely vague. She wanted to call Ivo. Maybe they could have dinner quickly somewhere nearby. She hadn't even seen him this morning. When she'd woken up, he was gone. He had left her a note that he had an early appointment. She was beginning to feel that they never saw each other and she didn't like it at all.

But when she called Ivo, he wasn't home. Mattie said he had called to say he'd be out for dinner, and Anthony seemed to be waiting behind her to use the pay phone. He heard the entire conversation despite her best efforts to be discreet, and when she hung up, he smiled disarmingly.

'Can I stand in for dinner, Bettina?'

She was going to say no, but in the face of those blue eyes she found herself saying 'Sure'. They wound up going somewhere for soup and a sandwich, and talking more about the play. And then almost imperceptibly he switched the conversation to her. He wanted to know everything about her, where she came from, where she lived, even where she'd gone to school as a girl. She told him about her father, whose work he knew. He seemed fascinated by every detail she told him. At last they walked back to the theatre, and they went their separate ways. But he found her quickly after the performance as she was preparing to leave. She had a feeling he was going to ask her for a lift again, so she hurried out to the car.

At home she found Ivo waiting up. They chatted for half

an hour about their respective days, and at last went upstairs. Bettina undressed slowly as they talked.

'I feel as though I've hardly seen you lately.' He looked at her with regret, but no reproach.

'I know.' She looked mournful, but he was quick to walk to her side. And a moment later he was helping her to undress, and then quickly he followed her to the bed. Their love-making was slow and gentle and fulfilling, but as they lay quietly afterwards Bettina found herself longing for their first fire. She turned to Ivo slowly, wanting to see a look of fresh passion lingering in his eyes. And instead she found him sleeping, his face turned to her and a small smile on his mouth. She lay on one elbow for a long time, watching him, and gently she kissed him on both eyes, but as she did so she realised her mind had strayed to Anthony, and relentlessly she dragged it back to the man at her side.

The friendship with Anthony continued to flourish as the success of the play went on. They had sandwiches together now and then backstage, and occasionally she had coffee with him in his loft. Several times a week he brought her small bouquets of flowers, but they were always presented to her casually, as though they meant nothing more than that he was her friend. Once or twice she tried to bring it up casually with Ivo, but it somehow never sounded quite right.

It was in the dead of winter when Ivo went back to see the play, as though he also needed to be there, to see, to try to reach out and grasp something that was nagging at the back of his mind. He had timed his entrance into the darkened theatre perfectly, sitting anonymously in the next-to-last row. And then, as the curtain rose and he watched him, he thought he knew. Anthony had the grace of a long sleek black leopard, moving hypnotically through the motions of his part. Ivo barely heard the words he was speaking. He only watched him, and then, with a terrible sensation of betrayal and aching, he understood. The betrayal was not

Bettina's, but that of the hands of time he had fought for so long.

It wasn't until spring that Bettina looked troubled. She had come home late one night, looking disturbed, and Ivo watched her, not sure whether to ask questions or leave her alone. Something was obviously bothering her, but for the first time in their marriage she didn't want to talk. She stared at Ivo absently, and eventually wandered upstairs alone. He found her staring out at the city from the terrace, frowning, with her hairbrush hanging useless in her hand.

'Something wrong, darling?'

But Bettina shook her head vaguely. 'No.' And then suddenly she turned to him, with a look of terror in her eyes. 'Yes.'

'What's the matter?'

'Oh, Ivo . . .' She sat down on a garden chair and stared at him, her eyes huge and luminous in the dark. Behind her was the soft light of the apartment, which caught the rich auburn glow of her hair. He thought that she had never looked more lovely, and he dreaded what she might have to say. All winter he had had a feeling of foreboding, and all winter he had been so dreadfully tired. It made him wonder sometimes if retiring had been a mistake. He had never felt that way while he had still worked.

'Darling, what is it?' He went to her, took her hand, and sat down. 'Whatever it is, you can tell me. Above all, Bettina, we're friends.'

'I know.' She looked at him gratefully with her huge green eyes, and slowly they filled with tears. 'They've asked me to tour.'

'What?' He looked at her with relief and amusement. 'Is that all?' Dumbly she nodded yes. 'What's so awful about that?'

'But, Ivo, I'd be gone for four months! And what about you? I don't know . . . I can't do it . . . but – '

'But you want to?' His eyes never left hers, and with one hand she began to play with her hair.

'I'm not sure. They've . . . oh, Jesus, it's crazy . . .' And then she looked at him, so unhappy, so obviously torn. 'They've asked me to be the assistant director. Me, Ivo, the errand girl, the pusher of scenery, the nothing, after all these years.'

'They're very smart. They know how much you've learned over the years. I'm proud of you, darling.' He looked at her with a warm glow in his eyes. 'Do you want to do it?'

'Oh, Ivo, I don't know . . . what about you?'

'Never mind about me. We've been together for almost seven years. Don't you think we could weather four months? Besides, I could fly out to see you now and then. After all there are advantages to being married to a man who's retired.'

She smiled bittersweetly and took a tight hold of his hand. 'I don't want to leave you.'

But he eyed her honestly. 'Yes, you do, darling. And it's all right. I've had my life, you know, a full one. I have no right to expect you to spend all of yours sitting here with me.'

'Would you miss me?' She looked up at him again with the face of a little girl.

'Outrageously. But if it's what you really need to do, Bettina' – there was a long pause as he looked at her – 'then I understand. Why don't you think about it for a while? How soon do they want an answer?'

She gulped almost audibly. 'Tomorrow.'

'Anxious, aren't they?' He tried to sound lighthearted. 'And how soon would you go?'

'In a month.'

'With the original cast?'

'Partly, Anthony Pearce is going, and the female lead.' She rambled on for a minute, but he didn't hear her, she had already told him all he wanted to know. He looked at her gently and shrugged softly in the warm night air. 'Why don't you sleep on it and see how you feel in the morning. Is Steve going to be the director by the way?'

She shook her head slowly. 'No. He got a job with a Broadway play.' She sat there for a while, saying nothing, and at last she got up and went inside. It was as though they both knew what was happening, but neither could speak. She left him there, on the terrace, drifting in his thoughts. Something had changed between them – without any warning, but it had. Suddenly she seemed so much younger, and he felt so old. Even their love-making had slowly changed over the past year. For a moment he wanted to rail at the fates for what was happening, it wasn't fair . . . but then he knew. He had had seven years with her. It was more than he had a right to.

He wandered inside. He made no move to make love to her that evening. He didn't want to confuse her even more. On her side of the bed Bettina lay wondering if she should stay with Ivo, or go. At last she heard his soft breathing and turned to look at him, so gentle, so loving, asleep on his side. She touched his arm as she watched him, and then she turned away and wiped the tears from her eyes. In the morning she would have to tell him. She had to do it. Had to. She needed to do it. She had no choice.

Chapter 17

'Ivo . . . you'll call me . . . promise?' She looked at him in the airport, her huge green eyes filling with tears. 'And I'll call you too. I swear . . . every day . . . and when you come for the weekend – ' But suddenly she couldn't go on. All she could do was reach out to him, blindly, barely seeing through her veil of tears. 'Oh, Ivo . . . I'm so sorry . . .' She hated to go. But Ivo was there, holding her, comforting as always, his voice gentle in her ear.

'No, stop it, darling. I'll see you in a few weeks. Everything is going to be fine. And you'll write a beautiful play after this. I'll be so proud of you. You'll see.' His voice was gentle and soothing as he held her in his arms.

'Do you really think so?' She looked at him, sniffing loudly, and then fresh tears came to her eyes. 'But what about you?'

'We already discussed that. I'll be fine. Remember me? I lived a hell of a long time before I was lucky enough to have you. Now just be a good girl and enjoy it. Hell, this is your big chance. Madam Assistant Director.' He was teasing now and she finally smiled. He pulled her into his arms and kissed her.

'Now, my little love, you have to go, or you'll miss your plane, and that is not the way to start a new job.' They were starting in St Louis, and the rest of the cast was already there. They had left that morning, but Bettina had wanted the last hours she could spare with Ivo in New York.

She glanced back at him as she ran towards the gate, feeling like a runaway child. Yet he was firm and kind and as loving as ever as he waved to her, and he stayed until he could see no more of the plane. As he left the airport Ivo Stewart walked slowly, thinking back to that morning, that summer, last year, and then the last twenty-five. A sudden tremor of panic ran through him as he wondered if this had just been goodbye.

Bettina landed in St Louis at 4.03 that afternoon. It was cutting it a little close for their first performance, but they had rehearsed so often that the cast was as tight as could be, and the director had flown out from New York with them, so Bettina felt safe coming in as late as she did. As the plane touched down she sighed to herself, thinking of Ivo, and slowly she forced her mind back to work. She left the plane hurriedly, anxious to pick up her bags, drop them at the hotel, and get to the theatre. She wanted to reconnoitre and make sure that everything was all right. She was already busy and distracted as she hurried past the other passengers on the way to her bags.

'Good God, lover, what's the rush? You're going to knock down an old lady if you don't slow down and watch out!' She started to turn in annoyance, and then suddenly she laughed.

'What are you doing here?' She grinned at Anthony in astonishment as she stopped in her tracks.

'Oh, let's see, I came out here to pick up a friend,' he grinned at her, 'who just happens to be the AD of our show. Anyone you know, green eyes?'

'Okay, smartass. Thanks.' But despite the teasing and the exchanges she was immensely glad to see him. She had felt suddenly very lost and alone as she got off the plane. 'How's everything going at the theatre?'

'Who knows? I've been hanging out at the hotel all afternoon.'

'Is everyone all right?' She looked genuinely concerned and he laughed.

'Yes, little mother, they're fine.' As they picked up her valises, his gaiety was contagious, and by the time they caught a taxi into the city, they were both laughing like two kids. He was teasing and playing and being silly. It was the closest she'd ever come to acting like a child. He brought that out in her, and she enjoyed it. It was a salute to all the moments that had passed her by as a little girl.

'This is it?' She looked at the hotel as they disembarked. The road show had put them in what had to be the oldest, and certainly the ugliest, hotel in town.

'Didn't I tell you, love? They had San Quentin moved all the way to Saint Louis just for us.' He looked delighted as he said it and Bettina cracked up.

'God, it's awful. Is it as bad inside?'

'No. Worse. Cockroaches as big as dogs. But not to worry, darlin', I bought a leash!'

'Anthony . . . please . . . it can't be that bad.'

'Yes, it is.' He reassured her with pleasure, and when she checked into her room, she realised that he was right. The walls were cracked, the paint was peeling, the bed was hard, the bedspreads looked dingy and grey. Even the water glasses in the bathroom were dirty. 'Was I right?' He looked at her cheerfully as she dropped her suitcase on the floor.

'Well, you don't have to sound so cheerful about it.' She smiled at him ruefully and sat down, but his spirits couldn't be dampened. He was a little boy on holiday as he jumped up and down next to her on the bed. 'Stop it, Anthony! Don't you ever get tired for chrissake?' She was suddenly hot and tired and fed up and she couldn't remember why she had left Ivo in New York. Surely not to travel around the country with this madman and to stay in fleabag hotels.

'Of course I never get tired. Why should I? I'm young! But I'm also not as spoiled as you are, Bettina.' His voice was caressing, and she turned to look at him.

'What do you mean "spoiled"?'

'I don't have a chauffeur or live in a penthouse. I've spent most of my life in dumps like this.'

She wasn't sure if she should be sorry or angry, and she didn't know what to say. 'So? Do you resent me for being married to a somewhat' – she hesitated – 'comfortable man?'

Anthony's eyes stared straight into hers. 'No. But I resent

you like hell for being married to a man almost three times your age.'

This time her eyes flashed. 'It's none of your business.'

'Maybe I think it is.'

Her heart pounded, and then she turned away. 'I love him very much.'

'Maybe you just love his money.' His voice was insinuating, and she turned in fury at what he had just said.

'Don't you ever say that again. Ivo saved me, and he's the only human being who ever gave a damn about me.' She had told Anthony the whole story about her father's debts one night as they shared coffee in the loft.

'That's no reason to have married him, for chrissake.' Anthony actually looked irate.

'I told you, I love him. Do you understand?' Bettina was livid. 'He's my husband and he's a wonderful man.'

But suddenly Anthony's voice grew softer, almost caressing her with his words. 'When I think of you married to a man forty-three years older than you are, it bloody breaks my heart.' He looked at her mournfully and she stared.

'Why?' Despite the throbbing in her temples, she tried desperately to calm down.

'It's not natural. You should be married to someone younger. You should be young and silly. You should have kids.'

She shrugged, and then sighed deeply, sinking into the uncomfortable bed. 'Anthony, I've never been young and silly. And I've known Ivo all my life. He's the best thing that could have happened to me.' But why was she doing this? Why was she justifying Ivo to him?

He looked at her sadly. 'I wish someone would say that about me.'

She smiled then, for the first time since they had started the discussion; her anger had begun to fade. 'Maybe someday someone will. Now, can we make a deal please?'

'What's that?'

'No more nonsense about Ivo, no more harping on me because he's more than twice my age.'

'All right, all right, it's a deal,' he said begrudgingly, 'but don't expect me to understand.'

'I won't.' But she did expect him to if he was her friend.

'Okay, now let's get the hell to the theatre before we both get fired.' And a few minutes later the bad feelings were gone. They had to be together too much to allow themselves the luxury of a fight.

They arrived together, they left together, they ate together, they talked together, they watched television in hotel rooms together, they fell asleep side by side in airports and ugly hotels waiting for rooms. They were inseparable. A tiny nucleus within a larger one. The entire cast and crew hung together as though they had been grafted, but within the group cliques and couples inevitably formed. Among them were Anthony and Bettina. No one quite understood, no one dared to ask questions, but after the first couple of weeks everyone knew that if you were looking for one, you'd find the other one too.

'Bettina?' He was pounding on her door early one morning. Usually now she let him have the spare key and he pounded her on the ass to wake her up, wherever they were. She was so exhausted that it almost took brutality to waken her. But the night before, in the hotel in Portland, she had forgotten to give him the key. 'Bettina! Dammit! Bettina!'

'Kick it in!' One of the understudies smiled and walked by as Anthony muttered.

'For chrissake, woman, wake up!' Finally she staggered to the door with a yawn.

'Thanks. Did it take long?'

'Jesus.' He rolled his eyes and sauntered in.

'Did you bring me coffee?'

'Would you believe they don't have any in this flophouse. We have to go two blocks down the street to the nearest coffee shop.'

Bettina looked at him blearily. 'My heart may stop before that.'

'That's what I thought.' He smiled at her mysteriously and returned to the hall. He was back a moment later with a small plastic tray with two cups of coffee and a stack of fresh Danish. 'Oh, God, you're wonderful. Where did you get that?'

'I stole it.'

'I don't give a damn if you did. I'm starving. What time do we leave, by the way? They hadn't decided when I went to sleep last night.'

'I wondered where the hell you snuck off to.'

'Are you kidding? If I hadn't gotten some sleep, I'd have dropped dead in my tracks.' No one had told them that they'd be performing every day. It was one of those little details that hadn't been mentioned. It was also why Ivo had not come out to see her yet, although she had already been gone for a month. But there was no point flying out to meet her if she would be working every day of the week. They called each other every day though, but she was getting increasingly vague with her news. Her whole existence centred around the tour. It was like being in Marine boot camp. It was becoming harder and harder to relate to anyone not living it with her. 'So what time are we leaving?'

He looked at his watch with a smile. 'In an hour. But, hell, look at it this way, Bett, we'll be in San Francisco by this afternoon.'

'So who gives a damn? Do you think we'll see it? No. We'll be stuck in some rotten hotel. And three days from now we fly out of there.' The charm of the road show was definitely wearing thin, but it was also a valuable experience. She told Ivo that every day.

'Not three days later, lover. A week. A whole week!' For a moment her face lit up and she wondered if she should tell Ivo and ask him to come out.

'Do we get a day off?'

'Not that I know of, but who knows? Come on, get

yourself ready. I'll keep you company while you pack.' She smiled at him as she climbed off the bed in her nightgown. By now it was almost like being married, and she had to remind herself to put on a robe.

'Did you get through to your agent today?' She called out to him from the shower and he shouted back.

'Yeah.'

'What did he say?'

'Nothing good. I've had my last bloody extension from immigration, and as soon as I leave the show, I have to get out.'

'Of the country?'

'Obviously.'

'Oh, shit.'

'Precisely. That was more or less what I said, give or take a few pungent expressions.' He smiled at the half-open door, and a few minutes later she turned off the shower and returned, wrapped in a towel, with another around her auburn hair.

'What are you going to do about that?' She looked concerned for him. She knew how much he wanted to stay.

'There's nothing I can do, love. I'll go.' He shrugged and looked into his coffee with a wistful look in his eyes.

'I wish there were something I could do for you, Anthony.'

But this time he only grinned lopsidedly. ''Fraid not, love, you're already married.'

'Would that do it?' She looked surprised.

'Sure. If I marry an American, I'm home free.'

'So marry someone just for the hell of it. You can always get a quickie Dominican divorce right afterwards. Hell, that's a terrific idea.'

'Not really. I'd have to live with her for six months.'

'So? There must be someone.'

But he shook his head. 'I'm afraid not.'

'Then we'll have to drum up someone for you.' But this time they both laughed, and she disappeared into the bathroom again. When she emerged, she was wearing a turquoise silk blouse and a white linen skirt. There was a matching jacket over her arm, and she was wearing high-heeled black patent leather sandals. She looked wonderfully crisp and summery, and Anthony smiled as he looked at her.

'You look lovely, Bettina.' He said it gently, with a mixture of affection, awe, and respect. And then later, as they were riding to the airport. 'How's your husband, by the way? Isn't he ever coming out?'

But Bettina shook her head slowly. 'He says there's not much point if we don't get a day off. I guess he's right.' She didn't seem anxious to pursue the subject, and after that there was chaos getting them all on to the plane. At last they were seated side by side on the aircraft. He read a magazine, and she read a book. From time to time he said something to her *sotto voce*, and she laughed, and then she shared something amusing with him from the book. To anyone who didn't know them, they looked as though they had been married for years.

The San Francisco airport looked like all the others, large, spread out, crowded, and chaotic. And at last they got everyone into the appropriate bus to the city, and then finally into cabs to the hotel. Bettina gritted her teeth to see one more ugly hotel room, and when the taxi stopped, she looked up in surprise. It wasn't the usual plastic commercial hotel she had expected. Instead it looked small and French, and it was perched on a hill with a breathtaking view of the bay. It looked in fact more like someone's home than a hotel where the road show would stay.

'Anthony?' She looked at him in astonishment. 'Do you suppose they made a mistake?' She got out slowly and looked around with a mixture of pleasure and dismay. 'Wait till the others see this.' And then she grinned at him as he paid the driver. She was suddenly very amused. But there was something in Anthony's eyes that she did not quite understand.

'The others aren't staying here, Bettina.' He said it to her very softly as they stood on the street.

'What do you mean?' She looked at him in confusion, not able or willing to understand. 'Where are they?'

'At the usual fleabag hotel downtown.' And then with a gentle look in his eyes, 'I thought you'd like it better here.'

'But why?' She looked suddenly frightened. 'Why should we stay here?'

'Because you're used to this kind of thing, and it's beautiful. You'll love it, and we're both sick to death of lousy hotels.' It was true. But why here? And why did he always talk about what she was used to? Why should they stay in a separate hotel, just the two of them? 'Will you trust me?' And then he turned to her with a look of challenge. 'Or do you want to go?' She hesitated for a long moment, sighed, and then shook her head.

'No, I'll stay. But I don't know why you did it. Why didn't you say something to me first?' She was tired and suspicious and she was suddenly unsure of what she saw in his eyes.

'I wanted to surprise you.'

'But what will the others say?'

'Who cares?' But she was hanging back again and he dropped the bags and reached for her hands. 'Bettina, are we friends or not?'

She nodded slowly. 'We are.'

'Then trust me. Just this once. It's all I ask.' And she did. He had already asked for adjoining rooms, and when she saw them, she had to admit that they were so pretty that suddenly she wanted to throw her arms around his neck and laugh.

'Oh, screw it, Anthony, you're right. God, it's lovely!'

'Isn't it?' He looked victorious as they stood on her terrace and enjoyed the view.

And then she looked at him sheepishly. 'I'm sorry I made such a fuss. I'm just so damn tired, and I . . . oh, I don't know . . . it's been so long since I've seen Ivo, and I worry about things, and . . .'

But he spoke softly with an arm around her shoulders, 'Never mind, love. Never mind.'

She smiled at him and walked slowly back inside to relax luxuriously on a pale-blue-velvet chaise longue. There was fabric on the walls, and lovely French furniture, a little marble fireplace, and a four-poster bed. When he walked back into the room, she smiled at him again. 'How did you ever find this place?'

'Luck, I guess. The first time I came to the States. And I always promised myself' – he looked down at his hands as he spoke – 'that I'd come back here with someone I care about a great deal.' And then his eyes rose to hers again. 'And I care very much about you.' He was barely able to say the words, and as he did Bettina felt her whole body grow warm. She didn't know what to answer, but she knew that she cared about him too.

'Anthony, I – I shouldn't . . .' She stood up, feeling awkward, and turned her back to him as she stood in the middle of the room. And then she heard him, next to her, and she felt him touching her shoulders gently until he had turned her to face him, and without saying anything more, he kissed her, with body and soul and fire and ecstasy, full on the lips.

Chapter 18

At first Bettina didn't understand how it happened, or even what led her to do a thing like that, except that it had been five weeks since she had seen Ivo, and being on the road with the show, she felt as though she were existing in a whole other world. And now she realised for how long she had been attracted to Anthony, and much as she hated to admit it, how exquisite it was to be joined with a youthful body and young flesh. They drank of each other endlessly, until it was almost time to go to the theatre. And Bettina left her bed almost in a daze, not knowing what to say to him, or what to think of herself. But Anthony was quick to see her expression and he sat her back down on the bed.

'Bettina, look at me . . .' But she wouldn't. 'Darling, please.'

'I don't know what to think. I don't understand . . .' And then she looked at him, agonised. 'Why did we – '

'Because we wanted to. Because we need each other and we understand each other.' And then he looked at her very hard. 'I love you, Bettina. That was part of it too. Don't overlook that. Don't tell yourself it was just bodies here in this bed. It wasn't. It was much, much more than that. And if you deny that, then you're lying to yourself.' And then, firmly, he brought her face up to his. 'Look at me, Bettina.' And slowly, agonisingly, she did. 'Do you love me? Answer me honestly. Because I know I love you. Do you love me?'

Her voice was barely a whisper. 'I don't know.'

'Yes, you do. You'd never have made love to me if you didn't love me. You're not that kind of woman. Are you, Bett?' And then more softly, 'Are you?' And this time she nodded, and then quickly shook her head. 'Do you love me? Answer me . . . say it . . . say it please . . .' She could feel his words begin to caress her body again and as she looked at him she heard herself speaking.

'I love you.' And then he put his arms around her and held her.

'I know that you do.' He looked down at her tenderly. 'Now we'll go to the theatre, and afterwards we'll come back here.' But just to remind her of what would happen, he made love to her again quickly, there on the bed. She was breathless and panting when he left her, and astonished at her own passion, her hunger. She was like an alcoholic guzzling wine. She couldn't get enough of him, of his body, so satiny smooth beneath her hand. But on the way to the theatre thoughts of Ivo began to press into her head. What if he called her? If he knew? What if he asked where they were staying? What if he came out to California as a surprise? What in hell was she doing? But each time she tried to tell herself it was madness, she thought of their love-making and knew she didn't want it to end. She could barely get through her work at the theatre that evening, and when they got back to the hotel, they made love all night. It made her wonder how long they had kept the friendship so platonic, and for so long.

'Happy?' He smiled down at her, in the crook of his arm.

'I don't know.' She looked up at him honestly, and then smiled. 'Yes, of course.' But in her heart was a terrible aching for Ivo. She felt pierced by a knife edge of guilt.

But Anthony knew. 'I understand, Bettina. It's all right.'

But she wondered if he did. She wondered if he had Ivo's genius for loving. He didn't have Ivo's experience or his years. There were benefits in loving a man that much older. He had used up his unkindness, learned his lessons long before. All he had left for her now was kindness and gentleness and loving. She grew very pensive as she thought of that. And then Anthony seemed to know what she was thinking. 'What are you going to tell him?'

'Nothing.' And then she turned to look at Anthony. He looked suddenly hurt. 'I couldn't, Anthony. It's not the same. If he were younger, it would be different. This way it just becomes an issue of his age.'

'But isn't that the issue? Partly?' Jesus, she was tough to convince. He suddenly realised what kind of fight he had in store.

'I don't know.' He didn't press the point that night. They had better things to do. But again and again Bettina found herself thinking first of Anthony, then of Ivo, then of Anthony again. It was a maddening circle, and her only escape from it was in Anthony's arms. In the course of the week she found herself not calling Ivo. Her guilt would have weighed on her too much. She couldn't pretend to him. She didn't want to lie. And she didn't want to tell him. So she simply fled. He called often, he left messages, and at last he reached her, in Los Angeles late one night. They hadn't spoken in nine days. And now there was no longer any pretence. She and Anthony were sharing a room.

'Darling? Are you all right?' There was a faint hint of desperation in his voice, and as Bettina heard him her eyes filled with tears.

'Ivo . . . I'm fine . . . oh, darling – ' And then suddenly she couldn't speak. But she had to . . . had to . . . or he would know. She was suddenly grateful that Anthony was already asleep. 'It's been so crazy, so much work . . . I haven't stopped. And I didn't want to call until I could tell you when to come out.'

'Is it still just as crazy?' His voice sounded oddly tense, and next to her in the bed Anthony stirred. She hesitated for a moment, and then nodded, squeezing the tears from her eyes.

'Yes, it is.' It was barely a whisper, but at his end Ivo understood.

'Then we'll wait, darling. I'll see you when you get home. You don't need to feel pressed. We have the rest of our lives.' But did they? He was no longer sure. Bettina felt as though she were being torn from him by hands stronger than hers.

'Oh, Ivo, I miss you so much . . .' She sounded like a

desperately unhappy child, and at his end Ivo closed his eyes. But he had to tell her. Had to. It was only fair.

'Bettina . . . little one . . .' He took a deep breath. 'This is all part of your growing up, little one. You have to do it. No matter what.'

'What do you mean "no matter what"?' She sat up in bed, straining to hear. Did he know? Had he guessed then? What was he saying or was he talking about the show?

'I mean that no matter what it costs you, if it's what you want, Bettina, it's right. Don't ever be afraid to pay the price. Sometimes we have to pay some pretty high prices . . . even if that means our not seeing each other for you to be with this play, even if that means – ' He couldn't go on. But he didn't have to. 'Just be a big girl, Bettina. You have to, darling. It's time.' But she didn't want to be a big girl. Suddenly all she wanted to be was a very little girl with him. 'Go to sleep now, Bettina, it's late.'

And then she realised. 'It's even later for you.' Back East it was three hours later, and it was two thirty in the morning in LA. 'Good Lord, what are you even doing up at this hour?'

'I wanted to be sure I got hold of you.'

'Oh, darling, I'm sorry.' Once again she was overcome with remorse.

'Don't be. Now be young, and have fun, and – ' He had been about to say And remember that you're mine, but he didn't want to say that. He wanted to let her fly free if that was what she wanted. Whatever it cost him. 'I love you, little one.'

'I love you, Ivo.'

'Good night.'

When she hung up, there were tears streaming down her face and Anthony was snoring softly. For a brief moment she hated him.

But three days later she wasn't sure if she didn't hate Ivo more. There was an article in an LA paper about the well-known star of the Hollywood screen, Margot Banks, spending the weekend in New York, visiting a very dear old friend, whose name she had refused to disclose to the press. The piece went on to mention however that she had been seen dining at Twenty-one with the retired publisher of the *New York Mail*, Ivo Stewart. Bettina knew full well that Margot had been one of her father's paramours, and later one of Ivo's, while Bettina was still growing up. Was that why he was being so understanding? Was that why he hadn't come out? Jesus, here she was crucifying herself every night for making love with Anthony when he had revived his old affair with Margot Banks. Was that what was happening? Was it he who felt like roving after their seven years? As she thought of it Bettina felt a wave of white-hot fury rise in her. The next time Ivo called her, she had one of the gophers tell him that she was out. And from where he sat, drinking coffee in his chair, Mr Anthony Pearce looked enormously pleased.

Chapter 19

For three more months it went on, until the road show closed. Anthony and Bettina passionately made their way from town to town, hotel to hotel, and bed to bed. They never saw anything of the cities they worked in. They spent their time rehearsing, performing, and making love. And more and more often now Bettina was seeing Ivo's name in the papers linked with one or the other of the women who had long ago populated his life. But mainly with Margot, the old bitch. Bettina almost snarled each time she saw her name. It only made Anthony laugh at her. She was hardly in a position to make jealous scenes. And she never mentioned the gossip to Ivo, but there was a definite strain between them now when they spoke on the phone. The four months away from each other hadn't done much good.

'So?' Anthony looked at her questioningly on their last day on the road. 'Now what?'

'What the hell does that mean?' She was exhausted and it was broiling out, on a summer day in Nashville, Tennessee.

'Don't get nasty, Bettina. But I think I have a right to ask you what I can look forward to now. Is it over? Is this it? Now you go home to your penthouse and your old man?' He looked at her bitterly. He was equally tired, and the heat was getting to him too.

Bettina seemed to wilt as she looked at him and slowly she sat down on the creaking bed. As it turned out the accommodations Anthony had made for them in San Francisco had been their only decent hotel rooms in four months. If for no other reason it was going to be good to get home, just so she could climb into her own bed. But the fact of it was that despite the gossip she was longing to see Ivo. So they had both been foolish. That was no reason to end what they had. And she had learned a lesson. She would never go on the road again. As much as she had enjoyed the affair with Anthony, it was time to go home.

'I don't know, Anthony. I can't give you any answers.'

'I see.' And then after a moment, 'I suspect that means you're staying with him.'

'I told you' – her voice rose ominously – 'I don't know. What do you want from me? A contract?'

'Maybe, love. Maybe that. Has it occurred to you that while you go home to your darling little elderly husband, I am out of a job, out of a romance, and possibly out of a country? I'd say I have good reason to be concerned.'

Suddenly she felt for him. He was right. She did have Ivo. And what did he have? From the sound of it he had nothing left. 'I'm sorry, Anthony.' She went to him and touched his face with her hand. 'I'll let you know what's happening as soon as I know myself.'

'Wonderful. This is beginning to sound like a job interview. Well, let me tell you one thing, Miss Assistant Director, whatever you may think, whatever I may or may not mean to you, I want to make one thing very clear before we go. And that is that I love you.' His voice quavered on the words. 'And that if you'll be so kind as to leave your husband, I want to marry you. Immediately. Do you understand?'

She looked at him, stupefied. 'Are you serious? But why?'

He couldn't keep from smiling at her words, and then softly he ran a finger around her face, down her neck, and slowly towards her breasts. 'Because you're beautiful, and you're intelligent, and wonderful, and' – he looked at her seriously for a moment – 'you're not the sort of girl one just plays around with. You're the sort of girl one marries, Bett.' She looked at him in amazement and he smiled. 'So, my darling, if I can pry you out of your existing situation' – he went down on one knee next to her and kissed her hand – 'I would like to make you Mrs Anthony Pearce.'

'I don't know what to say.'

'Just call me the day after we get to New York and say yes.'

But she knew that she wouldn't do that. She couldn't have done that to Ivo. What she hadn't counted on was Ivo doing it to her.

Chapter 20

'Ivo, you don't mean it.' As she stared at him her face turned an ashen grey. 'But why?'

'Because it's time. For both of us.' What was he saying? Oh, God, what did he mean? 'I think it may be time for both of us to start with lovers our own age.'

'But I don't want that!' And then with horror, 'Do you?' He didn't answer. But only because his guts were being torn apart. He was certain of what had happened. And he had availed himself of certain reports. She was involved with the actor. And she had been involved with him for months. Perhaps even before they left New York. Ivo wasn't going to stand in the way of that. She had a right to something more. She was so young. 'But I don't *want* to leave you!' She almost shrieked it at him as he sat calmly in his den.

'I think you do.'

'Is it because of the other women I've been reading that you're going out with? Is it because of them? Ivo, tell me!' She was suddenly frantic and frighteningly pale, but he held firm.

'I told you, this will be better for both of us. And you should be free.'

'But I don't want to be free.'

'But you are free now. I'm not even going to drag this thing out unbearably for both of us, I'm going to fly to the Dominican Republic next weekend and it'll all be over. Finished. You will be legally free.'

'*But I don't want to be legally free, Ivo!!*' She was shouting so loud, he was sure that Mathilde could hear everything through the door. Gently he reached out to Bettina and held her close to him.

'I will always be here for you, Bettina. I love you. But you need someone younger than I am.' And then, as though explaining to a very slow child, he told her, 'You can't be married to me any more.'

'But I don't want to leave you.' She was wailing now and almost hysterical as she clutched at his hand. 'Don't make me go . . . I'll never do it again . . . I'm sorry . . . Oh, Ivo, I'm so sorry . . .' Now she knew that he knew. He had to. Why else would he be doing this to her? As she clung to him she wondered how he could be so cruel.

And the tragedy of it was that inside he was dying, but he felt that it was the one thing he owed her. And yet it was the one thing she didn't want. He tried to explain to her through her hysteria that there would be a sum of money provided for her every month. He would never leave her penniless or stranded. He had also provided for her in his will. She could stay in the apartment until after he got back from the Dominican Republic, after which he suggested she move in with – er – a friend. And while she remained in residence, he himself would stay at a friend's club. Bettina listened to him in a stupor, she couldn't believe this was happening to her, this man who had rescued her, whom she had so desperately loved. But she had spoiled everything by sleeping with Anthony, and Ivo knew. Now she had to be punished.

The next days passed by her like a nightmare, and she could remember no more painful moment in her life. Not even the death of her father had left her feeling so broken, so abandoned, so desperately unable to turn the tides of what had come. She didn't even want to speak to Anthony, yet the day before Ivo returned from the Dominican Republic, she sat in her bedroom late at night, almost hysterical, and she could think of no one to reach out to but him.

'Who? What? Oh, my God, you sound awful . . . are you all right?' And then after a pause, 'Do you want to come over?' She hesitated for a moment, and then she said yes. 'Do you want me to come and get you?' It was a gesture of chivalry she appreciated but didn't feel was quite right. So she climbed into blue jeans, sandals, and a shirt, and a few minutes later she got in a cab and was on her way to him.

'He *what?*' Anthony was making them coffee as they sat in his comfortable kitchen on ladder-back chairs.

'He told me he wants a divorce, and he's in the Dominican Republic this weekend getting it.' She repeated it mechanically as fresh tears washed over her face.

Anthony stood there and grinned. 'I told you, ducky, he's senile, but who am I to complain? You mean he's divorcing you?' She nodded. 'This weekend?' She nodded again and he gave out a whoop.

'I might tell you, Anthony,' she sniffed loudly, 'I think your elation is in very poor taste.'

'Do you?' He grinned at her. 'Do you, my love? Well, I don't. I've never been so bloody happy about anything in my life.' And then with a polite bow he turned to her. 'Will you do me the honour of marrying me on Monday?'

She curtsied equally politely and said, 'I will not.'

He was momentarily taken aback. 'Why the hell not?'

She sighed and walked to the couch and sat down, blowing her nose again. 'Because we hardly know each other. Because we're both young. Because . . . Jesus, Anthony . . . I've been married to someone for seven years whom I cared about a great deal, he's gone off to get a divorce, and you expect me to get married the next day? I'd have to be crazy. At least give me a chance to catch my breath.' But catching her breath wasn't the point really. She didn't want to marry him. She wasn't sure of him. As a lover yes, but not as a mate.

'Fine. And you can write to me in England.' He looked suddenly sour.

'What's that supposed to mean?' She looked over at him and frowned.

'Precisely that. I have to be out of the country by Friday.'

'At the end of next week?'

'That's when Friday usually comes around.'

'Don't be cute, I'm serious.'

'So am I. Extremely so as a matter of fact. In fact I was about to start packing when you called.' And then he brightened. 'But if we got married, I wouldn't have to go anywhere, would I?'

She looked at him squarely. 'That's a hell of a reason to get married.'

But he moved close to her as she said it, and then he sat down and took her hand. 'Bett, think of our months with that damn road show. If we can stay happy and close through all of that, we can make it through anything. You know I love you. I told you I wanted to marry you, so what difference does it make if it's this week or next year?'

'Maybe a lot of difference.' She looked at him nervously and shook her head, and quickly he dropped the subject. A little while later they wound up in bed, and the subject didn't come up again until the next morning, when he reminded her that she was not only about to lose her husband, but her lover as well. That dismal reality had not yet fully come home to her, and she burst into fresh tears.

'Oh, for God's sake stop crying. There's a way to solve everything, you know.'

'Stop pushing for your own goddamn interests.' But he did, and he was brilliant at it. By the end of the afternoon, she was a nervous wreck. And then, checking her watch, she realised that she had to go back to Ivo's apartment. She had to finish packing the rest of her things and get them to a hotel. But when she told Anthony, he insisted that she stay with him. She wasn't absolutely sure that she ought to, but on the other hand it would be less brutally lonely for the first few days than a hotel. And as long as she had lived with him in hotel rooms all summer, there was no reason not to stay with him now. She also realised with a dull thud that she was no longer married. By that day Ivo would have gotten the divorce.

So at five o'clock she went uptown in a taxi to collect the rest of her things, and she was oddly reminded of when she had moved out of her father's empty apartment and come to stay at Ivo's. It was seven years later, and now she was moving in with another man. But only briefly, she promised herself. And then she reminded herself that she had only come to Ivo's to stay briefly too.

By Monday she was feeling more herself. On Monday evening he took her out to dinner. And on Tuesday he started to pack. By Wednesday the apartment was a shambles, and it was clear that in two days she was going to have to face another wrenching adieu. That morning she spoke to Ivo, and he was odd and cool and determined about what he had done. And when she hung up, she looked at Anthony, with fresh tears in her eyes. In two days he would be gone too. But he knew what she was thinking, and he had looked pointedly into her eyes. 'Will you do it?' She looked at him blankly. 'Will you marry me, Bettina? Please?'

And then she had to smile. He looked like a small boy as he asked her.

'But it doesn't make any sense. It's too soon.'

'No, it's not too soon.' And this time there were tears in his eyes. 'It's almost too late. If we don't get a licence today, we can't do it by Friday. And then I'm going to have to leave you. No matter what I feel . . . no matter what . . .' The words had an oddly familiar ring to Bettina and she remembered Ivo saying them to her on the phone when she was in California with Anthony. She also remembered his telling her to pay the price for what she believed in, 'no matter what'.

'And if it doesn't work?' She looked at him steadily.

'Then we get divorced.'

She spoke softly. 'I've already done that, Anthony. I don't want to do that again.'

He moved closer and reached out to hold her. 'We won't have to. We'll be together forever and always . . .' And then he held her tighter. 'We'll have a baby . . . oh, Bettina, please . . .' And as he held her she couldn't resist him. She wanted so desperately to cling to him, not to lose yet one more person who had meant something to her. And she wanted equally desperately to be loved. 'Will you?'

She held her breath for a moment and nodded. He could barely hear her answer. 'Yes.'

He got to City Hall before closing on Wednesday. They got the licence, the blood test, and Anthony got the ring. And on Friday morning, at City Hall again, they were married. And Bettina Daniels Stewart became Mrs Anthony Pearce.

Chapter 21

Anthony and Bettina spent the autumn months hibernating quietly after their September wedding. He hadn't gotten cast in another play and she hadn't returned to her job. She realised that she had the background she needed. And she certainly had the experience, the heartache to begin to write. Anthony didn't feel pressure to return either. Married to Bettina, he could stay in the States. And living on her alimony from Ivo, he decided that he could wait for the right part. Once or twice Bettina felt awkward about it, after all Ivo had provided the money for her. But it was obvious that Anthony felt embarrassed enough about his lack of employment, so she didn't press the point. And after all she wasn't working either. She decided she would take a break, get to know Anthony, every nook, every corner, every cranny of his mind. There were parts that she realised she didn't really know, parts of him that she knew he kept from her, however close they might seem.

So they tucked themselves into his apartment, read plays, cooked spaghetti, went for long walks, and made love. They laughed and talked and chuckled into the morning hours . . . when Anthony was at home. There were many evenings when he went to see other actors perform, and afterwards he and his friends talked far into the night. Alone in the loft, she understood how Ivo must have felt when she left him to work, at the theatre.

In fact she thought about Ivo a lot. She wondered what he was doing, if he was still so tired, if he was all right. She found herself wanting to turn to him, to hear his gentleness, his encouragement, and his praise. And what she found instead was Anthony's nonchalance and his humour, his warmth, and his passion, which spent itself so readily in her arms.

'What are you looking so glum about, love?' He had been

watching her for a while, gnawing at a pencil as she poised over some notes for her play. She looked up in surprise as she heard him. He had been out for hours and she hadn't heard him come in.

'Nothing. How was your evening?'

'Very pleasant. Yours?' he asked her casually as he unwound a long cashmere scarf from around his neck. Bettina had bought it for him at the first sign of winter. After he insisted that she sell her mink coat. They had been living on the proceeds for two months.

'It was okay.' But she was looking gloomy, and she hadn't been feeling well all day.

He smiled as he looked at her and came to sit down on the edge of the bed. 'Now, come on, lover. Tell me. Something's wrong.'

At first she only shook her head, and then she laughed softly and took his face in her hands. 'No. I was just thinking about Christmas. And I wanted to give you something wonderful. But I don't see how I can.' She looked at him regretfully and he pulled her into his arms.

'That doesn't matter, silly. We have each other. That's all I want.' And then he grinned mischievously. 'That and a Porsche.'

'Very funny.' But it was odd to remember that Ivo had given her a diamond bracelet the Christmas before. And she had given him a new cashmere coat, a four-hundred-dollar briefcase, and a gold lighter. But those days were gone forever now. All she had left was the jewellery, and that was carefully stowed in the vault. She hadn't even told Anthony. She had simply told him that she'd returned it all to Ivo when she left. As a matter of fact she had offered to return to him all the pieces that he'd given her, but he had insisted that she keep them, on the condition that she told no one where they were. He wanted her to keep them, like a nest egg, and she had followed his advice. Now, for a moment, she contemplated selling something, just for Christmas. But she knew that to do so would arouse Anthony's suspicions that she was hiding something more. And she was. Now she sighed as she looked at him. 'Do you realise that we can't afford to give each other anything?' She looked like a child who had just lost her most cherished toy.

But Anthony was undaunted. 'Sure we can. We can give each other a turkey and a Christmas dinner. We can write each other poems. We can go for a long walk in the park.' And he made it sound so lovely that she smiled and brushed away her tears.

'I wanted to give you much more than that.'

And then, reaching out for her gently, he whispered. 'You already have.'

But in the week that followed, her thoughts of Christmas were all but obscured. She became violently ill with some kind of flu that had her retching and gagging most of the day on the bathroom floor. By evening she would feel a little better. But it all started with fresh anguish in the morning. And by the end of the week she looked ghastly and wan.

'You'd better see a doctor, Bett.' Anthony looked at her one afternoon as she staggered out of the bathroom.

But she was hesitant about going to Ivo's doctor. She didn't want to have to explain to him, didn't want him to report to Ivo, or to pry. So she got the name of a doctor from a friend of Anthony's, some girl they had worked with on their last show. The waiting room was tiny and crowded, the magazines dog-eared, the furniture old, and the people all downcast and poor. By the time she got in to see the doctor, she was feeling not only nauseated but faint, and it was only a few moments later that she was retching violently into a bowl. But as she looked up at him his eyes were gentle, and with kind hands he helped her smooth back her hair.

'That bad, huh?' She nodded, trying to catch her breath. 'Has it been like this for long?' His eyes looked her over carefully, but they were nice eyes, and Bettina felt less frightened as she lay down on the table with a soft sigh.

'It's been almost two weeks.'

'Any worse? Any better? Or has it been like this the whole time?' He pulled up a stool on casters and sat down next to her with a small smile.

'It's been pretty much like this the whole time. Sometimes it's better in the evening, but not much.' He nodded slowly then and made a note on her chart.

'Has this ever happened before?'

She shook her head quickly. 'Never.'

And then he looked at her very gently and searched her eyes. 'Have you ever been pregnant before?'

But she only shook her head as she watched him. And then it dawned on her, and she sat up quickly. 'Am I pregnant now?'

'You might be.' And then, 'Would that be very bad?'

She shrugged pensively, and then a small smile dawned in her eyes. 'I don't know.'

'Is your husband an actor?' Most of his patients were. It was a world in which everything spread like wildfire, recommendations, referrals, gossip, diseases. And along with the rest, his name had been passed along. She nodded. 'Is he working right now?' He knew how that was also. Sometimes he had to wait to get paid for five or six months, if at all.

'No, he's not. But I'm sure he will be shortly.'

'What about you? An actress?'

She shook her head, smiling slowly. What was she? An assistant director? A budding playwright? A gopher? She was nothing now. She could no longer just say, 'I'm Justin Daniels's daughter' or 'I'm Ivo Stewart's wife.' 'I'm just Anthony Pearce's wife.' She said it as though by reflex as the doctor watched her, sensing that there was a lot more to her story than that. The sweater she was wearing was expensive, as was the tweed skirt. The loafers were Gucci, and although the coat she had been wearing had been oddly cheap in contrast, he saw that she was wearing a very fancy gold watch.

'Well, let's take a look at you.' And he did and he made an accurate guess. To confirm it they did a pregnancy test in his office, which showed that he had been right. 'I'd say you're about two months pregnant, Bettina.' He watched for her reaction and was touched by the broad smile. 'You don't look too unhappy.'

'I'm not.' She thanked him and made another appointment, although after that he said he'd have to refer her to someone else. He couldn't give her anything for the vomiting and nausea, but suddenly they didn't seem so bad, and he assured her that in another month it would probably disappear, or at least subside. She didn't even care now. It was worth it. She was going to have a baby! She was going to have Anthony's child! Suddenly even betraying Ivo didn't seem so terrible. It was worth it now. She was going to have a *baby*! She floated all the way home and almost raced up to the loft, and then suddenly she felt stricken. Maybe she shouldn't have run . . . maybe it was bad for the baby. She came roaring into the living-room like a tornado, brimming with her news, but Anthony wasn't there.

She drank bouillon, ate some crackers, got sick again, and tried to eat again. The doctor had told her that she should try it. And she had promised that she would. For the baby. And then suddenly, as she sat there, she had an idea. She wouldn't tell Anthony. Not yet. She'd wait till Christmas. That would be her gift to him. It was only another five days away. And she giggled to herself as she thought of her secret . . . she clapped her hands like a child as she thought of it . . . they were going to have a baby! She could hardly wait to hear what he'd say.

Chapter 22

On Christmas Eve Anthony surprised her and came home with a tiny little tree. They set it on a table, and she tied it with ribbons. They made popcorn, which she didn't eat, and they each put one tiny package under the tree. It reminded them both of an old movie, and they laughed as they kissed. She opened hers first. It was an old-fashioned fountain pen, a lovely one, and he smiled at her pleasure. 'To write your first play!' She hugged him and thanked him and he kissed her long and hard.

'Now yours.' She had given him a pair of silver cuff links that he had been drooling over for weeks in a nearby antique shop.

'Bettina, you're crazy!' He was delighted and ran to change shirts so he could put them on. And with a small smile she followed him and sat down quietly on the bed.

'Anthony?' Her voice was strangely soft as she spoke to him, and not knowing why, he turned around.

'Yes, lover?' His eyes met hers.

'I have another present for you.'

'Do you?' He tilted his head to one side, but neither of them moved.

She nodded. 'Yes. A very special one.' And then she held out her arms to him. 'Come here and sit down.'

Something very odd crawled up his spine. He came to her hesitating, with a look of anxiety in his eyes. 'Is something wrong?' But she shook her head quickly and smiled.

'No.' She kissed him then, tenderly, softly, and afterwards ran her fingertips across his mouth. In a whisper that only he could have heard, 'We're going to have a baby, darling.' And then she waited. But what she wanted never came. Instead he looked at her, frozen. It was as bad as he had thought. The possibility had crossed his mind with all

132

her vomiting, but he had forced it out of his head. It was more than he could cope with, and it would spoil all his plans.

'Are you kidding?' He stood up next to her and then looked down again. 'No, I guess you're not.' He threw the cuff links on the table and walked out of the room, and Bettina tried to fight an urge to cry and get sick all at the same time. Slowly she followed him out to the living-room and watched him as he stood at the window, his back to her, and running a distracted hand through his hair.

'Anthony?' She looked at him hesitantly, and slowly he turned around.

'Yeah.' He stared at her angrily, saying nothing for a time, and then the look of accusation came clear in his eyes. 'Did you do that on purpose, Bettina?' With tears in her eyes she shook her head. She had wanted him to be so happy. She wanted it to mean something to him too. And then, never taking his eyes from hers, 'Would you consider an abortion?' But this time she couldn't hold back the tears, and shaking her head, she fled the room. And when she emerged from the bathroom half an hour later, he was gone.

'Merry Christmas,' she whispered to herself softly with one hand resting gently on her still flat stomach and the other wiping her ceaselessly crying eyes. She fell asleep at last at four in the morning. But Anthony never came home that night.

He didn't return until five o'clock the next afternoon. Christmas was almost over, and for Bettina it had been ruined. She didn't ask him where he'd been. She didn't say anything. She was packing her bags. But that had been what he had feared. And it was what had brought him home. Three months into the marriage he couldn't afford to lose her. Not yet.

'I'm sorry.' He looked at her bleakly from the bedroom doorway. 'You just took me by surprise.'

'So I gathered.' She turned her back to him and continued to pack her bags.

'Look, Bettina . . . baby, I'm sorry.' He went to her and tried to hold her but she shook him off.

'Don't do that.'

'Look, dammit, I love you!' He turned her around to face him, and once again there were tears in her eyes.

'Just leave me alone . . . please . . . Anthony, I . . .' But she couldn't go on. She wanted him so badly. Wanted to share with him the joy of his child that she found herself melting into his arms and hoping that the dreams would come true after all.

'It's all right, baby. It's all right. I just couldn't imagine . . . I'm not . . .' And then at last when her tears had subsided, they sat down. 'But are we ready, Bettina?'

She smiled valiantly through red eyes. 'Sure. Why not?' For all those years with Ivo she had stifled that dream. She hadn't even known how much she wanted children. Until now. Suddenly this meant everything to her.

'But how will we feed it?' He looked bleak, but she was thinking of her jewellery. She'd sell everything if she had to, just to take care of the child.

'Don't worry. We'll manage. We manage now, don't we?'

'That's not the same thing.'

And then, sighing deeply, as though it caused him pain too, he looked at her regretfully. 'As much as I'd hate to do it, don't you think it would make more sense this time to have an abortion and then try again later, when we've saved some money, when we're both on our feet, when I'm not out of work?' But she was shaking her head determinedly.

'No.'

'Bettina . . . be reasonable!'

'Goddamn it, is that all you want? An abortion?' On and on the argument raged. In the end Bettina won. But Anthony looked grim for the next two weeks. She didn't leave him, but she thought of it often, and then suddenly one day he came home radiant and gave a loud whoop.

She came to find him in the doorway and smiled when she

134

saw his broad grin. 'What happened to you?' But she could guess.

'I got work!'

'What kind of work? Tell me!' She was happy for him and followed him to the couch; suddenly their hostility of the past weeks seemed to dim. 'Come on, Anthony . . . tell me!'

'I will, I will!' But for a moment he seemed too happy to talk. It was a beautiful part. 'I got the lead in *Sonny Boy*!' He looked at her triumphantly. It was the biggest hit on Broadway.

'On Broadway?' She looked stunned. She had recently heard a rumour that the star was leaving the show after its stellar fifteen-month run. But Anthony was shaking his head.

'On the road, my love, on the road. But not shit towns this time, my darling. All the best cities in the States. This time we travel with a little class! No flophouses, no cockroaches. We can even stay in some decent hotels for a change.' And then he told her how much they were paying him.

'Anthony! That's fabulous.' But she realised she had to tell him something then. She had noticed his 'we'. Regretfully she took his hand and spoke gently. 'But sweetheart, I can't . . .' She hated to say it, but she had to. 'I can't go along.'

'Of course you can. Don't be ridiculous. Why can't you?' He looked at her nervously and stood up.

But Bettina looked at him firmly. 'No, darling. I can't. The baby. That kind of travelling would be too much.'

'Bullshit it would, Bettina. I told you, we'll be staying in decent hotels. We're going to big cities. So what the hell is your problem? Christ, it doesn't even show!' He was shouting at her, and she could see his hands shake.

'Just because it doesn't show doesn't mean it isn't there. And it doesn't matter what kind of hotels we stay in, that's a lot of travelling.'

'Well, you'd better make up your mind to do it.' He

stalked across the room and looked back at her. 'Because if you don't go with me, I'm still out of work.'

'Don't be ridiculous, Anthony.' But she was momentarily touched. 'You mean you won't go without me?'

He paused for a long time, standing in the doorway. 'I mean that they want you as assistant director, sister. They want us as a pair. And they want us together. You don't do it, they won't hire me.'

'What? But that's crazy!'

'The producer saw us work together on the road and they think we make a good team. As it so happens their director on this one is kind of a figurehead, so he'll get the glory, but you'll be doing the work. It's not a great arrangement, but the money is good. Two fifty a week for you.' But she didn't seem to care.

'That's not the point, Anthony. I'm pregnant. Did you tell them that?'

'Hardly.' He spat the word at her.

But now she was angry too. It was starting all over again. 'I won't do it, damn you!'

'In that case, madam' – he swept her a low bow – 'allow me to thank you for destroying my career. I hope you realise' – he stood up very straight and faced her across the room with fury in his eyes – 'I hope you realise that if I turn this down I may not work for years.'

'Oh, Anthony, that's not so . . .' There were suddenly tears in her eyes again. But she also knew that was how it sometimes worked. Turn down a good offer, and word got around. 'Whose company is it?' She heard the name Voorhees and she cringed. They were one of the most hard-nosed outfits in the business. 'But, darling, I can't.'

He didn't answer, he simply walked out and slammed the door. Dammit. It was a ridiculous arrangement. Why did they have to insist on having her too? She had gotten all the experience she wanted in the last seven years. Now she wanted to read every play she could get her hands on, and then she would write her own. Her in-house training was over as far as she was concerned. But Anthony was a different story. If she blew it for him, he could be out of work for a very, very long time. After thinking it over for two hours, she called the doctor and discussed the matter with him.

'What do you think?'

'I think you're crazy!'

'Why? Because it would be bad for the baby?'

'No, the baby won't care. But the way you've been feeling, can you think of anything worse than travelling from hotel room to hotel room for the next five or six months?' She nodded grimly in silent answer. 'How long is the tour?'

'I don't know. I forgot to ask.'

'Well, let's put it this way, if you can stand it, I don't see any physical reason why you shouldn't go, as long as you get as much rest as you can, eat decently, stay off your feet whenever possible, and come back to home base in' – he looked at her chart – 'no more than five months. I want you back here when you're no more than seven and a half months pregnant. Any sensible obstetrician would tell you that. And I also want you to go to pre-natal clinics when you're on the road. Call the biggest hospital in every town you hit and get checked once a month. Think you can handle all that?' His voice smiled at her over the phone.

'I guess I'll have to.'

'Actually' – he sounded more gentle – 'once the nausea settles down, it may not be so bad. The old vaudevillians used to do things like that. You've heard the expression "born in a trunk"? They weren't kidding. I can think of easier ways to have a baby, but if you're sensible, it won't hurt you or the baby.' With a long sigh Bettina hung up the phone. She had her answer. And four hours later Anthony had his.

But the tour was even more exhausting than the last one, and she worked her ass off every day on the road. It turned out that the director had an ironclad contract with the company so they had to take him along, but he was an alcoholic who spent every day drinking in his room, which left everything on Bettina's shoulders. And by the second month on the road she thought she would collapse. The hotels were not nearly as lovely as Anthony had promised, the hours were endless, and with no director to lean on, and an inadequate staff, Bettina was hauling, yelling, working, running every hour of the day. She was losing weight instead of gaining, and she had constant pains in her legs. She hardly ever saw Anthony, who spent every day, when they weren't rehearsing, out playing with his friends. In particular, with a little blonde model from Cleveland who was making her debut in the show. Her name was Jeannie, and by the time they had left New York City, Bettina hated her guts. It made working with her difficult, as assistant director, but Bettina forced herself to be professional. She owed it to the girl, to herself, to the company, and to Anthony.

The second time she went to a clinic, the doctor told her where things stood. She was overworked, overwrought, and underweight, and if she didn't take things a little easier, she would lose the baby. She was almost four months pregnant. He suggested she ask her husband to help her a little, to reduce the pressure of her job. And that night after the performance she spoke to Anthony and asked him to help.

'Why, for chrissake? You planning to go up on stage and act for me?'

'Anthony . . . be serious . . .'

'I am serious. What do I care if you lose the baby? I never wanted it in the first place. Listen, lover, that baby is *your* kid. You don't want to lose it, find someone else to help you out.' And he had walked past her then and slid a hand into Jeannie's arm. He then informed Bettina that they were going out to dinner and not to wait up. She looked at him in stupefaction. What was happening to them? Why was he doing this? Was it just because of the child? She returned to her hotel room, troubled, and for the first time in two

138

months the urge to call Ivo was almost overwhelming. But she couldn't do that any more. She wasn't a little girl now. And she couldn't turn to Ivo just because this was hard. But she sat alone, alternately thinking and crying. Anthony never came home. She waited in her hotel room to confront him. But at noon the next day she finally had to leave for the theatre. And Jeannie was waiting for her there.

'Looking for Anthony?' she cooed at Bettina, and Bettina felt everything inside her go taut.

'No, I came here to work. Anything I can do for you?'

'Yeah. Act like a lady.' Jeannie hopped up on a stool, and it took all of Bettina's self-control not to knock her off.

'I beg your pardon?' Bettina's voice was like ice.

'You heard me, Betty.'

'The name's Bettina. And just exactly what do you mean?' Suddenly Bettina knew that there was something major happening here. What was this girl saying? And where was Anthony in all this? Bettina felt her guts ache, but she didn't waver as she looked at the pretty blonde girl.

'All right, Betty' – she had what the French call 'a face to slap' – 'why don't you just let Anthony do his thing now? His six months are almost up.'

'What six months?' She made it sound like a jail sentence, and Bettina looked stunned.

'Just why do you think he married you, sweetheart? Because he was so madly in love? Hell, no, he wanted his green card, or didn't he tell you that?' Suddenly Bettina was horrified. 'And you were the most likely candidate around. He knew your ex-husband would support you so he wouldn't have to worry about it. And he married you in September, right?' Bettina nodded dumbly. 'Well, he only has to stay with you for six months, babe, and he gets the green card. He can get rid of you after that. And if you think he won't, you're crazy. He doesn't give a damn about you, and he doesn't want that kid you were dumb enough to get knocked up with. And let me tell you something else' – she hopped off the stool and swung one well-formed hip – 'if you

139

think you're going to hang on to him when we get back to New York, you're nuts.'

All day she hid in the theatre, trying to concentrate on her work. And when at last Anthony arrived for the performance, she slipped into his dressing-room and closed the door. She was there waiting for him when he walked into it, and fortunately he was alone. He eyed her strangely, and then walked to the closet and hung up his coat.

'What do you want, Bettina?'

'To talk.' Her voice was firm, and he looked vague.

'I don't have time. I have to do my make-up for the show.'

'Fine. We can talk while you do it.' She pulled up a chair and sat down and he looked annoyed. 'I had a little talk with your friend Jeannie today.'

'What about?' He suddenly looked uncomfortable.

'Oh, let's see. Oh . . . that's right, she says that you married me just to get a green card, and that when the mandatory six months of living together are up in three weeks, then you're going to split. She also told me that you're crazy about her, more or less. She's awfully cute, darling. But is she accurate? That's what I wanted to ask you.'

'Don't be silly.' He avoided her eyes and dug around in his make-up box, but Bettina was right behind him, watching him in the mirror when he raised his eyes.

'What does that mean, Anthony?'

'It means that she may have gotten a little carried away.'

Bettina grabbed his arm. 'But that was more or less the truth, is that it? Is that what you're telling me, Anthony? Are you going to leave me after this show? Because if that's what you have in mind, I'd like to get used to the idea right now. I mean, after all' – she started to lose control of her voice and she sounded panicky – 'I am having a baby and it might be nice to know if I'm going to be alone.'

But suddenly he stood up and faced her, and he was shouting as he did. 'I told you not to have the fucking baby, dammit! Everything would have been perfectly simple if

140

you'd done as I said!' But he suddenly seemed to regret what he was saying and sat down.

'She was telling the truth, then?' Bettina's voice was grim. 'It was just for the green card?'

And then for once he looked at her honestly and nodded. 'Yes.' She closed her eyes as she heard him and sat back down.

'My God, and I believed you.' She looked at him and started to laugh as tears filled her eyes. 'What a brilliant actor you are after all.'

'It wasn't like that.' He hung his head sheepishly.

'Wasn't it?'

'No. I cared about you, I really did. I just couldn't see it forever . . . I don't know . . . we're very different . . .'

'You bastard.' She'd been had, then. She'd been had all along. She slammed the door to his dressing-room and hurried back towards the stage. The performance went smoothly and she left the theatre immediately afterwards, went back to the hotel, and asked for her own room. Not that it mattered, he probably wouldn't have come back to spend the night. But she didn't want to chance it. She wanted to be alone to think.

Now she was going to go home and write her play. And in another five months she'd have the baby . . . As she thought of it she closed her eyes tightly and tried not to cry. But it was hopeless. Each time she thought of having the baby alone, with no father, she panicked and wanted desperately to reach out to him . . . Ivo . . . anyone . . . she couldn't do it alone . . . couldn't . . . but she had to. Now she had no choice.

After hours of crying and mulling it over, at last she fell asleep, and it was four in the morning when she awakened with a strange sensation of cramps, and when she sat up in bed and looked down at the sheets, she saw blood. Her first instinct was to panic, and then she forced herself to calm down. After all, this was Atlanta. They had good hospitals. Two days earlier she had seen a doctor; now all she had to do was call the hospital and ask for him.

When she called, the nurse in the emergency room listened to the symptoms and told her to come in right away. She assured Bettina that it was probably nothing. Sometimes bleeding occurred, and with a few days of rest everything settled down. She told her to just have her husband bring her in. It was a nice assumption, but Bettina didn't even call his room. She dressed hastily, trying to stand upright in spite of the strange cramps, and she hurried to the lobby, and then out to the street to call a cab. But just walking from her room to the lobby had increased the intensity of the pain, and she was writhing badly in the backseat of the taxi as they hurried to the hospital. The driver caught sight of her in the rear-view mirror, and suddenly she gasped and then there was a small scream.

'Lady, you all right back there?'

She tried to reassure him but just as she did so, she was caught unprepared by another searing pain. 'Ohhh . . . God . . . no . . . I'm . . . oh, please . . . can you hurry . . .' But from the mild discomfort of only half an hour ago, she was suddenly in almost unbearable pain.

'Lie down on the seat.' She tried to lie there, but even lying down no longer helped. She couldn't lie still on the seat as he drove her. She kept having to turn and clutch, and suddenly she wanted to tear and scream.

'Oh, God . . . hurry . . . I can't – '

They got the information they needed about her identity and her insurance from the wallet in her handbag; Bettina was too far gone to make any sense. She could barely speak. All she could do was clutch the straps on the gurney, and every few minutes she writhed horribly and screamed. The three nurses hovering over her exchanged a look, and then nodded, and when the doctor came in she was rushed immediately to a delivery room. The baby came only half an hour later. A small foetus that shot out of her as she screamed uncontrollably. It was already dead.

Chapter 23

The plane touched down gently at Kennedy Airport, and Bettina stared out the window woodenly as they rolled towards the gate. She had just spent a week in the hospital, and she had only been discharged that afternoon. The day after her miscarriage she had called the theatre company and explained that she was in the hospital and the doctors had ordered her to rest for three months. It wasn't true but it got her off the hook, and a new assistant director was flown out from New York, a young man who was very sorry for her and delivered all of her things from the hotel to the hospital room. Anthony had only come once, looking uncomfortable. He said he was sorry, which they both knew was a lie. She kept the meeting businesslike and explained that she would call an attorney as soon as she reached New York the following week. She would give him the benefit of waiting to file for another three weeks, and he could keep his green card with her blessing. And then, looking at him with a look of bottomless revulsion, she asked him to go. He stopped at the door to say something to her, but he didn't say it. He only shrugged, and then walked out, softly closing the door. After that he didn't call her. Nothing more was said. And two days later, with Bettina still in the hospital, the road show moved on.

The rest of her hospital stay was uneventful. She felt sad and lonely, not for Anthony, but for the child who had died. It had been a baby girl, they told her, and day after day she lay in bed and sobbed. It wouldn't help, the nurses told her, but they understood she had to get it out. But by the end of the week Bettina realised that it wasn't just the baby. It was everything. She was crying for her father and the way he had left her, for Ivo and what she had done to him, and then the firm way in which he in turn had put her out, for Anthony and what he had done for his green card, and now at last for this lost child. Now she had nothing and no one. No baby, no husband, no home, and no man. No one wanted her. She had no one. And at twenty-six she felt like she was at the end of her life.

She still felt that way as she unhooked her seat belt in the plane and slowly wandered down the aisle. For her everything seemed to be moving strangely slowly. She felt as though she were underwater and she didn't really care. She picked up her bag at the baggage claim, got a porter, and went outside to find a cab. Forty-five minutes later she was unlocking the door to Anthony's apartment. She had promised herself that she would pack in a hurry and go to a hotel, but as she looked around the apartment again it was awful, and she started to cry. She fumbled in drawers, emptied cupboards, and packed the mountains of clothes in her closet. The job was done in less than two hours. She hadn't lived there that long with him. Not quite six months. And seven years with Ivo. Two divorces. She was beginning to feel like used merchandise . . .

She gathered all her bags near the doorway, and then slowly walked downstairs to find a cab. With luck she'd find one who could be bribed to climb up to the apartment and help her bring down all her bags. As it turned out, she was lucky and a young cabbie stopped when she waved. It took them four trips together, but they got everything, and when they reached the hotel she had asked for, she handed him a twenty-dollar tip. Leaving the loft had been oddly unemotional. Suddenly she just didn't care. All she cared about was herself. What a failure she was, what a fool she had been. Thinking of Anthony, she felt like a clown.

She should have been used to hotels by then after the road show, but she found as she sat in this one that all it did was make her cry more. She wanted to call Ivo, but she knew that wasn't right. There was no one for her to talk to, not even Steve, who was out of town. She tried to concentrate on the paper so she could find an apartment, but the paper blurred in front of her as she cried. Finally she couldn't stand it, she picked up the phone and dialled. She held her breath, feeling stupid. What if he hung up on her, what if he reproached her, what if – But she knew that Ivo wouldn't do that. She waited for Mattie's familiar voice, and then she was startled when she heard a voice she didn't know.

'Mattie?'

'Who is this?' the voice answered.

'I . . . it's . . . who is *this*? Where's Mattie?'

And after a pause, 'She died two months ago. I'm Elizabeth. Who are you?'

'I . . . oh, I'm so sorry . . .' Bettina could feel a fresh wave of tears coming on. 'Is Mister Stewart there?'

'Who *is* this?' Elizabeth was obviously growing annoyed.

'This is . . . Mrs Pearce, I mean Mrs Stewart, I mean – oh, never mind. Is he there?'

'No. He's in Bermuda.'

'Oh. When will he be back?'

'Not until the first of April. He's rented a house. Would you like the number?' But suddenly Bettina knew she didn't want it. It wasn't right. She hung up and sighed softly.

She spent a restless, anguished night in the hotel, and when she awoke the next morning, it had started to snow. It seemed odd to her because in the rest of the country, she had seen the beginnings of spring. Now she was suddenly plunged back into winter, with snowstorms, and nowhere to go. It made her suddenly reconsider. What if she left New York? If she went somewhere else entirely? But where would she go? She had no friends anywhere, no ties to any other city, and then, oddly, she found her mind wandering to California, to her fairy-tale week in San Francisco with Anthony, and suddenly she knew that what she wanted was to go there. Even without him, it was a place where she knew she could be at peace.

Feeling wildly adventurous, she called the airline, and then half an hour later she went to the bank. Carefully she put all the jewellery she kept there in a leather tote bag, and she smiled to herself. Maybe this meant she was never coming back. This time it was she who was leaving, she who had made a decision.

She took all of her bags with her to the airport; she had brought everything that she owned. And before leaving the hotel in New York, she called the hotel where she had stayed with Anthony and asked for a room with a view of the bay. Maybe it was foolish to stay in the same hotel, but she didn't really think so. It had been so lovely, and it didn't matter what memories she had there. They no longer meant anything to her. And neither did he.

The flight to San Francisco was uneventful, and by now she was so used to changing towns every few days that it didn't strike her odd to have left the snow that morning and find herself now in the midst of a blossoming spring on the West Coast. San Francisco was as beautiful as she remembered it, and she settled into her room with a contented smile. It was only that night that the ghosts began to assail her. She took two aspirin and a glass of water. And then in desperation, an hour later, she went for a walk. She came back to the hotel and took two more aspirin. And finally at three in the morning she took a sleeping pill from the bottle they'd given her when she left the hospital. They had predicted that she might have trouble sleeping for a while. But even the sleeping pill didn't help her, and she stared at the bottle for what seemed like hours. And then suddenly she knew the answer, and she wondered why she hadn't thought of it before. It was crazy to have come all the way to San Francisco when what she had wanted she had had with her in New York. But she hadn't thought of it. And suddenly she smiled to herself. Now she understood it all. And it was so simple . . . so simple . . . She walked into the bathroom, poured a glass of water, and then one by one she took all the sleeping pills in the bottle. There were exactly twenty-four.

Chapter 24

There were bright lights overhead, which seemed to zoom down on her and then fade and disappear. There were machines whirring, and she could hear someone retching, and there was a strange sensation of something hard pushed down her throat. She couldn't remember . . . couldn't remember . . . and then at last she did. She was in the hospital . . . she was having a miscarriage . . . and then again she drifted off to sleep.

It seemed years later when she woke up and found herself staring into the face of a strange man. He was tall, dark-haired, brown-eyed, attractive, and he was wearing a pale-yellow button-down shirt and a white cotton coat. And then she remembered. She was in the hospital. But she wasn't sure why.

'Mrs Stewart?' He looked at her questioningly, and she shook her head. She suddenly remembered, though, that she had not got around to changing her insurance card since she had married Anthony.

'No, Pearce.' She answered hoarsely, surprised at her own voice, and then she shook her head distractedly again. 'I mean . . . Daniels. Bettina Daniels.' But that sounded strange too. She hadn't used that name in so long.

'Quite a collection of names you have, isn't it?' He didn't look disapproving, only surprised. 'Mind if I sit down and we talk for a while?' And now she understood why he wanted to talk to her. 'Let's talk about last night.' Her eyes drifted away from his, and she looked out the window. In the distance all she could see was fog, hanging low over the Golden Gate Bridge.

'Where am I?' But she was stalling and he knew it. He mentioned Credence Hospital and she nodded with a small smile. And then nervously she looked at him. 'Do we really have to discuss all this?'

But he nodded soberly. 'Yes, we do. I don't know how long you've been out here, and I don't know what the procedures are in New York, but unless you want to be kept here for psychiatric treatment for a while, I think we'd better have a talk.' She looked at him sombrely and nodded again. 'What happened last night?'

'I took some sleeping pills,' she croaked. And then she looked at him. 'Why is my voice so funny?'

He smiled at her and for the first time he actually looked young. He was very good-looking, but also terribly serious, and he didn't look like much fun. 'We pumped your stomach. The tube we used will make your voice sound raspy for a few days. Now, about the sleeping pills, did you do it on purpose or was it an accident?'

She hesitated for a long moment, not sure what she should say. 'I – I'm not sure.'

He looked at her sternly. 'Miss Stewart . . . Daniels, whatever your name is, I'm not going to play games with you. Either we're going to talk about this or we're not. I want to know from you what happened, or I'm simply going to put on your chart that you stay here for observation for a week.'

Now she was angry. Her eyes blazed as she croaked at him, and he had to suppress a smile. She was really very pretty. 'I'm not sure what happened, Doctor. I flew out here from New York yesterday, and the day before that I was released from a hospital for a miscarriage. They gave me some pills and I either took too many of them or they were too strong for me . . . I'm not sure.' But she knew that she was lying. And suddenly she didn't care. It was none of his business what had happened. So what if she'd tried to kill herself? She hadn't succeeded, and it was still her own life. She didn't have to tell him everything. And it was none of his business either if she had 'quite a collection of names', as he put it. So what?

148

'What hospital were you in for the miscarriage?' He sat there with her chart, pen poised, sure that she was probably lying, but she was quick to supply the information about the hospital in Atlanta and he looked surprised. 'You certainly move around a lot, don't you?'

'Yes, I do.' She croaked again. 'I was Assistant Director of a Broadway play on tour, and I had the miscarriage on the road. I was in the hospital for a week, and I quit and went back to New York.'

'Are you out here on business?' Now he looked curious and she shook her head. For a moment she was going to tell him that she was there on a visit, but she decided not to. She could at least tell him the truth about that.

'No, I moved out here.'

'Yesterday?' She nodded.

'Married or single?'

'Neither one.' She smiled at him slowly.

'Sorry?' He looked naive, and Bettina found herself wondering if he ever laughed.

'I'm in the process of filing for divorce.'

'And he's ... let me guess' – this time he actually smiled at her – 'in New York.'

Now she smiled too. 'No. He's with the road show.'

'Now I begin to see. Married long?' For a moment she was tempted to shock him and say Which time? but she shook her head non-committally and let him think what he would.

He sighed for a moment, and then put down his pen. 'Now about the miscarriage.' His voice gentled, he knew how hard that could be. 'Were there complications? Was it difficult? Did it take very long?'

She looked away and the light went out of her eyes as she stared at the bridge. 'No, I don't think there were complications. They kept me in the hospital for a week. I ... it – it happened one night. I woke up in the middle of the night, went to the hospital, and it was pretty bad by then. I don't know how long it took after that. Not very long, I

149

think. And it' – she shrugged and wiped a tear from her face – 'it was very painful.'

He nodded gently, and suddenly he felt for this tiny red-headed girl. Not red-headed precisely, he thought to himself, her hair was more auburn, and as she looked at him he realised that she had bottomless emerald-green eyes.

'I'm sorry, Miss – '

He faltered and she smiled. 'Bettina. So am I. But . . . my husband didn't want it anyway . . .' She shrugged again, and he forgot about her chart.

'Is that why you left him?'

'No.' She shook her head slowly. 'There were some things I hadn't known about. A basic misunderstanding . . .' And then suddenly she wanted to tell him; she looked deep into his brown eyes. 'He married me to get a green card, his resident's permit. He was English. And apparently that was his only motivation.' She tried to smile but the bitterness showed in her eyes. 'It was something he didn't mention to me. Oh, I knew he needed the green card. But I didn't know that was why we got married, at least not exclusively. I thought that . . . well, anyway, it turns out that you only have to live together for six months, and' – she turned up both hands – 'it'll be exactly six months next week. End of marriage. And as it so happened, end of baby. It all kind of happened at the same time.'

He wanted to tell her that maybe it was for the best but he wasn't sure that he should. He had a way of being too blunt sometimes, and he didn't want to do that to her. She looked so small and so frail, propped up in the white hospital bed. 'Do you have family out here?'

'No.'

'Friends?'

She shook her head again. 'No one. Just me.'

'And you're planning to stay here?'

'Yes, I think so.'

'All alone?'

'Not forever, I hope.' She looked at him in amusement, and there was suddenly a twinkle in her eye. 'I just thought it might be a nice place to start over.' He nodded, but he was struck by her courage. She had come a long way from home.

'Your family's back East, Miss – er – Bettina?'

But she shook her head again. 'No. My parents are dead, and . . . there's no one.' Ivo didn't count any more. For her, he was gone too.

'Tell me the truth now, and I mean it, just between us, was that why you did it? Last night?' She looked at him and for an instant, just an instant, she knew that she could trust him, but she only shrugged.

'I don't know. I started thinking . . . about my – my husband . . . some other mistakes I've made . . . the baby . . . I got nervous . . . I took some aspirin, I went for a walk . . . all of a sudden it was like everything was closing in on me. But I've felt peculiar ever since I lost the baby, like I can't get my motors going any more. It's as if I don't care about anything, as if nothing matters . . . and . . . I – ' Suddenly she was looking at him and crying. 'If I hadn't – if I hadn't gone on the road with that show, I wouldn't have lost it, I wouldn't . . . I felt so guilty . . . I . . .' She was suddenly telling him things she hadn't even known that she felt, and unconsciously she had reached out to him, and he soothed her, holding her gently in his white-coated arms.

'It's all right, Bettina . . . it's all right. It's normal for you to feel like that. But I'm sure they told you that no matter what you'd have done, you'd probably have lost the baby. Some babies are just not meant to be born.'

'But what if this one was? Then, I killed it.' She looked at him miserably and he shook his head.

'When a baby is all right, you can do almost anything, ski, fall down the stairs, you can do just about anything and you won't lose it. Believe me, if you lost it, it wasn't right.'

She lay back slowly in bed and watched him with troubled eyes. 'Thank you.' And then with a look of sudden worry, 'Will you make me see a lot of shrinks now? Are you going to lock me up with the crazies because I told you about last night?' But he smiled at her and shook his head.

'No, I'm not. But I'd like to have you looked at by one of our gynaecologists just to make sure that everything's okay, and then I'm going to ask you to stay here for a few days. Just so you can catch your breath, get on your feet, get some rest, and take some of those sleeping pills, if you need them, under our supervision, not your own. But what you're going through is normal. It's just that usually a woman has a husband or a family to turn to with this kind of anguish. It's very hard to handle this alone.' She nodded slowly. He seemed to understand.

'And I'd like it if we could talk some more.' He said it very gently, with a small smile. 'Would you mind that very much?'

She shook her head slowly. 'No. What kind of doctor are you, by the way?' Maybe he was a shrink after all. Maybe she was being tricked.

'An internist. If you're going to stay in the city, you're going to need one of those too. And maybe right now, while you're settling down here, you could use a friend.' He smiled at her then and held out a hand. 'I'm John Fields, Bettina.' She shook his hand firmly, and then he looked at her again. 'And by the way, how did you come by so many names?'

She grinned at him then. If he was going to be her doctor and her friend, he might as well know the truth. 'Pearce is my most recent married name; Daniels is my maiden name, which actually I suppose I'll take back now; and Stewart was' – she hesitated for only a fraction of an instant – 'my first married name. I've been married once before.'

'And how old did you say you were?' He was still smiling as he walked to the door.

'Twenty-six.'

'Not bad, Bettina, not bad.' He saluted and prepared to leave, and then for a moment he stopped and looked at her. 'I think you're going to be just fine.' He waved then, and as he left he smiled at her in a way that told her everything just had to be okay.

Chapter 25

'And how are you today, Bettina?' John Fields walked into her hospital room with a smile.

'Fine.' She returned the smile. 'Better. Much better.' She had slept like a baby the night before, without the nightmares, the ghosts of old faces, without even a sleeping pill. She had put her head down on the pillow and fallen asleep. Life in the hospital was wonderfully simple. There were mommies and daddies in white uniforms who were there to take care of you, to keep all the bad dreams and bad people away, so you could relax. She hadn't felt this peaceful in a year. And as she thought it she looked up at the attractive young doctor sheepishly. 'I shouldn't say it, but I wish I didn't have to leave.'

'Why is that?' For only an instant a trace of worry crossed his smile. He had taken a lot on his shoulders, not bringing a psychiatrist in on the case. But he didn't really feel that she had deep-seated problems.

She was looking at him now with that childlike smile of hers and those devastating green eyes, which seemed to dance. She certainly didn't look like a crazy, but nevertheless he was going to keep an eye on her after she left.

She lay back again against her pillows, with a little sigh and a smile. 'Why don't I want to leave here, Doctor? Oh, because' – the eyes drifted towards him – 'because it's so easy and so simple. I don't have to look for an apartment, find a job, worry about money, go to the grocery store, cook for myself. I don't have to find a lawyer.' She looked at him, smiling again. 'I don't even have to wear make-up and get dressed.' But she had bathed for half an hour and there was a white satin ribbon in the long auburn hair. He looked at her and returned her smile. She looked pretty and young and as though life were terribly simple; she looked more like twelve years old than twenty-six.

'I think you've just given me all the reasons why some people stay in mental institutions for years, or even all of their lives, Bettina.' And then more quietly, 'Is that what you have in mind for yourself? Is it really all that much trouble to get dressed or to go to the store?'

She was suddenly startled by what he had just told her, and she shook her head. 'No . . . no, of course not.' And then she felt she had to explain to him. Just so he wouldn't really think her crazy after all. 'I – I've been' – she looked for the right words as she watched him – 'I've been under a lot of pressure for a long time.' Jesus. Then maybe she did have a major problem. He wondered as he watched her, wondering also if he should send her home.

'What kind of pressure?' Quietly he pulled up a chair.

'Well' – she stared down at her hands for a long time – 'I've been running houses, servants, kind of elaborate households for a lot of years.' She looked up with a small smile. 'Two husbands and a father have kept me busy for about the last fifteen years.'

'Fifteen? What about your mother?' His eyes never left her face.

'She died of leukemia when I was four.'

'And your father never remarried?'

'Of course not.' And more softly, 'He didn't have to. He had me.'

The doctor's eyes grew suddenly wide in horror, and she quickly shook her head and put up a hand. 'No, no, not like that. People like my father marry for all kinds of reasons, the convenience, someone to talk to or advise them, someone to keep them company when they're on tour, or to run interference for them while they're writing a book. I did all that for him.'

He watched her, suddenly fascinated by something in her face. She seemed oddly knowing and much older as she spoke of it, and she also looked more beautiful than any woman he had ever seen.

She was nodding slowly. 'I think most people marry for convenience and to combat loneliness.'

'Is that why you married?'

'Partly.' And then she smiled and laid her head back on her pillows with her eyes briefly closed. 'And I also fell very much in love.'

'With whom?' His voice was barely more than a whisper in the small room.

'A man named Ivo Stewart.' She continued to talk to the ceiling, and then she looked back at him. 'I don't know if it makes any difference, but he was the publisher of the *New York Mail* for years. He retired a little more than a year ago.'

'And you married him?' The young doctor looked more surprised than impressed. 'How did you meet him?' He still couldn't place her, couldn't understand her. He knew she had been with a theatrical road show. Yet there was something still more worldly, more regal about her bearing, and how did a little girl with a road show come to be married to the publisher of the *New York Mail*? Or was she lying? Was she really crazy? Maybe he should have checked on her further. Who was this girl?

But Bettina was smiling at him now. 'Maybe I should go back to the beginning. Have you ever heard of Justin Daniels?' It was a stupid question. Even she knew that.

'The author?' She nodded.

'He was my father.'

Then she gave him the unabridged version of her life, sparing no details. She really needed to talk it out.

And when she was finished with all the details, the hopes, the dreams, he said, 'And now what, Bettina?'

She looked him square in the eye. 'Who knows? I guess I start fresh.' But she still felt as though she had a load of bags on her back from years gone by. It was a heavy burden with which to travel into a new life, and even telling him hadn't really lessened the pain.

'Why did you choose San Francisco?'

'I don't know. It was a spur of the moment inspiration. I just remembered it as being very pretty and I don't know anybody here.'

'Didn't that frighten you?'

She smiled at him. 'A little. But by this time that was a relief. Sometimes it's nice to be anonymous, to go where you aren't known. I can start over here. I can just be Bettina Daniels and find out who she is.'

He looked at her seriously. 'At least you can forget who she was.'

Suddenly she looked at him and knew he didn't understand. 'That's not the point really. I've been several different people, but all of them meant something. All of them had a reason. In their own way each of those people was right at the time. Except maybe this last time – that was a mistake. But my life with my father – ' She hesitated, looking for the right words. 'That was an extraordinary experience. I would never give that up for anything else.'

But John was shaking his head. 'You've never had a normal moment in your life. No parents to love you, no simple home, no kids to bring home from school, no marriage to a boy you met in college, just a lot of nightmares, and odd, eccentric people, and show business, and old men.'

'You make it sound so sordid.' It made her sad to listen to him. Was that how it would sound to people now? Ugly and freakish? Was that what she was? She felt tears well up inside her and she had to fight them back.

And then suddenly he felt horrified at himself. What was he doing? She was his patient and he was badgering her. He looked at Bettina with guilt and horror in his eyes and reached out to touch her hand. 'I'm sorry, I – I had no right to do that. I don't know how to explain it to you though. It frightens me when I hear all that. It upsets me that you had to go through it. I'm worried about what will happen to you now.'

She looked at him oddly, the hurt still fresh in her eyes. 'Thank you. But it doesn't matter. You have a right to say what you think. As you said in the beginning, if I'm going to settle down here, I'm going to need more than just a doctor, I'm going to need a friend.' It was time she got out and discovered how the rest of the world lived, the 'normal people', as John would have said.

'I hope so. I'm really sorry. It's just that you have had a very, very hard life. And you have a right to much better now.'

'By the way, where are you from?'

'Here. San Francisco. I've lived here all my life. Grew up here, went to college at Stanford. Med school there too. It's all been very unexciting – peaceful and normal. And when you ask me what I think you have a right to, when I say that you have a right to better than you've had, I mean a nice, decent, wholesome husband, who's not four or five times your age, a couple of kids, a decent house.'

She looked at him with hostility for a moment. Why wouldn't he understand that some of that life had been beautiful, and whatever it had been, it was part of her?

He read something in her eyes. 'You're not planning to get a job in the theatre again, are you?'

Slowly she shook her head, holding his eyes with a firm look of her own. 'No. I was planning to start working on my play.'

But he shook his head. 'Bettina, why don't you get yourself a regular job? Something simple. Maybe something secretarial, or a nice job in a museum, or something in real estate maybe that lets you see nice, wholesome, happy people. And before you know it, you'll have your life back on the right track.'

She had never thought of being a secretary or a real estate agent before. It wasn't really her cup of tea. The literary and theatrical worlds were all she knew. But maybe he was right. Maybe it was all too crazy. Maybe she had to get away from all that. And then she remembered something else.

'Before I do that, do you have the name of a good lawyer?'

'Sure.' He smiled at her and pulled a pen out of his pocket. 'One of my best friends. Seth Waterston. You'll like him a lot. And his wife is a nurse. We all went to school together as undergraduates at Stanford.'

'How wholesome.' She was teasing but he didn't laugh.

'Don't knock it till you've tried it.' And then hesitantly he tilted his head. He paused for a long time as he considered, not sure if it was the right thing to do. But something was pushing him to do it. He had to. For her. 'As a matter of fact, Bettina – ' He seemed to hesitate for a long time as Bettina watched. 'I want to suggest something to you that may not be entirely ethical, but it might do you some good.'

'It sounds fascinating. What is it?'

'I'd like to take you to dinner with Seth and Mary Waterston. How does that sound?'

'Delightful. And why is that unethical? You said you were also my friend.'

He smiled slowly then, and she smiled in answer. 'Is it a date, then?' She nodded. 'Then I'll call them and I'll let you know before you leave when they can make it.'

'By the way, when am I leaving?' They had both forgotten as she told him her life story.

'How about today?' She thought briefly of the hotel to which she would have to return. It was not a very cheerful thought. It was the place where she had stayed with Anthony and suddenly she didn't want to go back there. 'Something wrong?'

But she shook her head briskly. 'No. Nothing at all.' She had to work it out for herself. And he was right. What she needed was a normal life, a simple job. She could wait another six months to start her play. All she needed now was an apartment, a job, and a divorce. She'd work out the first two and hopefully John's friend would help her with the last one. Now she understood she was divorcing more than just a person this time. John helped her see that. She had to divorce a whole life.

159

Chapter 26

Five days later Bettina had her own apartment, a tiny but quaint studio overlooking the bay. It had previously been the main parlour in a lovely Victorian owned by three men. They had fixed up the two top floors for themselves and had divided the bottom floor into two studio apartments, which they rented out. Bettina got the larger one, and it was a beauty. It had a fireplace, two huge French windows, a tiny balcony, a kitchenette, a bathroom, and a devastatingly beautiful view. She was enchanted when she first saw it, and the miracle of it was that it was something even she could afford. The rent was so low that she could have managed just on her monthly money from Ivo, which she would have, no matter what, for the coming years.

Two days after she found her apartment John Fields arrived to take her to dinner with his lawyer friend and his wife.

'Bettina, you're going to love them.'

'I'm sure I will. But you haven't told me. How do you like my place?' She looked at him as they left her apartment. He had commented only on the view. But now he looked at her squarely as he opened his car door. He drove a small American compact, in a subdued navy blue. There was nothing flashy or ostentatious about his clothes, his car, or his person. Everything was attractive, but quiet, like the tweed jacket he wore, the button-down shirt, the grey slacks, the well-polished loafers. In fact it was oddly comforting. He was predictable, in his style and taste. He looked like every good American ought to, he was every mother's dream of the perfect son. Handsome, bright, attractive, well-mannered, a graduate of Stanford, a doctor. Bettina smiled at him. He was really a damn good-looking man. She felt suddenly awkward in his presence. As though everything she had on was too expensive, too showy. Maybe he was right. She did have a lot to learn. 'Well, what about my apartment, Doctor? Isn't that some find?'

He nodded slowly with a smile. 'It is and I like it. But it still has the look of "Milady's Manor". I kept waiting for you to tell me you'd rented the whole house.'

He smiled to soften his words as he helped her into the car. The door slammed shut, and she wondered if she'd worn the wrong dress. She was wearing a white wool that she and Ivo had bought in Paris. It wasn't dressy, but it was easy to see that it was expensively made. It was a simple dress with long sleeves and a small collar, and she had worn it with a single strand of pearls and black kid Dior shoes. But when she reached the Waterstons' house in Marin County, she knew that she had made a *faux pas* again.

Mary Waterston came to the door, smiling broadly, her hair swept up on the back of her head with a leather thong. She was wearing a button-down shirt, a green V-neck sweater, bare feet, and jeans. And Seth arrived in almost the same costume. Even John looked overdressed, but he had come from the office. Bettina didn't have that excuse. She shook their hands with a faint look of embarrassment, but they were quick to put her at ease. Seth was a tall, handsome, sandy-haired man with a cowlick, a look of surprise, and seemingly endless legs. Mary was small, dark-haired, and pretty in spite of horn-rimmed glasses, and she was almost as thin as Bettina except that she had a somewhat noticeable paunch. A little while later she saw Bettina glance at her bulging midriff and she grinned.

'I know, isn't it awful? I hate this stage, everyone just thinks you're fat.' She patted it fondly, and then explained. 'Number two on the way. The first one is asleep upstairs.'

'Is she?' John had just joined them, the two men had been outside for a moment and had just returned. 'I had hoped we would see her.' He looked warm and kind as he said it, and for an odd moment Bettina felt something pull at her heart. Why hadn't she ever had a man who felt that way about children? It had been a closed door with Ivo. And Anthony had hated the baby from the start. For a moment she felt a terrible flash of pain as she looked at Mary. Only a few weeks before she had been about as pregnant as that.

'When is the baby due?' she asked her softly.

'Not till August.'

'Are you still working?' But Mary only laughed.

'No, that's a thing of the past, I'm afraid. I used to be an OB nurse until the first time I got pregnant. Now I seem to be a regular patient there.' The three of them grinned. And somehow Bettina felt left out. John had been right. It all seemed so normal. And she suddenly longed to be one of them.

'How old is your first one?'

'Nineteen months.' Bettina nodded and the other woman smiled. 'Do you have children?' But Bettina only shook her head.

They all drank red wine and ate steaks that Seth barbecued for dinner. And after coffee John offered to go out to the kitchen to lend Mary a hand. He had orchestrated that earlier with Seth, who looked at Bettina as soon as they were alone and gave her a warm smile.

'I understand you want a dissolution?' She looked at him in confusion and he laughed.

'I'm sorry, I didn't understand . . .'

'That's California legal jargon. I apologise. John mentioned that you're looking for an attorney to get a divorce.' She nodded, and then sighed. 'Can I help?'

'Yes, I'd like that very much.'

'Why don't you come to my office tomorrow? Say around two?' She nodded gratefully. A few minutes later John was back, but somehow she felt degraded by her exchange with Seth, by Mary's gently bulging stomach, by all of it. She had such a long way to go to be like them. And if they knew the truth, they'd never accept her. Look at them. Mary was thirty-five, the two men thirty-six, they all had respectable careers in medicine or in law. Seth and Mary had a house in the suburbs, one child, another on the way. How could she expect them to accept her? Later, when John took her back to her place, she told him mournfully what she had felt.

'You don't have to tell them. No one ever needs to know. That's the beauty of you starting out fresh here.'

'But what if someone finds out, John? I mean, my father was very well-known. Conceivably one day I could come across someone who once knew me.'

'Not necessarily. And that was so long ago, who would recognise you? Besides, no one needs to know about your marriages, Bettina. That's behind you now. You have to start fresh. You're still very young. No one would even suspect you had been married before.'

And then she looked at him hauntingly. 'Is it so terrible that I have?' But he didn't answer for a long moment.

'Bettina, it's just something no one needs to know.' But he hadn't said that it wasn't awful. He hadn't told her what she had needed to hear. 'Did you make an appointment with Seth?'

She nodded. 'Yes, I did.'

'Good. Then you can get that taken care of. And then you can find a job.' But it was odd. She really didn't want to. Except that she knew she should. She had to have the job for respectability because John thought so. She suddenly knew just how much it mattered to her what this man thought.

Chapter 27

A few weeks later she found a job in an art gallery on Union Street, and although it was neither exciting nor immensely profitable, it occupied most of her time. She worked from ten in the morning until six at night. And sitting at a desk smiling innocuously at strangers all day seemed to leave her exhausted, though she couldn't even remember what she'd done.

But she had finally become one of the great working class, working all day, and bored with it, and anxious to find a reason to get out of her job.

John took her out two or three times a week, for dinner or a movie, and they were beginning to spend some time together on the weekends. He loved to play tennis and sail. The time they shared was certainly healthful. Bettina was looking better than she had in a long time, and she had a deep honey-coloured tan. It set off the reddish lights in her hair, and her eyes looked more like emeralds than ever. The four months in San Francisco had been good for her in many ways.

Tonight he had cooked at his apartment and they were lingering over coffee.

'Want to stop by and see the Waterstons tonight? Seth says Mary's getting antsy and the doctor won't let her come to the city any more. She delivered last time in under two hours, and he's afraid that this time she won't make it to the hospital at all.'

'Oh, Jesus.' And then she looked at him thoughtfully with a half smile. 'That whole baby thing scares me to death.'

'But you were pregnant.' He looked surprised at her reaction. Having a baby was so normal. Why would any healthy woman be afraid?

'I know, and I was excited about the baby. But every time I thought about the rest of it, it scared me to death.'

'But why? Don't be silly. There's nothing to be afraid of. Mary's not afraid.'

'She's a nurse.'

And then he looked at her more gently. 'If you ever had a baby, Bettina, I'd be there with you.' She wasn't sure what he meant for a moment. As a friend? Or a doctor? Even though they'd been sleeping together for three months now, she wasn't quite sure what he meant. There was something so oddly uncuddly about their relationship that she was never sure if they were really lovers, or just friends.

'Thank you.'

'You don't sound very excited at the prospect.' He smiled at her and she laughed at him.

'It all seems very far off.'

'What, having children? Why should it be?' And then he smiled at her more tenderly. 'You could have one by next year.' But she wasn't sure she wanted one any more. She wanted to write her play.

'That doesn't mean I will.' It seemed a safe answer, and he laughed.

'Well, you certainly could. Let's see . . . when is your divorce final?' Suddenly she felt her heart racing. What was he asking her? What did he mean?

'In two months. September.' Her voice was oddly soft.

'We could get married then, get you pregnant immediately, and presto magic, next June you have a baby. How does that sound to you?' He was looking at her more closely now, and she felt his hand reach for hers.

'John . . . are you serious?'

And then very softly, 'Yes, I am.'

'But so – so quickly? . . . We don't have to get married the minute the divorce comes through . . . it's . . .'

He looked at her in consternation. 'Why not? Why would we wait to get married?'

And then, fearing his disapproval again, 'I don't know.'

People like John Fields don't live with someone. They get married. They have babies. Bettina knew that for sure now. He was not going to fool around. And not complying with his wishes meant fresh failure. It meant not measuring up, not being 'normal'. And she didn't want to do that any more.

'Don't you want to, Betty?' She hated the nickname, but she had never told him, because there were other things about him that she did love, his solidity, the way you could count on him, he was reliable and sturdy and handsome, and he made her feel like an ordinary, regular person, when they played tennis, or had dinner, or joined some of his friends for a Sunday sail. It was a life she had never known before. Never. Until she met Dr John Fields. But marry him? Get married again? Now? 'I don't know. It's too soon.' It was only a whisper.

He looked at her unhappily. 'I see.' And then he seemed to pull away.

Chapter 28

The next morning, on her way to the gallery, Bettina thought again about John's proposal. What more did she want? Why wasn't she ecstatic? Because, she answered herself slowly, what she wanted more than children or marriage was time. She wanted to find herself, Bettina, the person she had lost somewhere along the way while she was so busy changing names. She knew she had to find her, before it was too late.

She let her car idle at a stop sign, as she once again remembered his words, and the look on his face when she told him it was too soon. It *was* too soon. For her. And what about her play? If she married him now, she'd never write it, she'd get too caught up in his life and being Mrs John Fields. That wasn't what she wanted now ... she wanted – A horn bleated angrily as she remembered where she was and moved on. But she couldn't keep her mind on her driving, she could barely even keep her eyes on the road. She just kept thinking of the look on his face when she said – And then suddenly there was an odd thump against the front of her car, and she heard a woman scream. Startled, she stomped hard on the brake, and as she jolted forward against her seat belt she looked around. There were people standing, staring ... they were staring at her ... at ... what were they looking at ... oh, my God! Two men were bending down, talking to someone right in front of her car. But she couldn't see. What was it? Oh, God, it couldn't ... she didn't ... but as she flew from her seat she knew.

As she shakily ran to the front of the car, she saw him, a man in his early forties, lying prone on the street.

She felt panic rise in her throat. She knelt next to the man, trying to keep from crying. He was well dressed in a dark business suit, and the contents of his attaché case were strewn over the ground. 'I'm sorry . . . I'm sorry . . . isn't there anything I can do?'

The police were quiet and courteous when a few moments later they arrived on the scene. An ambulance appeared only five minutes after. The man was removed. Bettina's name and licence number were recorded. The police spoke to the eye-witnesses, their names written down in a careful little list compiled by a left-handed cop who looked barely older than a boy.

'Had you taken any medication this morning, miss?' The young policeman looked at her with wise eyes, but she shook her head and blew her nose in the handkerchief she had dug out of her bag.

'No. Nothing.'

'One of the witnesses said he'd seen you stop a few minutes before, and you looked' – he gazed at her apologetically – 'well, he said "glazed".'

'I wasn't . . . I was . . . I was just thinking.'

'Were you upset?'

'Yes . . . no . . . oh, I don't remember. I don't know.' It was hard to tell if she had ever been rational, she was so distraught over what she had just done. 'Will he be all right?'

'We'll know more after he gets to the hospital. You can call later for a report.'

'What about me?'

'Were you hurt?' He looked surprised.

'No, I mean – ' She looked up at him bleakly. 'Are you going to arrest me?'

He smiled gently. 'No, we're not. It was an accident. You'll get a citation, and this will have to go to court.'

'To court?' She was horrified, and he nodded.

'Other than the citation, your insurance company will probably handle most of it for you.' And then more gravely, 'You *are* insured?'

'Of course.'

'Then, call your insurance agent this morning, and your

attorney, and hope for the best.' Hope for the best . . . oh, God, how awful. What had she done?

When at last they had gone, she slipped behind the wheel of her car, her hands still trembling violently and her mind whirling, as she thought of the man they had loaded into an ambulance only moments before. It seemed to take her hours to get to the gallery, and when she arrived, she didn't bother to throw open the door or turn on the lights. She rushed right to the telephone after firmly relocking the door behind her. She called her insurance agent, who seemed nonplussed. He assured her that her twenty thousand dollars' worth of coverage ought to be adequate to take care of the accident unless it were terribly serious.

'Anyway, don't worry about it, we'll see.'

'How soon will I know?'

'Know what?'

'If he's going to sue me.'

'As soon as he decides to let us know, Miss Daniels. Don't worry, you'll know.'

There were tears rolling down her face as Bettina dialled Seth Waterston in his office. He came on the line only moments after she placed the call.

'Bettina?'

'Oh, Seth . . .' It was a desperate, childlike wail. 'I'm in trouble.' She began to sob out of control.

'Where are you?'

'At the . . . gall . . . ery . . .' She could barely speak.

'Now calm down and tell me what happened. Take a deep breath . . . Bettina? . . . Bettina! . . . now talk to me . . .' For a moment he was afraid that she was in jail. He could think of nothing else to cause hysterics on that order.

'I had an . . . accident . . .'

'Are you hurt?'

'I hit a man with my car.'

'A pedestrian?'

'Yes.'

'How badly is he hurt?'

169

'I don't know.'

'What's the guy's name and where did they take him?'

'Saint George's. And his name is' – she glanced at the little piece of paper given her by the police – 'Bernard Zule.'

'Zule? Spell it.' She did, and Seth sighed.

'Do you know him?'

'More or less. He's an attorney. You couldn't have hit some nice ignorant pedestrian? You had to hit a lawyer?' Seth tried to joke, but Bettina couldn't, and then as a wave of panic washed over her, she held the phone tighter.

'Seth, promise me you won't tell John.'

'Why not, for God's sake? You didn't do it on purpose.'

'No, but he'll – he'll be upset . . . or angry . . . or . . . please . . .' Her voice was so desperate that Seth promised, then hung up to call the hospital.

Four hours later Seth called her at the gallery. Zule was all right. He had a broken leg. It was a nice clean break. A few bruises. No other damage. But Bernard Zule was a very angry man. He had already called his attorney and he fully intended to sue. Seth had talked to him himself. He had explained that the woman who had hit Zule was a personal friend, she was terribly concerned, very, very sorry, and she wanted to know if he was all right.

'All right? That dumb fucking bitch runs me down in broad daylight, and then she wants to know if I'm all right? I'll tell her in court how all right I am.'

'Now, Bernard . . .' Seth's attempts at putting oil on the waters were of no avail, as Bettina learned three days later when she was served with papers for Zule's suit. He was suing her for two hundred thousand dollars for personal injury, inability to practise his profession, emotional trauma, and malicious intent. The malicious intent wasn't worth a damn, Seth assured her, she didn't even know Zule, after all. But it was a whopping big suit. He also told her that it could take a couple of years to come to court, by which time his fracture would be nothing but a dim memory. But it didn't make any difference. All Bettina could think of was the amount. Two hundred thousand dollars. If she sold every piece of jewellery she still owned, maybe she could pay it, but then what would she have? It reminded her of her panic after her father died, and it was all she could do to remain in control.

'Bettina? Bettina! Did you hear me?'

'Hmm? What?'

'What's wrong with you?' John stared at her in annoyance, she had been like that for weeks.

'I – I'm sorry . . . I was distracted.'

'That's an understatement. You haven't heard a word I've said all night. What is it?' He didn't understand. She had been that way since the night he had proposed to her. It hardly cheered him to acknowledge that. And then, finally, at the end of the evening when he brought her home, he looked at her sadly. 'Bettina, would you rather we didn't see each other for a while?'

'No . . . I – ' And then, without wanting to, she let herself be pulled into his arms, as long, terrified sobs wracked her soul.

'What is it? Oh, Betty . . . tell me what it is . . . I know something's wrong.'

'I . . . oh, John, I can't tell you . . . it's so awful . . . I had an accident.'

'What kind of an accident?' His voice was stern.

'In my car. I broke a man's leg.'

'You what?' He looked at her, shocked. 'When?'

'Three weeks ago.'

'Why didn't you tell me?'

And then she hung her head. 'I don't know.'

'Isn't your insurance handling it?'

'I'm only insured for twenty thousand. He's suing me for' – her voice dropped still lower – 'two hundred thousand.'

'Oh, my God.' Quietly they both sat down. 'Have you talked to Seth?' Silently she nodded. 'And not to me. Oh, Betty.' He pulled her closer into his arms. 'Betty, Betty . . . how could something like this happen to you?'

'I don't know.' But she did know. She had been thinking of the night before when he'd proposed, and of how much she didn't want to get married, but she didn't tell him. 'It was my fault.'

'I see. Well, it looks like we'll just have to face the music together, doesn't it?' He smiled down at her gently. She needed him, and that made him feel good.

But she looked horrified as her eyes met his. 'What do you mean together? Don'y be crazy! I have to work this out by myself.'

'Don't you be crazy. And don't get yourself totally insane over this thing. A two-hundred-thousand-dollar lawsuit doesn't mean anything. He'll probably be happy to settle for ten.'

'I don't believe that.' But she had to admit that Seth had told her something like that the day before. Not ten exactly, but maybe twenty.

And as it turned out, they were right. Two weeks later Bernard Zule accepted the sum of eighteen thousand dollars to balm his nerves and his near-mended leg. The insurance company cancelled Bettina's insurance, and she had to sell the small, inexpensive used car she had bought after she got her job. The sum of two hundred thousand dollars no longer shrieked in her head, but there was a feeling of defeat somehow, of failure, of having taken a giant step back, and not having been able to take care of herself. The pall of depression dragged on for weeks, and it was only two weeks before her divorce became final that John proposed to her again.

'It makes sense, Bettina.' And then, with rare humour, he grinned at her. 'Look at it this way. You could drive my car.'

But she didn't even smile. He pushed on. 'I love you, and you were born to be my wife.' *And Ivo's, and Anthony's* . . . She couldn't keep the thought from her mind. 'I want you, Bettina.' But she also knew that he thought she couldn't take care of herself. And in a way she had proven him right. She was incompetent. Perhaps dangerously so. Look at what she had just done. She had almost killed a man . . . she never let that thought slip from her mind. 'Bettina?' He was looking down at her. And then very gently he kissed her fingers and her lips, and then her eyes. 'Will you marry me, Betty?'

He could hear the sharp intake of breath, and then, with her eyes closed, she nodded. 'Yes.' Maybe he was right after all.

Chapter 29

With small measured steps Bettina approached the altar on the arm of Seth Waterston. She had asked him to give her away. There were close to a hundred people in the church, watching them happily as Bettina's white moiré whispered softly against the satin runner as they walked. Seth smiled down at her as she walked beside him, her face concealed by the delicate veil and the Renaissance coif. She looked beautiful and stately, yet she felt strange in the white wedding dress, as though she were in costume, or as though it were a little bit of a lie. She had resisted John's suggestion to have a white wedding until the end, but it had meant so much to him. He had waited so long after medical school to get married that she knew she had to do it for him. And, in the two brief weeks after she decided, he had promised that he would take care of everything, and he had. All she had had to do was go to I. Magnin's to shop for her wedding dress, and he had done the rest. He had organised the ceremony itself in the little Episcopal church on Union Street, and the reception afterwards for a hundred and twenty-five guests at the yacht club overlooking the bay. It was a wedding day that any girl would have died for, but somehow Bettina would have felt more comfortable going to City Hall. The divorce had come through only two days earlier, and as she walked down the aisle on Seth's arm she kept thinking of Anthony and Ivo. Suddenly she had a mad urge to giggle and shout at the dewy-eyed guests, 'Don't get too excited, folks, this is my third!' But she smiled demurely as she reached the altar and took John's arm. He was wearing a morning coat for the occasion with a little sprig of lily of the valley on his lapel. Bettina's bouquet was made of white roses, and they had given Mary Waterston a beige orchid corsage. John no longer had either of his parents, so there were no families to contend with, only friends.

The words seemed to drone on forever in the pretty little church, and the minister smiled lovingly at them as he spoke.

'. . . and do you, John . . . ?'

As she listened, suddenly that strange feeling came back to her. What if she said the wrong name when she made the vows? *I, Bettina, take you, Ivo . . . Anthony . . . John . . .* She wasn't going to louse it up this time. This was her last chance to do things right for herself. This was for real.

'. . . I do . . .' The words were barely more than a whisper as she said them. She was being given her last chance. Her eyes went quickly to John's and he looked at her seriously and repeated the same words loudly and firmly so the whole church could hear. He had taken her, Bettina, to have and to hold, to love and to cherish, in sickness and in health, for richer or poorer, until death did them part. Not misunderstanding, not boredom, not a green card or a road show, or a difference in age. *Until death did them part.* As Bettina listened she felt the impact of the words, she was aware of the smell of the roses. For the rest of her life she would smell those roses whenever she thought of those words.

'. . . I now pronounce you man and wife.' The minister looked at them, smiled at them both, and then leaned gently towards John. 'You may kiss the bride.' John did so quickly, while holding tightly to her hand.

The wide gold band was on her left hand now, the tiny diamond engagement ring on her right. She had wanted to show him her jewellery just before the wedding, but once he had given her the ring, she knew she couldn't do it, because she still had the nine-carat diamond from Ivo. And then, finally, she had decided to conceal his ring and show John the rest. The collection she had acquired from Ivo and her father was something she never showed anyone, and she never wore any of it any more. It sat safely in the bank, it was her nest egg, all she had left now of her own. And showing it to John, or wanting to, had been her final act of trust. But when she had told him that she had something she wanted to show him, something she kept at the bank, he had looked angry and suspicious until she finally explained.

'It's nothing . . . don't look like that, silly . . . it's just some jewellery I have from my other life . . .' She had grinned at him sheepishly and she had been stunned when he exploded in the tiny room at the bank.

'Bettina, this is disgraceful! It's outrageous! Do you realise how much money you have tied up here? . . . It's – it's – ' He had actually spluttered. 'It looks like a collection from some old hooker, for chrissake. I want you to get rid of it all!' But this time she had exploded. If he didn't like it, it was his business, and she would never wear any of it again. But they were beautiful pieces and they all meant something to her. And as they both stood there, angry, she promised herself again that she never would show him any part of her past. It was hers, just as the jewellery was, and it would stay that way, just as the jewellery would.

She had mentioned the money she still got from Ivo and would continue to get for her remaining years. But that had outraged John even more. What was wrong with her to stay on that man's payroll? Couldn't she live on her job? And she damn well better not plan to take any money from *him* after they got married, because he wouldn't stand for it. It was like a slap in his face. She didn't look at it that way and she tried to explain it to him, though unsuccessfully, that in some ways Ivo had always been like a father to her. He didn't give a damn, he told her. She was grown-up now, she didn't need a father any more. And this time it was not like the jewellery, which went unmentioned ever again. This time he drafted a letter himself to Ivo's lawyers and explained that Mrs Stewart – his teeth clenched as he wrote the word – did not wish to accept the monthly payment any more. She signed it, tearfully, but she signed it. And that was the end of that. She had severed her last contact with Ivo, even if it was only through his attorneys. And now, after the ceremony, she belonged wholly to John.

John and Bettina stood side by side outside the church for almost half an hour, smiling, kissing cheeks, shaking dozens of hands. And through it all Bettina watched them, his cousins, his classmates, his patients, his friends. And remarkably they all looked the same. They all looked healthy, youthful, smiling, wholesome. It was all so pretty and bland.

'Happy?' He looked at her for a moment as they stepped into his car. He hadn't hired a limousine. He said it was expensive and silly. He would drive himself.

She nodded as she looked at him. And remarkably she was very happy. There was something very refreshing about this new world. 'Very.' She didn't have to be sparkling and witty. Didn't have to be charming, or give the best dinner parties in town. She just had to be pleasant and make inane comments as she stood beside John. In many ways it was restful and undemanding after the years she had spent of being eternally 'on'. 'I love you, Doctor.' She smiled at him, and this time she really meant it.

He smiled back at her. 'I love you too.'

They went to Carmel on their honeymoon and spent three heavenly days wandering through shops and walking along the beach. They drove down to Big Sur one afternoon and held hands as they looked at the surf. They had long romantic dinners and spent the mornings in bed. It was everything a honeymoon should have been. And two weeks later, as Bettina sat in the gallery on Union Street, she felt desperately ill. She went home early and went to bed, where John found her later, curled up, looking ghastly, and trying to sleep. He frowned as he looked at her, enquired about her symptoms, and then sat down gently on the side of the bed.

'Can I have a look at you, Betty?' It still seemed funny to her when he called her by that name.

'Sure.' She sat up in bed and tried to smile at him. 'But I

don't think there's much to look at. I just have the flu. Mary said she had it last week.'

He nodded and examined her gently: he found her lungs clear, her eyes bright, and no fever. And then he looked at her, wondering, and smiled happily. 'Maybe you're pregnant.'

She looked at him, startled. 'Already?' It didn't seem possible. Two weeks after they had stopped using birth control? That had been his idea.

'We'll see.'

'How soon will we know?' Suddenly she felt anxious.

But John was smiling, pleased with himself. 'We can find out in about two weeks. I'll have them run a test in the office, and if it comes out positive, I'll send you to an OB.'

'Can I go to Mary's?' Suddenly everything made her feel anxious. What was happening to her? Who had made this decision? She was terrified just thinking about it, and she didn't want it to be true.

He kissed her forehead and left the room. He was back a few minutes later with a cup of tea and some crackers. 'Try this.' She did and a little while later she was feeling physically better, but still very much afraid. But she didn't dare tell him that.

Two weeks later John came home with a small bottle and put it in her hand before they went to bed. 'Use this tomorrow morning. First urine. Leave it in the fridge, and I'll take it to work.'

'Will you call me as soon as they do it?' She looked at him grimly; and he patted her arm and smiled.

'I know you're excited, baby. Just hang in. We'll know in the morning. And I promise, I'll call you as soon as we know.' And then after he kissed her, 'I'm pretty excited too, you know.' And she knew he was being honest. He had looked as though he had been floating on air for two weeks. It had made it that much more impossible to tell him how she felt. And then suddenly, in a burst, she had to tell him as they lay side by side in the dark.

178

'John?'

'Yes, Betty?'

She reached out and took his hand as she pressed herself into his back. 'I'm scared.'

He sounded surprised. 'Of what?'

'Of . . . you know . . . of' – she felt like an ass as she said it, it was so normal to him – 'of being pregnant.'

'But what are you afraid of, silly?' He turned around in their bed and faced her in the dark.

'Of . . . well . . . what if it's like the last time?' It was hard to get out the words.

'You mean you're afraid you might lose it?' She nodded, but in truth she was afraid of much more than that.

'A little . . . but . . . oh, I don't know, John, I'm just scared. What if it's awful . . . if it's too painful . . . if I can't stand it . . . I . . . what if I can't take the pain?'

There were tears in her eyes as she asked him the questions and he took her shoulders in both of his hands. 'Now I want you to stop this, Betty. Right now. Birth is a perfectly normal occurrence, there is nothing to be afraid of. Look at Mary. Did she die of the pain? Of course not.' He answered his own question with a smile. 'Now, just trust me. When you have the baby, I'll be with you every minute, and it'll be nothing, you'll see. Really, I promise you. This whole pain in childbirth thing is immensely over-rated. It just isn't that bad.'

She felt comforted, but there was still a thread of terror running through her soul.

She leaned over and kissed him gently. 'Thank you . . . for wanting the baby. Would we stay here?' She had moved into his apartment, which was spacious and pretty, but it only had one bedroom and a small den, which he used a lot. But there was a long silence after she asked him, and then a chuckle from his side of the bed. 'What does that mean?' He didn't often tease, and she looked surprised. 'Well?'

'It means mind your own business . . .' And then he couldn't resist. He had to tell her. 'Oh, all right, Betty, I'll tell you, but don't get excited yet. Nothing is sure. But' – he paused dramatically and she turned around to watch him, smiling – 'yesterday I put a bid on a house.'

She looked astonished. 'You did? Why didn't you tell me? Where? John Fields, you're impossible!' He grinned proudly at her and she looked thrilled.

'Wait till you hear. It's in Mill Valley. And it's next door to Seth and Mary's house.' He sounded triumphant and Bettina grinned.

'That's fabulous!'

'Isn't it? Just keep your fingers crossed that we get it.'

'Do you think we will?'

'I think we might. But first, let's find out if you're pregnant, madam. That's a lot more important. At least to me.' He put an arm around her and they snuggled in the bed.

Her old life forgotten, gone the penthouses, the lofts and the elegant co-ops, the quiet town house . . . all she could think of was her house in Mill Valley, her baby, her husband, and her new life.

Chapter 30

'Do you realise that this is the hottest June they've had since nineteen eleven? I heard it on the radio yesterday while I was lying on the bathroom floor trying to cool off.' Bettina looked at Mary in despair as she fanned herself in Mary's kitchen, and her friend and neighbour laughed.

'I have to admit, I can't think of anything worse than being nine months pregnant in the heat.' And then she laughed again as she looked at Bettina with sympathy. 'But I've done it both times.' Her children were three years old, and ten months now, but both were mercifully down for their naps.

Bettina grinned half-heartedly and picked at the dry tuna fish salad she'd brought. 'May I remind you that I am nine and a half months pregnant.' With a dismal sigh she looked down at the tuna fish and made a face. 'Yuk, I can't eat any more.' She pushed it away and attempted to settle herself more comfortably in the chair.

Mary looked at her sympathetically. 'Do you want to lie down on the couch?'

'Only if you realise that I may never be able to get up.'

'That's all right. If we can't get you up, Seth can push the couch out our back door into yours.'

And then Bettina smiled at her. 'Isn't it nice being neighbours?'

Mary smiled back. 'It sure is.'

They had had the house for six months. And it had meant commuting to the city to her job at the gallery for the first four, but finally John had let her off the hook when she had complained that she'd never get the house done unless she quit and stayed home. He had eventually relented, and she was ecstatic to be free. But the ecstasy had only lasted for a few weeks. In her last month of pregnancy she had been so tired, so bloated, so uncomfortable that she hadn't been able to get anything done.

Now as she stretched out on the couch she looked at her friend. Although they were neighbours, they hadn't seen each other in weeks. 'Is it always like this for you?'

Mary looked pensive for a minute. 'It's different for everyone, Betty. And it's different for every woman each time.'

Bettina grinned. 'You sound like a nurse.'

Mary laughed in answer. 'I guess I still am. Every time I see you, I find myself wanting to ask you questions about what's happening, are your ankles swollen, are you getting headaches, generally how do you feel? But I restrain myself. I figure you must be getting enough of that from John.'

But Bettina shook her head, smiling. 'Surprisingly he's very good. He never says much of anything. His feeling is that it's a natural process, it's no big deal.'

'And what does your OB say?'

Bettina looked relaxed as she answered. It had taken her the full nine months to dispense with the last of her fears. Now she knew they had all been groundless. And she knew that she was well prepared. 'He says pretty much the same thing.'

'Is that what you think?' Mary looked stunned.

'Hell, yes. I've worked my ass off with those breathing exercises in the classes I've gone to. I know I've got it down pat. Now, if I'd just have the baby.' She sat up awkwardly on the couch, and for a moment she flinched. 'Christ, my back is killing me.'

Mary handed her two more cushions and brought over a stool for her feet.

'Thanks, love.' She smiled gratefully, and carefully raised her feet. But even the pillows didn't seem to help her back. It had been killing her all day.

'Something bothering you?'

'My back.'

Mary nodded and went on. 'You know, I was scared

shitless before the first one. And actually' – she smiled openly
– 'I was kind of scared before my second one too.'

'And how was it?' Bettina looked at her frankly.

Mary smiled pensively in answer. 'Not bad. I was pretty
well prepared the second time, and I had Seth with me.'
And then she looked at Bettina pointedly. 'But I was not in
any way prepared for the first.'

'Why not?' Bettina looked intrigued.

'Because even though I was an OB nurse and I'd seen it a
thousand times, no one can really tell you what it's like. It
hurts, Betty. Don't kid yourself about it. It hurts a lot. It's
kind of like a long, hard race for a long time, and then you
get to a point when you think you can't take it, from about
seven centimetres on. Hopefully that doesn't last too long.
And then you get to pushing. That's exhausting, but it's not
so bad.'

She wanted to ask her how John had let her go to
McCarney. He was the coldest, cruellest doctor she had ever
assisted in OB. Twice she had left the delivery room in tears
after the patient had delivered. And after that she had
always disappeared when she knew he was bringing
someone in. 'Do you like him?'

Bettina seemed to hesitate for a long time. 'I trust him. I
think he's a very good doctor, but I don't . . . I don't love
him.' She grinned sheepishly. 'But John says he's an
excellent doctor. He teaches at the university, he's done a lot
of recent research papers. He's apparently working on some
fancy new equipment too. John says he's really tops. But he
isn't . . . well, he isn't warm. But I figured it didn't really
matter. If he's good and John's there, so what?'

Mary thought for a moment. There was no point
frightening her now. It was too late. 'McCarney is certainly
a very respected doctor, he's just not quite as warm and
friendly as mine. And you'll have John with you.' Thank
God. 'But try to be realistic about a first labour, Betty. It
could take a while.'

Bettina watched her in silence for a moment, and then

shook her head. When she spoke, it was very softly, with an old memory still lingering in her eyes. 'This isn't my first time, Mary.'

'It's not?' Now she was shocked. 'You've had another baby?' But when? With whom? What had happened to it? Did it die? She restrained the questions and Bettina went on.

'I had a miscarriage at four months a year and a half ago, before I moved to California. In fact' – she decided to tell the truth now, she felt oddly close to her friend – 'that was how I met John. I had the miscarriage and moved to San Francisco a week later, got depressed, and tried to commit suicide. They called John after they pumped my stomach, and' – she smiled softly – 'we got to be friends.'

'Well, I'll be damned. He never said a thing to us.'

This time Bettina smiled more broadly. 'I know. He didn't want me to either. But Seth knows.'

'Seth?' Mary looked at her in disbelief.

Bettina grinned. 'He handled my divorce.'

'You were married before too? Well, aren't you full of secrets. Anything else?'

Bettina laughed and shrugged. 'Not too many. Just a few . . . let's see . . .' Suddenly she wanted to make a clean breast of it to someone, and she had never felt as close to her friend. 'I've been married twice.'

'Including John?' Mary checked it out.

'Before John.' Bettina spoke softly. 'Once to a much older man, and once to an actor. I used to work in the theatre, my last jobs were as assistant director – '

'You?' Mary looked not only stunned but impressed.

'And my father was a writer. A well-known one.' She smiled and sat back against her pillows as Mary watched.

'Who was he? Anyone I've ever heard of?'

'Probably.' She knew Mary read a lot. 'Justin Daniels.'

'What . . . Of course . . . Bettina Daniels . . . but I never made the connection. Jesus, Bettina, why didn't you tell us?' And then she put both hands on her hips. 'Or does Seth know all of this too?'

But Bettina shook her head firmly. 'He only knows about my last marriage. He doesn't know all the rest.'

'Then why didn't you tell us?'

Bettina shrugged. 'John's not very proud of my chequered past, I'm afraid.' Momentarily she looked embarrassed. 'I didn't want to – to humiliate him.'

'Humiliate him? How? By being Justin Daniels's daughter? I would think he'd be proud. And as for the rest, your two marriages, so what, I'm sure they made sense or you wouldn't have done it, and your friends would love you no matter what. People who love you will always understand, or at least try to. The others . . . who cares? Your father must have known that. I'm sure people didn't always approve of the way he lived.'

'That was different. He was a genius in a way. People expect "eccentricities" of someone like that.'

'So write a book, your past will become exotic.'

Bettina laughed, and then sheepishly hung her head before looking back up at her friend. 'I've always wanted to write a play.'

'Have you?' Mary looked thrilled, and then sat back on her heels. 'Good Lord, Betty, do you realise I've always thought you were as dull as the rest of us, and now I find out you're not. When the hell are you going to write your play?'

'Probably never. I think it would upset John. And . . . oh, I don't know, Mary . . . that' – she seemed to struggle with her words – 'that world isn't very respectable. In some ways maybe I'm lucky I escaped.'

'Maybe. But you escaped with your talent. Couldn't you be respectable and exercise that too?'

'I'd like to try it someday.' She spoke as though dreaming, and then shook her head. 'But I don't suppose I will. John would never forgive me. I think he would feel I was dragging something unsavoury into his life.'

'Didn't it ever occur to you that maybe that was only *his* opinion, that maybe he was wrong? You know, sometimes without even knowing it, people are jealous. We all lead boring, ordinary, mundane existences, and now and then a bird of paradise comes along, and we all get scared. It scares us because we're not like that, our feathers aren't brilliantly hued in red and green, we're brown and grey, and seeing that bird of paradise makes us feel ugly, or as though in some way we've failed. Some of us love to watch that bird, and we dream that one day we might be birds of paradise too . . . others of us have to shoot at the bird . . . or at least frighten it away.'

'Are you saying that's what John did?' Bettina looked shocked.

But when Mary answered, her voice was infinitely kind. 'No. I think what he did was run around to find you brown and grey feathers and dress you up like one of us. But you're not, Bettina. You're exotic and beautiful and special. You are a very, very rare bird. Take off the brown feathers, Betty. Let everyone see how rich your plumage is. You're Justin Daniels's daughter, that in itself is a rare gift. How would your father feel about you hiding out here? Pretending you're not even his child?' Bettina's eyes filled with tears as she thought of it, and then suddenly she flinched. It was as though an electric shock had gone through her back. Mary leaned towards her and kissed her cheek softly, with a look of great tenderness in her eyes. 'Now tell me about those pains you've been having. It's started in your back, hasn't it?'

Bettina looked up at her in amazement, still deeply touched by all she had said. It was the first hint she had that she was still acceptable, in spite of her somewhat exotic past. 'How did you know about my back?'

'Because that used to be my business, remember? We can't all be birds of paradise, kiddo. Some of us have to be firemen and policemen and doctors and nurses.' She was smiling and holding Bettina's hand as she flinched again.

'I'm glad.'

'Do you want to start the breathing yet? Don't if it's not bad.'

'It is.' She was surprised at how quickly it had started to

hurt her. An hour before, it had only been a vague twinge and she hadn't known what it was. Ten minutes earlier it had been uncomfortable once or twice. Now it was cutting off her breathing.

Mary was looking down at her now, taking stock of the situation and still holding her hand as she had a new pain. But this one wasn't in her back, it ripped through her stomach, pulling at everything in its wake and tying it in a long razor-sharp knot that had her gasping and clutching at Mary's hand. The pain went on for over a minute as Mary steadily looked at her watch. 'That was a bad one.'

Bettina nodded and broke into a sweat as she lay back against the couch. She was almost speechless but managed to whisper, 'Yes.' And then suddenly her eyes grew frantic and she spoke hoarsely this time. 'John.'

'It's okay, Betty, I'll call him. You just lie still. And when you get another pain, just start the breathing.'

'Where are you going?' Bettina's eyes filled with panic.

'Just to the kitchen, to the phone. I'm going to call John and have him call your doctor. Then I'm going to call Nancy across the street and have her come over to sit with the kids.' And then she smiled at Bettina. 'Thank God they haven't woken up from their naps. And as soon as Nancy gets here, which should be in about two minutes, you and I are going to get in the car and drive over to the city and get you to the hospital. How does that sound?'

Bettina started to nod, but then she grabbed wildly at Mary's hand again. It was another long, rocky pain. 'Oh, Mary . . . Mary . . . it hurts awfully . . . it . . .'

'Ssshhh . . . now, you can handle it, Betty. Calm down.' Without saying more, she went to the kitchen quickly and came back with a damp cloth, which she put on Bettina's head. 'You just take it easy and I'll make those two calls.'

She was back in two minutes, wearing espadrilles with her jeans and T-shirt and carrying her handbag. She had asked Nancy, the neighbour, to stop in at John and Betty's and pick up the suitcase that she knew was standing in the hall. It was only five minutes later when Mary eased Bettina slowly into the car.

'What if we don't make it?' Bettina looked at her nervously and Mary smiled. She almost hoped they wouldn't. She'd much rather have delivered Bettina on the front seat of the station wagon than handed her over to McCarney when they arrived.

Mary grinned at her as she started the car. 'If we don't, then I'll deliver you myself. And think of all the money you'll save!'

They drove on in silence for a while as Bettina breathed doggedly through all of her pains, but they were coming much closer together and there was a glazed look of determination now in her eyes. Mary was surprised that it had gotten so sharp so quickly, but she hoped that would mean a quick delivery. Maybe she would be lucky, after all. And it wasn't her first child. As they drove, Mary found herself thinking back to what they had been discussing. It was extraordinary how you could know someone, and not know them at all.

'How's it going, kid?' Bettina shrugged and panted determinedly as they drove on. Mary waited until the pain had subsided, and then gently touched her arm. 'Betty, don't be a hero, love. I know you've prepared for natural childbirth, but if it gets to be too much, you ask for something, as soon as you want to. Don't wait.' She didn't want to tell her that if she waited too long they wouldn't be able to give her anything at all.

But Bettina was shaking her head at Mary. 'John won't let me. He says it'll brain-damage . . . the kid . . .' Another pain was starting and Mary had to wait again. But when the pain was over, she pressed on.

'He's wrong. Trust me. I was an OB nurse for years. They can give you an epidural, which is something like a spinal, and it will cut off all sensation below your waist. They can give you a little Demerol maybe, some kind of shot that will take the edge off the pain. They can do a lot of things that won't hurt the baby. Will you ask for it if you need it?'

Bettina nodded distractedly. 'Okay.' She didn't want to waste her breath arguing. She knew how John felt about it, and he had insisted that she would damage their child if she took anything for the pain.

Fifteen minutes later they drove up to the hospital, and Bettina could no longer walk. They put her on a gurney quickly, and Mary held her hand as she writhed in pain.

'Oh Mary . . . tell them . . . no! . . . Stop rolling!' She sat up, grabbing at the orderly, and then fell back and screamed. He waited patiently for the end of the contraction, and Mary tried to soothe her as she talked to her softly and held her hand. She was almost certain that she was now in transition and the pain was at its worst. But only three more centimetres, if that were the case, and she would be fully dilated, and then it would be almost over. She could start to push.

John was waiting for them at labour and delivery, with a look of excitement on his face. He looked at Mary happily and smiled at her and then down at Bettina, dripping perspiration and groaning as she lay huddled on the gurney. She clutched at him wildly and started to cry as she held on to his white coat desperately. 'Oh, John . . . it hurts . . . so much . . .' She was almost instantly torn apart by another pain as he watched. But he held her hand quietly and checked his watch as Mary looked on. An idea came to her suddenly then, and she quietly signalled John. When Bettina's pain had ended, he came to her with a look of peaceful satisfaction.

'What's up?'

'I just thought of something. Since I used to work here, they might let me scrub up to just be with you two. I can't assist, but I could be there for her.' And then she couldn't help adding, 'John, I think she's going to have a hard time.' Mary had seen it often. And things were rapidly getting out of control.

But John smiled gratefully at Mary, patted her shoulder, and shook his head. 'Don't worry, everything's going just fine. Just look at her' – he cast a glance over his shoulder with a smile – 'I think she's already in transition.'

'So do I. But that doesn't mean it's over.'

'Don't worry so much. You nurses are all alike.' She tried to insist for a moment longer, but he firmly shook his head. Instead he signalled to one of the waiting OB nurses to push her into an examining room. But Mary went quickly to her head.

'It's going to be okay, kiddo. You're doing great. All you have to do now is hang on. Kind of like a roller-coaster ride.' And then she bent down and kissed her gently. 'It's all right, Betty, it's all right.' But tears were pouring from Bettina's eyes as the nurse pushed her silently into an examining room. And a moment later Mary saw Dr McCarney disappear through the door, with John striding alongside. Mary almost cringed as she watched them, sure that no one had warned Bettina that he was going to have to examine her midpain. And tears filled Mary's eyes a moment later as the nurse came hurriedly out of the examining room, shrugged her shoulders, and they heard Bettina scream.

'They wouldn't let me stay with her.' The nurse looked apologetically at Mary, who nodded.

'I know. I used to work here. Do you know how dilated she is?'

'I'm not sure. They were guessing at seven and a half. But she just won't seem to progress.'

'Why don't they run an IV of Pitocin?'

'McCarney says there's no point. She'll get there in good time.' After that all Mary could glean from the hurrying nurses was that she was eight centimetres dilated, and McCarney and her husband had agreed that she shouldn't have anything for the pain. They figured it would be over pretty quickly, and either way, she'd be better off without doping herself up. The nurses were ordered out of the room almost as soon as they entered, and Mary paced the halls, close to hysteria herself. McCarney and John had decided to handle this one themselves while she was in labour, and the great Dr McCarney didn't want any nurses around until they went to the delivery room. Mary paced up and down the long halls, wishing she had Seth with her, wishing Bettina had a different doctor, wishing everything, and occasionally hearing the girl scream.

'She can't still be dilating, can she?' Mary looked woefully at the head nurse, who knew her well.

But slowly she nodded. 'It's just one of those bad-luck ones. She got to eight in a hurry and now she seems to be stuck right there.'

'How's she doing?'

There was a moment of silence before the head nurse answered. 'McCarney had us tie her down.'

'Oh, Jesus.' He was as bad as Mary remembered, and finally she put a call through to Seth. But he wasn't able to join her until after six o'clock. By then Mary was crying when she explained what had gone on. He put an arm around her shoulders.

'John's in there, he's not going to let the old guy be too rough on her.'

'The hell he's not. They tied her down three hours ago, Seth. And John told her he doesn't want her to have anything for the pain, or it'll brain-damage the child. What makes me crazy is that it doesn't have to be like that. You know that.' He nodded and for a moment they both thought back to how beautiful it had been for them ten months before when they shared the birth of their second child. And even their first one had been nothing like this. 'He's making it as awful for her as he can.'

'Just take it easy, Mary.' And then he looked at her gently. 'Do you want to go home?'

But she was vehement as she shook her head. 'I'm not leaving until that sonofabitch delivers her.' The head nurse chuckled as she walked by.

'Amen, Waterston.' The two women exchanged a small grim smile.

'How's she doing?'

'About the same. She's at nine now.' It had only taken seven hours for one centimetre, with yet another to go. It was just after ten o'clock at night.

'Can't you give her something to speed it up?'

But the head nurse shook her head and walked on.

At last, another four hours later, just after two a.m., the door to her labour room opened, and John, McCarney, and two nurses hurried out. One of the nurses was pushing the gurney, where a strapped-down, restrained, hysterical Bettina whimpered as she lay there, almost insane from the pain. No one had spoken to her for hours, no one had comforted or explained. No one had held her hand, helped her move more comfortably. They had simply let her lie there, tied down, hysterical, agonised, frightened as the pains tore through her body and mind. At first John had tried to help her with her breathing, but McCarney had been quick to suggest that he stay down at the far end. 'The work is happening down here, John.' He had pointed to where he was working. They had had her tied into stirrups so they could check her with greater convenience, for the past eleven hours. Once or twice she had tried to tell them how badly her back was cramping, but after a while she didn't care. And when John had hesitated another time as he heard her crying, McCarney had shaken his head firmly. 'Just leave her alone. They all have to go through it. She won't even hear you if you talk.' So John had done as McCarney told him and when Seth and Mary saw her being shoved into the delivery room, it was obvious that Bettina was almost out of her head.

'Oh, God, did you see her?' Mary began to cry as the door to delivery closed behind them and Seth took her into his arms.

'It's all right, honey. She's going to be all right.' But Mary pulled away from him, staring at her husband in horror.

'Do you have any idea what it's like to do that to a woman? Do you know what they've done to her mind? They've treated her like an animal for the last twelve hours, for God's sake. She'll never want to have a baby again. They've broken her, damn you! They've broken her!' And then, wordlessly, she reached for her husband and began to sob. He stood there, feeling helpless as he stroked her hair. He knew that what she was saying was right, but there was nothing he could do. He didn't understand how John had let McCarney deliver her. It seemed like a foolish thing to do. The man was competent, but he was a ruthless bastard. There was no doubt about that.

'She's going to be all right, Mary. By tomorrow she won't remember all this.'

But Mary looked at him sadly. 'She'll remember enough.' He knew it was true, and they stood there together, feeling helpless and unhappy, for another two hours. At last at four thirty in the morning Alexander John Fields came into the world, lusty and crying, as his father looked at him proudly and his mother just lay there, staring blindly as she sobbed.

Chapter 31

'Bettina?' Mary knocked softly on the open doorway, wondering if she was at home. At first there was no answer, and then there was a cheerful call from upstairs.

'Come on up, Mary. I'm straightening up Alex's room.'

Mary mounted the stairs slowly and smiled when she found Bettina at the top. 'I spend half my life doing that. Where's the prince?'

'Today's his first day at school.' And then she looked at Mary in embarrassment. 'I don't know what to do with myself, so I thought I'd clean up his room.' But Mary nodded in answer.

'That does me in every time.'

'What do you do to combat it?' Bettina smiled at her and sat on the brightly covered bed. The room was done in reds, blues, and yellows, with toy soldiers marching everywhere.

But Mary was suddenly laughing. 'What do I do? I get pregnant.' She was grinning broadly as Bettina looked at her.

'Oh, no! Mary, not again?'

'Yup.' They had had their third child two years before, and now there would be a fourth. 'I just got the call from the doctor's office. But I think this is going to be it for the Waterstons. Hell, kid, I'll be thirty-nine this month. I'm not a baby like you.'

'I wish I felt like one.' She had just turned thirty-one. 'But in any case for me pregnancy is not the solution.' She looked pointedly at her friend, and Mary looked at her sadly.

'I wish it was.' The experience of Alexander's birth had marked her. And she had made her stand to John very clear. There were going to be no more kids. But he had been an only child too, and he was satisfied with just one. 'You ought to rethink that decision some time, Betty. I told you three

194

years ago it doesn't have to be the way it was.' She remembered their conversation in the hospital right after Alexander was born. Mary had been tearful, angry, furious with John and McCarney. She had been the only one on Bettina's side.

Bettina shrugged. 'I have enough with Alexander. I really don't want any more.' But Mary didn't believe her. For a woman who hadn't even been sure she wanted children, she was a marvel with the boy. Creative, loving, gentle. For three years Alexander and his mother had been best friends. Now she stood up and walked towards Mary with a smile. 'But I must admit, I don't know what the hell to do without him today.'

'Why don't you go into town and go shopping? I'd take you along with me, but I just got a sitter and I promised Seth I'd meet him to help pick out our new car.'

'What are you getting?' Bettina wandered slowly downstairs in the wake of her friend.

'I don't know, something ugly and useful. With four kids who can drive anything lovely? We'll wait and buy our first "nice" car when we're too old to drive.'

'They'll be gone before you know it, Mary.' The oldest one was already six, and she had seen how time flew with Alexander. It was hard to believe he was three. And then suddenly she looked at her friend with a chuckle. 'Unless you keep having babies for another fifteen years.'

'Seth would kill me.' But they both knew that wasn't true. They enjoyed each other and their children. And after eight years of marriage they were still in love. Things were different with John and Bettina, they were very close, but they had never shared quite the same thing as Mary and Seth. And something had happened to Bettina. Part of her had closed up after the birth of the child. Mary had seen it happen to others. It came from being betrayed by people she had trusted. She would never trust anyone quite the same way again. It had often bothered Mary, but she had never dared to bring it up, just as she had never again dared to mention Bettina's play. But now that Alexander was starting school and Bettina would have more time on her hands, she wondered if now at long last she would start to write. 'So? You going shopping?'

Bettina shrugged. 'I don't know. Maybe I will go into town. Can I do anything for you?'

'Not a thing, Betty, but thanks. I just wanted to stop by and tell you the news.'

'Thank you.' Bettina grinned warmly at her friend. 'When's it due?'

'April this time. An Easter bunny.'

'At least you won't die of the heat for a change.'

Bettina watched her leave, then got ready to go to town. She was wearing grey slacks and a grey sweater, and she put a raincoat over her arm before she left the house. It was one of those mottled days of autumn when it could turn out to be beautiful and sunny, or it could turn out to be windy and foggy and cold. For a moment Bettina hesitated, thinking that she might call John and ask him if he wanted to meet her for lunch. The nursery school where they had put Alexander kept him in school from noon until four. But she decided to call John from the city. After she decided what she wanted to do.

She parked her car downtown below Union Square, and then walked across the street to the solemn St Francis and wandered through the elaborate lobby. She found a row of pay phones, called her husband, and discovered that he had already gone out for lunch. So she was left with a decision. To go shopping without eating, or stop somewhere for a sandwich by herself. She wasn't sure she was very hungry, and as she stood pensively for a moment she felt someone suddenly grab her arm. Startled, she jumped to one side, and then looked up to see who had grabbed her, and when she did, she fell silent, her eyes stunned and wide.

'Hello, Bettina.' He had hardly changed in the five years since she had seen him. But just looking at him again, she felt like a little girl. It was Ivo, as tall, stately, and handsome as

196

he had ever been, with as rich and full a head of snow-white hair. He looked scarcely older, and as she looked at him she was stunned to remember that now he had to be seventy-three.

'Ivo . . .' She didn't know what more to say. She was stunned into silence, but then, without saying more, she felt herself hold out her arms. There were tears blinding her eyes as he held her, and when he pulled away again, she saw that he was crying too.

'Oh, little one, how are you? Are you all right? I've worried and worried about you.'

But she nodded, smiling slowly. 'I'm fine. And you?'

'Getting older but not wiser.' And then, 'Yes, darling. I'm all right. You're still married?' He checked her left hand quickly and saw that she was.

'Yes. And I have the most wonderful little boy.'

'I'm glad.' His voice was gentle as the crowds ebbed around them in the lobby. But as he looked at her, she felt ashamed. Three husbands. It was disgraceful. She looked at him and sighed. 'You're happy?' he asked.

She nodded. In many ways she was. It was different than life had been with him. She wasn't a little girl living a fantasy life any more. It was a real life with lonely moments and hard spots. But through it all was the knowledge that she was respectable now, and there was always the joy she derived from her child. 'Yes, I am.'

'I'm glad.'

'And you?' She wanted to know if he had re-married, and he laughed when he saw her eyes.

'No, darling, I'm not married. But I'm perfectly happy as I am. Your father was right. A man should end his life as a bachelor. It makes a great deal more sense.' He chuckled softly, but the way he said it did not deny what they had had. He put an arm around her now and drew her to him. 'I always wondered what had happened when my lawyers told me what you'd done about the money. It took every possible ounce of effort not to set investigators on your trail

197

to find you. For a while I was going to do that, then I decided that you had a right to your own life. I had always promised you that.' She nodded, feeling oddly sobered and still overwhelmed to be standing there in his arms.

'Ivo . . .' She looked up at him happily and he smiled. 'I'm so glad to see you.' It was like going home. For years and years she had almost forgotten what she had come from and who she was, and now here was Ivo in San Francisco, with an arm around her shoulders. She was so happy, she wanted to dance. 'Do you have time for lunch?'

'For you, little one, always.' He glanced at his watch, and then excused himself and went to the phone. When he came back, he was smiling. 'I'm here to visit an old friend. Rawson. Remember him? He's the editor of the paper here now and I promised him some advice. But I have two free hours. Will that do?'

'Perfectly. After that I have to be home when my little boy comes home from school.'

'How old is he?' He looked at her gently.

'Three, and his name is Alexander.'

He looked at her for a moment. 'Have you given up the theatre?'

With a small sigh she nodded. 'Yes.'

'Why?'

'My husband doesn't approve.'

'But you're writing?'

And then gently, 'No, Ivo, I'm not.' He waited until they were seated at a comfortable booth deep in the rear of the restaurant. Then he took a deep breath and faced her.

'Now what's this nonsense about your not writing?'

'I just don't want to.'

'Since when?' He was scrutinising her carefully as she spoke.

'Since I got married.'

'Does this husband of yours have anything to do with that too?'

She hesitated for a long time. 'Yes. He does.'

'And you accept that?' She nodded again.

'Yes.' She thought for a moment. 'John wants our life to be "normal". He doesn't think that writing is.' It was painful but true.

And then he watched her. He was beginning to understand. Slowly he nodded and reached for her hand. 'You'd have been a great deal better off, my darling, if you had led a normal life from the first. If you had had a normal mother and father, if you had been allowed to be a normal little girl. But you weren't and you didn't. There has never ever been anything "normal" about your life.' He smiled gently. 'Not even your marriage to me. But sometimes normal can mean ordinary, or boring, it can mean run-of-the-mill, or banal. And nothing that has ever touched you, from the moment you were born until now, has been any of those things. You were an extraordinary woman, right up until now. You can't pretend to be otherwise, darling. You can't be something that you're not. Is that what you're doing here. Bettina? Pretending to be some nice ordinary man's ordinary wife? Is that what he wants you to do?' Silently she nodded and he let go of her hand with regret. 'In that case, Bettina, he doesn't love you. He loves a woman of his own creation. A painted shell in which he has forced you to hide. But you won't be able to do it forever, Bettina. And it isn't worth it. You have a right to be who you are. Materially your father left you nothing. All he left you was a piece of his genius, a flash of his soul. But those precious gifts you are denying each day you pretend to be someone you are not and refuse to write.' And then after a long pause, 'Can't you do both, Bettina? Couldn't you write and be this man's wife too?'

'I haven't allowed myself to consider that possibility.' She grinned at him mischievously. 'I'm considering it. What about you?'

'I'm doing my share. The intrinsic exhaustion you may remember turned out to be a bout of anaemia, which, thank God, they cleared up. I've written a book, and now I'm writing a second. But nothing like Justin's, of course. This is all non-fiction.' He smiled at her with pleasure.

'I'd love to read it.'

'I'll send you a copy.' And then, regretfully, he looked at her. Their two hours were over and he had to leave. 'I'm leaving tonight. Do you ever come to New York?' She shook her head slowly.

'I haven't been back in almost five years.'

'Isn't it time?'

'I don't think so. My husband doesn't like big cities.'

'Then come alone.' She rolled her eyes and laughed.

It gave him hope to see the spark in her eyes now. It hadn't been there before lunch.

'Maybe when I've written my play. I suppose it is time.' Seeing him made her realise with a start how much she had sacrificed, all along, for the play. It would all be for nothing if she never wrote it.

He nodded. 'What about your husband? Will you tell him you saw me today?'

She thought for a moment, and then sadly she shook her head. 'I don't think I can.' He was sorry for her then. She could always tell him everything. Except that foolishness she'd gotten into with the young actor at the end.

Bettina nodded slowly, and then she reached out and held Ivo close. 'This is all like a dream, you know. It's as though you're some sort of *deus ex machina* dropped from the sky to change my course.'

He chuckled softly. 'If that's how you want to think of me, Bettina, that's fine. Just be sure you do it. None of this nonsensical housewife routine, darling, or I'll come back and haunt you, and then you'll be up the creek.' They both laughed at that. 'Now, you promise you'll send me what you've written?'

'I promise.' She looked at him solemnly as they stood up and walked back to the lobby. It felt good to be with him again, to be tiny and elegant at his side. For a moment she longed for her old wardrobe, the expensive European clothes, and the jewels, and then as though he knew what she was thinking, he looked down at her and spoke softly.

'Do you still have the ring?' She knew he meant the big diamond, and she nodded with huge eyes.

'Of course, Ivo. I don't wear it. But I have it. I keep it in my vault at the bank.'

'Good. Don't ever let anyone have that. You keep that for you. It's worth a small fortune now, and you never know if you'll need it.' And then suddenly he remembered that he hadn't yet got her address or her new name. She gave it to him quickly, and then she giggled.

'They call me Betty Fields. Betty Fields.' But Ivo didn't look amused as he watched her.

'It doesn't suit you.'

And then in embarrassment, 'I know.'

'Will you write as Bettina Daniels?'

She nodded and it was obvious that he approved. And then he pulled her into his arms again and said nothing. He only held her, and for a moment she clung to him. It was Bettina who finally broke the silence. 'Ivo . . . thank you . . .'

His eyes were oddly bright when he looked down at her. 'Take good care of yourself, little one. You'll be hearing from me.' She nodded and he kissed her gently on the forehead, and she left him in the lobby, watching her go. He watched her until she had disappeared in the crowds outside the building, and at last with a small sigh he turned. How much she had changed in the five years he hadn't seen her. And how strong a hold this man must have on her to make her deny her other life, herself, and her old world. But Ivo wasn't going to let her disappear again so easily. On his way up in the elevator he took out a small black leather note-pad and made several notes.

Chapter 32

'How's it coming, Betty?' Mary smiled at her as she wandered slowly out into the yard. It was a warm, sunny April day.

'Not bad. How about you?'

'About the same.' They exchanged a grin, and slowly began to walk. Mary was once again hugely pregnant, but she always looked peaceful and happy like that. Despite the jokes and her pretence at complaining, being pregnant was something she didn't really mind. 'How long do you think it's going to take you to finish?' Only Mary and Ivo knew about the play. It was going well now.

Bettina squinted in the sunlight, thinking back on her afternoon's work. 'Maybe another two weeks. Maybe three.'

'That's all?' Mary looked impressed. Bettina had been at it for almost six months. 'You might even beat me to it after all.' The baby wasn't due until the end of the month.

'Whoever produces first owes the other a lunch.'

Mary grinned broadly. 'You're on.' They rambled on about the children then, and a little while later Alexander and Mary's two eldest came home. Bettina wandered slowly in after Alexander, confident that she had concealed all the pages of her work. But half an hour later she walked into her bedroom and found Alexander staring seriously down at her play.

'What's that, Mommy?'

'Something I've been doing.' She tried to sound non-committal. She didn't want him to tell John.

'But what is it?'

She hesitated for a long time. 'It's a story.'

'Like for kids?'

And then she sighed gently. 'No. Like for grown-ups.'

202

'Like a book?' His eyes widened in new respect, but she shook her head again with a gentle smile.

'No, sweetheart. And to tell you the truth, it's kind of a surprise for Daddy, so I don't want you to tell him. Think you could do that? Just for me?' She eyed him hopefully and he nodded.

'Sure.' And then he disappeared into his bedroom and she thought to herself that one day she would have to tell him about his grandfather. He had a right to know that he was related to a man like Justin Daniels. Even people who hadn't liked him had admitted that he was a great man. And his books were so lovely. Lately Bettina had read many of them again in the evening whenever John was working. She concealed them from him. As she did the calls she got from Ivo now, from time to time. He only wanted to know how she was doing. And she assured him that she was working and everything was fine. He already had an agent anxious to receive her first draft when she was finished, and the last time she had spoken to him she had promised that it would be soon. But it happened even sooner than she expected. And suddenly, a week after she had talked to Mary, she realised that the play lay completed in her hands. She stared at it for a long moment, her hair ruffled, her face smudged with pencil, and with a broad grin. She had done it after all! She had never been so proud in her life. Her pride wasn't even matched by Mary, who gave birth to a baby boy the next day, easily as always.

After carefully re-reading the play four more times, Bettina put it in the mail to Ivo.

'How is it?' He sounded as excited as she felt.

'Wonderful! I love it!'

'Good. Then I'm sure I will too.' He was going to send it to her agent.

A week later the agent called her and told her it needed more work.

'What does that mean?' She asked Ivo when she called to cry on his shoulder.

'Just what the man said. He told you where you should correct it. And it can't be news for you. You remember Justin doing his rewrites. It's not such a big deal. You didn't expect to have it right the first time, did you?' But he could tell from the disappointment in her voice that she did.

'Of course.'

'Well, you waited almost thirty-two years to write it, now you can give it another six months.' But she didn't have to. She had the corrections the agent wanted in three. She mailed it back to him over the Fourth of July weekend and two days later he was on the phone. Victory! She had done it! She had written a fabulous, wonderful, spellbinding play. She melted at the sound of his adjectives and lay on her bed for an hour, grinning at the far wall.

'What are you looking so happy about, Betty?' John came in from a game of tennis and looked at her with a smile.

She sat up on their bed and smiled at him, running a hand through his shining ebony hair. 'I have a surprise for you, darling.' She had had it bound for him when she'd had a copy made for the agent, but she had saved it until she heard if the play was any good.

'What is it?' He sounded intrigued as she walked across the room.

'Something I made for you.' She grinned at him over her shoulder, not unlike Alexander when he brought something home from school.

With a look of curiosity in his eyes, John followed her as she reached rapidly into a drawer, and then turned to him, with a large book, bound in blue.

'What is this?' He opened it slowly, and then stopped as though he had been slapped when he saw her name. He turned to look at her angrily, snapping the thin volume closed. 'Is this supposed to be funny?'

'Hardly.' She looked at him and felt her legs tremble. 'It represents nine months of work.'

'What is it?'

'It's a play.'

'Couldn't you have found something better to do with your time, Betty? The women's auxiliary at the hospital needs a chairman, your son likes going to the beach with you, I can think of a dozen things you could have done with yourself instead of that.'

'Why?' It was the first time she had challenged him.

He laughed derisively at her. 'This thing is probably drivel.' And then in a sudden burst of fury, he threw it at her. 'Don't give me this trash!' And then, without saying anything further, he slammed the bedroom door and hurried down the stairs, and a moment later she heard him slam out of the house. From their bedroom window she watched him drive away and wondered what he was going to do now. Probably drive for a while, or go for a walk somewhere, and then he'd come home and they wouldn't discuss it ever again. He'd never read it, never mention it. The subject would be taboo. But what if she sold it, she wondered, then what would happen? What would he do? Depressingly she realised that she'd probably never have to face that possibility, but it was still nice to dream.

Chapter 33

Right after the Labour Day weekend Alexander went back to school. The neighbourhood was suddenly oddly quiet. At least Mary had the baby, but Bettina had nothing to do. True to her silent prediction, John had never again mentioned her play, and the edition she had had bound for him in blue leather had been stuck back in her drawer for two months. He had never seen the dedication to Alexander and him. It had been two months since Bettina had sent it to the agent, and Ivo said it might take months before there was any news. But what news was there going to be? That someone had bought it? That there were a dozen backers? That the show was ready to go into production any day? She grinned at the unlikelihood of any of that happening and went down to the kitchen and put the dishes in the machine. From her kitchen window she could see Mary putting the baby in the carriage and she smiled to herself as she watched. Maybe Mary had the right idea. Because now that her play was written Bettina wondered what she was going to do with herself. As she put the last of the dishes mournfully in the dishwasher, she heard the phone ring.

'Hello?'

'Bettina?'

'Yes.' She smiled happily out the window. It was Ivo. 'I haven't heard from you in weeks.' She felt dishonest talking to him now and never telling John, but there was no harm in it and she knew that. There were some things she decided that she had a right to do without telling him. And what could she tell John anyway? That Ivo was calling to discuss her play?

'I just got back from the South of France. And Norton was going to call you.' Her heart skipped a beat. Norton Hess was his agent and now, of course, hers. 'But I told him that I wanted to call you myself.'

'What about?' She tried to sound nonchalant as she sat down on a chair.

But at his end Ivo was grinning. 'What do you think it's about, little one? The weather in California?' She chuckled and so did he. 'Not exactly, darling. As a matter of fact' – he drawled out the words and she almost groaned – 'it's about your brilliant little play.'

'And?'

'Not so impatient!'

'Ivo! Come on!'

'All right, all right. Norton has what looks like an army of backers. Some fluke happened and there's apparently an available theatre and it sounds almost impossible but they're talking about opening in late November or early December . . .' He was laughing happily. 'Need I say more? Norton wants you to come to New York on the next plane. You can discuss it all with him when you arrive.'

'Are you serious?'

'Of course I am. Never more so.'

'Oh, Ivo . . .' In all her writing and hoping and praying she had never really anticipated this. 'What am I going to do now?' She didn't know if she should laugh or cry. But Ivo understood immediately.

'You mean about your husband?'

'Yes. What'll I tell him?'

'That you wrote a play, there's a producer on Broadway who's interested, and with any luck at all it's going to be a smash.'

'Be serious.'

'I am being serious.'

'How soon do I really have to come?'

'The sooner the better. Norton will talk to you after I do, I'm sure. I just wanted the pleasure of breaking the news. But the fact is we're talking about an almost impossible opening date here, I gather. The only reason it's possible is because something happened to free this one theatre, and your piece requires almost no costumes and scenery, so it only becomes a question of the financial backing, casting, and rehearsing. But the longer you drag your feet out there, the longer it will take to open here. How about coming tomorrow?'

'Tomorrow?' She looked stunned. 'To New York?' She hadn't been there in five and a half years. There was a long moment of silence on the phone while Ivo let her digest it.

'It's up to you, little one. But you'd better pull yourself together right now.'

'I'll talk to John tonight, and I'll discuss it with Norton tomorrow.'

But Norton was not as gentle as Ivo. He called her half an hour later and insisted that she take the red-eye that night. 'I can't, that's ridiculous. I have a husband and a small child. I have to make arrangements, I have to . . .' He had finally settled on her arriving the next day, but that meant she had to reach John and tell him as soon as she could. She thought about going to see him at his office, but eventually she decided to wait until he came home. She wore something pretty, gave him a drink, and put Alexander to bed as soon as she could.

'What's on your mind, pretty lady?' He eyed her with interest and they both smiled, but Bettina's face grew rapidly serious as she put down her drink.

'There's something I have to discuss with you, darling. And no matter what you may think of it, I want you to know that I love you.' She faltered for a moment as she looked at him, dreading having to tell him about the play. 'Because I do love you very, very much. And this has nothing to do with loving you, it has to do with me.'

'And what does all this mean? Let me guess.' He was in a teasing mood tonight. 'You want to bleach your hair blonde.'

'But she shook her head sombrely. 'No, John, it's about my play.'

'Is that what it is? What about it?' His face was instantly tense.

She couldn't tell him that Ivo had sent it to an agent, because she hadn't told him that she had seen Ivo again. 'I sent it to an agent.'

'When?'

'Last July. No, actually before that, and he asked me to make some corrections and I did.'

'Why?'

She closed her eyes for a minute, and then she looked at him. 'Because I want to sell it, John. It's just . . . it's something I've always wanted to do. I had to. For myself, for my father. And in a funny way for you and Alexander too.'

'Bullshit! All you have to do for me and Alexander is be here for us, in this house.'

'Is that all you want from me?' She looked at him with enormous sad eyes.

'Yes, it is. You think that's a respectable profession, Madame Playwright? Well, it isn't. Just look at your father, the illustrious novelist. Do you think he was a respectable man?'

'He was a genius.' She was quick to defend him. 'He may not have been what you call "respectable", but he was brilliant and interesting, and he left contributions that millions have enjoyed.'

'And what did he leave you, sweetheart? His lecherous old friend? His buddy? That old fart who married you when you were nineteen?'

'You don't know what you're saying.' She was pale as she stared at him. 'John, this isn't the issue. The issue is my play.'

'Horseshit. The issue is my wife and the mother of my son. Do you think I want you traipsing around with people like that? What do you think that does to me?'

'But I don't have to go "traipsing". I can go to New York, sell it, and come home. I live here with you and Alexander, and three thousand miles away in New York they put on my play. You never even have to see it.' But as she heard herself

209

begging she began to hate him for what he made her do. Why would she have to tell him that he would never have to see her play? Why wouldn't he want to see it? 'Why are you so opposed to it? I don't understand.' She looked at him unhappily and tried to force herself to calm down.

'The reason you don't understand is because you had such a lousy, fucked-up upbringing, and that's not what I want for my son. I want him to be normal.'

She looked at him bitterly. 'Like you? Is that the only thing that's normal?'

He was quick to answer. 'That's right.'

And suddenly she was on her feet. 'In that case, John Fields, I'm not going to waste my time arguing with you. My God, you don't even understand where I come from, the fine people, the great minds. I spent my life before this among people that others would give their right arm to know. All except you, because you're frightened and threatened. Look at you, you won't even go to New York. What are you afraid of? Well, I am going back there now, tomorrow, to sell my play and come home. And if you can't accept that, then to hell with you, because by this weekend I will be right back here, doing what I always do, cooking your meals, making your bed, and taking care of our child.'

He stayed in his study for the rest of the evening and he said nothing to her when he came to bed. The next morning she explained to Alexander that she had to go away to New York. She told him why and she told him about his grandfather. And the little boy was fascinated and awed.

'Did he write story books for children?' He looked at her with the same huge green eyes as hers.

'No, he didn't, sweetheart.'

'Do you?'

'Not yet. I just wrote the play.'

'What's that?' He sat down and looked at her in fascination.

'It's like a story that people act out on a big stage. One day I'll take you to a play for children. Would you like that?' He nodded, and then his eyes filled with tears and he reached out and clung to her legs.

'I don't want you to go, Mummy.'

'I won't be gone for very long, sweetheart. Just a few days. And how about if I bring you a present?' He nodded, and she dried his tears as she disengaged herself from his grip on her thighs.

'Will you call me when I come home from school?'

'Every day. I promise.'

And then, mournfully, 'How many days?'

She held up two fingers, praying that would be all. 'Two.'

And then, sniffling loudly, he nodded and held out his hand. 'It's a deal.' He pulled her down towards him so he could kiss her cheek. 'You can go.' And together they walked out of the room hand in hand. She took him over to play at Mary's until the car came to take him to school, and half an hour after she left him, she was on her way to the airport alone in the cab. John had never discussed the matter with her further. And she left him a note, saying that she would be back in two or three days and leaving the name of her hotel. What she would never know was that when he got home that night he crumpled the note and threw it into the trash.

Chapter 34

She hurried off the plane with the others, wearing a black suit and a pair of pearl and onyx earrings she hadn't worn in years. They had been her mother's and they were large and handsome, as of course was the choker Ivo had given her so many years before. Ivo was there to meet her, wearing tweeds and a smile. And she sighed with relief as she saw him. She had been tense during the whole flight. She couldn't imagine what it would be like to be in New York again, if it would be a nightmare or a dream. As the plane had forged through the skies crossing the country, a thousand memories had danced in her head . . . with her father . . . with Ivo . . . at the theatres . . . at parties . . . with Anthony in the loft. It had been an endless film she hadn't been able to turn off. But now seeing Ivo in the crowded terminal came as a relief. At least it was real.

'Tired, darling?'

'Not really. Only nervous. How soon am I seeing Norton?'

He smiled at her. 'As soon as I get you to your hotel.' But there was no nuance, no impropriety. Ivo had long since relinquished his old role. He was back to being a friend of her father's, who in a way now stood in her father's stead. 'Are you very excited?' But he only had to look at her to know. She nodded nervously, and then giggled, and they waited for her bags.

'I can hardly stand it, Ivo. I don't even know what it all means.'

'It means that you're going to have a play on Broadway, Bettina.' He smiled happily with her, and then looked at her gently. 'What did your husband say?'

For an instant she looked serious, and then she shrugged and smiled again. 'Nothing.'

'Nothing? You mean he didn't mind?'

But Bettina shook her head and this time she chuckled. 'I mean he wouldn't speak to me from the time I told him until I left.'

'And your son?'

'He was much more understanding than his father.' Ivo nodded, not wanting to say more, but he had been wondering what Bettina planned to do with Alexander. If the play went into production, she would have to come to New York for several months. Would she bring the boy or leave him with his father? Ivo wondered, but he didn't want to stir up problems before the deal was closed. Instead they made idle chit-chat as her bags turned up on the turntable and a porter took them out to Ivo's car. He had a new driver.

'Does it look very different?' He was watching her as they crossed the bridge, but she shook her head.

'Not at all.'

'I didn't think it would.' And then he smiled at her. 'I'm glad.' He wanted her to find it familiar, to feel at home in her old town. For too many years she had lived like a foreigner with people who didn't understand what she came from, and with an almost alien man. Without knowing him, Ivo didn't like him. He didn't like the feelings he had bred in her, her distaste for her background, her father, her history, and herself.

As they sped up Third Avenue and then Park Bettina watched the crowds, the cars, the people, the action swirling about them in the early evening, people leaving offices, going to parties or dinner, hurrying towards restaurants, or hastening home. There was a kind of electric excitement that, even in the sanctuary of the limousine, they could both feel.

'There's nothing like it, is there?' He looked around him proudly and she shook her head, and then smiled at him.

'You haven't changed a bit, Ivo. You still sound like the publisher of the *New York Mail*.'

'In my heart I still am.'

'Do you miss it a lot?'

He nodded slowly, and then shrugged. 'But eventually everything has to change.' She wanted to tell him Like us, but she didn't. She sat very still, and a few minutes later the car swooped around the island of shrubbery and stopped at her hotel.

The façade was mainly gilt and marble, the doorman covered in brown wool and gold braid, the front desk marble, the concierge obsequious in the extreme. Only moments later Bettina was ushered upstairs and into her suite. She looked around her in astonishment. It was years since she had been anywhere like this.

'Bettina?' A short heavy-set man with bright blue eyes and a fringe of grey hair walked towards her. He wasn't handsome, but dignified, as he rose from the chair in her living-room and held out a hand.

'Norton?' He nodded. 'I'm so glad to meet you after all these months on the phone.' They shook hands warmly. She saw that her bag was deposited in the bedroom and that Ivo tipped the porter, so she called room service and ordered drinks.

And then Norton smiled at her. 'If you're not too tired, I'd love to take you to dinner, Bettina.' He looked at her questioningly with a warm smile. 'And I apologise for intruding on you so quickly, but we have a lot to discuss tonight. And I know how anxious you are to get home. Tomorrow we have meetings with backers, the producer, and I want some time with you to myself . . .' He looked apologetic and she held up a hand.

'I understand. That's perfect. And you're right. I want to do what I have to and get home.' For a moment his eyes travelled to Ivo's. He wondered if she realised that she was going to have to spend several months in New York. But there was no point pushing her on the first evening. That much would become plain to her the next day. 'As for dinner, I'd love it. Ivo, you too?'

'I'd be delighted.'

The three of them smiled at each other, and Bettina sat

down for a minute in one of the comfortable Louis XV chairs. It seemed extraordinary to be back in these surroundings after all those years. It looked like every hotel she had ever stayed in with her father. The only difference was that now they were there because of her. They chatted comfortably over white wine for Bettina and martinis for them, and an hour later she changed and ran a comb through her short chestnut hair. She once again wore her mother's pearl-and-onyx earrings, but this time she wore a new black silk dress. Seeing the new dress, Ivo noticed how plain her taste had become. The dress was good-looking, but compared to her old panache with a wardrobe, the little black silk dress was very dull.

At ten o'clock they went to La Grenouille for dinner, and as they sat down Bettina breathed a deep sigh of relief. It was as though for years she had lived in another atmosphere and now at last she was home. Ivo was thrilled as he watched her, and all she did was smile at him with her eyes. They all had caviar to begin with, rack of lamb, asparagus hollandaise, and soufflé for dessert. At the end of the meal both men ordered cognac and coffee and lit Cuban cigars. Bettina sat back and watched them, enjoying the sights around her and the familiar smells. It seemed years since she had eaten a dinner like this one or smelled the rich aroma of Cuban cigars. And as she looked around her for the hundredth time that evening, she marvelled again at the women, their make-up, their jewellery, their costumes, and their hair. Everything was put together to perfection, everything was designed to capture the eye and keep it both pleased and aware. They were a pleasure to look at, and beside them Bettina felt unbearably plain. Suddenly she realised more than ever how much she had changed in five years.

It wasn't until after the cognac that Norton seriously brought up the play.

'Well, Bettina, what do you think of our little deal?' He looked at her with satisfaction, clearly a man who had succeeded and was well pleased. He had a right to be. What had fallen together for Bettina was a most remarkable deal.

'I'm very impressed, Norton. But I don't know all the details yet.'

'You will, Bettina, you will.'

And by the next day she did. A remarkable sum of money, the best backers on Broadway, a producer people killed or died for, and a theatre that was nothing less than a dream.

It was one of those rare events in the theatre when absolutely everything falls into place. Normally her play wouldn't have been put on until at least six months later, but because of the simplicity of the production, the availability of the theatre, the backers, and the producer, everything was set to roll within three months. The producer was almost certain he could get the actors he wanted. The only thing lacking now was Bettina's okay. It all hinged on her.

'Well?' Norton asked her at the end of a gruelling day. 'Shall we sign it today and give everyone the green light, madame?' He beamed at her and waved at the mountain of contract forms on his desk. Technically she understood almost none of what was happening, all she knew was that if she agreed to accept a vast sum of money and come to New York until the play opened and the kinks had been worked out, and then kept an eye on what was happening with it for a little while, her play was in business and would open before Christmas. It was as simple as that. But she looked exhausted and nervous as she faced Norton across his desk. 'What's the problem?'

'I don't know, Norton . . . I . . . have to talk to my husband. I don't know what I'd do with the baby . . .' She looked terrified and he looked startled. The baby? She had a baby?

'The baby?'

She laughed nervously. 'My three-year-old son.'

Norton waved a casual hand and smiled again. 'Bring the baby with you, put him in school in New York for three or four months, and after Christmas you all go home. Hell, if you want to, bring your husband. For God's sake, they're paying you enough to bring all your friends.'

'I know . . . I know . . . and I don't mean to sound ungrateful. I'm not, it's just that . . . my husband can't come, he's a doctor, and –' She stopped, staring at Norton. 'I don't know, for God's sake. I'm scared. What the hell do I know about Broadway? I wrote a play, and now I wonder what I've done.'

'What have you done?' He looked at her for a moment with hard, beady eyes. 'You have done nothing. Zero. Zilch. You have written a play. But if you don't let someone produce it, if you don't take your chance when you get it, then, my dear, you haven't done shit. Maybe what you'd like better' – he paused for a moment, and then went on – 'is to take your play back to California and have it put on by some local playhouse, where no one will ever hear of it, or you, again.' The silence in the room was deafening after his brief speech. 'Is that what you want, Bettina? I'm sure if he could see it, it would make your father very proud.' He smiled at her benignly, unprepared for what happened next so that he jumped slightly when she slammed a fist down on his desk.

'Screw my father, Norton. And Ivo. And John. Everyone is always wanting me to do what suits their purpose, and invoking whatever names they have to to get whatever they want done. Well, I'm not doing this for my father, or my husband, or Ivo, or you. If I do it, I'm doing it for me, Norton, for me, do you hear me, and just maybe for my son. And the fact is I can't give you an answer and I'm not going to sign a damn thing today. I'm going to go back to my hotel and think it over. And in the morning I'm going to go home. And when I've thought it out clearly, I'll call you.'

He nodded calmly. 'Just don't wait too long.' But now she was tired. Of him and of them. Of everyone. And of being pushed around.

'Why not? If the play's any damn good, they'll wait to hear from me.'

'Maybe. But they may lose the theatre, and that could change the deal. You need everything going for you at one time, Bettina, and right now you have that. I wouldn't take too many chances with that if I were you.'

'I'll keep that in mind.' She looked troubled as she stood up and looked at him, but he smiled as he came around the desk to her.

'I know it's hard, Bettina. It's a big change. Especially after being gone for so long. But it's also a big chance, and good things are never going to happen to you if you don't take a chance. It could be a huge success, and I think it will be. I think it will make your career.'

'Do you really think so?' She looked at him in confusion. She didn't understand any of it. 'But why?'

'Because it's about a man and his daughter, because it says a great deal about our times, about men, about you, about dreams that get broken, and about hope that somehow pushes through the rocks and the shit and the weeds. It's a tough play, but it's a beauty. You said something you felt in your heart, Bettina. You paid a price for that understanding, and you felt every word you put down there, and the beauty of it is that others will too.'

'I hope so.' She whispered it as she looked at him sadly.

'Then give them that chance, Bettina. Go home and think about it. And then sign the papers and come back here. You belong here, lady. You have a job to do right here in this town.'

She smiled at him then, and before she left him, she kissed his cheek.

She didn't see Ivo again before she left New York, and she didn't speak to Norton again either. And as it turned out, she didn't stay in the hotel to sleep. Instead she called the airline and caught the very last flight home. She walked into their house in Mill Valley at two o'clock in the morning and tiptoed upstairs to their bedroom, where John was sound alseep in bed. Like all doctors though, he was a light sleeper and he sat up instantly as she closed the door.

'Something wrong?'

'No.' She whispered softly. 'Go back to sleep. I just got home.'

'What time is it?'

'Almost two.' As she said it she wondered if he appreciated the fact that she had hurried home to him and had made a point of spending only one night in New York. She could have stayed for another evening, another dinner, another night in a fancy hotel, but she wanted to get back to Mill Valley, to her husband and her son. As he lay back in bed slowly, watching her, she smiled and set down her bag. 'I missed you.'

'You didn't stay away for very long.'

'I didn't want to. I told you I wouldn't.'

'Did you make your deal?' He sat up on one elbow and switched the light on as slowly Bettina let herself into a chair.

For a moment she didn't answer, and then she shook her head. 'No. I wanted to think it over.'

'Why?' He looked at her coldly, but at least he was talking to her about the play. But she didn't want to tell him all the details. Not so quickly. Not in her first hour at home.

'It's more complicated than I expected. We can talk about it in the morning.'

But he was wide awake now. 'No. I want to discuss it now. This whole thing has been much too shrouded in secrecy from the start. You've been sneaky about it since you started writing that piece of garbage. Now I want it out in the open all around.' So it was back to that, then.

She sighed softly and ran her hand tiredly over her eyes. It had been an endless day, and by New York time it was already five a.m. 'I never meant to be sneaky, John. I didn't tell you about it, in part because I wanted to surprise you, and in part because I was afraid you'd disapprove, and it was something I had to do. It's in my genes maybe, what do

219

I know. I wish you'd try to see this thing a little more broadly. It would make it a lot easier for me.'

'Then you don't understand how I feel about this, Bettina. I have no intention of making it easier for you. I don't choose to. And if you were smart, Betty, you'd forget about all that. I gave you that chance five years ago. I don't understand why you have to go back now. Do I have to remind you that you tried to commit suicide, that you lost a baby, that you had been married twice and left destitute by your father, then you got swept up on the beach like an orphan out here.' It was not a pretty picture he painted, and Bettina hung her head.

'John, why don't we just stick to the issue.'

'What is the issue?'

'My play.'

'Oh, that.' He looked at her angrily.

'Yes, that. The problem, since you want everything out on the table, is that if I sell it, I'll have to spend the next few months in New York.' She gulped hard and went on, avoiding his eyes. 'Probably only until Christmas. I could come home right after that.'

'No, you couldn't.' His voice was like ice.

But her eyes flew innocently to his. 'Yes, I could. Norton, my agent, said that I don't have to be there for long at all after it opens and they want to open in late November or early December. So by Christmas I should be home.'

'You didn't understand me. If you go to New York to do this, I don't want you back.'

She looked at him with horror as he sat in rigid fury on his side of the bed. 'Are you serious? You'd give me a choice like that, John? Don't you understand what this could mean to me? I could be a playwright, for God's sake, I could have a career . . .' Her voice trailed off as she watched him. He didn't give a damn.

'No, you could not have a career, Betty. Not and remain my wife.'

'It's that simple, then? Go to New York with the play and

you throw me out?'

'Exactly. So that takes care of it, doesn't it? It's a very clear-cut choice. I thought you understood that before this.'

'I didn't or I wouldn't have bothered to go to New York.'

'Well, I hope you didn't waste your own money.' He shrugged and turned off the light, and Bettina went to undress in the bathroom, her shoulders silently heaving as she clutched a towel to her face to silence her tears.

Chapter 35

'I'm sorry, Norton, I can't help it. It's my husband or you.'
She felt laden as she sat holding the phone. She had cried all
night long.

There was a long pregnant silence, and then Norton told
her the truth. 'I think you ought to understand something,
Bettina. I'm not the issue here, you are. It's your husband or
you. That's a hell of a choice he's given you. I hope he's
worth it.'

'I think he is.' But as she hung up the phone she wasn't as
sure of it, and she was even less so as she wandered over to
Mary's and stared forlornly into her coffee as she shed fresh
tears.

Mary looked at her numbly. 'I don't understand it.'

'He feels threatened. He hates that part of my past.
There's nothing I can do.'

'You could leave him.'

'And do what? Start over again? Find a fourth husband?
Don't be ridiculous, Mary. This is my life here. This is
reality. The play is a dream. What if it's a bomb?'

'So what? Can you really give up your dreams for this
man?' She looked at Bettina angrily. 'He's my friend, Betty,
and so are you, but I think he's being ridiculous, and if I
were you, I'd take my chances and go to New York.' Bettina
smiled a watery smile and blew her nose.

'You're just saying that because you're tired of your kids.'

'I am not. I adore them. But I'm not you. Remember that
bird of paradise story I told you . . . well, you're starting to
look ridiculous with a grey and brown beak. You don't
belong here, Bettina. You know it, I know it, Seth knows,
even John knows it, that's why he's busting his ass, and
yours, to keep you here. He's probably afraid he'll lose you.'

'But he won't.' She said it with a mournful whine.

'Then tell him that. Maybe that's all he needs to hear, and if he doesn't shape up after that, screw him, pack your bags, take Alexander, and go do your play.' But as she watched Bettina walk back to her place, Mary knew that she wouldn't do it. She wouldn't leave him. She was too sure that he was right.

Bettina spent the afternoon alternately trying to read one of her father's books and staring out the window, and eventually the phone rang and it was Ivo this time.

'Are you nuts? Are you crazy? Why did you bother to come to New York if you were going back to hide again?'

'I can't help it, Ivo. I have to. Please . . . don't let's discuss it. I'm unhappy enough.'

'It's that moron you married.'

'Ivo, please – ' She faltered.

'All right, dammit, all right. But please, for God's sake, Bettina, reconsider . . . you've wanted this for your whole lifetime. Now the chance comes and you're throwing it away.'

She knew what he was saying was true. 'Maybe there'll be another chance later.'

'When? When your husband dies? When you're a widow? In fifty years? My God, Bettina . . . think of it . . . think of it . . . your play could have been on Broadway, and now you've doomed it to silence. You did it. No one else.'

'I know.' Her voice was little more than a whisper, and then her eyes filled with tears. 'I can't talk about it any more now, Ivo. I'll call you tomorrow.' But when she hung up, she was once again blinded by her tears. She wondered if John knew what it had cost her to deny her life's dream.

And then, pensively, wiping her tears on her shirt-sleeve, she went back to her book. Oddly enough it was one of her father's that she hadn't read in years, and Mary had had it in her bookcase. Bettina borrowed it months before and never read it. But it seemed comforting somehow today. As though he understood, as though he had written it knowing what she was feeling. She felt his presence as she continued to dry her tears and read. And then she found it. A folksy passage he had liked so well that he had often quoted it to her. Something his father had long ago said to him . . .

Don't give up your dreams or your dreaming. Don't let life cut your line as you reel in those dreams . . . hold on tightly . . . keep reeling . . . don't give up . . . grab that net . . . and if they look like they're about to leap out of the net after you've caught 'em, jump in after 'em, and keep on swimming, till you drown if you have to . . . but don't ever let go of those dreams . . .

Bettina slowly closed the book on her lap and this time she laughed as she gave way to her tears. She walked quietly to the kitchen and dialled Norton. And then she waited for her husband to come home that night. When he did, she told him, quietly, firmly, that her mind was made up.

Chapter 36

'Promise you'll at least call me once in a while?' Mary looked at her mournfully, the car filled with children, her eyes filling with tears.

'I promise.' Bettina held her friend tightly, she kissed everyone, then waved at them all as she scooped Alexander out of the car.

'Goodbye!' He waved at them frantically, and then marched into the terminal beside his mother, holding tightly to her hand. She had explained to him about going to New York for a few months and going to a new school, having a babysitter sometimes, and seeing a real play for children, and meeting some of his grandfather's old friends. He was sad that he couldn't take his Daddy, but he understood that Daddy had to stay to help sick people, and he was glad he was going with his Mom. He had left his Dad a big drawing, and then hurried to finish packing his favourite toys. And that had only been the night before. His Dad was already gone when he got up that morning. Someone must have been real sick for him to have to leave so early. And Aunt Mary from next door had driven them to the airport. It had been okay except that she and his Mom had cried a lot.

'You okay, Mommy?' He looked up at her with a hesitant smile.

'I'm fine, sweetheart. How about you?' But Bettina had been looking anxiously all over the airport on their way to the gate. John had been gone before she got up that morning also, and she was still hoping that he'd turn up to say goodbye. She had left him a letter telling him that she loved him, and she had called his office several times but even the nurse wasn't there, and the answering service hadn't been able to page him. He never showed up, and Bettina and Alexander boarded the plane.

It was Alexander's first trip on an aeroplane, and he had fun playing with the things they gave him and running up and down the aisle. There were three other children to play with, but eventually he fell asleep in Bettina's lap. This time when they arrived in the New York airport, Ivo had been unable to come, but he had sent his car.

Bettina was delighted with the comfort, and the driver took her to the hotel she had chosen, further uptown than the last one. She wanted Alexander to be able to go to the park. They had a pretty suite with bright-coloured fabrics and paintings and lots of sunshine. The autumn afternoon sun was streaming in the windows as the porter set down her bags. There were flowers from Norton, and Ivo, and a huge arrangement of roses from the producer of the show, which said only WELCOME TO NEW YORK.

That night Bettina spent settling in with Alexander, and before he went to bed, they tried to get John on the phone, but he wasn't there when they called him, so they called Seth and Mary and their kids instead.

'Homesick already?'

'Not really. We just wanted to say hi.' But Mary knew that Bettina was probably worried about John. She'd settle down once she started work on the play. And he would probably eventually come to his senses. And who knew, maybe he'd even go to see her in New York. She voiced her hope to Seth over dinner, but he only nodded vaguely.

Bettina tucked Alexander into his new bed in the suite's second bedroom, and then walked across the large pretty living-room to her own and sat down on the bed with a small sigh. She had rapidly done all her unpacking. All that remained to do the next day was meet Alexander's baby-sitter and check out the school she had selected for him.

She managed to accomplish both of those tasks before noon and turn up in Norton Hess's office by one for a quiet lunch his secretary brought in on trays.

'You ready?'

'Absolutely. My son's new babysitter is adorable, and he loved his first morning at school. Now I can get down to business, when do we start?'

He grinned as he saw her, she looked like a pretty young matron from the suburbs as she sat there in a camel's hair coat, black slacks, a sweater, her Goldilocks hair, and a little black hat. She had style, even as she sat there in the clothes she had worn to take her kid to school, but there was something so subdued, so quiet about her. It made him wish that she would tear off her clothes and jump on his desk.

'You know, I never thought I'd see you here, Bettina.'

'I know. I didn't really think I'd come.'

'What changed your mind? It couldn't have been anything I said?' His eyes asked a question, but she laughed and shook her head.

'It wasn't. It was my father.' His brows knit immediately in answer. What the hell did she mean? 'I was reading one of his books and it was something I saw there. I realised that I had no choice. That I had to come.'

'I'm awfully glad you came to your senses. You saved me an air fare.' His eyes twinkled.

'I did. How?'

'I was planning to come out to San Francisco and jump off the Golden Gate Bridge. After I beat you up.'

'I might have gotten there first. I was so depressed, I could hardly see.'

'Well' – he sat back and lit a cigar he plucked from his humidor – 'everything's worked out for the best. And tomorrow you get to work. Any other plans in the meantime? Anything you're itching to do? Go shopping, invite some friends in? My secretary will help you with anything you need.' But Bettina had started to shake her head quickly, and then slowly her eyes lit up as she tilted her head to one side.

'It's been so long since I've been here . . .' She mused

happily. 'Last time I was really only here for a day. I think maybe . . . Bloomingdale's . . .' She grinned.

'Women.' He rolled his eyes. 'My wife lives at Bergdorf's. She only comes home for meals.' She chuckled as she left him, and it was four hours later before she got back to the hotel, feeling guilty about Alexander left to a new sitter after he had been to a new school, in a new town. But when she got back to the hotel, buried under a stack of boxes, Alexander was eating spaghetti and had chocolate ice cream all over his face.

'We ate the ice cream first, then the spaghetti. Jennifer says my tummy won't know which came first as long as I eat them both.' He grinned happily at his mother, a portrait in red and brown. He certainly didn't seem to have missed her, and she had had a wonderful time.

A note from the desk told her that Ivo had left for London and that the producer would be at the hotel to see her at ten the next morning. It was obvious that John hadn't called. But she brushed her qualms away from her conscience and retired to her room to try on four new dresses, three sweaters, and a suit. She had spent almost a thousand dollars. But she could afford it now, and she had a ball. Besides she would need the wardrobe. Now that she was back in New York nothing she had brought with her looked even remotely right.

And she was gratified the next morning when she met the producer in a wonderful cream-coloured cashmere dress.

'My God, you look marvellous, Bettina. We ought to cast you.'

'Hardly, but thank you.' The had exchanged a warm smile and gone back to work. For the moment all she had to worry about was the smoothing of a few kinks; he had the mechanics to worry about and the hiring of everyone from actors to the director of the play. But they must have been living under a spell of magic, because all of the casting and hiring had been done by the end of a week.

'Already? That's a miracle!' Norton had told her when

she called to report to him. She had seen all the final try-outs and she loved the actors they had selected for the play. For a while she had been nervous that Anthony might show up for the auditions, but she didn't even know if he was still in the States, and six years was a very long time. It had been that long since she'd seen him last. But whatever the reason he never showed.

It was two weeks later when she got a call from Ivo. She had just sailed in from the theatre to dine with Alexander and she was wearing a comfortable old sweat shirt and jeans.

'Did you just get back from London?'

'Last night. How've you been?'

'Wonderful. Oh, Ivo, you should see how the play's going. It's just beautiful, and they've got the most marvellous actors to play the father and the girl.' It was easy to hear in her voice that she was thrilled.

'I'm glad, darling. Why don't you tell me about it over dinner? I'm having dinner at Lutèce with a friend.'

'Very fancy, Ivo. I'm impressed.' It was still the most expensive restaurant in town.

'Don't be. You should be more impressed with whom I'm dining with. The new theatre critic at the *Mail*.'

'Oh, God.'

'Never mind that, you ought to meet him, and he's very, very nice.'

'What's his name? Do I know him from way back when?'

'Unlikely. He's been at the *Los Angeles Times* for the last seventeen years. He just came to us –' He grinned at the slip and she laughed at him. 'To them, sorry, about six months ago. His name is Oliver Paxton. And he's both too young and too sensible to have been one of your father's friends.'

'He sounds dreary as hell. Do I really have to meet him?'

'He's not and you should. Come on, darling, it'll be good for you. You didn't just come here to work.'

'Yes, I did.' She was being immensely careful not to make the same mistake that she had made on the road show with Anthony seven years before. She wasn't hanging out with the cast or the crew or the producer, and she wasn't soliciting any close friends. She was doing precisely what she had told John she would do. Working, taking care of Alexander whenever possible, seeing her agent – but that was about it. Except for Ivo, but he was a special kind of friend. She was not risking any involvements. She wanted to do her play, but she wanted to keep her marriage too.

'So, will you join us?' She was thinking about it and watching Alexander play with his food.

'I was just eating with Alexander.'

'How exciting. Surely you can join us afterwards, Bettina. Besides, his menu can't be as wonderful as all that.'

'Not exactly.' He had ordered hot dogs and chocolate pudding, with a double order for her. 'As a matter of fact . . . what time are you dining?'

'I told Ollie I'd meet him at eight thirty. He had some sort of meeting he had to go to at six.'

'Sounds just like you in the old days, Ivo.'

'Yes, doesn't it? But he's not nearly as handsome.'

'And undoubtedly not as charming.' She was teasing now and he was laughing.

'I'll let you judge that for yourself.'

Chapter 37

Bettina stepped out of the taxi on Fiftieth Street, east of
Third Avenue, and hurried into the restaurant with an
expectant smile. This would be the first time she had seen
Ivo since she had agreed to do the play and had come to New
York with Alexander. She was happy to see him, although
she would have preferred to see him alone. But it didn't
really matter. It was amusing to be out for an evening,
instead of alone, poring over her notes in the hotel. She left
her coat with the girl at the cloakroom, and then waited for
the head-waiter so she could ask him if Ivo was already
there. But before he could reach her, she noticed several men
staring, and she wondered for a moment if what she had
worn was all wrong. It was one of the dresses she had bought
when she'd gone shopping, but she hadn't yet had occasion
to wear it anywhere. It was a pale lilac velvet that did
wonderful things to the creamy warmth of her skin and the
colour of her hair. It had clean, simple lines and it was a very
pretty mid-calf length. And the simplicity and the colour
reminded her vaguely of the beautiful Balenciaga outfit she
had owned years before, with a wonderful dark green velvet
tunic coat. But this was much simpler, and she wore it with a
single long strand of her mother's lovely pearls, and the
matching earrings in her ears. She looked wonderfully fresh
and demure as she stood there, tiny and delicate, with her
eyes very large and green. Ivo was watching from a distant
table and he signalled to her with a warm, friendly smile.
She saw him quickly and slipped past the head-waiter, to
where Ivo's table was, in a kind of canopied garden in the
back.

'Good evening, little one, how are you?' He stood and
kissed her and she gave him a warm hug, and then suddenly
she noticed the giant standing next to him. He had the look

of a friendly young man, with grey eyes, broad shoulders, and sandy California-blond hair. 'And this is Oliver Paxton. I've been wanting you two to meet for quite a while.' They politely shook hands and all three of them sat down at the table, as Oliver looked her over with considerable appreciation and wondered what lay between his friend and this girl. They seemed to have an odd, comfortable, almost family-like relationship, and then he remembered that he and her father had been close friends. And then suddenly he remembered what Ivo had told him before he went to London. This was Justin Daniels's daughter, the girl who had just written what was predicted to be the season's hit play.

'Now I know who you are!' He smiled broadly, and as she looked at him she grinned.

'Who am I?'

But he grinned. 'You're Justin Daniels's daughter and you've just written what is supposed to be a wonderful play. Does anyone call you anything besides Bettina?' He looked at her warmly, but she shook her head with a laugh and a smile.

'Not in New York they don't. In California some of my close friends get away with a name I hate. But I won't tell you.'

'Where in California?'

'San Francisco.'

'How long have you lived there?'

'Almost six years.'

'Like it?'

'I love it.' Her face lit up with a warm smile and so did his. The evening was off and running. He was from Los Angeles but had gone to school at the University of San Francisco, and had a warm spot in his heart for that city, though it wasn't a sentiment that Ivo shared.

The three of them ordered a special dinner, and the conversation was fast and heavy for the next three hours. It was close to midnight when at last Ivo signalled to the headwaiter for the bill. 'I don't know about you two children, but this white-haired old gentleman is about ready for his bed.' He stifled a yawn as he smiled at them. But he had had a lovely evening, and it was easy to see that they were enjoying themselves too. But now Bettina was laughing and looking at him with a teasing eye.

'That's not fair, Ivo. You've had white hair since you were twenty-two.'

'Possibly, darling. But by now I've earned it, so I can mention it as often as I like.' Oliver looked at him with frank admiration. He was a rare specimen in journalism, and someone he had respected for all of his life.

Ivo bid them a warm adieu as he got into his car just outside the restaurant, where it had waited for him all night long. And Oliver assured Ivo that he would get Bettina back to the hotel.

'You won't kidnap her or do anything vulgar?'

Oliver laughed warmly at the suggestion and there was a definite gleam in his eye. 'Kidnap her, no, Ivo, I promise not to, and I'd like to think that nothing I could do would be considered vulgar. At least not viewed by the right eye.'

'I will leave that entirely up to Miss Daniels.' He waved to them both, pressed the button that raised the window, and a moment later he drove off in his limo as the two of them waved and smiled.

Oliver looked down happily at Bettina as they walked slowly west, past brownstones, and then eventually apartment buildings, offices, and stores. 'How long have you known Ivo, Bettina?'

'All my life.' And then she smiled at him. Obviously he didn't know the rest of it. His next question seemed indicative of that.

'He was a friend of your father's?'

She nodded, still smiling, and then she sighed and decided to tell him the rest. But the smile hadn't fled. It was something she could tell easily now. It didn't shame her. It was something she remembered with tenderness and pride. 'Yes, he was a friend of my father's. But we were also married for six years . . . a long time ago.'

He looked at her in total astonishment, the handsome grey eyes amazed.

'What happened?'

'He wanted to think I outgrew him. But I didn't. In any case now we're just friends.'

'That is the most extraordinary story I've heard all night. You know, I never had any idea of it tonight at dinner.' And then he looked at her carefully. 'Do you . . . still see each other? . . .' He floundered painfully and she grinned. 'I mean . . . I didn't mean to . . . do you suppose he was angry when I said I'd take you home? . . .' He was in agony and all she could do was laugh.

'No, of course not.' In fact she suspected that there had been an ulterior motive for the introduction, but she didn't say that to her new friend. Either Ivo wanted him to feel kindly towards her new play or he figured she needed an escort while she was in town.

'Well, I'll be damned.' Oliver was still astonished, and for a while they walked along in silence, her hand slipped easily into his arm. And then he turned to smile down at her gently.

'Do you suppose it would be possible for us to go dancing?'

This time she looked at him in amazement. 'Tonight? But it's almost one o'clock.'

'I know it is.' He looked at her in amusement. 'But as Ivo said, things are different in New York. Everything is still open. Any interest?' She was about to say no to his outlandish offer, but something in the way he looked down at her amused her, and she found herself laughingly saying yes. They quickly jumped into a taxi, and he took her to a bar somewhere on the Upper East Side. There was live music and there were crowds of people, pressed together, swaying with the music, laughing and drinking and having a good time. It was a far cry from the elegant restraint of

Lutèce, but Bettina enjoyed it thoroughly, and an hour later they left, with regret.

As they travelled back to her hotel they spoke of her upcoming opening.

'I bet the play is brilliant.' He looked warm and solid as he looked down at her eyes.

'What makes you say that?'

'Because you wrote it – and you're a very special lady.' She laughed appreciatively. 'I wish you were something other than a critic.'

'Why?' He looked surprised.

'Because I'd like you to come and see my play and tell me what you think. But since you are who you are, Ollie' – she smiled up at him as she used the name – 'the producer would have a fit.' And then she had a thought and looked up at him again. 'Will you be the one who reviews it?'

'Probably.'

'That's too bad.' She looked woeful.

'Why?'

'Because you'll probably cream it, and then I'll feel awkward with you, and you'll be embarrassed, and it'll be awful . . .' But he was laughing at her predictions of woe and despair.

'Then there's only one solution to the problem.'

'What's that, Mister Paxton?'

'That we become fast friends before the play opens, so it doesn't matter when I review it what I write. How does that sound?'

'It's probably the only solution.'

When they got back to the hotel he asked if he could take her for a drink. She told him her son was upstairs and she wanted to make sure he was all right.

'A son – you and Ivo had a son? Oh, my, this is confusing.'

'No, the son is my child by my third husband.'

'My, my, what a popular lady. And how old is this son?' He hadn't looked particularly impressed by her three marriages, and she was relieved as they walked on.

'He's four and his name is Alexander, and he's wonderful.'

'And let me guess. He's your only child?' He smiled benevolently down at her as she nodded.

'He is.'

Then he looked at her carefully. 'And the young man's father? Has he been disposed of or is he in New York too?' The way that he said it made her laugh, despite her serious worries about John.

'Well, he's not too pleased about our coming to New York, which he is convinced is Sodom and Gomorrah. And he is furious that I'm doing the play. But I'm still married to him, if that was your question. He stayed in San Francisco. But I wanted Alexander with me.'

'Can I meet him?' It was the only thing he could have said that brought him closer to her heart.

'Would you like to?'

'I'd love it. Why don't we make it a very early dinner before the theatre tomorrow and take him. Then we can bring him back to the hotel and go out afterwards. Sound reasonable?'

'It sounds wonderful. Thank you, Ollie.'

'At your service.' He bowed impressively, and then hailed a cab. And it wasn't until she got upstairs that Bettina began having qualms. What was she doing going out with this man? She was a married woman, and she had promised herself she wouldn't go out with anyone while she was in New York. But he was a friend of Ivo's, after all.

She had heard nothing from John since the day they'd left. He answered none of Bettina's calls and letters, and his secretary always insisted that he had just gone out. Bettina let the phone at home ring again and again and again, but to no avail. He either never answered it or was never there. So maybe it wasn't so awful that she should have dinner with Oliver Paxton. And no matter how much she liked him, she was not going to have an affair.

And she told him that bluntly the next night after they left

236

the theatre and went to the Russian Tea Room for blini and drinks.

'So who asked you?' He looked at her in enormous amusement. 'Madam, it's not you I want, it's your son.'

'Have you ever been married?'

He smiled sweetly at her. 'No, I've never been asked.'

'I'm serious, Ollie.' He was rapidly becoming a real friend. And whatever their attraction to each other was, they both understood that it would go no further than the friendship they had. As far as Bettina was concerned, it couldn't. And Ollie respected that.

He was smiling at her now as their blini came and he dug in. 'I was being serious too, and no, I've never been married.'

'Why not?'

'There hasn't been anyone I wanted to get stuck with for the rest of my life.'

'That's a nice way to put it.' She made a face and tasted her blini.

He looked at her. 'So Number Three doesn't approve of all this?'

She began by trying to defend him, which told Ollie its own tale. And then slowly she just shook her head. 'No.'

'That's not surprising.'

'Why not?'

'Because it's hard for a lot of men to accept a woman with another life, either a past or a future, and you happen to have both. But you did what you had to do.'

'But how do you know that?' She looked so earnest that he couldn't resist reaching out and rumpling her soft auburn curls.

He smiled at her slowly. 'I don't even know if you remember it. But there's something in a book of your father's. I came across it one day when I was trying to decide if I should take the job at the *Mail* and come to New York. Your father would approve of your choice . . .'

She looked at him and her eyes widened, and they quoted

237

it together word for word. 'My God, Ollie, that was what I read the day I told them I'd come here. That was what changed my mind.' He looked at her strangely.

'It did that for me too.' And then silently they toasted her father, finished their blini, and walked back to her hotel arm in arm. He didn't come upstairs with her. But he made a date for Saturday to go to the Bronx Zoo with her and Alexander.

Chapter 38

By the end of October Bettina was working on the play almost night and day. She spent endless hours in the draughty theatre, and then more hours late at night making changes back at the hotel. Then back to the theatre again the next morning to try out the changes and change them again. She never saw Ivo, she hardly saw Ollie, it was all she could do to see Alexander for half an hour a day. But she always made time for him, and sometimes when she was at the theatre, Ollie came by to play with him. At least it gave Alexander a man to relate to. And they still had heard nothing from John.

'I don't understand why he doesn't call me.' Bettina looked at Ollie in irritation as she threw her hands up and hung up the phone. 'Anything could have happened to him, or to us, and he wouldn't know. I don't know. This is ridiculous. He doesn't answer my letters or my phone calls. He never calls.'

'Are you sure he didn't say anything more definite when you left home, Bettina?' She shook her head, and despite a strange premonition, he didn't dare say anything more. He understood that she considered herself married, and he respected what she felt. The subject changed quickly to her latest agonies about the play.

'We'll never be ready to open.' She looked slightly tired and thinner, but there was something wonderfully alive about her eyes. She loved what she was doing and it showed. And Ollie was always encouraging when she told him her woes.

'Yes, you will be ready, Bettina. Everybody goes through this. You'll see.' But she thought he was crazy as each week they drew nearer to the big day. At last there were no more changes to be made. They went to New Haven for three performances, Boston for two. She made half a dozen more changes after the try-outs, and then she and the director nodded in agreement. Everything that could be had been done. All that remained was to get one night of decent sleep before the opening and spend an agonising day waiting for night to come. Ollie called her that morning, and she had already been up since six fifteen.

'Because of Alexander?'

But she only chuckled. 'No, dummy, because of my nerves.'

'That's why I called you. Can I help keep you amused today?' But he couldn't. For that day and that evening he was The Enemy, a critic, a reviewer. She couldn't bear to spend the day with him and then have him lacerate her play. Because she was certain that he would.

'Just let me sit here and be miserable. I love it.'

'Well, tomorrow it'll be over.'

She stared gloomily into space. 'Maybe so will the play.'

'Oh, shut up, silly. Everything's going to be just fine.' But she didn't believe him, and after pacing nervously around her hotel suite and snapping at Alexander, she finally arrived at the theatre at seven fifteen. They had more than an hour until curtain but she had to be there. She couldn't stand being anywhere else. She stood in the wings, she walked into the theatre, she took a seat, she got up and walked down the aisle, she went back to the wings, then into the alley, back to the stage, back to the seat she had abandoned to roam down the aisle. Finally she decided to walk around the block and didn't give a damn if she got mugged, which she did not. She waited until the last of the stragglers were in the theatre, and then she walked in and slipped into an empty seat in the back row. That way if she couldn't bear the tension, she could always leave without making the rest of the audience think that someone hated it so much, they had left.

Bettina didn't see Ollie in the theatre, and when it was over, she didn't even want a ride in Ivo's car. She avoided everyone and left as quickly as she was able, hailed a cab, and went back to her hotel. She had the switchboard tell everyone she was already sleeping, and she sat in a chair all night, waiting to hear the elevator open and the man drop the morning paper outside her door. At four thirty she heard it and she leaped to her feet and ran to the door. Panicking, she tore open the paper, she had to see it . . . had to . . . what had he written . . . what had he . . . ? She read it over and over and over as tears poured slowly down her face. Trembling, she went to the phone and dialled his number, and shouting and laughing and crying, she called him names.

'You bastard . . . oh, Ollie . . . I love you . . . did you like it? I mean really like it? Oh, God, Ollie . . . did you?'

'You're a maniac, Daniels, do you know that? Crazy! Stark-staring crazy! It's four thirty in the morning and I tried to get you all night . . . now she calls me, now after I finally gave up and went to bed.'

'But I had to wait to see the paper.'

'You moron, I could have read you my review at eleven fifteen last night.'

'I couldn't have stood it. What if you had hated it?'

'I couldn't have hated it, you silly ass. It's brilliant. Absolutely brilliant!'

'I know.' She absolutely glowed at him, purring. 'I read the review.'

But he was laughing and happy, and he promised to meet her for breakfast in a few hours, whenever she called him after she got some sleep. But before she took off her clothes and went to bed, she asked the operator for another number. Maybe at that hour she'd find him at home, or he'd be caught unawares and he'd answer the phone. But still there was no answer. And she had wanted so badly to tell John that the play was a success. Instead she decided to call Seth and Mary, and they were thrilled for her as they

241

sat over breakfast with their kids. It was a quarter to eight in the morning on the West coast. And at last, as the sun came up, Bettina settled into her own bed, with a broad grin on her face and the newspaper spread out all over the bed.

Chapter 39

'So, kid, what now? Now that you're on the road to fame.'
Ollie grinned at her happily over poached eggs and a bottle
of champagne. They had met in Bettina's hotel for their late
breakfast and she still looked stunned and worn out and
elated and shocked all at the same time.

'I don't know. I guess I'll stick around for a couple of
weeks and make sure that everything goes smoothly, and
then I'll go home. I told John I'd be back for Christmas, and
I guess I will.' But now she looked a little vague. She had had
no contact with him for three months and she was seriously
worried about him, and about what she would tell the child.

'And professionally, Bettina? Any other stroke of genius in
mind?'

'I don't know yet.' She grinned at him slowly. 'I've been
playing with an idea lately, but it hasn't taken hold in my
head.'

'When it does, can I read it?' He looked almost as happy
as she.

'Sure. Would you really want to?'

'I'd love it.' And then, as she looked at him she realised
that she was going to miss him terribly when she left. She had
gotten used to their long chatty exchanges, their phone calls
every day, their frequent lunches, their occasional dinners
with Ivo and, whenever possible, alone. He had become
almost like her brother. And leaving him was going to be like
leaving home. 'What are you looking so morbid about all of
a sudden?' He had seen the look of anguish on her face.

'I was just thinking of leaving you when I go home.'

'Don't get yourself too worked up about it, Bettina. You'll
be back here before you know it, and you'll probably see me
more than you'll want to. I go back and forth to the Coast
several times a year.'

243

'Good.' She smiled at him a little more happily. 'By the way do you want to have dinner with me and Ivo, my last night in New York?'

'I'd love to. Where are we going?'

'Does it matter?' She grinned at him.

'No, but I figure it'll be some place wonderful.'

'With Ivo it always is.'

And it was. It was La Côte Basque, at his favourite table, and the dinner he had specially ordered was superb. There were quenelles to begin with, after they had had champagne and caviar; there was a delicate hearts of palm salad, filet mignon, wonderful little mushrooms flown in fresh from France, and for dessert a soufflé Grand Marnier. The three of them ate with a passion, and then sat back to enjoy coffee and an after-dinner liqueur.

'So, little one, you leave us.' He looked at her with a gentle smile.

'Not for very long though, Ivo. I'll probably be back soon.'

'I hope so.' But as Ollie walked her back to her hotel she thought Ivo had looked oddly pensive.

She turned to look at her friend then. 'Did you hear what he said to me when he kissed me goodbye? "Fly well, little bird." And then he just kissed me and got into his car.'

'He's probably just tired, and he's probably sad to see you go.' And then he smiled at her slowly. 'So am I.'

She nodded. She hated to leave him too. Hated to leave them both. Suddenly it felt as though she belonged here. She had put her roots back in the sod of New York in the last three months. It was cold, it was dreary, it was crowded, the cabbies were rude, and people never held doors open, but there was a bustle, a texture, an excitement. It was going to be tough to match in Mill Valley, waiting for Alexander to come home from school. Even Alexander had felt it, and except to see his father, he wasn't very anxious to leave.

Ollie took them to the airport, and he waved long and hard as Alexander reluctantly wandered towards the plane.

He blew a kiss to Bettina, and then he left the airport and went home and got roaring drunk. But Bettina didn't have the same luxury. She had to be sober to face John. She hadn't sent him a note to warn him that she was arriving, and she hadn't even warned Mary and Seth. She wanted to surprise everyone. And their bags were filled with Christmas presents for John, Mary, and Seth, and all the kids.

The weather was mild and gentle when they reached the airport. It was five thirty in the afternoon. They found a cab that would take them to Mill Valley and they both got in. Alexander was beginning to get very excited. He was finally going to see his Daddy, after three long months. And he was going to tell him all about New York, and the zoo, and his friends, and what they had done in school. He hopped all over Bettina, and she grinned stoically as he elbowed and kneed her, preparing all that he was going to say.

It seemed forever before they pulled into the familiar drive-way, and Bettina couldn't repress a smile. It did feel good to be home. The driver began to unload their luggage, and Bettina went to open the front door. But when she inserted the key in the lock, she found that her key would no longer fit. She turned it one way, then the other, pushed the door, jiggled the door-knob and then she looked up in astonishment, understanding what had happened. John had changed the locks. It seemed a very childish trick.

In a state of stupefaction Bettina hurried next door. She had paid the driver and told him to just push the bags into the garage. So she took Alexander by the hand and they crossed the backyard. She knocked on Mary's back door.

'Oh, my God! . . . Betty!' She took her quickly into her arms, and then Alexander, who was being loudly welcomed by his friends. 'Oh, have I missed you!' And then she called out behind her. 'Seth! They're back.' He came to the doorway, smiling, and held out his arms. But the warm welcome was quickly over and she looked from one to the other and explained about her key.

'I don't understand it.' And then softly, as they walked

245

into the living-room, she looked over her shoulder and faced them. 'I guess John had the locks changed.'

But Mary was looking unhappy, and Seth finally raised his eyes. 'Betty, sit down, honey. I've got some fairly stiff news.' Oh, God, had something happened? Had something happened to him while she was gone? But why did no one call her? She felt her face go suddenly white. But Seth shook his head slowly. 'It's nothing like that. But as his attorney, I had to respect his confidence. He came to me after you left and he insisted that I not say anything to you. It's been' – he seemed to hesitate awkwardly – 'it's been damn difficult, to tell you the truth.'

'It's all right, Seth. Whatever it is, you can tell me now.'

He nodded slowly, and then looked at Mary before he looked back at her. 'I know. I have to. Betty, he filed for divorce the day after you left.'

'He did? But I never got any papers.'

Seth shook his head firmly. 'You don't have to. Remember when you divorced your ex-husband? In this state it's called a dissolution and all that's required is for one spouse to want out. He did. And that was that.'

'How nice and simple.' She took a deep breath. 'So when is the final decree?'

'I'd have to look it up, but I think it's in about three more months.'

'And he changed the locks on the house?' Now she understood why he never answered her letters or phone calls while she was working on the play.

But Seth was shaking his head again. 'He sold the house, Betty. He's not there any more.'

This time she looked truly shocked. 'But what about our things? My things . . . the things we bought together . . .'

'He left you some boxes, and suitcases with your clothes, and all of Alexander's toys.' She felt her head begin to reel as she listened.

'And Alexander? He's not going to fight me for him?' She was suddenly grateful that she had taken the boy to New

York. What if he had disappeared with Alexander? She would have died.

But now Seth seemed to hesitate before he spoke. 'He – he doesn't want to see the boy again, Betty. He says he's all yours.'

'Oh, my God.' Slowly she stood up and went to the doorway, where she met the eyes of her son.

He looked up at her, his eyes filled with questions. 'Where's Daddy, Mom?'

But she only shook her head slowly. 'He's not here, sweetheart. He went away on a trip.'

'Just like us? To New York?' He looked intrigued and Bettina fought back tears.

'No, darling, not to New York.'

And then he looked at her strangely, as though he knew. 'Are we going back to New York, Mommy?'

'I don't know, sweetheart, maybe. Would you like that?'

He looked at her, smiling broadly. 'Yeah. I was just telling them about the big zoo.' It shocked her that he wasn't more anxious for his father, but maybe it was just as well. And then slowly she turned to face Seth and Mary, with tears in her eyes and a lopsided grin.

'Well, so much for Betty Fields.' But she hadn't been that for three months now. In New York, as a playwright, she had been Bettina Daniels. And maybe, she realised, that was who she should always have been. She looked back at her two friends. 'Can we stay with you for a few days?'

'As long as you like.' And then Mary held out her arms and hugged her. 'And, baby, we're so sorry. He's a fool.' But it wasn't the bird of paradise he had wanted. He had wanted the little grey and brown bird. Secretly Bettina had known it all along.

Chapter 40

Bettina and Alexander left San Francisco the day after Christmas, and after much soul-searching she sent the boxes filled with their possessions ahead to her hotel in New York.

'But I've been here for six years, Mary.'

'I know. But do you really want to stay here now?'

Bettina had thought about it endlessly for the two lonely weeks they were there, and by the time Christmas came, she knew that what Mary was saying was more than just a question of what city she wanted to live in. Everyone she had known in San Francisco was a friend of John's. Suddenly people who had been warm and friendly ignored her completely when they met her on the street. She not only wore the stigma of divorce, but of success.

And so, on the day after Christmas they got on the plane, and Ollie met them at the other end. It was odd, it didn't feel to Bettina as though she had just left home, instead it felt like she was coming back to it as she got off the plane in New York. Ollie swept Alexander into his arms and buried him in the folds of a huge raccoon coat.

'Where did you get that? It's super.' Bettina looked at him with a broad smile.

'My Christmas present to me.' And he had several for Bettina and Alexander in the back seat of the limousine he had rented to take her back to her hotel. It had snowed the day before Christmas, and there were still a few inches of snow along the side of the road.

But as they drove back to the city she had left only two weeks before, she sensed something different about Ollie, something quiet and tense. She waited until Alexander was busy with the teddy bear, the fire truck with the siren, and the set of battery-operated cars on the floor of the limousine, and then she looked over at him quietly.

'Is something wrong?'

Unconvincingly he shook his head. 'How about you, Bettina?'

She shrugged, and then smiled. 'It feels good to be back.'

'Does it?' She nodded. But there was still something sad in her eyes. 'Was it rough out there for you?'

She nodded slowly. 'Kind of. I guess I just didn't expect it. None of it.' She mused for a moment. 'When we got in from the airport, we went to the house, and I thought he had changed the locks.'

'Had he?'

She shook her head grimly. 'No. He had sold the house.'

'Without telling you?' Ollie looked horrified. 'How did he eventually break the news?'

Ruefully Bettina smiled. 'He didn't. My neighbours did.' And then she looked long and hard at Ollie. 'I never spoke to him while we were out there. Apparently he filed for divorce three and a half months ago, as soon as we left for New York.'

'My God . . . and he never told you?' She shook her head. 'What about . . . ?' He nodded his head towards Alexander and she nodded quick understanding.

'He says that's finished too.'

'He won't see him?' He looked deeply shocked.

'He says not.'

'Have you explained that?'

She looked pensive. 'More or less.' And then she sighed softly. 'It was an interesting two weeks. And that was just the bad news. The good news was almost worse. Every time I ran into someone I knew, acquaintances, or old friends, they stomped all over me, either bluntly or with kind of back-handed nasties.' She chuckled softly, relieved to have left it. 'It was a terrible two weeks.'

'And now what?'

'I look for an apartment tomorrow, put Alexander back in school after the Christmas vacation, and I go to work on my new play.'

249

Bettina watched while he stared out the window. At last she touched his arm gently and held his eyes with her own.

'Ollie . . . are you all right?'

He nodded slowly, but he averted his eyes. 'I'm fine.'

'Are you sure?'

This time he chuckled softly. 'Yes, Mother, I am.' And after a moment, 'I'm awfully glad you're back, Bettina. But I'm sorry you had such a hard time.'

'I suppose it was predictable. The only one who didn't predict it was me.'

He nodded slowly. 'I must admit, when he never got in touch with you here, I was afraid of something like that. But I just thought that maybe he was very angry. I figured maybe when he saw you he'd back off and you two would get a fresh start.'

'No such luck.' She looked glum for a moment and then looked back at him again. 'By the way, have you seen Ivo?' He started to say something, and then shook his head. 'I called him the day before Christmas and told him we were coming in. He said he was going to Long Island with friends for Christmas, but he's coming back tonight, and he asked me about lunch tomorrow.' She looked at Ollie happily. 'Want to come?' Again Ollie only shook his head. And he was spared further explanation as they pulled up in front of the hotel. The porter unloaded their bags, they reclaimed their old suite, which had been just vacated, miraculously, by two businessmen from London who had had it since she left.

'It feels just like coming home again, doesn't it?' Alexander had run off to his room, and Jennifer, his sitter, was due to return to them the next morning. Bettina was going to offer her a permanent job with them as soon as they moved. 'Want some dinner, Ollie?'

'No, thanks.'

She ordered a hamburger for Alexander and a small steak for herself, sat down on the long couch and ran a hand through her tousled hair. 'Tomorrow I start to look for an apartment.' But suddenly Ollie sat down next to her with eyes full of gloom.

'Bettina . . .'

'Good heavens, what is it? You look like you just lost your best friend.' Slowly he nodded, his eyes filling with tears. 'Ollie . . . what is it? . . . Ollie?' She reached out to him and he took her into his arms, but as he did so she could feel that he was not seeking comfort, but offering solace to her. 'Ollie?'

'Baby, I didn't want to tell you at the airport, but a terrible thing happened last night.' He held her close and felt her tremble as gently she pushed away.

'Ollie . . . ?' And then she looked at him, horrified, understanding. 'Oh, God . . . they closed my play?' He smiled gently, and then quietly shook his head.

'No, nothing like that.' And then he took a deep breath and took her tiny, frail hand in his. 'Bettina, it's Ivo.' He closed his eyes for only a fraction of a moment. 'He died last night.'

'Ivo?' She jumped to her feet and stared at her friend. 'Don't be silly. I talked to him two days ago, he was going to Long Island. He was – ' And then suddenly, trembling, she sank to the couch and stared at her friend. 'Ivo? . . . Dead?' Her eyes filled with an ocean of tears as she stared, and Ollie pulled her back into his arms where she cried. 'Oh, Ollie, no . . . not Ivo . . . oh, no . . . not Ivo . . . not Ivo . . .' He walked her slowly to the bedroom before Alexander could see her and gently closed the door, then he laid her down on the bed and let her sob. It was like losing her father all over again, almost worse because she was losing a lifelong friend, and he had always been so good to her, better than her father, and she had never stopped loving him, right till the end. 'But I was going to see him for lunch tomorrow, Ollie . . .' She stared at him, childlike.

'I know, babe . . . I know . . .' Gently he stroked her hair as she buried her face again. 'I'm sorry, I'm so sorry . . . I know how you loved him.'

As she glanced down at the floor she saw the newspaper

lying there and noticed Ivo's picture on the front page, with the story. She was glad she hadn't seen it before.

'He was responsible for everything good that ever happened to me,' she said to Ollie as she swung her legs at last over the side of the bed and dried her eyes. 'And now he's gone.'

Chapter 41

The funeral was two days later. Governors, senators, newspaper moguls, socialites, authors, playwrights, movie stars, everyone came. And in the front row was Bettina.

Ollie took her arm as they left the cathedral, and neither of them spoke a word after they got back into the car. She rode, silent and dry eyed, back to the hotel, holding tightly to his hand. She looked ivory-white as she sat there, her perfect features etched in cameo fashion against the grey silhouette of the sky.

'Do you want to come up for a cup of coffee?' She looked bleakly at Ollie, and then turned as he nodded and followed her inside.

But upstairs there was Alexander and she had to at least make the pretence of wearing a smile. And half an hour later after coffee and croissants and Alexander's stories to his mother about the joys of Central Park, the smile was more than just put on. Ollie was relieved to see her looking better.

'Bettina? How about a walk this morning? I think we could both use some air.' And then maybe lunch, and after that coffee at his place. Watching her, he had just decided not to leave her alone. 'How about it? You could put on some slacks, and we could go roam for a while. Sound inviting?'

It didn't really, but she knew he wanted to help her, and she didn't want to hurt his feelings by saying no. 'All right, all right.' She threw up her hands with a small grin.

They rode quietly down in the elevator and ten minutes later they were walking along the edge of the park. Traffic was less frantic than usual because it was Saturday, and now and then a hansom cab clopped slowly by. They wandered along for more than an hour, talking occasionally, and then falling silent for a while, and at last she felt a cosy arm around her and she looked up into his eyes.

'You're a good friend, you know, Ollie. I think that was part of my decision to come back to New York.' And then she hesitated for a moment. 'You and Ivo.' She brushed quickly at a tear with a white-mittened hand. And then softly she spoke again as they waited to cross the street. 'Life will never hand me another man like Ivo.'

Slowly he nodded. 'No, it won't.'

And then hand in hand they walked on. It was almost an hour later when they finally stopped to catch their breath.

'Can I interest you in lunch at the Plaza?' But she shook her head slowly. She didn't feel fancy and festive. She still wanted to be left alone.

'I don't think so, love, but thanks.'

'Too frenzied?' He understood perfectly.

'Kind of.' She smiled.

'How about tea and sandwiches at my place? Does that sound all right?' She brightened at the prospect, nodded, and he quickly hailed a cab.

They hurried up the steps of his brownstone, and he opened the door with his key. He had the garden apartment, and as he filled the kettle with water she took off her jacket and looked out into the tiny garden filled with snow.

'I'd forgotten how pretty this is, Ollie.'

'I like it.' He smiled at her as he started to make their sandwiches.

'I hope I find something as nice as this.'

'You will. It takes a while to find the nice ones, but it's worth the look.' He had a beautiful beam-ceilinged bedroom with a fireplace, a cosy living-room with the same, an old-fashioned kitchen with one brick wall, three wood-panelled ones, a wood floor, and a bread oven, and the garden, which was an unusual bonus in New York.

'How did you find it?' She looked at him happily as he worked.

254

He smiled at her. 'Through the *Mail*, of course. What are you looking for?'

She sighed as she thought of it. 'Something a lot bigger than this, I'm afraid. Like about three bedrooms.'

'Why so many?' He handed her a plate with a handsome sandwich filled with salami, smoked ham, and cheese.

She smiled at him and picked up the sandwich. 'I need a room for Alexander, some place to write, and a room for me.'

He nodded. 'Are you thinking of buying?'

She looked at him in confusion and eventually put down the sandwich and stared at her plate. 'I wish I knew.' And then she looked up at him. 'I don't know what's going to happen, Ollie. Right now I've got all this money from the play. But who knows if that's going to last.' She looked at him soberly and he grinned.

'I can promise you, Bettina, it will.'

'You don't know that.'

'Yes, I do. You wrote a great play.'

'But what if I can't write another one? What if it all stops?'

He rolled his eyes in amusement but Bettina didn't smile. 'You're just like the rest of them, kiddo. All writers seem to live with the same curse. They make a million bucks on their last book, they sit on the bestseller list for six months, and they cry to you about "what about tomorrow", can they still do it, what about the next one, what if . . . and on and on, and you're just like that with your play.'

Slowly she smiled at him. 'I'm not really sure any more, but I think my father was like that too.' And her eyes sobered again. 'But look at him, Ollie. He died without a penny. I don't want that to happen to me.'

'Good, so don't buy seven houses, nine cars, and hire twenty-three servants. Failing that, you should do just fine.' He smiled gently at her. She had told him all about her father's undoing and the four million dollars of debt when he died.

She looked quietly at Ollie, her head tilted to one side.

'You know, Ollie, all my life I've been dependent on men. My father, Ivo, that actor I was married to' – she didn't even like to say his name – 'then John. This is the first time in my life when I haven't been dependent on anyone except me.' She looked up at him with a small comfortable smile. 'I kind of like it.'

He nodded. 'You should, it's a good feeling.'

'Yeah,' she sighed, still smiling, 'and sometimes it's scary too. I've always had someone there, and now for the first time in my life, I don't.' And then more softly, 'I don't even have Ivo any more. All I have is me.'

He looked at her gently. 'And me.'

She touched his hand warmly. 'You've been a good friend. But you know something funny?'

'What?'

'I don't mind having to rely on myself. It scares the hell out of me sometimes, but it's a nice feeling too.'

'Bettina' – he eyed her with candour – 'I hate to tell you this, but I think you've just grown up.'

'Already?' She looked at him and started laughing, and he toasted her with his cup of tea.

'Listen, you're way ahead of the game. I'm nine years older than you are, and I'm not sure I've grown up yet.'

'Sure you have. You've always depended on you. You've never been dependent like I have.'

'Being independent has its drawbacks too.' He looked pensive as he stared into his garden. 'You get so hung up on what you're doing, on where you're going, and how to get there, that you never get too close to anyone else.'

'Why not?' She spoke very softly in the warm, cosy kitchen as he watched her.

'You don't have time. Anyway I was too busy getting important, wanting to be number one at the paper in LA.'

'And now you've almost made it here.' She smiled gently. 'Now what?'

'I haven't made it, Bettina. You know what I wanted? I

wanted to be like Ivo, to be the publisher of a major newspaper in a major town. And you know what's happened? All of a sudden I don't give a damn. I like what I'm doing. I'm enjoying New York, and for the first time in forty-two years, I don't give a shit about tomorrow, I'm just enjoying myself right now, right here.' She smiled at him in answer.

'I know just what you mean.' And as she said it she leaned almost imperceptibly forward, without even knowing she had, and Ollie suddenly moved towards her, and without thinking they kissed for a long, heady time. She pulled away finally, looking startled as she caught her breath. 'How did that happen?' She tried to make light of it, but he wouldn't let her. There was suddenly something very serious in his eyes.

'It's been a long time coming, Bettina.'

She was about to deny it, and then she nodded slowly. 'I guess it has.' And then after a moment, 'I thought . . . I kind of thought . . . we would always be just friends.'

He took her carefully in his arms again. 'We are. But there's a confession I have to make to you, Miss Daniels. It's something I've wanted to tell you for a very long time.' He smiled gently down at her and she smiled.

'Really, Mister Paxton, what's that?'

'That I love you . . . in fact I love you very much.'

'Oh, Ollie.' She buried her face in his chest with a sigh, but he reached under and caught her chin with his finger and gently made her look him in the eye.

'What does that mean? Are you angry?' For a moment he looked almost sad, but she was shaking her head with a look of chagrin.

'No, I'm not angry. How could I be?' Her voice softened still further. 'I love you too. But I thought . . . it just seemed so simple . . . the way it was.'

'It had to be simple then. You were married. Now you're not.'

She nodded, thinking, and then she looked him squarely

257

in the eye. 'I'll never get married again, Oliver. I want you to know that right now.' She looked deadly serious as she told him. 'Do you understand that?' He nodded. 'Can you accept it?'

'I can try.'

'You have a right to get married, you've never done it. You have a right to a wife and kids and all of that stuff. But I've done it, I've had it, I don't ever want that again.'

'What do you want?' He held her loosely in his arms and caressed her with his eyes.

She thought for a long moment. 'Companionship, affection, someone to laugh with and share my life with, someone who respects me and my work and loves my child . . .' She fell silent and their eyes met and held.

It was Ollie who finally broke the silence. 'That's not too much to ask, Bettina.' His voice seemed gentler by the moment as he stroked her soft coppery hair.

She nestled in his hand like a cat near a fire in winter, her eyes sparkling as she looked into his. 'And you, Ollie? What do you want?' Her voice was deliciously husky.

He seemed to hesitate for a long time. 'I want you, Bettina.' And as he said it his hands moved from the brilliant hair that framed her face and began to slowly peel away her clothes. She let herself be unravelled like a ball of twine, until at last she lay there, naked and shimmering, on his bed, a bare expanse of creamy satin beneath his soft, stroking hands. And then like a chorus to a song she had long dreamed of, he said it again and again and again. 'I want you, Bettina . . . my darling . . . I want you . . . my love . . .' And suddenly she felt the flames of her own long forgotten passion engulf her as he rapidly and expertly brought her body back to life. And suddenly she was leaping and surging in his arms, tearing at his clothes, until they lay there together, breathless and hungry, burning with an insatiable desire for each other's love. And at last the fires they had so quickly fanned burned gently to embers and they lay in each other's arms and smiled.

'Happy?' He looked down at her with a tender gleam in his eye that said that she was his now.

'Yes. Very happy.' Her voice was a sleepy whisper as she laced her fingers into his and nestled her head into his neck. 'I love you, Ollie.' It was the smallest and sweetest of whispers, and he closed his eyes and smiled.

He pulled her gently towards him and let his mouth hungrily seek hers once more, and his limbs and his soul and the very essence of his being reached out to her once again.

'Ollie . . .' This time she smiled when he took her. It was their game now. And they were both having fun and enjoying making love to each other at last. 'Is it really supposed to be like that?' She looked at him with a suspicious grin when it was over.

'Like what?' His smile was as mischievous as hers. 'You mean light-hearted?' He was grinning broadly as he reached around and held her behind in both his hands. 'Madame, has anyone told you lately that you have the best-looking fanny in town?'

'Do I!' She grinned wickedly at him. 'Maybe they ought to put that on the marquee of my play . . .' She appeared to ponder the possibility and Oliver laughed and tousled her hair.

'Come here, you . . .' But the hands were gentle even when the words were playful. 'Woman, you can't even begin to imagine how much I love you.' He fell silent for a long moment, and Bettina gazed up at him with a lifetime in her eyes.

She nodded slowly. 'Yes, I can, Ollie . . . oh, yes I can . . .'

'Can you?' He was smiling again. 'How?'

But she wasn't playing now. She reached out and held him with all of her strength, her eyes tightly closed, her heart held out to him as she whispered the words. 'Because I love you with my whole soul.' And as she said it she felt for a moment as though this were her last chance. Her eyes opened then and she looked at Oliver Paxton and smiled as he leaned down and kissed her again.

Chapter 42

Bettina stared at Ollie gloomily in his kitchen as he poured her more tea. They had been spending long hours in his apartment for the past two weeks. She was renting her suite in the hotel by the month now, but Ollie's place still felt more like a home.

'Don't look so cheerful, darling. I promise, I'm honest, hard-working, and very neat.' He waved at the total chaos around them, four days of newspapers, his bathrobe, and Bettina's clothes. 'See?'

'Don't be funny. And that's not the point.'

'Then what is?' He sat down comfortably at the oak table and reached for her hand.

'If we move in together, it's all going to start again, it'll happen. I'll get dependent, you'll want to get married. Now I have to think of Alexander. It's just not right.' She looked miserable and his eyes attempted to console. They had been discussing it all week.

'I understand your concern about Alexander, and I share that concern too. But this doesn't make sense either. You're running back and forth to the hotel, you never have time to work, and it'll be the same damn thing if you get your own apartment. You'll be spending at least half your time here.' He leaned over and kissed her and they both smiled. 'Do you know how much I love you?'

'Tell me.'

'I adore you.' He whispered it softly.

'Goodie.' She giggled and leaned forward to kiss him across the table as she felt his hand slide up her leg. It had been like that since the first time. He was so gentle and funny and easy to be with. He understood her, and her work, and he truly loved Alexander. But best of all, she and Ollie shared a special friendship. She wanted nothing more than

260

to live with him, but she didn't want the same nightmares to happen again. What if he started to resent her work? What if Alexander annoyed him? What if he cheated on her or she on him?

'So? Do we get an apartment together?' He looked at her triumphantly and she groaned.

'Has anyone told you that you're pushy?'

'Frequently. I don't mind it at all.'

'Well, Ollie' – she looked at him firmly – 'I'm just not going to give in.'

'Fine.' He shrugged easily. 'Then get your own apartment, don't get any sleep, stay here till five in the morning, and then rush home so your son doesn't know you were out, but that will mean another bedroom, you know.'

'Why?' She looked puzzled.

'Well, you'll have to have Jennifer living in the way she does at the hotel, but I assume she'll want her own room. You can't just run off and leave Alexander in the middle of the night.'

Bettina looked at him and rolled her eyes. 'Damn you.'

'You know I'm right.'

'Oh, shit . . . well, let me think it over.'

'Certainly, madam. Will five minutes be enough?'

'Oliver Paxton!' She stood up and shouted, but five minutes later he had her back in bed. 'You're impossible!'

Two days later Ollie solved the problem. He arrived at her hotel suite with a broad grin. 'It's perfect, Bettina.' He looked victorious as he entered and Alexander immediately threw himself at the large man's endless legs.

'Stop it, Alexander . . . what is?' Bettina was wearing two pencils in her hair. She was deep at work on the new play.

'I found the perfect apartment.'

She eyed him evilly and sat down on a chair. 'Ollie . . .'

'Now wait a minute, just listen. It's sensational. A friend of mine is going away for six months to LA, and he'll rent us his apartment. It's absolutely splendid, a duplex, four bedrooms, fully furnished, in a fabulous West Side co-op.

The rent is a thousand a month. We can afford it easily. So we take it for six months while he's gone, and try it out. If we like it, we find our own place together at the end of the six months, and if we don't, we each go our separate ways. And if it'll make you less nervous, I'll sub-let my own place while we try it, so you won't feel that you're stuck with me at the end of the six months. Sound reasonable?' He looked at her hopefully and she laughed. 'Besides, how long can you go on paying hotel bills?'

'I don't know if you're a magician or a charlatan, Ollie Paxton, but one thing's for sure, you come up with some damn fine ideas.'

'You like it?' He looked ecstatic.

'I sure do.' She got up and went to him, wrapping her arms around his waist. 'How soon can we take it?'

'I – uh – I'll have to ask him.' But suddenly as she looked at him, she knew the truth.

'Ollie!' She tried to look outraged but she only laughed. 'Did you already take it?'

'I – uh – of course not . . . don't be silly . . .'

But she knew him better than that. 'You did.'

He hung his head sheepishly as she grinned at him. 'I did.'

'We already have it?' She looked at him in vast amusement.

'We do.'

'But what if I'd said no to you?'

'Then I'd have had a very fancy apartment for the next six months.' They both laughed for a minute, and then Bettina's face grew stern.

'I want you to understand something though, Ollie.'

'Yes, ma'am?'

'We share the rent. And I have Alexander, so I'll pay two thirds.'

'Oh, Christ. Women's liberation. Don't you suppose you could let me handle it?'

'No, if that's what you want, then it's no go. Either we share or I won't move in.'

262

'Wonderful. But how about if you just pay half?'

'Two thirds.'

'Half.'

'Two thirds.'

'Half.' And he firmly grabbed her ass. 'And if you say another word about it, Bettina Daniels,' he whispered as Alexander went back to his own room, 'I will rape you right here.' But they were both laughing and still arguing as they hurried to her room and closed the door.

Chapter 43

'Do you like it?' He watched, hopefully.

'It's sensational, are you kidding?' She looked around her with delight and awe. It was one of those rare West Side apartments that was more than just elegant, it was absolutely grand. It was indeed a duplex, and the four comfortable bedrooms were all upstairs, but the living-room and dining-room were downstairs and the ceilings were the height of both floors. Both rooms were wood panelled, and even Ollie could walk in and out of the fireplaces with ease. The windows were long and handsome, and they had a view of Fifth Avenue across the park. There was also a small cosy den, which they could both use for their writing, and upstairs the bedrooms were all lovely and looked terribly French.

'Whose place is this?' She looked around again with fascination and sat on a beautifully sculpted French chair.

'A producer I knew years ago in the movies.'

'What's his name?'

'Bill Hale.'

'I think I've heard of him. Is he famous?' But she knew he would have to be to afford a place like this. When she looked at him, Ollie was grinning, and began reeling off the names of his movies and plays.

'He's not unlike you.'

'Very funny.'

'No, I mean it. He wrote one play and it was a hit, then he did several movies, then several more plays. Now he works mostly out of Hollywood. But it all started with one success, and then he was on his way.' And then he reached out an arm for Bettina and took her in his big loving grip. 'It'll happen to you. I'm just waiting to see it.'

'Well, don't hold your breath. What's he doing in Hollywood now?'

He grinned at her. 'Getting married. That's another thing he has in common with you. I think he's about thirty-seven, and this is his fourth wife.'

'I don't think that's funny, Ollie.' She looked suddenly very annoyed, and he tweaked her nose.

'Don't be so up-tight, Bettina. You can't lose your sense of humour about it.' He said it very gently and the smile returned to her eyes.

'Besides I only had three.'

'I could help you catch up with him.'

She looked over her shoulder despairingly. 'Gee, thanks.' She was on her way out to the kitchen, and when she got there she gasped. He heard her calling him as he was trying to help Alexander drag in a box filled with toys. 'Ollie, come in here!'

'I'm coming . . . just a second . . .' But when he did, he whistled too. The whole kitchen looked like a greenhouse, and there was a closed balcony outside filled with tulips, red, yellow, and pink.

'Isn't it gorgeous?' Bettina looked at him, enchanted. 'I wish we could keep it forever.'

But Ollie only smiled at her. 'I'm sure Bill does too.'

She nodded. 'At least we've got six months.'

But the months sped by amazingly quickly, and she finished her new play in late May. It was about a woman much like Bettina and she had called it *Bird of Paradise*. The title made Ollie smile.

'Do you like it?' She looked at him anxiously as he handed it back to her over breakfast. They were sitting in the kitchen, enjoying the spring sunshine and a bright blue morning sky.

'It's better than the first one.'

'Do you mean it?' He nodded. 'Oh, Ollie!' She threw her arms around his neck. 'I'll have a Xerox copy made and send it to Norton today.'

But as it turned out, he called her before the new play reached his desk.

'How about coming in to see me, Bettina?'

'Sure, Norton, what's up?'

'Oh, there's something I want to discuss with you.'

'Me too. I was just about to send you my new play.'

'Good. Then how about lunch?'

'Today?' She was surprised. He wasn't usually in a hurry, but by lunchtime, she knew why he was. They sat at a quiet table at Twenty-one, eating steak tartare and spinach salad, and Bettina looked at him in amazement as he told her what was on his mind.

'So, that's the offer, Bettina. What do you think of it?'

'I don't know what to say.'

'I do. Congratulations.' He held out a hand. 'I suppose you'll have to go out there. But you could wait a few weeks. They don't want to start getting organised until July.' It was perfect, that was when she and Ollie had to give up the apartment, but she still didn't know what to say. Everything Norton had just told her was still running around in her head. She managed somehow to get through lunch with Norton, and she hurried to the paper to find Ollie, writing his latest review.

'I have to talk to you.' She looked anguished and he was instantly worried.

'Something wrong? Alexander . . . Bettina, tell me . . .'

But she shook her head vaguely. 'No, no, nothing like that. I just had lunch with Norton.' And then she looked at him blankly. 'They want to make a movie of my play.'

'Which play? The new one?' He looked as stunned as she.

'No, the old one.'

But suddenly he was grinning at her. 'Don't worry, they'll wind up doing the new one too.'

'Ollie, stop that! Listen! . . . What am I going to do?'

'Do it of course, you moron. Do they want you to do the screenplay too?' She nodded and he whooped.

266

'Hallelujah, you've made it! This is the big time, baby!' But she wanted to ask him What about you?

And then she looked at him sadly. 'But I'll have to go to Hollywood to do it, Ollie. They're making the movie there.'

'So?' Then that was all it meant to him. Six months of pleasant cohabitation. Now she understood. And she had grown seriously attached to him in the last six months. 'Don't look like that. It's not the end of the world.'

'I know that . . .' She lowered her voice. 'I just thought – '

'What?' He looked puzzled.

'Never mind.'

'No, tell me.' He grabbed her arm, and she raised her eyes.

'Ollie, I have to go out there to do it. And I – I didn't really want to leave you.'

'Who says you have to?' He was speaking to her in a whisper as they stood in the busy room.

'What the hell does that mean?' She was whispering back at him. 'What about your job?'

'Can my job. So I'll quit. So what? It's no big deal.'

'Are you crazy? You're the lead theatre critic, you can't just walk out on that.'

'Oh, really? Well, watch me. I told you six months ago that all those boyhood ambitions of mine didn't mean a damn any more. You're the one with the booming career, and I happen to love you, so I quit and we go.'

She was shaking her head sadly. 'That's not right.'

But he grabbed her arm firmly again. 'Remember that line of your father's about hanging on to a dream?' She nodded and he increased the pressure on her arm. 'This is mine.'

She looked up at him gratefully. 'But what'll you do for work?'

'Don't worry. I'll find something. I can probably even get back my old job.'

'But do you want it?'

He shrugged easily with a smile as he looked at her. 'Why not?'

It startled her that he would give up his job so readily for her, but she was grateful to him too. She had realised in the four months they'd lived together that she was far more ambitious than he. What he had said about his aspirations had been true. All he wanted now was a decent job and a life with a good woman, and maybe eventually some kids. He was marvellous with Alexander and she knew he wanted some of his own.

'So you think I should do it?'

'Are you serious, Bettina? Call Norton this minute and tell him yes.'

But suddenly she hung her head sheepishly and grinned. 'That's what I told him after lunch.'

'Why, you little rascal. How soon are we going?' He lowered his voice as he asked her.

'Mid-July.' He nodded, and she kissed him, and a few minutes later she left.

That evening when he got home, he called his old boss at the LA paper, and two days later they called him back with the offer of a job. It was better than his last one with them, but not as good a spot as he had in New York. For an instant Bettina felt guilty but he was quick to see the look in her eyes. He held her for a long moment as they sat alone in the cosy wood-panelled library and he gently stroked her gold-flecked hair.

'Bettina, even if I couldn't have found something else, I'd have come with you.'

'But, Ollie, it's just not right.' She looked up at him, her eyes filled with worry. 'Your work is just as important as mine.'

'No, it isn't, baby. And we both know that. You have a great career ahead of you, and all I have is a job.'

'But you could have a great career too. You could be like Ivo . . .' Her voice seemed to trail off, and with a small smile Ollie shook his head.

'I don't think so, babe.'

'Why not?'

'Because that's not what I want. I'm forty-three years old, Bettina, and I don't want to knock myself out any more. I don't want to kill myself sitting in an office until eight thirty every night. It's not worth it. I want the good life.' So did she, but she wanted something more too. 'But you're going to make it very big, baby.' She smiled as she listened.

'Think so?' She liked the idea now. It was immensely appealing.

'Yes, I do.'

Chapter 44

At the end of July they reluctantly relinquished the apartment, and two days before Hale returned to take possession of it, Oliver, Bettina, and Alexander flew to LA, where a real estate agent had already lined up a small furnished house.

'Oh, Jesus . . .' Bettina looked around when they got there and grinned. 'I don't know whether to throw up or faint.'

Ollie looked at her, laughing. 'How about both?'

The outside of the house had been painted purple and the inside was mostly pink. There were gold touches and bits of fake leopard, and everywhere were collections of artifacts interspersed with shells. The only advantages it boasted were that it was in Malibu and that it was on the beach. Alexander was enchanted and immediately hopped off the terrace to play in the sand.

'Think you can stand it, Bettina?'

'After what we had in New York, it may be rough. But I guess I'll have to.' And then she looked at him blankly. 'How could they do this to us?'

'Just be grateful it's only for six weeks.' She nodded thankfully and wandered back inside, but in the weeks that followed they hardly had time to notice where they lived. Oliver was busy getting re-established at the paper and Bettina worked twelve and fifteen hours at the studio, for the first few weeks, establishing what would go into the screenplay as opposed to what had been done on the stage. But by the end of August, things began to settle down and Bettina turned her attention to the house. She called the real estate agent and discussed it. She knew what she wanted, but the question was could it be found. One thing was certain, she had had enough of living at the beach, and she was anxious to find something so she could hide there and get to work.

For the first few weeks she was hopeful, and after that she sank back in despair.

'Don't tell me that, Ollie, there's nothing.' She looked at him in desperation, and then barely missed sitting down on a shell. 'And I can't stand this goddamn place any longer. I have to get to work, and I'm losing my mind.' She looked at him desperately, and he held out his arms.

'Take it easy, baby. We'll find something. I promise.' She had re-established her friendship with Mary and Seth and commiserated with Mary over the phone one day about her problem finding a house.

'I'm beginning to lose hope. This place is crazy.'

'You'll find a place, honey. Meanwhile you're the bird of paradise again.' She smiled into the phone. She had seen houses that looked like palazzi with swimming pools indoors and out, places with Grecian statues, and one house with fourteen pink marble baths. But finally she found it, and she returned home with a gleam of victory in her eyes.

'I found it, Ollie. I found it! Wait till you see!'

He did and it was perfect. A beautiful but elegant house way at the back of Beverly Hills. It managed somehow to look both stately and lovely without looking pretentious, a rarity in that part of town. It was a little larger than she had wanted, but it was so pretty, she didn't care. There were five bedrooms upstairs, and a tiny den of her own; downstairs there was a solarium, a living-room, a dining-room, a huge kitchen, and another cosy den. Basically they could use all of it. She would work upstairs and Ollie down, and she had decided to hire someone to help her with Alexander, so one of the bedrooms could be for her, which still left two unused.

'What'll we do with all the bedrooms, kiddo?' Ollie smiled at her as he started the car.

'Just use them as guest rooms, I guess.' And then she looked worried. 'Do you think it's too much house?'

271

'No, I think it's perfect, but I had something in mind when I asked.'

'I already thought of that.' She looked at him proudly. 'The downstairs den is for you.'

But he only laughed softly. 'That wasn't what I meant.'

'It isn't?' She looked startled, and then confused as they drove back to Malibu. 'Then what did you mean?'

For a moment he seemed to hesitate, and then quietly he pulled the car off the road. He looked at her seriously for a long moment, and then he told her what had been on his mind for so long. 'Bettina, I'd like us to have a baby.'

'Are you serious?' But it was easy to see that he was.

'Yes, I am.'

'Now?' But she had to do the movie . . . and what if they put on her new play?

'I know, you're thinking about your work. But you said that you felt well when you were pregnant with Alexander. You could just write this screenplay while you're pregnant, and then I'll take care of it, and if we had to, we could hire a nurse.'

'Is that fair to the baby?'

'I don't know. But I'll tell you one thing' – he looked at her in dead earnest – 'I'd give that child all I have. Every moment, every scrap of laughter, every joy, every hour that I had to share.'

'It means that much to you?' He nodded and she felt the pain of regret slice through her, but she slowly shook her head.

'Why? Because of your work?'

She sighed softly and shook her head. 'No. I could probably manage that.'

'Then what?' He pressed her, his desire for a child urging him on.

'No.' She shook her head again, and then she faced him squarely. 'No one is ever going to make me go through that again.' For a long moment there was silence, and then gently he reached out and took her hand. He remembered the horror story she had told him only once.

'You wouldn't have to go through that, Bettina. I'd never let anyone do something like that to you again.' But she remembered too well what John had said. He was going to be there for her too.

'I'm sorry, Ollie. I can't. I thought I made that clear to you in the beginning.' She sighed as he started the car.

'You did. But I just didn't realise how much it would bother me.' He looked over at her with a half-hearted smile. He was hurt by her answer and he would be for a long time. 'You're a hell of a woman, Bettina, and there's nothing in this world I want more than your child.' She felt like a beast but there was nothing she could say as they drove home. Eventually the talk turned to the new house, and the next day she put in a bid. A week later it was theirs.

'A little expensive,' as she said to Mary over the phone, 'but wait till you see it, it's gorgeous and we love it. We've decided to stay out here.'

Mary was happy for her. Whatever she did. 'How's Ollie doing with his new job?'

'Actually it's his old job, but he likes it.' And there was a silence, as a shadow crossed Bettina's eyes. She hesitated for a moment, and then she sat down in the kitchen, the phone resting on her shoulder. She was alone in the house in Malibu for the morning, and she looked sadly out at the beach. 'Mary, I've got a problem.'

'What is it, love?'

'It's Ollie.' Mary frowned as she listened. 'He wants a kid.'

'And you don't.'

'That is the understatement of the year.'

'Why? Your career?' Mary didn't sound judgemental about it. She would have understood.

'No, it's not that, it's – '

'Don't tell me, McCarney.' Mary said it and almost snarled. But Bettina had to laugh.

'Jesus, I think you hate him more than I do.'

'I do.' And then her voice softened. 'But that's no reason not to have a baby. I told you five years ago it would never be like that again. Or, Jesus, Betty, even if it turned out to be a disaster, with a decent doctor he'd give you a spinal and a bunch of shots, you wouldn't even know what hit you; you'd be punchy and numb and the next thing you'd know you'd have a brand-new baby in your arms.' Bettina smiled as she listened.

'You make it sound nice.'

'It *is* nice.'

'I know. I love Alexander, and I know I'd love Ollie's child, but I just . . . oh, Christ, Mary. I couldn't . . .'

'I'll make a deal with you. What you do about this is your business, but if you get pregnant, I'll come down and be with you for the birth.'

'As a nurse?' Bettina sounded intrigued.

'Either way. As a nurse or a buddy. Whatever you want, and whatever the doctor says. I'd probably be more useful to you as a buddy, but whatever you like. And you could have Ollie with you. You know even in five years a lot of things have changed. With all this talk about babies, you two thinking about getting married?'

'Hell, no.' Bettina laughed.

'I didn't think so, but I just wondered.'

'That one, at least, he's given up.'

'Then maybe he'll give this one up too.'

'Maybe.' But Bettina didn't think so, and she wasn't totally sure that she wanted him to give it up. She had just turned thirty-four, and if she was ever going to have another baby, it was time.

Chapter 45

They moved out of the purple beach house a month after their six-week lease had expired and they moved into their lovely new stone one, and for a little while they lived with empty halls. But Ivo had left Bettina all of his furniture from the apartment in New York, so she called the place where it was in storage and had it sent out to the Coast. Then she and Ollie did some shopping, went to some auctions, bought some curtains, and spent a whole day picking out rugs. And three weeks later the place was off to a good beginning. Ollie's things had arrived from the little apartment he'd given up in New York.

He never again mentioned the baby, but Bettina thought of it as she closed the larger of the two extra rooms. She didn't have time to spend turning them into guest rooms, she had to sit down and get to work on the movie script of her play. It seemed to take forever, and four months later she was still buried beneath a mountain of notes, and changes, and rough drafts in her little sun-filled room. It jutted straight out from their bedroom, and Ollie could hear her typing late at night as he drifted off to sleep. But it wasn't till after Christmas that he noticed how tired she looked.

'You feeling okay?'

'Yeah. Fine. Why?' She looked surprised.

'I don't know. You look lousy.'

'Gee, darling, thank you.' And then she grinned at him. 'What do you expect from me? I'm working my ass off on this damn thing.'

'How's it coming?'

She sighed deeply and let herself fall into a comfortable chair. 'I don't know. I think I'm almost finished, but I won't admit it to myself. I keep playing with it and playing with it, until I get it right.'

'Have you shown it to anyone?' She shook her head. 'Maybe you should.'

'I'm afraid they won't understand what I'm doing.'

'That's their business, baby. Why not try it?'

She nodded slowly. 'Maybe I will.'

Two weeks later she took his advice and gave it to Norton and the producers. They congratulated her on the completed script. But instead of looking better, she was looking worse.

'How about going to the doctor?'

'I don't need one. All I need is sleep.' And apparently she was right. For the next five days she barely came out from between the covers, not even to eat.

'Are you that exhausted?' He looked frankly worried, but he had to admit that she had worked like a demon for four and a half months.

She nodded. 'More so. Every time I wake up, all I want to do is go back to sleep.'

But two days later he got nervous and insisted that she go to the doctor. He made the appointment for her, and she grumbled mightily when he picked her up and took her there after work.

'What's the big deal about going to the doctor?'

'I don't need one.' He had also noticed that she was snappish, and she hardly ever ate. 'I'm just tired.'

'Well, maybe he can do something to improve your mood.' But she no longer laughed at his humour, and when she went into the doctor's office, for a moment Ollie had thought she was near tears. When she came out of the office, he was sure of it, and she didn't say a word. 'Well?'

'I'm fine.'

'Terrific. What made him decide that? Your charming disposition or the healthy glow in your eyes?'

'I don't think you're amusing. Can't you just leave me alone?' But when they walked into the house, he grabbed her arm and pulled her into the downstairs study so they could be alone.

'I've had enough of this bullshit, Bettina. I want to know what the hell is going on.'

'Nothing.' But as she looked at him her lip trembled and her eyes filled with tears. 'Nothing! Okay?'

'No, not okay. You're lying. Now what did he say?' She started to turn away and he grabbed at her arm. 'Bettina . . . baby . . . please . . .' But she only closed her eyes and shook her head.

'Just leave me alone.' Slowly he turned her towards him. Maybe it was something awful. A tremor ran through him as he tried to hide from the thought. He couldn't bear to lose her. His life would never be the same.

'Bettina?' Now his voice trembled too, but at last she faced him, the tears streaming from her eyes.

'I'm three and a half months pregnant, Ollie.' And then, gulping, 'I was so wrapped up in that damn screenplay that I never noticed. All I did was work day and night, and I never thought . . .' She cried harder. 'I can't even have an abortion. I'm two weeks too late.'

He looked at her, momentarily in shock. 'Would you have wanted one?'

But she only stared at him. 'What does that matter now? I have no choice.' And then, wrenching free from his grip on her, she ran from the room. A moment later he heard the door to their bedroom slam shut, and Alexander came running down the stairs.

'What's wrong with Mommy?'

'She's just tired.'

But Alexander rolled his eyes in irritation. 'Still?'

'Yeah, tiger, still.'

'Okay, want to come play?' But Ollie was feeling distracted and he shook his head vaguely. All he wanted was to be alone.

'How about later?'

The boy looked disgruntled. 'But later I have to go to bed.'

'In that case' – Oliver stooped to give him a warm hug –

'you're just going to have to excuse me. Shall I give you a rain check?' The boy nodded happily. That was one of the things he loved best. With a flourish Ollie took out paper and pen and gave him a rain check. 'Will that do it?'

'You bet.'

As Alexander left the room to find his babysitter, Ollie sank slowly into a chair. He was still stunned about what Bettina had said about an abortion. Would she really have done it? Would she have told him? How could she? But he forced himself to understand that that wasn't what was happening. She was having his baby . . . his baby . . . He found himself smiling slowly, and then frowning again, agonised about her. What if it was as bad as the last time? What if she never forgave him? How could he do that to her? He felt himself begin to panic, and then almost without thinking, he looked for her phone book and dialled the number in Mill Valley. They hardly knew each other, but he knew that she would help.

'Mary? This is Oliver Paxton in Los Angeles.'

'Ollie?' There was a moment of silence. 'Is something wrong?'

'I . . . no . . . that is . . . yes.' And then, with a sigh, he told her the whole tale. 'I don't even know why I'm calling except that . . . oh, Christ, I don't know, Mary, you're a nurse, you're a friend . . . you were there last time . . . oh, Jesus, do you think it'll kill her? . . . I don't know what to say. She's hysterical. I have never seen her so upset.'

Mary nodded as she listened. 'She has a right to be.'

'Was it as bad as she remembers?'

'No. It was probably considerably worse.'

'Oh, my God.' And then, hating himself for the words, he grabbed at the only straw. 'Can't they do an abortion if she's three and a half months pregnant?'

'If they have to, but it's fairly dangerous.' And then after a moment, 'Is that what you really want?'

'It's what she wants. She said so.' He sounded near tears.

'She's just frightened.' And then slowly she told him what

it had been like. It almost made him squirm. 'She might have had a hard time anyway, but in essence it was all because of the doctor. He made it about as bad as it could get.'

'Does she know that?'

'In her head, yes. In her gut, no. She's panic-stricken about it. I know. We've discussed it before. She decided right then she'd never have another one. And if I'd gone through what she did, I'd have made that decision too. But, Ollie, this time it will be entirely different.'

'How do you know that?'

'Any doctor can tell you that. In fact hers probably did.'

'She doesn't even have an obstetrician yet.'

'Well, for God's sake, make sure she gets the right one. Have her talk to other women, other doctors, check the guy out in every way you can. Ollie, it's important. She shouldn't have to go through that again.'

'She won't.' He sighed softly into the phone. 'And, Mary, thank you. I'm sorry to bother you with our problems.'

'Don't be silly.' And then, with a slow smile, 'And Ollie . . . I'm so glad.'

He sighed again. 'So am I. But, God, I hate to put her through this.'

'She'll calm down in a while. Just get her a decent doctor.'

He took care of that the moment he hung up the phone. He called four of his close friends at the paper, who had recently had kids, or at least in the last few years. And miraculously three of the women had had the same doctor, and they all thought he was a dream. He hastily wrote the man's name down on a piece of paper, called information, and nervously dialled. Three minutes later he had him on the line.

'Doctor Salbert, my name is Oliver Paxton . . .' Laboriously he told him his tale.

'Just bring her in in the morning. Say around ten thirty?'

'Fine. But what'll I do in the meantime?'

The doctor chuckled. 'Give her a stiff drink.'

'That won't hurt the baby?'

'Not if she just drinks one or two.'

'What about champagne?' Oliver had never felt so ruffled and nervous, but the doctor only smiled.

'That'll be fine. See you tomorrow.'

'Absolutely . . . and thank you . . .' He hung up the phone and ran out the door.

'Where are you going?' Alexander called after him.

'I'll be right back.' And he was, with a huge bottle of chilled vintage French champagne. Five minutes later he had put the bottle, two glasses, and some peanuts on a large tray and he was knocking softly on their bedroom door.

'Yeah?' He could hear Bettina's muffled voice within.

'Can I come in?'

'No.'

'Good.' He opened the door gently. 'I love feeling welcome.'

'Oh, Jesus.' She rolled over in bed when she saw the champagne. 'This is not a celebration, Ollie.'

'Mind your own business, Daniels. I'll welcome my kid into this world any way I like. Besides which' – he put the tray down and looked down warmly at her – 'I happen to be madly in love with the kid's mother.' He sat down next to her and gently stroked her hair, but she pulled away.

'Don't . . . I'm not in the mood.'

But he just lay there and watched her, a lifetime of loving in his eyes. 'Baby, I know what you're feeling. I talked to Mary, and I understand what a nightmare it must have been. But it won't be like that again. Never, ever, I swear it.'

'You called Mary?' She looked at him with surprise and sudden suspicion. 'Why did you do that?'

'Because I love you, and I was worried, and I don't want you to be scared.' And suddenly the way he said it brought fresh tears to her eyes.

'Oh, Ollie, I love you . . . oh, darling . . .' She sobbed in his arms.

'It's going to be just fine.'

'You promise?' She looked like a little girl and he smiled.

'I promise. And tomorrow we're going to see a doctor that everyone loves.'

'You found me a doctor too?' She looked stunned.

'Of course, I'm terrific. Hadn't you noticed that before?'

'Yeah . . . as a matter of fact I had . . . How did you find this doctor?' She was smiling at him and she leaned over to kiss his ear.

'I asked some friends whose wives just had babies, and then I called him. He sounds nice.'

'What did he say?'

'That you should drink some champagne.' He sat up grinning. 'Doctor's orders.' He opened the bottle and handed her a glass of the sparkling wine.

'It won't hurt the baby?' She looked dubious as she held the glass and he smiled. John had forbidden her to drink while she was expecting Alexander.

'No, darling, it won't hurt the baby.' And the he looked at her, glad that she cared. 'It's going to be a lovely baby, Bettina.'

'How do you know that?' She was smiling broadly, a look of relief slowly coming to her eyes.

'Because it's ours.'

Chapter 46

'Hey, fatso, it's for you!' Ollie waved to her from the doorway as she played with Alexander in the backyard. She had just bought him a new set of swings, and with her enormous belly in front of her she was pushing him as high as she could.

'I'll be back in a minute, darling.' As best she could, she hurried to the kitchen door with a look of disapproval for Ollie. 'Don't call me that, you big-mouthed giant. As it so happens, I've only gained fourteen pounds.'

'You sure that guy knows how to read the scale?' But the doctor he had found her could do more than that. In the four months Bettina had been seeing him, he had established a relationship based on trust and confidence, and she was actually beginning to be less panicked by the birth.

'Never mind. Who's on the phone?'

'Norton.'

'What's he want?'

'I don't know. Ask him.'

She took the phone from him and they exchanged a friendly kiss. Their relationship was filled with joking and teasing. Ollie was ecstatic about the baby, and he was infinitely protective of her. Even Alexander had decided that maybe it wouldn't be bad after all, as long as it wasn't a girl.

'What?' Bettina was staring in disbelief at the phone.

Ollie glanced over at her, trying to mouth questions, but she shook her head and quickly turned her back. It seemed hours before she was finally off the phone. 'Well, what was it? Don't keep me in suspense.'

She sat down, looking pale. 'They're going to do my second play. Not only are they going to do it, but he already has a movie deal.'

'And you're surprised? I told you that months ago. The

only thing that surprises me is that it took this long.' It had taken almost a year to sell her second play. And then he looked suddenly worried. 'When do they want to start?'

She looked at Oliver in amusement. 'They had to be reasonable about it. Norton told them I was pregnant, so it's not for a while.'

'What does that mean?'

'October.' The baby was due in July. 'The contract says I only have to be in New York for three months.' And then she looked worried. 'Can you take a leave of absence for that long?'

'If I have to.' He didn't look concerned. 'Can we take a baby that young to New York?'

'Sure. It'll be two months old.'

'Not "it", "she",' he corrected. He kept insisting that he wanted a girl. He kept looking at Alexander proudly, saying that he already had a son. It was one of the reasons why he still wanted to get married, so he could adopt Alexander and give him his name. But Bettina was still firm in her refusal.

'It's more fun this way, we all have our own names, Daniels, Paxton, and Fields.'

'It sounds like a law firm.' But she wasn't moved.

Now she sat staring for a moment, thinking of her play, and Oliver smiled at her. 'How soon will they want to start work on the movie?'

'After Christmas. And figure it'll take six months, so that will bring me through June. All in all, it'll be about nine months of work.'

But he still looked worried. 'That won't be too much for you right after the baby?'

'It won't be "right" after. I'll have two months to rest. Believe me, afterwards isn't the hard part.' She still had some fears. But they had gone to classes together and they shared each session at the doctor. Ollie had waited too long for this event to miss even a moment of it now. At forty-four, he called it the event of his life.

Bettina found herself dividing her excitement between the

baby and the new play. It was only in the last month of her pregnancy that her excitement about the play was almost obscured. It seemed as though all she wanted to do was be with Ollie and sit peacefully in the shade, watching Alexander play. She went to bed early, she ate well, she read a little, but it was as though her mind was totally at rest. She didn't want to face any fresh challenges, didn't want to speak to Norton, or worry about making deals. Instead she was preparing for something very important that took all of her concentration. It seemed to absorb her whole life.

Two days before her due date Mary came down from San Francisco by plane. She had left all of the kids with her mother, and Seth had gone camping with a friend.

'Believe me, I'd much rather be here than out camping. So' – she looked at Bettina happily – 'what's been happening with you?'

'Absolutely nothing. I've turned into a vegetable. I may never write another play.' But she didn't even give a damn. All she could think about was the baby and the nursery. She wasn't even that concerned with Oliver any more. Just with her belly and the soon-to-be child. It was an oddly self-centred existence, and Ollie understood it, because the doctor had warned him that it was like that at the end.

'What does the doctor say?'

'Nothing. Just that it could be any day. I don't suppose it'll come on my due date though.'

'Why not?'

'Things just don't happen like that.'

'Sure they do.' Mary giggled as the three of them got in the car. 'What you have to do is plan something fancy, like a nice evening, dinner somewhere or an evening at the theatre, then you can count on it happening that night.' The three of them laughed at the thought, but Ollie decided that he liked the idea.

'How about dinner at the Bistro?'

'On my due date?' Bettina looked appalled. 'What if something happens?'

284

'If you ruin their carpet, then we never go back.' He chuckled and Bettina made a face. But he insisted when they got back to the house that he make a reservation for the following night.

'Oh, Jesus.' Bettina looked at him nervously and took Mary upstairs to unpack her bags. The deal they had with the doctor was that she would be at the delivery, just as a friend. But he was amenable to as many observers as they wanted, within reason. 'Just no small children or large dogs.'

So the following evening the three of them trooped out to the Bistro to eat. It was as lovely as ever, with soft lighting, cut-glass panels, and elegant decor. Bettina looked radiant, in a floating white summer dress, with a gardenia tucked behind one ear.

'You look very exotic, Miss Daniels.' And then he whispered softly, 'I love you too.'

She smiled and reached for his hand under the table, whispering the same thing. But it wasn't until they had ordered that Mary noticed an odd look on her face. At first she said nothing, but when it happened again five minutes later, she looked across the table and caught her eye.

'Was I right, Betty?'

'You might have been.'

Oliver didn't hear them. He was ordering the wine. 'Well, ladies? Everybody happy?'

'Absolutely.' Mary was quick to answer and Bettina signalled her quickly. She didn't want to say anything yet. But when the dinner came, she only picked at her food. She didn't want to overdo it, if she really was in labour she wanted to keep it light.

'You didn't eat anything, baby. You feeling okay?' He leaned towards her again as they waited for dessert.

But she smiled at him brightly. 'Not bad, for a broad about to have a kid.'

'When?' He looked at her blankly. 'Now?' He looked suddenly panicked and Bettina laughed.

'Not this minute, I hope, but in a while. I started having pains just before dinner, but I wasn't sure.'

'And now you are?' He quickly grabbed her arm and she laughed.

'Will you stop that, Ollie? I'm fine. Have dessert and coffee, and then we can go home and call the doctor. Relax.'

But it was impossible, and before the coffee had come, she was having trouble relaxing too. As they had the first time, the pains started to crowd her very quickly and grew rapidly intense.

Mary was timing contractions as they stood on the sidewalk, Bettina leaning heavily against Ollie, and she nodded her head. 'We'd better take you to the hospital, Betty. You may not have time to go home.'

'I should be so lucky.' She smiled softly, but from the look in her eyes Ollie knew she was in pain, and suddenly he felt panic clutch him. What if this time was as bad as the first? But Mary saw what was happening to him and grabbed his arm firmly just before she got into the car. Bettina was already lying down on the back seat.

'She's going to be fine, Ollie. Take it easy. She's okay.'

'Suddenly I couldn't help thinking – '

'She's probably thinking the same thing. But it's going to be fine.' He nodded and Mary slid quickly into the car. 'How's it going, Betty?'

'The same.' And then a moment later as Ollie moved the car away from the kerb: 'I'm having another one.'

He looked at Mary in terror. 'Should I stop?'

'Christ, no.' And with that the two women started laughing. Suddenly Bettina was no longer laughing, and by the time they got to the hospital, she no longer wanted to talk.

A nurse hurried away to call her doctor as two others ushered her gently into a small sterile-looking room. For a moment Bettina looked at Mary with a grim look in her eyes.

'I thought you said things had changed.' It was a room

286

just like the one where she had spent fourteen agonising hours strapped down while she screamed.

'Take it easy, Betty.' Slowly she helped her take off her clothes, but they had to stop constantly for the pains. And at last, as she held on tightly to Ollie, they helped her lie down.

'You okay, babe?' Suddenly he felt helpless and frightened, all he knew was that if they hurt her or his baby, he would kill them. He knew that for a fact. But slowly she smiled at him, holding tightly to his hand.

'I'm fine.'

'Are you sure?' She nodded, and then gulped as she felt another pain coming on. But this time Ollie remembered what they had learned together, and he coached her as she breathed. When it was over, she looked at him in amazement with a small smile.

'You know, it works?'

'Good.' He looked immensely proud and the next time they did it again. By the time the doctor joined them, everything was in control.

He told her that she was doing beautifully, and only the brief examination reminded her for a moment of the past, but there was nothing else he could do. At least this time no one had tied her down. The nurses were gentle and pleasant, the doctor was smiling, and Mary was somewhere in a corner of the room. Bettina felt surrounded by people who cared about what was happening to her, and through it all Ollie was with her, holding her hand, helping her breathe, and helping her to keep control.

Half an hour later the pains got harder and for a few minutes Bettina didn't know if she could go on. Her breath caught strangely, she felt herself trembling, she felt sick to her stomach, and she was suddenly violently cold. Ollie looked nervously at Mary, who was sharing a knowing look with another nurse. Bettina was in transition, and they both knew that this would be the worst. Half an hour later she clutched desperately at Ollie's arm and started to cry.

'I can't . . . Ollie . . . can't . . . no!' She cried harder as another pain came, and then screamed as the doctor examined her with his hand.

'She's at nine.' He looked pleased, and then suddenly he was encouraging her too. 'Just a few more minutes, Bettina. Come on . . . you can do it . . . you're doing great . . . come on . . .' As sweat dripped relentlessly down Ollie's sides, somehow they talked her on, and fifteen minutes later the doctor nodded and suddenly everyone around them began to run.

'Ollie . . . oh, Ollie . . .' She was holding on to him desperately and Mary saw that she was starting to push; it was time. They got her on to the delivery room table, and she grabbed willingly at the handles on either side.

'Do I have to have stirrups?' She looked at the doctor desperately, and he smiled.

'No, you don't.' He had a nurse on each side help with her legs and instructed Ollie to support her under her shoulders, and suddenly all she wanted to do was push. She had the feeling that she was climbing a mountain, shoving boulders out of her path with her nose, and now and then it all got too much for her and she slid a little way back down the hill. But all their voices were mingling, encouraging her and spurring her on, and then suddenly, with a last gasp and hard push, Ollie felt her whole body grow stiff as she strained and between her legs a little red face appeared and gave a wail. He looked at it in amazement, still holding her shoulders in his hands.

'My God, it's a baby!' And then everyone laughed with relief. Two more pushes and the rest of their daughter had appeared.

'Oh, Ollie . . . oh, Ollie, she's so pretty!' She was laughing and smiling, and this time she was crying with joy, and Ollie and Mary were too. Only the doctor was dry-eyed but he looked as happy as they.

Half an hour later Bettina was in a room with the baby, and Ollie was still shaken by what he'd seen. His wife looked calm and unruffled, and proud of what she'd done. The whole birth had taken less than two hours, and she looked at them as she held the baby and grinned.

'You know what? I'm starving.' Mary looked at her and laughed.

'I always was too.'

But Oliver could only sit and stare in rapt fascination at his daughter. 'I think you're both disgusting. How can you eat at a time like this?' But she did, she ate two roast beef sandwiches, a milk shake, and a doughnut. 'You're a monster!' He laughed at her as he watched her devour the meal. But his eyes had never been as tender, and at last she held out a hand to him with a small gentle smile.

'I love you, Ollie. I couldn't have done it without you. A couple of times I thought I was giving out.'

'I knew you never would.' But once or twice he had been frightened too, only because it had seemed so painful and so much hard work, but there she sat less than an hour later, her face washed, her eyes bright, her hair combed. It was all a little hard to absorb. Mary had gone downstairs for a cup of coffee, and to leave them alone. 'You were wonderful, darling. I was so proud.' They watched each other in endless, mutual admiration, and for an instant he wanted to ask her to marry him. But he knew better. And even then, he didn't dare. They had already chosen the name for the baby. Antonia Daniels Paxton. And that was enough.

Chapter 47

'Alexander, what do you think of your sister?' His mother looked at him in some amusement as he shrugged. She and the baby had been home for two days.

'Pretty cute, for a girl.' He had survived his initial disappointment, after Bettina had let him hold her.

'Boy, is she small!' But he kind of liked her, and he handed her back with a smile. And then later, when he was alone with his mother, he let one thing slip. 'I'm sure glad you were married to my Dad when I was a kid.'

'Are you? Why?' Bettina looked at him curiously, wondering why he had brought it up.

'Because what if people knew? Maybe they'd say something funny.' He looked at her, frowning. 'I wouldn't like that.' He had just turned six in June.

'I guess not. But would it really matter, darling?'

'It would to me.' Bettina nodded quietly and was lost in thought when Ollie came in to visit his wife and child. The doctor had let them leave the hospital quickly because the birth was so easy, but he wanted her to take it easy at home for about a week.

'What are you looking so serious about, madam?'

'Alexander. He just said a very strange thing.' She told him and he frowned.

'Maybe he's just sensitive about that right now.' He tried to look non-committal but there was a light of hope in his eye.

'What if she is too, six years from now?'

'Then we'll tell people we're married.'

She looked at him oddly. 'Maybe we should.'

'What? Tell people that we're married?' He looked confused, and she shook her head slowly.

'No, get married I mean.'

'You mean like now?' She nodded and he looked stunned. 'Do you mean it?'

She nodded slowly. 'Yes, I think I do.'

'Do you want to?'

She smiled at him more broadly. 'Yes, I want to.'

'Are you sure?'

'*Yes!* For heaven's sake, Ollie – '

'I don't believe it. I never thought I'd see this day.'

'Neither did I. So shut up before I change my mind.' Oliver rushed out of the room and a moment later they were laughing and drinking champagne. Three days later, after duly getting their licence, with Mary and Seth in tow, Bettina and Ollie went downtown, and in City Hall they took their vows.

She looked at the certificate suspiciously afterwards. 'At least it doesn't say you're my fourth husband.'

He grinned, but then he looked at her seriously. 'Bettina, you don't have to be ashamed of anything you've ever done. You've done it all honestly. There's nothing wrong with all of that.' He had always felt that way about her life, and she loved it about him. He made her feel proud.

'Thank you, darling.' And then, hand in hand, they walked down the stairs of City Hall. But when they got home, he was looking pensive and he gently held out a hand.

'There is something else I want to take care of, Mrs Paxton.' But she knew he was only teasing. They had agreed that she would keep her own name.

'What's that, Mister Paxton?'

But he looked serious when he answered. 'I want to adopt Alexander. Think I could?'

'If you mean would John let you, I'm sure of it.' They had never heard from him. She looked tenderly at her husband. 'Alexander would love it.'

Ollie smiled at her slowly. 'So would I. I'll call my lawyer tomorrow.' He did, and four weeks later it was done. They were four Paxtons living under one roof.

Chapter 48

On the first day in October all of the Paxtons flew to New York. Ollie had taken a three-month leave from work, they had found a nurse in New York to help Bettina with the baby, and they put Alexander back in his old New York school. By now he was a seasoned traveller. Ollie was quick to contact his old friends at the *Mail*. The play was hard work for Bettina, but she loved it, and she was fully recovered from Antonia's birth. When at last the play opened, it was another smashing success. They spent Christmas in New York in their suite at the Carlyle, and five days later they headed home.

'Feels good, doesn't it?' Ollie smiled at her happily as they lay in their own bed.

Bettina nodded happily. 'Yeah, it does.'

'I hope you wait awhile before you write another play.'

'Why?' She looked at him in confusion, he was usually so encouraging about her work. But he was laughing on his side of the bed.

'Because I'm tired of freezing my ass off in New York. Can't you stick to movies for a while?'

'For the next six months anyway.' But she hated to tell him that on the plane home she had been thinking about a new play. Her career was booming, and she had recently had several offers just to do films. Most ardent among her pursuers was Bill Hale, the man who had owned the first apartment they had shared in New York, but she had no desire to work with him and had never answered his calls.

'When do you start work on the movie?'

'In three weeks, I think.'

He nodded, and a little while later they were both asleep. And the next morning he went back to work while she re-organised their life. The baby was almost six months old and as cute as could be. Alexander was still on Christmas vacation and had turned out to be a big help with his sister. He loved to hold his little sister, and he was very proficient at feeding her and making her burp. Bettina was smiling, watching him do it at lunchtime, when she heard the phone. The sitter was hovering somewhere in the background, but Bettina nodded with a smile.

'I'll get it.' She picked it up on the third ring, still watching Alexander hold the baby with a smile. 'Yes, this is Mrs Paxton.' And then a long pause and; 'Why?' And then suddenly her face turned grey and she turned around so Alexander couldn't see her cry. 'Fine. I'll be right there.' They called her from the paper, but when she got there, it was already too late. The fire unit was double-parked on the street, and everyone stood around him as he lay lifeless on the floor.

'It was a heart attack, Mrs Paxton.' The editor looked at her mournfully. 'He's gone.' She knelt gently next to him and touched his face. It was still warm.

'Ollie?' She whispered it softly. 'Ollie?' But there was no sound, and the tears poured down her face. She heard someone urge the bystanders to go back to work or at least leave her alone, and she heard someone else say, 'Isn't that Bettina Daniels? . . . Yeah . . . that was his wife . . .' But the name of Bettina Daniels did her no good now. No success on Broadway, no movie, no screenplay, no money, no house in Beverly Hills would bring him back. At forty-five years of age, the man who wanted only the good life, who had wanted only to see the birth of his first child, had died of a heart attack on his office floor. Oliver Paxton was no more. It was the third man she loved that Bettina had lost in this way, and as she watched them bundle him carefully on to a stretcher, she sobbed in anger as much as in pain.

Chapter 49

Mary and Seth Waterston came down for the funeral, and afterwards Mary stayed with Bettina for another four days, while Seth went back to work. But there was very little they said to each other. She helped mostly with the children. Bettina seemed hopelessly withdrawn. She didn't move, she didn't talk, she didn't eat. She just sat and stared. Now and then Mary tried to bring her the baby, but even that didn't help. She just waved her away vaguely and went on sitting there, lost in her own thoughts. She was scarcely better the night before Mary left.

'You can't do this to yourself, Betty.' As always she was honest, but Bettina only stared at her.

'Why not?'

'Because your life's not over. No matter how hard this is.'

But then she looked at her friend angrily. 'Why isn't it, dammit? Why not me instead of him?' And then, sadly, her eyes slowly filled as she stared at nothing. 'He was such a good person.'

'I know.' Mary's eyes were damp too. 'But so are you.'

'When I had the baby' – her lip was trembling violently – 'I couldn't have made it without him.'

'I know, Betty, I know.' She held out her arms and Bettina went into them and seemed to cry out her soul. But she looked better when Mary left the next day.

'What are you going to do now?' Mary looked at her piercingly as they stood at the gate.

Bettina shrugged. 'I have to fulfill my contract. I have to write the screenplay for my second play.'

'And after that?'

'God only knows. They keep hounding me to make other deals. I don't think I will.'

'Will you go back to New York?'

But Bettina shook her head firmly. 'Not for a while. I want to be here.' Mary nodded, and they held each other for a long moment before Bettina kissed her cheek and Mary disappeared on to the plane.

Two weeks later, as promised, she appeared at the studio to begin discussing the initial work she was going to do in adapting her play. The meetings were dry, crisp, and exhausting. But Bettina never seemed to bend. She spoke to no one unless she had to, and at last she took refuge in her house to write the script. It took her less time than expected, and when it was completed, it was even better than they had hoped. They made her a lot of speeches about how gifted she was. And in short order Norton started getting an avalanche of calls. Bettina Daniels's reputation had been made.

'What do you mean you're not working?' He listened in shocked horror when he called her.

'Just what I said. I'm taking six months off.'

'But I thought you wanted to start a new play.'

'Nope. Not a new play. Or a new movie. Absolutely nothing, Norton, they can all go to hell.'

'But Bill Hale's office just – '

'Screw Bill Hale. I don't want to hear it . . .'

'But, Bettina – ' He sounded panicked.

'If I'm that good, they'll wait six months, and if I'm not, then too bad.'

'That isn't the point, but why wait when you can pull in anything you want at this point? Name the price, name the picture. Baby, it's all yours.'

'Then give it *all* back to them. I don't want it.'

He couldn't understand it. 'Why not?'

She sighed softly. 'Norton, five months ago I lost Ollie.' She sighed again. 'The wind has kind of gone out of my sails since then.'

'I know. I understand that. But you can't just sit there. It's not good for you.' But she knew it was also not good for him.

'Maybe it is. Maybe all this bullshit isn't as important as I thought.'

'Oh, Jesus, Bettina, don't do this. Don't do some kind of beachcomber routine. You are about to reach the summit of your life.' But she had already done that. When the baby was born . . . when she married Ivo . . . when she had shared some of her father's great moments . . . there was more than just work and success. But she didn't want to explain to him. Just trying to made her feel tired.

'I don't want to talk about it, Norton. Tell everyone I've left the country for six months and you can't get in touch. And if they bug me, I'll make it a year.'

'Terrific. I'll be sure to tell them. And look, Bettina, if you change your mind, will you call me?'

'Of course, Norton. You know I will.'

But she didn't. She spent the time peacefully with her children. Once she went up to visit Mary and Seth. But she seldom left her house, or her children, and she seemed to have grown oddly quiet since Ollie's death. On Thanksgiving Seth and Mary noticed it when they arrived with the entire brood. It was a lovely family Thanksgiving, but Oliver's absence was sorely felt.

'How's it going, Betty?' Mary watched her closely as they sat in the garden. Something deep down inside her seemed to have changed. She was quieter, colder, more remote, yet she was also more sure of herself. She seemed much older than she had a year before.

Bettina smiled slowly. 'It's going all right. I still miss him though. And there are things I still think about that I wish I could change.'

'Like what?'

'I wish I'd married him sooner. It made him so happy, I don't know why I had to hold out till the end.'

'You were still growing. He understood that.'

'I know he did. Looking back at it, I realise that he understood too much. Everything was for my sake, everything he did was for me. He gave up his job in New

York on the paper, took a leave of absence here so he could come to New York when I did the play. In retrospect it all seems so unfair.' She looked at Mary unhappily as she thought of it, but Mary shook her head.

'He didn't mind it. He told me that once. His career wasn't as important to him as yours is to you.' She didn't dare to tell her that what she needed now was a man as powerful and successful as she. Even her face had changed. There was a kind of angular beauty that commanded attention, and the simplicity of her black wool dress and her jewellery spelled success. She had finally unearthed all her old jewellery, from her father, from Ivo, all of it, and she wore it almost every day. She looked down at the large diamond, smiling now as Mary watched her.

'I don't know. Maybe I'm spending too much time reliving my past.'

'Are you just brooding about it, or do you understand it better than you did?'

'I don't know, Mary.' Her eyes looked dreamy and distant. 'I think I just accept it all better now. It has somehow become a part of me.' Mary watched her with a small smile of pleasure and nodded her head. That was what she had always hoped for. For Bettina to accept who and what she was. The only thing that made her unhappy was to see Bettina living a life behind locked doors.

'Do you see anyone?'

'Only you and the children.'

'Why don't you?'

'I don't want to. Why should I? So they can gossip that they finally met me, the playwright with four husbands . . . Justin Daniels's eccentric daughter . . . ? Who needs it? For a moment I'm a lot happier living like this.'

'I wouldn't exactly call it living, Betty. Would you?'

Bettina shrugged. 'I have what I want.'

'No, you don't. You're a young woman, you deserve more than solitude, Bettina. You deserve people and parties and laughter; you deserve to enjoy your success.'

Bettina smiled at her in answer. 'Just look at all this.' She waved at the beauty of the garden and the house.

'That's not what I mean, Bettina, and you know it. This is pretty, but it isn't a substitute for friends . . .' She hesitated, and then said it, '. . . or a man.' Bettina met her eyes squarely.

'Is that what it's all about, Mary? A man? Is that the whole story? That life isn't complete without a man? Don't you think that maybe I've had enough?'

'At thirty-six? I hope not. What do you have in mind for yourself? To just sit here and give up?'

'What are you suggesting? That I run out and audition all over again? Don't you think four husbands is an outrageously high quota for anyone, or are you suggesting that I try for five?' She looked very angry.

'Maybe.' And then after a moment, 'Why not?'

'Because maybe I don't need one. Maybe I don't want to get married any more.'

But Mary wouldn't be put off that easily. 'If I thought you meant that for the right reasons, I'd get off your back. No one has to get married, Bettina. That isn't the only name of the game. But you can't spend the rest of your life lonely because you're afraid of what people will say. And that's what it's all about with you, isn't it? You think that if you take your shirt off, someone will rush up and brand you with four letter A's. Well, you're wrong, for chrissake. Very much so. I love you, Seth does. I don't give a damn if you get married another twelve times, or if you don't, for that matter. But out there is someone, Bettina, someone who is as strong, as successful, as special, and as splendid as you. You deserve to find him, to let him know you, so you don't sit here for the rest of your life all alone. You don't have to get married if you don't want to, for God's sake, who the hell cares? But don't sit here, Bettina, behind your goddamn fortress doors.' Bettina looked at her sadly, and Mary saw that there were tears in her eyes. She thought that maybe she'd reached her, and when Bettina went inside without answering, she was almost sure.

They left at the end of the weekend, and before they got on the plane, Bettina held Mary close.

'Thank you.'

'For what?' And then she understood. 'Don't be silly.' Slowly she smiled at her. 'One day you may have to give me a good kick in the ass too.'

'I doubt it.' And then she smiled broadly too. 'But then again your life hasn't been as exotic as mine.' And for an instant, only an instant, Mary thought that Bettina looked proud.

'What are you going to do now, Betty?' Seth leaned over to ask her.

'Call Norton and tell him I'm getting back to work. By now I'm sure he's given up on me.'

'I doubt it.' Mary was quick to answer, and then hurriedly they boarded the plane.

Chapter 50

'Well, Rip van Winklé, coming out of hibernation, are you?'

'All right, Norton,' she said, chuckling softly, 'it was only six months.'

'It might as well have been six years. Do you have any idea how many people I've turned away since you decided to "retire", temporarily, thank God?'

'Don't tell me.' She was still smiling. It was the first of December and she was feeling good.

'I won't. Now what do you have planned before we cross wires again?'

'Absolutely nothing.'

'You're not starting work on a new play?'

'No, as a matter of fact, I don't want to. I want to stay out here for a while. It'll be too hard on the children if I start dragging them back and forth to New York every year.'

'All right, it doesn't make any difference. You have enough offers to write movies to keep you busy for the next ten years.'

'Like from whom?' She sounded instantly suspicious and he went down the list. When he was finished she nodded, approving. 'I'd say that's quite a few. Whom do you suggest I talk to first?'

'Bill Hale.' He answered instantly and she closed her eyes. 'Oh, Christ, Norton, not him.'

'Why? He's a genius. And he's doing producing now. As a matter of fact he's about as brilliant as you.'

'Terrific. So find me someone a little less brilliant who wants to talk.'

'Why?' He was intrigued.

'Because everyone says he's an asshole.'

'In business?' Norton was stunned.

'No, personally. He collects women, wives, mistresses, who needs it?'

'No one asked you to marry him, for chrissake, Bettina. Just discuss this movie idea he has in mind.'

'Do I have to?'

'Will you do it if I say yes?' He sounded hopeful.

'Probably not.' They both laughed. 'Look, I just don't want to put myself in an awkward situation. The guy has a legendary case of hot pants, which I hear he wears regularly to work.'

'So carry a tray of ice cubes and bring a pair of brass knuckles, but do me a favour, Bettina, after six months on your ass and not answering the phone, at least go to lunch with the guy. You and he are the two hottest people in the business these days. It's insane for you not to listen to what he has to say.'

'Okay, Norton. You win.'

'Do you want me to set it up from here? Or will you?'

'You do it. I don't want to be bothered.' Suddenly the voice of her father echoed in her own head. So that was how it had felt . . .

'Any place special you want to see him?'

'No. If he's as big a phoney as I think he is, he'll probably want to meet at the Polo Lounge at the Beverly Hills Hotel, so he can play Mister Hollywood and get paged every five minutes on the phone.'

'So I'll call you every five minutes too, all right?'

'Fine.'

And then suddenly he remembered something, but he didn't want to ask her. He was sure that she and Ollie had rented an apartment from him once, a long time before, in New York. But he figured it was just as well not to bring up Ollie. She had enough pain, and he knew that it had been a major blow when he died. She had had a lot of tough things happen, but on the other hand, he shrugged to himself as he dialled Bill Hale, she had had a lot of good things happen too. In some ways it was a story not unlike Bill Hale's.

He got through to Bill's secretary fairly quickly, and a moment later he was speaking to him. They agreed on the following Monday, but contrary to Bettina's prediction he asked if he might stop by her house after lunch.

'Is he kidding?' She was shocked when Norton called. 'Why does he want to do a thing like that?'

'He said it is less distracting than trying to talk in a restaurant with waiters and phones, and he thought that maybe you'd feel uncomfortable going to his place to see him.'

'So be it.' She shrugged and hung up, and the following Monday, she dressed slowly an hour before he was due. She was wearing a deep purple suit that she had ordered from London, and it was a wonderful anemone colour in a lovely thin wool. She wore a white silk blouse with it, and the amethyst earrings her father had given her. Her hair was soft and loose and the colour of autumn in New England, and as she took a last look in the mirror she heard the bell. It didn't really matter what she looked like, but as long as she was going back to doing business, she might as well look like who she was. Not Justin Daniels's daughter, or Ivo Stewart's wife, or Mrs John Fields, or even Mrs Oliver Paxton. She was Bettina Daniels. And whatever else she was, she knew she was a damn good playwright, and after a hell of a lot of pain and mistakes she knew one other thing. She was whole.

'Mister Hale?' She eyed him archly as he stepped inside. Like her, he had dressed for the occasion and he was wearing a dark blue pin-striped business suit, a dark blue Christian Dior tie, and an especially starched white shirt. She had to admit to herself that he was well dressed and good-looking, but she didn't really care. He nodded politely when he saw her and held out his right hand.

'Bill, please. Miss Daniels?'

'Bettina.' The formalities over, she led him into her living-room and took a chair. Her housekeeper appeared a moment later with a large handsome lacquer tray. There was both tea and coffee, a plate of little sandwiches, and cookies that Alexander had eyed longingly that morning before school.

'Good heavens, I didn't mean to put you to all this trouble.' She said something vague about it not being any trouble as she tried to decide if he was plastic or real.

After a few moments, as he drank coffee and she sipped her tea, they began to talk business, and it was two hours later when they stopped. She had to admit that she loved his idea and she was smiling as they slowly wound the meeting to a close.

'Should I call your agent and discuss the vulgar aspects of it with him?'

She laughed as he said it and nodded slowly, narrowing her eyes.

'You know, I like you a lot better than I thought I would,' he said.

She looked at him, torn between amusement and astonishment and she laughed. 'Why?'

'Well, you know, Justin Daniels's daughter . . .' He looked apologetic. 'You could have turned out to be one hell of a snob.'

'And I didn't turn out to be?'

'No, you're not.' And then, feeling bold as she looked at him, she chuckled too.

'I like you better too.'

'And what strike did I have against me? I didn't have a famous father.'

'No, but you have other sins from what I hear.' She eyed him frankly, and he nodded, meeting her green eyes with his blue.

'The bluebeard reputation?' She nodded. 'Charming, isn't it?' He didn't look angry, only lonely, and then he met her eyes again. 'People love to catch tidbits, there's a lot they talk about that they don't understand.' And then he told her honestly, 'I've been married four times. My first wife died in a plane crash, my second left me after' – he seemed to hesitate for a moment – 'after our life fell apart. My third was something of a dreamer, and six months after we got married she realised that what she really wanted was to join the Peace Corps, and my fourth,' – he stopped with a broad grin – 'was a raving bitch.' For a moment Bettina laughed with him, and then slowly something gentle fell over her eyes.

'I don't have any right to quibble with all that.'

'Why not? Everyone else does.' She was oddly touched by his honesty and embarrassed at what she had thought. But suddenly she was laughing and she hid behind her napkin. All he could see were the dancing green eyes.

'I've been married four times too.'

But suddenly they were both laughing. 'Why, you . . . and here I was feeling guilty!' He looked like a kid who had discovered a friend with something in common, but she had sat up with a girlish look on her face too.

'Do you feel guilty?'

'Sure, I do. Four wives, are you kidding? That's not wholesome!'

'Oh, Jesus . . . so do I!'

'You should. And you should feel a lot guiltier for not telling me sooner.' He nibbled a cookie, sat back in his chair, and grinned. 'So tell me about yours.'

'One lovely man who was a lot older than I was.'

'How much is a lot? You were sixteen and he was nineteen?'

She looked faintly supercilious. 'I was nineteen and he was sixty-two.'

'Ooo . . .' he whistled. 'That *was* older.' But his smile was gentle and there was no reproach. Only interest.

'He was a marvellous man, a friend of my father's. Actually maybe you knew him.' But he held up a hand as she started to say his name.

'No, no, please, this is marriage anonymous. Let's not blow it. The next thing you know we'll find out I was married to two of your cousins and you'll hate me all over again.'

304

She laughed, and then looked at him more seriously. 'Is this what everyone in Hollywood does? Sit around discussing their last four husbands and wives?'

'Only the sickoes, Bettina. The rest of us just make human mistakes, not that anyone would believe it. I mean four is a bit much.' They both grinned. 'Anyway, continue . . .'

'My second husband sounds like your wife who joined the Peace Corps. He wanted a green card. We were also married for six months.' But her face clouded briefly as she thought of the baby she'd lost. 'My third was a doctor in San Francisco, and for five years I tried to be a "normal" wife.'

'What does a "normal" wife do?' He looked at her with intrigue in his eyes as he took another cookie from the plate.

'To tell the truth I was never sure. I just knew that whatever it was, I was never doing it. One of my friends says that you have to be a little brown and grey bird.'

He looked at her, torn between laughter and compassion, as his gaze fell on the flaming hair and the deep-purple dress. 'You are very definitely not that.'

'Thank you. Well, in any case I blew it completely by writing my first play.'

'He didn't like that?'

'He filed for divorce the moment I left for New York, sold our house, and I found out when I came home.'

'He didn't tell you?' She shook her head. 'Charming. And then?'

'Then I moved to New York and' – she seemed to hesitate for a moment, and then she went on – 'I met . . . my fourth husband, and he was very special.' Her voice softened as he watched her. 'We had a baby, and almost a year ago he died.'

'I'm sorry.' They sat in silence for a moment, and then he looked at her gently.

'See, Bettina, that's what I mean. Other people, the rest of them out there, think that we just sit here laughing, collecting divorces, and paying alimony and that we're amused by our endless list of ex-wives, but what they don't understand is that it can happen to real people, tragedies and mistakes, and people you believe in who disappoint you . . . it's all terribly real, but no one understands.' They looked at each other for an endless moment. 'My second wife and I had two children, but she had a drinking problem I didn't know about when we got married. She spent most of our marriage in and out of hospitals, trying to deal with it, but eventually she lost.' He sighed for a moment, and then went on. 'She was driving one day with my two little girls in the car and – ' His voice caught, and without thinking, Bettina reached out to him, knowing what he was going to say, and he took her hand. 'She smashed the car up, and both of the kids died. But she didn't. And she was never the same after that. She's been in and out of institutions ever since.' He shrugged and his voice drifted away. 'I kind of thought we would make it, but . . . we never did.' And then he looked up at her kindly and pulled away his hand. 'How are you doing after losing your husband? Is that why you've been incommunicado for all these months?' Suddenly he understood.

She nodded slowly. 'Yes, that's why. And I'm doing better. At first it seemed so – so unfair.'

He nodded. 'It is. That's the bitch of it. The good people, the ones you could make it with – ' He didn't finish his sentence. 'My first wife was like that. God, she was so good and so funny. She was an actress and I was a writer. She got her first damn road show, and . . . end of the road. I was twenty-three and I thought it would kill me. I almost drank myself to death for a year.' And then he looked hard at Bettina. 'Isn't that incredible? That was sixteen years ago . . . and there have been three other women in my life since who were important enough for me to marry. If someone had told me that after Anna died, I'd have killed them. It's odd, time does such strange things.' He sat there musing for a moment, and then he smiled. 'Interesting stories, yours and mine.'

'I'm glad you think so. Once in a while I've thought it wasn't worth the trouble going on another day.'

'But it is, isn't it?' He smiled at her softly. 'The amazing thing is that it always is. There's always another event, another person, a woman you fall in love with, a friend you have to see, a baby you want to give birth to . . . something that makes you go on. It's been like that for me.'

She nodded, loving what he was giving her, because his words were setting her free. It fit all the pieces together and made the picture not only whole, but it allowed her to see that there was still more of the picture, a part she had yet to see. 'Do you have other children?' He shook his head slowly.

'No. Miss Peace Corps didn't stick around long enough to have a baby. And number four and I were married for three years, but – ' He laughed softly. 'They were the three longest years of my life.' And then suddenly she remembered.

'I remember when you were getting married.' She grinned broadly. 'I lived in your apartment in New York.'

'You did?' He looked baffled. 'When?'

'When you got married. You were on the West Coast. It was a beautiful place on the West Side.'

'My God.' He looked at her in stupefaction. 'I rented that to Ollie . . . Oliver Paxton . . . for chrissake . . .' He looked at her, stunned. 'That's who you are, Bettina! You're Ollie Paxton's wife!'

But as she looked at him, sitting very tall in her chair, she slowly shook her head. 'No, I'm not . . .' It was like hearing a dozen echoes and denying them all at last. Not even for Ollie could she be just that. 'I'm Bettina Daniels.'

For a moment he was startled, and then suddenly he understood, and he nodded, holding out a hand. She was not her father's or Ivo's or Ollie's any more . . . She was her own now . . . and he understood that, just as she knew it about him. Their eyes met as they shook hands carefully over the table. 'Hello, Bettina. I'm Bill.'

SEASON OF
PASSION

With all my love to
Beatrix and Bill,
and with special thanks
to Nancy Bel Weeks.

"How arrives it joy lies slain,
And why unblooms the best hope ever sown?"
                    "Hap" by Thomas Hardy

"Sweet are the uses of adversity,
Which, like the toad, ugly and venomous,
Wears yet a precious jewel in his head."
                    William Shakespeare

PART ONE

CHAPTER I

The alarm went off just after six. She stirred, reached an arm out from under the covers, and turned it off. She could still pretend that she hadn't heard it. She could go back to sleep. She didn't have to go . . . it wasn't as if . . . it wasn't as if . . . and then the phone rang.

'Damn.' Kaitlin Harper sat up in bed. Her long brown hair hung over her shoulders in the braids she had worn the day before, and her face was brown from the sun. The phone rang again, and with a sigh she answered it, crushing a yawn between her teeth. She had a delicate mouth, which smiled abundantly when she was happy, but today her green eyes already looked too serious. She was awake now. It was so much easier to sleep and forget.

'Hi, Kate.' She smiled at the familiar voice. She had known it would be Felicia. Nobody else knew where she was.

'What are you doing up at this hour?'

'Oh, the usual.'

Kate broke into a broad grin. 'At six o'clock? Some usual.' She knew Licia better than that. Felicia Norman could barely make it out of bed by eight, and at her office her secretary was carefully instructed to shield her from any undue shocks until at least ten. Six o'clock in the morning was hardly her hour. Except for Kate. For Kate, she would even get herself up at that ungodly hour. 'Don't you have anything better to do than check on me, Licia?'

'Apparently not. So what's new?' You could almost hear Felicia trying to force herself awake. The well-cut blonde hair, which hung straight to her shoulders, now lay flat on her pillow as a carefully manicured hand covered the ice-blue eyes in her chiselled face. Like Kate, she had the face of a model, but she was older than Kate by twelve years.

'Nothing's new, silly. And I love you. But I'm fine. I promise.'

'Good. I just thought maybe you'd like me to meet you there today.' There. An anonymous word for an anonymous place. And Felicia was willing to drive for two hours just to meet her friend 'there'. And for what? Kate had to do it alone now. She knew that. You couldn't go on leaning on people forever. She'd done that for long enough.

'No, Licia, I'm okay. Besides, the store will end up divorcing you if you keep running off in the middle of the day to baby-sit for me.' Felicia Norman was the fashion director of one of San Francisco's most elegant stores, and Kate had met her when she was modelling.

'Don't be silly. They don't even miss me.' But they both knew that was a lie. And what Kate didn't know was that Felicia had the Norell show to oversee that afternoon. The whole winter line. And Halston in three days. Blass next week. It defied the imagination. Even Felicia's. But Kate was removed from all that now. She wasn't thinking of seasons and lines. She hadn't for months.

'How's my little friend?' Felicia's voice softened when she asked, bringing a smile back to Kate's eyes. A real one this time, as she ran a hand over her full stomach. Three more weeks . . . three weeks . . . and Tom . . .

'He's fine.'

'How can you be so sure it's a boy? You've even convinced me.' Felicia smiled at the thought of the stack of baby clothes she'd ordered on the seventh floor last week. 'Anyway, it better be!' They both laughed.

'It will be. Tom said—' And then a silence. The words had slipped out. 'Anyway, love. I don't need a baby-sitter today. I promise. You can stay in San Francisco, get another two hours sleep, and go to work in peace. If I need you, I'll call. Trust me.'

'Where have I heard that before?' Felicia laughed a deep soft laugh into the phone. 'If I waited for you to call, I'd die of old age. Can I come down this weekend, by the way?'

'Again? Can you stand it?' She'd been there almost every

weekend for the past four months. But by now Kate expected her; Felicia's inquiry and Kate's response were only a formality.

'What can I bring you?'

'Nothing! Felicia Norman, if you bring me one more maternity anything, I'll scream! Where do you think I wear that stuff? To the supermarket? Lady, I live in a cowtown. You know — the men wear undershirts and the women wear housecoats. That's it.' Kate sounded amused.

Felicia did not. 'That's your own goddamn fault. I told you—'

'Oh shut up. I'm happy here.' Kate was smiling to herself.

'You're nuts. It's just this nesting instinct you've got comes from being pregnant. Wait till the baby comes. You'll come to your senses.' Felicia was counting on it. She was even keeping an eye out for available apartments. There had already been two or three gems in her neighbourhood on Telegraph Hill. Kate was crazy to stay down there. But she'd come out of it. The furore was already dying down. Another couple of months and she could come back in peace.

'Hey, Licia' – Kate looked over at the alarm clock – 'I'd better get moving. I have a three-hour drive ahead of me.' She stretched gingerly in her bed, hoping her legs wouldn't cramp and send her leaping out of bed – as best she could 'leap'.

'And that's another thing. You could stop going up there for the next month, at least until after the baby. There's no point—'

'Licia. I love you. Good-bye.' Very gently, Kate hung up. She had heard that speech before. And she knew what she was doing. It was what she had to do. What she wanted to do. Besides, what choice did she have? How could she stop going now?

She rolled slowly to a sitting position at the edge of the bed and took a deep breath as she looked at the mountains beyond her window. Her thoughts were years and miles away. A lifetime away.

'Tom.' She said it gently. Just the one word. She wasn't even aware she'd said it aloud. Tom . . . how could he not be there?

Why wasn't he running his bath, or singing from the shower, teasing her from the kitchen . . . was he really gone? It had been so little time since she could just call his name and hear his voice. He had been right there with her. Always. Big, blond, beautiful Tom, full of laughter and hugs, and a gift for making wonderful moments. Tom, whom she had met during her first year in college, when the team happened to be in San Francisco, and she happened to go to the game, and then happened to go to a party, and someone knew someone on the team . . . madness. And luck. She had never done anything like it before. She had fallen in love with him on the spot, at eighteen. And with a football player? The idea had seemed funny to her at first. A football player. But he wasn't just that. He was special. He was Tom Harper. Loving, warm, thoughtful in infinite ways. Tom, whose father had been a coal miner in Pennsylvania, and whose mother had worked as a waitress to help put him through school. Tom, who had worked nights and days and summers himself to get to college, and then had finally made it after all on a football scholarship. He had become a star. And then a pro. And then a real star. A kind of national hero. Tom Harper. And that was when she had met him. When he was a star. Tom . . .

'Hello, Princess.' His eyes had run over her like a trickle of warm summer rain.

'Hello.' She had felt so foolish. Hello . . . it was all she could think of to say. She had nothing to say to him really, but something small and tight had turned over in the pit of her stomach. She had had to look away. His bright blue eyes were too much for her, the way he searched her face, the way he smiled. Meeting those eyes was like trying to stare into the sun.

'Are you from San Francisco?' He had been smiling down at her from his immense height. He was a huge, powerfully built man, with the classic shape required for his profession. She was wondering what he was thinking about her. He probably thought she was ridiculous. A groupie, or just a kid.

'Yes. I'm from San Francisco. Are you?' And then they both laughed, because she knew he wasn't. Everyone knew where Tom Harper was from. And the team was based in Chicago.

'Why so shy?'

'I . . . it . . . oh damn.' And then they had laughed, and it was better after that. They had slipped away from the party and gone out for hamburgers.

'Will your friends be upset?'

'Probably.' She sat at the counter on a stool next to him, swinging one long leg, and smiling happily over her dripping hamburger. She had had a date, somewhere, back there at the party. But not anymore. She was out with Tom Harper. It was hard to get used to the idea. But he didn't seem to match the legend she had heard about. He was just a man. She liked him. But not because of who he was. Just because he was nice. No . . . more than that . . . but she wasn't quite sure what it was. She only knew that a strange tiny butterfly was soaring happily through her gut. It happened every time she looked at him. She wondered if he could tell.

'Do you do this often, Princess? I mean, ditch dates at parties.' He looked at her sternly for a moment, and they both laughed again.

'Never. Promise.'

'Better not do it to me.'

'No, sir.'

It had been a night of teasing and laughter, and she had instantly felt close to him, yet humbled at the same time. He could make her feel like a little girl, but he also made her feel safe, as though she had waited all her life for him to protect her. It was a strange feeling, but she liked it. They had driven to Carmel after the hamburgers, and walked along the ocean, but he hadn't tried to make love to her. They had only walked, and held hands, and talked until the sun came up, exchanging the secrets of childhood and youth . . . 'and wait till I tell you about . . .'

'You're a beautiful girl, Kate. What do you want to be when you grow up?' She had laughed at the question and delicately slid a handful of sand down the back of his shirt. He had retaliated in kind, and she wondered if he would kiss her, but he didn't. And she wanted desperately to kiss him. 'Stop that. I'm serious. What do you want to do?'

The question made her sit back with a shrug. 'I don't know. I just started college. I think maybe I want to major in political science, or maybe literature. You know, useful stuff like that. Who knows? I'll probably graduate and get a job selling cosmetics at Saks.' Or run away, or be a ski bum, or teach school, or be a nurse or a fireman or ... hell, how did she know? He was silly.

He was smiling at her again, that rich blue-eyed smile that melted the seat of her pants. 'How old are you, Kate?' He was full of questions, and he looked at her again and again as though he had always known her. The questions seemed only a formality. Somehow she thought he already knew the answers.

'I was eighteen last month. And you?'

'Twenty-eight, m'love. Ten years older than you are. I'm almost over the hill. In this business anyway.' His face tightened as he said it.

'And when you retire?'

'I'll join you selling cosmetics at Saks.' She laughed at the thought. He was easily six feet four or five. The idea of Tom Harper selling anything smaller than a battleship was absurd.

'What do retired football players do?'

'Get married. Have kids. Drink beer. Get fat. Sell insurance. The good things in life.' He sounded half ironic, half scared, and very serious.

'Sounds terrific.' She was smiling gently and looking out to sea as he put an arm around her shoulders.

'Not really.' He was thinking of the part about selling insurance, and then he looked at her. 'Do marriage and kids sound terrific, Kate?'

She shrugged. 'I guess. That stuff seems a long way off to me.'

'You're young.' He said it so soberly that it made her laugh. 'Yes, grandfather.'

'What do you really think you'll do after you graduate?'

'Honestly? Go to Europe. I want to spend a couple of years over there. Kicking around. Working. Whatever comes up. I figure I'll be pretty fed up with the discipline of school by then.' All that was still three years away.

'So that's what you call it. "Discipline".' He grinned to himself, thinking of the slightly rowdy crowd of rich kids he had watched her arrive with at the party. They all went to Stanford. They all had money, and fancy clothes, and there had been a Morgan and brand-new Corvette parked at the kerb. 'Where in Europe?'

'Vienna or Milan. Maybe Bologna. Maybe Munich. I haven't decided yet, but someplace small.'

'Tsk.'

'Oh, shut up.' The urge to kiss him was overwhelming again. It made her smile quietly in the night. Here she sat, virtually in the arms of Tom Harper. Half the women in the country would have drooled at the thought. And there they sat, like two kids, with his arm around her, and talking easily. Her parents would have been thrilled. She almost laughed at the thought.

'What are your folks like?' It was as though he had read her mind.

'Stuffy. But nice, I suppose. I'm an only child and they had me a little late. They expect a lot.'

'And you deliver?'

'Most of the time. I shouldn't though. I've given them bad habits. Now they expect me to toe the line all the time. That's part of why I want to go away for a couple of years. I might even do my junior year abroad. Or go next summer.'

'Subsidized by Daddy, of course.' He sounded smug, and she turned to look at him with anger in her green eyes.

'Not necessarily. I make my own money too. Actually, I'd rather pay for my own trip. If I can get a job over there.'

'Sorry, Princess. I just figured. I don't know ... that whole group you came in with tonight looked pretty well-heeled. I knew the type when I was at Michigan State. All of them were from Grosse Pointe, or Scottsdale, or wherever. It's all the same thing.'

Kate nodded. She didn't disagree with him, she just didn't like being tossed into the same basket with all those other kids. But she knew what he meant. Even though she had never rebelled, that way of life didn't appeal to her much either.

15

Everyone seemed to have so much of everything. And no texture, no pain, no questions, no qualms. They all had so much. And Kate was no exception. But at least she knew it.

'What do you mean, you make your own money?' He looked amused again.

She looked annoyed. 'I model.'

'You do? For magazines or what?' Now that was a surprise. She had the looks for it, but he just figured she didn't work. But modelling was a nice gig. He was almost impressed. He turned to look at her and the anger in her face softened.

'All kinds of stuff. I did a commercial last summer. Most of the time I just get called to do fashion shows at I. Magnin, Saks, stores like that. It's kind of a pain to go into the city just for that, but it pays decently and it gives me a little independence. And it's sort of fun sometimes.' He could just see her going down the runway, half colt, half doe, tall and thin in some five-hundred-dollar dress. Or maybe they didn't have her modelling stuff like that. But she had the style to pull it off. And though Tom knew little about fashion, he had guessed correctly.

'Is that what you're going to do in Europe when you finish school? Model?' He looked intrigued, as he kept a warm arm around her shoulders. She was comfortable there.

'Only if the alternative is starvation. I really want to do other things.'

'Like what?' He pulled her closer. He seemed older and yet not older at all. And for the first time in her life, she wanted a man to make love to her. That was crazy. She was a virgin, and she didn't even know him. Not yet. But he was the kind of man you'd want to be first. She couldn't imagine him being anything but gentle and kind. 'Come on, Kate, what kind of "other things" do you want to do in Europe?' He sounded a little bit teasing, and it made her smile. She had always wanted a big brother who would sound like that.

'I don't know. Work for a newspaper maybe. Or a magazine. Be a reporter. Maybe someplace like Paris or Rome.' Her face lit up and he rumpled her hair.

16

'Listen, kid, why not settle for modelling and live like a lady? What do you want to chase around after fires and murders for? Christ, you can do that over here. In English.'

'My father would have a nervous breakdown.' She giggled.

'So would I.' He held her close again, as though to keep her safe from unseen evil.

'You're a party pooper. Tom Harper. I'm a damned good writer. I'd be a good reporter.'

'Who says you're a good writer?'

'I do. And one day I'm going to write a book.' Damn. She'd said it. She looked away and stopped talking.

'You're serious about that, aren't you, Kate?' His voice was as soft as morning, and she nodded silently. 'Then maybe one day you will.' He tiptoed gently, trying not to step on any of her dreams. 'I used to want to write a book too. But I gave up the idea.'

'Why did you do that?' She was horrified, and he tried to keep his face serious. He loved her intensity.

'I gave up the idea because I can't write. Maybe one day you'll write one for me.' They sat quietly for a while, looking out to sea, enjoying the night breeze on their faces. He had lent her a spare parka, and they huddled together on the beach. It was a while before either of them spoke again.

'What do your parents want you to do?' he asked.

'Later?' He nodded. 'Oh, something "pleasant". A job in a museum, something at a university, or graduate school. Or best of all, find a husband. Boring stuff. What about you? What are you going to do after the newspapers stop telling us all what a fabulous football player you are?' She looked like a kid as she lay on the sand, but there was a woman lurking in her eyes, and Tom Harper saw her.

'I told you. I'll retire, and we'll write that book.' She said nothing more, and they sat in silence and watched the sun come up, and then drove back to San Francisco.

'Want to have breakfast before I drop you off?' They were in Palo Alto and he was already nearing her street in the little British sports car he had rented for his stay in the city.

'I should probably get back.' If her mother called and learned she'd been out all night, she'd have some very fancy explaining to do, but the girls would probably cover for her. She covered for them. Two of the four were no longer virgins. And the third was doing her damnedest to change her status. Kate didn't really care — or she hadn't anyway, till Tom.

'What about tonight?'

She looked crestfallen. 'I can't. I promised my parents I'd have dinner with them. And they've got tickets to the symphony. Afterwards?' Damn, damn, damn. And then he'd be leaving town and she'd never see him again.

There was something suddenly sad in her face and he wanted to kiss her. Not like a kid. Like a woman. He wanted to hold her close to him and feel her heart pounding against him. He wanted . . . he forced the thoughts from his mind. She was too young.

'Can't make it afterwards, Princess. We play tomorrow. I have to be in bed by ten. Don't worry about it. Maybe we can grab a few minutes together tomorrow before we fly out. Want to come to the airport with me?'

'Sure.' The look of despair started to fade.

'Want to come to the game tomorrow?' And then he laughed at something he saw in her face. 'Oh, baby, tell the truth. You hate football, right?'

'Of course not.' But she was laughing. He was on to her. 'I don't hate it.'

'You just don't like it much, right?' He laughed as he shook his head. It was perfect. A kid, a college girl, from some uptight fancy family. It was crazy. Totally crazy.

'Okay, Mr. Harper. So what? Does it matter if I'm not the world's hottest football fan?'

He looked down at her with a broad grin and shook his head. 'Nope. Not a bit.' In fact, the idea amused him. He was sick to death of groupies. And then, suddenly, they were in front of her house, and it was over. 'Okay, kiddo, I'll call you later.' She wanted to make him promise, to ask him if he was sure he'd call, to tell him she'd cancel the dinner with her parents. But hell, he was Tom Harper, and she was just another girl.

He'd never call again. She pulled a thin cloak of indifference around her, nodded, smiled easily, and slid out of the car. She was stopped before her feet touched the street. Tom Harper had a crushing grip on her arm. 'Hey, Kate. Don't go off like that. I told you I'd call you. And I mean it.' He understood that too. He understood everything. She turned to him with a smile of relief.

'Okay. I just thought . . .' The grip on her arm eased, and he ran a hand gently over her cheek.

'I know what you thought, but you were wrong.'

'Was I?' Their eyes held for a long moment.

'Yes.' It was the softest word she had ever heard. 'Now go get some sleep. I'll call you later.'

And he had. He called twice that morning, and once late at night, after she got home from the evening with her parents. He had been in bed, but couldn't sleep. They made plans to meet after the game the next day. But it was different this time. Too hurried, tense. They had won the game, and he was all keyed up, Kate was nervous. It wasn't the beach at Carmel, and it wasn't dawn. It was the whirlwind of Tom Harper's career, and a crowded airport bar before he flew to Dallas for another game. Other men from the team came and went, waved at them, two women wanted his autograph, the barman kept looking over and winking, and there was a constant turning of heads whispers, nodding . . . over there . . . Tom Harper? . . . yeah? . . . hell, yes! . . . Tom Harper! It was distracting.

'Want to come to Dallas?'

'Huh?' She looked shocked. 'When?'

'Now.'

'Now?'

He grinned at the look on her face. 'Why not?'

'You're crazy. I have to . . . I have exams . . .' A frightened little girl darted into her eyes, and suddenly he understood something else. Driving to Carmel with him had been an act of faith, of bravado, of something. She could handle that. But a trip to Dallas — that was something else. Okay. Now he understood. He would walk softly. This was a very special girl.

'Relax, Princess. I'm just kidding. But what about meeting

me somewhere else, sometime after exams?' He said it very gently and prayed that no one would turn up for an autograph, or to congratulate him on the day's game. No one did. He held his breath as she looked at him.

'Yeah. I could do that.' She was trembling inside, but it was a beautiful feeling.

'Okay. We'll talk about it.' But he didn't press the point. And it was laughter and teasing all the way to the gate. They stood there for a moment and she wondered if he would kiss her or not. And then, with a slow gentle smile, he bent down and kissed her, softly at first, and then as her arms went around him, he took her tightly in his and kissed her hard. It took her breath away and her head reeled. And then it was over, and he was gone, and she was alone at the gate.

He called that night. And every night, for a month. He invited her to various places where he was playing, but she couldn't get away, or his schedule was too tight, or she had a modelling job, or her parents wanted to do something with her, or . . . and she wasn't really sure if she wanted to "do it" yet. She thought so, but . . . She never explained that to him. But he knew.

'What are you telling me, Princess? That I'm never going to see you again?'

'Of course not. I just couldn't till now. That's all.'

'Bullshit. You just get that skinny little ass of yours on a plane to Cleveland this weekend, or I'm coming out to get you myself.' But there was always laughter in his voice, always that gentleness that let her know she was safe. He was the gentlest man she had ever known. And he was beginning to seem a little spoiled too. He kept insisting that he wanted her to come to him. But there was a reason for it. He wanted her away from home ground. Away from roommates and parents and guilt. He wanted to give her not just a night, but a honeymoon.

'Yes, love. Cleveland. Not Milan. Sorry.'

'You should be.'

But she had gone. And Cleveland had been hideous, but Tom was a dream. He had been waiting for her at the gate when she got off the plane, with the happiest smile she'd ever seen. He stood there, watching her walk towards him, and carrying one long-stemmed coral rose. And he had borrowed a house from the cousin of someone on the team. It wasn't a luxurious house, just a warm friendly one. It was what Tom was, unpretentious, tender, loving. And that was what he had been to her. He had deflowered her so gently that she was the one who wanted the second time. That was how he had meant it to be: he wanted her to want him. And from that moment on she was his. They both knew it.

'I love you, Princess.'

'I love you too.' She had looked at him shyly, with her long brown hair lying damp and soft over one shoulder. She was surprised at how unembarrassed she was with him, right from the first moment.

'Will you marry me, Kate?'

'Are you kidding?' Her eyes opened wide. They had been lying naked on the bed, watching the fire die in the grate. It was almost three in the morning and he had a game the next day. But this was the first thing in his life that had been more important than the game.

'No, Kate, I'm serious.'

'I don't know.' But there was a spark of interest in her eyes. Just enough. 'I've never thought about anything like that. That always seemed like such a long way off. I'm only eighteen, and . . .' She looked up at him with a mixture of gravity and mischief. '. . . my parents would freak.'

'Because of me, or your age?' But he knew, and she hesitated, looking for the right words. 'Okay, I read you.' He smiled, but he looked hurt too, and she quickly threw her arms around him.

'I love you, Tom. And if we did get married, it would be because I love you. I love who you are and what you are — I mean because you're Tom, not all the other stuff. And I wouldn't give a damn what anyone thought. It's just that . . . well, I've never thought of it. I kind of figured I'd float for a while.'

'That's bullshit, my love. You're not a floater.' And they both knew he was right. But this was crazy. She was the one

21

who was supposed to want to get married, and here he was, offering it to her on a silver platter. For a brief moment, there was a marvellous feeling of power. She was a woman now. And more than that, she was Tom Harper's woman.

'You know something, sir? You're terrific.' She lay back against him, and smiled with her eyes closed. And he smiled down at the delicately etched face.

'You're terrific too, Miss Kaitlin.'

She made a face. 'I hate that name.'

But when he kissed her, she forgot all about it. And then he suddenly bounded out of bed, and went to the kitchen to get himself a beer. She watched the broad shoulders and trim hips and long legs, as he walked easily across the room in all his natural splendour. He was an extraordinary-looking man, and then she found herself blushing and embarrassed when he turned and smiled at her. Her eyes darted away to the fire. She kept them averted, but the blush still hovered on her cheeks.

He sat down next to her on the bed, and kissed her. 'You don't have to be afraid to look at me, Princess. It's cool.' She nodded, and took a sip of his beer.

'You're beautiful.' She said it very softly, and he ran a hand slowly down her shoulder, gazing at her breasts.

'You're crazy. And I just had a wonderful idea. You don't want to get married yet, so how about if we live together for a while?' He looked pleased with the thought, and Kate, at first surprised, suddenly smiled.

'You know something? You're amazing. I feel like you're offering me the moon on a blue satin ribbon.' She held his eyes with her own.

'You wanted red velvet?'

She shook her head.

'Well, then?'

'Can we wait a little bit?'

'Why? Kate, we have something very rare and we both know it. We know each other better than either of us knows anyone else. We've spent the last month on the phone, sharing every thought, dream, hope, fear, that either of us has ever had. We know all we need to know. Don't we?'

She nodded, feeling tears start to her eyes. 'What if things change? What if . . .' And then he knew what was troubling her.

'Your parents?' She nodded. He'd find out soon enough.

'We'll handle it, Princess. Don't worry about it. And if you want to grow into it for a while, then you do that. Why don't we just relax till you finish the semester at school?' It was an easy wait. He had only another six weeks till the end of her first year. Then there was the summer. He knew it was settled. And secretly, so did she. And then quietly, gently, slowly, he let his lips run from her mouth to her neck, and play games with her nipples, his tongue darting around them and making her writhe slowly beneath his hands. He was afraid to try for a third time that night — he didn't want to hurt her. So, with all the tenderness he showed her in all things, he ran his tongue along the inside of her thighs, until he heard her begin to moan softly. It was a night she remembered with tenderness always.

She cried on the flight back to San Francisco. She felt wrenched away from him, torn from her roots. She needed him. She was his now. And when she got back to the house in Palo Alto, there were roses waiting for her, from Tom. He took care of her the way even her parents never had. They were so distant and aloof, so cool, so unaware of her feelings. Tom never was. He called two or three times a day, and they talked for hours. He seemed to be with her constantly. He flew back to San Francisco the weekend after Cleveland, and borrowed another apartment from a friend on the team. He was always careful and discreet. He wanted to shield Kate from reporters. And when school ended, she knew that she had to be with him. They had both zig-zagged across the country for six weeks, and it was an insane way to live. The week after school ended, he was traded to San Francisco. It was perfect. Now they could rent an apartment in San Francisco, and she could travel with him all the time. They would always be together. She was sure. He was the most important thing in her life. She could always finish school later — hell, maybe in a year or two she'd go back. This was only a hiatus. Maybe until Tom retired from the team. School was no big deal.

That was not, however, how her parents viewed it.

'Are you out of your mind, Kaitlin?' Her father stared at her in disbelief from his traditional stance near the fireplace. He had been pacing back and forth and had finally stopped there, with a look of desperation in his eyes. 'Leave school and do *what*? Live with this man? Have a baby out of wedlock? Or maybe someone else's baby ? I am sure there are other men on his team who'd be glad to oblige.' His eyes flashed as he went off on his own private tangent, and Kate saw Tom tense across the room.

'Daddy, that's not what we're talking about. I'm not having anyone's baby.' Her voice trembled.

'No? How can you be so sure? Do you have any idea what kind of a life you'll lead with this man? What kind of raucous, low-class, miserable life athletes lead? What exactly are you aspiring to? Sitting around in bars watching football on television and going bowling on Tuesday nights?'

'For God's sake, Daddy, all I told you is that I'm leaving school for a semester and I'm in love with Tom. How can you—'

'Very easily. Because you don't know what you're doing.' His tone held only condemnation, and her mother nodded silent agreement as she sat stiffly in her chair.

'May I interject a word, sir?' It was the first time Tom had spoken since they'd begun. He had accompanied Kate only to provide emotional support: he knew that the matter had to be handled between Kate and her parents. He had wanted to bolster her, not interfere, but there was no way to avoid interfering now. Kate's father was getting way out of hand, and enjoying it. It showed in his eyes.

Tom turned to her father now with a look of quiet concern. 'I think you have a somewhat frightening view of what my life is like. True, I don't work as a lawyer or a stockbroker, and there isn't anything very intellectual about playing football, but that's my life. It's an all-out, hard-working, physical job. And the people in it are like any other kind of people, there are good men and bad men, stupid ones and smart ones. But Kate's life will not be spent with the team. I lead an extremely

24

quiet private life, and I'd be very surprised if you could take exception to—'

Her father cut him off with a furious glare. 'I take exception to *you*, Mr. Harper. It's as simple as that. And as for you, Kaitlin, if you do this, if you leave school, if you dare to disgrace us in this way, you're finished. I don't want to see you in this house again. You may take whatever personal items you want now, and you may leave. I will have nothing more to do with you, nor will your mother. I forbid it.'

Kate's eyes filled with tears of pain and anger as she looked at him.

'Do you understand?' She nodded without taking her eyes from his. 'And you won't change your mind?'

'No. I won't.' She took a breath. 'I think you're wrong. And I think you're being . . . very unkind.' Her voice caught on a small throb lodged in her throat.

'No. I'm being right. If you think I have waited these eighteen years to banish my own daughter from my house, to stop seeing my only child, then you are greatly mistaken. Your mother and I have done everything we could for you. We have wanted everything for you, given everything to you, taught you everything we know and believe. And now you have betrayed us. It tells me only that we have had a stranger in our midst for these eighteen years, a traitor. It is like discovering that you are not ours, but someone else's child.' As Tom listened with growing horror, he suddenly agreed. She was someone else's now. She was his. And he would love and cherish her even more after this day. What bastards they were. 'You are no longer ours, Kaitlin. We could not have a daughter who could do these things.' He said it with ponderous solemnity, and a burst of almost hysterical laughter escaped from Kate's constricted throat.

'Do what things? Drop out of school? Do you have any idea how many kids do that every year? Is that the big deal?'

'I think we both know that's not the issue.' He glared at Tom. 'Once you have besmirched yourself, as you so determinedly plan to do, it will not matter whether you go to school or not. School is only part of it. It's a matter of your attitude.

your goals, your ambitions. Where you are going in your life ... and where you are going, Kaitlin, seems to have nothing to do with us. We are finished. And now' – he looked away from her to her mother – 'if you want to get some of your things, please do so quickly. Your mother has been through enough.' But her mother didn't look exhausted or shaken, she looked glazed and indifferent as she sat there, staring at her only daughter. For a moment Tom wondered if she was in shock. And then she stood up with an icy expression, and opened the living-room door, which had been carefully closed so the maid wouldn't overhear the exchange. In the doorway she turned to look at Kate, who was rising slowly and almost painfully from her chair.

'I'll wait while you pack, Kate. I want to see what you take.'

'Why? Are you afraid I'll take the silver?' Kate looked at her mother stupefied.

'Hardly, it's locked up.' She swept from the room then as Kate started to follow. And then Kate stopped. She looked at Tom, and then back at her father with an expression of revulsion on her face.

'Forget it.'

'Forget what?' For once, her father seemed at a loss.

'I don't want anything from you. I'll go now. You can keep whatever is in my room.'

'How kind of you.'

And then, without another word, Kate walked slowly from the room. Her mother was waiting for her in the hall, with her face set in hard, angry lines.

'Are you coming?'

'No, Mother, I'm not. I think I've had about enough.' No one said anything for a long moment, and then pausing for a last moment by the door, she turned to look at them and said only one word: 'Goodbye.' She was out the door as soon as she said it, with Tom next to her and his arm right round her shoulders. What he really wanted to do was go back and kill her father and slap her mother so hard her teeth would jangle in her throat. My God, what was wrong with those people? What were they made of? How could they do this to their only child?

26

Memories of his own mother's love for him brought tears to his eyes as he thought again about what Kate had just been through. He pulled her close to him as they reached his car and for a long, long time he just held her, as tightly as he could, letting his arms and his heart and the warmth of his body tell her what he could barely find words to say. He would never let her go through anything like that again.

'You're all right, babe. You're just fine, and you're beautiful and I love you.' But she wasn't crying. She was only trembling very slightly in his arms, and when she looked up at him, the much too serious eyes reached out to him as she tried to smile.

'I'm sorry you had to see that, Tom.'

'I'm sorry you had to go through it.'

She nodded silently and pulled slowly away from his arms. He opened the car door for her and she slipped inside.

'Well' – it was a tiny voice as he slid into the car next to her – 'I think that means it's just us. My father said he never wanted to see me again. He said I'd betrayed them.' She sighed deeply. Betrayed them. By loving Tom? By leaving school? Stanford was a tradition in her family. And so was marriage. 'Shacking up', as her father called it, was a disgrace. So was loving a 'nobody'. A coal miner's son. She was forgetting who she was, who her parents were, who her grandparents had been ... all the right schools and right clubs and right husbands and right wives. Her mother was then the president of the Junior League, and her father was senior partner of his law firm. And now she sat in the car next to Tom, looking stunned. He glanced at her again worriedly. 'He'll change his mind.' He patted her hand and started the car.

'Maybe he will. And maybe I won't.'

He kissed her very softly and stroked her hair. 'Come on, baby. Let's go home.'

Home that week was the apartment of another player on his new team. But Tom had a surprise for Kate the next day. He had been busy all week. He had rented a flat in a beautiful little Victorian house on a hill overlooking the bay. He drove her to the door, put the key in her hand, and carried her easily up three flights of stairs and over the threshold, while she laughed and cried. It was like playing house. Only better.

And he was good to her, always, even more so after they realized she would never again hear from her parents. Tom couldn't really understand what they were doing to her, or why. To him family was family; that meant love, and roots that couldn't be destroyed, bonds that couldn't be severed, people who never deserted you, no matter how angry they were. But Kate understood. Her parents had counted on her to be everything they were, and more, to be 'one of them'. She had committed the unpardonable error of falling in love with someone different, and daring to be different herself: daring to betray the rules, daring not to be bound by their restrictions or tiny hopes. She had hurt them, so they were hurting her. They would justify and inflate and dignify their actions until they were convinced her sins were beyond repair, until they wouldn't have to admit even to each other how much the loss of their daughter had hurt them. And if for a moment they doubted, her mother could speak to her bridge friends, or her father to his partners, and there would be instant reassurance: 'It's the only way . . . you did the only thing you could do.' Kate knew. So now Tom was everything to her — mother, father, brother, friend — and she flourished in his hands.

She travelled with Tom, she modelled, she wrote peoms, she took beautiful care of the flat, she saw some of her old friends now and then, though less and less often, and she came to like a few of the players on Tom's team. But mostly Kate and Tom were alone, and her life centred increasingly around him. About a year after they moved in with each other, they were married. Two minor happenings threatened to mar the event, but nothing really could. The first was that Kate's parents refused to attend the wedding, but that came as no surprise. And the second was that Tom got wound up in a heated discussion in his favourite bar and knocked a guy cold. He had been under a lot of pressure at the time. The San Francisco team was not what his old one had been, and he was one of the 'old men' on the team. Nothing came of the incident in the bar, but the papers made it sound ugly. Kate thought it was silly,

Tom laughed it off, the wedding took precedence over everything.

One of his teammates was their best man, one of her roommates from Stanford was her maid of honour. It was a strange little wedding at City Hall, and *Sports Illustrated* covered the story. She was Tom's now, entirely and forever. And she looked exquisite in a dress that was layer after layer of white organdie, with delicate embroidery and a little-girl scooped neck and huge, puffed, old-fashioned sleeves. It had been a present from Felicia, who was growing increasingly fond of the doe-like young model oddly paired with one of the country's heroes. For Kate she had chosen the cream of the store's spring line.

Kate looked like a beautiful child at the wedding, with her long hair swept up on her head in a gentle Victorian style, threaded with lily of the valley. She carried a bouquet of the same tiny fragrant white flowers. There were tears in her eyes and Tom's as they exchanged wide gold rings and the judge pronounced them married.

They spent their honeymoon in Europe, and she showed him all her favourite spots. It was his first time abroad, and turned into an education for both of them. He was growing in sophistication and she was growing up.

The first year of their marriage was idyllic. Kate went everywhere Tom did, did everything Tom did, and spent her spare time writing poetry and keeping a journal. Her only problem was that she didn't like being financially dependent on Tom. Felicia's position enabled Kate to get all the work she wanted, but her constant travelling with Tom made it hard for her to model as much as she felt she should. There was still the tiny income from a small trust her grandmother had left her, but that was barely enough for pocket money   it was impossible to reciprocate the lavish gifts Tom constantly gave her. On their first anniversary Kate announced that she had made a decision. She was giving up travelling with him to stay home and model full-time. It made sense to her. But not to him. It was hard enough travelling with the team he worked for now, without having to do it alone. He needed Kate with him. But she thought he needed a financially independent wife. He put up a fight, but he lost. She was firm. And three months later, he broke his leg in a game.

'Well, Princess, looks like the end of the season.' He was good-humoured about it when he flew home. But they both knew that it might be the end of his career. He was over thirty, the deathly magic number. And it was a bad break; the leg was a mess. He was getting tired of the game anyway, or at least that was what he said. There were other things he wanted more, like children, stability, a future. The move to the San Francisco team had made him professionally insecure; it was something about the chemistry of the team, or maybe the constant underlying threats of the manager, who called him 'old man'. The man's attitude drove Tom nuts, but he lived with it, hating the manager every inch of the way.

He also worried about leaving Kate when he travelled. She was twenty years old; she needed a husband around more often than he could be. He'd be home with her now, though, because of the leg. Or he thought he would be. As it turned out, *he* was home. Kate wasn't. She was getting a lot of modelling work, and she had signed up for a class on women in literature, at State. She went twice a week.

'And there's a super creative writing class next term.'

'Terrific.' She looked just like a kid when she talked about the courses. And he felt like what they called him on the team. Old man. A very bored, nervous, lonely old man. He missed the game. He missed Kate. He felt as if he were missing life. Within a month, he punched out a guy in a bar, wound up in jail, and the story was all over the papers. He talked about it constantly, he had nightmares about it. What if they suspended him? But they didn't. The charges were dropped, and he sent the man a big cheque. The leg still hadn't healed, though, and Kate was still out modelling most of the time. Nothing had changed. And a month later, he decked another guy in a bar, breaking the man's jaw. This time the charges stuck and he paid a whopping fine. The team manager was frighteningly quiet.

'Maybe you should go into boxing instead of football,

30

huh, sweetheart?' Kate still thought Tom's antics were funny.

'Look, dammit, you may think it's amusing, kiddo, but I don't. I'm going goddamn nuts sitting around here waiting for this fucking leg to heal.' Kate got the message. He was desperate. Maybe about a lot of things, not just the leg. The next day she came home with a present. After all, that was why she modelled – so she could offer him gifts. She had bought two tickets to Paris.

The trip was just what he needed. They spent two weeks in Paris, a week in Cannes, five days in Dakar, and a weekend in London. Tom spoiled her rotten, and she was thrilled with having bought him the trip. They came back restored, and Tom's leg had healed. Life was even better than before. There were no more bar fights and he began practising with the team again. Kate turned twenty-one, and for her birthday he bought her a car. A Mercedes.

For their second anniversary Tom took her to Honolulu. And wound up in jail. A fight in the bar of the Kahala Hilton resulted in a bad story in *Time* magazine and a worse one in *Newsweek*. And coverage in every newspaper in the country. Jackpot. Only the story in *Time* told Kate why the fight had really happened: apparently there had been a rumour that Tom's contact wasn't going to be renewed. He was thirty-two. He had been playing pro ball for ten years.

'Why didn't you tell me?' She looked hurt. 'Is it because of the fighting?' But he only shook his head and looked away, as the lines tightened around his mouth.

'Nope. That schmuck who runs the team has this mania about age. He's worse than anyone else in the business. The fights aren't such a big deal. Everyone fights. Rasmussen kicks ass on more people in the streets than he does on the field. Jonas had a drug bust last year. Hilbert's a fag. Everyone's got something. But me, it's my age. I'm just too old, Kate. I'm thirty-two, and I still haven't figured out what the hell to do with myself after football. Christ, this is all I know.' There were tears in his voice and in her eyes.

'Why can't you get yourself traded to another team?'

He looked at her finally and his expression was grim.

'Because I'm too old, Kate. This is it. Last stop. And they know it, which is why they hassle me all the time. They know they've got me.'

'So get out. You could do all kinds of other things. You could be a sportscaster, a coach, a manager ...' But he was shaking his head.

'I've been putting out feelers. It all comes back no.'

'Okay. So you'll find something else. You don't need a job right away. We could go to school together.' She tried to look cheerful. She wanted him to be happy, to share her youth with him, but her efforts only made him smile ruefully.

'Oh, baby, I love you.' He folded her into his arms. Maybe it didn't matter. Maybe all that mattered was what they had. And her support did help, for a while. A year, more or less. But after their third anniversary, things seemed to get worse. Tom's contract was under negotiation, and he started getting into fights again. Two in a row, and this time two weeks in jail and a thousand dollar fine. And a five thousand dollar fine imposed by the team. Tom sued for causes of injustice. He lost. He got suspended. And Kate had a miscarriage. She hadn't even known she was pregnant. Tom drove himself nuts. In the hospital, he wept more than she did. He felt as though he had killed their child. Kate was stunned by the sequence of events. The suspension would last for a year, and now she knew what was in store – bar fights, fines, and a lot of time in jail. And yet Tom was so good to her. So sweet, so gentle. He was all she'd ever dreamed of in a man. But she could see only trouble ahead.

'Why don't we spend the year in Europe?'

He had shrugged disinterestedly at her suggestion. He moped for weeks, thinking about the child they had almost had. But what really frightened him was what was happening to his career. When the suspension ended, so would his career. He was too old to make a recovery.

'So we'll start a business.' Kate was still so damn young, and her optimism only depressed him more. She didn't know what it was like – the terror that he'd be a nobody, have to drive a truck, or even work in the mines like his father. He hadn't

32

invested his money well and he couldn't count on that income. What the hell was he going to do? Commercials for underwear? Pimp for Kate's modelling career? Have her ghost-write his memoirs? Hang himself? Only his love for Kate kept him from the bleakest possibilities. The bitch of it was that all he wanted to do was play football. And none of the colleges were considering him as coach. He had earned himself a stinking reputation with all the fighting.

So they went to Europe. They stayed a week. He hated it. They went to Mexico. He was equally miserable there. They stayed home. He hated that too. And he hated himself most of all. He drank and he fought, and reporters bugged him everywhere. But what did he have to lose now? He had already been suspended and they probably wouldn't renew his contract anyway. The only thing he knew for certain was that he wanted a son. And he'd give His son everything.

Just before Christmas, they found out that Kate was pregnant again. This time they were both careful. Everything stopped. Kate's modelling, his drinking, the fighting in bars. They stayed home together. There was nothing but tenderness and peace between them, except for her occasional bouts of temper or tears. But neither of them took that very seriously; it seemed to be part of the pregnancy, and if anything, it amused Tom. He didn't even give a damn about the suspension anymore. To hell with them. He'd sit it out, and then he'd force them to renew his contract. He'd beg them. All he wanted now was one more knock-out year, so he could put the money away and take good care of his son. The next year he played would be for the baby. For Kate, he bought a mink coat for Christmas.

'Tom, you're crazy! Where'll I wear it?' She modelled it over her nightgown with a huge grin. It was heavenly. But she also wondered what he was trying to hide. What wasn't he facing? What didn't she know?

'You'll wear it to the hospital when you have my son.' And he had bought an antique cradle, a four-hundred dollar English pram, and a sapphire ring for Kate. He was crazy, and madly in love with her, and she was just as in love with him. But deep inside, she was afraid. They spent Christmas alone in San Francisco, and Tom talked about buying a house. Not a big house. Just a nice house in a good area for bringing up a kid. Kate agreed, but wondered if they could really afford a house. As New Year approached, she had an idea. They'd spend the holiday in Carmel. It would do them both good.

'For New Year's? What do you want to do that for, sweetheart? It's foggy and cold. Pizza, sure. Tacos, okay. Strawberries, what the hell. But Carmel in December?' He grinned at her and ran a hand over her still flat belly. But soon ... soon ... the thought made him warm inside. Their baby ... his son.

'I want to go to Carmel because it's the first place we ever went together. Can we?' She looked like a little girl again, although she was going to be twenty-three soon. They had known each other for five years. And of course he gave in to her wish.

'If the lady wants to go to Carmel, then Carmel it is.' And Carmel it was. The best suite at the best hotel, and even the weather smiled on them for the three days they were there. Kate's only worry was that Tom bought everything in sight for her and the baby, whenever they wandered past the shops on the main thoroughfare. But they spent a lot of time in their room, drank a great deal of champagne, and the worry faded.

'Did I ever tell you how much I love you, Mr. Harper?'

'I love to hear it, Princess. Oh Kate — ' And then he swept her up in a giant hug and held her close. 'I'm sorry you've had such a stinking time. I promise I'll shape up now. All that bullshit is over.'

'Just so you're happy.' She looked so peaceful lying in his arms, and he had never thought her more beautiful.

'I've never been happier.' And he finally looked it.

'Then maybe this would be a good time to quit.'

'What do you mean?' He looked shocked.

'I mean football, my love. Maybe now, we should just take the money and run. No more hassles, no more crap about your being an "old man". Just us, and the baby.'

'And starvation.'

'Come on, sweetheart. We're nowhere near starving yet.' But

34

she was startled. If he was so concerned about money, why the mink coat, the ring?

'No, but we don't have a real, solid nest egg. Not enough to do right by the baby in five or ten years. Another good year on the team will make all the difference.'

'We can invest my modelling money.'

'That's yours.' His voice sounded cold for a minute. 'You wanted that, and you earned it. I'll take care of you and the baby. And that's it. I don't want to talk about it.'

'Okay.'

His face had softened then and they had made love in the soft light of dusk. Kate was reminded of their first 'honeymoon' in Cleveland. But it was Tom who fell asleep this time, as he lay in Kate's arms, and she watched him for hours, thinking, hoping this year would be different, that they'd be decent to him, that the pressures wouldn't get to him as cruelly as they had done before. That was all she wanted now. She was growing up.

The day after they went back to San Francisco there was a story in the papers that reported that Tom Harper was 'through'. It was carried by every major paper in the country. Through. He went crazy when he read it, and a little careful digging brought him the information that the story had been planted by the team ... by the team ... the team ... the Old Man ... He had slammed out of the house without a word to Kate and she hadn't seen him until six o'clock that night. On the news.

He had gone to the home of the owner of the team and threatened his life, then he had got into a fight with the team's manager, who had walked in on the scene. Both men had realised that Tom was drunk and wildly irrational, and the owner claimed that Tom had been like a madman, raving about what they couldn't do to his son. In a careful monotone the newscaster explained that Tom Harper didn't have a son; he didn't need to add the conclusion that Harper was obviously crazy. And as Kate watched, her heart rose to her throat. The newscaster went on to explain that the two men had 'tried to subdue Harper as he ranted and swung wildly at them both.

But unexpectedly, Harper had pulled a gun out of his pocket, taken aim at the owner of the team, and then swung wildly on the manager and fired a shot. Miraculously, he had missed, but before anyone could move, he had then pointed the gun at himself, taken erratic aim, and fired twice. But this time he didn't miss. The manager and team owner were both unharmed, but Harper himself had been hospitalized in critical condition.' The newscaster stared sombrely from the television for a moment and gravely intoned, 'A tragedy for American football.'

For the tiniest moment Kate had the insane feeling that if she jumped up and changed the dial, none of it would have happened; all she had to do was switch channels and someone else would say it wasn't true. It couldn't be true. Not Tom . . . . . . please . . . she was whimpering softly as she turned around and stared at the room, wondering what to do. They hadn't said what hospital Tom was in. What was she supposed to do? Call the police? The team? The television station? And why hadn't anyone called her? But then she remembered – she had taken the phone off the hook for two hours while she took a nap. Oh God . . . what if . . . what if he was already dead? Sobbing, she turned off the television and ran to the phone. Felicia . . . Felicia would know . . . she would help her. Without thinking, she dialled Felicia's private line at the store. She was still there.

Felicia was stunned by the news and ordered Kate not to move. As she had her assistant call for a cab on one line, she called the police on another, and got the information. Tom was at San Francisco General. He was still alive – barely, but he was alive. Felicia fled from her office at a run, wondering for a moment why Kate had called her. Surely there was someone else. Her mother, a closer friend, someone? She and Kate were good friends through their work, but they'd never seen much of each other socially. Kate was always too busy with Tom. The hub of that girl's life was the man who lay dying at San Francisco General.

When Felicia arrived at the apartment, Kate was incoherent, but dressed. The cab was still waiting downstairs.

'Come on, put your shoes on.'

'My shoes.' Kate looked blank. 'My shoes?' Tears filled her eyes again and she looked greyish green. Felicia found the closet and a pair of black flats.

'Here.' Kate slid her feet into them and left the apartment without handbag or coat, but Felicia slipped her own coat over the girl's shoulders. She didn't need a bag, anyway, because she was in no condition to go anywhere alone. And she didn't have to. Felicia stayed with her day and night for four days, and at the end of that time Tom was still alive. He was in a coma, and the prognosis was poor, but he was alive. He had done a fairly thorough job when he fired, though. He would never walk again, and there was no way to tell yet how extensive the brain damage was.

When Felicia went back to work, Kate carried on like a machine, moving from Tom's bed to the corridor to his bed to the corridor, to cry alone. It was a treadmill which Felicia joined her on when she could, but there was no getting Kate away from the hospital. She was mourning for Tom. She just sat there, staring, or crying, or smoking, but she wasn't really there, and the doctor was afraid to give her anything, in case the medication hurt the baby. Felicia was amazed that she hadn't lost it.

While the newspapers tore Tom apart, Kate tore herself apart. Whey hadn't she seen some sign? Why hadn't she known? Could she have helped? Did she take his worries about the future – followed by those spending binges – seriously enough? It was all her fault. It had to be. With the egotism of grief, she tormented herself day after day. Football. It had been his whole life, and now it had killed him. The thought that he'd almost killed two other men was even more terrifying, but she didn't believe he could have done that. Not Tom. But what he had done was bad enough. He had destroyed himself. Poor gentle Tom, driven berserk at the idea of losing that last year of security he wanted for his son. Kate didn't let herself think about the baby though. Only about Tom. It was a nightmare that went on for seven weeks, while Kate paced and cried and was constantly haunted by reporters. And then he came to.

He was weak, broken, and tired, but little by little he grew

37

stronger. He would live now – what was left of him – they were sure of it. He would never walk again, but he could move. He could talk. And he could think. Just like a child. The long weeks of coma had moved him backward in time and left him there, with all his sweetness and tenderness and love intact. He was a little boy again. He remembered nothing of the shooting, but he recognised Kate. He cried in her arms as she stifled silent sobs which shook her tall, terrifyingly thin frame. The only thing he truly understood was that he belonged to her. But he wasn't sure how. Sometimes he thought she was his mother, sometimes his friend. He called her Katie. He would never call her Princess again ... Katie ... that's who she was now.

'You won't leave me?'

Gravely, she shook her head. 'No, Tom.'

'Never?'

'Never. I love you too much ever to leave you.' Her eyes filled with tears again, and she had to force ordinary thoughts into her head. She couldn't let herself really think of him when she said the words, or it would kill her. She couldn't let herself cry. She couldn't do that do him.

'I love you too. And you're pretty.' He looked at her with the bright, shiny eyes of a seven-year-old boy, and the wan tired face of an unshaven desperately sick man.

After a few weeks, he looked better again, healthy and whole. It was strange to see him, the ersatz Tom. It was as though Tom had left, and sent in his stead a small boy who looked like him. It would be that way forever. But Tom's condition settled the legal aspects of the case permanently. There was no case. Tom Harper was no more.

Three months after what Kate and Felicia called 'the accident', Tom was moved to a sanatorium in Carmel. Photographers had lunged at the ambulance as he was being wheeled inside. Tom had wanted to wave at them, and Kate had distracted him while he held tightly to her hand. She was used to them now. Some of the faces were even familiar. For three months they had torn her apart in story after story, exploded flashbulbs in her face, and crawled over the roof of their house to get a better view into the apartment. She had no one to turn to, to defend her. No family, no man. And they knew it. They even ran stories about how her family had disowned her years before because of Tom, and how they thought of her as dead. And she had lain in bed at night, sobbing, praying that the press would go away and leave her alone. But they didn't. Not for one day. Until he was moved to Carmel. And then, magically, it was as though they forgot. As though Tom no longer existed, or Kate, his wife. The two of them had left the magic circle. At last.

When Tom left San Francisco, so did Kate. The house was already waiting. Felicia had seen the ad, and the place turned out to be perfect. The owner lived in the East; his mother had died, leaving him a house he didn't need and didn't want to sell. One day he would retire there, and in the meantime it was Kate's hideaway, nestled in the mountains north of Santa Barbara. It was a three-hour drive from Tom's sanatorium in Carmel, but Felicia assumed that Kate would be back in San Francisco as soon as things calmed down, right after the baby was born. It was a pretty house, surrounded by fields and trees, with a little brook just down the hill from the house. It would be a good place to recover. It would have been a wonderful place to share with Tom. Kate tried not to think of that as she signed the lease.

After four months she was used to it; it was home. She awoke at dawn when the baby kicked and stirred, hungry for more space than she had to give him. She lay quietly, feeling him pound inside her, wondering what she would tell him one day. She had thought of changing her name, but decided not to. She was Kate Harper. No one else. She didn't want her father's name anymore. And Tom's baby would be a Harper. Tom didn't understand now about the swollen belly, or maybe he just didn't care. Children didn't, Kate reminded herself, as long as nothing changed for them. Nothing had. She went on visiting him, often at first, and only slightly less frequently as the pregnancy progressed. Nowadays it was twice a week. She was always there. She always would be, as he had been for her. There was no question of it. This was her life now. She

39

accepted it. She understood, as much as one can. 'Always,' whatever that meant. 'Forever,' whatever that was. It meant that each time she saw him, he was the same, always would be. Until one day, when he would quietly die. There was no way to say when. The doctor said he might live to be 'considerably older', though not what was normally thought of as old. Or it might all end in a year or less. At some point, Tom's body would simply fade and die. He would just let go. Unconsciously, but he would. And Kate would be there, for all the time in between, loving him. He still looked like Tom, and now and then there was still that magical light in his eyes. It allowed her to pretend that . . . but it was a futile game. Now she held him as he once had held her. She didn't even cry anymore.

Kate stood up after her call from Felicia, pushed open the window, and took a deep breath of summer air. She smiled to herself. There were new flowers in the garden. She would take him some. She could still love him. She could always love him. Nothing would change that.

The clock on the bedside table said six twenty-five. She had half an hour to get on the road if she wanted to be there before ten. It was a hell of a drive. A hell of a way to grow up – but she had. Kate Harper was no longer any kind of child. And the baby stirred in her belly as she slipped off her nightgown and stepped into the shower. She had a long day ahead.

CHAPTER II

The dark blue station wagon shifted easily into gear and Kate turned swiftly out of the gravel driveway. The little Mercedes Tom had given her was gone. She didn't need it anymore. This car suited her life now. The hills rolled away towards the horizon; they were still lush even this late in the summer. Here and there she noticed a brown patch, but there had been enough rain through the summer to counteract the heat. And there was a majesty to the scene that always took her breath away as she stood with the mountains at her back and the hills rolling ahead, blanketed with wild flowers and dotted with clumps of trees. She could see livestock grazing in the distance. It was the kind of scene you read about in storybooks, and it would be a beautiful place to bring up her child. He would grow strong here, he would feel free, he would play with the children of ranchers and farmers. He would be healthy and alive, not twisted like her parents, or tormented like Tom. He would run barefoot in the meadow near the house, and sit dangling his toes in the brook. She would make him a swing, would buy him a few animals, maybe one day a horse. It was what Tom would have wanted for his son. And if the child was a girl, she would benefit from the same life. And when she was older, she could go back to the world if she chose, but Kate wasn't going back. Let them forget. They would never touch her again. Not the press, nor her parents, no one. This was her home now. She had carved out a place for herself, she had chosen her role. The Widow Harper. It sounded like something in a bad Western, and it made her laugh as she flicked on the radio and reached for a cigarette. It was a rich summer morning, and she felt surprisingly good. Pregnancy wasn't as hard as she had expected it to be, but then, she'd had so many other things on her mind, so many decisions to make, changes to think out. Who had time to worry about heartburn and leg cramps and pains? But still, she had had surprisingly few of those. Maybe it was the easy life she led now in the country. And it was easy, except for the long drives to see Tom. And the way she felt afterwards.

The radio throbbed with the soft beat of ballads alternating with rock and roll, and the early morning announcer purred comments and snippets of news. It was summer time. Everyone was on vacation, taking trips, visiting, going to the beach. It was hard to remember that life now. Kate's life consisted of visiting Tom, then going home and writing. Sometimes she went into the nursery and sat in the rocking chair, wondering what it would feel like to hold the baby in her arms. Would it feel strange, or would she instantly love it? Being a mother was hard to imagine, even with the baby packed so tightly inside her. That she understood, but seeing it would be different . . . holding it . . . she wondered if it would look like Tom. She wanted it to. His name would be Tygue if a boy, and Blaire if a girl. She wanted an unusual name. She had wanted to pick something pretty, something special. Tom would have . . . a small sigh escaped as she put out the cigarette and turned the radio up louder. She'd had enough of her own thoughts. She rolled down the window and let the early morning wind play with her hair. She hadn't bothered with the braids today. Tom had always liked her hair loose. And the denim jumper was too tight now, but he wouldn't notice. The seams seemed to beg for release the way her own skin did now. But there was no give left in either her or the dress. She patted her stomach softly with one hand, as she turned onto the freeway and stepped on the gas. The baby was moving again, almost like a puppydog squirming in her lap. It made her smile as she edged the station wagon up to eighty-five. She wanted the drive to go faster. She wanted to see him now.

After another two and a half hours on the freeway, she knew the turnoff was near. All the signals were familiar now. A big green billboard advertising the restaurant another ten miles down the road. A white clapboard house with blue shutters. A sad-looking little motel, and then the turnoff. She automatically slid into the right lane and eased down her speed.

Nervously she flicked off the radio, lit another cigarette, and waited at the first crossroads for the traffic to pass. Another fifteen miles and she'd have been in Carmel. This area was more rustic, but prettier in its own way. It was inland from Carmel, but you could see the gulls overhead, endlessly looking for food.

Kate stepped on the gas again, and turned onto the first narrow road on her right. It led her onto another smaller road, more like a lane, overgrown with bushes and small trees. Here and there she could see berries ripe on the bushes, and she longed to get out of the car and pick some; she had done that as a child. But she didn't have time, she had to get there. She looked at her watch. It was already nine-thirty. He would be sitting outside now, or maybe just lying in his hammock, thinking. He did that a lot. She wondered what he thought. He never said. He just laughed when she asked, and sometimes he would look like Tom again, as if he still had things to think about. It was strange to see him that way, as though he were teasing, as though any minute he would stop the game. It made her love him even more; there was such sunlight in his eyes, such joy in his face. He was a beautiful boy.

The main building looked like any large well-kept house. It was painted a crisp white with freshly tended yellow trim, there were flower boxes at almost all the windows, and beautiful flowers planted at the edge of the lawns. A narrow, winding walk led to the front door of the main house, which bore a small brass plaque, carefully engraved. Mead Home. Only two words. They didn't need to say more; anyone who came there knew what the place was. There were several smaller houses visible nearby, all painted in the same yellow and white, and farther from the main cluster were a dozen small, cosy-looking yellow cottages, surrounded by flowers and adorned with white trim. The cottages were the more exclusive accommodation. Some were fitted for two residents, others for only one. And each cottage had its own resident attendant to care for his or her charge. Tom lived in one of the cottages, with a quiet older man in attendance – Mr. Erhard, who discreetly disappeared when Kate visited. The enormous

43

insurance Tom had had as a member of the team miraculously covered his stay at Mead, and would continue to do so for ten or twelve years. After that, Kate was going to have to make other arrangements, but by then ... who knew ... the doctors said he could go on for years the way he was.

The grass felt damp on her sandal-clad feet as she walked towards Tom's cottage. She didn't have to check in at the main house anymore. The residents were carefully protected, but she was familiar now. They saw her arrive from the ever-watchful windows of the main house, and she could come and go as she pleased. She simply arrived and went to find Tom. He was easy enough to find. But today when she reached the cottage, he wasn't there.

'Tom?' There was no answer to her knock. 'Mr. Erhard?' The attendant seemed to be gone too. Gingerly, she opened the door and looked around. The room was neatly kept and as bright and pretty as the rest of the facilities. It was why she had chosen Mead Home for Tom. She had been to see a number of places like it within driving distance of San Francisco, and all of them had looked bleak, full of despair. Mead had an aura of hope and sunshine about it. It was a place that time no longer touched, the way it no longer touched Tom. It was safe, tucked away. And it looked more like a school than a sanatorium; Kate always expected to hear children singing, or see them running off to play football.

'Tom?' She wondered where he had gone, as she sank into a chair for a minute to catch her breath. She was breathless today, more than she had been. The baby was crowding her increasingly. And she had driven the three hours straight through without stopping, despite her doctor's orders. But stopping took too much time. She always figured she could get the kinks out when she got to Mead. She stretched her legs for a minute, enjoying the comfortable rocking chair. It was upholstered in a bright print with little red flowers, and the quilts on the two beds matched the chair. The curtains were airy white dotted Swiss, and there was a small jar crammed full of bright yellow flowers on the table near the window. She knew Tom had picked them. Some of his drawings were tacked to

44

the walls, and his hand still had the maturity his head no longer had. There were delicate watercolours of flowers and birds. She had never known that he could draw until he had come to Mead. He had never done anything like it before. Only football. Now he didn't even remember he had played. It was as though he had had to go all the way back to childhood to get rid of it. But at last he had.

Actually this was the perfect cottage for anyone, sick or well, adult or child, and Kate liked knowing he was happy there. And he could get around easily in his wheelchair. Outside there was a hammock Mr. Erhard helped him into when Tom was content just to lie and watch the birds. Sometimes he even let him lie there for a while at night, covered with blankets, looking up at the stars. Mr. Erhard was good to Tom. He had been one of his fans for years, and he was pleased with the special assignment when Tom arrived at Mead.

There was a rustle outside as Kate pushed herself out of the chair, and then she heard Mr. Erhard's rich baritone, telling Tom a story. There was a pause for a moment, when he must have noticed the door to the cottage was slightly ajar. She heard his step on the narrow flagstone path, and in a moment the white mane of her husband's attendant was visible in the doorway.

'Yes?' It was a stern sound, and he looked like a man who brooked neither nonsense nor intrusions. But his face softened instantly when he saw Kate. 'Well, hello there. How are you feeling?'

'Fine. Fat.' They both laughed. 'How's our friend?'

Mr. Erhard nodded, with a satisfied look. 'Doing fine. He did a whole batch of new drawings yesterday, and we picked some flowers this morning. He'll tell you all about—'

'Hey! Andy!' It was Tom's voice from outside. The chair was stuck in the grass. 'Hey!'

'Coming, son.' Erhard was quick to leave the cottage and Kate was right behind him. It was crazy, that smile bursting into her eyes and onto her lips. Why did she still feel like this? As though he were still the old Tom, as though . . . she always felt the same thrill, the same excitement, the same pleasure in just looking at him, touching him, holding him, just knowing he was all right and still hers.

'Katie!' It was a burst of delight as Tom saw her coming towards him. His eyes danced, and his smile went on forever as he reached out his arms.

'Hi, sweetheart. How you be today?'

'Terrific! Wait till you see what we found!'

Mr. Erhard's wise old eyes twinkled as he rolled Tom gently toward the cottage and then inside. He was already gone when Kate turned around.

'Your new drawings are so pretty, love.' But she wasn't looking at the drawings, she was looking at him. He looked brown and strong and happy. The Tom Sawyer of Mead Home. And then he wheeled right up to her and she quickly bent down and took him in her arms. It was a good, clean, warm hug. That was all he understood now, but it carried with it the strength of everything she felt for him.

'You look pretty, Katie.' He looked almost embarrassed as he pulled away, and then wheeled his chair quickly to the table. He picked up the jar with the yellow flowers and then wheeled quickly back. 'I picked these for you.' Tears sprang to her eyes as she smiled at him and took the jar. But they were happy pregnant tears, not tears of grief.

'They're beautiful.' She wanted to hug him again, but she knew she had to wait. It would make him uncomfortable if she overdid it. He would come to her in his own time. 'Want to go for a walk?'

'Okay.'

She tossed her handbag aside and started to push his chair. It was heavier than she had realized, or maybe she was just exceptionally tired. The baby seemed to weigh a thousand pounds today. But Tom helped her as they got onto the walk. He guided the wheels with his hands, and they quickly found one of the smoother walks.

'Want to sit by the lake?' He looked back at her and nodded happily, and then he started whistling to himself.

The lake was tiny but pretty, like everything at Mead. Kate had brought him a model sailboat to use on the water, and he

46

went there often. Mr. Erhard said it was one of his favourite things to do. But they had left it at the cottage. Gently, she turned the chair around, and sat down heavily on the grass.

'So, what've you been up to all week?'

'How come you didn't come to see me this week?'

'Because I was too busy being fat.' There was still this foolish compulsion to talk to him about it, as though she could jog his memory, as though he would understand that the baby was his, or even that there was a baby at all.

'I bet it's hard to run.' He said it with a broad grin and a barely suppressed chuckle that made her laugh too. She reached for his hand, and the clear sound of her laughter rang out over the small lake.

'It sure is. I look like an old mother hen waddling along.' He laughed too then, and kept hold of her hand. They sat smiling for a long time and then he grew serious.

'How come I can't come home with you, Katie? I can do the chair myself. Or maybe we could take Mr. Erhard. Huh?' That again. Dammit.

Kate slowly shook her head, but continued to hold his big hand in hers. 'Don't you like it here, Tom?'

'I want to go home with you.' He looked so wistful that she had to swallow the tears in her throat. She couldn't discuss that with him. Not again. He didn't understand. He made her feel as if she were abandoning him.

'That would be kind of hard to do right now. Why don't we just leave it like this for a while, and then we can talk about it another time?'

'You won't let me then either. I promise I'll be good.' There were tears in his eyes now, and all she could do was rise to her knees on the grass and put her arms around him to hold him close.

'You are good, and I love you. And I promise, darling, if it's possible at all, one day I'll take you home.' There was a long sad silence, as they both held tightly to their own thoughts, worlds away from each other and yet never closer. 'And in the meantime, I'll visit and we'll play, and Mr. Erhard will take good care of you, and ...' It was impossible to go on as she choked back the tears. But Tom had already lost the thread of the conversation.

'Okay. Oh, look!' Excitedly, he pointed upward and she leaned back to look into the sun, wiping the dampness from her eyes. 'Isn't he pretty? I forget what you call it. Mr. Erhard told me yesterday.' It was a blue and green bird with a yellow tail and shimmering wings. Kate smiled slowly at Tom and sat down on the grass again.

'I brought you a picnic. How about that?'

'For real?'

She held up a solemn hand. 'For real. I promise.' It was fun doing things for him, even if it was only making a picnic lunch. She had brought salami sandwiches, and big fresh country potato chips, macaroni salad, beautiful peaches and a basket of cherries. And there was a thermos of lemonade and a slab of chocolate cake. He even ate like a kid now.

'What's it got?' His eyes were dancing again. The wanting to go home with Katie was already forgotten. For now.

'You'll see what's in the picnic when you get hungry for lunch.' She waggled a finger at him, and he caught it. It was a game they had played since they met. They still played it. It was one of the things that allowed her to pretend, for a moment, a minute, the flash of an eyelash, that everything was the same.

'I'm hungry.'

'You are not. You just want to see what's in the picnic basket.' She lay on the grass, feeling like an overturned whale, and grinned up at him.

'Honest, I'm hungry!' But he was laughing again, they both were.

'How can you be hungry? It's ten-thirty in the morning.'

'Mr. Erhard didn't give me any breakfast.' But the laughter danced right out of his eyes and he couldn't keep a straight face.

'Baloney. You fibber.'

'Come on, Katie. I'm starving.'

'You're impossible.' But she pushed herself up to a sitting position and thought about getting the basket. If he was hungry, why not? 'I brought you a present, by the way.'

'You did? What?'

'You'll see.'

'Oh, you're so mean!' He said it with the outrage of child-hood, and a fierce impatience for both the picnic and the gift. And with another slow smile, Kate got to her feet and then bent down to kiss the tip of his nose. 'Don't do that!' Gently, he swatted her away.

'Why not?'

'Because you're a meanie, that's why!' But his arm went round her waist, and for a moment they stayed there, he in his chair and she standing next to him. This time she moved away first.

'I'll go get the stuff.' There was smoke in her voice, and they still had the day ahead of them.

'Want me to help?'

'Okay. You can carry the picnic basket.' He wheeled himself to the car as she walked along slowly beside him in the sun-shine. They chatted, and he told her what he'd been doing, about the drawings, about a new game she'd brought him the week before, about a nurse he hated at the main house, and 'the best dinner I've ever had', while Kate listened as though it were all true, as though it mattered.

When they got to the car, she lifted the picnic basket care-fully onto his lap, and reached in beside it for a red- and white-striped package tied with a big bow.

'For you, my love.' She closed the car, and pushed him slowly back up the walk.

'Harry up!'

'We have a problem?' She'd need Mr. Erhard for that. Tom was far too heavy for her to cope with when he needed to relieve himself.

'No, dummy, I want to open my present.' He was holding it close, and had already dug a hand into the picnic basket and come up with a handful of cherries and a little tiny piece of cake.

'Stay out of that, Tom Harper, or I'll—'

'No, you won't, Katie, you love me too much.'

'You're right.' They both smiled then, and Kate settled him

49

under a tree outside his cottage. The grounds were fresh and bright. In time he might tire of them. But not yet.

'Can I open it now?' He looked at her for approval and she nodded, as he quickly tore off the paper. It had been a foolish thing to buy him, but she hadn't been able to resist when she'd seen it. And she'd bought one for the baby's room too. 'Oh, I love him! What's his name?' Tom held the big brown bear close, and squeezed it tight. Kate was surprised and pleased at his instant delight.

'I don't know his name. You tell me. I think he looks like a George myself.'

'Yeah. Maybe.' Tom looked him over thoughtfully.

'Lucius?' Kate was smiling again. She was glad she'd bought it for him after all. So what if it was silly? What difference did that make now, if it made him happy?

'Not Lucius, that's horrible. I know! Willie!'

'Willie?'

'Willie!' He leaned over with his arms held out and Kate gave him a hug, and a little kiss on the forehead. 'Thank you, Katie, he's beautiful.'

'He looks like you.'

He swatted her with the bear then and they both laughed.

'Want to sit in your hammock? I'll get Mr. Erhard if you want.'

'No, this is nice.' He was already elbow deep in the picnic basket and he stayed that way for the next half hour, with Willie sitting contentedly on his lap.

They rested quietly for a while after lunch, and Kate almost fell asleep in the warm summer air. There was the tiniest breeze ruffling her hair as she lay near Tom's wheelchair, and the baby was finally still for the first time all day. They passed the basket of cherries back and forth, shooting pits at the trees and then laughing.

'One day there will be a whole field of cherry trees here and no one will know why.'

'We will. Right, Katie?'

'Right.'

His voice was so soft, almost wistful, that she thought he

must know. But what was the point of his knowing? It was the one thing that always stopped her from trying to jolt him into remembering. If he ever returned to what he had been, he would have to stand trial for assault or attempted murder or whatever they decided to call it. He was better off in Mead Home, the way he was, than in a different kind of prison. There was no way to 'jolt' him back anyway. The doctor had explained it to her often enough. But the temptation was always there. Sometimes, just for a second, he sounded so much like himself, like the old Tom, that it was hard to believe the bullet had destroyed as much as the doctors said it had. It had been hard to give up hope, to stop trying.

'Katie?'

'Hm?' She looked up at him, a twig of cherries still in her hand; she had forgotten them for a moment.

'What were you thinking?'

'Oh nothing much. Just lying here, feeling lazy.'

'You look pretty when you think.' And then his eyes slid politely to her belly. He was sorry she was so fat, but it didn't matter much. He loved her, no matter what.

'Thank you, Tom.' She poured him a glass of lemonade, and lay back on the grass. There was a tall tree overhead, shading them from the bright sun, and in the air the wonderful stillness of a summer afternoon. The only thing missing was the squeaking of a screen door, somewhere in the distance, and then the banging of it as a child went in for a glass of cold water. 'It's pretty here, isn't it?' He nodded happily in answer and shot another cherry pit in the direction of the cottage.

'I need a slingshot.'

'My eye you do.'

'Not to hurt anyone with' – he looked offended – 'just for things like cherry pits. Or paper clips. You know – to shoot at trees.' But he was grinning again, the irrepressible, mischievous grin.

'How do you even know about those things anyway? They went out of style years ago.'

'I saw one on TV.'

'Terrific.'

'Maybe I could make one.' But she wasn't listening to him. The baby had just delivered a ferocious kick to her ribs. She took a deep breath, let it out slowly, and wondered if it was time to call it a day. She still had the long drive home, and it was almost two. She had been there for four hours. It wasn't long, but right now it was about all she could manage. She looked at Tom taking careful aim with another cherry pit. He still had a smudge of chocolate cake on one cheek. She sat up and wiped it off gently, then looked towards the cottage. She had seen Mr. Erhard go inside almost an hour before.

'I'm going to go inside for a minute, love. Want anything?'

He shook his head happily. 'Nope.'

Mr. Erhard was waiting, reading the newspaper and smoking a pipe. It seemed a wintry pastime for such a warm, sunny day.

'Ready to go?'

'I think I'd better.'

'I'm surprised your doctor even lets you come up here.' And then he smiled a fatherly smile. 'Or don't you ask him?'

'Well, let's just say we compromise on it.'

'You know, you really could skip a couple of weeks. I'll keep him busy. He may complain about it when you get back, but he won't notice it while you're gone.' It was depressing to realize Mr. Erhard was right.

'I don't know. I'll see how I feel next week.'

'Good enough.'

After another quick stop at the bathroom, she went outside and he followed her, walking towards Tom, waving his pipe in a greeting.

'So you're the one who's been pelting the house with cherry pits all day, is that it?' But he was grinning broadly and Tom laughed with delight. 'I'll bet you can't hit that tree.' But he was wrong. Tom hit it and squarely.

'You'd better watch out, Mr. E., he wants a slingshot.'

'Remember? Like the one on that show the other night? The one when the boy . . .' The tale was long and garbled, but Mr. Erhard fell into the discussion with ease, and Kate watched him. She always hated leaving him. It should have been a relief, but it wasn't. Getting there was a relief, seeing him was, leaving him still tore at her heart.

'Okay, love, I'm going to go now, but I'll be back soon.'

'Okay, Katie, so long.' He waved nonchalantly, and the discussion of the morning was long since forgotten. This was more home to him now than anywhere else. He didn't even flinch at her departure. She stooped to kiss him on the cheek and squeezed his shoulder.

'Take good care of Willie, my love.' She walked away with a wave and a smile and a rock settling on her heart, as he sat in his chair holding the teddy bear. She could still see him as she backed the car slowly out of its space. She rolled down the window for a last wave, but he was already engrossed in his talk with Mr. Erhard. 'Good-bye, Tom, I love you.' She said it to herself in a whisper as she drove away.

CHAPTER III

The drive home seemed longer than it ever had before. She kept seeing Tom with the teddy bear, and thinking of things he had said. She finally forced the visit from her mind, and flicked on the radio. She had cramps in her legs, and suddenly all she wanted was to get home. It had been too long a day, and she had that desperate feeling of exhaustion that swept up on her so quickly now, as though she hadn't the strength for another step. Maybe Mr. Erhard was right. Maybe she should stop coming for the next few weeks. It was only going to be three more weeks till the baby came. She didn't even let herself think of that though. Not the baby, not Tom. All she could think of was her bed, and getting out of the clothes that seemed to be strangling her whole body. It seemed a thousand years later when she finally pulled into her own driveway. She was so tired she didn't even see the little red Alfa Romeo parked at the side of the house. She just slipped out of the car, stood next to it for a minute, steadying herself and rubbing her calves, and began to walk slowly and stiffly towards the front door.

'You look like you're in great shape.' It was the deep, cynical voice of Felicia Norman, and Kate jumped a foot. 'Hey, lady, take it easy. I'm a miserable midwife.' And then Kate looked up and laughed.

'You scared the hell out of me, Licia.'

'I'm surprised you've got enough energy left to be scared. What do you think you're doing to yourself?' She took the basket out of her friend's hand and they walked slowly towards the house.

'Never mind that. What are you doing down here early?'

'I decided I needed a vacation and you needed a guest.'

'A vacation?'

'Well, a long weekend. I took four days.' And she was glad

she had come. Kate looked wiped out, and if that was what going up to see Tom did to her, maybe she could stop her from going for a while, or at least drive her up there. But this was lunacy.

'Do you realize what a miracle it is that you haven't been fired yet, thanks to me? But Kate was grinning. It was good to see her.

'They're just goddamn lucky I don't quit. If we do one more show this month, I'm going to have a nervous breakdown.' And so would her assistant. In order to be with Kate, Felicia had foisted all the week's shows onto her assistant again. That was going to cost her another Gucci bag, and a fat lunch at Trader Vic's, but she had had this feeling . . . she had to come down to see Kate. And she was glad that she had. She shoved the picnic basket onto the kitchen counter and looked around. It really was a pleasant house. It had been a good choice. 'So how's Tom?'

'Fine. Happy. Nothing new.' Felicia nodded solemnly and sat down in a chair. Kate followed suit.

'You know, Licia, you look worse than I do, but then, you drove further. Want the leftover lemonade?'

Felicia made a horrible face. 'Darling, I love you, but lemonade is not me. God, what a horrible thought.'

Kate looked at her with an apologetic smile. 'I don't have anything more interesting to offer you, I'm afraid.'

'The hell you don't.' Felicia grinned wickedly and walked towards a cupboard with glee. 'I left some vermouth and gin here last week. And I brought onions and olives.' She pulled the little jars out of her bag with a broad smile.

'You'd make a fabulous Girl Scout.'

'Wouldn't I though?' She retrieved her bottles and mixed herself a professional-looking martini, as Kate sat up a little straighter in her chair. 'Heartburn again?' Felicia knew the look on her face. She had been around enough to know all the looks, better than Kate herself did. Everything from heartburn to hysterics. And this looked like heartburn.

'I think I ate too many cherries at lunch. It feels more like indigestion than heartburn.' And cramps. Jesus, that was all she needed, a bellyache to go with her big belly. Poor baby, how could she have done that to him, and herself? Thinking of it made her giggle. 'Maybe I just need a martini.' But they both knew she didn't mean it. She hadn't had a drink in months.

'Why don't you go lie down? I'll have a shower, and then I can throw some dinner together.' Felicia looked matter-of-fact and very much at home.

'You came down here to cook for me, yes.'

'Yes. Now go get out of your dress and lie down.'

'Yes, mother.'

She felt better though when she had. And after a shower, she felt wonderful. She could hear Felicia starting to rattle around the kitchen, and she stopped in the nursery for a minute, and there it was. Willie. The same bear as Tom's. She wondered how his Willie was doing just then, if Tom was holding it, loving it, or had already forgotten it. She touched the bear gently and then left the room.

'What are you up to?'

'Spaghetti okay with you?' It was one of three things Felicia could cook. The other two were fried eggs and steak. Kate nodded.

'Wonderful. Spaghetti ought to be worth another five pounds, but at this point, what the hell.'

They ate dinner by candlelight, looking at the view, and it was refreshing to have someone to talk to. Kate was growing too used to silence, and to seeing only Tom. She needed Felicia to add a little pepper to the cream soup of her life. Felicia added lots of it. Pepper supreme. She was in the midst of regaling Kate with the week's gossip from the store – who was screwing whom, being promoted, getting fired, or had turned out to be a fag after all. But Katie wasn't listening as intently or laughing as hard as she normally would have.

'What's the matter, love? You look kind of green. My spaghetti?'

'No. I think it's those goddamn cherries again.' It was that same gnawing, grinding feeling she'd had before dinner, only slightly worse.

56

'Cherries, my ass. You wore yourself out. Why don't you lie down on the couch? Or do you want to go to bed?'

'I'm not really tired.' In fact, she felt jumpy, but she had felt like that before, just after seeing Tom. She lay down on the couch anyway, and then started to joke with Felicia again. 'Maybe it *is* your lousy spaghetti.'

'Up yours, lady. I happen to make the best spaghetti in the West.'

'Mama Felicia.'

Felicia concocted herself another martini and the two women bantered and laughed. But the indigestion grew worse rather than better.

'Maybe I'll go to bed after all.'

'Okay. See ya.' Felicia grinned as Kate went off to her room. The dishes had already been done. Kate had meant to say something about being glad her friend was there, but she had told her so many times before that she was no longer sure how to say it.

Kate was asleep before nine o'clock, and Felicia tucked herself onto the couch with a book. She wasn't tired and it had been a rough week at work. It was nice just to sit and unwind, nice to get away. She got engrossed in the novel and it was almost one o'clock when she heard Kate stirring in her room. She listened for a minute to be sure, and then she saw a gleam of light under the bedroom door.

'You okay?' Felicia was frowning as she called out. But the voice came back quickly.

'Yeah.' She did sound all right.

'You still have that bellyache?'

'Uh huh.'

It was two minutes later when Kate came out of her room, and stood in the doorway in a long pink and white nightgown. She looked like a strangely swollen child, and on her face was a bright wide-eyed smile.

'Felicia . . .' The smile broadened.

'Yeah? What's up?' Felicia didn't know what to make of the look on Kate's face. She looked ethereally happy, and Felicia had never seen her look like that before.

57

'I don't think it's a bellyache. I think maybe ... it's the baby.' Kate almost laughed. She felt elated. It was crazy — she was scared, and it was too soon, but she was excited. The baby! It was coming at last!

'You mean you're having it?' Felicia suddenly looked grey. Kate nodded. 'Maybe. I'm not sure.'

'Isn't it early?'

Kate nodded again, but she didn't look upset. 'I think eight months is safe. And it's been almost eight and a half.'

'Did you call the doctor?'

Kate nodded again solemnly, with a look of victory. She was going to do it. She was going to have the baby. Maybe tonight. She didn't have to wait anymore. It was over. It was beginning! 'He said to call him back in an hour, or if the pains got much harder.'

'You're having pains?' Felicia squeezed the book in her lap and stared at her friend.

. 'I guess so. I thought it was just indigestion, but they keep getting stronger, and then every now and then ...' And then, as though impatient with talking, she sat down suddenly and reached for Felicia's hand. 'Here, you can feel it.'

Without thinking, Felicia let Kate put her hand on the bloated belly. She could feel its hardness and tightness. It didn't even feel like a belly. It felt like a wall, a floor, something that could be cracked open, not squeezed.

'My God, how awful. Does it hurt?'

Kate shook her head, with that same excited look in her eyes, but there was a thin veil of sweat on her forehead. 'No, it doesn't hurt. It just feels very, very tight.'

'Can I get you something, love?' Felicia's hands were trembling and Kate laughed.

'No, and if you fall apart now, I'll kick your ass. I'm glad you're here.'

'So am I.' But she didn't look it and Kate laughed again.

'Relax.'

'Yeah.' Felicia sighed deeply and sat back against the back of the couch. 'I can handle almost any crisis. But babies have never been my thing. I've never been to one before. I mean ...

58

oh damn, I need a drink.' The unruffable Felicia Norman was ruffling badly, and Kate was strangely calm. This was what she had waited nearly nine months for.

'You don't need a drink. Licia. I need you.' That was a sobering thought and Felicia looked at her. Kate didn't look as though she needed anyone.

'You mean it?'

'Yes.' Her voice was tight again, and Felicia watched her. She knew what it was now.

'Another pain?'

Kate nodded, with a vague look, as though she were thinking of something else, and Felicia silently held out her hand. Kate took it and squeezed hard. The pains were starting to hurt.

CHAPTER IV

The pains were rising to a rapid crescendo now, and there was barely a moment to breathe between them. Felicia sat tensely in a chair near the bed in the bleak little hospital room. She was holding Kate's hand. The sun was just peeking over the hills with a golden halo around it.

'Want another piece of ice?' Felicia's voice was harsh in the quiet room, but Kate only shook her head. She couldn't speak now. She just lay there, panting determinedly as she had learned to do in the classes she had taken two months before. 'Aren't you tired of doing that?' Kate shook her head again, closed her eyes, and for ten seconds the panting stopped. She hardly had time for one normal breath before the pain crashed through her consciousness again. Her hair lay damp and matted around her face, and for what seemed the thousandth time that night Felicia stood up and wiped her forehead with a damp cloth. The exhilaration was gone from Kate's face. The only thing visible there now was pain.

'Hang in, love, it can't be much longer.' Kate showed no sign of having heard. She was panting again, and then suddenly she stopped and a soft moan gave way to a short startling scream. Felicia jumped in surprise, as Kate began to thrash in her bed and move her head from side to side.

'Licia ... can't ... I can't ... anymore ...' But even the time it took to say those words was too long. Already the pain was tearing through her again, and another moan escaped her, quickly capped by another scream.

'Kate ... hey, baby, come on ...' Jesus. She wasn't prepared for this. It was worse than anything she'd seen in the movies. Frantically, Felicia rang for the nurse, and Kate began to cry.

It was less than a minute later when the nurse opened the

60

door and stuck her head inside. 'How's it going, girls?' Felicia looked at her in icy fury.

'How does it look like it's going?' She wanted to kill her. Why the hell wasn't she doing something for Kate? The girl was in agony for chrissake. People died like that – didn't they?

'Looks just fine to me.' The nurse's eyes seemed to shoot sparks at Felicia. She walked quickly to Kate's bed and took the girl's hand. 'You're almost there, Kate. This is the hard part. You're in transition now. After this it gets lots easier, and pretty soon you can start to push.' Kate turned her head from side to side again, in a sharp frantic motion, and her tears mixed with the sweat running into her hair.

'I can't ... I can't ...' She retched as though to throw up, but nothing came.

'Yes, you can. Come on. I'll breathe with you.' And quickly, the nurse started the panting, holding firmly to Kate's hand. 'Come on, now, Kate ... now ...' She could see the pain starting to tear at Kate's face again. 'Now ... there ...' The panting was driving Felicia nuts, but Kate looked less panicky. Maybe she would make it after all. God, it was awful though. Christ, why would anyone go through that? Another soft moan, and then a sharp little scream burst in on her thoughts again, and the nurse's soft purring continued. She wondered how Kate stood it; she had always seemed so frail. No child was worth this. No man. No one. Felicia felt tears burn her eyes, as she turned to look at the rising sun. She couldn't bear to see her friend suffer anymore. She had already been through too much, and now this. When Felicia turned from the window she found the nurse's eyes meeting hers, this time more gently. 'Why don't you get a cup of coffee? The coffee shop should be open by now.'

'No, it's all right. I—'

'Go on. We're doing fine.' And she was right, Kate did look better. There was still that dogged look of pain in her eyes, but she was back in the fight again. And probably working too hard to care whether Felicia left for a few minutes. This was labour, in the real sense of the word.

'Okay. But I'll be back soon.'

'We'll be here.' The nurse smiled cheerily and went on breathing with Kate while timing contractions. And for the first time, Felicia felt left out. She wondered if that was how fathers felt as they watched their wives writhe in pain, straining towards a goal a man could see but never feel. Felicia knew she would never feel that pain. She would never love anyone enough for that. Not the way Kate had loved Tom. Thinking about it tore at her again, as she walked soberly towards the coffee shop. She didn't even want a drink now. What she really wanted was to know that it was over, and go home to shower and sleep. The long drive of the day before and the long sleepless night were beginning to catch up with her.

'How's Mrs. Harper doing?' A fat matronly nurse at the desk glanced up at Felicia. It was a very small town. Felicia wondered if the woman at the desk remembered everyone's name.

'I don't know. It looks awful to me.'

'Ever had a baby?' Felicia shook her head expressionlessly. Funny to be answering these questions for a stranger. The woman nodded. 'She'll forget all about it in a couple of days. She may talk about it a little, but she'll forget. You'll remember it longer than she will.'

'Maybe so.' For no reason she could fathom, she paused for a moment at the desk, as though expecting the nurse to say more. Just talking to someone was comforting. 'I hope it won't be much longer.'

'Might be. Might not. Hard to tell. It's her first one, isn't it?' Felicia nodded. Then that meant more pain, did it? The first one. And maybe her last. Poor Kate ... 'Don't look so sad. She'll be just fine. You'll see. As soon as the baby's born she'll be laughing and crying, and she'll call her folks and tell everyone she knows.' The woman's face clouded momentarily as she looked at Felicia. 'She's a widow though, isn't she?'

'Yes.'

'That's an awful shame. At a time like this. What did he die of?'

'Of ... in an accident.' Felicia's face closed quietly. Like a door. They had said enough.

62

'I'm sorry.' The nurse had sensed it, and sat silently for a moment, as Felicia gave her a small mechanical smile and walked away. The coffee would do her good.

She spent only five minutes in the coffee shop. She would have stayed for days if she could have, but she didn't want to leave Kate alone. She swallowed the hot coffee as quickly as her mouth could stand it, and considered an order of toast. But that seemed excessive. Kate was in agony, and she was going to eat toast? The thought of it made her feel sick. And then, suddenly, as she waited for her check, she found herself thinking of Tom. She wondered if Kate was thinking of him too, or only of her pain. Tom. He should have been here for this. It was incredible to realize that he would never see his child. He would never understand that he had one. The girl behind the counter slipped the check under Felicia's empty cup, and Felicia glanced at it and absentmindedly left two quarters on the counter. She had to get back to Kate. She didn't have time for this kind of thinking.

The black espadrilles she had worn the day before whispered silently down the corridor, and she looked down at how rumpled she was. The black cotton pant-suit she'd picked up on the third floor earlier in the week looked like she'd slept in it, and the heavy Indian silver bracelet was leaving a long red furrow on her arm. She wondered how much longer this waiting would go on, and how much more Kate could take. She had been in labour since a little after midnight, and it was now just after seven in the morning. But when Felicia gently pushed open the door, things had changed in the room. Kate's face was wet with sweat now, not just damp – she looked as though she had been standing under the shower. The blue hospital gown clung to her body, and her hand kept a white-knuckled grip on the nurse. But her eyes were brighter, her face was alive, and the rhythm of her movements had changed; it was as though she had moved from an agonized painful trot to a full-blown gallop. It was hard to tell if the pain had lessened, and even the nurse couldn't take time to talk to Felicia now. She was telling Kate about 'cleansing breaths' and giving orders with military precision. But Kate seemed to be totally

63

absorbed in what she was saying. And then Felicia noticed the free hand go quickly to the buzzer and press three times.

Felicia stood by, feeling useless, not knowing if things were going badly or well, and afraid to interrupt Kate's concentration by asking questions. But something had changed. Everything had. There was a light in Kate's face that Felicia had never seen before in anyone's face. It made her want to work too, want to help, want to run the race along with her and feel the winner's ribbon give way on her chest as she crossed the finish line and won. She was winning now. You could feel it in the room. She even smiled once, briefly between two mammoth pains. The smile darted away, but its aura remained.

The nurse buzzed again, and this time the door opened quickly and two nurses in what looked like blue pyjamas appeared with a gurney. 'Doctor's waiting for us in two. How's she doing?' They looked relaxed and unconcerned, and for a moment their attitude reassured Felicia, but Kate seemed not to notice them at all. The nurse at her side waited between pains to look at the two nurses in blue, and then gave them a wide, easy smile.

'We're ready. Very ready. Right, Kate?' Kate nodded, and for the first time in a while, her eyes searched for Felicia. She found her quickly, and started to talk. But she had to wait for another pain to pass before she could speak, and then the two nurses used the few seconds they had between pains to shift her to the gurney. But she was anxious for Felicia, who was quick to step to her side.

'Come with me . . . please, Licia . . .'

'Now?'

'I want you . . .' It was suddenly much harder to speak. As though all her air were cut off during the pains. Fresh rivers of sweat broke out on her face and ran down her neck, but she wouldn't let go of Felicia. 'Please . . . when the baby comes . . . you too.' Felicia understood. But, oh God, why her? The nurses were with Kate, they knew what they were doing. They could help her more than she could. But there was no denying that look in Kate's eyes.

'Sure, love. You just keep busy with what you're doing, and

I'll be right with you holding your hand.' She was already walking beside the stretcher, as it was rolled down the hall. The nurse striding quickly beside Kate raised an eyebrow in Felicia's direction.

'Are you planning to be in the delivery room?'

There was only the tinest second of hesitation, and then her answer was firm. 'Yes.' Oh Jesus. Her stomach turned over again, but she couldn't let Kate down.

'Then you'll have to scrub and change your clothes.'

'Where?'

'In there.' The nurse nodded at a door. 'The nurse on duty will help you. Meet us in delivery room two.'

'Two?'

The nurse nodded distractedly as Kate arched her back in pain and forgot Felicia's presence. 'Hold on, honey, we're almost there. Not yet. Not yet. Just as soon as we get you on the table.' And then she was gone, and Felicia disappeared into the appointed door to scrub and change.

She emerged less than three minutes later in sterilized blue pyjamas and rubber-soled 'grounded' shoes, and ran nervously down the corridor towards delivery room two. The nurse in the scrub room had told her where it would be. She pressed a floor buzzer and the door automatically swung open. She was careful to keep her hands and arms away from contact with any surfaces, as she had been told. Once in the delivery room she could hold Kate's hand, but she couldn't touch anything before that, or she'd have to scrub again, and she didn't want to keep Kate waiting that long. It had already seemed like hours. She caught a glimpse of herself in a narrow glass panel and almost grinned. She looked like a character in one of the medical shows on television, her hair tightly wound into a knot and covered with a blue cap that looked like a shower cap. She even wore a little mask. Christ, what if someone took her for a nurse? It was a horrifying thought as she walked into the delivery room, and then she realized that no one could take her for anything but a tourist. The pros were busy getting organized, and Kate was already draped with white sheets. Her legs had been strapped high in the air. To

65

Felicia it looked primitive and cruel, but Kate didn't seem to notice. She kept lifting her head now, as though there was something to see. And for a moment, Felicia felt a small thrill run through her as she realized that maybe there was. This wasn't just Kate's ordeal anymore. It was an event, a happening, a birth. In a few minutes a baby would be born, and the horror of it would be over for Kate. But Felicia had to admit that even now there seemed to be no 'horror' for Kate. For the first time in hours, Kate turned her head towards her and her eyes seemed to be laughing.

'Hi, cookie.' Felicia tried hard to sound more at ease than she was.

'You look ridiculous, Licia.' She could talk again. Felicia felt so relieved she wanted to hug her, but knew she couldn't. Instead, she started to reach for Kate's hand, and then realized that Kate's hands were busy now, pulling at two straps to give herself the leverage she needed to push. The doctor was at the foot of the delivery table, gowned and masked, and his eyes looked kindly behind horn-rimmed glasses.

'Okay, Kate, a nice big one now ... steady ... there ... that's it ... a little more ... come on, girl, harder ... there ... okay. Rest for a minute now.' For a moment Kate's face had been contorted with the effort, and the damp pallor gave way to a hot flush of bursting effort. She was breathless from the strain, and let her head fall back on the pillow, with a quick look at her friend.

'Oh Licia, I can't ... help me.' Felicia looked frightened and helpless for a moment and a nurse came rapidly up to the head of the table where she stood.

'If you'd support her shoulders while she pushed, it would help a lot.'

'Me?' It was the only word Felicia could think of, but Kate was looking like a tired child again – the joy and anticipation had gone. She was exhausted. And then another pain roared through Kate, and everyone seemed to tense with anticipation as the doctor did something between her legs.

'Licia ...' Without thinking, Felicia gently scooped Kate's shoulders into her arms, and held her as the labouring girl shook with effort. She had never worked as hard at anything in her life. 'I can't . . . it won't . . .'

'Harder, Kate! Come on, now!' The doctor sounded urgent and firm, the nurses seemed to be doing a lot of running and clattering, and Kate was starting to cry again.

'I can't . . . I . . .' Felicia felt sweat begin to run down her own face as she continued to support Kate's shoulder's. Even that was almost too much effort, and she knew it was nothing compared to what Kate must be feeling. Why the hell didn't they give her something to speed it up, or use forceps, or *something* dammit?

'Push harder!' The doctor sounded merciless, and Felicia hated him as she watched Kate's face contort with what she thought was pain. It was more work than pain, but Felicia couldn't know. And then suddenly the nurses were buzzing around them again.

'Come on, Kate. You can do it now. Just one more good hard push. That's it . . . come on . . .' There was no respite, and then suddenly Felicia realized the tension in the room had heightened. As she glanced at the doctor she saw a different look in his eyes, and one of the nurses was checking a monitoring system they had looped to Kate somewhere. And then Felicia heard it, softly, at the other end of the table. She prayed that Kate was too distracted to hear. 'Foetal heart monitor, Doctor.'

'Slowing?'

'Irregular.'

He nodded in answer, and another pain ripped into Kate.

'Okay, Kate, this is it. I want one nice big push from you. Now!' But this time she only flinched at the command, and fought against Felicia's arms behind her. She let her head fall back, and an endless sob burst from her.

'Oh, Licia . . . Tom . . . Tom! Oh Tom! . . . please . . .'

'Kate. Please, baby. Please, for us. For Tom. Just one more try.' Tears had begun to pour down Felicia's cheeks now and into her mask. She was blinded by them, as she held the frail shoulders in her trembling arms, and prayed that the ordeal would end. It had to. Kate couldn't take any more. Felicia knew that. But maybe for Tom . . . 'Please, baby, I know you can do it. Push as hard as you can.' And then a riot of sounds, the clattering of instruments, a grunt from the doctor, a little cry from a nurse, sudden silence from Kate, and a long, cackling little wail.

'It's a boy!' The doctor slapped him firmly on the bottom and Kate lay back with tears streaming from her eyes and smiled up at her friend.

'We did it.'

'You did it, champ.' Tears poured from Felicia's eyes too. 'Oh and he's so beautiful.' He was small and round and his face was an angry red as he wailed on, and then suddenly he stuck a tiny thumb in his mouth and the crying stopped as Kate laughed, watching her son. Felicia had never seen anything as beautiful as the way Kate looked. She couldn't stop crying, and Kate just grinned, silent and proud. And then without another word, they wrapped him carefully and handed him to his mother. The cord had been cut. He was free now. And he was hers.

Kate lay there with her son in her arms, tears still flowing from her eyes, and she looked up at Felicia again. And Felicia understood. She had seen it too. Tiny as he was, he looked just like Tom.

'What's his name?' The nurse who had been with Kate the longest came to look at the tiny pink face snuggled in his mother's arms. He was a big baby, just under nine pounds.

'His name's Tygue.' And then in the lull of activity, as the doctor looked on and smiled, Kate laughed a long happy laugh. She sounded like a girl again, and she picked up her head and looked around the room. 'Hey, everybody, I'm a mom!' They laughed with her, and Felicia couldn't stop laughing despite the tears still in her eyes.

CHAPTER V

'You're sure you'll be all right?'

Kate grinned across the room at her friend. 'No, I'm going to panic and call the Red Cross before noon.'

'Smartass.' Felicia grinned, and sipped the last of her coffee. It was a peaceful Sunday morning, and Tygue was almost nine days old. Felicia had gone back to San Francisco and had returned to the country for the weekend. Now she watched as Kate nursed the baby. 'Doesn't that hurt?'

Kate shook her head with a slow smile, and then looked down at her son, pink and white and shiny after his first week of life. 'No, it doesn't hurt. It sounds corny, but it almost feels like this was what I was made for. And I didn't really think I'd like it.'

'I never thought I would either. But you know, you're beginning to make me wonder about a lot of things. I always thought having a baby had to be the ultimate horror. Until Pipsqueak here came along.' Felicia smiled at him again; she still hadn't got over the beauty of the experience. 'I'm going to miss you two something awful.'

'It'll do you good. I haven't been to Europe in so long, I forget what it looks like.' Felicia was going over for a month, for the store.

'Want to come along on my next trip?'

'With Tygue?' Kate looked surprised, and Felicia smiled.

'Either way. It would be fun.'

'Maybe so.' But she looked away and her face was very closed.

'Kate, you're not really serious about staying down here, are you?' It was beginning to worry her.

'Very much so. I just signed another lease on the house.'

'For how long?'

'Five years.'

Felicia looked appalled. 'Can you get out of it?'

'I have no idea, love. I'm not planning to. Licia, I know you don't understand it, but this is my house now. I don't think I'd ever want to go back, no matter what. But with Tygue, I'm ready to start a new life. I'd have had to do it somewhere, and this is where I want to be. It's a good place for a child. He'll have a simple, healthy life. I can get up to see Tom. And in a town like this, Tygue never really needs to know what happened to Tom. Harper is a perfectly ordinary name. No one will ask questions. If we go back to San Francisco, one day – it'll all come out.' She sighed deeply and looked Felicia square in the face. 'I'd be crazy to go back.' Just thinking of the reporters still made her cringe.

'All right. Then what about Los Angeles? Someplace civilized for God's sake.' Kate grinned at Felicia's fervour, but she knew that she meant well. There was an even stronger bond between them now, ever since's Tygue's birth. They had shared one of life's most precious moments.

'Why Los Angeles, Licia? I have nothing there. It's just a city. Look, love, I have no family, no place to be, nothing I have to do. I have a little boy who will thrive here, and it's a good place for me to write. I'm happy here.'

'But you are planning to come up to the city from time to time, aren't you?' There was a long pause, and Felicia was finally seeing it all. '*Aren't* you?' Her voice was soft and sad. She was sad for Kate, who was gone for good. This was no place for her, but by the time she realized it, it would be too late. Maybe not until the boy was grown and gone. 'You will come up to the city, won't you?' She was pressing the point, but Kate's face was set when she looked up from Tygue's sleeping face at her breast. She buttoned her blouse.

'We'll see, Licia. I don't know.'

'But you don't plan to, is that it?' Dammit. How could she do that to herself?

'All right. I don't plan to. Does it make you feel better knowing that?'

'No, you ass, it makes me feel like shit. Kate, you can't do that to yourself, shut away down here in the weeds and the fields. That's nuts. You're beautiful, you're young. Don't do this!'

'I have nothing back there, Licia. Not anymore. No family, no memories I want to keep, nothing. Except you, and I'll see you here, when you can get away.'

'What about life and people? Theatre, opera, ballet, modelling, parties? Jesus, Kate, look what you're throwing away!'

'I'm not throwing it away. I've walked out on it. It'll all be there if I ever change my mind.'

'But you're twenty-three now. This is when you should be out there enjoying it all, taking advantage of everything life tosses at your feet.'

Kate smiled at the words and looked down at her son again, and then with a purposeful look she brought her eyes back to Felicia's. There was nothing left to be said. Felicia had lost.

Felicia closed her eyes for a moment and then stood up. 'I don't know what to say.'

'Just tell me you'll come to see us when you have time, and that you'll have a good time in Europe.' Kate wore a firm little smile that didn't invite argument or discussion.

'And what'll you do?'

'I am going to start work on a book.'

'A book?' Christ, it was like adolescence. Kate was throwing her whole damn life away, all because her husband had gone bananas and wound up in a sanatorium. But it wasn't *her* doing. Why did she have to bury herself alive because he was? The bracelets on Felicia's arms clanked as she nervously put her coffee cup in the sink. She wished she could talk sense into the girl, but she'd just have to give it another try when she got back from Europe. Something told her, though, that she would never win. Kate had changed a lot just in the few days since the baby was born. She seemed much surer of everything. And stubborn as hell.

'Why does it surprise you so much 'that I want to write a book?'

'That just seems like such a funny thing to do. And awfully lonely, frankly.'

'We'll see. And I've got Tygue to keep me company now.'

'After a fashion.' Felicia looked bleak. 'What'll you do with him when you go to see Tom?'

'I don't know yet. One of the nurses at the hospital thought she might know of a reliable sitter, an older woman who is wonderful with babies. Or I might take him with me. But it's really too long a trip, and . . . well, I'm not sure.' Tom wouldn't understand. It would be better leaving him home with a sitter.

'The sitter sounds like a good idea.'

'Yes, mother.'

'Up yours, Mrs. Harper. You know, you're going to give me more grey hairs than the store does.'

'On you, it'll look marvellous.'

'Such remorse!' But Felicia was smiling again. 'Just remember me in one of your books.' Kate laughed at the thought, and put the baby in the elaborate blue and white basket Felicia had brought down. And in another month she would start to use the antique cradle his father had bought, but it was still a little too big. He would have been lost in it. Felicia walked over, and stood looking at him for a long time. 'Is it neat, Kate?' There was infinite softness in her eyes.

'It's better than I ever dreamed it would be. It's perfect. Until the four A.M. feeding.' She grinned at Felicia. 'Then, I begin to wonder.'

'Don't. Just enjoy it.' Felicia couldn't shake off the mood of seriousness that had fallen over her. She felt as though she was saying good-bye to Kate for good. But Kate had already seen that in her face.

'Don't take it so hard, love.'

'I still think you're a fool to stay down here. But I'll be down the first weekend after I get back. And whenever I can after that.' But they both knew it wouldn't be every weekend anymore. They had their lives to get on with. Things wouldn't be the same. There were tears swamping Felicia's eyes as she picked up her bag, and Kate looked sobered as she opened the door. They walked slowly to Felicia's little red car, and then silently Kate hugged her tight.

72

'I'm sorry, Licia.' There were tears in her eyes now too. 'I just can't go back.'

'I know. It's okay.' She laughed through her tears and gave Kate another fierce squeeze. 'Take good care of my godchild, kiddo.'

'You take good care of you.'

And with that, Felicia saluted, tossed her bag into the car, and slid behind the wheel with a smile. She stopped for a moment and looked at Kate. Both women smiled a long quiet smile full of love and understanding. Their ships had set sail. And they waved to each other as Felicia faded from sight.

Kate looked at her watch as she walked back inside the house. She had another two and a half hours before Tygue woke up for his next feeding. That would give her plenty of time to work on the book. She had already written thirty pages, but she hadn't wanted to admit it to Felicia. The book was her secret. And one day – she smiled to herself at the thought – one day . . . she already knew.

PART TWO

CHAPTER VI

'Kate? Kate!'

Kate jumped in surprise at the sound of her name, as she sat barefoot at her desk in an old shirt and a worn pair of jeans.

'Hey, lady, is your hearing going too?'

'Licia!' She was standing in the doorway, looking as trim and fashionable as ever in a wine-coloured suede suit. 'You didn't tell me you were coming down!'

'I wanted to take a look at the Santa Barbara store, so I thought I'd surprise you. That's some outfit. Things getting as bad as that?' Kate flushed in embarrassment and zipped up her fly.

'Sorry. I was doing some work. I wasn't expecting guests.'

'How's it coming?' Felicia hugged her and cast an eye at the typewriter.

'Okay, I guess. It's hard to tell.' She shrugged and followed Felicia into the living room. She hadn't seen her since Christmas, two months before, when Felicia had spent a week with them, spoiling Tygue rotten.

'Don't be so hard on yourself. If you sold one, you can sell another one.'

'Tell my publisher that, Licia.'

'I'd be happy to. Care for a martini?' Kate grinned but shook her head. Felicia never changed. Her outfits followed the fashion of the moment, the men in her life came and went, and once every few years she rented a slightly larger, more expensive apartment, but essentially she hadn't changed in years. It was reassuring. The martinis, the husky voice, the style, the loyalty, the solidity, the good legs, none of them changed a bit.

'I don't know, Licia. I'm serious. The first book stank, even if it did get published. And they wouldn't even take the last one. I'm getting nervous.'

77

'Don't be. Three's a charm. And besides, your first one did not "stink". It sold very nicely, as I recall.'

'Bullshit.' Kate looked glum.

'Don't be so insecure. How many women your age have ever written two books?'

'Hundreds probably.' But Kate liked the reassurance; she had no one else to give it to her, no one to talk to, in fact. She was careful to avoid getting past the 'Hi, how are you?' stage with anyone in town. She had Tygue, and Felicia, and her work, and her visits to Tom. And no room for anything else. 'I'm just beginning to wonder if I have what it takes to write a successful novel.'

'Maybe you don't want to.' Felicia looked over her shoulder as she expertly poured her martini into a glass from the pitcher she kept in Kate's cupboard. Whenever Felicia arrived, it seemed to them both that she had just been there the day before. Kate loved that about their relationship. 'Maybe you just don't want the hassle of success. Wouldn't that force you into a lot of choices you don't want?' It was a question Felicia had long wondered about.

'What choices? Whether or not Tygue goes to college?'

'That's a benefit, love, not a choice. I'm talking about what would happen to *you* if your book was a smash. Could you go on living here? Would you expose yourself to publicity? Would you condescend to "visit the big city" for interviews? Those, my love, are choices.'

'I'll deal with them when I have to.'

'May it be soon.' Felicia toasted her with the martini, and Kate laughed.

'You never give up.'

'Of course not.' It had been three and a half years, and she still wanted Kate to come back. She admitted Tygue was thriving and happy, a beautiful child with healthy pink cheeks and his father's huge cornflower-blue eyes. He hadn't suffered yet from the cultural deprivations of the life his mother had chosen, but in time he would. That had been Felicia's latest tack, but it hadn't worked any better than the others. 'You are the stubbornest woman I know.'

78

'Thank you.' Kate looked pleased.

'Where's my godchild, by the way? I brought him a present.'

'If it weren't for you, Licia, the child wouldn't have a thing to play with. But thanks to you' – Kate grinned at her friend – 'he has more than all the kids in town. The train got here last week.'

'Oh did it?' Felicia tried to look innocent. Maybe he was a little young, but she'd felt he ought to have one. 'After all, living in this wasteland, the poor child needs something to amuse himself with. So where is he?'

'At nursery school.'

'Already? He's too young.'

'He started right after Christmas, and he loves it.'

'He'll get germs from the other kids.' But Kate just laughed at Felicia as she finished her drink. It was a sunny Friday afternoon in late February, and in Kate's part of the world, it already felt like spring.

'He should be home in half an hour. He goes from two to five, after his nap. Want to take a look at the new manuscript while you wait?' Felicia nodded acquiescence with a slow happy smile. 'What are you staring at?'

'I was trying to remember if I looked that good at twenty-six. But I just remembered. I didn't.'

'That's because I live here, and not in some wretched city.'

'Bullshit.' But maybe it was true. And in any case, Kate did look well. Even the visits to Tom didn't seem to weigh her down as they used to. Nothing had changed there, she had just adjusted.

Tom was still at Mead, and Mr. Erhard was still taking extraordinary care of him. Tom was still playing the same games, reading the same books, working out the same puzzles – it was like an eternity of first grade. Now that Kate had Tygue to compare him with, Tom's stagnation was more noticeable, but he remained gentle and lovable. She still saw him twice a week. Tygue thought she went away to work. It was just something his mother did.

Kate looked at her watch as she handed Felicia the manuscript. She still had a little time before Tygue came home, and she was anxious to know what Felicia thought of the new book. Licia made some surprisingly perceptive comments about her work. It was almost twenty minutes later when Felicia lifted her head with a look of surprise.

'How did you manage the sex scene?'

'What do you mean, how did I manage it?'

'You've been having more fun down here than I credit you with?' Felicia looked over with a sly smile, and Kate was annoyed.

'Don't be ridiculous. I just wrote it, that's all. It's fiction.'

'Amazing.' Felicia looked impressed, but there was mischief in her eyes.

'Why? Is it lousy?' She was worried.

'No. Surprisingly good. I'm just surprised you can remember that far back. You know, with the wonderful, normal, healthy life you lead down here, all the men you see . . .'

'Felicia Norman, up yours.' But she grinned as Felicia went back to the book. For a minute, she'd had her worried. Felicia was always bugging her about her sex life, or lack of it. Felicia might never have had a mad passion in her life, but there was always someone at hand to keep the juices flowing properly. Kate hadn't made love with a man in four years. She didn't even let herself think about it anymore. That wasn't part of her life. She put all her energies into Tygue, and the books. Maybe it even made the books better. Sometimes she wondered about that. The books were her lovers. And Tom and Tygue were her kids. It was an hour later when Felicia put down the manuscript with a serious look on her face. Kate trembled looking at her.

'You hated it.'

For a moment, Felicia only shook her head. 'No, I loved it. But kiddo, you're walking right into something you're refusing to look at.'

'What?' A plot problem obviously. Dammit, and she'd been so careful.

'Exactly what I warned you about – success.' Felicia's face remained grave, and Kate grinned.

'You mean it?'

'I do. But do *you* mean it?'

'Oh, stop being such a worrier. I'll face it when I get there.'

'I hope so.'

And then the conversation ended abruptly as the school bus arrived with Tygue. He came bounding into the house in blue jeans and a red flannel shirt, little cowhide cowboy boots, and a bright yellow parka. 'Aunt Licia! Aunt Licia!' He bounced into her lap, cowboy boots and all, and Kate cringed at what would happen to the suede suit, but Felicia seemed to mind not at all.

'Wait till you see what I brought you!'

'Another twain?' His face lit up like a spotlight, and both women laughed.

'Nope. Take a look. There's a big box in the car. Can you get it yourself?'

'Sure, Aunt Licia.' He went thundering outside again, and Kate watched him go. He was growing so fast . . . and then she caught a funny look on her friend's face.

'Okay, you, warn me now – what did you bring him? A live cobra? White mice? Tell me the truth.'

'Nothing like that. Kate. Really.' But she could already hear the squeals from outside the house. Felicia had been nervous about it since she'd arrived. She'd even sneaked out to the car once with a saucer of water. But he had been asleep. He wasn't asleep now though, he was being passionately squeezed by Master Tygue.

'It's weal!'

'Of course it's weal!' Felicia grinned at the look on the boy's face, and for a minute Kate rolled her eyes, but she was smiling too. 'Is he yours, Aunt Licia?' It was the droopiest sad-eyed basset hound puppy Kate had ever seen, and just looking at him made her want to laugh. Tygue put him on the floor, and the dog's legs seemed to slide out from under him. His ears fanned out and he looked mournfully up at the little boy and wagged his tail.

'Do you like him, Tygue?'

Tygue nodded ferociously and then sat down next to the

little black and white dog. 'You're so lucky. I wish we had one too. I want one, Mommy.'

'You've got one, Tygue.' Aunt Licia was on her knees next to her godchild, holding both the boy and the dog.

'I got one too?' Tygue looked confused.

'This one's yours. Just for you.' She kissed him softly on the top of his blond head.

'For me?'

'For you.'

'Oh! Oh!' It was all he could say for minutes, and then he threw himself on the dog with delight. 'What's his name?'

'That's up to you.'

'I'll have to ask Willie.' Willie, the treasured teddy bear, had become his best friend. Tom still had his too, and it was hard to decide which one looked more loved and weather-beaten, Tygue's or his father's. Tygue bounded out of the room a minute later and Kate stooped down to pet the little dog.

'Are you furious, Kate?' Felicia looked only slightly remorseful.

'How could I be, you nut? Just don't bring the kid a car next time you visit. Save that till he's six.' The dog was irresistible though, and she lifted him happily into her lap. Tygue was back in a minute with Willie.

'Willie says his name is Bert.'

'Then Bert it is.'

Tygue squeezed him again, and Bert wagged his tail. The family was complete. And Felicia had even liked the beginning of her new book. Kate felt as though good things were in store. And Licia was crazy with that bullshit about success. Hell, if the publisher just accepted the book, that would be enough. It didn't have to be a best seller. That only happened one time in a million, and she knew it wasn't for her. She could feel it. This was her life.

CHAPTER VII

'Going to teach today, Mom?' Kate nodded and handed Tygue another piece of toast. 'I thought so. I can always tell.' He looked pleased with himself, and Kate watched her son with a warm glow. Graceful and sturdy and thoughtful and bright, and so pretty, but in an appropriately boyish way. He looked a little less like Tom now. And he was nearly six.

'How can you always tell when I'm going to teach?' They had long since established a chatty rapport over breakfast, and on this beautiful spring day she was feeling playful. Tygue was the person she spoke to most. Now and then it made her respond to him on his own childlike level, but most of the time they found a mutually acceptable middle ground.

'I can tell 'cause you wear gooder clothes.'

'I do, huh?' She was grinning at him, and there was a fierce sparkle of mischief in his eyes, not so very different from her own. 'And the word is "better", by the way.'

'Yeah. And you wear that goopy stuff on your face.'

'What goopy stuff?' She was laughing with a mouthful of toast.

'You know – the green stuff.'

'It's not green, it's blue. And it's called eye makeup. Aunt Licia wears it too.' As though that would make it okay.

'Yeah, but she wears it all the time, and hers is brown.' He grinned broadly at her. 'And you only wear yours to teach. How come you only wear it then?'

'Because you're not old enough to appreciate it, hot stuff.' But neither was Tom. Anymore. She just wore the eye makeup and the 'gooder' clothes, as Tygue called them, because she felt she ought to, for visiting Tom at Mead. It seemed suitable. There she was 'Mrs. Harper'. Here she was only 'Mom', and occasionally 'ma'am' at the supermarket.

She had long ago explained to Tygue that she taught writing at a school in Carmel for disturbed children. It allowed her to talk about Tom sometimes, or some of the others she saw. She had often told him stories of Tom, of his drawings, of Mr. Erhard – the stories were dusted off just enough so that she could tell Tygue and feel some relief. Or sometimes when Tom had had a moment of great victory, done a wonderful drawing, learned a game, or completed a puzzle that had seemed so much beyond him – sometimes then, she could share the triumphant feeling with Tygue, even if she shouldn't have. And by telling him that she taught at a school for disturbed children, she could also provide an excuse for going to her room and closing the door after a rough day. Tygue understood that. He felt sorry for the children she told him about. And he thought she was a good person for going there. Sometimes she wondered if that was why she had told him that story . . . poor Mommy . . . good Mommy . . . she drives all that way to work with retarded children. She shrugged off such thoughts. It was crazy to need strokes from a six-year-old child.

'How come they don't ever get vacation?' He was slurping through his cereal now, and Kate's thoughts had already drifted ahead to Tom.

'Hm?'

'How come they don't get vacation?'

'They just don't. Want to bring Joey home from school today? Tillie will be here when you get back.' But she didn't need to tell him. He knew that. 'She could drive you guys over to see the new horses down at the Adams ranch, if you want.'

'Nah.'

'No?' Kate looked at him with astonishment, as he ploughed through the cereal with a blasé look on his face, but that same bright little flame in his eyes. He was up to something. 'What's with you? Other plans?'

He looked up with a quick smile and a faint blush, but a vehement shake of his head. 'No.'

'Listen, you, be a good boy for Tillie today. Promise?' Tillie had the phone number at Mead, but Kate was on the road so much of the time that she still worried a little, even after all these years. 'Don't do anything wild or crazy while I'm gone. I mean it, Tygue.' The voice was suddenly stern, and his eyes met hers with a promise.

'It's okay, Mom.' As though he were a thousand years old. And then suddenly the staccato honking of his car pool, and she could see the big yellow jeep in the driveway.

'They're here!'

'Gotta go. See ya!' The spoon flew, a last grab at the toast, his favourite cowboy hat, a stray book on the table, a wave as she blew him a kiss, and he was gone. As she took another swallow of coffee, she couldn't help wondering what he was up to, but whatever it was, Tillie could handle it. She was a large, grandmotherly, affectionate woman, but she had been a widow for too many years herself to take any nonsense from Tygue. She had brought up five boys and a daughter, managed a ranch by herself for years before turning it over to her eldest son, and she had been baby-sitting for Tygue since he was born. She was rough and ingenious, and they had a marvellous time together. She was a real country woman, not an immigrant like Kate. There was a difference, and probably always would be. Besides, Kate was a writer, not a woman of the kitchen and garden. She enjoyed the country around her but she still knew little about it.

She looked around the kitchen for a minute before grabbing her jacket and handbag, wondering what she'd forgotten. She felt a strange tug this morning, as though she shouldn't be going. But she was used to that too. She no longer listened to those feelings. She just steeled herself and went. Tillie was unquestionably reliable. She shrugged into the jacket and looked down at her slacks. They still fitted her as they had eight years before when she'd bought them after modelling them. They had been beautiful then and were still beautiful, a soft caramel-coloured gabardine, and the jacket was a tweed she had worn riding years before. The only thing new was the pale blue sweater she'd bought in town. She smiled again as she thought of what Tygue had said about what she wore. She liked looking pretty for Tom. She almost wondered if she should make

85

more of an effort for Tygue too. But at six? That was crazy. What did he know? Or did he? The thought of dressing up for a six-year-old boy made her laugh as she walked out to the car.

She put her mind into automatic pilot all the way up to Carmel, and it turned out to be one of those days when she stayed on automatic throughout the day. The road had been tedious and all too familiar. Tom was dull and listless, the day turned foggy. Even the lunch was one she'd had hundreds of times before. Some days with Tom stood out like rare gems, their facets gleaming and brightly hued, casting rainbows of dancing light. Other days were dark and cold and had the taste of ash. And some days she felt nothing at all. Today she felt nothing, except fatigue as she left. She was anxious to hit the freeway as soon as she could, and drive back to the little house in the hills, and Tygue, and the silly sad-eyed basset hound who had become a member of the family. She had missed them all day. Maybe she should have stayed home after all. The speedometer hit well over ninety as she drove home. It often did, but she seldom got caught. Only twice in six years. The trip was so boring, only shortening it by speeding made it bearable. Now and then a pang of conscience toward Tygue would make her slow down, but not often. Fifty-five was intolerable. She cruised at eighty-five most of the time.

It was almost five as she drove, still too fast, over the back roads that led to the house. Why had she had this damn uneasiness all day? She ground across the gravel on the driveway, keeping an eye out for the dog, but anxiously combing the area around the house for Tygue. And then she saw him, and smiled as she stepped on the brakes and slid into park. He was filthy and smiling and beautiful and she had been crazy to worry. What the hell was wrong with her? She made the trip all the time. What had made her think that anything would be wrong today, or that anything would come up that Tillie couldn't handle? Tillie, in fact, was looking as filthy as Tygue, and even Bert looked as though he needed a bath. The three of them were covered with mud. Tillie even had a great smudge of it on one cheek, and there was lots of it matted in Tygue's hair, but they looked delighted with themselves.

Tygue was waving frantically now and shouting something. It was time to move. To get out of the car. To be Mom again. And Tillie was peeling a pair of overalls down from her shoulders. The outfit she was wearing underneath was scarcely more elegant, and as always when returning from Carmel, Kate instantly felt overdressed. She grabbed her handbag and stepped out of the car. Her day as Tom's Kate had ended. It was Tygue's turn now. She took a deep breath of the fresh country air, and then sighed as she reached down to pat Bert, snuffling happily at the cuffs of her slacks.

'Hi, guys. What've you been up to?'

'Wait till you see, Mom! It's terrific! I did it! I did it! Tillie didn't do nothing!' Anything. To hell with it. 'Nothing' was good enough. She was too tired to correct him, and too happy at seeing him safe and sound.

'She didn't, huh? Well, guess what?' She had already scooped him into her arms, mud and all, and he was squirming to be free.

'Come on, Mom, you gotta come look.'

'Can I have a kiss first?' But she had already given him one, and was holding him close, as he looked up at her with that heart-melting smile of a boy of six.

'Then will you come look?'

'Then I'll come look.' He bestowed a perfunctory kiss and pulled ferociously at her arm. 'Wait a minute, what am I going to look at? Not snakes again . . . right, Tillie?' She cast a rapid eye in the older woman's direction. Tillie had said nothing yet. She was a woman of few words, particularly with other women; she had more to say to Tygue than to Kate. But there was a certain warmth and respect between them. Tillie didn't really understand what Kate did at the typewriter, but the one published book she could tell her friends about had impressed her. It hadn't been much of a book, sort of a nonsense novel about fancy people in San Francisco, but it had been published, and that was something. And she said she had another one coming out in a month. Maybe she'd be famous one day. And anyway, she was a good mother. And a widow too. They had that in common. There was something different about her, though,

87

that kept a distance between them. She wasn't a snob, and she didn't have anything anyone else didn't have. There was just a feeling one got about her. It was hard to explain. Refined. Maybe that was it. It was a word Tillie's mother had used. She had said Kate was refined. And smart. And pretty maybe, but too thin. And there was always that sad, hidden look in her eyes. But Tillie knew that one, she had seen it in the mirror for years after her own man had died. Not for as long as she'd seen it in Kate's eyes though. The look was still as fresh in her eyes as it had been when she'd first met her, after Tygue was born. Sometimes Tillie wondered if the writing kept her pain alive. Maybe that was what she wrote about. She didn't really know.

Tillie watched now as Kate rounded the corner of the house, impatiently pulled along by her son, and then they both stopped and Tygue grinned broadly and held tightly to his mother's hand. He was still such a little boy, yet now and then he seemed very grown up, probably because his mother often talked to him as though he were already a man. But that wouldn't do him any harm. Tillie had done that to her own boys, after their father died. It brought back memories, watching the boy look up at his mother in front of the patch of garden they'd worked on all day while she was gone.

'We made it for you. Half of it's flowers and half of it's vegetables. Tillie said we should do vegetables so you could make salads. You know, peppers and stuff. And next week we're gonna do herbs. You like herbs?' He looked suddenly dubious. Herbs sounded like girl stuff to him. 'I want to plant pumpkins. And coconuts.' Kate grinned, and bent to kiss him again.

'It's beautiful, Tygue.'

'No, it isn't. But it will be. We planted all kinds of flowers. We bought all the seeds last week. And I hid them.' That was what that look of mystery had been about this morning. It was his first garden.

'He did all the hard work too.' Tillie walked up to him and patted his shoulder. 'He's going to be mighty proud when he sees what a fine garden he planted too. Won't be long.'

'Tomatoes too.'

For a moment, Kate felt herself fighting tears, and then suddenly she wanted to laugh. She had worried about him all day, and he had been planting her a garden. What a beautiful world it was. No matter how fast she drove on the freeway.

'You know something, Tygue? This is the most beautiful present anyone's ever given me.'

'For real? How come?'

'Because you worked so hard at it, and because it's alive. And because we'll watch it grow, and get good things to eat from it, and pretty flowers. That's quite a present, sweetheart.'

'Yeah.' He looked around, doubly impressed with himself, and then shook hands soberly with Tillie, as the two women tried not to laugh. It was a beautiful moment, and then Tillie looked up, as though she had just remembered something.

'You got a call.' Felicia obviously. Kate nodded, pleased but not overly interested. 'From New York.'

'New York?' For a moment, there was a tiny catch somewhere in her heart. New York? It couldn't be. Probably something stupid like the main office of her insurance company. Something like that. She'd got wound up over nothing before. She knew better now. After six years, she knew.

'They want you to call back.'

'Too late now.' It was already five-thirty in the West, three hours later in the East. Kate didn't look particularly upset.

Tillie nodded in her easy-going, never-hurried country way. 'Yeah. He said it might be too late. Left a number you could call in L.A.'

The something in her heart caught again. Harder this time. This was ridiculous. She was playing games with herself. Why was she so damn jumpy today?

'I wrote it all down inside.'

'I'd better go take a look.' And then she looked down at Tygue with a tender smile, and her voice softened again.

'Thank you for my beautiful garden, sweetheart. I love it – and I love you.' She stooped for a moment and held him tight, and then hand in hand they walked towards the house, with Bert loping along beside them as best his stumpy legs would allow. 'Want a cup of coffee, Tillie?' But the older woman shook her head.

'I've got to get home. Jake's kids are coming by tonight for supper, and I've got some things to do.' The usual understatement. Jake had nine kids. There would be dinner for twelve. More, if assorted boy friends and girl friends came too, which they often did. Tillie was always prepared.

She got into her truck with a wave, and then hung out the window. 'You going up to teach again this week, Kate?' It was funny she should ask, and Kate looked at her with a barely perceptible frown. She always went twice, but she had wondered the same thing herself on the way home today. She just didn't feel like going the second time this week.

'Can I let you know tomorrow?' It wouldn't alter what she paid Tillie – a set amount, once a month, to baby-sit twice a week. It was easier just writing one cheque a month, and the arrangement suited them both. If she decided to go to a movie in the evening, she just dropped Tygue off at Tillie's place on the way, and picked him up on her way home. Tillie didn't charge her for that, he was just like one of the 'grand-kids'. But Kate hardly ever did that. She spent her evenings at the typewriter. And going out at night still made her long for Tom. It was easier to stay home.

'Sure, call me tomorrow, or the day after if you want, Kate. The day's yours, one way or the other.'

'Thanks.' Kate smiled and waved, as she gently pushed Tygue ahead of her into the house. Maybe she would take the a day off, and skip seeing Tom later in the week. Maybe she could plant some more things in the garden with Tygue. What a super idea Tillie had had. Why didn't she think of things like that?

'What's for dinner?' He threw himself on the kitchen floor with Bert, spewing mud around him on the clean floor as his mother grimaced.

'I'm going to make you eat mud pies, kiddo, if you don't get into the bathroom and get clean in about fourteen seconds. And take Bert with you.'

'Come on, Mom ... I wanna watch ...'

'You'd better watch some soap and water, mister, and I mean it!' She pointed determinedly towards the bathroom and then Tillie's message caught her eye and she remembered the call from New York. It turned out to be from the New York office of the agency she used in Los Angeles to see her books. All the publishers were in New York, so her agent just shipped her manuscripts there and let the eastern office handle it. Her Los Angeles agent did hold her hand a lot, and would get into the act if she ever sold a film, but the very thought of selling a film made her laugh. That was the stuff of writers' fantasies. Only novices believed they really had a chance. She knew better now, and she was just damn grateful to sell a book now and then, even if it was only for a lousy two thousand bucks every three years. It helped pad out the small income she still got from Tom's investments.

So she wrote her book, and sent it to the agent in L.A., who would then mail it on to New York. And then New York would take two months even to tell her they knew she was alive, and after that – with any luck at all – they sold the book. Then she got a cheque from them, and twice a year she got royalty statements from the publishers. It was no more exciting than that. The first time it had taken them almost a year to sell her book, the second time it had taken them that long to tell her the new book stank and they couldn't sell it. This last time they had told her they were 'hopeful'. But they had taken almost two years to sell it. That had been a year ago. And it finally would be out in another month. All of which was reasonable by publishing standards. She knew that publishers sometimes sat on a book for two or three years before publishing it. She had been given an advance of three thousand dollars, and that could be that. It didn't even disappoint her anymore. Just a nice polite print run of five thousand books, and eventually she would see it in her local bookstore if she took the trouble to go down there to look for it. And a year later it would be out of print. It would go as quietly as it had come. But at least she'd have written it. And she was pleased about this one. It was a little unnerving to think this book might actually sell. Its subject was a little too close to home. She had almost hoped it wouldn't sell, in case someone remembered her. But how could they? Publishers didn't advertise the work of relatively unknown authors. And who was Kaitlin Harper? No one. She was safe. The book was a novel, but there was a lot in it about professional football, and the kind of pressure that was put on the players and their wives. Writing it had done her good. It had freed her of some of the old ghosts. There was a lot in it about Tom, the Tom she had loved, not the Tom who had snapped.

'Mom, did you start dinner yet?' His voice woke her out of her reverie. She had been standing by the phone for almost five minutes, thinking about the book, and wondering what the agency had wanted. Maybe something was wrong. A delay. They wouldn't bring it out in a month after all. They'd make her wait another year. So what? She'd got her advance. And she had been playing with an idea for another novel anyway. Besides, her real life was car pools for Tygue and mud on the kitchen floor. What difference did it make that she was a writer? Except to her.

'No, I haven't started dinner yet.'

'But I'm hungry.' He was suddenly whining and dirty – a tired little kid. He had worked hard all day, and it was starting to show. But she was tired too.

'Tygue' – the word was a sigh on her lips – 'Will you please take your bath, and then I'll get dinner. I have a phone call to make first.'

'Why?' From child to beast in one quick minute. But he was only six. She had to remind herself of that at times.

'It's for business. Now come on, sweetheart. Be a sport.'

'Oh ... all right ...' He left, grumbling, with Bert sliding along behind him, nibbling at his heels. 'But I'm *hungry*!'

'I know. So am I!' Damn. She didn't want to snap at him. It was twenty to six. She dialled the agency's number in Los Angeles, wondering if anyone would even be there. If not, she'd call New York in the morning. But the phone was answered quickly, and the receptionist put her through to the man she normally dealt with: Stuart Weinberg. She had never met him. But after speaking for years on the phone, they felt like old pals.

'Stu? Kate Harper. How've you been?'

'Fine.' She always imagined what he looked like, young, short, thin, nervous, and probably good-looking, with very dark hair and expensive Los Angeles clothes. Tonight he sounded as though he were in a good mood. 'How've you been, out there in the boonies?'

'We're not that far from L.A. The boonies, what a thing to say!' But they were both laughing. It was a game they played whenever they spoke.

'Listen,' she went on. 'I got a call from Bill Parsons in New York. The message is a little garbled, but it says to call him, or call you if I got back too late to call him, which I did. I didn't even think you'd be in this late.'

'See how hard we work for you, madam? Burning the midnight oil, working our fingers to stumps . . .'

'Stop. You're making me sick.'

'Sorry. I just thought I deserved a little sympathy.'

'Mom! I'm hungry!' The voice warbled out from the bathroom with suddenly loud splashing sounds, and Bert started to bark. Jesus.

'Cool it in there!'

'What?' Weinberg sounded momentarily confused, and Kate laughed.

'Crazy hour around here, I'm afraid. I think my kid is drowning the dog.'

'Fine idea.' He chuckled and Kate fumbled for a cigarette. She didn't know why, but he was making her nervous.

'Stu?'

'Yes, ma'am?' There was something funny in his voice. The way Tygue had sounded at breakfast, before planting his surprise garden.

'Do you know why Parsons wanted me to call you?'

'I do.'

'Well?' Why was he doing this? It was killing her.

'Are you sitting down?'

'They're not going to publish the book?' Her heart sank. She could already feel tears well up in her eyes. Another bomb.

She'd blown it again. She'd never publish another one. And this one had been so good.

'Kate—' There was an interminable pause as she squeezed her eyes closed and tried to force herself to listen to him. 'Today has been a fairly incredible day, love. Parsons closed a deal in New York. And I closed one out here. Your publisher sold your paperback rights, and I sold your movie.' Her mouth opened, her eyes filled, and no sound emerged. And then suddenly everything happened at once. Tears, words, confusion, chaos. Her heart was pounding and so was her head.

'Kate, you won't remember a thing I tell you, but we'll talk again tomorrow. In fact, we're going to be doing a whole lot of talking in the next weeks and months. Contracts, plans, publicity. Lots of talking. And I think that you should come to Los Angeles so we can celebrate.'

'Can't we do it over the phone?' Panic had crept through the elation. What was happening?

'We'll discuss everything later. Anyway, the paperback rights sold for four hundred and fifty thousand dollars. And' – there was another endless pause – 'I sold the movie for one twenty-five. You have to split the paperback money with your publisher fifty-fifty, but that's still one hell of a figure.'

'Good lord, Stu, that still makes – two twenty-five?' She was dumbstruck. What did it all mean?

'All told, you stand to make three hundred and fifty thousand dollars. Not to mention royalties, the exposure, and what this could mean for the future of your career. Baby, this could be a quick ride to success. In fact, I'd say you're already there. Parsons spoke to the hardcover publisher today, and they're upping the second print order to twenty-five thousand copies. For hardcover, that's beautiful.'

'They are? It is?'

'Mom, I need a towel!'

'Shut up!'

'Take it easy, Kate.'

'Yeah I don't know what to say. I never thought this would happen.'

'This is just the beginning.'

94

Oh God, and then what if someone remembered about Tom? What if someone made the connection between her and what had happened six and a half years ago? What if . . .

'Kate?'

'I'm sorry, Stu. I'm just sitting here, trying to absorb it.'

'You won't be able to. Just sit there and relax, and we'll talk tomorrow. Okay?'

'Okay. And Stu . . . I don't know what to say. I . . . it just knocks me out . . . it's . . . you . . .'

'Congratulations, Kate.'

She blew out a long sigh and grinned at the phone. 'Thanks.' It took another minute to get to her feet after she hung up, and even begin to gather her thoughts. Three hundred and fifty thousand dollars? Jesus. And what about the rest of it? What did he mean, this was only the beginning? What . . .

'Mom!' Oh Lord.

'I'm coming.'

And there, in the bathroom, was the reality of her life. Tygue Harper was sitting in the bathtub with his dog, wearing a cowboy hat, and splashing three inches of water into the hall.

'What the hell are you doing?' She could hardly stand up on the wave of soap and water swishing under her feet on the bathroom tile. 'For chrissake, Tygue.' Anger exploded in her eyes and the boy looked suddenly hurt.

'But I made you a garden!'

'And I sold a movie! I . . . oh Tygue . . .' She sat down in the river on the bathroom floor, grinning at her son, with tears spilling from her eyes. 'I sold a movie!'

'You did?' He looked at her sombrely for a moment, as she grinned through her tears and nodded. 'Why?'

CHAPTER VIII

'What do you mean, it makes sense to you?' It had been three days since the news, and she was on the phone to Felicia for at least the seventeenth time.

'Kate, for chrissake, you're talking about making a fortune. He's not just going to mail those contracts to you. He wants to explain them to you.' Felicia was trying to sound soothing, but she was failing dismally. She was too excited to sound anything but elated, and pushy.

'But why here? All these years we've dealt perfectly happily at this distance. And ... oh shit, Licia. I should never have written the damn book.' She sounded agonized.

'Are you crazy?'

'What if someone finds out? What if there's more of that bullshit that almost drove me nuts six years ago? Do you have any idea what it was like to be constantly hunted by reporters? They lived outside the house, they squeezed into my car with me, Jesus, they practically knocked me down the stairs. Why the hell do you think I came down here?'

'I know all that, Kate. But that was a long time ago. It's not news anymore.'

'How do you know that? How does anyone? Maybe those maniacs would revive it. What if they found out where Tom was? What would that do to Tygue? Just think of it, Licia!' She paled at the thought, but in her office in San Francisco Felicia was unsympathetically shaking her head.

'You should have thought of that when you wrote the book. The fact is, it's a damn good book, and it's a *novel*, Kate. No one is going to know it's true. Will you please relax for chrissake? You're driving yourself into a frenzy for nothing.'

'I won't see Weinberg.'

'You're being impossible, dammit.' But Kate had already

96

hung up, and was frantically dialling the agency in L.A. He might not have left yet. He said he'd arrive around three. It wasn't quite noon. But his secretary told her he had left an hour before.

'Damn.'

'Sorry?'

'Nothing.'

She dialled Felicia back in San Francisco, and her friend sounded grim. 'You'd better get a hold of yourself, Kate. You're getting out of hand. I told you this would happen when I read the book.'

'I thought you were just saying it. And who gets known with a book, dammit? Who sells paperback *and* film? Jesus, I know writers who sell on the back shelves of the dime store forever.'

'And you're crying that that's not you?' Felicia was exasperated and Kate sighed again.

'No, I'm not crying that that's not me. I just don't know what to do, Licia. I've hardly seen anybody in six years, and this guy is coming up here from L.A. to discuss hundreds of thousands of dollars with me. I'm so damn scared I can't see straight.'

'Come on, baby, you can deal with this.' Her voice softened as she thought of Kate. 'You're a pro. You're a hell of a writer, a beautiful girl, you're twenty-nine years old, and you're on the threshold of success. Christ, you could meet this guy wearing burlap and a mudpack and you'd do fine.'

'That's about all I've got to wear.'

'That's your own goddamn fault. You haven't let me send you anything in years.'

'I don't wear anything. Anyway, what to wear is not the problem. What to say . . . what to do . . . he wants to talk publicity. Jesus, Licia, I can't deal with it.' She was near tears and chain-smoking nervously.

'What exactly did he say about publicity?' Felicia sounded intrigued.

'Nothing exactly. He just mentioned the possibility of it. But he didn't explain.'

'You're damn right he didn't.' The deep, husky laugh rang in

97

Kate's ears. 'Has it ever occurred to you that he doesn't know if you have three heads or two, or if you wear curlers and pink suede sneakers to church.'

'Which means that I have about two and a half hours to come up with curlers and pink sneakers. Wait, I have an idea.' Now Kate was laughing too. 'I'll get Tillie to stand in for me.' Felicia laughed.

'Nope. You face the music. You meet the guy. He is your agent, after all. He isn't going to throw you to the lions, and he can't make you do anything.'

'What'll I say to him?' It had been six and a half years since she'd been alone with a man.

'He's not going to rape you, Kate. Not unless you get very lucky.'

'You're terrific. Dammit, how did I get myself into this?'

'Your big mouth, your fine mind, and your typewriter. But it's a hell of a good combo.' Kate sighed again in answer, and Felicia shook her head with a grin. The earthquake was just beginning. And the aftershocks might be felt for months. Even years.

'Anyway, I'd better get off the phone and find something to wear.'

'Yeah. And Kate?'

'What?'

'Zip up your fly.'

'Oh shut up.' She was smiling when she hung up, but the palms of her hands were drenched. What if he did put the make on her? What if he was a pushy jerk? What if . . . She sat outside in the sunshine for half an hour, trying to calm down, thinking. Of the book, of Tom, of Felicia, of Tygue. Why had she written it? Because she had had to. Because the story had been tearing her up inside and she had needed to get it out, and she had. It was a beautiful book and she knew it. But she hadn't expected this. She had wanted the book to sell, but she hadn't expected it to affect her life. And now what? Once she opened the door to publicity, her secluded life would be over, all her efforts to protect Tygue futile. But it was too late now and she knew it. She had just finished dressing when Stu Weinberg rang the bell. She took a deep breath, stubbed out her cigarette, looked around the living room, and walked to the door. She was wearing black slacks and a black sweater, and a pair of expensive Italian suede loafers that had survived the years. She looked very tall and very thin, and very serious as she opened the door.

'Kate Harper?' He looked a little uncertain, and not at all the way she'd pictured him. He was about her height, and had bright red hair. He was wearing jeans and a beige cashmere sweater. But the shoes were Gucci, the briefcase Vuitton, the watch Cartier, the jacket slung over one arm was the classic Bill Blass. All the status accoutrements of Los Angeles. But he had the face of a kid, and ten thousand freckles. It made her smile and she had to laugh at the idea that this was the guy she had entrusted her career to for six years. Maybe if she had seen him, she wouldn't have. He looked about twenty-two. But he was forty-one, the same age as Felicia.

'Stu?' She smiled at him from the doorway.

'I know. I know. You want to see my driver's licence and you want to tear up your contract immediately. Right?'

'Hardly. Come in.' She waved him inside, wondering if the house looked shabby or merely comfortable. She watched him summing her up, and then casting a quick eye around the room. He looked intrigued. 'Coffee?'

He nodded, and put his jacket and briefcase on a chair as he looked out the window. 'It's a beautiful view here.' She stood very quietly for a minute, and was surprised at how peaceful she felt. He wasn't the enemy. He was a harmless man who wanted to help her make money. And he looked like a nice guy.

'It is pretty. And I'm glad you came all this way to see me.'

'So am I.'

She poured him a cup of coffee and they both sat down.

'Kate, can I ask you a crazy question?' The way he smiled made her like him more. He looked like one of Tygue's friends, not like an agent.

'Sure, what's the crazy question?'

'What the hell are you doing here?'

'You said it when you looked out the window. It's pretty. It's peaceful. It's a good place to bring up kids.'

'Bullshit.'

She laughed at his bluntness and took a sip of coffee. 'Not at all.'

'Tell me something else? Would you have come to L.A. if I hadn't come here?' With a small smile, she shook her head. 'That's what I thought. Why?'

'Because I'm a hermit, and I like it. When I lost my husband, I just . . . I stopped going places.'

'Why?'

'I'm busy here.' He was coming too close. Suddenly she was scared again.

'What do you do?' The eyes were quick, busy, probing, but not unkind.

'I write. I mother. I teach. I'm busy, that's all.'

And scared. Oh, Jesus, was she scared. But of what? He couldn't figure it out. Men maybe? People? Life? Something. He couldn't put his finger on it. But it was in her eyes.

'You don't look the part. Did you ever model or act?' Bingo.

'No.' She shook her head nervously, smiling as she lit another cigarette. Dammit, there was something about her. And he knew she was lying. The way she sat, moved, walked, all of it spoke of something else. Breeding. Training. Modelling? Or maybe she'd been a stewardess. But she hadn't sat in this nowhere town all her life. And he noticed her shoes. Eighty-dollar shoes. In Shit Town, U.S.A. But whoever she was, she was going to thrill the publishers, if he could pry her out of her shell. That was why he had come up to see her, to find out just how marketable a property she was. And now he had his answer. Very. If she'd co-operate. He smiled gently at her, and sipped his coffee, thinking she'd look great on TV.

'How many kids do you have?'

'Nine.' She laughed at him nervously again. 'No, seriously. One. He just acts like nine.'

'What's his name?'

'Tygue.'

'How does he feel about his mom being a huge success?'

'I don't think he's figured all that out yet. As a matter of fact,' she sighed and let her shoulders relax for a minute, 'neither have I.'

'You don't need to worry about it for a while, Kate. In fact, you don't need to worry about it at all. We'll handle it for you. All you need to do now is to look over the contracts, and then spend the next month enjoying yourself. You know, buy new curtains, a new ball for the kid, a bone for the dog . . .' He glanced around innocently and she laughed. He had got the message: she liked the simple life. But she also knew that he was refusing to take that seriously.

'What happens when the book comes out?'

'Nothing for a couple of weeks.' He was stalling her.

'And then?'

'Then you make a few appearances for the book, do a couple of interviews. No more than you can handle.'

'And if I don't?'

'The book suffers. It's as simple as that. It's statistically proven.' He looked serious as he said it.

'Is it in my contract that I have to?'

Regretfully he shook his head. 'No. Nobody can force you to do any of it. But it would be a big mistake for you not to, Kate. If you had buck teeth, a big nose, and crossed eyes, well, then I'd say that maybe you ought to consider skipping any appearances, but under the circumstances' – he looked at her with a rueful smile – 'you could do a hell of a good job, Kate.' And he didn't give a damn what she said, when he watched her walk across the room again, he knew she'd been a model. What intrigued him most, though, was the impenetrable shield around her. He had never sensed that on the phone. Now he wondered why he had never been curious about meeting her. He had to confess, though, that he had never expected her to be a biggie, not until the last book. *A Final Season.* He hadn't thought she'd been capable of a book like that. 'We can talk about the publicity stuff later. Why don't we check out some of the points they'll want in the contract first?'

'Okay. More coffee?'

'Thanks.' He devoured five cups of coffee in the two hours it took to sort out the contracts. And now she knew more than ever why she liked him as her agent. He was suddenly the same man he had been on the phone for all these years. He explained every possible inference, statement, danger, benefit, every line, every word, every nuance. He did one hell of a good job.

'Jesus, you should have been a lawyer.'

'I was. For a year.' The kid? Howdy Doody with the freckles a lawyer? When? She grinned at the thought. 'I hated it. This is a lot more my speed.'

'Mine too.' She thought of the three hundred and fifty thousand dollars again.

'You've got that look, Kate. Just don't let it go to your head.'

'Not a chance, Stu. Not a chance.' She said it with a rocklike certainty and a faintly bitter smile. 'This is strictly for new curtains and a bone for the dog.'

'Glad to hear it. But just in case you pull up outside my office in a new Rolls, say in three months – what do I get for being right?'

'A kick in the pants?'

'We'll see.' He grinned broadly.

She heard the car pool roll up outside then. It was already five fifteen. They had worked hard. 'Would you like to stay for dinner?' Dinner. Meat loaf, macaroni and cheese, carrots and Jello. The idea made her want to laugh, but he was shaking his head and looking at the flat-faced Roman-numeraled watch that looked like a Dali painting draped over his wrist.

'I'd love to, Kate. But I have a dinner date at eight in L.A.'

'Beverly Hills, I hope.'

'Is there anywhere else?' They laughed together, and Kate walked to the door to greet Tygue. Stu Weinberg watched the boy come in, throw a quick hug around his mother, and then come to a sudden halt when he saw him.

'Hi, Tygue. My name's Stu.' He reached out a hand but the boy didn't move.

'Who's he?' Tygue looked almost stricken.

'This is my agent from Los Angeles, sweetheart. Don't you have a better hello than that?' Tygue looked as frightened as his mother, and Stu instantly felt for the boy. He looked as though he were as unaccustomed to strangers as Kate.

Tygue grudgingly approached and held out a hand. "'Lo.' His mother glowered, and Stu slowly put the contracts back in the briefcase.

'Well, Kate, nothing left for you to do but relax.' She had signed everything.

'What about the other matter?'

'What?' But he knew. Let her say it. Let her try it out.

'The publicity.'

'Don't worry about it.'

'Stu . . . I can't do it.'

'Can't or won't?' His eyes were very hard on hers.

'Won't.'

'Okay.' He sounded very calm. Too calm. And all the while Tygue watched silently.

'You mean it?'

'Sure. I told you. No one can make you do it. You're foolish if you don't. But it's your book, your decision, your royalty cheque, your career. It's your trip, baby. I just work for you.' He made her feel small somehow, stupid and cowardly. If he had known, he'd have been pleased.

'I'm sorry.'

'Then think about it. And I'll keep the publicity directors of both the publishing houses off your back until you decide. Okay?'

'Okay.' He let her feel that she had won something, but she wasn't sure what. They shook hands at the door, and she watched as he backed a long plum-coloured Jaguar out of her driveway.

She waved from the doorway, and Tygue watched her as Stu smiled at them both from the car. All three of them suddenly knew that everything was about to change.

CHAPTER IX

'You survived it?' Felicia called after Tygue had gone to bed.

'Yes. I survived it. Actually, he's a very nice guy. I suspect that underneath the veneer, he's a pushy sonofabitch, but I like him.'

'Damn right he's pushy. How do you think he got you that fortune you just made?'

Kate laughed at the thought. 'Good point. If I'd looked at it that way, I'd really have gotten nervous. You know what's amazing though, Licia?'

'Yeah. You.'

'No. Seriously. After all these years, I wasn't that scared talking to him. We sat here like regular people, drinking coffee, looking at the contracts. It was really very civilized.'

'You're in love?' Felicia sounded amused.

'Christ, no. He looks like Alice in Wonderland's kid brother, with carrot-red hair yet. But he's a good agent. And I didn't have a heart attack from talking to a man.' Felicia was pleased for her.

'Okay. So now what?'

'What do you mean, now what?'

'I mean what happens next?'

'Nothing. I put the money in the bank. I send Tygue to college. Stu suggested we buy Bert a new bone' – she grinned – 'and I might just buy those pink suede sneakers we discussed this morning.'

'You're leaving something out, dear one.' Felicia sounded sarcastic and determined again. Kate knew that voice only too well. 'What about publicity for the book?'

'He says I don't have to.'

'I don't believe you.'

'That's what he said.'

'Didn't he ask you to?' Felicia was floored.

'Yes.'

'So?'

'I said I wouldn't do it.'

'You know, you're an ingrate and a bitch, Kate Harper, and if I were your agent, I'd kick your ass from one side of the room to the other.'

'That's why you're not my agent, and he is.'

'He let you off the hook that easy?'

'Yup.' Kate sounded like her son as she grinned.

'Then he's crazy.' Either that, or very very smart. She suddenly wondered.

'Maybe so. Anyway, I signed the contracts and I'm all through. Finished. Until the next book.'

'What a drag.' Felicia was smiling to herself.

'What do you mean "what a drag"?'

'I mean just that. You crank them out, stay up late, smoke a lot, drink a lot of coffee, and you don't even get to do any of the fun stuff. You don't even get to spend the money.'

'Why the hell not?'

'On what? Groceries? What a drag. The least you could do for yourself is go on a spree somewhere civilized. L.A., here, Santa Barbara. Hell, you could even go shopping in Carmel.'

'I don't need anything new to wear.'

'Obviously. You don't go anywhere.' And why did that make her a failure? Why did she have to go, dress, do, be in order to not 'be a drag'? Why wasn't just writing the book enough, dammit? Besides, maybe she would do some shopping in Carmel the next time she saw Tom. And that was another thing. She had to go tomorrow.

'Listen, Licia, I'm not going to get into a hassle with you about this. Anyway, I've got to get off the phone.'

'Anything wrong?'

'No. I have to call Tillie.'

'Okay, love.' Felicia sounded cool and distant when they hung up, and she wondered if she'd got through at all. But maybe . . .

At her end, Kate made plans with Tillie for the next day, and then took a hot bath and went to bed. It had been a nerve-wracking day, and she had none of the feelings she wanted to have. She wanted to feel proud of herself, and instead she just felt annoyed, as though she had failed at something. At last she fell asleep. Until the alarm woke her at six.

'You teaching again, Mom?' Tygue looked at her over breakfast, only this morning he whined the question, and it annoyed her.

'Yes, love. Tillie'll be here for you.'

'I don't want Tillie.'

'You can work on the garden. You'll have a good time. Eat your cereal.'

'It's not crunchy enough.'

'Come on, Tygue.'

'Yerghk! There's a bug on my toast!' He pushed it away and Bert grabbed it off the edge of the table with a contented smacking of his lips.

'Goddammit, Tygue!' And then suddenly there were tears in his eyes, and she felt awful. It was a hell of a way to start the morning. She sat down again and held out her arms. He came to them slowly, but he came. 'What's up, love? Something bothering you?'

'I hate him.'

'Who?'

'Him.'

Now what? 'Who, for heaven's sake?' She was too tired to play games.

'The man . . . the one in that chair.'

'You mean yesterday?'

He nodded.

'But he's my agent, sweetheart. He sells my books.'

'I don't like him.'

'That's silly.' Tygue shrugged and the car pool honked. 'Never mind about him. Okay?' He shrugged again, and she grabbed at him and held him fast. 'I love you and only you. You got that, mister?' A small smile crept back to his face. 'So relax and have a good day.'

'Okay.' He grabbed his jacket, patted Bert, and headed for the door. ''Bye, Mom.'

"Bye, love.' But when he left, she realized that she was angry at him. What was his problem? Jealous of Stu Weinberg? But it was hardly surprising. He had never seen a man in their house before. And it was time he got used to at least an occasional stranger. But still his recalcitrance made her feel pushed. He was pulling her one way, they were pulling the other. Everyone wanted something from her. And what did she want? She wasn't sure. And she didn't even have time to ask herself. She had to get going if she wanted to see Tom ... wanted to see Tom ... wanted ... what an amazing idea. It suddenly made her stop dead in the middle of the kitchen. *Did* she want to see Tom? She hadn't thought of it that way in years. She *went* to see Tom. But did she *want* to see him? Probably. Of course. She picked up her bag, patted Bert, and left, without answering the phone.

CHAPTER X

Kate stood up and stretched. She had only been with him for two hours and she was already tired. Tom was in a tiresome mood. Even Mr. Erhard looked worn out.

'Come on, love. Why don't we take a walk to the boat pond?' There was silver threaded into his hair now, but he still had the clear, happy face of a child. Happy most of the time anyway. But sometimes he had the fretful nervousness of a child in distress.

'I don't want to go to the boat pond. I want Willie.'

'Then let's go get Willie.'

'I don't want Willie.'

Kate tightened her jaw and closed her eyes for a minute. Then she opened them again with a bright smile. 'Want to lie in your hammock?' He shook his head in answer, and looked as though he was going to cry. In fact he looked just the way Tygue had that morning. But Tygue had been jealous of her agent. What was Tom's problem? And, dammit, he was so easy sometimes, so lovable. Why did he have to be like this today? She had enough on her mind.

'I'm sorry, Katie.' He looked up at her and held out his arms. It was as though he suddenly understood, and she felt guilty as she took him in her arms, leaning down to reach him in his chair.

'It's all right, sweetheart. I guess you just need some new games.' It had been months since she'd brought him any. And then she had brought him the ones Tygue had just outgrown. Cast-off games and puzzles from his son. But she didn't see it that way. It was just cheaper buying one set than two. She held him close as she leaned over him and she felt him tighten his grip on her. For the strangest moment, she had an urge to kiss him. Like a man, not like a little boy.

'All I need is you, Katie. You don't have to bring games.'

Just hearing him say that gave her the oddest feeling. She pulled away suddenly and looked into his eyes. But there was no one there. No one but Tom, the child. Not the man.

'I love you too.' She sat down on the grass next to him, holding his hand, and the irritation of the first half of the day started to fade. For a moment she wanted to tell him what was happening. The book, the movie, what it all meant . . .

'Want to play Bingo?' He looked down at her sunnily, and she smiled a small tired smile, with her head tilted to one side. She had worn an old lavender wool skirt, and soft matching cashmere sweater. He had bought them for her shortly after they were married. He had loved them. Once. Now he didn't notice or remember. He wanted to play Bingo. 'Want to?'

'You know what, love?' I'm kind of tired. In fact . . .' She took a deep breath and stood up. She had played enough games for one day. With Tygue, with Tom, with herself. 'In fact, I think it's time for me to go home.'

'No, it's not!' He looked heartbroken. Oh Jesus. No! She didn't want him pulling at her too. 'It's not time to go!'

'Yes, it is, my love. But I'll be back in a couple of days.'

'No, you won't.'

'Yes, I will.' She smoothed the soft lilac skirt and looked up at him as Mr. Erhard approached. He had Willie and some books under one arm. 'Oh, look what Mr. Erhard has for you.' But Tom looked like a sad, angry little boy. 'Be a good boy, darling. I'll be back soon.' He held her close for a minute, and for the first time in a long time it tore at her soul again. She needed him now. And he wasn't there. 'I love you.' She said it softly and then backed away with a wave and a too bright smile in her eyes. But Tom was already holding Willie and reaching out for his books.

Kate walked back to the car with her head bowed and her arms tightly crossed, as though giving herself the hug she suddenly felt she needed so badly. And then as she slid into the car, she sighed and looked up at the trees. It was crazy. She had so much. She had Tygue, in a way she still had Tom, and she had just sold a book and a movie. She had just made three hundred and fifty thousand dollars, and she felt like a kid with a busted balloon.

'This is crazy!' She said it out loud and then laughed and lit a cigarette as she started the car. And then she had a better idea. She sat back for a minute with a mischievous smile, forgetting where she was and why she was there. Or rather, remembering where she was in a way she hadn't in years. Carmel. For six and a half years she had come to see Tom, and she had never driven the last twelve miles into town. Never gone to see the shops. Never had lunch there. Never walked along the main street. Never sat on the beach for an hour to unwind. Six and a half years and she had travelled the same well-worn path back and forth. And suddenly, she had a wild urge to drive into town. Just to see it. To wander along a little bit ... the shops ... the people ... she looked at her watch. She was early. She had cut the visit short by almost two hours today. Two hours. With a grin she released the brake and turned left when she reached the road. Left. The road to town.

It was a pretty road bordered with palm trees, and eventually little pastel cottages dotted the road. She was coming closer to Carmel. Nothing looked familiar yet, but her heart was pounding horribly. God, what was she doing? Why now? In two days she was venturing farther out into the world than she had in almost seven years. She had let Stu Weinberg come up to see her from L.A., and now she was going into Carmel. Such tiny acts, but they were a chink in the wall she had built. And then what? What would come next? A torrent? A flood? Or a slow trickle of the outside world over a long period of time? What if it got out of hand? What if ... she couldn't go on. She pulled the car off the road, and stopped. She was almost out of breath, and the road suddenly looked menacing instead of inviting.

'I can't.' Her voice trembled as she said it, and there were tears backed up in her throat. 'I can't ...' But she wanted to. Dammit, she wanted to. For the first time in years, she wanted to see what the place looked like, what they were wearing, how their hair was done. It was crazy to care about nonsense like that. But in the town where she had made her home they were still wearing teased beehives and mini-skirts ten years past their prime on bodies thirty years past theirs. She wanted to see people who looked like people she had known. But what about all the decisions she had made, everything she had chosen? It was threatened now. She had written a book that told more than it should have, of Tom, of herself, of her life. And the damn thing was going to be splashed all over the country. Hundreds of thousands of copies, and a movie . . . and . . .

'Bullshit.' She opened her eyes wide and looked around as she eased the car back on the road. She *had* sold a book and a movie, she had a right to an hour in Carmel. Her face set into a mask of determination and she stepped on the gas. And suddenly things started looking familiar. Nothing had changed very much in all the years since she'd last been there. The pastel-coloured cottages looked the same, the bends in the road, the quaint little hotels, and then suddenly the main tree-lined street leading right to the beach two blocks away. And along those two blocks, dozens of tiny boutiques. A few tourist traps, but for the most part they were elegant stores. A world she hadn't seen in six years. Gucci, Hermes, Jourdan, Dior, Norrell, Galanos, Givenchy . . . names, labels, scarves, perfume, shoes, she saw it all as she drove slowly down the street and slid into a parking place. It felt good now. She was glad she had come. She was even smiling broadly to herself as she hopped out of the car.

The first thing that caught her eye was an exquisite cream-coloured silk suit in a shop window. They were showing it with a peach-coloured blouse, and cream-coloured shoes with a tiny gold chain that looped around a naked heel. She felt like a little girl again. She wanted the bride doll and the teddy bear and the doll with the stockings and the bra and . . . she practically giggled as she walked into the shop. She was suddenly glad she had worn the old cashmere sweater and skirt. They had weathered well. And she had worn her long hair in a loose ladylike knot at the nape of her neck. Today, she hadn't even let it down for Tom.

'Madame?' The woman who ran the shop was obviously French, and she looked at Kate with a measuring glance in her eyes. She was a small, trim woman with greying blonde hair, and she was wearing a grey silk dress and a rather staggering triple strand of pearls. But Kate still remembered that side of Carmel. People dressed. Shopkeepers, restaurateurs, visitors, natives. Only a handful of 'artists' in the area looked artsy craftsy. Everyone else looked as though they were going to Maxim's for lunch. 'May I help you?'

'May I just look?'

'But of course.' The woman was gracious, and turned her attention to the latest copy of *L'Officiel* on her desk. Kate remembered modelling for them once. A thousand years ago. And then the suit in the window caught her eye. The woman in the grey silk dress looked up with a smile. She hadn't wanted to suggest it, but she had thought of it immediately. And then their eyes met and Kate laughed. There was laughter dancing in the other woman's eyes as well.

'May I?'

'I'd love to see it on you. We just got it in.'

'From Paris?'

'New York. Halston.' Halston. How long had it been since she'd felt those kinds of fabrics? Seen the clothes? And what the hell did it matter, dammit, except somehow . . . it did. Now it did. She needed to celebrate her success.

She grabbed three dresses and a skirt as the owner of the boutique got the suit off the mannequin with the help of an assistant. Kate was loving every minute of it, and when she tried on the suit, she loved it even more. It was made for her. The peach blouse turned her pale, delicate skin to a warm rosy blush, and her green eyes danced as she looked at the suit. It flowed over her body. The skirt was mid-calf and draped itself around her like a caress, the jacket was long and feminine and graceful. She tried the shoes on too, and she felt like a princess, or maybe even a queen. The suit was two hundred and eighty-five dollars. The shoes were eighty-six. Shameful. Sinful. And where in God's name would she wear it all? It was what she had been telling Felicia for years. Where would she use stuff like that? At the supermarket? In the car pool, taking Tygue and his little buddies to school? Bathing Bert?

'I'll take it.' And in a hasty gesture she added the red wool skirt and print blouse and the high-necked, long-sleeved black dress she had tried on first. It looked terribly grown up and almost too serious, but it was so damn elegant. And subtly sexy. Sexy? That was crazy too. Whom did she need to look sexy for? Willie the Bear? What in hell was she doing? She was spending just slightly over five hundred dollars on clothes she would probably never wear. Maybe she could get away with the cream silk suit at Tygue's college graduation. But even then, only if he went to Princeton or Yale. The idea made her grin as she wrote out the cheque. She was going nuts. It was all that money those lunatics in Hollywood and New York were going to be paying her. It was a delicious kind of craziness though, and she revelled in it. She even added a tiny bottle of perfume, the kind she had worn years before. And it was only as she walked back to the car with her arms full of bundles that she noticed where she had parked. The hotel where she and Tom had stayed on their last visit to Carmel . . . their hotel . . .

'Not anymore.' She said it softly and looked away as she put the packages in the trunk. Maybe she'd leave them there. Maybe she'd sell them with the car. She didn't need them after all. But as she thought of them again, she couldn't wait to try on the suit again when she got home. And the black dress. Tygue would think she was crazy. She'd wait until he went to bed.

She drove home faster than she ever had before. This time, she didn't even feel guilty. And the funniest part was that no one knew she had done anything different; no one had to know. Maybe she could even do it again. The idea made her laugh as she turned into the driveway. Right on time. She had used the extra two hours well. She waved at Tillie as she parked the car behind the house. They were busy in the garden again, and Tygue looked a lot happier than he had that morning. He waved at her frantically as he burrowed into his planting.

'Hi, love!' She left the packages in the car and went to kiss him, but he was too busy. Even Bert had a new bone and was off by himself. Kate wandered happily into the house. Everything was just fine. And there was a message from Felicia, saying she'd be down for the weekend.

And she was. She came down with three bottles of champagne, and an armload of presents. Silly presents, fun presents, things for Kate's desk, for her house, for her room, and then from the bottom of the bag of goodies she handed Kate a small silver-wrapped box.

'Not another one!' Kate was still laughing, but Felicia's face had grown quiet and serious and there was a look of tenderness in her eyes. 'Oh Jesus, something tells me this one's for real.'

'Maybe so.'

There was a small neat card stuck into the ribbon of the silver box. Kate opened the card carefully, and read it as tears filled her eyes. 'To the lady with the golden heart, all you need is courage. The Cowardly Lion discovered that he had the courage all along. All he needed was a medal to remind him of it. You are hereby reminded that you are not only brave, but able and good and wise and much loved.' And it was signed 'The Good Witch of the North'. Kate smiled through her tears.

'From *The Wizard of Oz*?'

'More or less.'

Kate opened the package, and inside, on a blue velvet lining in a red satin box, was a gold watch with a watch chain. It was like a man's, except that the watch was in the shape of a heart, and as Kate turned it over, she saw that on the back was inscribed 'For courage, for colour, with love'. Kate held the watch tightly clasped in one hand and threw her arms around Licia in a tight, crushing hug. And Licia hugged back. It was a hug Kate had longed for so badly, from someone who would tell her that everything was all right.

'What can I say?' The tears trickled down her face.

'Just say you'll be a good kid and give yourself a chance. That's all I want for you.' For a minute, Kate almost wanted to tell her about the shopping spree in Carmel. But she couldn't. Not yet.

'I'll try. Hell, with a watch like that, I almost feel like I have to. Licia, I'd be lost without you.'

'No, you wouldn't. You'd relax, and nobody would bug you anymore. It would be heavenly.'

'Horseshit.'

They both grinned at each other and talked about the book and the contracts and the store. For Kate the romance of success was just beginning. They finished the bottle of champagne just after 4 A.M., sleepily said good night, and went to their beds.

It was a cosy wonderful weekend. Kate wore the new watch pinned to her favourite tee-shirt the next day. They had a picnic, and then took Tygue to the Adams ranch, where all three of them took out horses and rode over the hills. On Sunday, Licia slept late, while Kate took Tygue to church, and they had a leisurely lunch on the grass after they got back. It was five o'clock before Licia even started to think of leaving. She was lying on the warm grass, looking up at the sky, holding Tygue's hand, and trying to fend off Bert.

'You know, once in a while, Kate, I can understand why you love it here.'

'Mmhm.' Kate's mind had been a thousand miles away, but she smiled at her friend.

'It's so goddamned peaceful.'

Kate laughed at the look on her face. 'Is that a complaint or a compliment?'

'Right now a compliment. I really hate to go back. And it'll probably be several months before I can come down again.' Kate was looking straight at her as she said it, and there was a strange look in Kate's eyes. 'Something wrong?' Felicia had never seen that look before.

'Just thinking.'

'What about?'

'Some stuff I've got in the car.'

'So?' She wasn't making any sense.

'What are you doing tomorrow, Licia?'

'Oh Jesus. Don't ask. I've got three meetings before lunch, we're coordinating all the fall shows, and the whole winter look.'

'And then?'

'What do you mean "and then"?' Kate was making her nervous. What the hell was she getting at?

'Are you busy for lunch?'

'No. Why? Can I do something for you?'

'Yeah.' Kate was grinning now. She just sat there and laughed at Felicia. To hell with it. 'As a matter of fact, Miss Norman, there is something you can do for me.'

'What?'

'Take me to lunch.'

'But I have to go back, you dummy.' Felicia sat up now too. And she was smiling, but confused. It was just a silly Sunday.

'I know you have to go back. I'll go with you.'

'To San Francisco?' Felicia was grinning broadly now too, with a look of astonishment on her face as Kate nodded.

'Yeah. What the hell.'

Felicia threw her arms around her friend and the two women exchanged a ferocious hug of joy, as Tygue watched wide-eyed, with a look of dismay.

'Who'll stay with me?'

Kate looked over at him in surprise, and drew him into the hug. 'Tillie, sweetheart. And maybe one of these days I'll take you to San Francisco too.'

'Oh.' But he didn't look impressed, and in a moment Kate left him with Licia. She had things to do. Tillie to call ... things to get out of the car and pack ... things to do. San Francisco. It had been six and a half years.

'Hallelujah!' She could hear Felicia shouting as she walked into the house with a wide grin and her arms full of the clothes she'd bought in Carmel. Kate was going to town.

CHAPTER XI

They had driven along in silence for almost an hour, after the initial excitement and burst of conversation. They were already more than halfway there, and Kate had just noticed her turnoff in Carmel. Felicia had noticed it too.

'Kate?'

'Hm?'

It was dark in the car, but Felicia could see her profile as she glanced over. She looked no different than she had six and a half years before when Felicia had driven her down to her 'retreat'. If she had known then how long Kate would hide there, she would never have agreed to find her the house.

'What's bugging you, Licia?' Kate turned to her with a quiet smile.

'What made you change your mind?'

'I don't know that I have, on the whole. I just . . . oh damn. I don't know, Licia. Maybe this crazy thing with the book has thrown me off. I was so damn happy with my life down there, in the hills. The kid, the dog, all of it.'

'Bullshit.'

Kate glanced over at her sharply. 'You don't believe me?'

'No. I think you've been bored a long time. You wouldn't admit it to me, but I think you knew it. You can't bury yourself alive like that. You have a whole fantasy life in your books, but that's not real and you know it. You're young, Kate. You need people, places to go, trips, men, clothes, success. All of it. You gave up too soon. Tom had his big time. He lived it, he enjoyed it while it lasted. I think that if he . . . if he were still the same, it would kill him to see you locked up like some old woman. You're not Tillie for chrissake. Anyway, you've heard all that from me before. I'm sorry. I didn't mean to make a speech.'

117

Kate was still smiling in the darkness. 'I'd think you didn't love me anymore if you stopped doing that. Anyway, in answer to your question, maybe you're right. Maybe I did know I was bored. Bored isn't really the right word, though. I like my life. I just . . . all of a sudden I just got hungry for more. I wanted to see people. *Real* people. Friday, when I went to see Tom, it was kind of a lousy day and I left early. And for no reason at all, I just got the itchies and drove into Carmel.'

'You did?' Kate nodded with guilty pleasure. 'You little wretch. You didn't say a thing. What did you do?'

'Spent a fortune.' Kate's cackle made Felicia grin.

'On what? I'm dying to know.'

'Ridiculous stuff. Clothes. Nothing I need. Jesus, I don't even know where I'll wear them. Or rather, I didn't know where I'd wear them till tonight. Maybe that's why I decided to come up to the city with you. To wear my new clothes.' She was only half teasing. She still wasn't entirely sure herself why she'd come. Except that there was this new little demon in her that was beginning to shout 'Go! Move! Live! Dream! Spend! Be!' And then she had a sobering thought. 'Do you think it's an awful thing to do to Tygue?' Her eyes loomed large in the darkness as Felicia glanced over at her.

'What, go away for a couple of days? Don't be ridiculous. Most parents do it all the time. It'll do him good.'

'Maybe I should have taken more time to prepare him.'

'You'd just have backed out.' Kate nodded silent agreement and lit a cigarette.

It seemed only moments later when Felicia looked over at her with a smile. 'Are you ready?'

'For what?' Kate looked vague and then suddenly she realized what Felicia meant. She had been so engrossed in her own thoughts that she had missed the first landmarks. They were nearing it now.

They were already past the airport. Yes. She was ready. Another two miles, and the freeway rounded the last obscure bend and there it was. Kate sat in silence, smiling slowly, as tears filled her eyes. It was home. The skyline was a little taller, a little more jagged, but in essence it was the same. San Francisco was a city that never changed that much. It always kept the integral part of its personality intact. And its beauty. The TransAmerica spire pointed sharply into the air from downtown. And suddenly Kate allowed herself to think of places she had blotted from her mind for years. The tree-lined streets of Pacific Heights, the little Victorian houses, the yacht club on a summer's night, the Marina on a Sunday morning, the majesty of the Presidio, the sweep of the Golden Gate Bridge, and all the tiny hiding places she had shared with Tom. Just seeing the skyline, as Felicia raced toward the city, brought back a thousand memories she had long since put away in musty old trunks. Now she held them in her hands and they smelled faintly of old familiar perfume. She rolled down the window and let the night air whip her face.

'It's chilly. The fog must be in.' Felicia smiled at her and said nothing. Kate really didn't want to talk. She wanted to watch and listen and feel. They were already on the off ramp into the city.

They were on Franklin Street heading north towards the Bay. As the car crested the hills, you could see the lights twinkling on the other side of the Bay. Even the traffic looked sophisticated. Jaguars and Mercedes and Porsches hobnobbing with vans and VWs and an occasional motorcycle zooming by. Everything seemed to be moving very quickly, and everything looked bright and alive. It was ten o'clock on a Sunday night.

Felicia turned right on California Street, and a block later they found themselves following a cable car up the hill as Kate started to laugh.

'Oh God, Licia, I'd forgotten. I love this town. It's all so pretty.' Felicia wanted to stand up and shout. Victory! She was back. Maybe she'd even come back for good.

Felicia swooped carefully around the cable car at the top of Nob Hill, and Kate fell silent again as she took in the sober splendours of the cathedral, the Pacific Union Club, the Fairmont and the Mark, and then they were speeding down the other side of the hill into the financial district, with the Ferry Building straight ahead. And Kate was laughing again.

'Okay, Licia. Confess. You did this on purpose, didn't you?'

'What?'

'The guided tour. You know what I mean, you bitch.'

'Me?'

'You. But I love it. Don't stop.'

'Anything else you want to see?'

'I don't know.' So many feelings were being awakened at once that she couldn't decide what she wanted to see next.

'Are you hungry?'

'Sort of.'

'Want to stop for something to eat at Vanessi's?'

'Like this?' Kate looked down in horror at the blue jeans, red shirt, and fading espadrilles.

'On a Sunday, who notices? And it's late.'

'I don't know, Licia.' She looked nervous again, and Felicia waved a hand as she sped up Kearny towards where it met Broadway. And then suddenly they were catapulted into the uproarious vulgarity of Broadway. 'Teen Age Co-Ed Wrestlers Topless Here,' and the usual promises delivered by barkers – 'Virgins, all virgins' – side by side with Finocchio's and its female impersonators. In the midst of the madness, the traffic and the trucks coming off the Bay Bridge, Enrico's sat with artsy courage, offering one of the city's first *al fresco* sidewalk cafés. Somehow, with the roses on the pink marble-topped tables, the friendly noise, the colourful passers-by, it all felt very Via Veneto, and not quite so Broadway. And to maintain the illusion, across the street, sat Vanessi's, catering to the beautiful and the nearly beautiful, the important and the soon-to-be and the never-was-but-thought-they-were. Governors and ghouls, matriarchs and madams, portly men in blue suits, women in black with great chunks of gold bracelets, and then at the next table jeans and wildly frizzy hair. It was a place to get lost in, a place to be found in. It was, simply, Vanessi's. Kate and Tom had loved it. At first they had found it too noisy for their romantic evenings alone, but after a while it had grown on them. And Tom was always left in peace there. A few autographs, a couple of handshakes, a wave, but no hassles. No kisses and grabs. Vanessi's.

'You up to it?' Felicia had come to a screeching halt in the parking lot next door. She hated to give Kate a choice, but it seemed only fair. There was a long pause as Kate looked around and then absently, her hand went to the heart-shaped watch pinned to her shirt. For valour, for courage.

'Okay.' She stepped out of the car, stretched her legs, and almost cringed from the noise and the bustle. But even she knew that what she now considered 'bustle' was still half-dead for San Francisco.

Felicia got her stub for the car, and arm in arm they strolled towards the restaurant. 'Scared?'

'Terrified.'

'So are most people about ninety percent of the time. Don't forget that.'

'They don't have anything to hide.' It was out then. That was it. That was always it. Damn.

Felicia stopped walking and faced her, still holding her arm. 'You don't have anything to hide either, Kate. You have a lot of pain in your past. But that's it. It's the past. And it's someone else's past. It's his past, not yours. You have a child, a book, a nice clean life in the country. That's all.' Kate closed her eyes with a smile and took a deep breath.

'I wish that's what I felt, Licia.'

'Then make it what you feel.'

'Yes, sir.'

'Oh shut up.' The moment of seriousness had already passed and Kate giggled as she sprinted along on her long coltlike legs.

'I'll race you!' They ran the last few steps, laughing and choking, and the headwaiter opened the door for them, and even at ten o'clock they were instantly swallowed up in the noise and bustle and avalanche of smells that was Vanessi's. Waiters shouting at the grill, people laughing in the bar, political battles being waged, romances being begun, all of it. It was fabulous. Kate just stood there and smiled. To her the noises sounded like an orchestra playing 'Welcome Home'.

'Table for two, Miss Norman?' Felicia nodded with a smile,

and the headwaiter looked blankly at Kate. He was new there. He didn't know her. He didn't know Tom. He only knew Felicia. And Kate wasn't anyone anyway. Just a girl in jeans and a red shirt.

They were seated in the back, and the pinkish lighting made everyone look rosy and young. The waiter handed them menus. Kate handed hers back. 'Cannelloni, house salad, zabaglione for dessert.' The zabaglione was a warm runny feast of rum and egg whites.

Felicia ordered steak, salad, and a martini, as Kate looked at her watch. 'Already have a date?'

'No. I was wondering if I should call Tillie.'

'She's probably asleep.'

Kate nodded, as a wave of guilt tried to creep into the evening, but she wouldn't let it in. She was having too good a time. And dinner was just as good as it had always been. Afterwards they walked for a few minutes through the narrow colourful streets of North Beach. Hippie boutiques, artists' hangouts, coffee houses, and the smell of marijuana heavy in the air. Nothing had changed there either. After a few blocks they wandered back to Felicia's car. It was just midnight, and Kate was beginning to yawn.

'Just call me Cinderella.'

'You can sleep late tomorrow.'

'What time do you leave for work?'

'Don't ask. You know how I feel about mornings.' Kate yawned all the way home, suddenly overwhelmed by the feelings her return to San Francisco had brought back. She could hardly keep her eyes open as Felicia pressed a button in the car as they reached the top of Telegraph Hill, and a garage door half a block away swung open.

'Good Lord, Licia, how fancy.'

'Just safe.'

Kate was looking at the building with amusement. It was even more elegant than the one Felicia had lived in when Kate had left town. It was the typical older bachelors' building. Expensive, well-run, quiet, one- or two-bedroom apartments with extraordinary views of the port and the Bay. Not a place for children, and really not much warmth or charm. Just expensive.

'You disapprove?' Felicia looked amused as they slid into the garage.

'Of course not! What made you say that?'

'The look on your face. Remember me, I'm the city mouse. You're the country mouse.'

'All right, all right, I'm too tired to fight you.' Kate grinned again through a yawn, and then they were in the elevator and rapidly upstairs. Felicia unlocked her apartment door right from the elevator, and they were immediately let into a hall with delicate French wallpaper in a rich dusty rose and thick creamy beige rugs. There were watercolours on the walls, two large palm trees and an antique English mirror. It was all done in exquisite taste. And perfectly Felicia.

'Should I take off my espadrilles?' Kate was only half teasing.

'Only if you plan to shove them up your ass. I'm not prissy for chrissake, Kate. You can roll on the floor if you want to.'

'I'd love to.' The foyer alone would have made a beautiful bedroom.

But Felicia was already turning on the lights in the living room, which was done in the off-white silks and creamy damasks, with dark oriental inlaid tables. There was a breathtaking view and the room's decor was wonderfully stark. The dining room beyond it was much the same with a black and white marble floor, numerous crystal sconces, and a small chandelier. Kate was sure Felicia's life-style hadn't actually been as grandiose six years before. Elegant, but not as spectacular. And there was a terrace that wrapped itself around the apartment and was covered with lush flowers and plants. Kate knew it for the work of a gardener, not her friend.

'You like it?'

'Are you kidding? I'm overwhelmed. When did life get like this?'

'With the last big promotion.' She smiled and then sighed softly. 'I have to do something with the money. And you won't let me buy Tygue a car for a while. So this is it.'

'It sure is.'

'Thanks, love. I'll show you your room.' She was pleased that Kate liked it, though actually she was getting a little bored with it herself. It has been two and a half years now. She was almost ready for something else. Something even more elaborate, another step up.

The guest room was in keeping with the rest of the apartment – a blue and white room in another delicate French print. There was a tiny fireplace with a white marble mantel, more plants, a door onto the terrace, a little French desk, and a Victorian love seat.

'I just want you to know that I may never leave.' And then she laughed as she had a horrifying thought.

'What's so funny?'

'The thought of Tygue here. Can you imagine our old peanut-butter pal plonked down on that love seat?'

'I'd love to imagine just that.' Felicia looked almost annoyed and then shrugged. 'Well, maybe ...' And then they were both laughing again like kids. Talking about Tygue made Kate miss him a little though. This was the first night since he'd been born that she had been away from him. What if he needed her? If he had a nightmare? If he couldn't find Willie? If ...

'Kate!'

'Huh?'

'I can see what you're thinking. Stop it. You'll talk to him tomorrow.'

'I'll go home tomorrow. But in the meantime ...' She tossed herself onto the bed with a happy smile. 'This is sheer heaven.'

'Welcome home.' Felicia strolled out of the room and across the hall to her own room as Kate called after her, 'Can I see it?'

It was white and stark and very cold, much like the living room. Kate was disappointed.

'You expected mirrors on the ceiling perhaps?'

'At least.'

'Want a drink, by the way?'

But Kate only smiled and shook her head. She knew exactly

what she wanted, and after they had said good night and she had heard Felicia's door close, she got it. She stood barefoot on the terrace, in her nightgown, watching the fog hang low over the Bay, looking at the ships below, the Bay Bridge and the cars whizzing across it. She stood there for half an hour, until she was trembling so hard from the cold that she had to go inside. But when she went inside she was still smiling.

CHAPTER XII

When Kate got up, she found a plate of croissants and a left-over pot of coffee from Felicia, with a note, 'Meet me at the office at noon. Shopping with discount before or after if you want. Love, F.' Shopping with discount. It was not her most pressing wish. She wanted to see the city again. Only the city. Places, memories, moments. Squealing with delight as she raced over the top of Divisadero with Tom, with the bay breeze whipping their hair into their faces as they swooped down again towards the tiny lip of beach, or headed out on the freeway across the Bay Bridge. Walks down narrow brick-paved streets in the upper part of town, browsing along Union Street, wandering down around the piers, or nibbling shrimps among the tourists at Fisherman's Wharf.

She stretched lazily as she stood barefoot in the kitchen, her brown hair showing soft red highlights in the sun as it hung long and loose down her back. Felicia even had a view from the kitchen. Kate stared at it happily as she nibbled at a peach, waiting for the coffee to warm. The phone rang just as she finished the peach. Probably Licia for her.

'Lo.'

'Well, hello. You're back.' For a moment her heart stopped. Who was he?

'Uh ... yes.' She stood very still, waiting to hear his voice again.

'And enjoying a lazy morning, I see. Is it a shock to be back?'

It was now. 'No, it's very pleasant.' Jesus, who was this guy? He seemed to know her, but she had no idea who he was. His voice was deep and interesting. It rang no familiar bells though. Still, something inside her was shaking. It was like being seen without being able to see.

'I tried you for dinner last night, but you weren't home yet. How was your friend?'

And then Kate let out a long sigh. So that was it. But he couldn't know Felicia very well, if he had mistaken Kate's voice for hers. 'I'm sorry, I think there's been an awful mistake.'

'There has?' Now he sounded confused, and Kate laughed.

'I'm the friend. I mean, I'm not Felicia. I'm sorry. I don't know why on earth I thought you knew who I was, but you seemed to.'

'I just assumed.' He sounded amused too, and his laughter was as pleasing as his voice. 'I'm sorry. You're the friend from the country?'

'The country mouse. At your service.' Well, not exactly, but it was fun talking to him, now that she knew that she wasn't on the spot. This had to be one of Licia's current men, if he knew about the trips to the country. 'I'm really very sorry. I didn't mean to mislead you. Can I give Felicia a message? I'll be seeing her at lunch.'

'Just tell her, if you would, that I've confirmed this evening. I'll pick her up at eight. The ballet's at eight-thirty, and we have a table at Trader Vic's for dinner afterwards. That ought to meet with Miss Norman's approval.'

'Hell, yes.' Kate laughed again, and then was embarrassed. Maybe he was more formal than that.

'I'll tell her you approved.'

'I'll tell her you called.'

'Thanks very much.' They hung up, and then Kate realized with horror that she had never gotten his name. How awful. But it had been so strange to talk to a man again. That made two in one week. But she assumed that Felicia would know who he was. If not, she was being taken to the ballet by a total stranger. The idea amused Kate, and she laughed to herself as she poured a cup of coffee. Men. She still liked her celibate life, but it was fun playing with them again. Fun hiding in a telephone, or just talking business with Stu. For some reason, she felt like playing again. Not 'doing', just playing. She was still grinning to herself when she went to get dressed.

She pulled the new dresses out of her suitcase with a look of mischief and excitement. The black was out, it was too dressy.

The red skirt would be about right. She had also brought a pair of grey flannel slacks from the year one, with a white shirt and a big soft grey shetland sweater. But she didn't want to wear something like that. She wanted to wear the suit. The creamy silk suit with the peach blouse, and the delicate little shoes with the gold chain at the heel. She almost wanted to jump up and down with excitement. And half-an-hour later, she was delighted with herself as she stood in front of the mirror. Bathed, made up, perfumed, and draped in the divine suit she had bought in Carmel. Her hair was loosely swept up in a Gibson Girl knot that looked wonderfully ladylike, and she had brought little pearl earrings, 'just in case'. As she looked in the mirror, she felt like a model again. But a much older one. She was almost thirty, and she was ready for the high-fashion look. She had never owned anything quite like the cream suit. She grinned at herself again and twirled on one heel. Who was this person? Was she a celebrated writer stopping in San Francisco for a day to have lunch? Was she a quiet young matron, up from the country for a visit? Was she the mother of a small boy, a teddy bear, and a basset hound named Bert? The heartbroken wife of . . . no, that she was not. Not now. But she was all the others, and none of them. Was the woman she saw in the delicate peach silk blouse really Tygue's mother? Did he even exist? Where? What country? She was in San Francisco now. This was real. How could anything else be?

She picked up the flat little beige suede bag she had brought up to go with the suit, and tucked it under her arm. It had a coral clasp and had been her mother's long ago. In another life. Now it was just a bag. And it was a beautiful day in a beautiful town, and she had things she wanted to do. She walked down Telegraph Hill from Felicia's apartment and found a cab in Washington Square. From there she reached a car-rental place and then she was on her own. Up Broadway into Pacific Heights, past all the great houses, and into the Presidio. Then back. Divisadero and over the hill, with a broad grin and an irresistible squeal. And then back into the Presidio until she reached the cliffs that looked out to sea, with the Golden Gate

Bridge stretching out, seeming to be only inches away, in all its rust-coloured splendour, and with the majesty of the cliffs on either side. It was a view that had always taken her breath away and still did. And it was a place she suddenly knew she had to bring Tygue. He had to know the town where they had lived. He had a right to this. To the excitement, the beauty, the cable cars, the bridge, the people, all of it. Just thinking about him confirmed in her mind the decision she had really made when she'd left him the day before. She was going back that night. She had answered her own questions. She *could* do it. She *had* faced it. No photographers were lurking in corners. No one knew or cared who she was. This was a new era, filled with new people, in all the most beloved old places She wanted to share it with Tygue. She would tell him all about it that night.

Feeling at peace, she slid into the rented car and headed downtown. Even that was fun now. She could remember a time when, just before she left for good, it filled her with dread. Terror. She would get claustrophobia everywhere she went. Pregnant, frightened, alone, with her whole life having fallen apart, just the simple act of going downtown had been a nightmare. Now it was funny. All those busy little people in gem-coloured dresses running in and out of buildings, dodging cars, hopping cable cars, as the dowager queen, the St. Francis Hotel, looked benevolently out upon Union Square. For a moment Kate stopped and smiled. Nothing had changed here. It had barely changed since she was a child, and certainly not in six years. The green of the square was as pretty, the pomp of the big stores just as apparent, the pigeons were as plentiful, the drunks equally so: all was well with the world. She rounded the bend into Geary, and slowed the car in front of the store. For a moment she thought maybe that had changed, but no – the doorman rushed out to help her.

'Leave the car, miss?'

'Thank you.'

'Be long?'

'I'm seeing Miss Norman.'

'That's fine.' He smiled pleasantly as she handed him the

keys and a dollar. It was simpler and cheaper than a garage. He'd do something with it. God knows what. The store probably had an arrangement with the garage across the street, or the police department, but one always got one's car back.

With a feeling of trepidation, Kate pushed open the heavy glass door, and walked inside the pale cocoa marble halls. Hallowed halls. Sacred halls. Bags to the right, jewellery to the left, men's department to the extreme right only bigger now, and cosmetics and perfume in the alcove at the far left. The same, all the same. Gloves had vanished now. Stockings seemed to have moved, but nothing essential had been displaced. And God, it was pretty. Incredibly so. A riot of wares that no woman could resist. Red suede shoulder bags, black lizard clutches, marvellous great chunks of gold and silver, purple threaded with gold to weave around one's waist in the evening, thick rich capes in wonderful pastel colours, Lanvin scarves, and the smell of perfume heavy in the air ... silk flowers ... suedes ... satins ... an endlessly abundant palette of colours. It made you feel you could never be beautiful without all of it. She smiled to herself as she watched the women devouring whatever they could touch. She wanted to do it herself, but she wasn't even sure she knew how to play the game anymore and she didn't want to keep Felicia waiting and besides, she felt extravagant enough in the suit she was wearing.

As the elevator carried her upstairs, it stopped for a moment on the second floor, then the third. She had lived on those floors, worn the dresses, shown the minks, been the brides. She saw new faces now in the moments the elevator door was open. Fresh faces. No one left from her time. She was grown up now. The others were gone too. Twenty-nine. Was that really old?

The elevator stopped on the eighth floor, and she stepped out. She was no longer sure exactly where Felicia's office was, but she was quickly informed by a guard. A corner office naturally. The fashion director for all the company's stores in California would have to have a corner office. At least. Kate smiled to herself again as she walked into a small anteroom and was instantly stopped by two very stylish-looking young women, and a man wearing pale blue suede pants.

'Yes?' He hissed it though perfect teeth and delicate lips.

'I'm Mrs. Harper. Miss Norman is expecting me.' The young man checked her out, then rapidly disappeared. In a moment, Felicia came stalking out of a huge white room behind her. Everything was white, glass, or chrome. It was cold but exquisite. And white definitely seemed to be Felicia's colour these days.

'Good God! You're for real!' Felicia stopped dead in the doorway, and looked at her friend. If she had ordered a model's setup for their biggest show, she would have done nothing differently. And suddenly, looking at her, she was proud of Kate. And pleased that the new watch was carefully adjusted on the delicate suit.

'Do I pass?'

Felicia rolled her eyes and practically dragged her inside. Kate was even walking differently, with a kind of sway of the hips and swagger all at the same time, as though she felt as beautiful as she looked. It made Felicia want to sing. 'Is that what you bought in Carmel?'

'Yup.'

'It's divine. Did you get stopped by every man in the store?'

'No.' Kate grinned at her. 'But you're going to the ballet tonight with a nameless stranger who is picking you up at eight, and then taking you to dinner at Trader Vic's.'

'My, my. Peter.'

'Then you know him.'

'More or less.' Which meant physically more and mentally less, but so what. That was Felicia's business. She looked pleased with the announcement about dinner. 'Want to join us?'

'I'm sure he'd be thrilled. Anyway, love, I'm going home.'

'You are? Why?' Had something happened? Felicia looked horrified. 'Already?'

'No, this afternoon. And I've already done a lot. A lot more than you know.' But Felicia did know. When she looked into

Kate's eyes, she knew. Kate looked confident again, in a way she hadn't in years.

'Will you come back again?' Felicia held her breath.

She nodded quietly, and then smiled. 'With Tygue. I think he ought to get to know the place a bit. He's old enough to enjoy it.' And then there was a pause as her smile broadened. 'And so am I. Maybe.'

'Maybe my ass. Come on, let's go to lunch.'

She took Kate to a new restaurant tucked in between the piers, and again they had champagne to celebrate. Every day seemed like a celebration now. The restaurant served a lavish lunch, and catered to the cream of the downtown clientele. It was kept locked, and considered itself more or less a club. 'By reservation only,' and they were extremely careful about who got reservations. Felicia always did. She brought the right people, looked marvellous, gave them good publicity. 'Miss Norman' was a venerated figure at Le Port, as they had called themselves. But Kate was beginning to realize that Felicia had become something of a personality around town.

'Does everyone know you?' It seemed as though everyone at this place did, and all the best-looking men.

'Only the right people, darling.'

Kate shook her head and laughed. 'You're impossible.' But Felicia had also grown. In Kate's years of hiding out, Felicia had been busy. She was important now, whatever that was. There was a certain aura around everything she touched. Success. Money. And style. Felicia had vast quantities of the latter, and had been quietly earning and amassing the former for years. Watching her in her own milieu, Kate had a new respect for her.

'Did you talk to Tillie, by the way?' Felicia asked the question nonchalantly, but Kate's heart almost stopped.

'Did she call?'

'Of course not. I just thought you might have called.' Felicia was sorry she'd brought it up.

'No. I was going to, but Tygue had already gone to school when I got up. I'll talk to him tonight. I'm going to try and get home in time to see him.'

'It'll do him a lot of good to see you like that, Kate. He needs to know more than torn blue jeans, kiddo.' She looked momentarily stern.

'That's why I thought I'd bring him up here. So you could teach him the facts of life. Right, Aunt Licia?'

'You bet, sweetheart.' They toasted each other with the last of the champagne, and Felicia regretfully looked at her watch. 'Dammit, I hate to go. When are you coming back?' She was going to pin her down. Now. Before she changed her mind.

'I thought I'd bring him up next month, when his school closes for the summer.' Then she meant it. Felicia beamed.

'Oh God, Kate, I can hardly wait till you tell him!'

'Neither can I.'

CHAPTER XIII

Kate had made it home in just under five hours, and without a single speeding ticket. That in itself was a miracle. Ninety-five, ninety-eight. But she wanted to see Tygue before he went to bed. She wanted to tell him about San Francisco. About taking him up there. About cable cars and the bridge. She had brought him chocolate from Ghirardelli Square, and she would tell him about that too. She had so much to tell him. Just the thought of it made her jumpy as she turned into the gravel drive. She had worn the red skirt and bright print blouse to come home in. Maybe Licia was right. Maybe it would do him good to see her looking pretty. She wanted to share the newness with him. The excitement.

The house looked cheerful and well lit as she pulled the car slowly into the parking space. There were no calls of hello, no barking, but she knew they were all cosily tucked inside. She unlocked the door with her key, and there he was, at the kitchen table, doing a puzzle with Tillie. He was wearing soft blue flannel pyjamas and the little yellow robe Licia had sent God knew when. He looked cosy, and comfortable, and warm, and all hers. She stood there for a moment, watching him, while Tillie smiled at her, and Tygue stayed intent on his puzzle.

'Hi, guys.' Silence. Tillie raised her eyebrows but said it had nothing to do with her. But it didn't come. No 'Hi Mom'. Only Bert sleepily wagging his tail at her feet. 'Hey, tough guy. Aren't you going to say hello?' She walked quickly over to him and folded him into a hug, but he ignored her.

'Yeah. Hi.' And then Kate's eyes found Tillie's. So that was it. He was pissed. Kate slowly sat down in one of the kitchen chairs and watched him. He still hadn't looked at her. And Tillie got up and went to find her things. One thing about Kate, she always came back when she said she would. No fooling around. She had said she'd be home Monday night and she was. Tillie liked that about her. She also knew that Kate was going to have some serious fence mending to do. Tygue hadn't been himself since she had left. 'Overnight, Tillie! She went overnight!' The boy had been shocked.

'Where'd you get the new puzzle?'

'Tillie. We bought it today.'

'That's nice. Aunt Licia sends you her love.' Silence again. Jesus. It was going to be a long thawing out, at this rate. She almost wondered if it was worth it. But as she thought back over the last twenty-four hours, she knew it was. He was just going to have to understand. 'Hey, guess what.' She snuggled up to him and tried to kiss his neck, but he made himself stiff and hard to reach. 'I have a surprise for you.'

'Yeah?' It was the least curiosity he had ever shown about a surprise. 'What is it?'

'A trip.' He looked at her with horror. But she went on. 'How would you like to come up to San Francisco with me sometime, to see Aunt Licia?' She waited for the intake of breath, the widened eyes, but it didn't happen that way. Instead he shrank from her and his eyes filled with tears.

'I won't go! I won't!' He ran away from the table, and a moment later she heard the door to his room slam shut. Tillie watched her as she slipped into her coat, and Kate let out a long tired breath.

'I knew he'd be mad at me for going, but I didn't expect this.'

'He'll get over it. It's a big adjustment for him.' Tillie sounded sorry for them both, but it irritated Kate.

'A big adjustment that I leave him for one night?' Hell, she had a right to that much, didn't she? Well, didn't she, dammit? She knew she did. He was only a kid. He couldn't expect all her time. But he had always had it before. That was the bitch of it.

'How often have you left him overnight before, Kate?' Tillie already knew the answer to that, of course.

'Never.'

135

'Then that's a big change for him. He'll get used to it, if you plan to go on doing it. I think he senses a change. Maybe he's confused by it.'

'Oh damn, Tillie. So am I. I made a very big deal on one of my books last week. It means a lot of nice things for us, but it also means some things I don't understand yet. I've kind of been experimenting with how I feel about it all.'

'He doesn't understand that. He feels it, but he doesn't understand. All he knows is what he's always known. He hasn't gone very far from here, you know. And now you're off for the night, and you're telling him that you're taking him to San Francisco. You and I know it's exciting. He just thinks it's scary. And to tell you the truth, it would scare a lot of older folks from around here.'

'I know. It scared me for a lot of years too.' For whatever the reasons. 'I guess I'm expecting too much of him.'

'He'll come around. Give him time. You know' – she looked at Kate apologetically – 'probably even seeing you dressed like that scares him a little. Maybe it tells him he's losing you, or that you're changing. You never know with kids. They think the craziest damn things. When my husband died, my youngest son thought that meant we'd put him up for adoption. Don't ask me why, but he thought we were sending him away too. He cried for three weeks until he finally came out and said it. Maybe Tygue is afraid you'll leave him, all dressed up like that. You look awfully nice though.'

'Thanks, Tillie.'

'Take it easy. Oh, and are you going up to teach tomorrow?'

'I think I'd better wait a couple of days before I tackle that.'

'Nice that they can be that flexible.'

'Yeah.' Oh Christ, Tillie. Don't challenge me on that too. Please. But she didn't. She just waved and quietly shut the door.

Kate suddenly felt alone in the house. Only Bert made his presence known, wanting to play with the shiny gold chain on her new shoes.

'Not for eighty-six bucks you don't, Bert, m'boy.' She swatted him away with her hand, and noticed how empty the house sounded with only her voice in it. She sat very still for a moment, and then stood up and slipped off the skirt. She unzipped the valise she had taken to the city with her, and fished out the jeans and red shirt as she tossed the new skirt and blouse over the back of a chair. 'So long for now.' She carefully put the shoes in the suitcase, or Bert would have eaten them for dinner. And then, on stockinged feet, she walked softly toward Tygue's room and knocked. 'Can I come in?' There was a silence and then finally his voice.

'Yeah.' He was sitting in the dark, and the bright moon of his little face looked tiny in the dark room.

'Don't you want a light on?'

'Nope.'

'Okay. Have you got Willie?'

'Yeah.'

'I'll bet that feels good.'

'What?' His voice was so little and wary.

'I'll bet having Willie feels good. You know you've got him. He's all yours forever.'

'Yeah.' The voice was softer now in the dark, as she lay across his bed and tried to watch what she could see of his face.

'Do you know you've got me, just like you've got Willie? Only more so. Forever and ever. Do you know that?'

'Sort of.'

'What do you mean, "sort of"?' It wasn't an accusation. It was a question.

'I mean, sort of.'

'Okay. What happens if you tie a red ribbon on Willie? Does it make him different?'

'Yeah. It makes him look silly.'

'But do you love him less?' Vehement shaking of the head as he held the bear closer. 'Okay, so no matter how funny-looking I may seem to you, or what I wear, I'm still old Mum, right?' A nod. 'And I love you just the same no matter what I'm doing, or what I look like, or where I am.'

'Willie doesn't leave me.'

'Neither do I. I never leave you either. Sometimes I may

go away. But I don't leave you, darling. And I never will. Not ever.'

'But you go-ed away.' The voice was trembling and full now.

'Only for one night, and I came back. Just like I said I would. Didn't I?' Reluctantly, he nodded.

'Why did you do it?'

'Because I needed to. Because I wanted to. Sometimes grown-ups need to go places, without kids.'

'You never needed to before.'

'No. But I did this time.'

'Did that man send you away?' She knew instantly whom he meant.

'Stu Weinberg?' He nodded. 'Of course not. I sent myself away. And was it really that bad, for just one night?' He shrugged noncommittally and then suddenly he was crying and holding out his arms. She was stunned.

'I missed you! And I thought you didn't love me anymore!'

'Oh, darling, oh baby . . . how could you think a thing like that? I love you so much. And I missed you too. But . . . I just had to. But I'll always, always, always come back. And next time I go, you'll go with me.' She wanted to promise him that she wouldn't do it again. But she knew that she would. How could she give that up, now that she'd just found it again?

He cried for almost half an hour, and then slowly it stopped. And he looked up at her with the tiniest smile.

'If I squeezed my shirt, we could give Willie a bath just with your tears. Did you know that?'

He chuckled hoarsely and she gave him a kiss as she smoothed the blond hair falling over his forehead. 'Can I interest you in some chocolate?'

'Now?'

'Sure.' She had bought a huge bar of it wrapped in gold. It was the size of a hardcover book. And she had also brought him a box of chocolate lollipops and a chocolate pistol. Better than Easter or Hallowe'en. When he saw the gold foil-wrapped chocolate gun, his jaw dropped and his eyes grew as he held out his hands.

'Wow!'

138

'Not bad, huh, hotshot?'

'Wow, Mom, it's terrific!'

'So are you.' She pulled him back onto her lap as he gobbled the chocolate from the large bar. But he was saving the pistol to show his friends in school.

'What if somebody breaks it?'

'Then we'll buy some more when we go up to San Francisco together.' Something deep inside trembled for a moment, but he looked at her with a big grin and a look of greedy glee.

'Yeah. That must be some place.'

'It is.' She held him close that evening for a very long time.

CHAPTER XIV

'Okay, now close your eyes, sweetheart.' Tygue sat very still in the seat next to her, with his eyes closed. She had recognized the last bend in the road before the skyline would come into view. She wondered what he would think of it. He had never seen anything like it. She took the bend smoothly, and smiled to herself at the zigzag of buildings that lay ahead. 'Okay. You can open your eyes now.' He was very quiet as he did. He took it all in, but said nothing. Kate was surprised. 'Well? What do you think?'

'What is it?'

'San Francisco, silly. Those are all the big buildings downtown.' Tygue had never seen anything taller than four stories. It was amazing to realize that. At his age she had already been to New York, and gone to the top of the Empire State Building.

'I thought it had hills.' He sounded disappointed. And a little scared.

'It does. You can't see them from here.'

'Oh.'

She didn't know what to say to him, as he sat there looking straight ahead. He wanted to go home. And she wanted him to love San Francisco. She and Felicia had planned everything. They would be there for a week. A whole week! Fisherman's Wharf, Sausalito, cable cars, the beach, the zoo, a ferry ride, bike riding on Angel Island, they had thought of everything. Felicia had even got the location schedules of the local TV shows, so he could watch them filming chase scenes on the hills. Inevitably, there was one scheduled on Divisadero.

'Want to see the crookedest street in the world?'

'Sure.' He held Willie tightly on his lap and Kate was about to snap at him. He was in San Francisco. It was exciting. It was the first trip he had ever taken. Why wasn't he happy?

Why didn't he feel what she did? And then she felt mean for what she was thinking, and she turned right off Franklin Street, so that she could pull over. 'This is it? Aunt Licia's house?' He looked up at the ramshackle hotel with unconcealed horror, and Kate laughed. It had been a long drive, and she realized suddenly how tense she had been about what he was feeling.

'No. And I love you, you silly kid. C'mere and give me a hug.'

His little freckled face melted into a smile and he reached out to her. She wound up hugging both her son and his bear. Tillie was keeping Bert for them until they got back. 'Tygue Harper, I promise you that you're going to have a good time here. Okay? Will you trust me a little?' He nodded as she looked down at him and kissed the top of his head.

'It's so big.' There was real awe in his voice. 'And so . . .' He looked around the dreary neighbourhood she had temporarily parked in and the disappointment was clear on his face.

'Yeah, it's big. Bigger than we're used to now. But you know E street, in town?' He nodded sombrely. E street was horrible. Way past the old railroad tracks, near the dump. There were drunks and old deserted cars there. It smelled bad, and it was the kind of place you never wanted to go to. He knew E Street. Everybody did. He looked up at his mother with big eyes. 'Well, where we are right now is just like E Street. But there are beautiful places here. And we're going to see all of them. Okay? Deal?' She held out a hand with a smile and he took it in a hard businesslike little shake. 'Ready to roll?'

'Ready to roll!' He sat looking ahead, but he was holding Willie less ferociously now, and Kate smiled to herself as she started the car again.

'Hungry?' She knew they weren't far from the Hippo on Van Ness, but he shook his head. 'Ice cream?' The head turned, and there was a smile in his eyes. A small nod. 'Then ice cream it is.' That was perfect. She'd stop at Swensen's on Hyde Street on the way to Licia's. Licia was waiting for them at the apartment. And she was as anxious as Kate.

Kate parked the car outside Swensen's on Union and Hyde,

and as they got out and stretched, two cable cars came clanking down Hyde. 'Look!' Tygue jumped up and down waving his bear. 'Look, Mom! It's a . . . a . . .' He could hardly stand it, and his mother grinned. Everything would be all right after all. And the ice cream was terrific. A double scoop of rocky road and banana, sugar cone, and chocolate dip. Tygue was already wearing most of it on his nose and chin when they left the store, and another cable car came down the hill. She could hardly get him back in the car.

'We'll go for a ride later.' But first, she had another idea. Two of them. The steepest hill. The crookedest street. They were near both.

The steepest hill did not impress him, but he loved the crookedest street as they inched their way down the narrow, winding brick road banked with flowers and bordered with pastel-hued Victorian houses. Tygue loved it so much he almost forgot the ice cream dripping on his bear. He happily licked a gob of chocolate off Willie's ear.

'Tygue, yerghk!'

'Uh uh, yummy!' He was happy again. 'What's that?' He settled back in his seat and pointed ahead to Coit Tower on Telegraph Hill.

'That's a memorial to the fire department. It's called Coit Tower, and it's right near Aunt Licia.'

'Can we go see it?'

'Sure. But first let's see what Aunt Licia has planned.'

'This is fun.'

And so was the rest of the trip. They did everything. Hippo dinners, picnics at Stinson Beach, the wax museum, Fisherman's Wharf, ten or fifteen rides on the cable car, the aquarium, the planetarium, Chinatown, and the Japanese Garden in the park. It was sheer heaven, and by the following Saturday, Tygue knew San Francisco better than most children who had lived there for years.

'Well, champ? What do you think? Gonna ditch your Mom and come live with me here?' They were all sprawled out on Felicia's impeccable, white, living-room rug eating popcorn. For the first time all week, they had been too tired to go out.

Felicia had agreed to order pizza. It had been totally Tygue's week, and both women were exhausted. They smiled at each other over his head.

'You know, Aunt Licia.' Tygue was looking thoughtfully out at Bay Bridge just beyond the terrace. 'When I grow up, I might come up here and work on the cable car.'

'Great idea, champ.'

'And if you buy him his own real one for Christmas, Licia, I'll kill you.' Kate laughed at the thought, as she shoved a handful of popcorn into her mouth.

'When do you think you guys'll be back?'

Kate shrugged, looking down at Tygue. 'I don't know. We'll see.' She had been neglecting Tom lately, and she had some ideas for a new book. 'I really ought to do some work. And I've got Tygue set up with a group that's going to ride every day at the Adams ranch until school starts in the fall.'

'And the book?' Leave it to Felicia to bring that up. She had been trying not to think of it. Publication date was only a few days away.

'That's their problem now. I wrote it. Now they can sell it.'

'That simple, eh?' Felicia raised an eyebrow and looked pointedly at Kate. 'You wrote it, and that's it. Did it ever occur to you that they're going to want your help selling it?'

'How about door to door?' Kate lay on the floor with a giggle.

'You know what they want.' Felicia was not going to be pushed off the track. Not that easily. She had waited weeks to bring it up.

'How do I know what they want? And that's not the point.'

'Oh really? Then what is the point? What *you* want?'

'Maybe. I don't see why I should do anything that makes me uncomfortable.'

'Don't be an ass, Kate.' Tygue got up and snapped on the TV. He was bored. He removed the bowl of popcorn and took it with him, and there was nothing left for Kate to hide in. She looked up at Felicia, and then out at the view. 'You heard me. And you're crazy if you don't do promotion work on the book. This is your big chance. You've made it. This time. If you

143

capitalize on that now, your next book will be even bigger. And then you'll be a permanent fixture in the realm of literary successes. But this is your tryout, kiddo. Blow this one, and you'll never have the chance again. You can't afford to ignore it.'

'How do you know that's what they want? The book can sell itself.'

'You're crazy. You're throwing your career away. And you know as well as I do that that's what you want. And you can do it, dammit. You've got everything it takes to make it. Everything. Looks, brains, and talent.'

'But no balls.'

'Bullshit. You're just so busy hiding them from yourself, you've forgotten you have them. And you know that's true. Besides, look what you've done in the last month. You've been up here twice. You're not a hermit anymore, Kate, and you know it. You don't even want to be.'

'This is different though, Licia. This isn't public. I'm not sticking my face out there on television, asking for someone to throw a pie in it. Or worse, put a knife through my heart. Or Tygue's.' She said it softly, so the boy wouldn't hear. But he was wrapped up in the programme he was watching on the huge colour TV. 'I'm just not going to take that chance, Licia.'

'You're a tough woman to argue with, damn you. Because if you did do it, and something went wrong, I'd feel like shit.'

'So would I. That's why I won't do it.'

'But think how much fun it would be.'

'Would it? I'm not so sure. It wasn't really fun for Tom.'

'Yes it was.'

'Not really.'

'Maybe not for you. But it was for him. It's got to be. It's got to be the biggest high in the world.'

'I'm happier without it.'

'And lonelier too.'

'Licia, my love, success is no antidote for loneliness.'

'Maybe not. But doesn't it turn you on to see all the ads for your book? Christ, lady, it'll be out in three days. Doesn't that knock you on your ass?'

Kate grinned up at her friend sheepishly. 'It sort of does.'

'See what I mean. And think what would happen if you did some publicity appearances!' Felicia was at it again, and Kate held up a hand with a grin and a shake of the head.

'Enough. Basta! No more!' But Felicia would never stop . and they both knew it.

'Maybe Weinberg will change your mind.'

But this time Kate shook her head with a look of assurance. 'Not a chance. And he's too smart to try.'

Kate and Tygue left San Francisco early Sunday afternoon. Felicia had taken the week off to be with them, but she was going back to work the next day, and Tygue was scheduled to start his riding group the following morning. And there was Tom. Poor Tom. He hadn't had a visit in almost two weeks. She had been so busy before she left. She would go up to see him first thing the next morning. It was a little crazy driving all this way down on Sunday, and then halfway back up on Monday. But there was no other way to do it. She couldn't take Tygue with her to Mead.

'Mom?'

'What, sweetheart?' They were just easing into the Sunday-afternoon traffic leaving the city.

'Can we come back?'

'I told you we could.'

'Soon?' She smiled over at him and nodded.

'Soon.'

And then he giggled to himself and she looked over at him again.

'What's up?'

'I can't wait to see Bert.'

She laughed at the thought too. 'Neither can I.' It would be good to get home. All these expeditions were exhausting. For a minute, she was reminded of the travelling she had once done with Tom. That had been exhausting too. She wondered how how she had done it. Constantly packing, flying, driving, staying in hotels. But he had always made it fun. An adventure. A honeymoon.

145

'What were you thinking?'

'How much fun I used to have taking trips with your dad.' She was surprised at herself for saying it. She rarely spoke of Tom to Tygue. The subject was better left alone. And he knew she didn't like to talk about it. All he knew was that his father had died. In an accident. Before he was born. He had never even asked what Tom did for a living. But one day he would. She'd cross that bridge when she came to it. She'd come up with some lie like all the others. She'd have to.

'Did you take a lot of trips?'

'Some.' She was closing up again.

'Like to where?' Now he was all boy, settling down in his seat with Willie, wanting to hear about her adventures. The way he looked made her laugh.

'Lots of places. We went to Cleveland once.' Their first weekend together. Why had she told him that? Why had she thought of it? She felt a wave of pain turn over slowly in her heart.

'Was it neat?'

'Yes, very neat. It's not a very pretty place, but your father made it pretty.' Tygue looked bored. Pretty was for girls.

'Did you ever go to New York?' Felicia was going there soon, and he had heard them talk about it.

'Yes, with my mom and dad. Never with your dad.'

'Mom?'

'What, sweetheart?' She prayed it wouldn't be a tough one to answer. Not today. Not now. She felt so good, she wanted the mood to last.

'How come all your people are dead? Your mom and dad and my dad? How come?' And the strangest part of it was that none of them really were – but they might as well have been.

'I don't know. It just happens that way sometimes. But I have you.' She smiled over at him.

'And Willie and Bert, and Aunt Licia. And we're never gonna die. Maybe Aunt Licia will. But we won't. Right, Willie?' He looked down at the bear seriously, and then up at his mother. 'He says right.' She smiled at them both, and reached over a hand to rumple his hair.

146

'I love you a lot, hotstuff.'

'I love you too.' But he said it in a low little voice, as though afraid someone might hear. It made her laugh, and feel good about life as she brought her eyes back to the road. They rode on in silence for a while, and the next time she looked at him, he was asleep. They had just passed Carmel, and three hours later they were home. They picked up Bert on the way, at Tillie's place, and had a comfortable dinner at their own kitchen table.

Right after dinner Tygue was ready for bed, and less than an hour later, so was she. She didn't even bother to unpack or open her mail. She just took off her clothes and piled into bed. And it felt like only an hour later when the phone rang, but the sun was already shining brightly, and she could hear Tygue clattering around somewhere in the house. It took her four rings to get to the phone. It was Stu Weinberg.

'I thought you said you didn't go anywhere.'

'I don't.' She tried to force herself awake and at the same time sound pleasant.

'I've called. I've written. I thought maybe you died. I would have committed hara-kiri on my desk.'

'Bad as that, huh? Anything wrong?' Jesus. What if they were cancelling those contracts? Suddenly she was wide awake.

'Of course not. Nothing's wrong. Everything's right. The book is coming out in two days. Or had you forgotten?' No. But she was trying to.

'I hadn't forgotten.' But she sounded wary now.

'We have something to talk about, Kate.' Oh God. And the first thing in the morning yet. Before coffee.

'Oh?'

'You've had a wonderful offer.'

'Another one?' Her eyes opened wide. Good Lord. What now? The movie rights in Japan? She grinned.

'Yup. Another one. We got a call from the "Case Show".'

'Jasper Case?'

'You bet. And they'd like you on it. It's a marvellous opportunity for the book. We're all very excited.'

147

'Who's "we're all"?' She sounded distant and suspicious.

'The people who care about the book, Kate.' He rattled off the names of her editors, and the publishers. 'Not to mention the movie guys. This could do beautiful things for the book.' Silence. 'Kate?'

'Yeah.'

'What are you thinking?'

'About what I told you.'

'I think you'd be wrong not to do it. I kind of think this is one of those things you have to grit your teeth and do. For the sake of God and country, lady. And the book.' The book, the book, damn the book. 'Case is a hell of a nice guy. He's a good place to start. Easy-going, mellow, very correct. He's English.'

'I know. I watch the show.' It was the best latenight show on, and the whole country watched it. And Jasper Case was a gentleman. She had never seen him make anyone uncomfortable. But what about the people who watched it? What if someone saw her and remembered? Oh Christ. Who the hell was going to remember a tall skinny brown-haired kid who'd dragged around behind Tom Harper? Who knew? Who cared? 'I'll do it.'

'I'm so glad, Kate.' He rolled his eyes and wiped a thin veil of sweat off his forehead. 'They've made some terrific arrangements. They've scheduled you for a week from today. And they thought you might like to come down and stay at the Beverly Hills Hotel. They booked it for that Monday night. You can come down in the morning and relax a little bit. Someone from the show will join us for lunch, and give you an idea of who's on the show that night, what to expect. They'll get a feel for what you want to talk about and what you don't. You call the shots. And then you sit around the swimming pool all afternoon or get your hair done or do whatever you want to do. The show is taped at seven, and shown later. But after the taping, at nine, your time is your own. We'll have dinner or something, to celebrate. And that's it. You spend the night, you go home the next day. Painless.'

'Sounds like a damn pleasant way to lose my virginity.' She was smiling at her end of the phone. Weinberg had done it.

And they both knew it. He'd had her pegged from the start, had known just how to handle her. Damn.

'Kate, trust me. You're going to love it.' Now they were both laughing.

'If I don't, do I get my money back?'

'Sure, baby. Sure. Don't forget. A week from Monday. Oh, and by the way, the L.A. *Times* wanted an interview. How do you feel about that?' She hesitated for a long moment.

'No.'

'*Vogue*?'

'Jesus. What the hell is happening, Stu?'

'A lot more than you realize, m'dear.' Or want to. 'All right, what about this one?' He mentioned an inane women's magazine. 'No photographs, just a nice quiet interview over lunch on Tuesday.'

'Okay, okay. You drive a hard bargain. How many more of those do you have to throw at me? Tell the truth now!' She sounded as though she were talking to Tygue.

'Nine magazines, five newspapers, and three other talk shows. And one radio show in Chicago. They'll tape it by phone. If you read your mail, love, you'd know all about it.'

'I've been away.' She said it sheepishly.

'Any place fun?'

'San Francisco.'

'Terrific. We can have an interview up there, if you want it. You can go back whenever you want.'

'Christ, Stu. I'm not ready for this.'

'That's what I'm here for. You let me be the buffer. Right now all you have to deal with is one thing — "The Jasper Case Show". The rest can wait. Try your wings out with Case. And then we'll see. Sound reasonable?"

'Very. Oh God.' She was panicking again. 'What'll I wear?'

Stu Weinberg started to laugh. They had it made. If she was worrying about what to wear, they were home free. 'Sweetheart, go naked if you want to. Just enjoy it.'

Five minutes later, Kate was on the phone to Felicia, who sat at her desk with her mouth open and her eyes wide. 'You're going to be what?'

'On "The Jasper Case Show".' Kate almost sounded proud. What the hell had that man done to talk her into it? Mentally, Felicia took her hat off to him. 'What the hell should I wear?'

But Felicia only smiled at the phone. 'Kate, baby, I love you.'

CHAPTER XV

The car slowed to a halt in front of the covered entranceway to the hotel. Instantly, a doorman and three porters approached the car. Three? For a station wagon? Kate glanced around nervously. She had brought only one very small bag. She smiled uneasily at one of the porters, but he remained expressionless as she got out. He slid behind the wheel of the car as the other porter grabbed her bag. The third disappeared, and the doorman stood there looking impressive as a bright red Rolls Royce and a black Jaguar sedan pulled up behind her. A veritable fleet of porters appeared for them. And at the same time there was a constant hum of activity. Suitcases, golf clubs, armsful of mink whizzing by, anonymous cars arriving and departing, and a constant touching of hands with the doorman. As Kate fumbled in her handbag, she looked up quickly to see what the man nearest her was giving the porter, and she gasped as she thought she saw ten dollars changing hands. Ten dollars? Oh God, she prayed she hadn't said it aloud. Another glance to her left and she caught a glimpse of a five. It was insane. It had been ten years since she'd handled this sort of thing when she travelled with Tom. But five and ten bucks to the porter? Things couldn't have changed that much in seven years. But this was Hollywood. The outfits alone told her that. The people disembarking from their cars were wearing blue jeans that seemed to be soldered to their souls, equally tight shirts left open to the waist, vast quantities of gold jewellery, and a fair amount of bright, flashy silk, which clung and dripped and draped over starlet bodies and middle-aged men. And here and there, a dark suit hurrying into the hotel, presumably to launch into metamorphosis and emerge again in jeans.

'Reservation, ma'am?'

'Him?' She was startled from her staring by the porter. She realized that she looked out of place. She had worn a simple white cotton dress from the batch of 'possibilities' Felicia had sent her from the store. It had a careful V at the neck, which she had thought too low, but down here didn't even count, delicate little white sandals, and her hair was looped into an easy knot on top of her head. She looked deeply tanned and relaxed, and as though she were going to have lunch next to the tennis courts in Palm Springs, not compete with the sex symbols of Hollywood. The thought made her smile. And then she remembered the porter again. 'Sorry. Oh yes, I have a reservation.' He walked quickly inside and she followed him along the open but protected breezeway flanked by pillars on either side. Between the pillars frothed tiny jungles of exotica, strewn there in the thirties, when the women slithered into the hotel in ermines and diamonds instead of blue jeans and mink.

She found herself almost instantly crossing miles of green carpet, in sharp contrast to the washed-flamingo façade that had assaulted her outside. Here again people were bustling past, going to meet or discover or be discovered, discuss or disdain, destroy a career, their own or someone else's. One sensed that the business of Hollywood was being conducted nearby. One could almost feel the pulse; the building throbbed with the power inside it.

'Yes?' The man at the desk looked up at her with a smile. There were seven men at the desk.

'I'm Mrs. Harper. I believe—'

'But of course.' He smiled again as he cut her off mid-sentence, and disappeared somewhere behind the desk. But of course? How did he know who she was? He reappeared only to wave vaguely at the porter and hand him a key. 'We hope to see you here often.' You do? Kate felt like a kid in a dream. Who were they? Who was she? And where was the Mad Hatter in all this? Surely he belonged here. But she was already following the porter down a wide hallway bordered with shops. Jades, emeralds, diamonds, maribou-trimmed bed jackets, satin nightgowns, a little white mink bolero, Vuitton luggage, suede handbags, a lizard briefcase. She wanted to stop and

152

stare at it all, but she felt obliged to look unimpressed, to be grownup. And beneath it all, there was a wild urge to tug at someone's arm and whisper, as they raced along the hall, 'Look ... over there ! ... and there! ...' As she thought of it, she noticed three familiar faces from the movies. Even she knew who they were. Her head snapped around as she watched them laughing together, and she almost bumped into someone else, a face from television. It was fantastic! She was smiling to herself as she walked along, wondering suddenly if this was what it had been like for Tom, living in a world of celebrities. No, it couldn't have been. This was fabulous! And unique.

They were passing a pool now, surrounded by tables and white-jacketed waiters. Women in bikinis strolled by wearing perfectly browned skins and hairdos that had not been affected by the water. Kate watched them in fascination as they too disappeared, and she suddenly found herself standing in front of a small, manicured-looking cottage. For the tiniest moment, it reminded her of Mead, and she had a wild urge to giggle, but she didn't, she couldn't, not with the porter standing there, waiting for what. A fifty-dollar bill? Surely if that other porter could make ten dollars just by opening a car door, this one would expect fifty or a hundred for walking her down all these halls, and past all these exotic sights. He opened the door to the bungalow, as he referred to it, and she handed him a five dollar bill as she stepped inside, feeling ridiculous for having given him so much money. The door closed softly behind her, and she looked around. It was indeed very pretty. Flowery prints, chaise-longues that seemed to invite one to recline on them in one of the satin nightgowns she had seen in the shops. With a long cigarette holder undoubtedly. There was an entirely mirrored dressing room and a vanity table worthy of two hours of makeup. A pink marble bathroom and a separately lit tub set into an alcove. She was grinning to herself again. And then the phone rang, startling her. She found it on a bedstand next to the huge double bed. She noticed then that there was another phone, in a little sitting room beyond. And there was yet another entrance to the cottage. Two entrances? Why? To make a fast getaway? She laughed as she picked up the phone.

'Hello?'

'Welcome to Hollywood, Kate. How's it going?' It was Stu sounding as even and unruffled as ever, with the smile built his voice.

'I just got here. This place is amazing.'

'Isn't it though?' He laughed too. He was relieved that she hadn't panicked and already left. When they had booked her into the Beverly Hills Hotel he had worried a little. For a neophyte, this was a stiff dose. 'How's your bungalow?'

'I feel as though I should dress up as Jean Harlow. At least.' This time his laugh was less restrained. Katharine Hepburn maybe. But Harlow? He chuckled again.

'You'd sure surprise the hell out of the people on the "Case Show". They're expecting something else.'

'They are? What?' She sounded nervous again.

'You. Just as you are.'

'That's good, Stu. 'Cause that's all I got. God, I'd love to have a swim before lunch, but I take it nobody swims here.'

'Sure they do. What makes you say that?'

'Their hair.' She said it like a mischievous kid, as she remembered what the women at the pool had looked like. But Stu was already laughing again.

'Sweetheart, I wish I'd been there when you arrived.'

'So do I. Do you realize what people tip around here?' They were both laughing now. 'Why do they do it?'

'To be remembered.'

'Are they?' She was fascinated.

'Not for that reason. If they are remembered, it's because they're already somebody. If they're not, no one'll remember them anyway, no matter how much they tip. Do you realize, by the way, that your preferences and foibles will all be marked down on a little file card at the desk, and the next time you arrive you'll have everything your little heart needs and desires, without your even asking for it?'

'What the hell do you mean?' She suddenly felt uncomfortable, as though people were watching her through the walls.

'I mean, like if you'd brought that ridiculous hound of yours with you and he only ate pink grasshoppers and lemonade, next time you showed up, they'd have a full plate of pink grass-hoppers and lemonade for him. Or special towels for you, or martinis very dry, or satin sheets, or nine pillows on the bed, or only French gin and English scotch, or ... name it, love, and you got it.'

'Good God. Do people really get away with that here?'

'They don't get away with it. They expect it. It's all part of being a star.'

'Which I'm not.' She said it with relief, and he smiled again.

'Which you are.'

'Does that mean I have to order pink grasshoppers and lemonade?'

'Whatever you like, Princess. The palace is yours.' But a stiletto of pain pierced her heart. Princess. Tom had always called her that. There was something in her eyes that Stu couldn't see when she spoke again.

'It feels more like "Queen for a Day".'

'Just enjoy it. By the way, we're meeting Nick Waterman in the Polo Lounge at twelve-thirty. That's at your hotel.'

'Who's Nick Waterman?'

'The producer of the "Case Show". Himself, my dear. No assistants, no feeling around. He's coming to meet you and brief you about the show.'

'Will it be scary?' She sounded like a kid dreading a trip to the dentist, and he smiled. He wished she'd sit back and enjoy it. But in time she would.

'No, it won't be scary. And there's a party tonight after the show. They want you to go to it.'

'Do I have to?'

'Why don't you just see how you feel after the show?'

'Okay. What am I supposed to wear to the Polo Lounge, by the way? Everyone around here seems to be wearing denim and mink.'

'In the morning?'

'Well, they're wearing denim, but they're carrying mink.'

'Is that what you wore?' He sounded amused.

'I wore a cotton dress.'

'Sounds refreshing. Lunch might be a little dressier than

that. But it's up to you. Be comfortable, be yourself. Waterman is a very nice, easygoing guy.'

'You know him?'

'We've played tennis together a few times. Very pleasant. Just relax and trust me.' He could hear her starting to get nervous.

'All right. I guess I'll go order my pink grasshoppers and lemonade and relax by the pool.'

'You do that.' A moment later they hung up. He was relieved that she sounded relatively calm. The 'Case Show' was important, a lot more so than Kate realized. She was about to be catapulted into the eye of the American public, and she was either going to be loved or hated — or they'd decide they didn't give a damn. But if they decided that she was someone they cared about, someone who made them laugh and cry and know she was human, then every book she wrote would sell. She had talent, but it took more than that. They had to love *her*. And Stu Weinberg knew that if she let herself go, they would. The big If. He had taken a big chance levelling with Waterman. Maybe he was crazy to trust the guy. But he had a gut feeling about him, and he hoped he wasn't wrong. He rarely was. They had played tennis the evening before, and had had a long round of drinks after the game. He had told Waterman that Kate had been something of a recluse, a beautiful one, but a recluse nonetheless. And he suspected that she had been that way since the death of her husband. It was important that no one hurt her now, or frighten her back into her cave. Stu didn't want Jasper Case playing with her on the show, or setting her up side by side with some Hollywood bitch. This had to be done gently or not at all. Her career depended on it. And Waterman said he'd take care of it himself. He had even agreed to come to lunch himself, instead of sending the woman who usually went. And there had been a quick shuffling in the seating for the show. The cancellation of the big female star this morning would be a break for Kate too. Stu was just praying that all would go well. And he was counting on Waterman. It was going to be an interesting lunch, watching Kate slowly step out into the world.

CHAPTER XVI

She waited in the bungalow until twelve twenty-five, tapping her foot nervously on the thick beige carpet in the little sitting room. Should she be on time? Or was she supposed to be late? Should she leave her room now? Or in five minutes, at exactly twelve-thirty? And what if what she was wearing was totally wrong? She had tried on three of the outfits she'd brought, and she still wasn't sure. She was wearing a white linen pant-suit Felicia had insisted was 'very L.A.', white sandals, and no jewellery other than her wedding band and the watch Licia had given her 'For courage, For valour'. She pressed her hand to it for a moment as she sat there and closed her eyes. She could still smell the flowers that had arrived for her. A huge arrangement of spring flowers, with big bright red and yellow tulips, and all the flowers she loved. The arrangement was from the 'Case Show'. And the hotel had delivered a bottle of Bordeaux, Château Margaux '59, and an exquisite bowl of fresh fruit. 'With our compliments.' She liked the idea of wine rather than champagne, it seemed simpler. The thought made her smile. There was nothing simple about Margaux '59.

'Well, this is it.' She said it aloud as she got to her feet with a sigh and took a look around the room. She was terrified. But it was time to go. It was exactly twelve-thirty. But what if he was a jerk? What if he hated her and didn't want her on the show? Or what if he did, and they were awful to her on the air? 'Oh shit.' She said it aloud again and then grinned as she left the room.

The walk back to the main building of the hotel seemed endless, and she caught a glimpse of the pool and the tennis courts again, and wished she were there. The suit felt cool on her back as the breeze played with her hair softly framing her face, and she wondered again if she should have worn a dress, or maybe something more glamorous-looking. Felicia had sent her a navy-blue chiffon halter dress too, but she'd never dare wear it on the show. She felt so naked in it. She just couldn't. Maybe tonight, if she went to the party. The party . . . she felt as though she were running along a railroad track, with an express train rushing up behind her.

'Madam?' She was already there, staring into a black pit. The Polo Lounge was a well of darkness she couldn't see into. A glimpse of pink tablecloths, a tiny bar, a series of red banquettes. After the bright sunlight she could only guess at who was there and what she saw. She could hear them though. It sounded like hundreds of people, eating and talking and laughing and asking for phones. Just outside the room there was a bank of unoccupied pay phones. Obviously they were never used. No one would dream of going outside, when you could ask for a phone at the table and impress passers-by . . . 'Four hundred thousand? You're crazy . . .' The phones at the table were more fun. 'Madam?' He said it again, looking her over. She looked pretty but not glamorous. He was used to dazzling women, like the actresses and subtly noticeable call girls she thought she glimpsed threaded into the group at the bar.

'I'm meeting Mr. Weinberg, Stuart Weinberg, and . . .' But the headwaiter was already smiling.

'Miss Harper?' She nodded, incredulous. 'The gentlemen are waiting for you outside on the terrace. Mr. Waterman is already with Mr. Weinberg.' He carefully led the way, as Kate followed him, still barely able to see. But she didn't need to see the faces. Even their voices sounded important. And there seemed to be a lot of long, blonde hair, a lot of clanking of bracelets, and a lot of men with clinging, open shirts and clusters of gold around their necks. But she barely had time to look more closely in the gloom, as the headwaiter sped towards the back and led her out to the terrace with a look of enormous decorum. It was nice to be out in the sunshine again, and it was good to see someone familiar, as she caught sight of Stu.

'Well, well, you made it. And don't you look pretty!' She blushed beneath her tan as Stu stood up and hugged her in a warm brotherly way. He looked into her face approvingly and they exchanged an easy smile.

'I'm sorry I'm late.' She glanced around the table, not really allowing herself to see the other man, and looking at the chair which a waiter quickly pulled out for her. And then she was seated, and Stu swept an easy hand in the direction of the man to his right.

'You're not late. And Kate, I'd like you to meet Nick Waterman. Nick, Kate.' Kate smiled nervously and let her eyes stray to Nick's face as she shook his hand. It was a large, very firm hand, and the eyes were a fierce tropical blue as they held hers.

'Hello, Kate. I've been anxious to meet you. Stu gave me a copy of the book. It's terrific. Even better than your last.' He showered her with what felt like a torrent of sunshine from his eyes, and she felt herself start to relax.

'You read my first one?' He nodded and she looked at him, stunned. 'You *did*?' He nodded again and laughed as he sat back in his chair.

'Didn't you think anyone read them?' He sounded vastly amused.

'Not really, I guess.' How do you explain to someone that you haven't been anywhere to find out if anyone was really reading them? Tillie had read her book, and Mr. Erhard, but she always figured they did it because she gave them free copies. It was incredible to meet a stranger who had read her too.

'Just don't say that on the show.' Stu looked at her with a grin and signalled to the waiter. 'What'll you have?'

'Pink grasshoppers.' She said it in a careful whisper and grinned. Stu started to laugh again, and Nick looked bewildered as the waiter rapidly made a note.

'A grasshopper for the lady?'

'No, no!' And then she was laughing too. 'I don't know. Iced tea, I guess.'

'Iced tea?' Stu looked surprised. 'You don't drink?'

'Not when I'm nervous. I'll pass out over lunch.'

Stu glanced over at Waterman with a smile and patted Kate's hand.

'I promise I won't let him attack you till after dessert.' And then they were all laughing again.

'Actually, I think I'm drunk already. Oh, and by the way, the flowers were beautiful.' She turned to Nick Waterman and felt herself blush again. She wasn't sure why, but he made her faintly uncomfortable. There was something magnetic about him, that made you want to seek out his eyes, made you want to reach out to him, but it frightened her. It was terrifying to be drawn to a man after all these years, even if only in conversation. And he was so big, so *there*. It was impossible to avoid him. And she didn't really want to. That was what frightened her.

'What do you think of Hollywood, Kate?' Standard, ordinary question, but she felt herself start to blush again under his gaze and hated herself for it.

'After two hours, I'm already overwhelmed. Is this really it? Or is the hotel some sort of mad oasis in the midst of a saner world?'

'Not at all. If anything, this is the mainstay. It becomes crazier and crazier the further away you get.' The two men exchanged a sympathetic glance and Kate smiled.

'How do you stand it?'

'I was born here,' Stu said proudly. 'It's in the genes.'

'How terrible, can they operate?' Kate gave him a serious look. Nick laughed and she bravely turned to look at him too. 'What about you?'

'I'm clean. I'm from Cleveland.'

'Gawd,' Weinberg said derisively as the waiter set the iced tea down in front of Kate. She smiled softly.

'I went to Cleveland once. It's very pretty.' She was lost in her iced tea.

'Lady, I hate to tell you this.' The voice at her side was a deep, baritone caress. 'But you didn't go to Cleveland.'

'Oh yes, I did.' She looked up at him with a told-you-so smile, and his blue eyes flashed at her.

'Not if it was pretty you didn't.'

'All right, let's just say I had a good time.'

'That's better. Now I believe you.'

They ordered huge bowls of shrimp on ice, and asparagus vinaigrette, and there was delicious hot French bread.

'Well, Kate, shall we talk about the show tonight?' Nick looked over at her with a gentle smile.

'I'm trying very hard not to.'

'That's what I thought.' The smile broadened. 'You don't have anything to worry about. Not a thing. All you have to do is what you just did.'

'Stuff my face?' She grinned at him and he wanted to reach out and ruffle the carefully done hair. But he wouldn't do anything to surprise her, or she would run like a frightened doe back into the forest. He had listened carefully to what Weinberg had said. When she spoke, there was no trace of skittishness about her. In fact, she was kind of ballsy, and he liked it. But there was something different in her eyes. Something frightened, something sad, something older than her body or her face. Wherever she had been hiding, it had not been a happy place. It made him want to reach out to her and take her in his arms. That would have blown it for sure. Weinberg would have killed him. He grinned at the thought and brought his mind back to what she was saying about the show.

'No, Kate, I'm serious. All you have to do is chat, laugh a little, say what comes to mind – but no four-letter words, please!' He rolled his eyes. They had had to bleep two 'shits' and a 'fuck' the night before with that goddamn comic Jasper had been so hot to have on. He had enough problems without a night full of language. 'But all you have to do is be you. Relax. Listen. Jasper is a master of the art. You'll feel like you're at home in your own living room.'

'I can't imagine feeling that way, between worrying about whether I'm going to pass out or throw up.'

'You won't. You'll love it. You'll never want to get off.'

'Bullshit.'

'Say that, and I'll get you off myself.'

'Is it live?' She looked horrified but he shook his head.

'Nope. So all you have to do is look pretty and have fun. Is there anything you particularly want to talk about?' He looked serious now and she liked him better than ever.

She thought about it for a minute, and then shook her head. 'Think about it, Kate. Any particular aspect of the book that means a great deal to you? Something that would make it more real, bring it closer to our viewers? Something that will make them want to run out and buy it? Maybe something that happened to you while you wrote it? In fact, why did you write it?'

'Because I wanted to tell that story. I guess it was just something I cared about, so I wanted to write about it for other people. But that's not very remarkable. The decay of a marriage and a love affair is hardly hot stuff.'

'Bleep that!' Weinberg rolled his eyes. 'Whatever you do, love, don't talk them *out* of buying the book!'

'Seriously, Kate.' Nick was watching her again as he talked. The eyes, the eyes, there was something in her eyes. What the hell was it? Fear? No, something else. Something deeper. He wanted desperately to know what it was, to reach out to her. The feelings were wildly inappropriate at this lunch, and she was looking away from him now, down at her hands, as though she sensed that he saw too much. 'All right then, why did you write about football?'

She didn't look up. 'I thought it would provide background. And that men might relate to the book too. Good commercial value.' He didn't know why, but he didn't believe her, and when she looked up at him, he knew he didn't. Almost as if something had clicked.

'You put some beautiful insights into that, Kate. I almost got more excited about that than about the rest. You know the game. Not just football, the sport, but the *game*. I loved that.'

'Did you play in college?' She felt as though they were alone now. Stu Weinberg knew he was forgotten, but he didn't mind.

Nick was nodding in answer to Kate's question. 'All through college, and one year of pro. I tore up both knees in my first season, and had to call it quits.'

'You're lucky. It's a shitful sport.'

'Do you really think that? That's not what I heard in the book.'

'I don't know. It's a crazy savage way to kill people.'

'How do you know all that, Kate?'

Her answer was quick and very smooth, and delivered with a Hollywood smile. 'Careful research for the book.'

'That must have been fun.' He was smiling too, but still searching, still watching. She wanted to hide from him again, but she couldn't. And the bitch of it was that she wished she didn't have to hide. But she couldn't afford to get to know this man. He knew football. He was dangerous. She couldn't afford him even as a friend. 'Would you talk about the research on the show?'

She shook her head and then shrugged. 'It wouldn't be very interesting. Some games, some listening, some interviews, some reading. That really isn't the main point of the book.'

'Maybe you're right.' He wasn't going to push. 'Well then, what about you? Married?' He looked at the thin gold band still on her left hand, and remembered what Weinberg had said about her being a widow. But he didn't want it to look as though he knew too much. As far as he could tell, he didn't know enough.

'No. Widowed. But for God's sake, don't say that on the show. It'll sound so melodramatic.'

'Good point. Kids?'

Her face lit up at the question and she nodded, but hesitantly. 'Yes. One. But I don't really want to talk about him either.'

'Why not?' Nick looked surprised. 'Hell, if I had a kid I'd talk about nothing but.' Maybe there was a bitchy side to her after all, but he didn't think so.

'I take it you don't have kids.'

'Brilliant deduction, madam.' He toasted her with the last of his bloody mary. 'I am totally pure and untouched. No kids, no wife, no nothing.'

'Never?' She was surprised. What was a man like that doing wandering around on the loose? Gay? He couldn't be. Maybe he had a heavy starlet habit. That seemed the only answer. 'I guess that makes sense around here,' she said. 'There's so much to choose from.' She looked around the terrace with a mischievous grin and he threw back his head and laughed.

'Ya got me.'

Weinberg smiled at them both, and then sat back with pleasure. She was doing just fine. He didn't need to say a word.

'So why don't you talk about your kid? Boy or girl, by the way?'

'A boy. He's six. And terrific. A real little cowboy.' She looked as though she were sharing her best secret and Nick smiled again as he watched her, and then her face grew serious. 'I just don't want to expose him to what I do. He leads a nice, simple life in the country. I want to keep it that way. Just in case . . . in case . . .'

'In case Mom becomes a celebrity, huh?' Nick looked amused. 'What does he think of all this?'

'Not much. He was barely speaking to me when I left. He's . . . he's not used to my being away. I . . . he was pissed.' She looked up with a broad smile.

'You'll have to take him back something he wants.'

'Yeah. Me.'

'And you spoil him rotten, don't you?'

'No. A friend of mine does that.' A friend. So that was it. There was somebody. Dammit. But nothing showed in his face.

'So, let's see, where does that leave poor Jasper tonight? You won't talk about football or your research, and you won't talk about your kid. How about a dog?' He was grinning at her and Stu rolled his eyes and got back into the conversation.

'You shouldn't have said that. You just blew it.'

'She has a dog?'

'I have a Bert.' Kate looked prim as she said it. 'Bert is not a dog, he's a person. He's black and white with long ears. And a fabulous face.'

'What does that make him? A cocker spaniel?'

'Of course not!' She looked offended. 'A basset hound.'

'Great. I'll be sure to tell Jasper. Okay, lady, be serious, what'll you talk about? Marriage? How about marriage? Any views on marriage?'

'I love it. It's very nice.' So why didn't she marry the 'friend' who spoiled her kid? Or was she still carrying the torch for her dead husband? He hadn't figured that one out yet. But he would.

'Living together? Any feelings about that?'

'That's nice too.' She grinned and finished her iced tea.

'Politics?'

'I'm not political. And, Mr. Waterman' – she looked up mischievously again – 'I must tell you that I am very boring. I write. I love my kid.'

'And your dog. Don't forget your dog.'

'What about your teaching?' Stu stepped into it again with a serious look on his face. 'Don't you teach retarded kids or something?' He had gotten Tillie on the phone a few times when she was visiting Tom.

'I promised the school I wouldn't mention it.' That was a lie she was still good at, and Nick Waterman sat back with a smile.

'I've got it! Weather! You can talk to Jasper about the weather!' He was teasing but Kate looked suddenly crestfallen.

'Is it really that bad? Jesus. I'm sorry.'

But instantly his hand covered hers and his face softened from laughter to something that almost looked like love. It startled her, it happened so quickly. 'I'm only teasing you. It's going to be just fine. We never know what's going to come up. Subject may come up that you never knew you cared about. You may end up carrying the whole show. But no matter what, you're bright enough and pretty enough and amusing enough to carry the ball for as long as you have it. Just relax. And I'll be out there waving at you, and grinning, and making terrible faces to keep you amused.'

'I'll never make it.' She practically groaned as she thought of it.

'You'd better, sweetheart. Or I'll kick your ass.' It was Weinberg again and they all laughed. But she had to admit that she felt better now. At least she knew she had a friend on the show. Nick Waterman was already a friend.

'What are you doing this afternoon?' Nick was looking at his watch as he asked. It was already ten after three, and he had things to do back at the studio.

'I thought I'd take a swim and relax for a while. I have to be there at a quarter to seven?'

'Better make it six-fifteen or six-thirty. We tape at seven. You can check your make-up, chat with the other guests in the

Red Room, and just kind of settle in. Oh, and before I forget, you can't wear white. It'll glare on us.'

'I can't?' She looked horrified. 'What about off-white?'

He shook his head.

'Oh my God.'

'That's all you brought?' He said it the way a husband would looking over his wife's shoulder as she dressed, and she felt awkward at the intimacy.

'I was going to wear a cream-coloured suit with a peach-coloured blouse.'

'Sounds gorgeous. I'll have to take you to dinner sometime just to see it. But not on the show, Kate. I'm sorry.' He looked sorry, too, and she looked sick. She should have listened to Licia, and gotten a bunch of things from the store, but she had been so sure about the suit. And the only other thing she had to wear was that half-naked, navy-blue, chiffon halter dress. And she didn't want to be that bare on national television. Christ, they'd think she was a hooker. 'Do you have anything else? You can always go shopping, you know.'

'I guess I'd better. I brought something else, but it's too naked.' Weinberg perked up his ears, and Waterman glanced at him. They had both been afraid she'd wear something too serious.

'Whatcha got?' Waterman asked.

'A navy-blue halter dress. But I'll look like a tart.' Weinberg whooped and Waterman grinned.

'Believe me, Kate, you wouldn't know how to look like a tart.'

'Is that a compliment?' She had a feeling it wasn't, but Nick looked around with an air of acute boredom at the over-decorated women at the surrounding tables.

'In this town, Kate, that's a compliment. Is the dress sexy?'

'Sort of. It's more just dressy.'

'Glamorous?' She nodded again, almost apologetically, and he beamed.

'Wear it.'

'You mean it?'

'I mean it.' The two men exchanged a smile, and Nick Waterman signed the check.

CHAPTER XVII

Kate took a last look in the mirror as she got ready to leave the bungalow. She had been planning to order a cab, so she wouldn't get lost driving herself around L.A. But Nick's secretary had called an hour before to tell her he was sending a car for her. At six. And the desk had just called to tell her it was there. She had already phoned Felicia twice, in a panic. Talked to Tygue. Gone for a swim, washed her hair, done her nails, and changed earrings and shoes three times. She was finally set. She still felt like a tart in that dress. But a very high-priced one. The dress bared her narrow, elegant shoulders and showed off her long, delicate neck. It had a high-necked halter, and there was very little fabric at her back, but no one would see that on the air - she'd have her back against the chair. The dress nipped in carefully at the waist and then flowed gracefully away again. She had decided finally on the navy silk sandals Licia had suggested she wear with it, pearl earrings, and her hair swept up in a carefully done knot. It was the same hairdo her mother had been wearing, years ago, the last time she'd seen her, but Kate didn't remember that anymore. The hairdo just looked right to her. And other than the pearl earrings, the only jewellery she wore was her wedding band. She looked striking and understated and the mirror told her that everything worked. She hoped Nick thought so too, and then she blushed again at the thought. Not Nick as a man, just Nick as the producer of the show. But there was an overlap in her mind between Nick's functions as mentor, advisor, friend, man. It was a confusion of feelings for a man she'd known only since noon. But she was anxious to see him and know that she looked all right for the show. And if she didn't, she was up shit creek. She hadn't gone shopping that afternoon. She had decided to take a chance on the one

167

suitable dress she had. If they hated it for the show, she was stuck. But Felicia said they'd love it. And she was usually right.

Kate wrapped a midnight-blue shawl of web-thin crochet around her shoulders, picked up her bag, and opened the door. This is it; she couldn't get the words out of her head. This Is It. She wouldn't let herself listen to that feeling as she walked quickly to the main lobby and then down the breezeway under the awning until she stood next to the doorman at the kerb.

'Miss Harper?' How the hell did he know? There were armies of people passing by. It was amazing. She noticed a floor length chinchilla coat on a very old, very ugly woman, followed by three middle-aged fags, and she forced her attention back to the doorman.

'Yes. I'm Mrs. Harper.'

'The car is waiting.' He signalled to a limousine parked to one side, and an endlessly long ·chocolate-brown Mercedes sped to her feet. For me? Talk about Cinderella! She wanted to laugh but she didn't dare.

'Thank you.' The driver held open the door for her, having leapt out almost before the doorman could reach it, and the two uniformed men stood there as she slipped inside. Once again, she had the wild urge to poke somebody, to collapse, giggling, in the back seat. But there was no one else to giggle with. She was suddenly dying to see Nick and say something to him. And then she realized that she couldn't. To him this was everyday. To her, it was once a lifetime.

The car sped through unknown neighbourhoods, past mansions and palm trees, and into uncharted areas of freeway she knew she would have been lost on forever, and then they reached a long, unpretentious, sand-coloured building. The studio. The car stopped, the driver opened her door, and she stepped out. It was difficult not to make An Exit. Difficult not to look·imperious just for the hell of it. But she reminded herself that Cinderella had lost the glass slipper and almost broken her ass on the stairs.

'Thank you.' She smiled at the driver, and was pleased that

the voice still sounded like Kate's, not 'Miss Harper's'. But she was getting to like the 'Miss Harper' stuff. It was a riot. Kaitlin Harper. The author.

Two security guards stood just inside the door, and asked for her identification when she got inside. But before she could give it to them, a young woman with sheaves of blonde hair appeared and smiled at the guards.

'I'll take you up now, Miss Harper.' The two guards smiled now too, one of them looking appreciatively at the blonde girl's ass. She was wearing the standard pair of jeans, with Gucci shoes, and a little see-through white top. Kate felt like her mother. The girl was probably only twenty-two, but she had an air about her that Kate hadn't had for years, if ever. Maybe, way back when, a thousand years ago ... it was hard to remember.

'Everything's all set in the Red Room.' The girl continued to chat amiably as they took an elevator to the second floor. They could have walked just as easily but Kate sensed immediately that would not have been the thing to do. This was a town where everything one did reflected one's status.

They emerged into an anonymous corridor, and Kate tried to glance at the photographs mounted on the walls. They were faces she had seen in major movies, in newspapers, in news reports on television, even some faces from the backs of book jackets. She wondered if one day they'd have her face up there too, and for one mad heavenly moment she wanted her face up there. Kaitlin Harper ... Ha! That's me! See! Me! I'm Kate! But the girl was already holding open a door. The inner sanctum. A ring of guards protected it outside and in, and the door opened only by key. A long white-carpeted hall now. White? How impractical. But obviously nobody gave a damn. It was beautiful. More photographs. These were more personal, and in all of them there was Jasper Chase. He was an attractive man in the photographs, silver-haired and very tall. He had a certain elegance about him. And she knew from watching the show that his English accent added to the distinguished image. and he got the best interviews on television, because he was never pretentious, never vicious, always warm, thorough, interested, and he somehow managed to draw the viewer into the conversation. The man sitting at home drinking Ovaltine and watching Jasper before he went to bed felt as if all Jasper's guests were sitting in his own living room and including him in the party.

Kate was still engrossed in the photographs when she heard another door open with one of the girl's magical keys, and she found herself looking into what appeared to be a guest room. It was done in dusty rose and looked very glamorous. There was a couch, several easy chairs, the now standard chaise longue, a vanity, a jungle of orchid plants, and other leafy wonders hanging from the ceiling. It was the kind of room Kate would have dreamed of as an office, instead of the grubby hole where she, and most writers, did their work.

'This is your dressing room, Miss Harper. If you want to change or lie down. Whatever. When you're ready, just press the buzzer and I'll take you down to the Red Room.' You will? You promise? But do I gotta? Kate liked the Pink room. Who needed the Red Room?

'Thank you.' They were the only two words she could think of. She was too busy being overwhelmed. And when she stepped inside and the door closed, she noticed a delicate bouquet of pink roses and baby's breath, with a little card. She walked over to it, wondering if the flowers were for someone else. Surely someone more important. But her name was on the envelope. She opened it with curiosity and trembling fingers. Stu maybe?

But they weren't from Stu. They were from Nick. 'Don't forget the dog and the weather. Nick.' She laughed at the card, and sat down and looked around the room. She had nothing to do there, except gape. She felt the shawl fall away from her shoulders as she sat in one of the large comfortable chairs and let it swallow her. And then, nervously, she jumped up and looked in the full-length mirror. Did she look all right? Was the dress awful? Was she . . . did she . . . should she . . . there was a soft knock which interrupted her glaring at herself in sheer panic.

'Kate?' It was a man's voice, a deep one, and she suddenly

smiled. She wasn't alone after all. She pulled open the door, and there he was, tall and smiling. Nicholas Waterman. He was even taller than she had remembered from lunch, but his eyes were just as she had left them, warm and kind, the eyes of a friend. 'How're you doing?'

'I'm a wreck.' She beckoned him inside and shut the door like a fellow conspirator, and then she remembered the roses. 'Thank you for the flowers. How do I look?' Everything was coming out staccato and bumpy and she wanted to lie face-down on the floor and hide. 'Oh, I can't stand it.' She sank onto the couch and almost groaned. Nick laughed.

'You look beautiful. And you're fine. Just remember. The dog and the weather. Right?'

'Oh shut up.' But then she noticed him looking at her and squinting. 'What is it?'

'Take your hair down.'

'Now? I'll never get it back up.' She looked horrified.

That's the whole point, silly. Come on. That dress needs long hair.' He sat back on the couch next to her and waited, as she looked at him with an astonished grin.

'Do you do this with everybody who comes on the show?' What a disappointing thought. She hoped he didn't.

'Of course not. But not everybody comes on this show on the strength of her dog and the weather.'

'Will you stop that!' She was grinning broadly now. And she had just decided again that she loved his eyes.

'Take your hair down.' He looked like a big brother trying to teach her a new sport. She was going to resist, but she decided to let herself be persuaded.

'Okay. But I'll look a mess.'

'You wouldn't know how to.'

'You're crazy.'

It was bathroom patter. He shaves while she dries. She combs her hair while he does his tie. She looked at him with a smile as her hair cascaded past her shoulders in soft, loose, gentle waves. He grinned. He had been right.

'Some mess, gorgeous one. Take a look in the mirror.'

She did, and frowned uncertainly. 'I look like I just woke

up.' There was something he wanted to say to her, but he didn't say it. He just smiled.

'You look perfect. And you have just sold your book to half the men in America. The other half are either too old or too young. But if they're awake for the show, Kate – you've sold 'em.'

'You like it like this?'

'I love it.' And he loved the dress. She looked exquisite. Tall and delicate, elegant and sexy. There was a kind of naïve glamour about her. She didn't know it, but she was the kind of woman men were going to crawl over each other to get to. It was the subtlety, the hint of shyness behind the humour, the reserve mixed in with the mischief. Without thinking, he took her by the hand. 'Ready?' She had to pee, but she couldn't tell him. She just nodded, with a smile.

'Ready.' She was so breathless she could hardly say it.

'Then on to the Red Room.'

There was champagne there, and coffee. There were sandwiches, and a plate of *pâté de foie gras*. There were magazines, aspirins, and assorted other remedies for minor ills, including several rather ferocious hangover remedies. And there were faces Kate had never expected to be in the same room with. A journalist from New York, a comedian she had heard of all her life, who had just flown in from Las Vegas to do the show, a major singing star, an actress, and a man who had spent four years in Africa writing a book about zebras. She had heard of them all, seen them all. There were no unknowns there. And then she grinned to herself. She was the unknown.

Nick introduced her to everyone and handed her the ginger ale she had asked for. At exactly a quarter to seven he left the room. The zebra man was sitting away from her, making inane conversation in his almost unintelligible Etonian accent, and the female singing star was looking Kate over.

'Looks like the producer's got the hots for you, darling. Old flame or new one? Is that how you got on the show?' She filed a clawlike crimson nail and then grinned over at the actress, who was her friend. There was a new face in town and they didn't like it. Kate smiled at them, wishing she were dead.

What the hell did you say? Fuck off? May I have your auto-graph? She continued to smile inanely and crossed her legs, wondering if they could see her knees shake. And then the comedian and the journalist saved her, as though they had been dropped from the sky just for that purpose. The journalist insisted that he needed her help with the *pâté*, and the comedian immediately pelted her with funny remarks, and the three of them wound up together for the duration, on the other side of the room, while the other two women seethed. But Kate didn't notice. She was too nervous, and too busy chatting. Nick had been right; every man in the room would have given his right arm to go home with her. But Kate was too worried about the show to notice the effect she was having on them.

'What's it like?'

'Like falling into a bed of marshmallows.' The comedian looked at her with a smile. 'Want to try that sometime?' She laughed at him and sipped her ginger ale. Oh Jesus, what if it made her burp? She put it down, and squeezed the paper nap-kin with her damp hands. 'Don't worry, baby. You're gonna love it.' The comedian whispered it to her gently with a warm smile. He was old enough to be her father but she could feel his hand on her knee. She wasn't sure if she was going to love it or not. And then suddenly, it was air time. A sudden current of electricity seemed to pass around the room, and everyone fell silent.

The singing star went on first. She did two songs, and left after five minutes of chatting with Jasper, who was 'enormously grateful that she could stop by, and knew she had a special to tape'. Kate was enormously grateful when she left five minutes later. The journalist was next, and was surprisingly amusing. He was almost a regular on the show. Then the actress. The comedian. And then ... oh my God ... no! Only she and the zebra man were left, and the man at the door with the ear-phones on his head was beckoning to Kate. Me? Now? But I can't. But she had to.

It felt like walking into a jet stream, or off a cliff. She was numb. She couldn't hear what he was saying. And worse yet, she couldn't hear herself. She wanted to scream as she sat there, but she didn't. She heard herself laughing, chatting, admitting to the appalling outfits she wore when she wrote, talking about her feelings about living in the country. Jasper's boyhood had been spent in a place that he said was much like the place she described. They talked about writing, and the discipline of the profession, and even about how funny it was to come to L.A. She found herself cracking jokes about the women she'd seen around the pool, and the droopy-assed old men squashed into their jeans and body shirts with their dangling doodads of gold around their necks. She almost made an outrageous allusion and then backed off, which made it even funnier, because the audience caught the allusion without her having to say it. She was fabulous and she was Kate. And somewhere out there, in the lights and electric lines and confusion and cameras, was Nick, making victory signs and grinning at her with pride. She had done it! And then there was the zebra man, and by then Kate was right at home, laughing and loving it, part of the jokes and the conversation. The journalist and the comedian kept aiming good lines at her, and she and Jasper looked as though they'd been dancing together for years. It was one of those shows that jelled from beginning to end, and Kate was the diamond in the night's tiara. She was still flying high when they went off the air, and Jasper kissed her on both cheeks.

'You were marvellous, my dear. I hope we see you again..'

'Thank you! Oh it was wonderful! And it was so easy!' She was blushing and breathless and loving it and then suddenly she found herself in the comedian's arms.

'Want to try that bed of marshmallows now, baby?' But she even laughed at him, too. She loved them all. And then, there was Nick, smiling down at her, and she felt her insides turn to mush.

'You made it. You were terrific.' His voice was very soft in the wild confusion of the studio.

'I forgot to talk about the dog and the weather.' They exchanged a slow smile. She felt shy with him now. She was Kate again, not the mythical Miss Harper.

'We'll have to have you back then.'

'Thank you for un-scaring me.' He laughed and put an arm around her shoulders. He liked the feel of her skin on his arms.

'Anytime, Kate, anytime. We have about ten minutes until we ship out for that party, by the way. All set to go?' She had almost forgotten it. And what about Stu? Wasn't she supposed to see him?

'He called before you got here. He'll meet us there. It's Jasper's birthday, you know. Everyone will be there.' Cinderella at the ball. But why not? She was dying to celebrate.

'Sounds wonderful.'

'Do you want to go in one of the brown bananas, or shall we escape the crowds?' He looked away to sign a paper on someone's clipboard and then glanced at his watch.

'The brown bananas?' She looked at him in confusion.

'That's what I sent to pick you up. The brown limo. We have two of them. Everyone is going to the party in the two limos. All the guests from the show, and Jasper. But we could avoid the rush and go in my car.' It sounded simpler, but also a little unnerving. She would lose the safety of the group. On the other hand, Kate had a feeling the comedian would find some way back to her knee. It would be easier to go with Nick.

'May I bring my flowers?' He smiled at her question. She had remembered. No one ever did. They left them in the dressing rooms and the maids took them home. But Kate had remembered. She was that kind.

'Sure you can. What's a little water all over the car?' They both laughed as he led her back to the dressing room. There was a slowing of the pace around them, a feeling of winding down, in direct contrast to the mounting tension Kate had sensed before the show. What a way to live. Getting jacked up like that every day. But what a high too. She had never felt as good in her life. Or not in a long time at least. A very long time.

She carefully picked up the vase with the little pink roses and the baby's breath. She had long since slipped the card into her bag. A souvenir of her Cinderella evening. 'Thank you for these, too, Nick.' She wanted to ask him if he was always this thoughtful, but she couldn't. It would have been rude.

It was over now. The performance was finished. They were both real people again. He was no longer The Producer, and she was no longer The Star. She felt a little awkward as they walked quietly out to his car, and then she stood back and whistled. The sound was incongruous with the way she looked.

'Is that yours?' It was a long, low, dark-blue Ferrari with a creamy leather interior.

'I confess. I gave up eating when I bought that.'

'I hope it was worth it.'

But judging by the way he looked at the car, she knew it had been. In his own way, he was a big kid too. He held the door open for her and she slid inside. The car even smelled expensive, a rich mixture of good leather and expensive men's cologne. She was glad it didn't reek of perfume. That would have upset her.

It was comfortable there in the dark, as he pulled into the constant flow of traffic, and she sat back and started to unwind.

'Why so quiet all of a sudden?' He had noticed.

'Just unwinding, I guess.'

'Don't do that yet. Wait till you see the party.'

'Will it be a madhouse?'

'Without a doubt. Think you can stand it?'

'This is some debut for a country girl, Mr. Waterman.' But she was loving it, and he could see that.

'Something tells me, Kate, that you were not always a country girl. None of this is new to you, is it?'

'On the contrary, it's all new. Or at least, I've never had the limelight on me before.'

'But on people near you?' She jumped in her seat, and he looked at her, startled. What had he said? But she looked away and shook her head.

'No. I led a very different sort of life from all this.' But he had almost lost her and he knew it. She had hidden again. And then unexpectedly, she looked at him with a warm smile and a sparkle in her eyes. 'I certainly never rode around in Ferraris.'

'Where did you live before the country?'

'San Francisco.' She hesitated only for a fraction of a second.

'Did you like it?'

'I loved it. I haven't been back in . . . in years, until about a month ago and then I took my little boy up a week ago, and he fell in love with it too. It's a neat town.'

'Any chance you'll move back there?' He looked interested.

She shrugged. 'I can't see it really.'

'That's too bad. We're thinking about moving the show up there.' She looked surprised.

'And away from the mecca of Hollywood? Why?'

'Jasper doesn't like it here. He wants to live someplace more "civilized". We suggested New York. But he's tired of that. He was there for ten years. He wants San Francisco. And I suspect' – he looked at her with a rueful grin – 'that if he wants it badly enough he'll get it.'

'How do you feel about that?'

'Okay. I guess. I've had my kicks here. But it gets old very quickly.'

'Quick, bring in the Vestal Virgins!' She laughed at him, and he ran a hand through her hair playfully.

'Vestal Virgins, eh? You must think I use 'em up a dozen a day.'

'Don't you?'

'Hell, no. Not anymore! Try as I might, I can't get past eight or nine ladies a day. Must be old age.'

'Must be.'

They were playing, feeling each other out. Who are you? What do you want? What do you need? Where are you going? But what did it matter? She realized with a little sinking feeling that she'd probably never see him again after tonight. Maybe in another five years, if she had a book that was a big success, if he was still with the show, if there still was a show . . . if.

'Scared?'

'Hm?'

'You looked so serious. I wondered if you were nervous about the party.'

'A little, I guess. It doesn't really matter. I'm an unknown. I can be invisible.'

'Hardly, love. I don't think you could ever manage that.'

'Bullshit.'

They laughed again and he pulled into a palm-lined drive-way in Beverley Hills. They had been passing mammoth palaces for the past ten minutes.

'Good lord. Is this Jasper's house?' It looked as big as Buckingham Palace. Nick shook his head.

'Hilly Winters.'

'The movie producer?'

'Yes, ma'am. Shall we?' Three attendants in crisp white jumpsuits were waiting to take the cars, and the door to the house was being opened by a butler and a maid. One could just glimpse a brilliantly lit hallway before the door closed again. Kate couldn't decide whether to look inside or out at the non-stop stream of Rolls Royces and Bentleys rounding the bend into the drive. It was easy to see why Nick had bought the Ferrari. He moved in a world that resembled no other.

The door opened again, and they were instantly sucked into the eye of a glittering storm. There were easily three hundred people, and Kate had a blurred impression of chandeliers, candles, sequins, diamonds, rubies, furs and silk. She saw stars from every film she had ever seen, read of, or heard about.

'Do people really live like this?' Kate whispered to him as they stood at the edge of the crowd in the ballroom. The house had a fully mirrored, magnificent ballroom, which had been brought over piece by piece from a château on the Loire. How could this be real?

'Some people live like this, Kate. Some of them do it for a while, some forever. Most don't do it for very long. They make a fortune in the movies, spend it, blow it, give it away.' He eyed a pack of rock stars at the other side of the room. They stood in skin-tight satin, and the wife of the lead singer was wearing a very bare skin-coloured dress and floor-length sables with a hood. A little warm for the ballroom, but she looked happy. 'That kind comes and goes quickly. People like Hilly will be here forever.'

'It must be fun.' She looked like a little girl peeking through the banisters at a Mardi gras ball.

'Is that what you want?' But he already knew it wasn't.

'No. I suppose I don't really want anything different from what I have.' Yeah. The friend who spoils your kid. He remembered that, and suddenly felt bitter. She had more than anyone in that room. And much more than he had. Lucky bitch. But she wasn't a bitch. That was what bothered him. He liked her. Too damn much. And she was so naïve. He wondered what would happen if he just grabbed her and kissed her. She'd probably slap him. Marvellous old-fashioned gesture. The thought of it made him laugh as he put an empty glass of champagne back on a tray. And then he noticed that she was gone. She had drifted off in the throng, and he could see her twenty feet away, being harangued by some guy in a maroon velvet dinner jacket. He was one of the local hangers-on. Somebody's hairdresser, somebody's boy friend, somebody's son. There were a lot of guys like him around Hollywood. Nick started to move slowly through the crowd to get back to her. He couldn't hear the conversation, but she didn't look happy.

'Harper? Oh yeah. The writer on Jasper's show tonight. We saw you.'

'That's nice.' She was trying to be polite, but it wasn't easy. The guy was drunk for a start. She still couldn't understand how she could have got pushed this far from Nick, but there were so many people, and the ballroom was becoming the big attraction. The band was beginning to play some hot rock.

'How come a broad like you wrote a book about football?'

'Why not?' She looked at Nick. It was hopeless to try to get to him. But he was slowly making his way towards her. Another two minutes maybe.

'You know, there was a football player years ago with the same name as yours. Harper. Bill Harper. Joe Harper. Something like that. Went nuts. Tried to kill somebody and shot himself instead. Nuts. They're all nuts. Killers. You related to him?' He looked up sloppily at Kate and burped. It would have been funny except that suddenly she knew the clock had struck twelve. It was over now. It had happened. Someone had remembered. Someone. That was all it took. From where he stood. Nick could see panic break out on her face. 'You related to him?' The guy was persistent, and smiling ghoulishly.

'I . . . what? No. Of course not.'

'I don't think so.' But Kate didn't hear his last words. She pushed herself in the direction of Nick who forded the last clump of bodies between them, and finally reached her. There was terror stamped all over her face.

'Are you all right? Did that guy say something out of line to you?'

'I . . . no . . . no, no, nothing like that.' But there were tears swimming in her eyes, and she looked away. 'I'm sorry, Nick. I'm not feeling well. It must be all the excitement. The champagne. I . . . I'll call a cab.' She was squeezing her handbag and looking around nervously as she spoke.

'The hell you will. Are you sure that guy didn't say something?' He'd kill him if he had. What the hell had he done to her?

'No, really.' He knew she wouldn't tell him the truth, and that made him madder still. 'I just want to go home.' She said it like a child, and without another word, he put his arms tightly around her and led her out into the main foyer, and and quietly out of the house, after collecting her shawl.

'Kate' – he looked down at her as they waited for the car – 'please tell me what happened.'

'Nothing, Nick. Nothing. Really.' He tilted her face up to his without saying a word, and in spite of herself, two tears spilled out of her eyes and onto her cheeks. 'I just got frightened, that's all. I haven't been around . . . around people for a very long time.'

'I'm sorry, baby.' He folded her into his arms and held her there until the car came. She stood there, feeling his jacket and breathing the scent of him in the night air. He smelled of spice and lemons and he was warm and solid next to her. When the car came, she pulled away slowly, took a deep breath, and smiled.

'I'm sorry to be such a fool.'

'You're not. I'm sorry that happened. This should have been your big night.'

'It was.' She looked at him as she said it, and then slipped into the car. She had done it at least. Done the show. Gone to the party. It wasn't anyone's fault that someone had remembered Tom. But it was heartbreaking to know that some people still did. Why couldn't they remember the good years? The happy times? Why did they remember only the end? She looked up and realized that Nick was watching her. He hadn't started the car yet. He wanted to take her home, to his place. But he couldn't, and he knew it.

'Want to stop off someplace for a night cap?' But she shook her head. He'd known she would refuse. He didn't want one either. And he didn't know what else to suggest. A walk? A swim? He was at a loss. He wanted to do something simple with her, not something Hollywood. There were times when he hated this town, and tonight was one of them. 'Back to the hotel then?' She nodded regretfully, but with a small, grateful smile.

'You've been wonderful, Nick.' A dismissal. He wanted to kick something. And she didn't understand his silence all the way back to the hotel. She was afraid he was angry. But he didn't look it, he looked sad. Or maybe hurt. He was feeling helpless.

'Sure I can't talk you into something glamorous, like an ice-cream cone?'

'Do people indulge in simple pleasures like that here?'

'No, but I'd find you one.'

'I'll bet you would.' She said it warmly, and she wanted to touch his face as they drove up in front of the hotel. 'I'm afraid Cinderella has had her big night at the ball. And if I were you, I'd beat it before this jet plane of yours turns into a pumpkin.' They both laughed at the thought, and she picked up her bouquet of roses from the floor. 'See, they didn't even spill.' He was watching her, and she found his eyes again. 'Thank you, Nick. For everything.' He didn't move, and for a moment neither did she. She hesitated. She wanted to touch him. His hand. His face. To hold out her arms again and let him hold her. But this was different. She knew she couldn't do that. And she knew, too, that she wouldn't see him again.

'Thank *you*, Kate.' He said it very carefully. As though he meant it, but she wasn't sure why.

'Good night.' Gently, like a quiet whisper of air, she touched his hand and then opened the car door and was gone. The doorman closed the Ferrari door behind her, and Nick watched her go. He didn't get out, or call her back, or even move. He just sat there, for a very long time. And when he called her the next morning, she had already checked out. It took all his connections through the show to find out from the manager that she had checked out a little after 1 A.M. That was when he'd brought her home. It didn't make any difference, but he wanted to know. It was that sonofabitch at the party. Damn. And he didn't even know where she lived. He wondered if Weinberg would tell him.

CHAPTER XVIII

'Tygue, I said no!'

'You always say no. Besides, I don't care what you say!'

'Go to your room!' There was a moment of fierce glaring between them and Tygue gave in first. It was fortunate for him because his mother was in no mood to fool around. She had got in just after four in the morning. Tillie had left at six-thirty. And it was now only seven. Kate had had two and a half hours of sleep. This was not the day for Tygue to decide to give Bert a bath before school, with her best soap from Licia. Any other day, Kate would have laughed. Today, she wasn't laughing. And her head was still full of what had happened in L.A. She called Tygue back when breakfast was ready. 'Are you going to be reasonable now?' But he said not a word as he sat down to his cereal. She drank her coffee in silence, and then suddenly she remembered something. It was in her suitcase. 'I'll be right back.' It wasn't really the right time to give it to him, but maybe it was what they both needed. A silly moment. Of her spoiling him and his feeling loved. She had felt so lonely driving home last night. As though she had lost. But she had forced herself out. No one had sent her away. The whole thing was stupid. So what if the guy remembered a football player named Harper? Why did she have to leave like that? And she knew Stu would be angry at her. She had arranged for the hotel to deliver a message to him first thing in the morning: 'Was called home unexpectedly, please cancel magazine interview. Terribly sorry. Thank you for everything. Love, Kate.' But he'd be mad anyway. She knew it. And she was angry at herself as well. And then with a soft whisper of pleasure she remembered the feel of Nick's hand when she'd said good-bye to him in the car.

'What are you thinking about? You look silly.' Tygue had

wandered into her room and was watching her from the doorway, his bowl of cereal in his hand, tilting at a precarious angle.

'Don't walk around with your breakfast. And what do you mean, I look silly? That's not a nice thing to say.' She sounded hurt, and he looked down into his bowl.

'I'm sorry.' He was still mad at her for leaving.

'Go put that in the sink and come back here.' He looked up at her and then vanished, clomping loudly along the floor. He was back in seconds with an expectant look on his freckled face. 'Wait till you see what I brought you.' It was totally outrageous. She had found it in the children's shop at the hotel, and she had had to have it. She had bought it at a scandalous price, but why not? He was the only son she had, and he was never going to have another outfit like this.

'What is it?' He looked suspiciously at the fancy dress box, and the pale blue curlicues of ribbon put him off.

'Go ahead. It won't bite you.' She grinned to herself, thinking of the dusty blue velvet suit they'd had too. The idea of her son in that getup had made her laugh right there in the shop, much to the salesperson's horror. But blue velvet on a boy of six was pushing it. Tygue wouldn't have worn it at two. She watched him as, gingerly, he pulled off the ribbons, and then stared at the box for one brief moment before yanking off the lid, pushing aside the tissue paper, and then gasping as he saw it.

'Oh, Mom! Oh! . . . Mom! . . .' There were no words to describe what he felt, and tears burned her eyes as she watched him. They were still tears of fatigue and excitement, but they were tears of joy too. He pulled it out of the box and held it up. A miniature cowboy suit in leather and suede. There was a fringed vest, and chaps. A cowboy shirt, a belt and a jacket. And when he tore off his clothes and tried it on, it fitted him perfectly.

'Well, hotshot? You look gorgeous.' She beamed at him from her seat on the bed.

'Oh, Mommy!' She hadn't heard 'Mommy!' in a while. Only 'Mom'. Now 'Mommy' was saved for special occasions, when no one else was around to hear. He ran up to her in the little cowboy suit and threw his arms around her with a huge mushy kiss.

'Am I forgiven?' She hugged him close with a smile.

'For what?'

'Going away.' She cringed at the precedent she was setting, but her son was smarter than she was.

'No,' he said matter-of-factly, with a big smile. 'But I love the suit. And I love you best of all.'

'I love you best of all too.' She sat down on the bed, and he piled into her lap. 'You should take that off. It's a little fancy for school, darling, isn't it?'

'Awww, Mommm . . . please . . .'

'Okay, okay.' She was too tired to argue. And then, unexpectedly, he looked up at her.

'Did you have a good time?'

'Yes, I did. I was on TV, and I stayed in a big hotel, and I had lunch with some people, and went to a party with some other people.'

'It sounds terrible.' She laughed and looked at him. Maybe he was right. Maybe it had been terrible. But she couldn't really make herself believe that. 'When are we going back to San Francisco?'

'Soon. We'll see. Do you want Tillie to take you down to the Adams place today, so you can ride in your new suit?' He nodded vehemently, looking down at the vest with delight. 'I'll leave Tillie a note.'

But the boy looked up in terror. 'Are you going away again?'

'Oh Tygue . . .' She held him tight. 'No, sweetheart. I'm just going to see . . . to teach.' Jesus. She had almost said it. To see Tom. She was exhausted. She was really too tired to drive up there too. But she felt that she had to. It had been days. 'I'll try to come back early today and we'll have a nice quiet dinner. Just us. Okay?' He nodded warily, but the terror had left his eyes. 'I told you, silly. I'm not going to run off and leave you. Just because I'm gone for a day, or even a couple of days, doesn't mean I'm leaving you. Got that?' He nodded, silent, his eyes huge. 'Good.' And then the honking of his car pool threw them both into chaos. Lunch pail, books, hat, big kiss, squeeze, good-bye, gone. Kate sat in the kitchen for a moment, trying to summon enough energy to get her jacket and go. She was crazy to make the trip on two hours' sleep. But it was never the right time to go to Carmel anymore. There was always something else she wanted to do. She picked up her bag and her jacket, wrote a note for Tillie, and left as it started to rain.

The soft rain continued as she drove up to Carmel, and it pattered gently on the roof of the cottage as she visited with Tom. It was the kind of gentle summer rain that made her want to turn her face to the sky and run barefoot through the long summer grass, feeling twigs tickle her toes. She didn't do that though. She was too tired to do more than walk to the cottage and sit down. She had nothing much to tell him. She couldn't tell him about L.A., he wouldn't understand. But he was in a peaceful mood. The rain seemed to soothe him, and they sat hand in hand, side by side, he in his wheelchair, she in a cosy rocker, and she told him stories. They were the stories she had known as a child, the same ones she had told Tygue for years. Tom loved them too. And shortly after lunch, he fell asleep. The rhythm of the rain soothed them both and she had to jolt herself a few times to keep from falling asleep too. But once Tom had drifted off, she sat for a moment, watching his peaceful face, letting the rush of memory drift over her . . . the thousand times she had seen that face asleep before, in other places, other days. It made her think of Cleveland, so long ago, and then unexpectedly of Nick Waterman. She didn't want to think of him here. This wasn't his place, it was Tom's. She kissed him gently on the forehead, ran a hand softly over his hair, put a finger to her lips as she looked up at Mr. Erhard, and tiptoed carefully from the room.

It was a long drive home. The roads were fairly deserted and she was anxious to get back, but she didn't dare drive as fast as she normally did. And eventually she had to open the windows and turn on the radio to keep awake. Twice she had to pull over to the side of the road to shake the cobwebs out of her head. She was pushing it and she knew it. She was tempted just to stay there and sleep for a while, but she knew Tillie would want to get home. It was Friday and there was always some member of her family coming for dinner, or the weekend. She only had another fifty miles to go, and she decided to make a run for it, as the thunder clapped and the lightning flashed, and the rain splashed in over the top of the window and washed her face. It made her smile as she felt it. It felt good just being back in her part of the world again. She didn't belong in L.A., but it had been fun for a visit, for a moment. And never again. What totally mad people. She let her mind drift back to the pink dressing room, the tension of the Red Room, and then the opulence of the party in Beverly Hills . . . and then the feeling of Nick Waterman holding her as they waited for his car. She pushed that from her mind with the rest of it, and turned up the radio. L.A. was their world. Not hers.

She turned off at the familiar exit and followed the back road until she reached her driveway. There was a rainbow over the hills. And there was a car in her driveway. As she saw it her foot hit the brakes, hard, and she jolted forward. How . . . but how did . . . where . . . it was a dark-blue Ferrari, and Nick Watergate was standing in the driveway next to Tygue. Tillie waved sheepishly from the door. And with her heart pounding, Kate pulled slowly into the drive. The sound of the gravel startled them both and they turned to look at her. Tygue ran towards the car, waving, with a big grin of excitement, and Nick simply stood there and watched her, with that endless smile of his. She stopped the car and stared back. What could she say? And how had he found her? Weinberg, of course. That was easy. She should have been angry at Stu, and normally she would have been. But she wasn't. Suddenly all she wanted to do was laugh. She was so goddamn tired, all she *could* do was laugh. And Tygue was reaching into the car window and talking as fast as he could.

'Hey, you, wait a minute, slow down. Wait till I get out of the car.' But the child certainly looked happy.

'Did you know Nick was a football hero? And he worked in a rodeo?'

'Oh, really?' What had happened to him? When Weinberg had been there for only an hour, Tygue had instantly detested him. But Nick was a football hero and a rodeo star. Apparently, he had the touch. She stooped to kiss Tygue and looked across at Nick. He hadn't moved. He just stood there. She walked slowly towards him with a careful smile on her face. Her eyes looked tired, but there was still laughter in them, and the smile was turning into the mischievous one he remembered from lunch.

'How was teaching?'

'Fine. Should I ask what you're doing here?'

'If you like. I came to see you. And Tygue.'

She was standing in front of him now, and he looked down at her as though he wanted to kiss her, but Tygue and Bert were already underfoot.

'You make a terrific detective.'

'You're not hard to find. Are you angry?' For a moment, he looked worried.

'I suppose I should be. At Stu, not at you. But' – she shrugged – 'I'm so damn tired, I couldn't get mad at anybody if my life depended on it.' He put an arm around her shoulders and pulled her closer.

'You couldn't have gotten much sleep, Mrs. Harper. What time did you get home?'

'About four.' She liked the feel of his arm around her. It was heavenly as they walked slowly back to the house. For a moment she worried about Tygue, but he didn't seem to notice. She couldn't understand how Nick had put the boy so quickly at ease.

'Why did you leave like that?'

'I wanted to come home.'

'That badly?' He still didn't believe her.

'The party was over. Cinderella had been to the ball. And what was the point of spending the night in a strange hotel, when I could have been here?'

He looked around and nodded. 'I see your point. But I didn't feel that way about it this morning when I called. I got this sinking feeling that ... that I'd never see you again.' His face sobered as he remembered it, and they walked into the house. 'Weinberg was damn close-mouthed about it too.'

'What changed his mind?' Kate peeled off her damp rain-coat. She was wearing jeans and a blue gingham shirt. It was a far cry from the lady in the navy halter dress of the night before. Cinderella was just Cinderella again.

'He changed his mind because I threatened never to play tennis with him again.'

'Now I know where his allegiance lies, not to mention his priorities.' Kate looked at him and laughed. This was crazy. She had met him yesterday at lunch and now he was here? In her house? With Tygue leaping at his feet? Suddenly it all seemed ridiculous. She sat down in a chair and started to laugh, and she couldn't stop till tears ran down her face.

'What's so funny?' Nick looked blank.

'Everything. You, Weinberg, me, that damn crazy party you took me to last night. I can't even begin to sort out what's real and what isn't.' And then Nick started to laugh too, but now there was mischief in his face and he went to his briefcase. He hoped he had guessed right.

'What are you up to over there, Waterman?'

'Well, Kate' – he had his back to her, but there was humour in his voice and Tillie was smiling broadly as she watched the proceedings – 'I know what you mean about not being able to sift what's real from what isn't, so ... to figure things out' – Kate was already grinning as she listened – 'I thought I'd come up here once and for all and find out if you were really Cinder-ella, or just one of the ugly stepsisters.' And with that he wheeled around, and produced a glass slipper, reposing on a gold-bordered red velvet cushion. It was a life-sized shoe, the best plastic made, and it had taken his secretary three hours to locate it through the prop department at Paramount. And now she was sitting there, in her blue jeans, laughing again.

'Well, Cinderella, shall we give it a go?' He walked over to where she sat, and she saw that the slipper was a high-heeled, pointed-toe number with a glass rosette. He kneeled at her feet while she broke into fresh whoops of laughter, as she stuck out the 'dainty' red rubber boot she had worn in the rain.

'Nick Waterman, you're crazy!' But the entourage was loving it. Tillie couldn't stop laughing. Tygue was hopping around like a flea, and even Bert was chasing and barking as though he knew what was going on. But the boot came off, the shoe slid on, and Nick sat back on his heels with a grin.

'Cinderella, I presume.' He couldn't help feeling victorious and looking it. He had guessed exactly the right size.

She stood up on it gingerly and broke into laughter again. 'How the hell did you guess my size?' Practice, obviously. But whatever else he did, he certainly didn't do *this* every day. 'And how did you find it?' She sat back down in the chair with a thud and a grin and looked into those magical blue eyes of his.

'God bless Hollywood, Kate. But it did take us a while.'

'What time did you get here?'

'About three. Why? Was I late?' He laughed again, and sat down hard on the floor, narrowly missing Bert, who then crawled onto his lap, leaving two muddy footprints on his clean beige linen trousers. But Nick didn't seem to care. He was more interested in Kate, who was looking at him in astonishment.

'You got here at three? What have you done all this time?' It was already past five.

'Tygue took me down to look at the horses. With Tillie o course.' He smiled in her direction, and she blushed, not unlike Kate. There was something about him, so open, so direct; there was no avoiding him, no shying away. 'Then we went for a walk down by the river. We played cards for a while. And then you came home.'

'Just call me Cinderella.' She glanced down at her foot again, and wondered if she could keep the shoe. 'You came up here just for this?' She couldn't get over it, but he averted his gaze.

'I was coming up this way anyway, as a matter of fact. I rent a house in Santa Barbara from time to time. I have it this weekend.' Something made her doubt him, but she wasn't quite sure what. Why would he lie to her? 'May I invite you two over to visit tomorrow?' He looked hopeful, but Tygue immediately jumped in with a fierce shake of his head.

'No!'

'Tygue!' Now what? The man had come all the way up from L.A. with a glass slipper, and Tygue was going to keep her from seeing him? But she wanted to see him! To hell with Tygue.

'But Joey's mom invited me for the weekend! And they have two new goats and his dad said he might get a pony tomorrow!' It was the best news Kate had had all day.

'Hey, podner, that's dynamite!' Nick looked enormously impressed, and Tygue looked at him as though they were the only two people in the room who made any sense.

'Can I go?' He looked imploringly at his mother.

'Why not? Okay. And tell Joey he can come here next weekend. I may regret that, but I'll take my chances.'

'Can I call Joey and tell him?'

'Go ahead.'

Tillie took her leave as Tygue dashed into the kitchen to use the phone, and Kate held out a hand to Nick. He took it in his, as he sat down more comfortably near her chair.

'I'd like to know what you did to win him over. It must have cost you a fortune.'

'Nope. Not yet anyway.'

'What does that mean? Nicholas Waterman, what have you been up to? Any man who can show up here with a glass slipper, and in the right size, is a man to be reckoned with.'

'I'll accept that as a compliment. No, honest, I didn't do a thing. I just promised to take both of you to Disneyland.'

'You did?' She was stunned. He carefully took off the glass shoe, and she wiggled her toes.

'Yes, I did. And your son accepted. He thinks Disneyland is a terrific idea. And he invited me to San Francisco to meet his Aunt Licia. I hope you don't mind.'

'Not at all. "Aunt Licia" would love you. Which reminds me, would you like a martini?'

'That's it? The whole shot? A martini?' He laughed again. 'All or nothing, huh?'

'You can have coffee. But the only booze I have right now is the stuff Licia leaves here to make her martinis.'

'Your sister?' He was only slightly confused, but he liked the chaotic family scene he was seeing. And he loved the boy.

'Felicia is my best friend, my conscience, and my alter ego.

And she spoils Tygue rotten.' That rang a familiar bell with Nick, but he wasn't sure why. 'Anyway, a martini?'

'I think I'll opt for coffee. By the way, am I totally disrupting your life?'

'Yes.'

'Good.' And then his face grew serious and he stopped teasing for a moment. 'I mean it though. I asked Weinberg if he thought I'd get punched in the mouth by some six-foot-nine sumo wrestler when I got here, and he said he didn't think so, but he didn't really know. He suggested I take my chances, and proceed at my own risk. Which I did. But all kidding aside, am I going to make trouble for you by being here?' He seemed upset at the thought. She had looked so unhappy at the end of the party the night before. He didn't want to see her that way again. But he had had to see her, even if only once more.

'Of course you're not going to make trouble. Who would you make trouble with? Tygue seems to approve of you. He's the only sumo wrestler around here.' She knew what he meant, and she liked him for asking. As she got up to make him coffee, she was wearing one red boot and one stockinged foot and her hair was tangled and loose, the way he liked it. He thought she looked even more beautiful than she had on the show.

'Let me just get this straight. Tygue is the only one around here to object?' He said it slowly and carefully, as though she might not understand.

'That's right.'

'Seems to me you said something about a friend.' She looked at him quizzically and then shrugged. 'Someone who spoils the boy. You said it at lunch yesterday.' And then they both grinned and they said it together, as Nick suddenly understood.

'Aunt Licia.'

He smiled broadly and followed her out to the kitchen, where Tygue hung up the phone.

'Okay, Mom. All set. His dad'll pick me up tomorrow morning. And he'll even bring me home Sunday afternoon.' He looked up at both of them matter-of-factly, as though he'd known Nick forever. 'What's for dinner? Did you know Nick is going to take us to Disneyland? Right, Bert?' Bert wagged his tail, and Tygue left the room in search of Willie, without waiting to hear what was for dinner.

'He's a riot.'

'Sometimes.' Kate smiled at his retreating back as he left, and then looked up at Nick. 'He's a nice kid and I love him a lot.'

'You're a good mother. What is for dinner, by the way?'

'Does that mean you'd like to stay for dinner?'

'If it's not too much trouble.'

It was amazing. She hardly knew him, and here he was, hanging out in the kitchen, and asking to stay for dinner. But it felt good. Her defences were not what they should have been; she was just too tired.

'It's not too much trouble. And you made it here just in time for Tygue's favourite gourmet treat.'

'What?'

'Tacos.'

'That's my favourite too.'

She handed him a mug of coffee and sat down at the kitchen table. It was a long way from Carmel right now. A long way from Tom.

'What were you thinking just then?'

'When?'

'Just now.'

'Nothing.'

'You're lying.' He was suddenly very intense as he reached out again for her hand. 'Are you happy here, Kate?' She looked up at him honestly and nodded.

'Yes. Very.' Then what was the shadow? Why the fleeting lightning bolts of pain?

'Are there good people in your life?' he wanted to know. Suddenly it mattered to him.

'Yes. Very. You've met them all now. All except one. Licia.'

'That's it?' He looked shocked. 'Just the boy?'

'And Tillie, the woman who was here with Tygue when you got here. And Bert, of course.' She smiled, remembering her threat to talk about him on the show.

'Of course. But you're serious? This is it?'

'I told you. I'm a hermit.' No wonder she had freaked at the party. 'I like it this way.'

'Was it like this when you were married?' She shook her head, but her eyes gave nothing away.

'No, it was different.'

'Does Tygue remember his dad?' His voice was very soft as they sipped their coffee in the quiet kitchen, and she shook her head again.

'He couldn't. His dad died before he was born.'

'Oh God, how awful for you, Kate.' He looked at her as though he understood what it must have been like. It was the first time in a long time that she had thought of it.

'It was a very long time ago.'

'And you were alone?'

'Nope. I had Felicia, she was here with me.' Maybe that was it. All that incredible aloneness. Maybe that was the pain he saw.

'No family, Kate?'

'Only what you see. This is it. It's a lot more than most people have.' And more than he had. She had hit close to home, without even meaning to. All those chicks with the big tits that he'd been taking out for the last twenty years, and where was that? He was thirty-seven years old and he had nothing.

'You're right, Kate.'

'What?'

'Will you come to Santa Barbara tomorrow, for the day?' She was the sort of woman he felt he had to say that to. For the day. If he even hinted at more, she wouldn't come. But she nodded slowly, watching him, as though weighing something, considering.

'Okay.'

CHAPTER XIX

She found the house easily with the map he had drawn her. She hadn't let him come to pick her up. She wanted to drive there on her own. It was only half an hour away, but the drive gave her time to think. She wasn't sure why she was going, except that she liked Nick. And he was easy to talk to. He had stayed until almost eleven the night before, when she had started to fall asleep on the couch. She was exhausted, and he just kissed her chastely on the cheek when he left. But it had been a lovely evening. They had built a fire, and he had popped corn for Tygue, and the boy had shown him the new cowboy suit. Nick was in awe of it.

'Where did you ever find that?'

'At the hotel.' Other people bought jade and maribou bed jackets, she bought her son the kind of outfit every little boy dreamed of.

'I wish I'd been your kid.'

'No you don't. I'm a monster. Ask Tygue.' But Tygue had only chuckled and shoved another handful of buttery popcorn into his mouth.

'Some monster.' He had wanted to kiss her then. But not in front of the boy. He knew she wouldn't like that. And he didn't want to do it that way either. He wanted a lot from this woman. Her love as well as her body, and even more than that. He wanted her time, her life, her children, her wisdom, her gentleness, her compassion. He saw all that was there. But she saw what was in him too. She had begun to see it that first day. He had cared enough to come looking for her, to find her, to bring her a silly plastic slipper. But he cared enough to be good to Tygue too, to see what was in her eyes, to hear what she didn't say. She had to be careful of that, she reminded herself, as she pulled into the driveway of the address he had given her in Santa Barbara. Nick Waterman saw too much.

It was a white house, with well-tended black trim and beautiful large bronze fixtures. There was a carriage light, and an enormous bronze sea gull hovered on the door as the knocker. She flapped its wings to knock, and then stepped back. The house was on a little hill overlooking the water, and three willow trees stood nearby. It was in sharp contrast to her own simpler house. But this one had less warmth, only beauty.

He opened the door barefoot and wearing cut-off jeans, and his shirt was an old faded tee-shirt that matched his eyes.

'Cinderella!' His face lit up when he saw her, in spite of the teasing words.

'Should I have worn the slipper just to be sure you'd recognize me?'

'I'll take your word for it. Come on in. I was outside painting the deck.'

'Sounds like you work hard for your rental.' She followed him into the house, and noticed the stern Early American decor. It was as she had thought, all beauty and no warmth. It was a pity, because the house was filled with beautiful things.

'I enjoy puttering around here. The guy who owns it never gets out of L.A. So I dabble around when I have time.' He was painting the deck a breezy sky blue, and he had painted two gulls in flight in a corner.

'You need clouds.' She said it in a business-like way, as she looked at the deck.

'Huh?'

'Clouds. You need clouds. Do you have any white paint?'

'Yeah. Over there.' He grinned at her, and she smiled back as she rolled up the sleeves of her shirt, and then the cuffs of her jeans. 'Want some of my old clothes to wear, Kate? I'd hate to have you wreck your stuff.' He was serious but she only laughed at him. She had worn comfortable old clothes to lie on the beach. And underneath it all was a little orange bikini. But that was for later. Maybe. She wasn't sure yet.

'How's Tygue?'

'Fine. He said to say hi. He left at the crack of dawn to see those goats. Now he wants one too.'

'He should have his own horse.' Nick was painting another gull in the far corner.

'That's what he tells me. Maybe you'd like to buy him one.' She was teasing, but she got worried when she saw his face.

'Nick, I'm only kidding. Now, seriously, don't you dare. I've been fighting Felicia off on that one for two years.'

'Sounds like a sensible lady. I'll have to meet this Felicia of yours. How long have you known her?'

'Oh, for years. I met her when I was modelling for—' And then she looked up as though she had said something she shouldn't have.

'You think I didn't know?' He smiled at her from his corner. 'Come on, love. I'm a producer. I can tell when people have modelled, or done ballet, or lifted weights.'

'I lifted weights.' She looked over at him with a broad grin and flexed an arm as he laughed at her.

'Great clouds you're painting, Cinderella.'

'You like 'em?' She looked pleased.

'Sure do. Especially the one on the tip of your nose.'

'Creep. I lied to Weinberg, you know. I told him I'd never modelled. I thought if I admitted it, he'd sell my body to the highest bidder and make me do a lot of publicity stuff.'

'That's my girl. Chicken Little.' He made rude clucking noises and she threatened to splash paint in his direction.

'Can you blame me for not wanting to do all that crap? I'm happy here, away from all that crazy stuff. Nick, I don't belong there.'

'Nobody does.' He sat down on the railing and looked at her. 'But I'll tell you something else, babe, you don't belong here either. You're wasting yourself. One of these days you're going to have to get ballsy and get back out there, at least part of the time.' She nodded sombrely.

'I know. I've been trying. But it's rough.'

'Not as rough as you thought though, is it?'

She shook her head, wondering how he knew. He seemed to understand so much. She had the feeling he really knew her.

'And there are compensations in getting out in the world.' he said. She laughed at that one.

'There certainly are.'

'Hungry?'

'Not really. You? I can go out to the kitchen and make you some lunch if you like.' They had finished the deck, and agreed it was a work of art. 'I hope the guy who owns this place appreciates your improvements. He ought to pay you to stay here.'

'I'll tell him you said so.' He put a casual arm around her shoulders, and they wandered out to the kitchen together, barefoot and brown. Nick had bought prosciutto and melon and a roast chicken that morning. And another package yielded peaches, strawberries, and watermelon. There was a long baguette of French bread and a beautiful slice of ripe Brie.

'That's not lunch. It's a feast.'

'Well, Cinderella, for you, only the best.' He swept her a low bow, and then straightened to stand very close to her. He held out his arms. She felt a pull like nothing she had ever felt before, and slowly she melted towards him. She couldn't have resisted if she'd wanted to, but she didn't want to. She just wanted to be there, next to him, feeling the warmth of his skin and the strength of his arms, and smelling the scent of lemon and spices that was already so familiar to her. Nick.

And then gently he put a hand under her chin and lifted her face to his and kissed her, softly at first, and then harder, his arms holding her close, his mouth holding tightly to hers.

'I love you, Kate,' he said as he stood there, breathless, wanting her, watching her. But he had spoken the truth. She said nothing, not knowing what to say. He couldn't love her. He didn't know her. It was too soon. He said that to everyone. She couldn't do this. She couldn't let this happen to her.

'I love you. That's all. No questions, no demands. I just love you.' And this time she reached out to him, and when she let go of him she said it, with a soft smile and a mist over her eyes.

'I love you too. It's crazy. I hardly know you. But I think I love you, Nick Waterman.' She looked down at her feet. Seven years. Seven years. And now she had said it to a stranger. I love

198

you. But he wasn't a stranger. He was Nick. There had been something infinitely special about him from the first moment she'd met him. As though he'd been waiting for her. As though they both knew he was there to stay. Or was she crazy? Did she only *want* to think that? She looked up at him searchingly and he smiled gently and made light of the moment to make it easier for her.

'You "think", huh? Boy, that's a gyp. You "think" you love me.' But the look in his eyes was teasing and he gently swatted her behind as he put their lunch into a basket. 'Let's go eat on the beach.' She nodded and they went off together, hand in hand, as he carried the basket with one powerful arm. He had the same kind of shape as Tom had had years ago. Tom had none of that left anymore. He had diminished over the years of sitting in his chair. But this man had never been diminished by anything. He was throbbing with life. 'Want to go for a swim, Cinderella?' She grinned to herself. That name was going to stick.

'I'd love it.' She had decided to trust him.

'So would I.' He was leering unabashedly at the tiny orange bikini that had suddenly appeared, with a great deal of skin, as she peeled off her shirt and jeans. But his leering was so open and friendly that it only made her smile. 'You expect me to go swimming with you looking like that? I'd drown for chrissake.'

'Shut up. I'll race you.' And she was off in a flash of orange and brown, long graceful legs dashing towards the water, as he followed appreciatively and then streaked out ahead, flashing past her and diving into the first wave. But she was close behind him, and they surfaced together a good distance out. The water was brisk and delicious on their sun-baked skin. 'Beats the hell out of the pool at the hotel, doesn't it?' He laughed at her remark and tried to dunk her, but she was too quick. She slipped quickly under the water and darted between his legs. An attempt to catch her almost removed the top of her bathing suit, and she surfaced spluttering and laughing.

'See, smartass. You're going to lose that little Band-Aid you're wearing if you don't watch out.' It was barely decent and she knew it. But all her bathing suits were like that.

Felicia sent them to her, and the only one who ever saw her was Tygue. 'Show-off,' he accused.

'You're impossible.'

'No. But I will be if I have to look at you like that much longer.' She laughed again as, side by side, they set out for shore. It has been a long time since anyone had talked to her like that. And Nicholas did it in a way that amused her.

'I'm starving.' She collapsed on her towel on the beach and looked hungrily at the basket.

'Go ahead, silly, dig in. Don't be so polite.' He sat down next to her, and gave her a salty kiss. 'Your family must have been very strait-laced. You're a very well-behaved young lady.'

'Not anymore.'

'Kate, are your folks dead too?'

She looked at him for a minute before answering, and then decided to tell him the truth. About that at least.

'They disowned me.'

He stopped unwrapping the lunch to look at her.

'Are you serious?' He looked so shocked that it made her want to laugh. It didn't matter to her anymore. It was too long ago.

'Yes, very serious. I disappointed them, so they crossed me off their list. Or I suppose it would be more honest to say that they felt I had betrayed them.'

'Do you have brothers and sisters?'

'Nope. Just me.'

'And they did that to you? What kind of people are they? You were an only child and they threw you out? What the hell did you do?'

'Marry someone they didn't like.'

'That's it?'

'That's it. I dropped out of college after my freshman year and went to live with him. And then we got married. They never came to the wedding. We never spoke again. They crossed me off the family tree when we started living together. They didn't think he was good enough.'

'That's a hell of a price to pay for a man.'

'He was worth it.' She said it very softly and without regret.

'That's a nice thing to say about somebody. He must have been a very special guy.'

She smiled again then. 'He was.' They didn't talk for a few minutes, and she helped him unpack the lunch. And then she saw something in Nick's face. Something a little bit hurt, or left out. 'Nick?'

'Yeah?' He looked up, surprised. He had been lost in his own thoughts.

She reached out and took his hand in hers. 'All of that was a long time ago. Some of it hurts, some of it doesn't. It all mattered then. A lot. But it's gone now. All of it. And . . .' She couldn't say it, but she had to. She knew she had to. No matter how much it hurt. '. . . So is he. He's gone too.' Her eyes shone too brightly for a moment and Nick pulled her into his arms.

'I'm sorry, Kate.'

'Don't be. There've been such good times too. Tygue. The books. Licia. You . . .' She said it in a tiny voice and he sat back from her for a minute with a tender smile.

'Lady, one day . . .' But he didn't dare say it. He just sat there smiling at her.

'What?'

'Just – one day . . .'

'Nicholas, tell me.' She propped herself up on one elbow and smiled at him.

'One day, Cinderella, I'd like to make you Mrs. Charming.'

'As in Prince Charming and Mrs. Charming?' She looked at him wide-eyes and he nodded. 'But you're crazy, Nick. You don't even know me.' Who was this man? Why was he saying all this?

'Yes, I do, Cinderella. I know you to the tip of your soul, and I'm going to know you better. With your permission, of course.' He handed her the bread and kissed her softly on the lips. But she was looking more serious than he liked. 'Does that upset you?'

'No, not the thought behind it. But Nick – I'm never getting married again. I'm serious about that.'

'Famous last words.' He tried to make light of it. He was sorry he'd brought up the subject. It was much too soon.

'I mean it. I couldn't.'

'Why not?' Because my husband's not dead. Jesus.

'I just couldn't. Once, but not again. Up until two days ago, I could never even imagine loving a man again, and now I can imagine that, but not getting married.' Then there was hope after all.

'Then let's just take one step at a time.' She could tell that he wasn't taking her seriously, but she didn't know what else to say to him. 'Prosciutto, melon?'

'You're not listening to me.' She looked unhappy but he ignored her.

'You're absolutely right. Besides which, I'm an optimist, and I love you. I refuse to take no for an answer.'

'You're a lunatic.'

'Absolutely.' He sat back happily with a hunk of bread and Brie and smiled at her. 'And you are a fairy princess. Care for some Brie? It's terrific.'

'I give up.'

'Good.' And then even he had to smile, when he thought of all the women over the years who would have given anything to hear him propose marriage, and the third he'd seen them yet.

They polished off most of the lunch and then lay side by side in the sun for a time before going back to the water. And by then it was after four. 'Had enough of the beach, Kate?'

'Mmm . . .' She was lying in the sunshine again, and tired from swimming. The salt water was running in little rivers from her temples to her neck and he leaned over and kissed them off with his tongue as she opened her eyes.

'Let's go home. We can get rid of all this sand. And oil, and salt, and bread crumbs, and watermelon seeds.'

She laughed as she stood up and looked at the mess they'd left on the blankets.

'Looks like it was quite a party.' She wrapped up the towels, he picked up the basket, and they walked slowly back to the house.

'We'd better go in the back way. He'll have a nervous breakdown if we get sand all over the house.' It seemed a crazy way to live at the beach, but no crazier than anything else people from L.A. did.

'Yes, sir.' She followed him in the back way, to a brightly decorated little yellow room. It had a striped circus awning, and three separate shower stalls, a half-dozen director's chairs, and a marvellous old-fashioned wicker chaise longue with a huge striped parasol overhead.

'The dressing rooms, Miss Harper. They're usually not co-ed, but if you trust me—'

'I don't.'

He grinned at her. 'You're right. Tell you what. Leave your bathing suit on.' And laughing along with him, she complied and climbed into the shower with him. She was still laughing as he told her funny stories about the show while he washed the sand off her back, and then suddenly the chattering stopped and he turned her slowly around to him. And slowly, hauntingly, under the spray of warm water, they kissed. She felt his arms go around her, and his body press against hers, and suddenly she was as hungry for him as he very plainly was for her, and they couldn't get enough of each other as the water rained down on them.

'Wait, I'm drowning!' She giggled as he moved and the shower ran full in her face. And laughing down at her, he turned off the water.

'Better?'

She nodded. It was very still without the purring of the shower in their ears. And the shower stall was filled with steam. Their hair hung loose in dripping strands, and there were beads of water on her eyelashes, which he gently kissed as he slowly peeled down the top of the bikini. He whispered gently in her ear as she ran her hands over his chest. 'You just lost your Band-Aid, Cinderella.' She smiled but her eyes were still closed when she kissed him, and then he stooped to kiss her breasts. He did it so gently that her whole body cried out for him.

'I love you, Prince Charming.'

'Are you sure?' His voice was very serious as he stood up again, and she opened her eyes. 'Are you sure, Kate?'

'Yes, I'm sure. I love you.'

'It's been a long time, hasn't it?' He had to know, though in his heart he already did. She nodded. He had sensed that about from the first, once he had realized the extent to which she had been cloistered for years. In an odd way, it pleased him. It made him feel special, and made him know just how special she was. 'Very long, darling?'

She nodded again, and he loved her all the more for it. 'Since before Tygue.'

'Oh, sweetheart . . .' And then he pulled her close and held her very tight for a long time. He wanted to make up to her for years without loving, without a man. But he couldn't give her those years back. He could just give her now. And ever so gently he wrapped her in an enormous pink terry-cloth towel and carried her upstairs to the room where he slept. It was a lovely airy room that seemed to sail out over the sea. There were big picture windows, and fine old Early American pieces, and there was a sombre-looking brass bed. It was not the room he would have chosen for her, but it was the room where he first loved her, and he loved her gently and well, caressing and stroking and entering her again and again, and at last she slept in his arms as he watched her. When she awoke it was dark.

'Nick?' She remembered what had happened but not where they were.

'I'm right here, darling. And you can't even begin to know how much I love you.' It was a beautiful way to wake up, and she smiled as she cuddled back into his arms. And then suddenly she stiffened.

'Oh my God.'

'What's wrong?' Had she remembered something painful? He was suddenly frightened.

'What if I get pregnant?'

He smiled and kissed the end of her nose. 'Then Tygue has a baby brother. Or sister, as the case may be.'

'Be serious.'

'I am serious. I'd like nothing better.'

'Good lord, Nick. I've never even thought of having another

child.' She sounded so subdued in the darkness, and he held her closer.

'There are a lot of things you haven't thought of for much too long. We'll do something about all that next week. But this weekend, we can take our chances, And if something happens ... we'll live with it.' And then he had a thought. 'Or would you hate that very much?' Maybe she didn't want his child. He'd never even thought of that, and he looked down at her in that darkness. He could see her face clearly, and her eyes.

'No, I wouldn't hate it at all. I love you, Nick.' He was all that mattered in the world as she kissed him again, and he slipped the covers away from her body and let his hands roam across her skin, as she smiled a long, slow, womanly smile.

CHAPTER XX

It felt as though they'd been together forever. They had got up at seven and puttered around the house together. Gone into town for the paper, taken a walk down the beach, and had a huge breakfast which they concocted as a team. Even that went smoothly, as though someone had catalogued their abilities and figured out how each could complement the other. And there was such ease and comfort between them – it was that that astounded Kate. After years of celibacy, she did not even feel uncomfortable wandering around naked under his tee-shirt, and now the two of them were lying naked on a towel behind the dune nearest the house, concealed from any eyes but theirs. She marvelled again at his beautiful body, as she propped herself up on one elbow and looked at him.

'Do you have any idea how extraordinary all this is? Or do you do this all the time?' The words embarrassed her as soon as she had said them. It was none of her business what he did 'all the time'. But perversely, she wanted to know. The unexpectedly hurt look on his face as he sat up told her a great deal.

'What do you mean by that, Kate?'

'I'm sorry. I . . . it's just . . . you live in a different world, Nick. That's all. Things are very different for you than they are for me.' She said it softly and regretfully. Maybe she didn't want to know after all. He reached out and gently took her shoulders in his hands, and looked at her until she looked back at him.

'You're right. Things are different. Kate. Or they have been. In some ways, anyway. When I was much younger, I ran my ass off. I chased every woman who turned me on, and a few who didn't. I ran and ran and ran, and you know what? I ran myself out. I finally realized that there was nothing left to run after. Things got a lot quieter after that, and a lot saner, but a lot lonelier too. There aren't many women worth the trouble out there. Hollywood seems to be a mecca for stupidity, selfishness, and vacuousness. Women who'll sleep with you to further their careers, to get closer to Jasper Chase, to be seen at the Polo Lounge at the right hour of the day, to get to the best parties, or maybe just to get a free meal and get laid. You know what I got out of all that? Zero. So why bother? Most of the time I don't. In a lot of ways, Kate, I've been as lonely as you have. And you know what I've wound up with? A slick apartment, a few rooms full of expensive furniture, a couple of good paintings, a fancy car. And all added up, my love, it's not worth shit. And then, once in a lifetime, one moment, one face, one tiny speck of time, and you know you've seen every dream you've ever had. It's like that feeling of waking up in the morning, dazed and bleary-eyed but you don't quite know why, and suddenly in the middle of your coffee, you remember a dream. A flash of it and then a corner of it, and then a whole chunk of it. And suddenly you know the story and the place and the people you dreamed about. You know the whole thing, and all you want to do is get back there. But you can't. No matter how hard you try you can never get it all back. But it haunts you. Maybe for a day. Maybe for a lifetime. I could have let that happen to me, Kate. I could have let you haunt me for a lifetime. But I didn't want to do that. I decided to run like hell and get back to the dream before it was too late, for both of us. That was why I came up to see you. I couldn't lose you, not after all these years of waiting. I didn't even know I was waiting for you, but by Thursday night, I did. And so did you.' He was right too. She had. She had tried to avoid seeing it. She had told herself she'd never see him again. But she had known something, that strange feeling deep in her soul . . . a whisper . . . a promise . . . 'I love you, Kate. I can't explain it. I know it's only been a few days. But I just know this is right. I'd marry you today, if you'd let me.' She smiled at him and let her head rest on his shoulders, as she gently kissed his neck.

'I know. It's incredible though, isn't it?' She lay back on he blanket and looked up at him as he watched her with those rich morning-blue eyes. The sky behind him was exactly the same colour. 'It's all moving so quickly. I don't know what to make of it. I keep thinking I can't be feeling like this. I keep thinking – I *kept* thinking,' she corrected herself with an apologetic look and a smile, 'that maybe you did this all the time. But that didn't explain how *I* feel. How can I feel this way about you so quickly? After all these years . . . I don't understand myself.' But she did not look unhappy. In fact, it was the first time he had seen her without the shadows haunting her eyes. That darting look of pain had been gone when they'd woken up that morning. She looked like a new person. And she felt reborn.

'Maybe that's how it happens though. Over the years, I've heard stories about people who've lived together for five or ten years, and then suddenly – zap – one of them meets someone else and gets married in two weeks. Maybe if you had to wait all that time to check it out, you knew it wasn't right all along. Maybe when it really happens, when it's right, when it's the person you were meant for, maybe then it just happens, bang, and you know it. That's what happened to me.'

He lay down next to her on his stomach and kissed her on the mouth. 'Kate?'

'What, love?'

'Were you really serious about never remarrying?'

She nodded and looked hard at him before answering. 'Yes.' He could hardly hear the word, but he was sorry when he did. 'Why?'

'I can't explain it. I just know I can't.'

'That's not fair. And it doesn't make sense.' Or maybe it was just too soon to push. He searched her face and saw something pained come into her eyes again. He was sorry he'd brought it up. 'Maybe you don't owe me any explanations.'

'There are none to give.' She ran a hand softly down his back and looked at him in a way that made his insides tie into a satiny knot. 'All I can tell you is that I'll do anything you want, but not marriage.' She said it intensely, and he gave her a lecherous smile.

'Given what I'm thinking at this very moment, Cinderella,

208

that suits me just fine.' And he did not mention marriage again. He made love to her on the towel, in the sand, and then bobbing in the waves in front of the house.

'Nick, you're indecent!' She ran laughing and breathless back to the towel and lay down, smiling up at him, as he fell carefully on top of her, catching himself on his arms.

'Look who's talking. I didn't do it by myself, you know.'

'Nicholas ... Nick ... N ...' Her voice faded away as he kissed her again and spread her legs softly with his in the warm sand. It was well into the afternoon before they went back to the house, tired and brown and happy, and as though they'd been lovers for years. And then with shock, Kate looked at a clock on the wall in the kitchen. 'Oh my God!'

'What's wrong?' He looked over his shoulder with a mouthful of grapes.

'Tygue. He'll be home at four. I totally forgot!' It was the first time in six years she had done that. She had even forgotten Bert, but at least she had fed him before leaving the house the day before. He only ate once a day, and he could get in and out through his own special door.

'Relax, darling. It's only three.'

'But ...' He shut her up with a kiss, and shared one of his grapes passed delicately and uncrushed through his lips. 'Will you stop that? I have to ...' But she was laughing now. 'I'm serious.'

'So am I. I packed this morning. All I have to do is shower, and strip the bed, and we'll get back in plenty of time. Do you want to call Joey's parents?'

'Maybe I should. Christ, I probably should have done that last night. What if something happened to him, or ...' He kissed her again while picking up the phone, which he handed to her with a smile.

'It's not a sin to have a good time yourself for a change.' He kissed her again. 'Call. I'll start the shower.' She joined him in it five minutes later. 'Everything okay?'

'Fine.' She looked sheepish. 'He doesn't even sound like he missed me.'

'Of course not. Not with two new goats to distract him. Did

Joey's dad get the pony?' He lathered himself and handed her the soap. It smelled of carnations.

'Two of them. One for Joey's sister.'

'Sounds like a good man.'

'So are you.' They kissed again under the spray, with the smell of carnations all around them.

'No funny stuff, young lady. We have to get home.'

'Well, listen to you.' But she was amused. He seemed to be good at all things. Being a lover, being a father, being a friend. He was right to want to get married. He would have made a marvellous husband ... would have made ... she thought the words with regret as she handed back the soap, and let the spray of hot water rinse her clean.

They were dressed and the house was closed twenty minutes later. She had packed up the kitchen while he finished dressing, and she stood next to him with a sorrowful look as he locked the front door. He turned and saw her, and then pulled her into his arms with a smile.

'Aw, sweetheart, come on. It's not over. This is just the beginning.' It was crazy but there were tears in her eyes. The weekend had been so lovely, she didn't want it to end. She wanted it to go on forever. And now she had to go back to being Tygue's mother, and driving up to see Tom. She wanted to stay in Santa Barbara with Nick forever. But he had to get back to reality too.

'But what happens now?' She sagged against the railing for a moment, and looked into his eyes. But there was nothing frightening there at all, only oceans of love.

'Why don't we just see what happens? I can have this house every weekend for as long as I like. The guy who owns it never uses it. It's not flashy enough for him so he just lets it sit here and rents it out. So it's all ours if we want it. And I can drive up from L.A. every night if you want me to. After the show. I could be there by midnight, and gone by the time Tygue gets up.'

'Nick, that's crazy. You'll be a wreck.' But she had to admit she loved the idea.

'We could give it a try, and you can come down to L.A. and

try it on for size. Ease into it, if you want. There's a whole lot we can do, Cinderella. I told you, this is just the beginning. The glass slipper fit, didn't it?' He leaned over and kissed her, brushing the soft, flying hair from her eyes. 'I love you. That's all.' That's all. So simple. And everything he said sounded wonderful ... except that she had her own decisions to make. She had to move at her own pace, in her own time. And there was Tygue to think of too.

'What do we do about Tygue?'

'Let him grow into things too. Trust me. I think I can manage that.'

'I think you can too.'

'So, is it settled then? Are you satisfied?' She nodded happily as she slid a hand into his arm and walked down the steps to their cars. Nothing was settled, but it all sounded damn good.

'Do you want to follow me back?' It seemed obvious that he'd come home with her, but he shook his head and unlocked his car as she stood next to hers with a look of surprise.

'No. I think you need some time with Tygue. How about if I come by around six? I have some things I could do in Santa Barbara.'

'For two hours?' He nodded, and she felt a sudden wild stab of jealousy. What if he had a woman in town? What if that was why he usually came to this house? What if ... but he saw the look in her eyes and started laughing.

'Darling, you are perfect and I adore you.' He walked over to her and took her tightly into his arms. 'You looked like you were about to kill somebody.'

'I was.' She looked over his shoulder with an embarrassed smile.

'Not me, I hope.'

'No. The woman I imagined you were seeing.'

'Kate, my love. I can honestly tell you that I don't have a single woman friend in this town. I usually come up here to get away from it all. And as for the rest of them, I will happily hold a public burning of my little black book in front of city hall at high noon on Monday.'

'Why wait that long? I'm sure I've got a match.' She

fumbled with the pockets of her shirt and he tweaked her nose.

'I'm sure you do. We'll use it later. Now get your ass back to your kid, you jealous bitch, before I rape you right here on the front steps.'

'In front of my *station wagon*?'

'Anytime.' He held the door to her car open and she slipped inside. He shut the door carefully and leaned inside for a last kiss. 'Drive carefully, please.'

'Yes, sir. See you at six.'

'On the dot.'

He waited until she had pulled away, and then got into his own car and turned towards town.

CHAPTER XXI

'Hey, Mom! It's Nick!' His shouts of glee echoed precisely what she felt, and the two of them raced outside with Bert as the long blue Ferrari came to a gravelly stop. The two exchanged a quick look over the child's head, and then Nick's attention was entirely Tygue's. He hopped out of the car and swept the boy into his arms with ease.

'How were the goats?'

'Great! And Joey's got two ponies. Well, one is supposed to be for his sister. But it isn't. She's a creep, and she's scared of it. What a dumb girl, it's a great pony.'

'I'll bet it is.' He put the boy down and turned to reach into his car. 'Tygue, when you visit a lady, when you grow up, it is always a good idea to bring her flowers and candy. So ...' He pulled out an armful of lilac and tulips, and handed Tygue a huge box wrapped in gold. 'Your mom gets the flowers, you get the candy.' Tygue looked immensely pleased with the arrangement, and his mother looked equally so.

'You're spoiling us, Nicholas.'

'Anytime, Cinderella.' He put an easy arm around her shoulders, and held out a hand to the boy, and together they walked inside. It was a warm summer night, with only a slight breeze to bring a chill to the air. Tonight it was too warm for a fire. Instead, they sat on the floor and sang songs and ate hot dogs and potato salad until Tygue went to bed. He was already half asleep when he got there, deposited by Nick, and tucked in by his mother. He was sound asleep when they left the room. And Nick took her into his arms as soon as she closed the door. 'Okay, sexy one, which way to yours?' And then he stunned her by picking her up off her feet. 'Next.' She was laughing softly as she gave him directions, and he deposited her on her bed. It was a cheery room done in bright flowered prints. Licia had given her the matching bedspread and curtains and beautifully covered chairs as a house warming present six years ago, but they looked as pretty and cheerful as ever.

'It looks like a garden.' He looked surprised and pleased. There were flowers and plants all over the room, and lots of white Victorian wicker.

'What did you expect? Black satin?'

'Jesus. I'd have dropped you on your ass in the doorway.'

'Is that so?' She was smiling broadly as she unbuttoned his shirt. 'And what did you do in Santa Barbara, monsieur?'

'Shopped a little, walked a little, and missed you a lot.' And with that, he sat down carefully on the bed and took her in his arms. She forgot all about what he had done in Santa Barbara.

Until the next day, when a message arrived. He had called her three times that morning after going back to L.A. He had left at six thirty, half an hour before she got Tygue up. And so far so good, the system worked, but she wondered how long he would be able to stand it. It was a hell of a commute to L.A., three hours each way. But he had sounded chipper on the phone, and he hadn't said anything to prepare her for the arrival of a message shortly after three. It came just after Tygue got in from school. The message said that there was a package for Tygue Harper at the post office in Santa Barbara. It gave the address of a branch Kate didn't know, and said he had to pick it up in person. Kate suspected Licia was at it again. Now what? Maybe a car. She had jokingly promised to wait till he was six. Kate grinned to herself as she started the car. He had insisted on setting out at once, and he'd have been impossible to live with if she hadn't.

It took them half an hour to reach the address, but when they did, she knew there must be some mistake. It wasn't a post office, it was a house, with a tidy-looking white barn out back, and a few small corrals. Kate was about to drive away when she saw a man wave with a cowboy hat and a grin. Tygue waved back, and then the man hurried towards them, as Kate sighed. She wanted to get on with it. They still had to find the post office before it closed. But the man was already abreast of the car and looking in at them purposefully with the same big smile.

214

'Tygue Harper?'

'Yes!' He practically shouted it.

'We have a package for you.' He winked at Kate, who was totally at a loss.

'Is this the post office?' Tygue looked excitedly from his mother to the man.

'No. But we do have the package for you.' And then suddenly Kate knew. She would have groaned, but she didn't dare. He had done it. She put her face in her hands and started to laugh as Tygue jumped out of the car and ran off excitedly with the man. Kate got out of the car more sedately and followed them to one of the corrals. She saw the man in the cowboy hat open the gate, and still holding tightly to Tygue's hand, lead him over to a beautifully groomed brown and blonde Shetland pony. 'See that, son?' Tygue nodded in awe-struck silence as his mother and the man in the hat looked on. 'That's your package, Tygue. He's all yours.'

'Oh ... Oh! ... OH! MOM!' And then he ran towards the pony and threw his arms around its neck. It was wearing a bright red bridle and a spanking new saddle. Kate watched his face, wishing Nick could see it too. Then the man in the cowboy hat reached into his pocket and fished out two letters, one for Tygue and one for his mother.

'Want me to read it to you, sweetheart?' She knew he was too excited to be able to read his own name. He was cooing and stroking the little pony, who seemed enchanted with the attention.

'What does it say?'

'It says ...' She opened the letter carefully and smiled at the message. 'It says, "Thought this would look nice with the new cowboy suit your mom got you in L.A. He's all yours. Give him a good name, and I'll be seeing you in the rodeo real soon. Nick."'

'Wow! Can I keep it?' He looked at her imploringly and she nodded.

'I guess so. Nick said he's all yours, didn't he?'

Tygue nodded ferociously.

'Then you can keep him. What are you going to call him?'

215

But in the pit of her stomach there was suddenly a squeamish twinge. This was an enormous gift. Just what did it mean?

'His name is Brownie.' This time he didn't need to ask Willie. He knew instantly.

And then she had a minute to open her own letter from Nick. 'Fifteen minutes to buy flowers. Ten minutes to buy chocolates. Five minutes looking in the phone book for name of stables. Twenty minutes getting here. Sixty-five minutes to choose pony and make arrangements. Five minutes to dream of you. Two hours, all accounted for. I love you, darling. See you later. Love, Nick.' And then he had added a P.S. explaining that he'd made all the necessary arrangements to leave the horse there, unless she wanted him taken over to the Adams ranch, but they could discuss that later – 'among other things.'

The 'other things' took priority when he reached the house at midnight. When he arrived, they went straight to the bedroom and Nick unravelled his tired body on the bed with a sigh and a smile.

'Long night?' Kate smiled over at him, still a little startled at the newness of seeing a man on her bed.

'Not really. I was just anxious to get back here all day. And it felt like it took forever to tape the show tonight and drive up here.'

'That's quite a commute, Mr. Waterman.'

'I think you're worth it, Mrs. Harper.' He sat up on the bed and held out his arms as she stood for a moment and watched him. And then slowly she walked towards him and sat down next to him as he pulled her closer. 'Feeling shy tonight, Kate?'

'Maybe a little.' They smiled again, and he pressed his lips down softly on hers. She didn't feel shy a moment later when he slid his hand into her shirt and ran it over her breast until her nipple was hard in his fingers. She felt an urgency begin to build in her loins as his mouth pressed harder on hers, and his hand found her other breast. The years of celibacy seemed to melt from her body once again, as his hands searched the silk of her flesh, and then finally moved downward until he found what he wanted.

216

It was hours before they had had enough of each other, and they lay side by side amid the rumpled sheets. He was smoking a cigarette and she was drawing circles on his chest with a lazy finger. He turned to her then and for the first time in hours, he remembered Tygue.

'What about the pony? Did he like it?'

'Are you kidding? He almost died on the spot.' But there was a moment of silence before she said anything further, and Nick glanced over at her with a smile.

'And? . . . There's more in your voice, Kate. Angry at me?'

'Angry? How could I be? No . . .' But he was right. There was something more. She looked at him squarely and her brow furrowed for a moment. 'I don't know how to say this, Nick, it sounds so ungrateful. He was thrilled with the pony, and it's an unbelievable present for a little boy. It's like a dream come true. You're like a dream come true. Maybe that's what's bothering me, though. What I'm trying to say . . . I don't want all of this to be just a dream. I don't want *you* to be a dream. I want all of this to be real. And maybe . . . maybe if . . .'

'Maybe if I just vanish, then where will you both be? Is that it, Kate?' He looked as though he understood all that she felt, and she was relieved that he didn't look angry.

'I guess that is it, Nick. What would happen if suddenly you weren't here anymore? One minute ponies and presents and promises of Disneyland, and the next . . .' She didn't want to finish the sentence, but she looked truly worried. And the business of spoiling Tygue worried her too. It was too much like Tom's grandiose generosity . . . near the end.

'I'm going to be here, Kate. For a long, long time. As long as you'll let me be here. I'm not going anywhere.' That was what Tom had said. But life wasn't like that. She knew better now.

'You don't know that. You have no control over that. You may want to be here, but you never know what fate has in store for you.'

'Darling' – he leaned carefully towards her and took her worried face in his hands – 'what I love most about you is your optimism.' She grinned sheepishly up at him and shrugged.

'I guess it'll just take me time to adjust to all the good things that are happening to me.'

'It may take Tygue a little while to adjust too. Don't kid yourself, even the bearers of ponies and promises of Disneyland can be viewed with suspicion.'

'I think you've gotten off lucky though. I was all set for him to resent you like crazy, but he doesn't.' She was still amazed.

'He probably will, when he figures out that I'm here to stay.' He kept saying that – 'here to stay.' How did he know? How could he be so sure? What if it didn't work out? In a way, it frightened her that he was so sure of himself.

'Come on, Kate, you look tired. Enough of all this worry-wart shit. I love you, and I think Tygue is terrific, and I'm not going to run out on either of you. And I also won't spoil him rotten if you don't want me to. No more ponies.' He grinned at her and tugged at a lock of her hair. 'Not for at least a week anyway.'

'You sound just like Licia.'

'Christ, I hope I don't look like her.'

'Not in the least, my love.' And with a slow happy smile, Kate forgot about her son and stretched out her arms to her lover again. It was almost four o'clock in the morning when they stopped making love, and Kate lit a cigarette with a contented sigh. She glanced over at her alarm clock and winced.

'You're going to be so tired tomorrow.'

'What about you? Can you go back to bed after Tygue goes to school?' He looked worried about her. She did a lot in a day too. He could always sleep when he got back to L.A. Except on rare occasions, he didn't have to be at the studio until three. Most of the show's procedures were pretty well set, so he rarely left his house before two, except when he had a date for lunch.

Kate sighed in answer to his question about going back to bed. 'No. I'm going up to Carmel tomorrow.'

'To teach?'

She nodded. But she hated lying to him.

'Could I go with you sometime? I'd like to see what you do.'

But she looked away and stubbed out the last of the cigarette before answering. He couldn't see her face, and when he could, he wasn't sure what he saw. Distance more than anything else. It surprised him. And he saw something hidden in her eyes, which bothered him more.

'They don't let me bring anyone with me. It's kind of a difficult place.'

'Do you like it?' He was searching for something as he looked at her, but he wasn't sure what.

She closed her eyes. 'As those places go, yes.' Oh God, she wanted to get off this subject, but she had to sound convincing. She had to make it sound like a *job*. She couldn't tell him about Tom. Not yet. Not even Nick.

'Can't you do something like that closer to home?' She shook her head. He almost hated to ask any more questions, and besides, they were both tired. He had other things on his mind, too. He ran a hand softly up her leg, and she looked at him in surprise. She was glad he wasn't pushing the subject of what she did in Carmel. The hand on the inside of her thigh travelled up and she smiled and reached out for him.

'Again?'

'Is that a complaint?' He was smiling softly too. Something happened between their bodies that had never happened to him with anybody else, not quite like that. It was a kind of ecstasy neither of them had ever known. And when the alarm rang at six neither of them regretted their night without sleep.

CHAPTER XXII

'Did you teach today?' He looked at her carefully as he sat down in a chair by the fire. He had just come in, and with a smile at Kate he loosened his tie. She looked almost as tired as he did.

'Yeah, I taught.' There was a moment's pause. 'How was the show?' It had been a hard day with Tom too. He had a cold and sore throat and twice he had cried.

'The show was a killer.' He named three of Hollywood's top stars, two of them female and known to be at war with each other. But he didn't want to talk about the show. He wanted to talk about the one thing she wasn't telling him. And he wanted to know why. Something had continued to bother him for weeks. Discrepancies, little threads. Something. It had gnawed at him on the drive back to L.A. that morning. It had been gnawing at him ever since he met her. Just tiny, tiny pieces of the puzzle that were always left out. Things she didn't say, years she didn't talk about. And some of the things she did talk about had bothered him too. The way her parents had abandoned her, her distrust of 'fate', her years alone with Tygue, and the 'teaching job' where she couldn't bring anyone along. As he sat over his third cup of coffee on his terrace in L.A., he had felt a sudden urgency about knowing the answers, and he had plenty of sources for the answers he wanted. Maybe yet another night without sleep was giving him crazy ideas, but what the hell, he had nothing to lose by looking for an explanation, and she didn't have to know. He wasn't even sure what he was looking for, but he knew there was something. And his first question had to do with her name and the book. That was the first coincidence that didn't sit right. She knew too much about football, about ... the answers had come back over a period of days and had finally tied into one solid story one afternoon, just before five o'clock as he sat in his office at the studio. The answer didn't surprise him at all. The man at the studio research office was his friend, and Nick had already told him that the inquiry was highly confidential and entirely personal. He wasn't worried about a leak. But he hated what he heard. For her sake.

'I found out just about all I can on the girl you had me check out. But first, let me tell you what else I found.

'Funnily enough, I didn't even remember the guy until we came across the clips from the show. I called the papers and the newsroom archives at the network after that. Tom Harper, he was a big football star about ten years back. We had him on the show three or four times, when Jasper still worked out of New York. Before your time, Nick. Anyway, he was a nice guy, I think. America's number one hero. I don't know why the name didn't click when you asked me this morning. He was a pro hero for eight or nine years until his career started to slide. I don't remember the details but he started getting into trouble, his career was on the rocks, he was getting too old for pro football. Did some crazy thing like try to shoot the team owner, or manager or something, and wiped himself out instead.'

'Killed himself?' But now Nick was remembering the story too. He had even met Harper once or twice when he himself was starting out in pro football. How quickly they had all forgotten. Six, seven, maybe eight years before, it had been big news, and now it took a research office to jolt the name back into mind. Kate would have been pleased to know that.

'I don't think he died, not right off, anyway. I couldn't get you all the details on that, but originally he was only critically wounded, paralyzed, something like that. Eventually they moved him down to some fancy sanatorium in Carmel, and I guess everyone forgot him after that. No one seems to know if he's still alive or not, and I couldn't find out the name of the sanatorium or I'd have called. But that's about all we got on him. One of the newsroom guys had a story that explained that Harper was paralyzed from the waist down, and permanently impaired mentally when they moved him to Carmel, but that's about it on Harper. As for the girl, she was his wife. There's not much on her. Some footage of her coming and going from the hospital. They sent it over here and it made me sick to watch it. She has that godawful look of people living in a nightmare, and there was another clip of when they were unloading him into the ambulance for the trip to Carmel. He looks like he doesn't know what's happening, kind of childlike and dumb. There's absolutely nothing on either of them after that. I got a little background on her, but damn little. She went to Stanford for a few months, went to live with Harper after her first year there, travelled everywhere with him, but stayed pretty much out of the limelight. She was a model or something for a while. Kind of a pretty girl, then at least, but that was quite a while ago. And the only bit of scandal about her was that apparently her parents disowned her or something for marrying him. They were your basic staunch upper-middle-class snobs, who couldn't stand the idea of their princess marrying a jock or something. Anyway they cut her off.

'That's all I know, Nick. What happened to him, if he's still alive, or what happened to her, I couldn't tell you. There's just no press record on any of that. If you can find the name of that sanatorium in Carmel they'll probably be able to tell you if he died, but the name of the place may have been kept out of the press. I don't know. Want me to work on that?'

'No, I can do that myself. And listen, thanks a million. You got me everything I wanted to know.' And more. He knew everything now. The rest he could figure out for himself. Obviously, Tom was alive, and still in Carmel. That was the mysterious 'school' she went to. It had happened seven years before. And Tygue ... Tygue was six. Kate must have been pregnant when Tom Harper shot himself. What an incredibly long time for Kate to live the way she had. He felt subdued for the rest of the evening as he mused over what he'd heard, and thought about her. He wanted to talk to her about it, to air it out, to hold her in his arms and let her cry if she still needed to after all these years. But he knew he couldn't say a word. Not until she did. He wondered how long it would take.

He looked at her now as she sat across from him, watching

222

him, and he looked at the circles under her eyes. She was pay-
a price, too, for their happiness and her double life.

'How did it go in Carmel, Kate? Difficult today?' He hated
that look of pain in her eyes. It told him the rest of the story,
the part the research office didn't know. He wondered just
how bad off Tom Harper still was. He had gathered from the
research material that the mental damage had been irreparable.
That had to be an incredible strain. But he still couldn't
imagine what it was really like, dealing with someone like that
on a regular basis. Someone you had loved.

'Yeah, it was difficult today.' She smiled and tried to shrug
it off, but he wasn't letting her. Not just yet.

'Are they very demanding?' He was asking her about Tom,
not about 'them', but he hoped she'd tell him the truth anyway. Some kind of truth at least.

'Sometimes. People like that can be very sweet, and very
childlike, or very difficult, like children too in that respect.
Anyway, never mind that, tell me about the show.' The subject
was definitely closed. He saw it in her face.

'The people on the show can be "very sweet and very childlike" too, or total shits and equally childlike. Maybe most
actors and celebrities are retarded too.' He smiled at her and
sighed.

'Did you get the house for this weekend, by the way?' She
was happily unbuttoning his shirt and he nodded.

'Yes. And you know, I was thinking. How about if all three
of us stayed there this time?'

She thought about it for a long moment and then looked
up at him. 'Why not here?'

He shook his head carefully. 'Not yet. This is Tygue's turf.
I don't want to crowd him.' He thought of everything, and he
cared about everything. Just as she cared about him. Enough
to worry about the way he looked. Exhausted.

'Nick?'

'What, love?' He lay back against the couch, his eyes closed,
holding her hand. He was trying not to feel hurt that she
wouldn't tell him about Tom. But he knew he'd just have to
wait until she was ready.

'What are we going to do?'

'About what?' But he knew. He was wondering the same thing. Neither of them had had a full night of sleep in three weeks.

'You can't go on running around like this forever.'

'Are you telling me I'm over the hill?' He opened an eye and she grinned.

'No. I'm telling you I am. And if it's killing me, I can imagine what it's doing to you. I'm not driving to Los Angeles every day.'

'Never mind. Why don't we just ride out the summer? And then we'll see.'

'But then what?' She had worried about it all the way back from Carmel. The drive gave her an idea of what Nick was doing every morning and every night. The distance was the same. 'What the hell are we going to do after the summer?'

'I could buy a plane. A helicopter maybe.' He was only half teasing and she kissed him softly on the cheek. It was all her fault too. But there was Tygue, and she couldn't just ... 'Hang in there, darling. And then we'll see. I'm waiting to find out what Jasper wants to do about the show. That might change everything. And he has to make up his mind in the next two weeks.'

'What do you mean, it'll change everything?' She looked even more worried.

'Never mind. Now stop worrying about it, Kate. And that's an order.'

'But ...'

'Shh!' He pressed his mouth against hers, and met every objection with a kiss until at last she was laughing, and they fell into bed. But tonight they didn't even make love. They just slept, wrapped around each other, exhausted. And Nick was already gone when Kate woke up the next morning.

'Where'd you get this?' Tygue picked up a huge white tee-shirt and held it in the air with a look of suspicion, as his mother covered herself with the sheet. This was the first time Tygue had appeared in her bedroom before she'd wakened to put on a nightgown, and she felt oddly defensive. And they had been so tired that Nick had forgotten his undershirt under the bed.

'I used that yesterday to do some gardening in.'

. 'It smells like Nick.' He eyed her fiercely. Jealousy was beginning to set in. Nick had been right. The initial glow had been too good to be true, or to last.

'Nick gave it to me. What do you want for breakfast, cereal or eggs?' And why was she making explanations to him, dammit? She had a right to have anyone's undershirt under her bed. Jesus.

'I want French toast or pancakes.' He said it in a tone of argumentative accusation.

'That's not on the menu.' She looked at him sternly.

'Oh all right. Eggs. When's Nick coming up to see Brownie again?' The funny thing was that he sounded anxious to see Nick, and yet angry too, and as though he was looking for a fight with his mother.

'He said he'd be up this weekend. In fact' – she held her breath – 'he invited us both to stay at his house in Santa Barbara. How does that sound?'

'Okay. Maybe. You coming too?'

'Sure. Any objection?'

'Nick doesn't like to talk about horses when you're around. When we're alone he talks about better stuff.'

'Well, maybe you two could go off to the stables alone, or for a walk on the beach or something. How about that?'

'Okay.' There was the first glimmer of a smile. 'Can I bring Joey?' She hadn't even thought of it, but it wasn't a bad idea. It would keep him busy, and give her and Nick more time alone.

'I'll ask, but I suspect Nick will say yes.' Nick said yes to everything Tygue wanted. Sometimes that bugged her. He had kept his promise about not spoiling Tygue too much, but still he indulged the boy, and it irritated her. It made it harder for her to control Tygue. It made Nick look like the good guy, and made her look like a louse when she disciplined him. Besides, it was new to her to have someone else become the source of special treats for Tygue. Tygue had looked to her for everything for so long that it was a little hard to share the

225

glory. She didn't like to admit it, but she knew it was true. There had been Felicia of course, but Felicia's trips were a rare event, Nick was becoming part of every day, and with familiarity came a certain assumption of authority that was also a little hard to take. Tygue wasn't the only one with some adjusting to do. Kate had some new things in her life to accept too, but the lessons were worth learning, for Nick.

'Don't forget to ask Nick about Joey.' Tygue muttered the reminder over his shoulder as he left the room.

'I won't. Now go get dressed for school.' He vanished into his room and she scooped the large white undershirt into a drawer, but she sniffed it first. It smelled just like him, lemons and spice. Just holding the shirt made her want him.

But that morning, he didn't call. Stu Weinberg did.

'I have a surprise for you, Kate.' He sounded immensely pleased with himself.

'Good or bad?'

'I only have good surprises.' He tried to sound insulted but couldn't.

'Okay, tell me.'

'Well, m'dear, we have just been asked to invite you to spend eight days at the Regency Hotel in New York, three days in Washington, two days in Boston, and a day in Chicago on the way back. It's a tour for your book, and you're on the best possible shows in all four cities. You're being offered first-class accommodations everywhere, and strictly four-star treatment. Miss Harper, you've made it.'

'Oh God.' Another mountain to climb. And she was so happy at the plateau she had just reached. Why did she have to move up now? 'Do I have to?'

'Are you kidding?' He sounded horrified. 'Look, Kate, to put it bluntly, do you want a best seller or a bomb? Baby, if you like your royalties, you have to do some of this too.'

'In other words, sing for my supper.' She didn't sound pleased. 'How many days does that make altogether?'

'Exactly two weeks. Now that's not so bad, is it?'

She sighed deeply. 'I guess not. Can I let you know though? I have to see if I can get someone to stay with Tygue.'

'Sure, love. That's fine. I'll call you back later.'

'How soon would I have to go?'

'Monday.' He didn't even apologize.

'In four days?' It was already Thursday.

'He didn't give me much notice for chrissake.' And then he stopped. Dammit.

'Who didn't?'

'The guy in the publicity department at your publisher.'

'Oh. Well, I'll call you later.' She wanted to call Nick, and at his end, Stu let out his breath softly. Jesus. He'd almost blown it. And he had promised Nick he wouldn't. It must have been going great guns for Nick to call and make a request like that. Why couldn't he just ask her himself? But Stu knew why. If Nick had asked her, she wouldn't have gone. This just might get her going.

She got Nick at his apartment, and he sounded sleepy. 'Did I wake you up?'

'No, just daydreaming. What's up, love?' She could hear him yawn, and imagined him stretching.

'You forgot your undershirt.'

'No place outrageous, I hope.' He smiled to himself as he remembered how she had looked that morning sound asleep when he left.

'It was under the bed. Tygue found it.'

'Oops. Any problems?'

'Not with Tygue.'

And then he noticed that she sounded worried. He sat up in bed with a frown.

'Stu just called me.' The frown deepened. And he waited.

'He has a two-week tour for me. New York, Boston, D.C., and Chicago. Eight days of it in New York. Oh Jesus, Nick, I don't know what to do. I'm scared to death.' She sounded near tears, and he wondered if he'd done the right thing. Maybe he had no right to meddle.

'Don't get excited, darling. We'll talk about it. What's he booked you on?'

'I don't know. I forgot to ask. And it's for Monday. And . . . oh Nick, what'll I do?'

227

'I have an idea.' He forced his voice to sound cheery as he closed his eyes, feeling as if he were pushing her off a cliff.

'What?'

'Why don't you go on the show with Jasper again?'

'I can't for chrissake. I just told you. Stu wants me to go to New York.' She sounded nervous and exasperated.

'That's where Jasper is doing the show for the next two weeks.' And then he opened his eyes wide and waited for a moment. There was no sound. 'Would you go to New York with me, Kate? I know it's hard for you, darling, but I'll be there, I promise. I'll be right there with you.'

'Did you tell Stu to do this?' She sounded incredulous.

'I . . .' Crap. He had blown it. But there was no point lying to her. He would swear never to meddle again. 'I did. I'm sorry. I shouldn't have, I . . .' But suddenly she was laughing. 'Kate?'

'You jerk. You did that? I thought it was for real. I thought my publisher had a tour for me that I had to do, or *else*. I thought . . .'

'He does. Only they didn't line it up until I told Stu I thought you'd do it. You can fly in and out of Boston and D.C., and keep on staying with me in New York.'

'What about Chicago?' She was still laughing. Thank God.

'Did they do that too?' Nick sounded amazed.

'Oh yes.'

'Zealous, aren't they?'

'You know something? You're crazy, that's what you are. Totally crazy. Did you know about all this when you got home last night?' Her house was home now to both of them.

'Okay, I confess.'

'How long have you known?'

'Since Monday. Jasper sprang it on us.'

'Terrific.'

'So what are you going to do now?' He was more than a little curious. 'I mean, other than give me a black eye when I come home tonight.'

'Are you sure you want me to tell you over the phone?' The voice was pure Mata Hari, and he started laughing too.

'Never mind that. Will you go with me?'

'Do I have a choice?'

He waited for a long moment, wondering what he should say, but he decided to take a chance. 'No. You don't have a choice. I need you too much. Get Tillie to stay with Tygue, and we'll buy out F.A.O. Shwarz for him.'

'He accepted your invitation for the weekend, by the way, and he wants to bring Joey.'

'Wonderful. I don't care if he brings King Kong. I want to know if you're coming to New York with me.'

'Yes, dammit, yes! Okay? Are you happy?'

'Very!' They were both smiling.

'Do I still have to do all that publicity bullshit?'

'Of course.' Nick sounded shocked. 'And I meant what I said. I'll put you back on the show with Jasper.'

'Do I gotta?' She was lying in bed grinning at the phone.

'Yes. You gotta.'

'Hey, Nick?'

'What, sweetheart?' The voice was suddenly soft in answer to hers.

'Any chance you could come home?'

'You mean now?'

'Uh huh.'

He had a mountain of work to do, a thousand things to arrange . . . and a woman he adored.

'I'll be there.'

And he was.

CHAPTER XXIII

'Kate?'

'Mm?' She was asleep next to him on the plane. It had been a hectic few days. She had insisted on 'teaching' on Friday, but the trip to Carmel had given her a chance to shop. They had all spent the weekend at the house in Santa Barbara, Joey included, and on Sunday night Nick had driven her down to L.A. with him, so that they could leave together Monday morning. This was the first time he hadn't flown with Jasper. He wanted to be alone with her. A glance at his watch told him they would land in New York in an hour. He kissed her softly on the top of her head and folded her hand into his.

'Miss Harper, I love you.' He said it more to himself than to her but she surprised him by opening one eye, and looking up with a yawn that crept into a smile.

'I love you too. What time is it?'

'Two o'clock our time. It's five o'clock there. We'll get in at six.'

'And then what?' She hadn't even thought to ask him. She stretched her long legs out ahead of her and looked down at the now familiar cream-coloured suit. She was getting more wear out of it than she'd ever expected to when she'd bought it. 'Oh my God.'

'What?'

She was looking up at him with horror in the big green eyes he loved.

'Is it Tygue? Did you forget something?'

'No. Licia. I forgot to tell her I was going. If she calls and Tillie tells her I've gone to New York, she'll have a stroke.'

'Will she disapprove?' He was curious to meet this character who was the only important person in Kate's life besides Tygue. Maybe she'd hate him, be jealous of his role in Kate's life. He looked at Kate curiously.

'Licia? Disapprove?' Kate snuggled in next to him with a soft laugh. 'She'd give you the Legion of Honour for dragging me out of my cave.'

'Have you told her about me yet?'

Kate shook her head slowly. She hadn't. And she wasn't sure why. Maybe because she was afraid the magic would all fade away and telling Licia would make it that much harder to live with the loss when he was gone. 'No. Not yet.'

'I'd like to meet her. She sounds like a character. Would I like her?'

'I think so.' And what if he didn't? She loved Felicia, always would. But she already felt herself slipping into Nick's world. Nick had a special place in her life now.

He looked down and saw the serious look in her eyes, and he held her close. 'You look so pensive sometimes, love. One day you won't look like that anymore.' When she looked like that, he knew she was thinking about Tom.

'Like what?'

'Like your only friend in the world is about to walk out.'

'Are you sure he won't?'

'Positive.'

She could feel it in his arms, and she felt peaceful as she closed her eyes. She was so happy with him. But it couldn't last forever. Nothing did. No matter what he said. Tom had made those promises too. But she hadn't had the same worries then. She hadn't realized how quickly things come to an end.

'Scared about New York?' He forced her mind back to the present, as he tilted her face up to his. He was smiling at her again, and she smiled back.

'Sometimes. Once in a while I panic and want to hide in the ladies' room, and then I forget all about it and get curious. It's been so long, I hardly remember it.'

'Good. I want to give it to you brand new.' He looked pleased. They were going to stay at the Regency, only three blocks from Jasper's hotel. Jasper was addicted to the Pierre. But Nick wanted to stay somewhere else, so Kate wouldn't feel awkward. 'I ordered separate rooms for us, by the way.'

'You did?' She looked disappointed, and he laughed.

'Don't look like that, you dummy. They're adjoining, and we can use one of them as an office. I just thought it would look better in case some nosy reporter gets wind that you're staying with me. This way, you're just staying at the same hotel. A cosy coincidence.' She looked pleased again.

'How did you manage to think of all that? Glass slippers, separate rooms to protect my lily-pure reputation – is there anything you don't think of?'

'That's why I've managed to stay the producer of Jasper's show all these years, my love. It's all part of the job.' But she knew it was part of the man. They exchanged another smile and looked out over the city. It was still bright daylight outside, and would be for several hours, but already there was the softened hue of late afternoon. 'It's going to be hotter than hell, by the way. Did you bring lots of naked clothes?' She laughed as she accepted the glass of champagne he was handing her from a passing tray. First class was delightful. Champagne coast to coast.

'I did what I could. I didn't have a lot of time to shop.' And Carmel was not San Francisco. But she hadn't done badly. And when they got off the plane in New York she understood what Nick meant about the heat. She had never been to the city in mid-summer, and it was blistering, even at six o'clock.

Nick had arranged for them to be met by the airline's special customer service cart, and they were whisked right to the door of the terminal. Their bags would be separated from the others and brought out to the car. And the little golf cart whizzed through the terminal, ploughing through countless bodies. Everyone looked hot and tired and grey, not brown and healthy the way they did in California. It had been a long time since Kate had seen people looking like this, and so many of them. She felt breathless as they launched through the crowds in the ice-cold terminal. The air conditioning was blasting full force on the hot, tired, sweaty crowds.

'It's a wonder they don't all die of pneumonia.' She held tightly to his hand as she watched them from the cart. It was all so busy and so loud. It was terrifying and fascinating at the same time. Like visiting another planet.

'It's a wonder they don't all die from lack of air, you mean. Have you ever seen so many people?'

She shook her head as he watched her. He had made all the arrangements very carefully, so she wouldn't be overwhelmed right from the first. They were already at the terminal door, and the driver was waiting for them at the kerb.

They were shoved through the revolving door by the force of the crowds, and Kate found herself pushed outside, into what felt like a vacuum. It was white-hot and humid, without so much as a breath of air.

'My God.' It was like being punched in the stomach by an elephant.

'Lovely, isn't it?' He grinned as she rolled her eyes, but the driver was already holding open the door of the air-conditioned car, and Nick was urging her gently inside. It was all wonderfully quick and efficient. And five minutes later, the driver had their bags, and they were on their way to the city. She looked back over her shoulder through the smoky glass of the limousine and she could still see the people in line for cabs. There was a short fat cab driver waving a cigar in another man's face, and as they sped away she started to laugh.

'Isn't it crazy?'

'It's like the circus.' She didn't remember the city as quite so intense. Everything had seemed more sedate when she had been there on Easter vacation with her parents when she was seventeen. They had stayed at the Plaza and had tea in the Palm Court and at a place called Rose-Marie. That all seemed a thousand years ago. And Tom had never let her go to New New York with him. He hated it, and usually stayed outside the city with friends. Now she could see why. This wasn't Tom's scene. And it wasn't really Nick's. But he handled it perfectly. He had shielded her from everything unpleasant, even the heat.

She watched the constant fury of the traffic on their way to the hotel. Even on Park Avenue, the cars moved along as though they were angry. Jerk, bump, stop, screech, honk, shout, and jerk on again. The noise was deafening even in the carefully sealed car.

'How do they stand it?'

233

'I don't know. Either they don't notice it, or they love it.'

But the crazy thing was that she loved it too. She loved the aliveness of it. The frenzy and the sparkle, the crackle of electricity as everything moved at breakneck speed. She suddenly wanted to get out of the womblike car and walk. But she was afraid that if she told Nick, he would think she was crazy. And ungrateful. He had gone to such lengths to protect her from her fears. And yet, there she sat, dying to push and shove along with the rest of them.

They had arrived at the Regency, and the driver helped her into the doorman's hands, from whose protective grasp Nick took her and led her quickly inside. They knew him there. He signed the registration card and they were instantly led to their rooms. Hers was a suite, his a large double room with a door that adjoined her living room. They decided to use his as the office, and hers as their 'house'. The bags were stacked on elaborate little gold and white stands, and Kate looked around as her feet sank into the thick carpet, and then with a sigh she settled onto the rose-coloured silk couch. Everything was very subtle and very lovely. It looked like an English watercolour painting. And they had a beautiful view of the city facing south. She looked around the room again and then at Nick with a smile and a sigh. She felt like the poor little rich girl, shielded from everything that was fun, like dirt and noise and all the crazy people she was dying to gape at, and run along on the sidewalk with. Nick meant well by shielding her from it all, but she felt as if he were keeping her from the fun. Maybe it was nuts to feel that way. But she did. Suddenly she wanted to break loose from her shell, and even from Nick . . . from the past . . . from Tom . . . from Tygue . . . from all of them. She wanted to be free.

'Want a drink?' He loosened his tie, and smiled down at her. He had already made reservations for them at Caravelle. He had had his secretary do that from Los Angeles that morning. The reservations were for nine. He didn't think they'd be hungry until then. That would give them time to have a drink and relax, maybe have another drink in the bar of the hotel, and go off to a quiet dinner. But Kate only shook her head at the offer for the drink. 'What's up, Cinderella? You look like those wheels are turning a mile a minute. Want to call Licia now?'

'No.' And she didn't really want to call Tygue either. Not yet.

'Then what would you like to do?' He sat down next to her on the delicate couch and put his arms around her as she started to laugh. And he loved the fire he saw in her eyes. New York was doing good things to her. Already. It was as though she were coming to life in a way he had never seen before. 'Name your pleasure, milady, and it's yours.'

'You mean it?'

'Of course I mean it.'

'Okay. I want to go for a walk.'

'Now?' He looked stunned. At seven o'clock, it was still ninety-five, and the humidity was close to the same figure. 'In this heat?' She nodded excitedly and he threw back his head and laughed. He understood. Kate, who had hidden for years, almost since she was a girl, was suddenly young again and hungry for life. 'Okay, Cinderella, you're on. Do you want to change first?' She shook her head with a grin and looked just like her son. 'In that case' – he held out an arm and she slipped a hand through it as they both stood up – 'we're off.'

And it was just what she wanted. They wandered up Madison Avenue as she looked into all the shops, and then over to Central Park, where people were still playing games on the grass. Balls were being thrown, radios were blaring, buses zoomed by, and hansom cabs clopped along behind tired, flower-bedecked horses. It was as though someone had assembled every possible moving part, every face, every car, every smell, every colour, and jammed them all into one town and called it New York. 'God, I love it.' She took a deep breath of the polluted air and sighed with delight as Nick laughed.

'I think I've created a monster.' But he loved seeing her like that. She was so alive. It was what she should have had for years. Fire, and excitement and success. He was glad he could share them with her now. He looked at his watch. It was already after eight, and they were nearing Sixty-first Street and Fifth. It was only two blocks to the hotel. But they had walked at least twenty, drinking everything in – Kate watching the city with passion, and he watching her with delight. 'Ready to go back and get dressed?'

'Where are we going?'

'To the best restaurant in town. All for you, Cinderella.' He swept a wide arm towards the skyline, and she beamed. She smiled all the way back to the hotel, and when he closed the door to their room, she advanced on him with a purposeful gleam in her eye.

'Does this mean what I think it means?' He was grinning at her from the bathroom door, and she suddenly reached over and unzipped his pants.

'It certainly does.'

'Lady, I don't know what this town does to you, but I love it.'

They didn't even make it to the bedroom, but made love on the richly carpeted floor of their room, as her tongue and delicate hands brought soft moans from Nick. This time it was Kate who took the lead, and Nick who lay back spent when they had both come. Kate lay on the floor, in the twilight, smiling victoriously at her life.

CHAPTER XXIV

'Miss Harper?' The woman in the expensive black dress and the Cinandre-sculptured hair walked into the room and extended a hand. Kate shook it nervously, and smoothed her dress. 'You'll be on in a minute.' It was her first television appearance in New York, and she was terrified. But prepared. She had gone over what she would say with Nick that morning. And the dress was a new one she'd bought in Carmel. It was a warm coral linen that set off her deep tan. She wore it with some of the coral jewellery Felicia had brought her from Europe the year before, despite her protests. Now she was glad Felicia had insisted she keep it. 'You never know.' Kate remembered the words with a smile. Her hair was pulled back. She hoped she looked like a writer. At least she felt like one.

'I've been admiring the view.' It was breathtaking. They were in the southwest corner of the thirty-something floor of the General Motors Building, with a sweeping view of Central Park if you looked uptown and an unbroken panorama of Wall Street downtown. 'It must be fabulous living in this town.'

The woman in the black dress laughed, shaking the well-coifed hair and flashing a large emerald ring. 'I'd give my right arm to live on the Coast. But Audrey does the show here, so . . .' She threw up her hands. This woman was the biggest female producer in daytime television, and her job was not unlike Nick's. Now Kate better understood what it entailed.

'Ready?'

'I think so.'

She held open a door and Kate walked through it. The door to the studio showed a brightly lit sign: 'On the Air.'

She was on for almost an hour, with three other prominent women, a representative from the United Nations, a nationally known lawyer, and a woman who had won the Nobel Prize in biochemistry the year before. Good God. She felt breathless as she looked at them. What was she doing there? But as they looked at her, she realized they were wondering the same thing. She was an unknown.

'How does it feel to write your first best seller?' Audrey Bradford, the host of the show, smiled at Kate, and the other women looked interested but hardly overwhelmed.

'It hasn't quite gotten there yet, but I must admit so far it feels awfully good.' She laughed and Audrey smiled with her. This was the biggest high in the world. The ego trip of the century. Success. Public success. On national television. But still she could feel an undercurrent from the other guests. Envy? Suspicion?

'Our research shows that you're in your third printing and have sold fifty thousand copies in five weeks. I'd say that's a best seller, wouldn't you? In fact, it's starting to show up on the national charts.' It is? It had? ... It was? Why hadn't anyone told her? Jesus. Fifty thousand copies? She almost gasped, but instead she smiled.

'In that case, I concede.' After a few minutes of nervousness, Kate was surprised at how easy the show became. The other women were fascinating, and Audrey was good at what she did. She turned a potentially chilly situation into a cordial one. And Kate was still riding high when she met Nick at Lutèce for lunch, and swooped down on him at his table in the little garden.

'Hi, darling. God, it was scary.' And then, all in one breath, she heard herself telling him how tense she had been, how terrifyingly successful the other women had been, how impressive Audrey Bradford was, how well put together the woman producer was, how ...

'Hey, hey, wait a minute. Slow down there, lady, or you'll pop your girdle. Relax.' He was amused at her excitement. She was suddenly as hyper as everyone else in New York.

She sat down with a sheepish grin and took a breath. 'I don't wear a girdle, by the way.'

'Thank God. Now, did you make sense on the show?'

'Didn't you watch me?' She looked stunned.

'My darling, you are about to discover what my life is like in New York. I sat down peacefully in Jasper's suite to watch you there, and all three phones started to ring at once. He's had two extra lines put into the suite for his stay. The secretary he brought with him ran in with a major crisis on her hands. Our big name for the first show here is in the hospital with a stroke, it'll be front page by tonight. The additional secretary he hired here walked in and quit. Jasper's oldest boy called from London, had run over some kid with his car and was in jail. And meanwhile, I had calls in to nine different people to try and make a substitution for tonight's show. No, my love. I did not see your show. But I'm sure you were splendid.' He looked at her with a grin and she tried to hide her disappointment. Sometimes she forgot how much he had to do. 'By the way, Jasper was thinking that you might like to come back on the show. Maybe at the end of the week?'

'Already? He just had me on.'

'That's all right. You're getting to be a hot property these days, with the book doing as well as it is, and with the daytime exposure you're getting, the women in his audience will like seeing you on our show.' For a moment, he wasn't even Nick. He was a producer, a stranger, a nervous man with the nation's most important talk show to run. He hadn't even had time to watch her on her first New York show. 'I'll have Stu talk to your publisher about putting you on. Jasper definitely wants you.' He pulled out a little book, jotted something down, and then looked up, surprised, as the headwaiter brought him a phone.

'Call for you, Mr. Waterman.' What followed were ten minutes of unintelligible conversation with someone on his production staff as Kate looked around at the other tables nearby. She was having lunch at one of the most expensive restaurants in New York, surrounded by the illustrious and the powerful. Nick signalled to the waiter and pointed at his watch midway through the conversation. The waiter nodded and hurried back with a menu for Kate. It was another five minutes before he was off the phone.

'I'm sorry, love. Some days are just like this, I'm afraid.'

239

More than he let on to her in fact. She never realized just how busy he was. But she was getting a ringside view of it in New York. He looked at his watch again. 'Damn.'

'Something wrong?'

'No. Except that I'm going to have to leave you in about twenty minutes. I've got about thirty-seven things to discuss with Jasper before tonight.'

'Lucky man, sounds like he's going to be seeing more of you than I am.' She was almost miffed, but not quite. She didn't have a right to be too demanding; they were both here to work not just play.

'I'm sorry I missed your show, Kate. I really am. Next time I'll watch, no matter what. I promise. If I have to bolt all the doors and take the phones off the hook.'

'Okay, then I forgive you.' They kissed just as the Louis Roederer arrived. It was an exquisite champagne, 1955.

They had caviar on paper-thin slices of white toast, quenelles Nantua, endive salad, fresh raspberries and whipped cream, and knocked off the whole bottle of champagne in less than half an hour. The result was that Kate sat back against the banquette, looking slightly drunk.

'You know . . .' She looked at Nick philosophically and he smiled as he signed for the check. Thank God for expense accounts. 'You know,' she started again, 'sometimes it's hard to remember that all of this fun can lead to disaster.'

'Now what's that supposed to mean?' He looked at her and was about to laugh, and then suddenly he remembered Tom. 'Only if you let it go to your head, Kate. There are ways of having the success without the insanity.'

'Are you sure?' She looked worried. She hadn't forgotten what all of this had done to Tom – and to her.

'I've seen people handle it well. You just can't lose your perspective. You can't let yourself forget what *you* really care about. And maybe you have to know too that it's nice while it lasts, but it's not everything. You're lucky, Kate. You have something real to go home to. You have Tygue, the house . . .'

'You forgot something.' She was looking very subdued.

'What did I forget?'

'You forgot that I have you to come home to, Mr. Waterman. There's that too.'

'Yes, there is. And don't *you* forget it either, Mrs. Harper.'

And she didn't. She thought about it at great length as she walked back to the hotel, still feeling the effects of the champagne. It was so easy to be intoxicated by one's own self-importance, by expensive meals in lavish restaurants, by adulation and attention and acclaim. She had to admit she was enjoying it, but it frightened her too. Suddenly, for the first time, she understood all that had tempted Tom. And especially Tom, because his life had been so simple before all that. It was impossible for him to resist all the glitter that came along. But was she much different now? Was she making more sense? She wasn't sure.

She went back to the hotel to sleep off the wine, and was awakened by the hotel operator at four. She had left a wake-up message just in case she overslept. She had to be at a radio station on the West Side at six. And this time, the taping was horrendous. The interviewer asked her all the wrong questions, and prodded interminably about how a woman knew so much about football; he was a pushy, aggressive sexist, and she hated every minute of the interview, but she told herself that the exposure would be good for the book. Her publisher had also promised her a car and driver to take her back to the hotel, but they never arrived after the show, and she found herself walking down some of the more dangerous streets of Manhattan, praying for a cab. It was nine by the time she got to the studio to meet Nick. He had had a hectic evening, and problems for the next day's show had already begun to crop up. It was ten-thirty before they got out for something to eat, and then, hot and bedraggled, they wound up at La Grenouille, where even the elegant fare no longer appealed to her. She was hot and tired and she wanted to go to bed. Instead a photographer from *Women's Wear Daily* snapped her photograph on the way out, and she found herself almost snarling as the flash bulb went off in her face.

'Now, now, take it easy, Kate. It's all in a day's work.' She sighed briefly and then smiled at him.

'I don't know. I'm beginning to think that running after Tygue and Bert wasn't so bad.'

'I told you so, madam.'

They strolled up Fifth Avenue arm in arm, and Kate was exhausted when they fell into bed at one o'clock. She was almost as tired when she woke up the next day, and when he handed her a copy of *Women's Wear* her face puckered into an immediate frown. There was a photograph of them leaving the restaurant the night before, mention of who they were, mention of the book, and a catty remark about her dress.

'Christ, it was a hundred and four degrees and I'd been running my ass off all night. What do they want from me anyway?'

Nick laughed and shrugged as he sipped his coffee. 'This is the big time, baby. In New York, they don't pull any punches.'

'Well, they can go to hell. And I don't like being in the papers.' She looked decidedly nervous as she lit a cigarette. It was a lousy way to start the day.

'How do you know? Have you ever tried it?' She only stared at him, saying nothing. 'What's the matter, baby?' He sat down quietly on the bed and took her hand. 'It's just a little blurb in the paper. It's no big deal.'

'I just hate that kind of thing. It's none of their goddamn business.'

'But they're interested in you. You're new, you're intelligent, you're beautiful. Your book is a smash. This is all part of it.'

'I hate it.' She looked at Nick again and her eyes filled with tears. It was all going to start again. They were going to spoil everything. She wanted to go home.

'Hey ... come on, love ... it's nothing.' He folded her into his arms, and then looked down at her. 'And if it bothers you that much to be in the papers, we'll be more careful. We'll go someplace quiet for lunch.' He wrote down the name of a French restaurant on Fifty-third Street, where they wouldn't be noticed, gave her a last kiss, and left for a meeting with Jasper. But when they met for lunch, there was still a thread of fear woven into the tapestry of excitement. She found herself looking around warily, and Nick watched her closely.

'What's up?'

'Nothing.'

'Worrying about the *paparazzi* again?'

'Yeah. Sort of.'

'Well, don't. None of them would be seen dead here. And as far as *Women's Wear* is concerned, anyone who eats here isn't worth mentioning.'

'Good.' She looked relieved and took his hand. 'I just hate that stuff.'

'Why?' Why wouldn't she tell him? Didn't she trust him yet? Even now?

'It's such a violation. It's like rape. They tear your clothes off, stare at your body, and take what they want.' She looked mournful, and he laughed and leaned closer.

'Can I be first?'

'Oh shut up.'

'Well, stop worrying about it. It's all part of the package. We all get used to it. I've been called everything from a male nymphomaniac to a faggot. So what?' She grinned up at him.

'They called you that?'

'Yup. Especially the former.' But he didn't say it with pride. Anyway, that was over now. He hadn't looked at another woman since he'd met Kate. Six weeks exactly, to the day. 'Hey, today is our anniversary.'

'I know. Our sixth.' She beamed up at him and forgot the papers. To hell with them. This was all that mattered now.

They dined that night at '21' with Jasper and a well-known New York theatrical producer. And Kate watched them tape the show. It was nice getting to know Jasper better, and she didn't mind his knowing what was happening with Nick. He seemed to approve wholeheartedly and treated her like someone very special.

The next day they all met for lunch in his suite at the Pierre, and that afternoon she and Nick went shopping for Tygue at F.A.O. Schwarz.

'Want to try out the boat?'

'Now?' She laughed at him as they left the store. It was the only thing they had carried. The rest they had sent back to the hotel. All kinds of cowboy equipment, a fabulous little bike, and Kate had had to fight Nick not to buy him a boy-sized log cabin. Nick wanted to buy it all. But she didn't want him doing that and he knew it. She had wanted to buy something for Tom too, but didn't know how to do it without Nick knowing. Now he was looking down at her, holding tightly to the elaborate remote-controlled boat. Tygue was going to use it on the lake.

'Listen, there is the most fabulous model-boat pond here in Central Park. All these old guys hang around there with models of windjammers and schooners. We'll be outclassed. But it's terrific.'

And it was. They spent two hours there, chatting with old men, watching the boats, smiling at the nannies passing by with large lace-laden English prams. New York gave one the impression that everyone was either terribly rich or terribly poor, and the people in between were banished somewhere else. To New Jersey perhaps. Or the Bronx.

They walked slowly out of the park past the zoo, and Kate stopped for a moment at the pony rides. 'I wish Tygue were here. He'd love it.'

'Maybe next time.' He pulled her hand more tightly through his arm and thought of the boy, and then looked down at Kate again. 'Want a pony ride, Cinderella?'

'Are you kidding?' She burst into laughter. 'I'd break the cart. Or kill the horse.' It was designed for very small children.

'Answer the question.'

'Just what do you have in mind?'

'You'll see.' He strolled her out of the park and right to the hansom cabs lined up at Fifty-ninth Street. There, he paused for a moment, spoke to one of the top-hatted drivers, and then turned to hand her inside. 'This is a little more our speed.' It was still blazingly hot, but she was almost used to the temperature now. And it was five o'clock as they strolled lazily through the park in the musty old carriage. People looked up and smiled, children waved. It was like living a fairy tale. Nick bought them both ice creams at a red light farther into the park. It was an hour later when he had the driver deposit them at the hotel.

'I smell like the horse.' She whispered it to him with a giggle as they walked sedately past the marble desk.

'I love it.' He grinned at the smudge of ice cream on her chin. 'You're a mess.' But he could hardly wait to close the door behind them. They spent an hour in bed, and then they both had to run. He had to do Jasper's show, and she was scheduled on a rival talk show on another network.

It went very well, as did one of the two radio shows she did the next day. The second one was a bomb where no one seemed to know who she was or why she was there. And there had been nothing more in the papers. She was enjoying the trip, despite the frantic pace, and she was amazed at how quickly one adjusted to the interviews and the cameras. She was much less nervous this time when she did Jasper's show. And she let Nick help her pick out a dress, a clinging pearl-grey Halston. It was the sexiest dress she had ever seen, yet it was ladylike too. It was perfect for her. Even Jasper was a little startled when she appeared. She was a very striking-looking girl. And her appearance on the show was the climax of her trip.

'So, Mr. Waterman, what's on the agenda for today?'

'I don't know. Want to go to the beach? It might be nice to see some sand again.' It was Saturday.

'Is there any around here? I thought they didn't approve of that sort of thing.'

'Southhampton.' He lay on his side and looked at the woman he loved, just as the phone rang. 'You get it. This is your room. Remember?' He thought of everything.

'Hello?' She expected it to be Licia, or maybe Jasper for Nick. Who else would call? But it wasn't. It was Tillie. 'He is? He did? What . . . oh, my God. Is he all right?' She sat up very straight, and Nick's face puckered into a worried frown. 'Now? Why did they keep him there? Can't he come home?' The one-sided conversation was driving Nick nuts and he started asking questions, but she waved him back to silence. 'This afternoon? All right. I'll see what I can do.' She hung up with a frown, looked at Nick, and then at her lap with a sigh. 'Damn.'

'What happened, for chrissake?'

'Tygue fell off the gate at the Adams ranch and broke his

arm. Tillie said he was just swinging on it with Joey, but he fell over backward. They thought he might have a concussion, so they kept him in the hospital overnight. She said she tried to call us last night, but we weren't home, and she was afraid to leave a message and scare me half to death. Godamnit.' She got off the bed and stalked across the room.

'Poor little thing. Are they sure there's no concussion? And what kind of a hospital did Tillie take him to?' Nick looked suddenly very worried and Kate smiled.

'He's in Santa Barbara and he's fine. He can go home this afternoon. All he has is a cast on his arm.'

Nick looked at his watch. 'If I put you on a plane in an hour, you could be there at noon California time, catch a plane to Santa Barbara ... hell, Kate, you could be there by two.' He smiled helpfully and she sank into a chair.

'Yeah. I know.'

'What's with you?' Nick stared at her in confusion. 'You're going back, aren't you?'

'I don't suppose I have much choice.' But she looked as if she wanted one.

'What's that supposed to mean?' It was the first time she had ever seen him look disagreeable. In fact, he looked shocked.

'It means that I know I should go, but I don't want to. I was having such a good time. And Tillie says he's fine, but I know that if I don't go back, I'll feel awful and he'll hate me, and ... oh, Nick. I haven't done anything with my life in seven years and this has been so much fun.'

'It's not his fault you locked yourself in a closet for all those years, for chrissake. You're his mother!' He was actually shouting. It stunned her.

'Okay. I know that. But I'm me too. I'm Kate, not just Mom. I'm almost thirty years old, and I've been Mom non-stop for six years. Don't I have a right to more than that?'

'Yes, but not at his expense, lady. Never at his expense.' He was stalking the room now, furious. 'Let me tell you something, Kate. I've seen a lot of assholes come and go from where I sit. They screw up their lives, they fuck over their children, they cheat on their husbands, they break up their marriages, and

246

you know why? Because they're so goddamn in love with themselves they can't see straight. They love the noise, and the
lights, the introductions and the applause, the cameras and
the microphones, and you know what else? I can see you falling
for that bullshit too. Well do yourself and Tygue and me a big
favour, kiddo – don't. There's nothing there. Fame is a nice
place to visit, but that's it. And now, your kid broke his arm,
and you're going home, and that's it.' He leaned past her,
grabbed the phone, and asked the hotel operator for TWA,
but before he could finish his sentence, Kate's finger was on
the button, disconnecting his call. He looked at her in astonishment. Her eyes were blazing, but when she spoke, her voice
was soft.

'Don't ever do that again. When I want to call the airline, I'll
do it. When I decide to go home, I'll let you know. And when
I need your advice about my maternal responsibilities, I'll ask
for it. In the meantime, mister, keep your ideas and your
threats and your righteous indignation to yourself.' She stood
up and walked across the room with her back to him. When she
reached the window, she turned to look at him, and he had
never seen such fury in a woman's face. 'I have given everything to that child for years. Everything I have, everything I
am, everything I know how to give has been his. But it's my
turn now. And I know better than anyone the price to be paid.
I watched someone I loved grow cancerous with that bullshit
fame trip. I know all about it, thank you. And I'm scared to
death of it. But that doesn't mean I want to be buried alive
either. I've done that to myself for years and I've had enough
of it. I have a right to this. I have a right to my time with you,
my career, my own life, and if I'm disappointed because I have
to go back to reality now, then I have a right to that too. But
don't you ever try to guilt-trip me out, and tell me what I owe
that child. I know what I owe Tygue, and believe me, I've
paid my dues. And don't you ever tell me what to do again.
I've been there. I've tried that. I've relied on a man until there
was no me left. I let him make all my decisions, and I loved it
and I loved him, but it almost killed me when he wasn't there
to do the telling anymore. So I grew up. I make my own

decisions. And I like it that way. I love you, Nick, but you will never tell me when to go home. I'll make that decision. Is that perfectly clear?' He nodded silently and she walked back across the room with her head bowed. She stopped when she stood right in front of him.

'I'm sorry if I said too much, Nick, but it's been a long hard road from there to here, and I've paid a hell of a price for everything I have. I don't know how to deal with anyone messing with that. I'm not even sure I know how to deal with someone helping me. And there's an awful lot happening to me right now. I need time to absorb it . . . maybe going home isn't such a bad idea after all.' Her voice was deep and gruff as she ended the words and reached for the phone. She asked for the same airline Nick had asked for only a moment before. He said nothing now. He only listened as she made a reservation on the next flight. He stood up when she was through on the phone, and they both remained still for a moment, neither of them speaking, neither of them sure what to say, both of them shaken by what they had felt and said. It was Kate who spoke first. 'I'm sorry, Nick.'

'Don't be. I had no right . . .' He pulled her gently into his arms and sighed. He wanted to do everything for her, because he knew that no one had for so long, but he knew she had to grow into this new life herself. He wanted to spare her the pain and the price, but he couldn't. He held her tight for a long moment and then swatted her behind and pulled away. 'You'd better go get ready, or you'll miss your flight.'

'No, I won't.' She was smiling now. A small, womanly smile, and it evoked a real smile from him.

'Listen, you . . .'

'Oh shut up.' She led him gently by the hand into the bedroom they had shared during their stay in New York and she pulled him onto the bed and began to laugh. 'Don't be so serious, Nick. The world hasn't come to an end.' As a matter of fact, she felt as though it was just beginning. And as he carefully pulled off her shirt, she reached out to him with a longing and hunger she could barely control. She pulled him down to her, her mouth and her body aching for his.

CHAPTER XXV

'Tillie, can you stay with Tygue for a few hours?'

'Sure. I'll be over right away.'

Kate smiled as she hung up. Nick was coming back from New York. It had only been a week, but it felt more like years. Tygue's cast made his arm itch and he was constantly restless. She had been up to see Tom twice and he seemed in poor form too. He looked tired and gaunt, and she could see that he was losing weight. And he cried the second time when she left. Everyone was pulling at her. But it was no different than it had been before. Only she was different. The past week had been like a living reminder of what her life had been like before Nick. But now he was coming home. And she had two chapters of a new book to show him.

'Where are you going?' Tygue looked worried as she pulled out the coral dress she had worn in New York.

'To meet Nick. I'm going to surprise him.' And then she knew she shouldn't have said it, because he'd want to come too. The boy's face lit up like a firecracker on the Fourth of July.

'He's coming home?' She nodded, with a smile. She felt the same way.

'Can I come?' She paused for a long moment, and then sighed.

'Okay, tough guy, you win.' Motherhood, Inc. And suddenly she wanted so much to be alone. But she knew Nick would be happy to see him. She called Tillie back and told Tygue to change his clothes. He could manage pretty well with the cast now.

They were in the car half an hour later. Tygue had on his new cowboy boots and his favourite hat, and she felt pretty again in the coral dress. It felt nice to wear good clothes. She sick of blue jeans and old shirts.

249

They had three and a half hours to get to the airport, and they made it just in time. They ran to the gate just as Nick walked off the plane. Tygue shouted his name, and Kate stood there, breathless. It had been a mad dash through the building.

'Hey, Tiger!' Nick looked at the boy in astonishment and then at his mother. It had been years since anyone had met him at a plane. He just stood there and beamed, with the child in his arms. But the hug he gave Kate told him what her surprise meant.

'We brought you a present!' The boy was ecstatic too. All three of them were, as they stood there blocking traffic.

'You did?'

'Yup. A picture of Brownie with me on it. Mom had it framed for your desk.'

'That's terrific.' He put an arm around Kate's shoulders and they walked slowly along. 'Hi, darling.' He said it just for her and she reached up and kissed him again.

'I missed you something awful.'

He rolled his eyes in answer, pulled her closer, and turned his attention back to Tygue.

'I missed you too, Nick. And I can ride Brownie, even with my arm.'

'Is that a good idea?' He looked at Kate with a frown.

'The doctor says it won't hurt him, as long as he doesn't go galloping around. They just walk.'

'Okay.'

They collected his bags as the three of them charged in and out of the conversation, and then went to get the car. They chatted all the way home, where even Bert seemed happy to see Nick.

'Now the whole family is together again!' Tygue said it with a fervour that tore at Kate's heart. He was getting so attached to Nick. But he wasn't alone in his affection. Nick could hardly wait to get his hands on the boy. They tried out all his new toys before dinner.

'And wait till you see the boat go! Your mom and I tried it out in New York.' They exchanged a smile at the memory.

'They have a lake there?'

'A boat pond. And a zoo. And pony rides. We'll take you there sometime. As a matter of fact, young man, I have another trip in mind for you now.'

'You do?' Tygue's eyes opened wide. Nick was always full of surprises, and Kate stood by waiting to hear about a weekend in Santa Barbara. But this time she was surprised too.

'Do you know what we're all doing tomorrow?'

Tygue shook his head wordlessly.

'We're going to Disneyland!'

'We are?' His eyes couldn't open wide enough, and Kate and Nick laughed.

'We are. All three of us.'

'How on earth did you manage that?' Kate walked over and put an arm around him.

'Jasper went to the South of France for a week. So I'm all yours. If you can stand me.' And after a week in New York, busting his ass for the show, now he was taking them all to Disneyland. Kate looked at him in amazement.

'Mr. Waterman, I must be the luckiest woman alive.'

'Nope. I'm the luckiest man.'

The trip to Disneyland was perfect. They came home three days later, exhausted and happy, spent a day at Kate's place, and then went to Santa Barbara for the weekend. Kate hadn't been up to Carmel all week, but she didn't even care. She was happy where she was. And Tom had Mr. Erhard. For once, that would have to be enough. She had her own life to lead now.

'I'll see you next weekend, Tiger.'

'But I want to see you sooner than that.' Nick would be there every night, but Tygue didn't know that.

'Maybe you will.'

Nick didn't know how honest the promise was, until the next day. He started the drive back to Kate's at four o'clock, and got there at seven. She was surprised to see him at first, and then worried. There was something brutally unhappy in his face, but he insisted that they'd talk when Tygue went to bed.

'Okay, tell me. I can't stand it.' They had just closed Tygue's door.

'I talked to Jasper today, Kate. And ... he's made up his mind.' Had he been. fired? God, he looked awful. Kate reached for his hand.

'What about?'

'The show moves to San Francisco.'

'When?'

'In six weeks.'

'Is that awful?' She didn't quite understand.

'I think so. Don't you? That's a five-hour drive, at best. Sometimes six. I can't drive that every morning and every night. Not even for you.' Now what would they have? Weekends? But she was smiling at him and took him into her arms.

'Is that why you're upset? God, I thought you'd been fired.'

'I might as well have been.' He had been thinking all day about quitting. Hell, any one of a dozen shows in L.A. would love to have him. But she was looking at him in astonishment.

'Are you crazy? What's the big deal?'

'I'll never see you, for chrissake. Doesn't that matter to you?' He looked as if he were going to cry, but Kate was smiling.

'So I'll move to San Francisco. So what?' She looked at him as though he were being ridiculous, and he closed his eyes and then opened them with a tired smile.

'You'd do that for me, Kate?'

'Sure. Or would that only make problems for you?' Maybe it wasn't what he wanted after all. Maybe he still wanted some freedom. But so did she. They could still have freedom and each other.

'Problems? Lady, you are amazing.' And then he had a thought. 'But what'll you do with the house?'

'We can use it on weekends. And the timing is perfect for school. We'll just enrol Tygue someplace up there, and he can start the school year next month, along with everyone else.' She had thought it all out the last time he'd mentioned the possibility of the move. But she hadn't said anything to him, and he had been worried sick.

'Are you serious about all this, Kate?' He still couldn't

believe it. But she looked serious. He didn't know whether to laugh or cry, or dance.

'Of course I'm serious, Mr. Charming.'

'Oh Kate . . .' He held her in his arms for hours. The weeks of worry had been for nothing. It was going to be a whole new life. Together.

CHAPTER XXVI

Her heels clattered through the empty room, leaving an echo behind her. It was a large open room with an endless span of picture window looking out on the Bay. The floors were a beautiful dark inlaid wood and there were bronze sconces on the wall. To the left, they could see the Golden Gate Bridge, to the right Alcatraz, and Angel Island sat straight ahead.

'It's really a remarkable view.' Kate nodded pleasantly, but said nothing. It was a beautiful view ... a splendid view ... but it reminded her a little of the house she had shared with Tom. But that was silly. That had only been an apartment. This was a whole house. And a lovely one. Nick said he wanted a house.

She stood in the dining room with the same view of the Bay, her back to the fireplace. It was a warm room with beam ceilings and bay windows instead of the flat picture window of the living room. She squinted, seeing white organdie curtains and plants, inviting cushions in the window seats, a soft white rug, and a rich, dark wood table ... She squinted again, seeing it all, and started to smile.

'I'm going to take a look at the upstairs again.' The realtor nodded silently this time. She was tired. They had been doing this for three days, and there was nothing left to show. Kate had seen everything. Sunken living rooms, sweeping views, seven bedrooms, and only three, wood panelling, marble floors, crooked Victorians in need of work. She had seen everything from the decrepit to the divine in Pacific Heights and Presidio Heights, along the Presidio Wall and on Lake Street, and even on Russian Hill. But she seemed to know exactly what she wanted, and she apparently hadn't seen it yet. Her kind was the worst. She wasn't going to settle for anything less than the house she had laid out in her head. The realtor sat down heavily in the window seat, and flipped through her book for the thirtieth time in three days. This was it. It was the last suitable rental she had. She could hear Kate wandering around the uncarpeted rooms above, and then she noticed her footsteps stop.

Upstairs, Kate was looking out at the view from the master bedroom. The Bay again, and the same cosy window seats that she had seen downstairs in the dining room, a tiny fireplace with a marble mantelpiece, and a dressing room just big enough for a flea to change shoes in. But there was a friendliness to the place. She could imagine Nick passing her in the hall, squeezing past her in the dressing room and pinching her behind as he reached into his closet. She could imagine sitting in the window seat with Tygue looking out over the Bay at twilight, talking about something important, like baseball or snakes. She could even see Bert here, clattering between the rooms. There were two other bedrooms on the second floor. A large one, which faced the garden at the front of the house, with lots of sunshine and tall French windows. That room could be Tygue's. And another equally pretty bedroom. A guest room perhaps. They didn't really need one, but it was always good to have a spare room. And there was a tiny maid's room behind the kitchen which she could use as an office. It wasn't pretty, but at least it would give her a room in which she could write.

The kitchen she'd seen downstairs was open and warm, a room to have dinner in when they didn't have guests. It had two brick walls and a built-in barbecue, and the rest of it was painted yellow with a bright yellow ceramic floor. The tiles had been brought over from Portugal by the last tenants. It was perfect . . . all it needed was copper pots, and a wrought-iron hook with salamis and peppers . . . glass jars filled with spices . . . curtains, and the butcher-block table Nick had in his kitchen now. She was bringing very little up from her place in the country. Only a few treasured things, the pretty pieces she had acquired over the years. The ordinary, functional things Nick said they could buy. It would be a little strange setting up housekeeping with him, without being married. What would

255

belong to whom? And who decided what they bought? But Nick seemed to be comfortable with the arrangement, and was giving her carte blanche.

She looked around the bedroom that could be Tygue's again, and down at the well-tended little garden. It was surrounded by a high hedge which would give them privacy, and there was a gate, so Bert couldn't get lost. In fact, the house seemed to have everything they needed. The view and fireplaces and high ceilings Nick had said were a must, an elegant sweeping staircase that led upstairs, and three bedrooms, which even gave them a spare. And a small, dark room, near the kitchen in which she could work. She didn't love the workroom, but the rest seemed to be just what they wanted. She sat on the top stair and looked up. Directly over her head there was a skylight, and to her right a slightly open door. More closets maybe. She leaned backwards to take a look. It looked like a stairway. She frowned and got up, calling down to the realtor still waiting downstairs.

'Is there more upstairs?'

There was the sound of shuffling through the now familiar book, and then a vague 'I'm not sure'. And then as Kate walked towards the door, the realtor came to the foot of the stairs. 'Maybe some kind of an attic. But it doesn't say in the book. It just says here "three bedrooms, den, and maid's".'

'Den?' She hadn't seen a den. There was a den?

The stairway was narrow but carpeted, and the walls were still tapestried with a new-looking beige silk. It hardly looked like the kind of thing you'd put on the way to the attic, and as Kate reached the top of the stairs, she saw why. This was no attic, it wasn't even a den, it was an oasis, a dream. A small, well-proportioned wood panelled room with a fireplace and a 360-degree view of San Francisco. The Bay, the Presidio, downtown, and the hills leading south. The rooms were well-carpeted, boasted the now familiar bay windows, and there was even a little extension to it, a kind of solarium, which would be heavenly when it was filled with plants. And there would still be room for a desk and her file cabinets. The extension had two discreet glass French doors, which did not impair the view, but still allowed one to shut oneself off ... the perfect office. And a wonderful room to sit quietly in with Nick, after he did the show. They could light the fire and look out at the city. Their special hideaway, a room to fill with beauty and children and love. The whole house was that way. It was exactly what she had wanted. Better than that. It was exactly what she had dreamed, and known they would never find. Beauty, elegance, simplicity, warmth, privacy, and convenience. The realtor had thought she was crazy when she'd ticked them off. But she'd found them all in one house. And it didn't look a bit like the house she'd had with Tom.

'We'll take it.' She said it in a decisive voice as she turned to the realtor, who had followed her upstairs.

'It's a remarkable place,' the woman agreed.

Kate nodded victoriously. 'It's perfect.' She was beaming. She could hardly wait to show Nick. 'How soon can we have it?'

'Tomorrow.' The realtor grinned. They had done it after all. She couldn't get over it. She had been sure this one was hopeless. The woman wanted everything and wouldn't settle for less. But that upstairs room did make the house an incredible find. Why the hell hadn't someone else snatched it up? Maybe no one else had noticed the upstairs room before. It wasn't on the listing. 'It says here that it's available immediately. We can draw up the lease and it's yours.'

'I really ought to show it to ... to my husband. But I'm absolutely sure. This is it. In fact, just to be sure of it ... how much do they require as a deposit?' The realtor checked her book again and came up with a most unexceptional figure. Kate wanted to shriek 'That's all?' but she kept quiet. This one was too good to blow. She hastily wrote out a cheque and handed it to the woman. 'I'll bring him back tonight.'

She did, and he fell in love with it too. 'Isn't it super?' With him she could be exuberant. 'Oh Nick, I love it!' She plonked herself down in one of the window seats with a grin.

'I love you.' He walked over to her with a peaceful smile, and then looked out at the bay. 'But I love the house too. It's going to look terrific with you and Tygue running around in it.'

'And Bert.' She corrected him with a serious look.

'Excuse me. And Bert. But not Brownie, if you please. I've already called the stable in the park. They'll give Brownie a very comfortable stall. At about the same price we'll be paying to rent this house.'

'God, how awful. Maybe we should leave him in Santa Barbara.'

'Hell no. You can't do that to Tygue. Besides, I think I can still manage it.' He was looking around what Kate was already calling 'the Ivory Tower', the wood-panelled room on the top floor. He could already imagine nights in front of the fire, Kate in his arms, the lights across the Bay twinkling just past Angel Island, and Tygue sound asleep downstairs. Or he could see Kate busy at her desk on the other side of the glass doors, oblivious to anything but her work, concocting a new book on the typewriter with three pencils and a pen stuck haphazardly into her hair. He loved what he saw, in his mind and around him.

'Do you think we should take it?' She was smiling at him like a child, anxious and excited and proud.

He laughed. 'You're asking my advice? I thought that was already settled, Cinderella. I owe you for that deposit, by the way.'

'The hell you do. That was my share.'

'What share?' He looked at her in surprise.

'You don't expect to support me, do you? We go fifty-fifty on this. Don't we?' She suddenly looked embarrassed. They had not yet discussed the financial aspect of the move.

'Are you serious?' Nick looked offended. 'Of course I expect to support you.'

'But you're not marrying me, for chrissake. We're just living together.'

'That's your decision, not mine. Tygue is your responsibility, if you like, but you're mine. I'm not going to have you paying rent to live here.'

'That doesn't seem fair.'

'Then mind your own business. And I'd happily support Tygue too, if you'd agree.' He looked at her seriously, but she shook her head.

'Nick . . .' She looked across at him with a tender look in her eyes. It had been only two months, and he was offering her everything. He was offering to support her, entertain her, take care of her, take on her son. It was all very much like a dream. 'Why are you always so good to me?'

'Because you deserve it, and I love you.' He sat down next to her in the window seat. 'I'd do more, if you'd let me.'

'What more is there?' She looked around with a twinkle in her eye, but he was looking unusually serious.

'Marriage.' He said it very softly, and she looked away. 'You still won't even consider it, will you?' But hell, it had been only two months. And she still hadn't told him about Tom. In time . . . he knew that in time . . . at least that was what he hoped. And he liked the idea of the spare bedroom next to Tygue's. He had an excellent idea of how to fill it, and not with friends from L.A. or New York. But Nick was looking at her very carefully in the twilight and she finally lifted her eyes to his. And then very carefully she put her arms around him and held him very tight.

'I'm sorry, Nick. But I can't think of marriage . . . I can't.' She sounded as though something were breaking inside of her.

'Are you still hung up on your husband?' He didn't want to push, but he couldn't let this go.

'No. Not in the way you mean. I accept what happened. I told you. He's gone. Part of another life, another century. And the funny thing is that you already know me better than he ever did.' And then she felt like a traitor for saying that. Tom had known her perfectly, but she had been a girl, a child, not yet a woman, not until the end. She hadn't even known herself then. But she did now, and Nick knew her too. It was a very different relationship.

'But you still hang on to him, don't you?'

She started to say no, but then nodded. 'In some ways.'

'Why?'

'Maybe out of loyalty. Out of what we once had.' It was a strange double-edged conversation. She was answering his questions with more truth than she thought he understood.

259

'You can't live like that forever, Kate.'

'I know. I just always knew I'd never remarry.'

'That's ridiculous.' He stood up with a sigh then. 'We can talk about it later. In the meantime, Cinderella' – he looked down at her with the smile that never failed to melt her – 'welcome home.' He took her face in his hands and kissed her very gently.

Three weeks later, they moved in, amidst chaos and laughter and loving. Tygue ensconced himself in his room, Bert took over the entire house, the kitchen became everyone's favourite meeting place, and the maid's room became an instant depository for ice skates, bicycles, and skis. Nick was teaching Tygue to skate, and he was going to take them both skiing as soon as the first snows came. The dining room looked just as she had envisioned it, with a table they found at an auction, with eight rustic old ladder-back chairs, and white organdie curtains. The living room was a little grand for everyday, in brown velvets and beige silks, but it would be perfect for entertaining Nick's friends, or people from the show. And the room upstairs became just what they had dreamed. A love nest. When they were not tucked into their cluttered Victorian blue and white bedroom, they were to be found hiding out in the wood-panelled room upstairs. Kate filled it with plants and books, some old paintings she loved, the leather chairs Nick liked best from his apartment, and his most treasured private things – trophies of his boyhood, favourite photographs, and the stuffed head of a lion smoking a hysterically oversized cigar, one eye sewn into a wink. There was also a tuba hanging from the wall, in memory of a past even more distant than that commemorated by the trophies or the lion, and there were endless baby pictures of Tygue. Her past seemed to go no further back than that. But before Tygue had come her parents, and Tom, and both of those eras were now closed. This was a new life. And she made it that when she moved up from the country. Just as she had when she'd moved down there. She closed a door behind her with each move.

Tygue loved his new school, and the show was going well. Even Kate's new book was progressing nicely. She was sure she would finish it before Christmas. And *A Final Season* was already in its fifth printing.

'You know, I can't get over this place.' Felicia was their first dinner guest. She sat down in the living room after dinner and looked around. 'Some of us just happen to hit it lucky on the first try.' Or the second, but she didn't say that. She looked warmly at Nick. 'You've managed to accomplish in a couple of months what I couldn't push the kid into in almost seven years. Mr. Waterman, hats off.' She smiled at Nick, and he executed a neat bow. Their affection was mutual. He liked what she did for Kate, the way she had stood by her for so long.

Nick grew serious for a minute. 'I think she was just ready to come out of her shell.'

'*Come out?* I was *blasted* out.'

Felicia concealed a grin with another sip of her coffee. Even their belongings had combined well to make a home. Felicia looked around, and shared another smile with Nick, and then he glanced at his watch.

'Ladies, with deepest regrets, I'm afraid I'll have to leave you.' They had eaten dinner early so he could get to the taping on time. The 'girls' were going to stay home and chat. 'I'll be back after nine. Stick around, Licia. We can play poker or something when I get home. Or I'll take you two out for a drink.'

'I'll take a raincheck, love. I've got half a dozen early meetings tomorrow. It'll really be a bitch of a day. I don't hang around in bed till noon the way you two do.'

'The hell I do. I spend half my life car-pooling Tygue and his pals around here.'

'Oh you do.' Nick arched an eyebrow and she laughed guiltily.

'All right, all right. I'll do it next week, I swear.'

'Kate Harper, you are spoiled.' Felicia looked at her in amazement. 'Nick even car-pools for you?' Kate nodded guiltily, but with a grin. 'Jesus. You don't deserve the gold mine you got.' She looked at her friend in mock horror, but Kate's happiness was exactly what she had longed to see for years. And this new living situation obviously suited Kate perfectly. Just enough domesticity and just enough sparkle.

Nick hugged Felicia and kissed Kate, and they heard the Ferrari pull out a moment later after he had gone upstairs to say goodnight to Tygue, who was playing with Felicia's train in the spare room.

'Is there anything that man doesn't do for you, Kate?' Felicia looked over at her, sitting peacefully at the other end of the brown velvet couch.

'Nothing I can think of.' She looked totally content. 'I know. I'm spoiled rotten.' But he wasn't all teddy bear either. They had their moments and their fights, but she liked that about him too.

'You deserve it, love. He's really an extraordinary man.' And then after a pause, she looked up with a question in her eyes, and Kate looked away. 'He still doesn't know, does he? I mean about Tom.' But Kate had known what she meant. She looked up at her and shook her head, with a look of pain and sorrow. 'Have you stopped going?' She hoped ... she hoped ... but she didn't get her wish. Kate shook her head again and sighed.

'Of course not. I can't stop going. How could I stop? What could I say? "I'm leaving you now. I've found someone else." You don't say that to a seven-year-old boy. You don't walk out on him. You don't stop, Licia. You can't. I'll never stop as long as he's alive.'

'Will you tell Nick?'

'I don't know.' She closed her eyes for a moment and then looked at the fire. 'I don't know. I guess I should. But I don't know how. Maybe in time.'

'You'll have to, if this goes on for a long time. Where does he think you go?'

'To teach.'

'Doesn't he get sick of that? I mean, all the way to Carmel to teach is pushing it a little, isn't it?'

Kate nodded again. 'I just don't have any choice.'

'You don't want to have a choice. I think he'd understand.'

'But what if he didn't, Felicia? He wants to get married, to have children, to have a normal life. How can you have a normal life living with a married woman? A woman who's married to a seven-year-old physical and emotional cripple. What if I tell him and he decides it's too much for him?' She closed her eyes for a moment at the thought.

'And you think not telling him would change that, Kate? What if he finds out eventually? What if he presses you about getting married? What if you tell him in five years, or two years, or ten years? What do you think he'll say then? He has a right to know the truth.' And so did Tygue. She had thought so on and off for years. Now and then she had been wooed by Kate's insistence that not telling Tygue had been the right decision, but in her gut she had always thought that the boy might be better off if he knew. But she wasn't going to tackle that one with Kate again. And if only Nick knew, he could help Kate deal with the issue of telling Tygue. 'I think you're playing with dynamite by not telling him. You're also not showing a lot of faith in him, and you're not being very ballsy.'

'My, my, that's quite a speech, Licia.'

'I'm sorry, Kate. But I think it needs to be said, before you make a big mistake.'

'All right. I'll see.'

'Doesn't he ask you about Carmel?'

'Sometimes. But I cut him off.'

'You can't cut him off forever, Kate. And why should you? It's not fair. Look what he's doing for you, what he's giving you, how much he loves you. You owe him the truth.'

'All right, Licia, all right. Just let me work it out for myself.' She stood up and walked to the fire with her back to her friend. She didn't want to hear it. She knew that Licia was right. She did have to tell him. Eventually. But not yet. And Licia was also right that she couldn't stall him forever. She was already getting nervous about the days she went away. She had tiptoed downstairs three days before, hoping he wouldn't be up. But he had been. And she hated the act she had put on as she left.

'How often do you go?' Felicia, as usual, wouldn't let up.

'Same as always. Twice a week.' And with a sigh she realized that she was going again the next day. Maybe Nick would sleep late.

CHAPTER XXVII

She closed the door as the car pool rounded the corner. A last wave before the little blond head in the back seat disappeared from sight, and Tygue was off to his day. And she to hers. She walked softly into the kitchen for a last sip of her coffee. She didn't want to wake Nick.

'You look awfully done up for a foggy Tuesday morning.' He looked at her from the large kitchen table and she jumped.

'Hi, darling. I didn't know you were up.' She tried to sound light as she bent to kiss him. 'Want some coffee?' He nodded. 'Eggs?'

'No thanks. I'll make my own when I can open my eyes. You teaching again?'

She nodded, looking into the coffee she was pouring.

'Your schedule seems to vary a lot.' There was something strange in his voice. An accusation. A suspicion. Something she didn't like. She looked up at him, but she couldn't quite tell what it was. 'Last week you went Monday and Thursday. Didn't you?'

'I guess so. I don't know.' She poured in the two sugars he liked and busied herself at the sink.

'Come here a minute.'

Her heart was pounding, but she tried to think empty thoughts as she turned towards him. She didn't want him to see anything, know anything . . . know she was lying. She stood looking at him, but there was no smile in his eyes.

'Why won't you tell me what you really do down there?'

'Are you serious?'

'Very.' And he looked it. Her heart only beat faster and seemed to fill her ears.

'I told you. I teach retarded children and adults.'

'Can't you find something comparable in the city? Surely San Francisco has lots of retarded kids who'd love you. Why Carmel?' And why not the truth, dammit? Why?

'I've been going there for years.' That much he knew.

'While you were married?'

'No.' And then there was a strange silence and she looked hard at him again. 'What difference does that make?'

'I don't know, Kate. Maybe I should ask you that.'

'What the hell difference does it make, dammit? I don't bother you. I leave at eight. I'm back at five. Sometimes four-thirty. It doesn't take anything away from you.' She was angry now, and frightened. She had never seen him look like that before.

'It does take something away from me, Kate.' He looked at her in a way that shrivelled her soul. It was a cold, angry look. 'It takes you away.'

'For a few lousy hours?' Christ, she owed Tom that much. He had no right to . . .

'Have you ever looked in the mirror when you get back?' She stared at him silently. 'You look like a ghost. You look haunted and hurt and tired and sad. Why do you do that to yourself?' He found himself staring at her even harder, but found no answers. 'Never mind. It's none of my business.' She said nothing, but walked out of the kitchen. She should have gone to him, hugged him, kissed him. She knew it. It would have been smarter. But she didn't want to be smart. And she didn't want to be pushed. She wasn't going to tell him until she was ready to, if ever. And she would never let him stop her from going. Those two days a week were sacred. They were Tom's.

'I'll see you at five.' She said it from the front door, with her eyes closed, wanting to go to him, but afraid he'd do something to stop her from going or worse, force the truth out of her. Why the hell did he have to wake up? It was so easy when he was asleep. She hesitated a moment and then spoke again. 'I love you.' She heard him walk softly out of the kitchen and into the dining room. He stood there with the Bay at his back and looked at her for what felt like an aeon.

265

'Do you, Kate?'

'You know I do.' She walked slowly towards him and took him into her arms. 'Darling, I love you so much.'

There was a long pause as his arms held her too, and then he pulled away.

'Then tell me about Carmel?' He almost prayed that she would. God, how long could he go on pretending not to know? But Kate only looked at him, with wide sorrowful eyes.

'We've already talked about Carmel, Nick.' Her eyes never left his.

'Have we? Then why don't I feel more comfortable about your going there?' What else could he say, dammit? Jesus, if she'd only give him an opening.

'There's nothing for you to worry about.'

'Isn't there, Kate? Wouldn't it worry you if I went somewhere every week without telling you more about it than you tell me?'

She was silent for a moment and then she looked away. 'But I tell you about it, Nick. You know why I go.' She tried desperately to sound soothing.

His eyes held a penetrating quality she didn't understand. He wanted to tell her that he *did* know. He felt almost compelled to tell her, but he couldn't. He had to hear it from her. She had to want to tell him. 'Never mind, forget it. Have a nice day.' He wheeled around then and walked back towards the kitchen, as she stood there wondering if she should run after him. But she couldn't. He wanted answers that she was not yet ready to give him.

She walked out the door and to the car, but she felt as though she were dragging chains around her feet. Should she go? Should she stay? Did she owe him an explanation? Should she tell him the truth? What if he left her? What if ... and then, as she started the car, she forced him from her mind. She owed the trip to Tom, she owed him these visits, these days ... but did she owe it to him to lose Nick? The thought made her step on the brakes and think for a minute. Was she really playing for those kinds of stakes? Could Felicia be

266

right? Could she lose Nick if she didn't tell him and he eventually found out?

'Shit.' She muttered the word to herself as she let herself gently into the traffic outside their house. She just couldn't tell him yet. Not yet . . . but maybe soon.

CHAPTER XXVIII

It was pouring as she drove back to San Francisco from Carmel. Where was all this gorgeous October weather Felicia always talked about? Christ, it had been raining for days. It had rained the last three times she had gone there. It was even raining in Carmel. And the rain was so hard on Tom. He looked so pale now, and he wasn't eating well. There was a lost quality about him lately, like a tired sick child hatching some terrible illness. He would hold her hand for hours and beg her for stories, looking at her with those eyes that seemed to see her, really see her, but never did. Those eyes still remembered nothing. And the arms still reached out for her as he called out 'Katie', the way Tygue shouted 'Mom'. He seemed so helpless now though. He had been this way for so long, and something about him seemed to be slipping away. The teasing was gone. The laughter had dimmed. Mr. Erhard looked concerned too. But the director of Mead said it was 'normal'. Normal ... what the hell was normal about a man who thought like a child? A man who had once been so alive and had now lived in a wheelchair playing with paper aeroplanes for seven years? But the doctor insisted that people in Tom's condition did 'fade' from time to time, and eventually, one day ... but that could be years away. In the meantime, he could have these 'spells' and still rally, as long as one kept his interest up and 'challenged him'. Although, the director admitted, that didn't always change things. He admitted, too, that Tom might have these spells more and more frequently over the next years, until the end. It was neurological, and inevitable, but it wasn't acute. And she didn't understand it any better than anything else that had happened in the past seven years. Whatever it was, Tom hadn't been right for almost a month. And she could sense that Nick wanted her to stop going to Carmel. Christ. She sighed as she drove off the freeway onto Franklin

Street. It was going to be good to get home. She was so tired. And thank God Nick hadn't been up when she left that morning. She had been getting up earlier for the past two weeks, in order to avoid him. And she was making special efforts to keep his mind off her trips to Carmel.

She turned left on Green Street and followed it west until she almost reached the Presidio, then unexpectedly she swooped up a narrow, curved, brick-paved street, and there, hidden amidst the sculptured landscape, concealed by the hedges, trees, and bushes, nestled their house. After little more than a month in it, she already loved it more than any house she had ever lived in, maybe because she was so happy there.

She let herself into the house with a sigh of relief. It was only four-twenty. Tygue was at his special art class, and would be delivered by the car pool at four forty-five. She had just made it. And the Ferrari had been nowhere in sight. Safe. No explanations, no excuses, no little bits of chatter to cover up the worry and the pain. It was always so hard confronting Nick after all that. He hated it too. And he always saw too much. She slipped off her wet shoes and left them on a mat in the front hall. She hung up her umbrella in the kitchen, and then with another sigh she sat down at the kitchen table, and rested her head on her arms.

'Hi, Kate.' The voice was only inches away from her and she leapt from her seat at the table with a look of terror in her eyes. 'Oh, darling. I'm sorry.' His arms went instantly around her as she sat there and trembled. She was speechless, and not at all prepared for the usual games. She had thought he wasn't home. But he had been sitting there, watching her, from the corner, and she hadn't even noticed.

'You scared the hell out of me.' She smiled shakily. It had been a long day. 'I didn't know you were home. How was your day?' The efforts at chitchat were futile, Nick refused to be diverted. He looked strangely serious and walked to the stove without even bothering to answer her question.

'Tea?'

'That would be nice. Anything wrong?' She hated the way he looked. He reminded her of the way her father looked when her report card arrived. She could feel her heart pounding as it had during their last confrontation over Carmel. Only this time was worse. She wasn't sure why, but she could sense that it was. 'Something wrong?' He still hadn't answered her.

'No, nothing's wrong.' The words were carefully measured. 'I missed you today.' He turned to look at her and there was already a cup of tea in his hand. He had even had the water boiling and she hadn't noticed the steam. When she had walked into the kitchen, she had been exhausted. Now she was terrified. And she still wasn't sure why.

'I missed you too.'

He nodded and picked up a second cup. 'Let's go upstairs.'

'Okay.' Her smile went unanswered as she took her cup and followed him meekly to the den on the third floor, where he settled slowly into his favourite chair. It was a big red leather one that was satiny smooth and wonderfully soft with the rich smell of good leather. It had a matching ottoman, but he pushed it aside with one foot. He wasn't planning to relax. And then he did the unexpected and set down his tea and held out both arms to her. She came to them willingly, kneeling next to his chair. 'I love you, Nick.'

'I know. I love you too. More than I've ever loved anyone.' He looked down at her, smiled tiredly, and then sighed. 'And we need to have a talk. I have a lot to say. I don't know where to start, but maybe the best place is where we just did. I love you. And I've waited a hell of a long time for you to level with me, but you haven't. So it's time we just sat down and let it all out. What bothers me most in all this is that you don't trust me.' She felt her blood turn to ice.

'That's not true.' She sounded hurt, but her heart was pounding with terror. What did he mean? Did he know? How? Who had told him?

'It *is* true. If you trusted me, you'd have told me about Carmel. About Tom.' An interminable silence filled the room as her eyes flew to his.

'What about Tom?' She was stalling and they both knew it, as she put down her cup of tea with a trembling hand.

'I don't know much, Kate. I had some vague suspicions in

270

the beginning. What you knew about football in your book, the behind-the-scenes stuff, things you said. I did a little research, very little in fact. Just enough to find out that you'd been married to Tom Harper, *the* Tom Harper, and that he had shot himself and become paralyzed and mentally, well ... I don't know the right words. I know he was moved to a sanatorium in Carmel after a lengthy hospital stay, but I wasn't able to find the name of the home. I knew then that he hadn't died, and I think he's probably still alive now. I think that's what you do in Carmel. Visit him, not teach retarded children. I could understand that, Kate, I could even accept it, I could understand a lot of things. What I don't understand is why you won't share it with me. Why you wouldn't tell me the truth in all these months. That's what hurts.' There were tears in her eyes and his when he stopped speaking, and Kate let out a long rattling sigh.

'Why didn't you tell me you knew? I've made an ass of myself all those months, haven't I?'

'Is that what bothers you now? Making an ass of yourself?' He looked suddenly angry and she shook her head and looked away.

'No. I ... I just don't know what to say.'

'Tell me the truth, Kate. Tell me what it's like. What kind of shape he's in, whether you love him, is it any kind of a life for you, where does it leave us ... I don't know what hope there is for our future, or for his. I have a right to know those things – I had a right to know them from the first. But I didn't tell you I knew because you had to trust me enough to tell me yourself. You never did. I had to confront you.'

'I think I was trying to protect both of you.'

'And maybe yourself.' He turned away from her and looked out at the Bay.

'Yes.' Her voice was very quiet in the room. 'And maybe myself. I love you, Nick. I didn't want to lose you. We have something with each other that I've never had before, with anyone. Tom knew me as a girl. I was a child with him, until ... until the accident. And now he's the child. He's like a little boy, Nick. He plays games, he draws, he's a little less grown up than Tygue. He cries ... he needs me. And he gets about as

271

much from me as he wants. I can't take that away from him. I can't leave him.' Her voice caught on the words.

'No one is asking you to, Kate. I never would have asked you that. But I just wanted to know. I wanted to hear it from you. Will he go on that way for a very long time?'

'Until the end, whenever that comes. It could be days, or months, or years. No one can know. And in the meantime ... I visit.'

'How do you stand it?' He turned to look at her again and there was pain and compassion in his eyes.

She smiled a small wintry smile. 'I owe it to him, Nick. Once he was everything to me. He was all I had, after my parents closed the door on me. He gave me everything. Now all I can give him are a few hours a week. I can spare those hours. I have to.' She said it defiantly as she watched him.

'I understand that.' He went to her and put his arms around her with a sigh. 'It's something you have to do. I respect that. I wish I could make it easier for you though.'

'It's not that hard anymore. I got used to it a long, long time ago. If you ever really get used to that sort of thing. At least it doesn't shock me anymore – or break my heart the way it once did.'

'Was Felicia around then, darling?' He cuddled her close and she looked up at him with a small smile. It was a relief to tell him, and she hated herself for not doing it sooner.

'Yes. She was around through the whole thing. She was marvellous. She was even in the delivery room with me when Tygue was born.'

'I wish I'd been there then.'

She smiled tiredly. She had a peaceful feeling she hadn't had in years. He knew everything now. There were no more secrets. No more dreading he'd find out. 'I was so afraid of what you'd think if you knew.'

'Why?'

'Because I'm married. Because I'm not free. That's not really fair to you.'

'It doesn't make any difference. One day you won't be married anymore. There's time for us, Kate. We have a lifetime ahead of us.'

'You're an incredible man, Nicholas Waterman.'

'Bullshit. You'd feel the same . . . Kate?'

'Mm?'

'Your parents never contacted you after he . . . after the accident?' He had understood that that was the euphemism she used for the shooting.

'Never once. They made up their minds when I went to live with Tom, and that was it. What he did just confirmed everything they'd thought about him, I guess, and as far as they were concerned I was no better than he was. I'd gotten what I deserved. They were just very black and white in their thinking. There were acceptable people and unacceptable people . . . I was no longer acceptable because of Tom, so they felt justified in cutting me out of their lives.'

'I don't know how they could live with themselves.'

'Neither do I, but that's not my problem anymore. It hasn't been for a long, long time. It's all very remote. And I'm glad. It's really all over. The only thing that isn't, that never will be, is my obligation to Tom.'

'Tygue doesn't know, does he?' He was sure that he didn't, but there was always a chance that the boy had been hiding it from him too.

'No. Felicia says I'll have to tell him one day, but I haven't figured that out yet. It's too soon now anyway.'

Nick nodded and then looked at her strangely. 'Can I ask you an odd question?'

'Of course.'

'Do you . . . do you still love Tom?' He made himself say it. He had to know.

Her voice was full of astonishment when she answered him. 'Do you think I could love you as I do, live with you like this, be yours, if I did? Yes, I love him. As I love a child, as I love Tygue. He's not a man, Nick. He's my past . . . and only a ghost . . . the ghost of a child.'

'I'm sorry I asked.'

'Don't be. You have a right to all the answers now. And I suppose it's hard to understand. There's no man there to love. Oh, before you came along, once in a while, I'd pretend to my-

273

self that there was a glimmer of something. But there wasn't. There hasn't been in seven years. I go to see him because that's what I do. Because once he was good to me, because a long time ago I loved him more than anyone I'd ever known or loved before, and because Tygue is his son.' Suddenly she was crying again, and the tears were streaming down her face. 'But I love you, Nick, I love you . . . as . . . I never loved him. I've waited such a long time for you.' He reached for her then and pulled her into his arms so hard that they were both stunned by the force of his grip on her. He needed her just as desperately. He had needed her for years.

'Oh darling, I'm so sorry.'

She pulled away with a sigh. 'I've been so afraid, ever since the book's been a success, that someone would find me out. That someone would dig up all that shit and spread it all over my face.' He cringed again at the thought of what she must have been going through. It was a wonder she had gone to Los Angeles at all. 'And when you said you'd played football, I almost died.' She laughed as she looked up at him, but his face was still almost grey.

'The funny thing is that I knew him. Not well. I was in and out of football too fast, and he was already on top when I came into it. But he seemed like a nice guy.'

'He was.' She looked sad at the words. He was.

'What made him do it? What broke him?' The papers he'd read hadn't really given him any insight. It was as though the reporters didn't care why.

'Pressure. Fear. He was being shoved out and it drove him crazy. He had nothing else in his life, only football. He didn't know what else to do. And he had also invested his money pretty badly and he wanted everything for Tygue. That was all he could think of. "His son." He wanted one more season so he could sock away a fortune for Tygue. And they canned him. You read the papers. You know the rest.'

He nodded sombrely. 'Does he know about Tygue?'

'He wouldn't understand. I visited him the whole time I was pregnant. He had no more interest or understanding than any kid that age. I think he just thought I was fat.'

'Has there been any change over the years?' He was embarrassed to ask.

But she only shook her head. 'No. Except in the past few weeks. He's not himself. But the doctor says it's nothing unusual.'

'Is it a decent place?'

'Yes, very.' She reached out to him then and he came to sit next to her on the floor. 'I love you, Mr. Waterman, even if you did scare the hell out of me. I thought you were going to tell me we were through.'

'What do you mean, you crazy woman? Did you think I'd really let you go?'

'I'm a married woman, Nick.' She said it with a tone of despair. She knew how badly he wanted to get married. And there was no chance. Not as long as Tom as alive.

'So what? Does it bother you that you're married, Kate?'

She shook her head very simply. 'I thought it out very carefully before I drove to Santa Barbara to see you this summer. In my heart, I'm not married to him anymore.'

'That's all that matters. The rest is nobody's business but ours. Is that the only reason why you didn't tell me, Kate?'

'No ... I ... well, that's part of it. The other part was just cowardice, I suppose. I had kept everyone outside the sacred walls for so long that I couldn't imagine telling anyone the truth. And by the time I *could* imagine telling you, it seemed impossible to start from the beginning and admit I had lied. How do you say to someone, "Oh, remember when I told you I was a widow, well, actually, I was lying. My husband is in a sanatorium in Carmel and I go to see him a couple of times a week." I don't know, Nick, it sounded nuts, and admitting it, talking about it – it's like reliving it. It's like feeling it all over again.'

'I'm sorry about that.' He held her closer.

'Maybe I'm not. Maybe it's time the whole thing was aired. But you know what else I was afraid of? I was afraid that once you knew, you'd make me stop seeing Tom. I couldn't do that, Nick. He means too much to me. I owe him a debt until he dies.'

275

'Is that the only reason why you do it? Because you "owe" him?' She shook her head.

'No. For a lot of reasons. Because I loved him, because of the strength he gave me at times, because of what we shared ... because of Tygue ... I could never stop going, and I didn't think anyone could understand that. Not even you. Does that make any sense?'

'A great deal of sense, Kate. But I have no right to take that away from you. No one does.'

'But can you live with it?'

'Now that it's out in the open between us, I can. I respect what you're doing, Kate. My God, if something like that ever happened to me ... What an incredible thing to realize that someone cared enough to keep on visiting like that, for years and years and years.'

She sighed. 'It's not as noble as you make it sound. Sometimes it's damn hard. Sometimes it's exhausting, and I hate it.'

'But you do it anyway, that's the point.'

'Maybe it is. And I have to go on doing it, Nick.'

'I understand that.' It was a sober moment between them, a moment of peace that sealed a pact of understanding. He took a sip of his tea, and then looked down at her again. 'What are you going to do, though, if someone does find out? If they unearth the past? I assume you've faced that possibility?'

'Yes and no. The only way I make myself get out there is to pretend it won't happen. If I really thought it might, I'd never leave the house again.'

'That might be very pleasant.' They exchanged the first real smile in an hour. 'I'm being serious though.'

'I don't know, love.' She sighed deeply and lay back on the rug. 'I don't know what I'd do, really. Run, panic, I don't know. Maybe it won't matter as much now that you know. Of course there's still Tygue.' She sighed and then remembered something as she looked across at Nick. 'Remember that party you took me to in L.A., after I was on Jasper's show?'

He nodded. 'That guy who said something that upset you? He knew?' Jesus. No wonder she had freaked.

'Not really. He just picked up on my name. Harper. And told me all about a football player named "Joe or Jim or someone", who'd gone crazy, and, well . . . he knew the story, more or less. He asked if I was related to him, as a big joke. And of course I panicked.'

'Poor baby. No wonder. Why the hell didn't you change your name after all that, though?'

'It didn't seem right, because of Tygue. Tygue was his son. He was meant to be Tygue Harper. Changing names seemed such a shoddy thing to do to Tom. Not that he'd have known. I don't know. I just always had such a feeling of loyalty about that.'

'What about Tygue now though? You can't keep this from him forever. And if someone tells him one day that his father almost killed two men and virtually destroyed himself instead, it'll screw up his whole life. You owe him the truth, Kate. Some kind of truth, at an age where he can begin to digest it. Will he ever see him?'

'Never. That would be impossible. Tom wouldn't understand, and it would break Tygue's heart. That's not a daddy. That's a strange helpless child in a broken man's body. He doesn't even look well anymore. Tygue would have to be a grown man to be able to withstand it. And why should he? He doesn't know him. It's better that way. And by the time Tygue is old enough to understand, by then—' She paused and there was a small, sobbing sound. She looked up at Nick, but his face was grave and not tearful as he looked at her. 'What was that?' She sat very still. And Nick cocked his head.

'Nothing. Why?'

'I heard . . . oh God . . .' And then she realized. They had both forgotten the car pool bringing Tygue home. The clock behind Nick said five-fifteen. He had been home for half an hour. Long enough to . . . and then without thinking, she wheeled around, and saw him standing there, silent, with tears pouring down his face. Tygue. They both moved towards him at the same time, and he darted away down the stairs, his sobs echoing as he shouted back at them, 'Leave me alone . . . leave me alone . . .'

CHAPTER XXIX

'Is he all right?' Nick looked at her sombrely as she came out of Tygue's room. It was six-thirty, and it had been a long hour. He had hidden from them in the garden, and had been soaked to the skin when they brought him inside, clutching an equally soaked Willie. Kate had put him in a hot tub while Nick made hot chocolate, and she had sat for a long time in his room. Nick had waited on the stairs.

'I think he's okay. It's hard to tell. Anyway, he's asleep.' She looked exhausted.

'What did you tell him?'

'The truth. What choice did I have? He had heard most of it already, standing at the door. I don't think he meant to eavesdrop. He says he came upstairs to tell me he was home, and he heard us talking about Tom.' She motioned to the open door of their bedroom, and Nick nodded, and followed her inside. They closed the door, and Kate sat down heavily on the bed as Nick handed her a cigarette. She looked more like she needed brandy and a hot bath. All they could think of was Tygue.

'I stirred up some fucking hornet's nest, pressing you about Tom.' It was all he could think of as he waited on the stairs. But she shook her head through the small cloud of grey smoke.

'Don't do that to yourself. Painful as it is, I think you've done us all good. I feel relieved. And Tygue will live through it. This way I can tell him the good stuff too. Tom Harper was a beautiful human being. Tygue has a right to know that, and he can't unless he knows the rest. So now he'll know both. It's a fair trade.' She hesitated for a moment and then spoke again, with a sigh. 'There have been times when I've wondered about the way I've played God. I kept a very important part of himself away from Tygue. I kept him from knowing who and what his father was. I thought that would be easier for him.' She sat down slowly and looked very hard at Nick. 'But there were other reasons too.'

'They couldn't have been bad-reasons.'

'Maybe they were. I wanted him to be mine. I wanted him to be totally free of all that. I didn't want him to be ... like Tom.' Nick waited for her to go on, without saying a word. 'I didn't want him to fall in love with the image of Tom Harper, the glory of the albums and the clippings and the adulation. Tom loved all that stuff. What man wouldn't? I think maybe I was always a little bit afraid that Tygue might want it too, maybe even to prove something for Tom. To leave the Harper name "clean". God only knows what crazy ideas might have gone through his head ... I was afraid of all those possibilities. It was just a lot easier the way it was.' And then, remembering Nick again, she smiled a tiny smile. 'But it wasn't right, Nick. It's right that he should know. One day I'll probably even have to tell him about my parents. I let him think the whole world around him had died, except me. But that's not the truth. I suppose everyone has a right to the truth.' Nick had had a right to it too. For a moment, she felt as though she had betrayed them all, and she felt a wave of exhaustion sweep over her at the thought. 'Anyway, darling, things have a way of working out for the best.' She held out a hand to Nick, but he didn't take it and he looked suddenly stricken again.

'Does Tygue think so?' Nick said it bitterly as he looked at her and then out at the Bay. He should have minded his own business.

'He's confused. He doesn't know what the hell to think. The only thing he was positive about was that he wanted to see his dad. I told him he couldn't.' She sighed again. 'And right now he hates me for it, but he'll get over it. He has you.' She smiled at Nick's back, and then moved towards him and put her arms around his waist.

'I'm not his father though, Kate.'

'That doesn't matter. You give him more than most fathers would – emotionally and in every other way. And I don't know, Nick. This is our reality. Tom was who he was and he did what he did. For whatever reasons. Maybe it's just time we both faced the truth. It won't kill either of us. So stop looking like somebody died.' He turned to face her and tried to smile, but it was not an overwhelming success. He felt as though the world had fallen in on him, and he didn't know what to do to make it up to them. 'By the way, aren't you working tonight?' She looked at the clock in surprise.

'I called in sick while you were in with Tygue.'

'I'm glad.' She smiled up at him and stretched out on the bed. 'I'm so tired I could die.'

'I can't imagine why, Cinderella.' He sat down and started to rub her feet and then her legs. 'I mean, after all, you only drove about three hundred miles today, came home and were forced to confront me with all the skeletons in your closet, after which, I was kind enough to tear the guts out of your son, forcing you to rescue the child from the pouring rain, bathe him, comfort him, and generally save the day. Why the hell are you tired?' She was grinning at the description.

'Do I get a national award for all that? It sounds exemplary.'

'You really should. And me, I should get a kick in the ass.'

'Would you settle for something else?' She sat up as he rubbed her legs and slid her arms around his neck.

'I don't deserve it.' He hung his head like a wicked child and she laughed.

'Just shut up and relax.' He did and they did, and it was nine o'clock when Kate went in to run a bath. 'Will you keep an eye on this for me for a minute? I want to check on Tygue.'

'Sure.' He stopped her for a moment, for a long tender kiss. She had given him everything that night, he knew that. Her body, her soul, her heart, everything she had to give had been his. As though to soothe his pain for what he'd done. 'I love you, Cinderella. More than you know. By the way' – he looked down at her gently and smoothed a stray lock of hair from her face – 'far be it from me to snoop into your life or question your motives, but it seems to me that you forgot something tonight.' She looked up at him with a confused little smile. She knew he was teasing but she wasn't sure about what.

'I did?' And then she grinned broadly. 'Oh damn. Dinner. Oh darling, I'm sorry. Are you starving?'

'No, I'm not starving. I couldn't even eat. I meant something else.' He pulled her back into his arms and felt her body bring his to life again as they both smiled and kissed. 'You forgot the flying saucer – you know, the magic baby catcher.' He looked at her with a grin. He had forgotten it too. Until afterwards. Everything had been so topsy-turvy all night. And when he looked at her now, she was frowning with a look of irritation but not panic.

'Shit. My diaphragm.' She had left it sitting virginally in the drawer.

'Is that a disaster?' He felt an obligation to ask, although for him it was anything but a disaster. He still wanted her child. Tygue as well as his own. 'Would you freak out?'

'No. But I won't get pregnant anyway. It's the wrong time of the month.'

'How do you figure that?' Not the way he understood things.

'I had my hair done yesterday.'

'Huh? You're crazy. And you haven't answered my question.'

'What is it?' But she was teasing him and he knew it.

'The question is ... oh to hell with you. Get pregnant, so what. I'll drop you off at the unwed mothers' home, and go to Tahiti with Tygue.'

'Be sure you send me a postcard. And don't bother watching my bath.' She grinned as she turned it off, and grabbed a white terry-cloth robe to go check on Tygue. 'I'll be back in a sec.'

'Do that.' He said it with a smile. And she did. She was back in a second but without a smile. She walked back into the bathroom with her robe flying wide, showing her long thin naked body, and her face deathly white.

'Tygue's gone.'

Nick felt as though the earthquake had hit. She silently handed him a note, and as he read it, she bent over the john and threw up.

CHAPTER XXX

'No, we don't know where he went. All we know is what he left in this note.' Nick looked across at Kate. They had discussed it all before the police arrived. They were not going to say anything about Tom. It wouldn't help.

'Let's have another look at that note.'

The note was painfully simple. 'Iym goang to fine mie fathere.' Nice plain seven-year-old English. He was going to find his father. The plainclothesman looked up at Nick and Kate.

'You're not his father, Mr . . . er . . . Waterman?'

'No. He's Mrs. Harper's son. But Tygue and I are very close.' After he said it, he felt like an ass. But who was thinking straight? Kate was beginning to look strangely translucent and grey. She had barely spoken to the police, and Nick was afraid she was going into shock.

'Do you know where his father is? Seems like it would be pretty simple to give him a call.' Kate looked agonized, and Nick shook his head.

'I'm afraid not. The boy's father died before he was born.'

'Was he angry at you then?' The cop came back at him quickly and this time Kate revived.

'No, I think, if anything, he was angry at me. I think mostly he's just under a lot of new pressures. We just moved to San Francisco, and he's in a new school, and . . .' She faltered and Nick squeezed her hand.

'Does he have any money?'

Kate shook her head. 'I don't think so.'

'Did he take anything?'

'Yes. His teddy bear.' Her eyes filled as she said it. 'It's a large brown bear with a red tie.' She looked down at Bert, who wagged his tail and approached, and she only cried harder.

'What's the boy wearing?'

She didn't know. And she would never be able to guess. But she went to the hall closet and discovered his slicker was gone.

'A yellow slicker. And probably jeans and cowboy boots.'

'Anyone in town he would go to?'

'Felicia!' She ran for the phone, but there was no answer when she dialled. Sombrely, she gave the officer Licia's number. And Tillie's. And Joey's back home. And ... 'And I think he might have tried to get to Carmel.' She looked miserably at Nick.

'Does he know anyone there?' The policeman looked up.

'No. But he likes it.' Damn. What could she tell him? He went to find his retarded, crippled, once-famous father, whom he didn't even know was alive until this afternoon? 'What are you going to do?' She squeezed Nick's hand as the police closed their little brown books.

'Comb the area until we find him. Now we need some pictures.' They brought out dozens of them. Colour, close-up, distance, in every possible outfit, on his pony, with his dog, at Disneyland, on a cable car with Licia. They shoved the makings of an album into their hands. 'We'll only need one or two.' Kate nodded numbly as they went out into the rain. 'We'll call you every hour to report.'

'Thank you.'

'Hang tough.' They looked encouragingly at Nick as they left. Expensive house. And the kid looked happy enough in the pictures. They obviously weren't abusing him. Maybe he was just one of those funny little kids who needed to run away. They'd seen that kind before. The girls tended to stand dramatically in the doorway, giving their parents every opportunity to beg them to stay home. The boys just packed up and split.

'Oh God, Nick, what'll we do?'

'Just what they said, darling. Hang tough.'

'I can't ... oh God ... Nick, I can't. He could be kidnapped. Run over. He could be ...'

'Stop it!' He grabbed her by the shoulders and then pulled her tightly into his arms. 'Just stop it, Kate. We can't do that. We have to know he'll be okay.' Kate nodded numbly as she cried, and then clutched hopelessly at Nick. There was something agonized in her eyes that tore at him, and finally as she sobbed, he began to understand. There was more than just fear and worry in her heart.

'It's my fault, Nick . . . it's all my fault.'

'I said *stop it*, Kate. It's not your fault.' He wanted to tell her it was his own fault for bringing up the whole mess that afternoon, but it was pointless for either of them to blame themselves now. What they had to do was get Tygue back and tell him about his father, talk about the past, try to explain Kate's reasons for keeping him in the dark. And they would love the boy more than they had before. He needed that. Tonight proved it. But breast-beating was a futile act. Nick held tightly to Kate and gently pushed her chin up with one hand until her drenched eyes met his. 'It's no one's fault, darling. We can both torment ourselves with that for the next hundred years, but maybe it was just meant to come out. Maybe he had to know.'

'I know he did. I should have told him years ago and then this wouldn't have happened.'

'But you didn't, and you can't know now if that made any difference. Maybe he couldn't have handled it till now. Whatever the case, you just have to let the past be. You didn't tell him. Now he knows. Those are the facts we have to deal with.'

'But what if something awful happens to him?' Her voice was a plaintive wail again as her eyes flooded again.

'Nothing will. We just have to believe that, Kate.'

'I wish I could.' She blew her nose loudly and closed her eyes.

The police had called every hour, as promised, but they still had no news. It was after midnight when they reached Felicia.

'Oh my God.' Felicia gasped and sat down as Nick explained. Kate was in no condition to talk. She had stopped crying, but she only sat there, staring, and thumbing through the pictures. Nick had finally stopped trying to take them away from her. 'Should I come over?'

'It might help. You've been through worse things with her before.'

'Yeah. And Nick' – she hesitated for a moment, and then decided to say it – 'I'm glad you know. She needs to be free of all that. She can't hide forever.'

'I know. But this is a rough way to go.'

'Maybe there's no other way.' Nick nodded silently and they hung up. Felicia came right over, and they sat there together, drinking coffee and going crazy until five. And at five-thirty, the police called again. Nick braced himself for the same dismal news. No news.

'We've got him.'

'Where?'

'Right here.' The cop grinned down at the kid.

And Nick closed his eyes and shouted into the room. 'They've got him.' And then into the phone again, 'Is he okay?'

'Fine. He's tired, but fine. Willie the Bear looks a little forlorn though.' The kid was very quiet. Probably sobered by the experience.

'Where was he?'

'Sitting around the Greyhound bus station, trying to talk someone into taking him to Carmel. His mother was right. They usually are. We'll have him home to you in ten minutes.'

'Wait. Can I talk to him?' He was going to put Kate on, as she stood there next to him sobbing and laughing and squeezing his arm while Felicia looked on through her own tears.

The policeman came back on in a minute. 'He says he's too tired to talk.' Ornery little bugger. But that was their problem. He'd make out the report, give the kid a speech about the evils of running away and the dangers of bus stations, and take the boy home.

'What do you mean he was too tired?' Kate looked stunned after Nick hung up, and then she understood. 'He's still pissed.'

Nick nodded. 'I assume so.'

He assumed right. When Tygue got home he was subdued, and he waited until the policeman had left before speaking to them. He had dutifully hugged his mother when he came in, but it won her no warmth and no comfort, only the puddle Willie had squeezed onto her shirt. He was still soaking. Tygue had dried off in the bus station. It was amazing he had got there at all. He said he'd had a nickel and had taken the bus. Bus drivers all along the way had given him directions.

'Do you have any idea what could have happened to you?' She was starting to scream at him out of relief. He hung his head, but he did not look contrite. And then finally he spoke.

'I'm going to do it again.'

'*What?*' She shrieked as Nick tried to calm her down.

'I'm going to find my father. I want to see him.' And then she sat back with a sigh and looked at her son. How could she tell him without breaking his heart that there was no father to see? There was a man, and he had been his father, but he was gone now. And Tygue couldn't see him.

'You can't do that.' She said it very softly.

'I'm gonna, Mom.' He looked at her with determination all over his face.

'We'll talk about it.'

She put him to bed and this time he stayed there. But it had been a very long night, and as Felicia drove home at six-thirty in the morning, she had a feeling that it wasn't over yet. Maybe this time. But Tygue meant what he said. He was going to see his father. She hoped Kate understood that. But at that moment, Kate was already sound asleep in Nick's arms. She got three hours' sleep. Stu Weinberg called at nine-thirty.

'Hm?' In the deep haze of sleep, she couldn't figure out who it was. Nick had promised to leave a note out for the car pool, and they would all sleep late. All day, if she could. Nick had said he'd deal with Tygue until she got up.

'Did I wake you?'

'Hm? What? . . . No . . .' But she was already drifting off again. Nick walked into the room and shook her shoulder.

'Wake up. You're on the phone.'

'Huh? Who is this?'

'It's Stu Weinberg, for chrissake. What the hell is going on there? Did you go to a wild party last night?'

'Yeah. Very.' She sat up in bed, squinting, feeling sick. Her head churned as though she had the worst hangover of her life, but at least now she was functioning. 'How's the book?'

'Making you and me both a fortune. In fact, that's why I'm calling. You've got another tour.'

'Oh no. Did Nick fix this one too?' She tried to smile, but her face wouldn't comply. What was Nick up to now? But Weinberg insisted Nick had nothing to do with this one. And he sounded sincere. 'Then what is it?'

'A week in New York. Your publisher wants you there for promo to keep the book hot on the lists. It's a must, kiddo, especially if you want to hit them pretty soon with the one you're working on now. You'd better stay in their good graces.'

'I can't now.' There was too much to cope with at home.

'Bullshit, Kate. You have to. You have an obligation to these people. They're making your career.' He began to tick off the shows they had booked her on. Too many, maybe. It was going to be an incredible week.

'I told you. I can't.'

'You're going to have to. I told them you would.'

'How could you do that?' She was ready to cry. And she was still so unbearably tired from the night before.

'I did it because you have no choice. Ask Nick. He knows what this means.'

'Never mind that. All right, I'll see. From when to when?'

'You leave in three days. You'll be gone for a week.'

'I'll do my best.'

'You'll have to do better than that.' He was relentless. 'I'll call you later to confirm it.'

'Okay.' She was too weak to argue. She lay back on her pillow and tried to think.

'Who was that?' Nick looked down at her with concern.

'Weinberg.'

'Something wrong?'

She nodded. 'He called to tell me that my publisher booked me on tour in New York. For a week.'

'When?' Nick looked stunned.

'I leave in three days.'

'Sonofabitch. I'll kill him.' Nick sat down and ran a hand through his hair. 'You can't go.'

287

'He says I have to. And he didn't do it. I told you. My publisher did.' And besides, dammit, Nick couldn't tell her what she could and couldn't do.

'I don't care who did it. You know goddamn well you can't go now. You told him that, didn't you?'

But she hadn't. Even with everything that was happening, she hadn't. Stu had made it sound as if her career were on the line, as though she had to 'or else'.

'What the hell did you tell him?' Nick looked down at her, shocked.

'I told him I'd see what I could do.'

'You mean you're going?'

'I don't know. I don't know, dammit. I can't even think. How do I know what I'm doing three days from now?'

'If you have any sense, three days from now you'll be trying to straighten out this mess with your son. That ought to be the number one priority.'

'It is, but . . . godamnit, leave me alone.' Would they never get off her back? Nick with his righteous indignation and ideas of perfect parenthood, and Tygue with his overwhelming needs and demands. Jesus, she had a right to some kind of life too. She had a right to the success that was coming her way.

'Falling in love with yourself, aren't you, Kate?' It took every ounce of control not to slap him. 'It's not so much fun being a mommy now, is it?'

'Will you leave me alone, damn you?' She was shrieking and her voice didn't sound like her own. 'What do you want from me? Blood?'

'No, some reality. You have a child who is facing a major crisis in his life. He doesn't need you to go gaily off on tour.'

'Well, what about what *I* need? What about my career? What about what I've given him all these years? Doesn't that count for anything? Don't I get a little time off for good behaviour?'

'Is that how you feel about it all, Kate? Is that how you feel about him? About me?' For an insane moment, she wanted to say yes, but she didn't dare.

288

Her voice was suddenly very quiet. 'I just need some time to think. That's all. Just let me work this out for myself.' She sat down on the bed and ran a hand through her hair.

'I just don't think you've got much choice.'

'I've never had much choice. Maybe right now I need to be able to choose, to make my own decisions.'

'You've made decisions before, Kate.' Why was he pushing so hard? Why didn't he get the hell off her back? But she didn't say any of what she was thinking. She was suddenly lost in her own thoughts.

'Yeah. I've made decisions before.' Like the decision not to tell Tygue about Tom. That had been some great decision, as it turned out.

'What's eating you, Kate? Are you feeling guilty again? Is that it?'

'Dammit, Nick, yes!' She jumped to her feet as she shouted at him again, and this time her eyes were blazing with fury. 'Yes, I feel guilty. Okay? Does that make you feel better, to hear me say it? Yes, I feel like this whole mess with Tygue is my own goddamn fault. And you know what? It doesn't make me love him any more than I did before. It just makes me want to run away. Because between his being pissed off at me and not understanding anything I've done, and you shoving it in my face, I want to get the hell away from both of you. How does that sound to you, mister?'

'Just dandy.' He turned on his heel and left the room, and she slammed into the bathroom, to emerge ten minutes later looking tidy but still wan. Tygue was still asleep, but Nick was sitting at the breakfast table with a cup of coffee. She poured herself one and looked over at him. He looked like hell too.

'I'm sorry I yelled.'

'It doesn't matter.' His voice was subdued now too, but he looked at her as though examining a visitor from another planet. 'Are you going?'

'I don't know.'

'It's happening to you, Kate.'

'What is?' But she knew what he meant.

'The star trip. The Me-Fabulous-Me syndrome. You have

to do what you have to do for your career. Do you have any idea what's happening to that kid right now?' Nick was seething again.

'Do you have any idea what's happening to me? How many ways I'm being pulled?'

'I'm sorry. But you're a grownup. You can deal with it, Kate. He can't. I know you've had a lot of rotten breaks, but that's no reason to pass them on to him. He can't help it. And he is totally confused right now about his father.'

'And I can't change that. I can't wave a magic wand and make Tom whole again. He's not. And Tygue can't see him. It would be terrible for both of them.' She was shouting again.

'I understand that' – he made an effort to lower his voice – 'but Tygue doesn't. I just can't believe you'd go to New York now.'

'I didn't say I would.'

'No, but you will.'

'How the hell do you know?' She wanted to throw her coffee at him, as he sat there glaring at her, angry and self-righteous. She hated him.

'I know you'll go because you've already been suckered into that whole horseshit game of success. The shows, the interviews, the money, the best sellers, all of it. I can see it happening to you, Kate. And I'll tell you something, I'm goddamn sorry I had anything to do with it. I'm sorry they put you on the show.'

'What does that have to do with it? Look at the money I've made in the last four months. It comes to over a quarter of a million dollars. Me. I made that, all by myself, with one lousy book, with or without your lousy show. Tygue will go to college because of that, he'll go to a good school before college. He'll have everything he needs.'

'Except his mother.'

'Fuck you.'

'You know something? I don't give a damn what you do. I just don't want to have to sit here and watch when you tell him you're going to New York.'

'Then don't. I'll tell him while you're out.'

'You're going, aren't you?' He pushed and he pushed and he pushed . . .

"Yes!' It was a long angry wail that seemed to fill the whole house. They were both startled, mostly Kate. She hadn't even been sure she was going. At least, she liked to think that. Actually she had known all along. As soon as Weinberg had told her how important it was for her next book. She wanted that one to do even better than the first. It told her a cold hard empty thing about herself as she sat in the kitchen alone, after Nick had quietly left the room. Maybe he was right. Maybe it was starting to happen to her. The success trip. But not at Tygue's expense . . . no . . . not Tygue.

She tried to explain it all to him that afternoon, but Tygue didn't want to talk. She tried to make him understand about Tom, about the books, about her work, about what had happened to Tom, about . . . but he was only seven. He didn't understand very much. And all he could think about was his father. She gave him an album of Tom's old clippings from the golden years of success. Tygue left to devour those in his room. And Kate called Tillie.

Tillie would come to stay in the guest room for the week she was gone. It would ease the burden on Nick, whom Kate barely saw before she left. He came home late both nights, when she was already asleep. And he was out all day. She tried to explain what she felt to Felicia, but she was unsympathetic too. No one understood. Even Tillie seemed cool when she arrived, but perhaps she was only intimidated by the city. Kate was grateful she had come. And Tygue seemed thrilled to see her. In fact, Kate felt suddenly shut out: Tygue was happier to see Tillie than he was to be with her.

'Want me to take you to the airport?' Nick looked at her coolly.

'I can grab a cab. I want to leave Tillie my car here at the house. But it's no big deal.'

'Don't be a martyr. I'll drive you.'

'I couldn't stand the speeches.' There was a chill between them that had never been there before, and it terrified her, but she wouldn't let that show.

'I've made all the speeches I'm going to make. Except for one. You look tired, Kate. Try not to overdo it in New York.'

'It's been a rough couple of days. For everyone.' She looked over at him and something softened in his eyes.

'Just don't forget that I love you, Cinderella.' It was the first time she had seen him soften like that in several days. 'What time's your plane?' He smiled a slow smile and she told him what time she had to leave. They both looked at each other with regret. 'Damn.' She slipped into her dress. He zipped her up instead of down, and five minutes later they left. It was a quiet trip out to the airport and she was sorry they hadn't had time to make love. It would have done them both good. A reminder of what they had. A peaceful bond before being cannonballed into the madness of New York. But when he kissed her, she knew how much he cared. She waved to him as she boarded the plane, and felt as though she had never been as lonely in her life. She drank a great deal too much wine before reaching New York, but it took the edge off her loneliness, and she slept the last two hours. It was a hell of a way to get to New York. Tired and rumpled and hungover. A honeymoon this wasn't. It was for real. And she was alone in the big city. She knew it as she stood on the sidewalk fighting for a cab. The limo they'd sent for her hadn't shown up, and she couldn't find one of her bags. It was a perfect beginning. But things got better after that. In desperation, she shared a cab into the city with a very nice-looking, well-dressed man, an architect from Chicago, somewhere in his late forties. And he was staying at the Regency too.

'How convenient. Do you always stay there?' He made no effort to discover her name, and made pleasant conversation all the way into the city. She looked over at him casually. His hair was grey, his face well-chiselled and fine-featured but worn. His body looked taut and young though. He was attractive, but in a very quiet way. He looked nothing like the healthy athletic men of California. He looked cosmopolitan and a little pale, but interestingly so.

'I stayed there the last time I was in town.'

'I manage to get here about once a month.' He glanced at

her casually and smiled. They chatted about the buildings, the view, San Francisco, and inadvertently she let slip that she was a writer.

'What a marvellous profession. You must love it.' He looked at her with frank envy and she laughed. He made it sound even better than it was.

'I enjoy it a lot.' And then, somehow, he drew her out and she found herself telling him about her next book.

'You know, it has a feeling, not a similar plot pattern, but just a family resemblance in terms of mood, to a marvellous book I just read, *A Final Season*.' She began to laugh.

'Have you read it too?' He looked amused as she grinned.

What the hell? Why not admit it to him? 'Well, not recently. But I wrote it.' It took a moment to register and then he looked at her in amazement.

'Did you? But it's a wonderful book!' He looked stunned.

'Then I'll send you a copy of the next one!' She said it teasingly but he immediately whipped out his card and handed it to her with a smile.

'I'll expect you to keep that promise, Miss Harper.'

And now he knew her name. She put the card away just as they reached the hotel.

CHAPTER XXXI

It was a far cry from her trip to New York with Nick. Gone were the limousines, the hansom cab rides, the secret adventures, the lunches at Lutèce and dinners at Caravelle. And gone the buffer of his loving. This time she was confronted with New York in all its bold brassy reality, pushing, shoving, fighting for cabs, fighting stiff winds as newspapers and litter swirled around her feet. And the bookings her publisher had made were almost inhuman. She had three radio shows to do the first day, no time for lunch, and at four that afternoon she taped a television talk show, where the host had paired her with a sportswriter who was openly condescending. She was numb with exhaustion and anger when she reached the hotel at six, and it was the wrong time to call Nick or Tygue. Nick would be setting up the show, and Tygue would still be in school. She called room service and asked for a glass of white wine, and then sat back quietly to wait until she could call Nick. Even the room was less pretty this time. It was more elaborate, in white and gold, but smaller and colder, and the bed looked sad and empty. She smiled as she remembered the love-making of their last trip.

She sat back on the couch with her glass of wine and tucked her long legs under her. She was three thousand miles from home, alone in a strange hotel, and she couldn't talk to anyone she knew. She felt unloved and suddenly frightened, and she desperately wanted to go home. This was it. The wild fabulous high rise of fame. But it was a lonely empty building and no one else seemed to live there. She longed to be back in the house hidden in the hedges on Green Street. If he even wanted her back. Maybe it was almost over. It felt as though they had just begun, and she and Tygue had only just moved to San Francisco the month before, but maybe it would all be too much for Nick. Maybe her career would be too great a conflict for him, with his own work, or maybe he just couldn't accept her. Kate started to call room service for a second glass of wine, and then with a frown she put down the phone. This was ridiculous. She was in New York. She was a star. She grinned to herself at the word. All right, so she wasn't a star, but she was successful. She could go anywhere she liked for dinner. She didn't have to sit in her room. It was absurd. She reached into her handbag and pulled out the sheet of paper where she'd written a list of restaurants Felicia had given her. The first on the list was someplace called Gino's. Licia had told her she could go there alone, and that it was crawling with models, ad men, and writers, a smattering of European society types, and 'beautiful people'. 'It's a good show. You'll love it.' And it was only two blocks from her hotel. She could walk.

She ran a comb through her hair, washed her face, and put on fresh makeup. She was ready. The black dress she had worn all day would do fine. Felicia said it wasn't dressy. By New York standards, anyway, that meant blue jeans, Guccis, and mink, or your latest Dior. As she picked up the long red wool coat off the back of a chair where she'd flung it, she remembered the gruelling heat of only two months before. She looked down at the black lizard shoes, and then around the room again . . . so empty. God, it was so empty. It was going to feel good to get out. Even the view didn't delight her this time. The whole city looked very tall and frightening and dark. And it was chilly and even windier when she stepped outside. She turned up the collar of her coat and turned east towards Lexington Avenue. She had rejected the doorman's offer of a cab, and walked rapidly away. She had already picked up the pace of New Yorkers. Run, dash, fly, bump into someone on street, grunt, shove, and run past. She laughed to herself as she thought of it. She had only been in town for a day and she already felt corroded by the pace. Her mind wandered back to Nick as she walked, and she was annoyed at herself. And at him. What right did he have to make her feel guilty about her success? She had worked hard for it. She deserved it. And she wasn't short-changing Tygue, or Nick, for that matter. All right, so the timing wasn't perfect for a trip, but Christ, she'd only be gone for a week. And she had a right to this... she had a right to it ... the words kept echoing in her head as she turned south on Lexington Avenue, her high heels beating an even staccato against the subway grille beneath as she avoided fleets of pedestrians clattering by. She was almost thirty years old now, and she had a right to this ... right to this ... She almost missed the restaurant, and looked up in surprise as two men bumped into her. They were just leaving Gino's. They didn't even say sorry, they merely looked her over, seemed to approve, and walked on, stepping off the kerb to grab a cab from two other men. Standard New York. In California, the men would have been knocking each other cold for something like that. In New York, the two men who'd lost their cab simply hailed another, and grabbed it, just before the woman who'd flagged it first from the kerb. Kate smiled to herself as she slipped inside Gino's double, yellow, swinging doors. It would take years to develop a style like that on the streets of New York, or maybe it happened very quickly. Maybe one got that way without noticing it. It still seemed funny to her.

'Signora?' A dapper Italian in a grey pin-striped suit came to her side with a smile. 'Table for one?'

'Yes.' She nodded with a smile. She could hardly hear him in the din as she looked around with amusement. The walls were a hideous colour, covered with zebras chasing each other diagonally up and down the walls. Plastic plants flourished in several locations, and the lighting was dark. The bar was jammed seven deep, and the tables were covered with white cloths and well populated by '*le tout* New York'. Just what Felicia had promised. Models still wearing the day's makeup and the latest Calvin Klein, ad men looking suave, married and unfaithful, actresses and society matrons of some note, and a certain uniform look to the men. There were two kinds: European and American. The Americans all looked very Madison Avenue, in striped suits, horn rims, white shirts, and ties. The Europeans had them beat by a mile – better tailors, better shirts, softer colours, more scandalous eyes, and their trousers were all the right length. The laughter of women darted in and out of the conversations of men, like chimes in an orchestra, and thickly woven into the background was a constant caw and clatter provided by the waiters. They made as much noise as possible with their trays, all but destroyed the crockery as they sent it sailing into the hands of the busboys, and shouted to each other as loudly as they could from as far away as they could manage in the crowd. The kitchen itself would have produced lightning and thunder, and for lack of that they did the best they could with the materials at hand. They managed very nicely with metal pots and heavy utensils. And all of it combined to produce Gino's, a rich tapestry of sounds and sights, and the luscious smells of Italian cuisine.

'We'll have a table for you in a moment.' The maitre d' in the grey pin-stripe suit looked her over in a manner worthy of Rome and waved her graciously to the bar. 'A drink while you're waiting?' His accent was perfection, his eyes were a caress. She had to force herself not to laugh. Gino's was a heady experience. It catapulted her instantly from her earlier mood of gloom to a feeling of fiesta.

With only the slightest hesitation she walked to the bar, ordered a gin and tonic, and heard the man just in front of her order Campari. Obviously an Italian She could tell by the way he said 'Campari soda' and then carried on a few sentences of conversation in Italian with the bartender. Kate looked him over from just behind him, where she stood. He smelled of a rich European men's cologne ... something French ... she couldn't remember it, but it was familiar. She had tried it out once at I. Magnin's, thinking of buying it for Nick. But it wasn't Nick, it was too rich, too sophisticated. Nick's lemon and spice suited him better. But not this man. The collar she saw was a warm Wedgwood blue, the back of his suit looked like a blazer, and it too had an Italian flair to it, from what she could see. The hair was grey, the neck slightly lined ... forty-five maybe ... forty-eight .... and then suddenly he turned to face her and she felt herself blush and then gasp in surprise.

'Oh, it's you!' It was the man from the cab she'd taken from the airport. The architect from Chicago. 'I thought you were Italian.' And then she was even more embarrassed to have admitted considering the matter at all, and laughed again as he smiled at her.

'I lived in Rome for seven years. I'm afraid I'm addicted to scungili, antipasto, Campari, and all things Italian.'

His front view was even more impressive than the rear view had been, and she realized now that he was much better-looking than she had first thought him. She hadn't paid much attention to him in the cab.

'How is New York treating you, Miss Harper?' He smiled at her over his drink and made room for her at the bar.

'All right, for New York. I worked my tail off today.'

'Writing?'

'Nothing as easy as that. Doing publicity.'

'I am impressed.' But he looked more amused than impressed, and his eyes somehow embarrassed her. It was as though he saw too much through the black dress, yet he said nothing inappropriate. It was just a feeling she got. There was something raw and sexy beneath the well-tailored clothes and the businesslike manner. 'Will I see you on TV?'

'Not unless you stay in your hotel room and watch daytime television.' She smiled at him again.

'I'm afraid not. I've been doing my New York number too. We started with breakfast conferences at seven today. They work like madmen in this town.' And then together, they looked out at the room. 'They do everything like madmen. Even eat.' She laughed with him and for a few minutes they just watched the scene. Then she felt his eyes on her again, and she turned towards him. She said nothing. They only looked at each other, and he smiled and held up his drink.

'To you, Miss Harper, for a book that meant a great deal to me. How did you ever get those insights into what makes men tick? The crawl for success, and the heartbreak if you stop just shy of the top - or get there, and fall off.' He looked into his glass and then back at her, and she was surprised at the seriousness she saw in his face. The book really had meant something to him, and suddenly she was glad. He understood. It was as though he understood Tom.

'You handled it very well. Even from a man's point of view. I would think it would be difficult for a woman to really understand what it's like. All the macho nonsense about making it, and then the heartbreak of it when you don't.'

'I'm not so sure it's all that different for women. But I watched my husband go through it,' she said, looking into her drink. But she was very aware of this man's gentle voice, like a soft summer breeze in the winter storm of the noise around them.

'He must be very proud of you now.'

She looked up at him unexpectedly and shook her head. 'No. He's dead.' She didn't say it to shock him. She just said it, but he was stunned nonetheless. And then she was the one who apologized. 'I didn't mean to say it that way.'

'I'm sorry for you. But now I understand the book better than I did. That makes a lot of sense. Did he make it, in the commercial sense of the word, before he died?' It seemed to matter to this man a lot. And Kate had decided to be honest with him. He was a stranger, and she had had two drinks. The wine at the hotel, and now the gin. She was feeling unusually honest, and cut off from everyone she knew. Here, no one knew her. She could say anything that popped into her head.

'Yes, he made it. And he blew it. That's what killed him. He had to have another chance, "or else". He got the "or else".

'Heart attack?' It was his worst fear.

'More or less.' And then she realized what she was doing to this man, and looked up quickly. 'No. Not a heart attack. Something else. His soul died. The rest just sort of went with it. But no, it wasn't a heart attack.' He looked only slightly relieved.

'I wonder what the answer is. To refuse to play the game? To refuse to run the race for success? But it's so damn tempting, isn't it?' He looked at her with that warm, sexy smile, and she smiled back.

'Yes, it is. I'm beginning to understand that better now myself. You always end up having to choose, having to make decisions about what matters, hurting somebody. Somehow one shouldn't have to make those choices.'

'Ah, Miss Harper, but one does.' He smiled ruefully.

'Do you?' She was shocked at her own question, but she liked talking to him. He was worldly and bright and very good-looking, and he wanted to talk about the things that were bothering her now.

'Yes, I have to make those choices. I have a wife who says she needs me in Chicago. For dinner parties, or something like that. A son who thinks I'm a capitalist asshole, and a daughter with cerebral palsy. They need me. Probably very much. But if I don't run after the almighty dollar, then my wife can't give her dinner parties, and my son can't sit on his lazy ass and espouse his saintly causes, and my daughter ... well, she needs it most of all.' He grew very quiet and looked into his drink, and then back at Kate again. 'The bitch of it is that my reasons for running all sound good and righteous and proper, but the truth of it is, that isn't even why I do it anymore.'

'I know.' She understood. Only too well. 'You do it because you enjoy it. Because you have to. Because now it's part of you, and ...' She said the last words very softly, as though to herself, '... because you have a right to it. To the good stuff. To the excitement, the success ...' She looked up at him again and he held her eyes for a long time with a small ironical smile.
. 'That's why I loved your book. Because you knew.'

And then she smiled too. 'The funny thing is that when I wrote the book, I knew all about it. Or I thought I did. But I knew it from seeing it, not feeling it. I knew it from where your wife sits. Now I know it differently. Now I'm confronted by the same things myself.'

'Welcome to the land of the successful failures, Miss Harper.'

'Do you consider yourself a failure?'

'Depends on how you look at it. I suspect that to them, my family, I probably am. I don't know. To the business community, I'm certainly not a failure.' Far from it. He had won several major international awards in the past five years. But he didn't tell Kate that, he merely smiled the small ironical smile. 'One pays a very high price, just like all the songs say.'

'Is it worth it?'

'Ask your husband.' Ouch. She almost flinched at the words. 'You ought to know the answer to that.'

'I suppose so, but I see it differently now. I'm enjoying what I'm doing. I don't see why you can't have both. A real life, a family life, a life with some meaning and integrity, and a successful career.'

'I suppose so.' He waved to the barman to refill their drinks and she didn't object. 'But it depends on what you call successful and what you call a career. Your career is by no means of small proportions, I would think. In a sense, you're a celebrity. That must take its toll.'

'And you?' She wanted to know more about him. She liked him.

'I'm not a celebrity. I'm just an architect. But I play in the big leagues.'

'Are you happy?'

'No.' He said it very simply as though it were something he accepted, not something he cried about. 'I suppose it's very lonely for all of us.' He looked at her pointedly.

'And your wife?' Kate's eyes bored into his with the question.

'I suppose she's unhappy too.'

'Doesn't she say?'

'No. She's a very well-behaved woman. And' – he hesitated for only a moment – 'I don't ask her. We knew each other as kids, and we got married young. We had both just finished college. I was going to be a commercial artist. She wanted to play around with fine arts. Instead, my father suggested I go to graduate school at Yale. I did and studied architecture, got my degree, and that was the beginning. We both forgot about the dreams. The small dreams anyway. The big dreams came easy. Too easy.' And then he looked up at Kate with a broad smile that belied everything he'd said. 'And now you know my entire life story, Miss Harper. From beginning to end. The dismal failure of my marriage, the pains of my soul, even my fears about a heart attack. You can use it all in your next novel.' He finished his drink and then looked up at her again with irony and laughter in his eyes. 'And I'll bet you don't even remember my name.'

She still had his card somewhere but she hadn't looked at it. And now she gave him an embarrassed smile. 'I hate to admit it, but you're right. Besides, I'm awful with names.'

'So am I. The only reason I remembered yours is because I liked the book. Kaitlin, isn't it?' She liked the way he said it.

'Kate.'

'Philip. Philip Wells.' He held out a hand, and she solemnly shook it.

And then suddenly the headwaiter in the pin-stripe suit was standing discreetly next to them. 'Signor, signora, your tables are ready.' He waved towards the centre of the room, and Philip looked at Kate.

'Could we consolidate them into one? Or would I be intruding on your time alone?' It never even occurred to him that she might be meeting someone, but she liked the idea of eating dinner with him. She didn't want to eat alone.

'No, that would be very nice.'

The headwaiter nodded instant acquiescence, Philip paid the bartender for their drinks, and they moved on towards the main dining area in the centre of the room, between the diagonally fleeing zebras. Kate looked up at them with a dubious expression and winced as Philip held out a chair for her and laughed at the look on her face.

'I know. Aren't they awful? The best of it is that every time they've redecorated, they've gone to fabulous expense to reproduce the exact same decor. Right down to the plastic greenery and the zebras. They're probably right. The natives expect them.'

'Do you come here that often?'

'I'm in New York fairly often, and I always come here when I am. I told you, I'm addicted to all things Italian.' Especially the women, but he omitted telling her that. She suspected it anyway. He didn't look like a man who was faithful to his wife, and he had told her enough to let her know that he was unhappy. That was the usual prelude. But she

302

didn't care. She liked him anyway. And he was an intelligent person to talk to. It was better than watching television in her room. Much better. And besides, Nick wasn't home either ... she felt the same gnawing worries again as Nick crept into her thoughts.

'When did you live in Rome?' She forced herself to think of Philip and not Nick, at least for the duration of this meal.

'We came back ten years ago. We were there while the children were small. My daughter was born there. It's a marvellous city.'

'Do you go back often?'

'Once or twice a year. I have more business in Paris and London than I do in Rome.' She could see what he meant about being successful. Paris, London, Rome, New York. It sounded exciting. She wondered if she'd ever have to go to Europe to tour for the book. Nick would probably kill her. If he was still around.

The conversation moved on easily through dinner. No more baring of souls or heartrending secrets. She told him amusing stories about San Francisco, and he told her tales of his adventures abroad. There was a great deal of teasing, right through dessert. They finished the dinner with zabaglione.

'You should come to San Francisco. We have a restaurant there with zabaglione that makes this one look sick.' The rest of the dinner had been fabulous, but at dessert she missed Vanessi's oozing rum-kissed treat.

'I might surprise you.' She laughed at the thought. That would be a surprise. But she knew he didn't mean it. 'Actually, I haven't been out there in about twenty years. Most of my business is in the East or in Europe. We do very little work on the West Coast, and usually when we have something out there' – he looked at her in embarrassment – 'I send out one of the underlings.'

'That's nice. Don't you consider California worthy of you?' She was teasing, and he laughed.

'I confess. I guess I never did. Business isn't as high-powered there.'

'Maybe that's a virtue.'

'I never thought so. But maybe you're right.' He smiled at her warmly and reached for the check, as she frowned.

'I don't think we ought to do it that way, Philip. Let me pay my half.'

'How modern! Don't be absurd.' He smiled benevolently as he put several bills on the plate.

'Please don't. After all' – she grinned at him mischievously – 'I have an expense account.'

'In that case, I'll let you pay for drinks. Can I lure you up to the Carlyle for an hour of Bobby Short?'. It was a tempting invitation, but she looked at her watch with regret.

'Would you settle for a quick drink at our hotel? I'm afraid I have to be up and out at an ungodly hour tomorrow. I have to be at the studio by seven-fifteen.'

'I have to be at a breakfast meeting on Wall Street at seven-thirty myself. The hotel sounds fine.'

And it was better than fine. It was lovely. A pianist was playing, and the room was uncrowded and surprisingly romantic for a hotel bar.

'I didn't remember this bar was so nice.' She looked around in surprise and he laughed.

'Is that why you suggested it? You thought it would have neon lights and a jukebox?'

She laughed at the thought. 'What a shame it doesn't. Wouldn't that be fun at the Regency?' They both laughed and sipped their brandies. She had had a lot to drink, but she didn't feel drunk. They had shared half a bottle of wine with dinner, but they had eaten well, so the food had balanced out the wine. Only the brandy was finally beginning to make her feel a little bit high, but not very. It only heightened the softness of the music, and the warmth of Philip's leg next to hers.

'What are you doing at the studio tomorrow?'

'Giving guided tours.' She said it with a serious expression and he laughed at her.

'I'm serious. I'm fascinated by all this celebrity stuff.'

'Don't be. It's exhausting. And most of it's very dull. I'm beginning to find that out. I was here in August and it all seemed very glamorous. Two months later, it's terribly tedious and a lot of hard work.'

'Do you have to prepare for the shows?'

'Not really. They ask me ahead of time what I'll be willing to talk about. And you have some idea of what each show wants. But that's about it. After that it's ad-libbing and being charming and terribly witty.' She said it with a face Tygue would have made, and Philip laughed at her.

'I see you take it very seriously. By the way, Kate, could I talk you into lunch tomorrow? Mine has been cancelled and I'm free.'

'I wish I were too.' She said it mournfully and he looked disappointed. 'I'm going to some kind of women's literary luncheon. Can you think of anything worse?'

'Can you get out of it?'

'Not if I plan to publish my next book.' He smiled regretfully. And he couldn't offer her dinner. He had a big business dinner he had to go to, and she was having dinner with her editor and her publisher anyway, and some guy from the New York office of her agency.

'How long will you be in town?'

'Till the end of the week.'

'Good. Then we can do it another day. Day after tomorrow? Lunch?' He was even free for dinner, but he thought he'd wait to suggest that at lunch. Lunch was always a good way to start things. They could work their way towards the evening slowly.

'I'd love it. Where shall we meet?' She was actually beginning to feel drunk now, and was suddenly anxious for bed. She looked at her watch and was horrified to realize that it was after one. They had spent a long time together. And she was going to get only about four hours sleep. Very New York.

He looked at her with a smile and put down his empty glass. 'Let's see ... what's fun for lunch? Quo Vadis?'

'Where is it?'

'Just up the street. It's very pleasant.' It also had the

305

advantage of being a block away from the hotel, in case their lunch together went unusually well.

He held her arm as they walked to the elevator, and his eyes watched her hungrily as she got off at her floor. He held the door open for just a moment and looked at her. There was no one else in the elevator, and they were automatically run after midnight. 'Good night, Kate.' His voice was a caress, and she almost shivered. 'I'll miss you tomorrow.'

'Thanks.'

He let the door close then and she felt foolish. 'Thanks.' How unglamorous. How unsophisticated. How stupid. Christ, he was way out of her league. She had never met a man quite like him before. He was more European than American, and very, very smooth. And then she laughed as she let herself into her room. In some ways, he was very much like her father. And not at all like Nick. That was a relief at least. She was so damn sick of Nick and Tygue and Tom and all they wanted from her. Sick of the guilt trips and confusion and conflicts. She lay down for a moment on the bed, promising herself she'd get up in a minute and take off her clothes. But she never did. They called her from the desk at six, and she had to rush to get ready. They wanted her on the air at seven-thirty for a show where they were going to get her name wrong and liberally misquote her book.

CHAPTER XXXII

Kate didn't get back to her room at the hotel again until after eleven that night. She hadn't had a moment to herself all day. That damned women's luncheon, the shows, the dinner with the people from the agency and the publishers ... it seemed endless. A carousel crawling with asparagus and smoked salmon, and heartburn, and she was sick of it all. She had missed the chance to talk to Tygue again, but every time she'd been near a phone, it had been the wrong time for him with the time difference. And now it was after eight in San Francisco and he'd be asleep. And she couldn't even talk to Nick. He was doing the show. And by the time he finished it, she'd be asleep. There had been no messages from him anyway, and that was message enough. She knew he was still angry. She vowed to herself just before falling asleep that she'd find time to call both him and Tygue the next day. No matter what. She needed to talk to them, or they'd never forgive her.

But she was gone first thing in the morning again, and she ran all morning until she reached Quo Vadis at noon. Philip was already waiting for her, and she was breathless as she swept out of the cab and into the restaurant. It was freezing outside, and her cheeks were bright from the cool air. She looked striking in the red slacks with her mink coat, and her eyes looked like emeralds. It was the first time she had worn the mink since she'd put it away when she moved to the country. It was the coat Tom had told her she'd wear to the hospital to have his son. And it was a beauty. Long, rich, and full in lustrous bittersweet chocolate-brown fur. Its classic lines were still very much in style. She looked dazzling, and Philip could hardly wait to get his hands on her.

'Am I late?'

'Not at all. I just got here.' He helped her off with her coat

307

and felt engulfed in her perfume. It made him want to nuzzle her neck, but not now ... later. Their eyes met, and with a faint blush she looked away. 'So how is New York? I didn't even see you at the hotel yesterday.' The headwaiter led them to a quiet table, and Philip took her hand. The gesture surprised her a little, but so did her reaction. There was something very electric about this man, and her response to him made her feel oddly naive.

'I was never at the hotel. I ran around all day. And when I got home, I went right to bed.'

'What a splendid idea.' He looked at her teasingly and she laughed as he reached for the wine list. He ordered a dry white Bordeaux that was tart, strong, and wonderful. She had never drunk anything like it. Along with everything else, Philip knew his wines.

They had lobster for lunch, and *mousse au chocolat* for dessert, followed by small delicate cups of espresso. And then he surprised her by ordering something called '*poire*'.

'What is it?' It arrived looking like water, but even one sip scorched her mouth with a hot, pungent taste of pear. He smiled at the look on her face.

'It's pear brandy. And I can see, Mademoiselle Harper, that you need to spend some more time in Europe. Have you been recently?' She smiled at the distant memories. She hadn't been since her last trip with Tom.

'Not in a very long time. I went quite a lot with my parents. But that was part of another lifetime. I haven't been in' - she thought for a moment - 'more than seven years. And I was awfully young. No one was offering me pear brandy.' And Tom certainly wouldn't have known about *poire*. He was perfectly happy with German beer. She hadn't even got him to try *kir*, or Cinzano, or some of the local wines as they travelled around Italy and France. Beer.

'Drink it carefully, by the way. It's strong stuff.' He said it in a conspiratorial tone and seemed to edge closer to her on the banquette.

'How can I drink it any way but carefully? It burns the hell out of my mouth.' She sipped again, and almost winced, but

308

Philip didn't seem to be having any trouble with it. He smiled at her as he lit a Dunhill Monte Cristo. Philip Wells was a man of taste. She was sitting back against the banquette, watching him carefully light the full tip of his cigar, when her glance strayed just past him, and she thought she heard herself gasp. But she hadn't, there was no sound. She was only staring . . . but it couldn't be . . . it . . . but it was. She hadn't seen him in twelve years, but it had to be. Her father.

'Is something wrong?' Philip looked at her inquisitively through the delicate blue smoke. 'Kate?'

She nodded distractedly, but didn't look at him. 'I'm sorry. I see someone I know.' Had he changed? No, she didn't think he'd changed a great deal. His hair was whiter, and maybe he was a little thinner. But he was sitting very close to a young woman almost her age. Where was her mother? Who was that girl? And why the hell did she care after all these years? She forgot all about Philip, but he was concerned as he watched the colour drain from her face.

'Kate, do you want to go?' He signalled the waiter for the check without waiting for her answer. But she only shook her head, and then slid quickly off the seat.

'I'll be right back.' That was crazy. She couldn't go over there. He'd laugh at her. He'd tell her to go to hell. He . . . but she had to . . . had to . . . had to . . . She felt her feet moving rhythmically, and then suddenly she was standing there, looking at him, and saying one word. 'Daddy?' There were tears in her eyes, and he looked up at her, shocked, and rose slowly to his feet, with only a glance down at the woman beside him. He was as tall and distinguished-looking as ever and his eyes were riveted to Kate. She had grown to be quite a woman. But he did not hold out his arms. They only stood there, separated by a table and a lifetime.

'Kate.' She nodded in silent answer, as the tears ran down her cheeks. But she was smiling, and there were tears in his eyes too. He didn't know what to say. 'I read your book.'

'You did?' He read her book but he didn't call or write or reach out to her when . . . he had read her book. Why?

'It's a beautiful piece of work.' Another fan. Only he

wasn't supposed to be that. He was supposed to be her father. 'Kate, I . . . I'm sorry about all that. We . . . we thought it was best if we didn't' – he almost choked on the word as she stared at him – 'if we didn't interfere. We thought it would only make it harder. It would have been awkward.' Awkward? Christ. All these years later and still an excuse. They had read the papers, they knew what was happening to her, and they never held out a hand. Slowly, her tears stopped. And she could see her father had more to say. He was looking well. She could see that now. He had aged, but he had aged well. And she had been right. He did look like Philip Wells. For a moment, she found herself thinking that her father was a successful failure too. Who was that girl sitting next to him and what was he doing in New York?

'I live in New York now.' He looked down at the girl and then back at Kate. 'Do you?' He was visibly uncomfortable, and in her guts, Kate finally felt something very old slip from its moorings and drift away. Finally. It was really gone.

'No. I'm just here on business. For a few days.' It would save them the embarrassment of having to see her, or finding excuses not to. It must have been awkward having a famous daughter who had the bad taste to turn up. She suddenly looked down at the woman lunching with her father, and found herself looking into a young, rich-girl face. 'I'm sorry to interrupt your lunch. We just haven't seen each other for a while.'

'I know.' The girl spoke very quietly, as though with understanding. She wanted to tell Kate she was sorry, but it wasn't her war. It was theirs.

Her father was looking at her uncomfortably again, as he still stood there, the centrepiece in the drama between the two so much younger women. The woman at the table was three years younger than Kate.

'Kate, I . . . I'd like to introduce you to my wife. Ames, this is Kaitlin.' Kaitlin . . . he still called her that. It rang emptily now. Kaitlin. It was a name on a book. Nothing more. But this woman . . . this woman was his wife? The words suddenly got through to her.

'Your wife?' Kate looked at him in astonishment. 'You and

mother are divorced?' God, whole lives had gone on, on their separate continents. But he was slowly shaking his head.

'No, Kate. She died.' He said it so softly she could barely hear him. And for a fraction of a moment she closed her eyes, but when she opened them again she did not cry. She only nodded.

'I see.'

'I tried to find you, to let you know, but there was no trace of where you were.' And then he had to ask. 'Is . . . did Tom . . .' But she shook her head and cut him off.

'No. He's still alive.'

'I'm sorry. That must be very hard. Or don't you . . .' He still remembered everything he had read in the papers. But he couldn't . . . they had said . . . they had decided to stick to . . . but had they been wrong? He could feel the reproach of his young wife as she sat next to him. He and Ames had argued about it often, especially after she had read the book.

'Yes, I still go, Father. He's my husband.' And you were my father. That was what the words said. And then she looked down at Ames again, with the faintest of smiles in her eyes. 'I'm sorry to do this to you. It's a hell of a way to have lunch.' Ames only shook her head. She wanted to reach out to Kate, to be her friend. God, what bastards they had been to her. She had never been able to understand it when he tried to explain it to her. If he ever did that to their son, she'd kill him. But he'd never do that again. He knew that too. This child would be his forever.

'I . . . you had . . .' It was unbearable, standing there, asking those questions, but they seemed to be frozen into a Greek play, a tragedy, with a phalanx of waiters off in the distance somewhere as the chorus. 'You had a child?'

'A little boy. He's six.' It was her first real smile. And then she looked pointedly at her father. It was as though she already knew. 'And you?'

'We have . . . we also have a son. He's two.' Poor little bastard. For only a second, she hated this man, and then she looked at Ames and knew she could not.

'Would you . . . would you like to sit down and join us?'

He waved helplessly at the unoccupied chair, but Kate shook her head.

'No, but thank you. I really . . . have to go.' She stood there for a moment, not sure whether to reach out to him, or just leave, and then slowly he held out his hand. It was like a scene in a very bad movie. Across a span of twelve years he held out a hand, only to shake hers. No hug, no kiss, no tenderness, no warmth. But it was fitting. They were strangers now.

'Good-bye.' She looked at him for one last moment, and said it in a whisper as she started to walk away. And then she looked back, and saw his wife crying. She wanted to tell her it was okay, but that was his problem, not hers. She walked quietly back to Philip and he stood looking at her with concern. He had paid the check ten minutes before, but he had sensed that a drama was unfolding and he hadn't dared to approach. He had suspected that the tall, distinguished man who had stood there looking so unhappy was a past lover, and it was clear that the meeting hadn't been a joyful one. The woman seated at the table was obviously upset. His wife? It stunned him a little that Kate had had the balls to go over and talk to him, if that was the case. He hoped it wasn't, as he thought of Margaret in Chicago.

'Are you all right?'

'Yes. Can we go?'

He nodded and took her arm. It was a relief to get out in the chilly wind. It whipped her hair and squeezed fresh tears from her eyes. But they were clean tears, tears from the cold, not old, rancid tears that had waited years to be shed.

'Kate?'

'Yes.' Her voice was very deep and hoarse as she looked up at him.

'Who was that, or shouldn't I ask?'

'My father. I hadn't seen him in twelve years.'

'And you just ran into him like that? In a restaurant? My God, what did he say?'

'He told me that my mother had died, and he has a two-year-old son. He's remarried.' Philip looked at her with horror. It was an incredible story.

312

'That woman was your sister, the one who was crying?'
Kate shook her head. 'His wife.'

'Jesus.' And then he looked at Kate again, and simply took her in his arms. They walked a few steps away from the restaurant, and slowly, painfully, she started to sob. She had nothing to say, but she had to get it out. It was twenty minutes later before he walked her slowly back towards the hotel. And the bitch of it was that he had to be somewhere at three. He would be late. The lunch had taken much longer than planned.

'He didn't even ask to see me again.' She said it like a heart-broken child, but he looked down at her, sensing something else too. A woman who understood.

'Did you really want him to?'

And then she smiled up at him through her tears. 'He could at least have asked.'

'Women. You wanted him to ask so you could tell him to go to hell, right?' She nodded and wiped her eyes with the handkerchief he handed her. It was fine Swiss linen mono-grammed with PAW. Philip Anthony Wells. 'Listen, I hate to say this.' He hated it more than she knew. He had had such sweet plans for after lunch. 'But I have a meeting at three, and' – he looked at his watch with a grin – 'it's five past. Do you think you'll be all right, and we'll kind of put back the pieces over dinner?' He gave her another quick hug and she smiled. There were no pieces to put back. She had done that years ago. With Tom's help. She was only crying at the funeral. But for her they had all been dead for so long. Maybe Tom had been right after all. The old bastard was a hypocrite. There he was married to some kid in her twenties, and with a son.

'Can you make dinner?' She had forgotten all about Philip and looked up in surprise.

'Sure. I'd love to.' She needed someone to talk to, and he was easy company. 'I'm sorry you got mixed up in all this. I don't usually drag my life around in front of strangers.'

'I'm sorry to hear that.'

'Why, are you fond of dirty linen?' She smiled at him as they walked briskly towards the hotel.

'No, but I didn't think we were still strangers. I hoped you

313

thought of me as a friend.' He put an arm around her shoulders again and she sighed.

'I do.' And then he surprised her and simply stopped, there on the sidewalk. He looked down at her, and holding her tightly in his arms, he kissed her. She started to pull away, but what surprised her more was that she didn't want to. She found herself responding to him, kissing him back. Her arms were around him now too, and she felt him press his body close to hers. She wanted to feel more of him, but she couldn't through their coats. And she was sorry when he took his lips from hers.

'Dinner at seven?' They were almost under the canopy of the hotel as she nodded, with a serious look in her eyes. She was shocked at what she had just done. There was something powerful and magnetic about Philip Wells. She wondered if he did that often. But she knew he did.

'Seven will be fine.'

'Then I'll leave you here.' He kissed her very gently on the cheek and started towards a cab stopped at the corner of Park Avenue. He looked back over his shoulder once with a smile and a wave. *'Ciao, bella.* See you tonight.' And then he was gone, and she stood there, too stunned even to feel guilty. Then she walked slowly past the doorman and into the hotel. And as she waited for the elevator, she heard someone call her name. A man at the desk was gesticulating wildly as she turned around.

'Mrs. Harper! Mrs. Harper!' She walked towards him, confused. And he was almost breathless with excitement when she arrived at the desk. 'We have been trying to reach you everywhere. Mr. Waterman had us calling every restaurant in New York.'

'Mr. Waterman?' Why' Maybe because she hadn't spoken to him in three days. She looked down at the message they handed her. 'Call Mr. Waterman immediately. Urgent.' It gave her home phone number.

She waited till she got to her room to call back. Nick answered the phone.

'Hi. I got the message. What's up?' She sounded strangely

314

unconcerned to Nick, who didn't realize it was only that she was numb. She had been through too much in two hours. Her father, Philip, and now this wildly urgent call from the Coast. All of that and daytime television too. It was more than she could cope with. And all the wine she'd drunk at lunch didn't help. But she was sober. That she was.

'Where the hell have you been?'

'Out, for chrissake. Shows, interviews, lunches, dinners.'

'With whom? Nobody knew where the hell you were.' He had called her publisher and the agency.

'I'm sorry. I was having lunch.' She felt like a truant child apologizing to an irate father. But she was beginning to pick up something more in his tone, and she sat up straighter in her chair. 'Is something wrong?'

'Yeah.' He took a deep breath, and closed his eyes. 'Yes. Something's wrong. Tygue is gone again.'

'Oh God. Since when?'

'I don't know. Maybe last night. Maybe this morning. Tillie put him to bed last night, and I checked on him when I got home. He was fine, but he was gone this morning. He could have left anytime.'

'Did he leave a note?' But they both knew where he was going.

'No. Nothing this time. Can you come home?' It stunned her that he would even ask, and her heart melted. He sounded frightened and exhausted, and all she wanted in the world was to see him again. She had had enough of New York.

'I'll get on the first plane out. Did you call the police?' It was almost a familiar routine now.

'Yes. Same old routine. I know we're going to find the little bugger on the way to Carmel somewhere.'

'Yeah.' She knew he was right.

'I want to drive down there myself.'

'Now?'

'I'll give the cops a few more hours, and wait for you. We can go down there together.'

She smiled softly as she listened to him. Nick. It was like hearing a whole family in one voice, and she knew they'd find

Tygue. They had to. He had to be all right. 'What are you going to do when we find him? We can't go through this every two days.'

'I'll think about it on the flight.' He was right, of course. He had been right all along, about her going to New York. She should never have gone. If it hadn't been . . .

'Hey, Kate . . .' She waited as tears filled her throat. It had been a rough day. 'Baby, I'm sorry I gave you such a rough time before you left. I know you're going through a lot.' And then the sobs engulfed her again. Everything was happening at once, it was all swirling around her like a nightmare. 'Come on, baby, it's all right. We'll find him. I promise.'

'I know. But I shouldn't have come here.'

'Was it rough?' She nodded, and then squeezed her eyes shut, thinking of Philip. Christ, what if Nick found out? She prayed that he wouldn't. She'd only kissed him. But . . . she thought of the dinner date they had for that night. At least she wouldn't be there now. The fates had intervened. She forced her mind back to Nick.

'Yeah, it was rough. And I . . . I just saw my father.'

'Just now? You were having lunch with him?' Nick sounded stunned.

'No, he was in the same restaurant. With his wife.' She said it very softly.

'Your parents got divorced?' He was almost as stunned as she had been, and he didn't even know them.

'No, my mother died. He's remarried to some very young girl and they have a two-year-old son.'

'Sonofabitch.' Just hearing about it made Nick want to kill him, but Kate got control of her voice and dried her eyes.

'It doesn't matter anymore, Nick. It's all over.'

'We'll talk about it when you get home. Call when you know your flight.'

She did, and left the message with Tillie. Nick was busy talking to the police, but there was nothing new. Tillie was beside herself, but Kate felt strangely calm. She knew Tygue was all right. He had to be.

And she left a note for Philip Wells in an envelope at the

316

desk. 'Sorry to do this to you, but an emergency has come up and I have to go back to S.F. Will send you that copy of the new book when it comes out. And I'm awfully sorry about the dramatics today. Bad luck. Take care, and thank you. All the best, Kate.' It was a perfectly innocuous note.

CHAPTER XXXIII

Nick was waiting at the gate when she arrived, staring tensely at the faces drifting by. And then he saw her, and pulled her tightly into a vast hug. She clung to him for a moment and then sought his face.

'Did they find him?'

He shook his head. 'No, but we will. I want to hit that road to Carmel. I don't think they realize how intent he is about that.'

'Did you tell them?' He knew what she meant, and he shook his head.

'I didn't think I had to. We'll find him.'

'What if we don't?'

'Then we call out the FBI or whoever we have to. We'll find him.' They picked up her bag, and walked quickly to the car, saying little. But it felt good just to be near him again. To have his arm around her, to be home. She sighed deeply as she got in the car. 'You okay, babe?' He looked at her nervously, and she smiled.

'Sure.' And then he stopped with the keys in his hand and he reached out for her very gently and held her close.

'I'm sorry I've been such an asshole. I just love you two so damn much.'

'Oh Nick.' She was crying again. It seemed to be all she had done all day. But there was just too much happening. 'I've been so crazy. And you're right, that star trip is crap. It just went to my head for a while. The money, the excitement, it's a goddamn ego trip.'

'There are nice sides to it, sweetheart. You don't have to throw the whole thing away.'

'Right now I want to.'

'That's stupid. If it weren't for all that, we'd never have

met.' He released her gently and started the car as she sat back comfortably on the leather seat. Even the car smelled familiar, like home, and it was full of their things. Tennis rackets, the Sunday paper they had shared only four days before. It was so good to be back. With him anyway. Now they had to find Tygue. She talked to him about her father on the trip south. 'I don't know how you managed not to slap the sonofabitch.'

'I didn't want to.'

'Didn't he at least say he was sorry?'

'Not really. He tried to explain it. He thought it would be "awkward" if he got in touch with me when everything was happening with Tom. I don't know, love, it's a whole other world. He lives in New York now.'

'Good. I'd kill the motherfucker if we ever ran into him.'

There was a long silence then as they careened down the freeway. And then suddenly Nick had a thought. 'You know, maybe we should take the coast road. That might just be it.'

Kate lit another cigarette and then handed one to him. It felt as though they had been driving forever, and it had been only an hour. Eight hours before, she'd been having lunch in New York. It was only six o'clock as they hurtled down the old coast road. There was no sight of him yet. And then suddenly, Kate pulled at Nick's sleeve.

'Over there ... back up, Nick ... I saw a flash of yellow jacket.' It was already almost dark, but she could have sworn it looked like Tygue's jacket. Nick moved over onto the shoulder of the road and shot into reverse.

'Here?'

'Over there, near those trees.' She unlocked the door and jumped out. She ran quickly over the twigs and leaves towards the clump of trees where she had thought she'd seen the jacket. And there he was. Standing there. Watching her. Not sure of what she'd do. He seemed to shrink backwards for a moment, and then he just stood there and sagged. She went to him very slowly and pulled him into her arms. She didn't say anything to him. She didn't have to. He was crying softly in her arms as she stroked his hair. She was thanking God that she had come back from New York and Nick had thought to take that road.

319

Anything could have happened. The force of it came crashing in on her again. She hadn't let herself think of it in the hours on the plane. But there had been a sense of mounting panic as they drove along. Now it was over.

She heard Nick walk up behind them, and he put his arms around them both and spoke softly to Tygue. 'Hi, Tiger. You okay?' The boy nodded and looked up at Nick.

'I wanted to go to Carmel. And nobody's stopped for me for hours.' Poor little thing. He was tired and cold, and probably hungry. When he looked up at his mother, the defiance was gone, but the pain was still there. 'I have to see him. I have to. He's my father.'

'I know, love.' She ran a hand across his hair again, and nodded. But there was no smile in his eyes. 'I'll take you to see him.' Nick looked surprised but said nothing. 'We'll go tomorrow.' The boy nodded too. There were no shouts of joy, no glee, no excitement. They were simply doing something they had to do. Like Kate shaking hands with her father before she left New York. Sometimes just knowing wasn't enough.

'What do you want to do, Kate? Do you want to go back to the city or spend the night in Carmel?'

'Don't you have to do the show?'

He shook his head. 'Called in sick again.'

'Jesus. Won't Jasper get pissed? You want to try and get back?' He shook his head. He'd deal with all that when he went back to his office. This mattered more.

'No, but I think we ought to call the police. They're going to be revving up their engines now that it's dark. It's only fair to let them know.' She nodded and looked at Tygue.

'Okay. Let's stay in Carmel.'

And there was no way of avoiding it. Nick pulled up in front of the hotel where she had stayed with Tom. But she just didn't care anymore. There were no landmarks, no shrines. It was too late for that. Much, much too late. Tygue was asleep in her arms, and she looked at Nick. She wanted to tell him how much she loved him, but she didn't know how. He just watched her, and finally smiled. But there was worry in his eyes too.

'You're really going to take him?'

She nodded. She had to. For everyone's sake.

'Do you want me to come?'

'I'd like you to be there. But I don't think he should see you. It'll confuse him, scare him. Tygue will be enough.'

'I wish you didn't have to go through that.'

'It'll be okay.'

He kissed her then, and came around the car for Tygue. He carried him inside the hotel, and the boy didn't wake up again. They notified the police that they had found him. And Nick quietly made an appointment with the lieutenant for the following Monday. He wanted to make sure that Kate wouldn't be hassled with social workers and investigations. This was a family matter, but dragging the police into it twice on a statewide alert was going to cause some embarrassment. He wanted to handle it before it got out of hand.

'What did they say?' Kate looked nervous as she sipped a cup of tea in their room. She had just checked on Tygue again. He was still asleep. He would be all night. He was too tired even to eat. He had come a long way in a short time. Hadn't they all. She stifled a yawn.

'They said everything was fine. Don't worry about it. And you should get some sleep.'

'I'm fine.'

'You look it.' She was a pale greyish green, and there was no makeup left except smudged mascara beneath her eyes. He sat down next to her on the bed and held her close. 'God, I'm glad you're back, Kate. I've been worried sick about you.'

'I thought you hated me when I left.'

'I did.' He smiled down at her. 'But I did some thinking. What we have is too special to throw away.'

Jesus, and she almost had thrown it away, with that jerk in New York. It was horrifying to realize that she might have been in bed with him at that very moment if she hadn't had to come home. In a way, Tygue's flight for Carmel had been a blessing. She closed her eyes as she lay in Nick's arms. Only for a moment. She just wanted to lie there and feel him next to her. Her eyes closed and when she opened them again, it was morning.

She looked around, stunned, as the sun poured into the room. 'Nick?' He laughed at her from the other side of the bed. He was already drinking a cup of coffee. 'What happened?'

'You passed out, Cinderella. Zap. Gone.'

'That must have been fun.' She grinned at him and stretched. He had taken off her clothes.

'Yeah, best it's ever been.' They exchanged a playful smile, and she reached out for his coffee.

'Where'd you get that?'

'Your son and I had breakfast, my love.'

'When?'

'About an hour ago.'

'Jesus, what time is it?'

'Almost nine o'clock.' She nodded, and then they both sobered. They knew what lay ahead.

'How's Tygue?'

'Okay. Quiet. He was hungry as hell.' She bent over to kiss Nick quickly and then went into the other room to see Tygue. He was sitting quietly near the window with his bear. She walked over to him softly and sat down.

'Hi, love. How's Willie?'

'He's okay. He was kind of hungry this morning, though.'

'He was, eh?' She smiled and pulled Tygue close. He felt so soft and warm in her arms. It reminded her of all the years when they'd had only each other. 'Are you ready for today?' He knew what she meant. He only nodded, holding tightly to Willie. 'It won't be much fun. In fact' - she made him look at her - 'it may be the hardest thing you ever did. He's not like a daddy, Tygue.'

'I know.' Tygue's eyes were even larger than hers.

'He's kind of like a little boy. But a sick little boy. He can't walk. He's in a wheelchair, and he doesn't remember things.' She was almost sorry that she hadn't brought him earlier, when Tom had looked bronzed and healthy. Now he always looked so tired and unhappy. It would be harder for Tygue. 'And I want you to know ...' She hesitated, fighting back the tears. 'I want you to know now ... that before he got like this, he loved you very much. Before you were born.' She took a deep breath and held her son tight. 'And I want you to know that I love you too, with all my heart, and ... and if it's too hard you don't have to stay. Is that a promise? You'll tell me if you want to go?'

Tygue nodded, and gently wiped the tears from her face as she fought back more. All she could do then was hold him.

'Is Nick coming too?'

She pulled back to look at him. 'Do you want him to?'

Tygue nodded. 'Can he?'

'He can't see T ... Daddy, but he can be there.'

'Okay.' And with an imploring look, he turned his face up to hers. 'Can we go now?'

'In a little bit. I'll have some coffee and get dressed.' He nodded, and sat where he was.

'I'll wait here.'

'I'll hurry.'

Nick looked up when she walked back into the room. This was going to be another brutal day. But maybe this would be the last one. He hoped so. 'Is he all right?'

'Yes. He wants you there.' And then she looked at him again, with those big bottomless green eyes that he had loved from the first. 'So do I.'

'I'll be there.'

'You always are.'

'That's a nice thing to say.' He handed her a cup of coffee and a piece of toast, but she couldn't eat. Even the coffee made her feel sick. There was a knot in her stomach the weight of a coconut. All she could think of was Tygue. And his father.

CHAPTER XXXIV

Nick drove up the driveway and pulled into the spot she pointed out to him behind the main house.

'Should I wait here?' He looked as nervous as she felt, and Tygue was sitting silently on her lap, watching everything.

'You can come closer to the cottage. There are other people around. You won't stick out.' He nodded, and they all got out of the car. She took Tygue's hand, and smoothed his hair. He was still carrying Willie. Kate had called ahead to warn Mr. Erhard. He said Tom was in good form. At least there was that.

The silent trio followed the pathway, and then Kate pointed to a little white wrought-iron bench. 'Why don't you wait there, love? You can see the cottage from here.' She pointed again, and he looked. This was how she had spent all those years. He still had to fight back tears when he thought of it.

He looked down at the boy then, and gently touched his cheek. 'You're okay, Tiger.' Tygue nodded, and Kate took his hand and walked on. Mr. Erhard was waiting in the doorway, and he looked down at Tygue with a warm smile. Kate had already forgotten Nick. She was in Tom's world now. And she was holding tightly to Tygue's hand. She wanted him to know how much they had loved him, how much they had loved each other. She wanted him to see something of Tom that was no longer there to see. But above all, she wanted Tygue to survive it. She put an arm around his shoulders and forced a smile.

'Tygue, this is Mr. Erhard. He takes care of your daddy. He has for a very long time.'

'Hi, Tygue. That's a beautiful bear. What's his name?'

'Willie.' Tygue's eyes looked enormous. And Mr. Erhard's eyes sought Kate's.

'We have a Willie too. Would you like to see him?' Tygue nodded, trying to look past him into the cottage, and then Mr. Erhard stepped aside, and Kate walked slowly inside. Tom was staying in the cottage today, despite the good weather, and when she saw him she realized how much time he must have been spending inside lately. He looked ghostly and pale, and seemed to have lost twenty pounds in the past two weeks. But there was a warm light in his eyes today, and he smiled a smile she hadn't seen in years as he caught sight of Tygue. Kate had to clench her teeth so as not to cry. It was Tom who spoke first.

'You have a Willie too! So do I!' He instantly held up his bear and Tygue smiled. 'Let me see yours.' He very gently held out a big hand and Tygue let him have Willie, and for a few minutes they compared bears, while Tygue stole glances at his father. They decided that Tygue's was in better shape. 'Want some cookies?' He had saved some from the night before, and produced a plate for Tygue, as Kate and Mr. Erhard hovered. The two 'boys' ate cookies, and Tygue crept quietly into the rocking chair as they talked. 'What's your name?'

'Tygue.'

'Mine is Tom. And that's Katie.' He glanced over at Kate with a broad smile, and she found herself smiling back. 'She comes to see me a lot. She's a nice lady. I love her. Do you love her too?' Tygue nodded silently and it almost seemed to Kate as though Tom was forcing himself to speak like a child, to put Tygue at ease. As though he could have behaved as a grown-up if he wanted to. 'Want to see my boat?' Tygue looked up in surprise and smiled.

'Yeah. I've got a boat too.' They talked about their boats for a minute, and then Mr. Erhard stepped in.

'Do you two want to take a walk to the pond? We could try out Tom's boat.' Father and son looked enthusiastic, and Kate smiled as he wheeled Tom outside and Tygue walked along beside him. He looked almost proud as he walked next to his father. And the half hour at the boat pond brought laughter to everyone. Even Tom looked better than he had at first. And then Kate could see him starting to tire, and Mr. Erhard suggested they go back inside.

For once Tom didn't argue, and he reached out for Tygue's hand as they started back. He was being rolled along by Mr. Erhard, and Tygue was once again at his side. The little boy held tightly to the shrunken man's hand, as Kate watched them. She was glad she had brought him. And when they reached the cottage door, Tom leaned over and picked two bright orange flowers. One for Kate, and one for his son. He looked hard and long at the boy as he handed him the flower and held his hand.

'Why did you come to see me?'

Kate felt her heart stop, but Tygue looked at him and didn't waver.

'I needed to see you.'

'I needed to see you too. Take good care of Katie.'

Tygue nodded sombrely and she could see his eyes fill with tears as quickly as her own. Tom had never said anything like that before.

'I will.'

'And Willie? Always take good care of Willie.' But this time Tygue only nodded, and then unexpectedly he leaned over and kissed Tom on the cheek as he sat in his chair. Tom smiled at him and hugged him for a moment.

'I love you.' The words were Tygue's.

'I love you too.' And then he laughed, the clear, open laugh of a boy, and Tygue laughed too. It was as though they understood each other, as though they had a secret between them. As though they felt the moment in a lighthearted way that no one else understood. They were both little boys. Tom was still laughing as Mr. Erhard wheeled him inside. 'Is it time for my nap?' Mr. Erhard nodded, looking at Kate. It was enough. Better to stop now.

'Yes, it is.'

'I hate naps.' He made a face and looked at Tygue.

'So do I.' Tygue laughed back and picked up his bear again. Tom watched him with a funny look in his eyes, but he was smiling.

'I'll trade you.'

'What?'

'Willies. I'll give you my Willie, and you give me yours. Want to? My Willie is so tired of being here.' Tygue's face lit up then, as though his father had offered him the most precious gift in the world.

'Sure.' He held out his bear with a look of awe, and Tom wheeled over to his own and handed it to Tygue.

'Take good care of Willie.'

'I will.' Tygue stooped to kiss him again, and Tom only smiled.

''Bye.' Tygue watched him for a long moment, as though wondering what to say, how to end it, but he only smiled and walked to the door.

''Bye.'

Kate walked towards Tom, and stood next to him, holding his shoulder with her hand. Together, they looked at their son, smiling in the doorway with his bear. He had seen his father. He had won.

Tom looked up at her with a tired smile. The visit had cost him something, but he looked as though he had won too.

''Bye, Katie.' Something about the way he said it tore at her heart, and she couldn't say good-bye. Tygue was still watching them from the doorway.

'I'll see you soon.'

He only nodded, though, with a quiet, happy smile. He was still watching the boy. And Kate could still feel his eyes on them after they'd left, and were out in the warm autumn sun. She looked down at Tygue, and wiped her eyes. 'I'm glad you came.'

'Me too.' And then, with a smile, he walked over to the bench where they had left Nick. Kate had totally forgotten him. And she followed slowly behind Tygue, trying to recover from the hour they'd spent with Tom. 'Hi.' Tygue stood in front of him with a broad grin. 'I've got a new Willie.'

'Looks like the old Willie to me.' Nick smiled, trying to search the boy's eyes, but he didn't see anything there but peace and love, and a warm glow. The visit had done him no harm.

'You mean he has one too?' Nick looked at Tygue warmly as he nodded. 'That's neat.' And then he looked up at Kate, as she stood near them. She was still holding the two flowers Tom had given them after their walk. 'How are you?'

'Okay. I kind of forgot you were here.' She smiled, looking wistful and tired, but relieved.

'I know. But I'm glad I am.'

'So am I. Nick . . .' She looked down for a moment and then back into his eyes. 'Could we go down to my place for a few days? I mean all three of us. I kind of want to . . .' She didn't know how to say it, but it was as though she had to see that too. As though she needed to get away from the city, and the book, and everything that had been happening. 'Can you get away?'

'We're going to have to stop and buy some tee-shirts and Jeans, but I can get away. I think it would do us all good.'

'So do I.'

'Are you lonely for the country, darling?' He looked at her curiously as they walked back to the car. He hadn't thought she was.

'No. I don't know. I just need to be there. Just for a few days.'

'Okay.' He put an arm around her shoulders, and another around Tygue's, and the three of them walked back to the car. Kate was glad when they drove away from Mead. She didn't want to leave Tom, but it was time that she did.

CHAPTER XXXV

Going back to Kate's house in the hills for a few days had been a good idea. It gave them all the time they needed to absorb the past week. Nick and Kate needed the time together, and with Tygue. He was whole again, and at peace. He was quiet for the first day, sitting outside with the teddy bear he'd gotten from Tom. But he wasn't unhappy, only pensive.

Kate looked down at her son as they sat in the sunshine the second day. Nick was doing something in the house.

'Maybe I should have told him about my horse,' Tygue said.

'He never really liked horses very much.' Kate was looking off at the hills, thinking back. For a moment she almost forgot the child. He was looking up at her incredulously.

'He didn't like horses?' Tygue looked shocked, and she smiled and looked down into the sunny little face. He looked better again. Rested and happy, like the boy she knew, not the waif they had picked up under the trees on the road to Carmel. 'How could he not like horses?'

'He loved football. That was his whole life.'

'That's 'cause he was such a big star.' Kate smiled at the pride in the boy's voice.

'Yes, he was.'

'Are you a big star, Mom?'

She looked down at him with a grin. 'No. I wrote a book that a lot of people are buying, but that doesn't make me a star. Nobody knows who I am.' She lay back and stretched out the long legs that had modelled so long ago. 'But everyone knew who your dad was. Everywhere we went people wanted autographs, they wanted to touch him, ladies wanted to kiss him.' She grinned and Tygue started to laugh.

'Did he let them?'

'Not when he was with me.'

'It must be neat though, having everyone love you like that.'

'Sometimes. Sometimes it's very hard. People expect too much of you. People won't leave you alone. They won't let you be yourself.'

'I wouldn't like that.' He picked up a leaf and studied it.

'He didn't either. That's what made him sick. All the people pushing him. And all he wanted to do was play football. For the rest of his life.'

'Couldn't he?'

She shook her head. No, love. You can only play professional football for a few years. And then they make you retire.'

'What's that?'

'Stop playing.'

'Forever?'

'Forever.'

'That's terrible!' He threw the leaf away and stared at her.

'That's what your dad thought too. He didn't want to do anything else. And they made him quit. And then a lot of people bugged him about it. Like newspapers and stuff.' It was the best explanation she could give him, and it was true.

'And he went crazy. Right?'

'That's about right.'

'Does he remember that he played football?'

'No. I don't think he remembers anything except where he is now, and Mr. Erhard and me. And now he'll remember you.' She smiled at him with a mist glistening in her eyes, and she heard Nick come out of the house. He was carrying a blanket and two apples. He handed one to each of them, and looked down at them with warmth in his eyes. 'Thanks, love.' Kate smiled him a kiss.

'Do you guys want to sit on this?'

'Nah.' Tygue looked up at the blanket disparagingly and then he remembered something . . . those words his father had said . . . 'You want to, Mom?'

'Okay.' She remembered the words too . . . Take care of Katie . . .

The three of them spread out the bright plaid blanket and sat down and munched apples. Kate and Nick shared theirs, and Tygue attacked his with glee. They were fresh country apples. They had gotten them from the market the day before.

'You want to go down to the Adams place later and see what kind of new horses they've got?' Nick looked over at him, as he crunched his way to the core, but the boy shook his head.

'No. They've got better horses in the park.'

'In San Francisco?' Nick looked surprised, and Tygue nodded insistently. Kate smiled as she listened to him. They had outgrown this place, both of them had. It made her smile to think that four months before he had never left town. She was remembering his first trip to San Francisco in June . . . and hers the month before that . . .

'And what are you thinking about, Cinderella?' Nick handed her their apple and she took a bite and handed it back.

'I was thinking about last spring. Neither of us had been anywhere then. And suddenly it all started to happen.'

'That's what it does.'

'What were you doing last spring, Mr. Waterman?' She looked at him with a curious grin.

'None of your business.' He grinned back and finished the apple.

'As bad as all that?'

'Up yours.' He said it softly as he nibbled her neck. They worried less about Tygue observing them now. He was used to them. And then Nick had another thought. 'Want to go see Joey?' But Tygue shook his head again. He had already said good-bye. He had new friends. A new life.

They spent a peaceful afternoon together, as they had the day before. They bought steaks in town and Nick barbecued them in the late-afternoon sun. That evening they watched television together, and made popcorn in the fireplace, as they had the first few times Nick had come up from L.A. And like the old days, they waited until Tygue went to bed, and then rushed into the bedroom, laughing, hungry for each other, aching to make love.

'My, my, aren't we the anxious one tonight,' he teased as she kissed the inside of his thighs and tugged playfully at his shorts.

'You didn't exactly drag your feet getting in here either, Mr. Waterman.' She sat down on the floor next to him in her bra and pants, laughing up at him as he smiled down at her. She had seemed younger and freer since they had seen Tom.

'Kate? You're glad we went to see him, aren't you?'

She nodded quietly for a moment. 'I feel relieved. There's no more secret to hide, not from you, not from Tygue. It's all out now. I feel free again.'

'But what about him?' They hadn't talked about that yet, but there were still questions that Nick felt he had to ask.

'What do you mean, Nick?' She looked very peaceful as she looked up at him, and he slowly knelt down next to her.

'I mean, what happens to Tom now? You can't very well stop seeing him after all these years, I understand that, but . . . well, it takes a lot out of you, Kate.'

'I don't think it will anymore. I'm not carrying the weight alone anymore. I can share it with you and Tygue. I can tell you what I feel, what it's like, what's happening to him, whenever I go.' There was a moment's pause and then she lowered her face and looked silently at the wedding band on her hand. And then, carefully, she slipped the ring from her finger and held it tightly in her palm. 'It's all over, Nick. I won't be going as often anymore. I'm not even sure he'll notice very much. He may at first, but he has so little sense of time. I think if I go once every couple of weeks, it'll be fair to everyone. What do you think?' She turned her eyes back to his, and they were bright and full, but she didn't look unhappy.

'I think you're a remarkable woman, and I've never loved you more. Whatever you want to do, Kate, however you want to handle it, I can accept it.'

'That's all I need to know. It means, though, that we can never get married as long as he's alive. I . . . I couldn't do that to him. I know he wouldn't even know I'd divorced him, but I just wouldn't feel right.'

'We don't need the papers, Kate, we have each other. And

when the time is right, we can get married. In the meantime
...' He grinned broadly; she had just given him the only gift he
had ever wanted from her - a promise of marriage, even if a
remote one. He looked at her again and there was mischief in
his eyes. 'In the meantime, young lady, I had no idea that
you'd even been considering marriage. I thought you were
going to carry on this independent act of yours well into your
nineties.'

'Well, why not?' She glared at him sheepishly for a moment,
and then defiantly. 'I can't let you make all my decisions for
me, Nick. Even if we do get married one day. I did that with
Tom, and it just wasn't right.'

'I understand that. I think we've been handling that fairly
well.'

'So do I.' She softened again. 'And that's not the only thing
you've been handling well.'

'Oh?' The mischief danced in his eyes again, and she
laughed.

'No, you lecher, I meant Tygue. You've gotten him over all
the rough spots. I don't think he resents you even a little anymore.'

'I think that seeing his father will help even more.'

'Probably. But you've done a beautiful job, darling. I'm
afraid neither of us was too easy at first.'

'My God, a confession. Quick, the tape recorder ...'

'Oh shut up.' She reached over playfully and tweaked the
hair on his chest. 'And by the way, I'm closing the house.'

'What house?' Life with Kate was full of surprises. For all
he knew, she was closing the San Francisco house and moving
them all somewhere else.

'This house, silly. I don't need it anymore.'

'You mean you're giving up your ace? The retreat where
you can always flee from me?'

'That's not how I looked at it.' She tried to sound insulted,
but she was already giggling. 'How did you know?'

'Because I'm not as dumb as you like to think I am.'

'I would never think such a thing.'

'Good. Then tell me the truth about why you're closing the

house, and explain to me what you mean by "closing" it. You mean giving it up completely?'

'Completely. We don't need it. We never come down here, we're not going to, and I wouldn't want to anyway. This is a part of my life that's over.' And then her face grew sober again, and she slowly opened her hand and looked at the wedding ring she had slipped from her finger moments before. 'It's over. Just like this.'

And then, wordlessly, she put the ring down on a table and came into his arms. She had never been as free with him as she was that night. It was as though something in her had been uncaged, and she gave herself to him in ways she never had before, her body arching and writhing in ecstasy beneath the expertise of his hands and his tongue.

The next morning, they had a quiet breakfast alone in the kitchen before they woke Tygue and told him that he was leaving that morning with Nick.

'Without you, Mom?' She expected a few moments of protest and was surprised by the look of delight on his face.

'Don't look so heartbroken about it, you creep.' But in fact she was relieved. It was as though their little family had solidified in the past few days.

'How long do we get to be alone?' His eyes danced at the prospect and Nick laughed.

'As long as it takes me to pack up this house. Speaking of which, young man, I want you to go through your games and toys this morning and decide what you're giving away and what you want in San Francisco.' There wasn't too much left in his closet and cupboards, but enough to keep him busy for a couple of hours.

They all rolled up their sleeves and started packing that morning, but by late afternoon Kate was working alone. After lunch, Nick and Tygue had piled into the car and driven back to San Francisco. And Kate was surprised how comfortable it was to be alone in the house. She did a lot of thinking as she packed up the boxes she and Nick had got at the supermarket before lunch.

He had been right, she *was* giving something up by letting go

334

of the house. But it was something she didn't want anymore anyway, an emergency exit, a place to hide, a place where she could keep herself from Nick. She had liked knowing that she had that, but she didn't need that anymore. If she needed to get away from him, or express her independence, she could do it with words, or a long walk, or a trip alone somewhere for a weekend, but not by coming back to the place where she had lived for seven years, mourning the past. There was nothing left to mourn. And if she found herself frightened or bothered or bugged, sometime in the future, she could handle that too – without running away. It was a nice thing to know about herself.

It took her three days to pack up the house. She gave a lot of things away, labelled some boxes for Tillie, and left them in the garage. And she collected what amounted to a small truckload of odds and ends and useful items that she arranged to have sent up to the city. After that there was nothing left. She sent a letter to notify the landlord that she was leaving, and wondered if it wasn't time for him to retire there anyway. Maybe he would finally use the house himself one of these days. It had served her well. It had kept her secret safe for all those years. She remembered how happy she had been when she first got there. Happy just to be away from the hell she had lived through, happy as she lay on the grass in the springtime, feeling Tygue grow inside her, and so happy when he had been born and she brought him home. She stood in the bedroom on the last morning, and remembered looking out over those same hills, all those years ago, with Tygue in her arms. And then solemnly, she turned on her heel, and walked out of the house.

CHAPTER XXXVI

'I'm home!' It was four o'clock in the afternoon when she arrived. And everyone was there, even Bert, wagging his tail in the front yard as she got out of the ugly little rented car. Tygue was clattering around on a new pair of roller skates and Nick was just getting some papers out of the car. It seemed as though everyone converged on her at once, talking and laughing and hugging and kissing. Nick was holding her so tight she could hardly breathe.

'Woman, if you go anywhere in the next six months, I'll go stark staring crazy, and furthermore, I'll . . .' He grinned. 'I'll set fire to your new book!'

'Don't you dare!' She looked at him in horror. She was hungry to get back to that too. She hadn't touched it in weeks.

'If you do that, I'll burn all your jockstraps, and . . .'

'What's a jockstrap?' Tygue said it at the top of his lungs and they both laughed. They laughed for the rest of the afternoon. Nick urged Kate to disappear for a 'nap' and Tillie shepherded Tygue off down the block to break in his new skates. And when he got back, Nick and Kate were both roaming around in their bathrobes, making tea.

'Want to come to the show tonight, Kate?'

She looked up in surprise. 'Like this?'

'No, I kind of thought you'd get dressed.' He looked prissy and she made a face at him.

'I mean, you want me on it without my hair done and all that?' She looked horrified, and he sat back in his chair and laughed.

'Listen, Miss Ego, you happen to live with the producer of that show. I wanted to know if you'd like to come and hang out and keep me company while we tape it.'

'And not be a guest on the show?' She looked shocked, but her eyes were dancing.

336

'What do you think you are, some kind of celebrity or something?'

'Hell, yes, Mr. Waterman. I'm a best-selling author!'

'Oh yeah?' He slipped his hand into her robe, and then leaned across the table to kiss her.

'You're impossible. But since you invited me' – she looked up with a smile – 'I'd love to come keep you company while you tape. Will it bother anyone there?'

'That's their problem. I run the joint. Remember?'

'Oh that's right, you do.'

'Sounds to me, young lady, like it's time you came home and settled down. You've forgotten how things run around here.'

She let her fingers play along the inside of his arm, and he got goose flesh and looked at her with a gleam in his eye.

'If you do that for much longer, I'm going to get a lot more serious than you bargained for.'

'In the kitchen?' She was grinning again. It was just the way they had been in the beginning. The honeymoon was on again.

'Yes, in the kitchen, Cinderella. I will make love to you anytime, anywhere, any way, for the rest of your life. I love you.'

She kissed him very softly on the mouth, and they made love very quickly, in the kitchen, before Tygue got home. And they laughed like two outrageously naughty children as they hurried back into their robes, and tried to look as though they'd been drinking tea.

'You've got your robe inside out,' she whispered to him as they giggled, and he laughed even harder when he looked at her. She had her belt tied through the sleeve.

'You're a mess.'

It went on that way for weeks. Clandestine meetings in what she jokingly called 'the attic', making love in the upstairs den, sharing long lazy breakfasts in the kitchen, taking Tygue to the zoo. She watched him tape the show almost as often as he did it, and he sat peacefully in his favourite leather chair as she worked on the new book. It was a kind of Siamese-twin existence but they loved it. They both knew it couldn't go on forever, not like that – she'd have things to do for the new book, and he had a lot of extra work he needed to do for Jasper's show. But right now they both needed what they were getting. Each other.

'Don't you ever get tired of sitting up here while I clack away on this silly book?'

'Darling, any woman who is making the kind of money you are does not write silly books.'

'To what do I owe this renewed respect for my talent?'

'Your last royalty statement. I saw it on your desk this morning. Christ, what are you going to do with all that money?' He was glad she was doing so well. He knew it meant something to her. Security for Tygue, things for herself, gifts she'd like to buy him. But it also meant that she felt independent, and he knew that she needed that.

She was sitting back in her chair, looking at him, wondering what she would give him for Christmas. It was only a month away. 'What do you want for Christmas, by the way?' She lit a cigarette and took a sip of cold tea. He had been reading the paper while she worked.

'You know what I'd really like for Christmas?'

'What?' She was grinning, thinking that she knew what he'd say.

'Don't look like that, you dirty old woman. What I'd really like is to see a little colour in that pale face of yours. Want to go to Acapulco or someplace for the holidays?' She looked surprised at the thought.

'I've never been there. That might be fun.' She was turning the idea over in her mind as he looked at her, but he didn't answer her smile.

'Kate?'

'Hm?'

'Are you feeling all right?' Worry had crept into his face.

'Sure. Why?' But they both knew why. She was tired all the time, her appetite was lousy, and she was always pale. The rings under her eyes had become part of the decor. She was pushing hard on the book though. She had blamed it on that.

'Would you go to see a doctor?' It was the first time he had asked, and it frightened her that he was that worried.

'You mean it?'

'Yeah. I do.'

'Okay. I'll see. When I finish the book.' And what was he going to tell her that she didn't already know? That she had been under a lot of pressure? That her whole life was altered and her son had run away twice? That she was finishing a five-hundred-page book? None of it was news to her. So what was the point of seeing a doctor? 'He's not going to tell me anything new. He's just going to say I'm working too hard, or I've been through a lot of changes, or some other bullshit like that. Why spend money to listen to that?'

'Do me a favour, and save your money someplace else.' He looked at her seriously and stood up. 'I mean it, Kate. Promise me you'll go. And not six months from now.'

'Yes, my love.' She said it too sweetly, and he frowned.

'Promise?'

'Promise, but only if you promise not to worry about it.'

'Sure.' Both promises were equally empty. She was not a fan of doctors and he was a devoted worrier, at least about her. But none of that changed how she looked. Felicia had noticed it too. But Kate had brushed her off.

'What are you doing today by the way?'

'I'm meeting Felicia for lunch. Want to come?'

'No. I have to talk to a couple of guys at the Press Club over lunch. And then we've got a meeting at the studio. 'He looked at his watch, and then stooped to kiss her. 'In fact, I'm almost late for lunch. I'll be home around three.'

'I'll try to be too.' She tried. But she didn't make it till five. She went shopping for an hour, after lunch at Trader Vic's with Licia, and then she'd wandered over to Saks. Just 'for a minute' to see what was new. But the store had been crowded and she had got tired, and the elevator had taken forever to come, and when it had she was pressed near the back. And when they reached the third floor, they found her crumpled in the rear of the car. She had fainted. They had wanted to call home for her, but she wouldn't let them. She had sat there at Saks for an hour feeling like a fool, with smelling salts under her nose, and she'd taken a cab home. She hadn't wanted to drive. She'd have to tell Nick she'd had a problem with the car. Dammit. And she still felt light-headed and a little dizzy when she got home. She was fully prepared to be amusing and distracting, and get upstairs as fast as she could, to go to bed. He had wanted to take her to the taping of the show, but she'd beg off.

She slid her key into the door, and turned it. The door opened easily, and for a minute she hoped that he wasn't home. But he was. And he was sitting in the living room, waiting for her, his face rigid with rage.

'Have a nice lunch?'

'Very. How was your . . .' But she stopped when she saw his face. 'What happened to you?'

'Who's Philip?'

'What?'

'You heard me.' He glared at her and she started feeling dizzy again. She slowly sank down in a chair. 'Who the hell is Philip?'

'How do I know? Is this some kind of a game?' She felt weak but she sounded angry. She was scared. Philip? Philip from New York?

'As a matter of fact, I'm beginning to wonder the same thing. *Is* this some kind of a game? Every couple of months I find out something new about you.'

'What's that supposed to mean?'

'This.' He walked across the room and threw a piece of paper at her. 'It was in an unmarked envelope tucked into the front door. I thought you'd left me a note. I was wrong.' The paper was a sandy beige, the ink was brown and the hand-writing distinctive. And then she saw the monogram at the top. PAW. Philip Anthony Wells. She felt her heart slide into her heels. Jesus. And the letter itself did nothing to help. 'Sorry you had to leave so suddenly. It was a beautiful lunch, a beautiful evening before that. The music was never the same after you left. I've come West, at last, to see two promises fulfilled. Yours, and that of the zabaglione at Vanessi's. Join me tonight? Call. I'm at the Stanford Court. Love, P.' She almost gasped.

'Oh Jesus.' She looked up at him with huge eyes that instantly filled with tears.

'That's what I said. It's quite a letter. And don't let me stop you from having dinner with him, darling.' His voice dripped hurt and anger. He had felt as though someone had punched him when he read the note. 'Just exactly what went on in New York?'

'Nothing. I had dinner with him, by accident, at Gino's.'

'By accident?' He looked at her nastily and she jumped to her feet and peeled off her coat.

'Oh for chrissake. I couldn't get a goddamn cab from the airport, so we shared one. We happened to be staying at the same hotel. And that night I went to Gino's for dinner, by myself, and he was there. We chatted at the bar, and then we just decided . . .' It sounded terrible in the telling and his face was looking anything but relieved. But she decided to press on. 'We just decided to share a table. Big deal! So what?'

'And then what?'

'What do you mean "and then what?"'

'Whose room did you go to?'

'Mine for chrissake. And he went to his. What do you think I am, dammit? A whore?'

'We were hardly speaking to each other that week, if I remember correctly.'

'So? You think I run out and get laid by a stranger every time we have a fight?'

'No, but apparently you have dinner with one.'

'Goddamn you!' She grabbed her coat again and stared at him. Now she was blazing. Fuck him. She'd tell him the whole story, and if he didn't like it he could take his whole goddamn life and shove it. 'Yeah, so I had dinner with him. And I had drinks with him after that. And I had lunch with him two days later. And if Tygue hadn't run away that day, I'd probably have had dinner with him that night. But that's all I bloody did. No, as a matter of fact, come to think of it, I kissed him. Whoopee. I'm twenty-nine years old and I kissed him. But that's all I did, you sonofabitch, and I don't need you to play watch-

341

dog. I can keep myself out of other men's beds all by myself. And as a matter of fact, smartass, I spent days being grateful that Tygue had run away. Because I was just unhappy enough at that point, and insecure enough about us, that maybe I would have gone to bed with him. But I didn't. And I was so glad I hadn't. Because I didn't want to. Because I love you, you stupid sonofabitch, not anyone else.'

She was screaming and trembling and the sobs were starting to shake her voice, but she stood up, waving the letter and advancing on him. Nick was feeling greatly subdued by his effect on her. He had never seen her get like that. Never. She looked as though she were going to have a stroke and fall dead at his feet. And he suddenly felt foolish for making such a stink of it. He knew she was telling the truth, he'd just been upset when he came home and found the letter. He knew she was faithful to him, though he was upset by the kiss. But he could live with a kiss, and he was glad, too, that she hadn't done more. But it was too late to be glad. She stood over him waving the letter. 'And you know what you can do with this? You can take it to Philip Wells and cram it down his throat. And then you can both go to Vanessi's and eat the fucking zabaglione for all I care. But get the hell out of my life!' And then, sobbing, she reeled around, threw the letter on the floor, grabbed her bag and coat and walked out. She stopped in the doorway for a moment, afraid she was going to faint again and he looked at her. Something was terribly wrong with her.

'Are you all right?'

'Mind your own goddamn business.' And with that she slammed out of the house. Tygue was visiting a friend, so she knew she didn't have to be there, and now she didn't want to be there with Nick. Fucking Philip Wells. She hated them both. And then, she suddenly realized she'd left her car downtown. She set off towards the Bay, on foot, crying like a child. Why had Philip done this to her? And why had Nick read the letter? And why had she kissed him that day in New York? She sat down on a secluded garden wall a few blocks away, and stayed there for a while with her face in her hands, sobbing, and wishing she were dead.

At home, Nick was still sitting in the living room, staring at the letter she had thrown on the floor, wishing he'd handled things differently. He had never seen her that emotional. And then she had stopped in the doorway, looking absolutely green. He had to get her to a doctor. Maybe it was her nerves. The phone broke into his thoughts, and he scooped the letter up on the way. He scrumpled it and threw it into the waste basket next to the phone.

'Mrs. Harper? No, I'm sorry, she's out. Is she what? What do you mean is she all right? She what? ... Oh my God ... No, no, it's all right. I'll take care of it.' He sat very still for a moment, and called Felicia. He was lucky to catch her, it was almost six. But she agreed to come over right away. She could hear in his voice that something was wrong.

'Where's Tygue?' She looked around as she came in. The house seemed unusually quiet and dark.

'Spending the night at a friend's. It's not Tygue, Licia. It's Kate. I think something terrible is wrong with her.' He sat down in the living room again, and held his head in both hands. Felicia sat down across from him and looked at him for a minute.

'You don't look so hot either. What happened?'

'I made an ass of myself.' He walked to the wastebasket and scooped up the letter and handed it to her. 'I found that when I came home, in an unmarked envelope. I thought it was for me.'

'Oops.' She looked up at him with a wry smile, and he wasn't smiling.

'I confronted her with it when she got home, like a total ass. And she told me the whole story. It's nothing. But what totally wiped me out is what happened to her. Jesus, Licia, I've never seen her do that. She just fell apart. She screamed and shook and she looked like she was going to pass out. She's been looking horrendous lately, and she won't see a doctor. She's working too hard, she's not sleeping enough, she's tired all the time, she cries when she thinks I don't know it. I think she's sick. Or something. I don't know what the hell it is.' And then he looked over at Felicia with the clincher. 'Customer

343

Relations at Saks just called. She passed out in the elevator there this afternoon. I'm worried sick.'

'I take it she's not home now?' Felicia looked worried too.

He shook his head. 'No. She blazed out of here ... over this ...' He waved the letter and then crumpled it again.

Felicia hated to ask. But Kate was not really one for intrigues. Even though the little minx had said nothing about New York. And then she did remember a gleam in Kate's eye when she had asked her about Gino's. But that didn't explain the histrionics and the fainting. 'Is it possible ... could she be with that guy?'

Nick shook his head again. 'Not in the state she was in when she left here. And ... no, I know she's not.'

'I don't think she is either. And she's a grown woman. She'll just have to be reasonable and go to a doctor. She didn't eat a thing for lunch. But she's not losing weight.' And then she sat back in her chair and narrowed her eyes.

'What is it?' He looked more nervous than ever. Was there something else he didn't know?

'Something rings a bell.' She looked back into his eyes. 'I'm afraid I have no experience with it myself, but methinks I've seen this one before with Kate. Then, I thought it was just what was happening – because of Tom.' Felicia frowned, wondering. It would be a hell of a relief.

'Her nerves?'

'No. Not exactly.' She looked at him with a small smile. 'Far be it from me to pry into your private lives, but is it possible that she's pregnant?'

'Kate?' He looked stunned.

'Not Tillie, I hope.' He shared a laugh with her at the thought.

'I don't know. I hadn't thought of it. I always figured that if something like that happened, she'd know, and —'

'Don't rely on that. Half the women I know never figure it out till they're about three months pregnant. You figure the flight to New York threw you off, the food, your sex life, god knows. Anyway, for whatever the reasons, people seem not to notice a lot these days.' Jesus. The very idea of 'not noticing' made her break out in a sweat. But Kate was the kind not to. 'Any chance that's it? She had some incredible temper tantrums when she was pregnant with Tygue. Usually about the press, so they were justified, on the surface anyway. But when you thought about it later, you knew she'd gone way overboard. She fainted a couple of times too. And for the first couple of months, she looked dreadful. But' – she looked at him sombrely – 'she was going through a lot then.'

'She's gone through a lot in the last couple of months too.' He sat back and tried to think. He was still trying to shake off the idea that she was either having a nervous breakdown or dying of cancer. Pregnant? He hadn't thought of it, and then suddenly he remembered.

'Jesus. I forgot. The night Tygue ran away, the first time . . . we kind of kidded about it . . . she forgot her diaphragm.' He looked over at Felicia apologetically, for regaling her with the details. 'Anyway, it's certainly possible. So much has happened since then, I think we both forgot. Or I did anyway. You really think she doesn't know, if it's that?' He looked suddenly elated.

'She might not. But don't get excited. I may be wrong. By the way, have you got anything to drink?' She lit another cigarette and stood up. 'It's been a bitch of a day.'

'Yeah.' He echoed the sentiment and walked over to the bar. They always kept the fixings for a martini close at hand, in case she dropped by. 'Now what do I do?'

'Wait till she comes home, and ask her.'

'What if she doesn't come home? What if she goes out with that guy?' He paled at the thought, and then he flushed as he viciously mixed her martini.

'Don't take it out on my drink, Nick. She'll come back. Did she take the car?' But it was a dumb question. Of course she had. But Nick was looking at her strangely again.

'That's right. She came home in a cab. She must have left her car downtown.' Felicia didn't like the sound of that. She must have been feeling like hell to do that.

'I think you're just going to have to wait this one out and ask her. And will you do me a favour' – she finished her drink

345

and set down the glass — 'will you please let me know? If she's sick, I want to know about it.' He nodded his head miserably, and Felicia stood up. 'I hate to do this to you, but I have to get moving. I'm being picked up at eight and I have to do a lot of repair work before then.' She was going to the symphony. With someone new.

'Yeah. I'll call you.' And then he looked at his watch too. 'Damn. I'm going to have to leave in a minute too. I have to do the show.'

'Maybe she'll be at home when you get back.' Felicia patted his shoulder as he walked her to the car, and she wondered to herself what he'd be like in bed. Beautiful and strong. She had decided that before. Kate was a lucky girl. She looked up at him and smiled. 'She'll be all right. And hell, you may even wind up a daddy.'

'God, Felicia, I'd love it.'

'Just do me a favour, and stick around. I couldn't go through the delivery number again.' But the gruffness of her voice told him she could. For Kate.

'Don't worry, Licia, this time you won't have to. I just hope it's that.' As he walked back into the house, he found himself thinking back, and suddenly he was almost sure of it. He'd have been ready to celebrate as he drove to work, if only he'd known if she was all right. She could have done anything, the way she was acting when she left the house. Anything.

But all she had done was sit on the wall she had found and cry. And at last she sat there and just shivered. She wanted to go home, but not until she knew he was gone. And at twenty after seven, she walked back to the house, went upstairs, took off her clothes, and went to bed. She was exhausted. She didn't wake up until she felt Nick gently shaking her shoulder.

CHAPTER XXXVII

'Kate?' She felt him shaking her softly, and it was still dark outside when she looked up. It was almost dark in the room. There was only one lamp lit, in the far corner, and it gave off a soft glow. 'Hi babe.' He rubbed her back softly and she closed her eyes again. His hands felt so good. But she was mad at him. She remembered that as he started to wake up.

'What do you want?'

'To talk to you.'

'What about?' She refused to open her eyes, but she could hear a fire burning in the grate.

'Open your eyes.'

'Go away.' But she was starting to smile now, and he saw it. He bent down and kissed her cheek.

'Stop that.'

'I want to ask you something.'

She opened an eye. 'Not that again.' She was frowning.

'No, not that again.'

'Then what?'

'What happened at Saks today?' He was smiling down at her and speaking very softly, but his eyes still looked worried. He hadn't been able to think all night, as they taped the show. And he had raced home to see if she was there. He had almost cried with relief when he saw her huddled form under the covers. He didn't care if she hated him; at least she was home, and not dead somewhere, sick, or mugged, or hysterical. But she hadn't answered him. 'Tell me about Saks.'

'Is there anything about me you don't know?' She sat up and looked at him in astonishment. 'Are you having me followed?' She looked stunned, but he shook his head with a small, rueful smile.

'No, they called. They wanted to make sure you got home all right. So what happened?'

'Nothing.'

'That's not what they said.'

'All right, so I passed out. I ate too much for lunch.' That wasn't what Felicia had said either, but he didn't want to make her feel totally boxed in, so he didn't say it.

'Are you sure it was that?' He reached out carefully and held her face in his hands. Her eyes instantly filled with tears, and she started to relax in his hands.

'What do you think it was, Nick?'

'I think maybe . . . I hope . . .' He looked at her so tenderly that the tears only came more quickly, and he smiled. 'Is it possible, Cinderella, that you're pregnant?' He watched her very closely and she pulled slowly away from his hands.

'Why would I be pregnant?' But like Felicia earlier, there was a look about her, as though she were mentally running her fingers through file cards, remembering, matching events, and then suddenly she looked at him with a sheepish grin. 'Maybe. I hadn't even thought of that.'

'Possibly more than maybe?' He looked at her hopefully.

'Maybe a lot more than maybe. Jesus, I don't know how come I didn't think of that.' She had begun to wonder if she had some rare disease. She grinned at him and he kissed her softly, and then hungrily, feeling carefully in her nightgown for her breasts. 'I would be about seven weeks pregnant. It was the night Tygue . . . wasn't it?'

'I don't know. Is it too soon to find out if you are?'

'No. This is just about right.'

'Want to try again?' She laughed as he lay next to her on the bed.

'Try again, huh?'

'Sure. Why not?'

But they didn't need to. She was pregnant. The test was positive the next day.

'Are you sure?' He was beside himself when she hung up the phone after getting the results of the test. The nurse's voice had been unemotional. 'Harper? Oh, Here it is. Positive.'

'You're pregnant?'

'Yes I am, and yes I'm sure. That's what the lady said any-

348

way.' She slid her arms around his neck and he beamed at her.

'Oh Kate, I love you.'

'I love you too.' She said it softly, her voice muffled in his arms. 'And I'm sorry about New York.' She hadn't said that to him the night before, and she had wanted to.

'It's all right. Nothing happened. But if you ever go back there, I'm sending an armed guard.' And then suddenly he looked at her seriously, as he held her gently in his arms. 'I don't want you to tour while you're pregnant. Not at all. Is that clear?'

'Yes, sir.'

'What about your new book? Will you be willing to wait before you go anywhere? It won't hurt your career to wait a few months.'

'It won't be out for another year anyway. Perfect timing.' She grinned up at him and ruffled his hair. He was taking it all so seriously. She didn't feel as nervous about this pregnancy as she had with Tygue, but that had been a long time ago too. In some ways, this felt new. And it would be so nice to have Nick there. She held him very tight for a few minutes, and they each smiled at their own thoughts. And then he looked down at her again.

'Promise me you won't push while you're pregnant.'

'Push what?' She tried to make light of it.

'Kate ... please ...' He wanted this child more than anything. She understood.

'Relax, darling. I promise.' She could feel him relax as he held her close again, and the phone rang next to them. She looked at him with a grin. 'Maybe they changed their minds.'

'Tell them it's too late. We accept.' She smiled at him and answered the phone, but her face clouded instantly.

'Hi, Stu.' She could feel Nick tense beside her.

'That's a surprise. When? ... I don't know.' She looked at Nick and smiled, but he was already panicking. He had started stalking the room, his face filled with despair. It was starting again. Weinberg and his fucking trips.

'You promised!'

'Relax!' She whispered it with a hand over the phone, and

349

tried to continue the conversation with Weinberg. And then finally to him a vague 'I'll see'. But suddenly Nick couldn't take anymore. He grabbed the phone away from her and put his hand over the receiver.

'You tell him that the person he's trying to exploit is pregnant, and he can take his next fucking tour, or whatever the hell he's calling about, and shove it up his ass.' He looked at her in desperation, but she was grinning as she retrieved the phone.

'Sorry, Stu.' She grinned at Nick and his face lightened a little as she said the words. 'He won't play in the tournament with you. He thinks you're trying to exploit him. And he's pregnant. Very temperamental.' Nick rolled his eyes and sat down with a grin. 'No, he said you could shove it up your ass. That's what he said ... Fine, I'll tell him.' She hung up and stood looking at Nick. 'You worry too much, Mr. Waterman.' She was grinning broadly.

'You're a spoiled brat, Cinderella. Has anyone told you that lately?'

'Not since this morning. By the way, when am I going to get the other glass slipper?' She smiled at him as she sat down on his lap.

'When you promise me that you're not going on tour, and not going to wear yourself out while you're pregnant. If you promise me that, you can have anything you want.'

'I may hold you to that.'

'You didn't answer my question.'

'Was it a question? It sounded more like an order to me.' She raised an eyebrow and ran a finger around his ear.

'I'm serious, Kate. This means a lot to me.'

'It does to me too. But you don't have to coerce or threaten to get me to take it easy. Trust me a little.'

'Not when it comes to your work ... and our child.' He looked at her with a small worried frown. 'Is that going to be very hard on you, Kate? Handling both, I mean?'

She shook her head, but she didn't answer for a moment. 'No.' She hoped not anyway, but if so, they'd work it out.

'Had you thought of ... of ...'

But she cut him off before he could say the words. 'No, I wouldn't do that.' And then she pulled him closer into her arms. 'I want your baby, Nick. I think I've always wanted that. Tygue is special, and he has always been just mine. I never got to share him, the waiting, the getting born, all those special moments that come later ... I never had anyone to share that with. With us, with this baby, everything will be different.'

'Including the fact that we're not married.' He sounded a little embarrassed as he said it, and searched her face again. 'Will that be very hard on you and Tygue?'

'Of course not. Tygue's too young to care, and do you really think *I* care what people think about that? Besides, we'll get married someday.' She looked down at the pale line on her left hand where the wedding ring had once been. 'In the meantime, it doesn't really matter. Unless ... will it matter to you? On the show, I mean. Could it cause you problems?' She had to think about that too. Her reputation wasn't the only one at stake, but he was already grinning in response.

'In that crazy world I work in? Are you kidding? They'd think we were strange if we *were* married and having a baby. But you know, I thought of something last night.' He looked memomentarily embarrassed and then decided to go ahead and tell her his idea. 'If it does bother you, or Tygue, we could tell people that we are married. Who's to know that we're not? We could say we went off somewhere quietly and got married. And then ... later ... we could do just that. Nobody has to know if we're really married or not.' But she was already shaking her head with a look of negative determination.

'Nope. No way, Mr. Waterman, I won't do that.'

'Why not?'

'Because when we finally do get married, I am not going to sneak off anywhere to marry you, sir. I am going to do it with more pomp and ceremony and noise and style than you've ever seen. And the whole world is going to know. How about that?'

'You know what, Cinderella?'

'What?' She was smiling as broadly as he.

'For that, you get your other glass slipper.'

351